SWORD A ORD
FROM THE
EMBERS

SHE WILL FLY

A SWORD FROM THE EMBERS

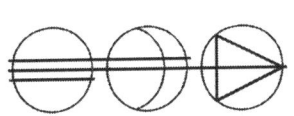

CHLOE C. PEÑARANDA

DEDICATION

For you my dear reader,

From the heart of Agalhor Ashfyre,
"It's easy to forget the leaps we've taken when the steps forward become so small. But never forget you are still moving. You are challenging yourself with every day you decide to face your reality."

A Sword from the Embers
Copyright © 2022 by Chloe C. Peñaranda
All rights reserved.

This is a work of fiction. Names, characters, places, and incidents either are the product of the author's imagination or are used fictitiously. Any resemblance to actual persons, living or dead, events, or locales is entirely coincidental.

No part of this book may be reproduced in any form or by any electronic or mechanical means, including information storage and retrieval systems, without written permission from the author, except for the use of brief quotations in a book review.

Published by Lumarias Press
www.lumariaspress.com

First Edition published January 2023

Map design © 2022 by Chloe C. Peñaranda
Cover illustration © 2022 by Alice Maria Power
www.alicemariapower.com
Cover design © 2022 by Lumarias Press
Edited by Bryony Leah
www.bryonyleah.com

Identifiers
ISBN: 978-1-915534-04-0 (eBook)
ISBN: 978-1-915534-03-3 (paperback)
ISBN: 978-1-915534-02-6 (hardback)

www.ccpenaranda.com

AUTHOR NOTE

My dear reader,
 In case there was any confusion, I don't want you to begin this book with the impression book four, A Clash of Three Courts, was a spin-off and not needed for the core storyline. If you have skipped book four, A Sword from the Embers contains major spoilers for Nik, Tauria, Jakon, Marlowe, and Tarly. I hope you enjoy reading as much as I did writing.
 All my love.

Please read with care. This next part of the journey touches on some darker themes.

CONTENT WARNING
<u>*Not core themes but mentions/ depictions of*:</u>
Depressive thoughts
Suicide ideation
Torture
PTSD
Heavy grief/loss
<u>*More prominent themes/longer scenes:*</u>
Graphic fantasy violence
Adult language
Multiple explicit sexual scenes

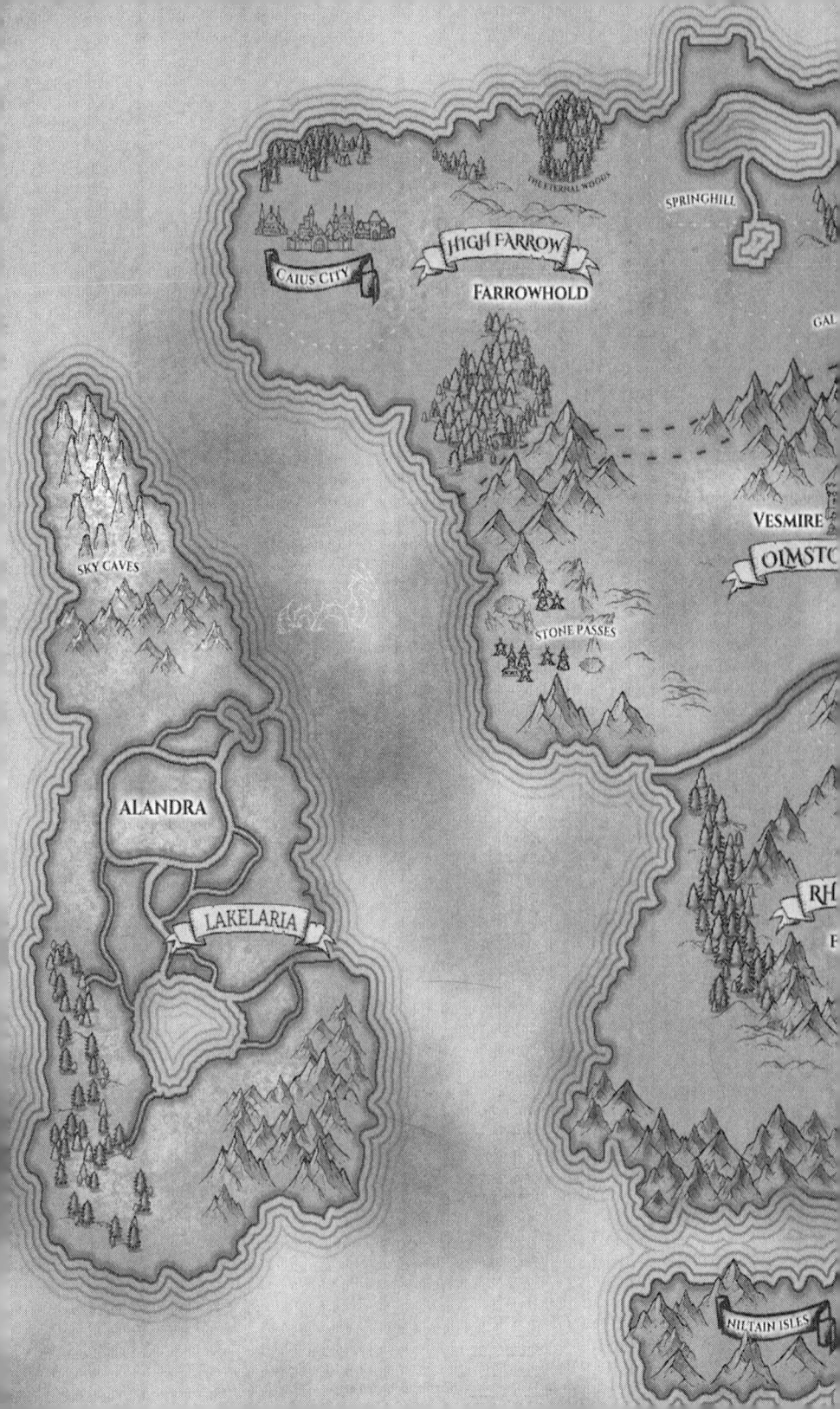

PROLOGUE

S HE DIDN'T OFTEN wander so late, but tonight the stars were restless.

Hopping between rooftops, she kept alert, at one with the shadows. She had no clue what would become of her hasty decision to leave the warmth and safety of home, only needing the air to breathe since being pulled from sleep as if the night called to be ventured.

She sat staring at the moon for some time, thinking it might open her mind to an explanation as to why they sought each other's company. As she shook her head, a huff left her, tugging at the corner of her mouth. If this peaceful moment was all she achieved, it would be enough of a reward. Though she should be at home where she'd sworn to remain, and she shuddered to the thought of her mother's scolding if she were caught. She didn't like to defy her, but the pull to leave had tightened in her throat the longer she resisted it.

A shuffling from the street below awakened her senses. The disruption spiked her adrenaline at the discovery she was no longer alone despite still being hidden. Curious, she shuffled stealthily across the narrow flat and down the slanted side, where she peered out over the street, inconspicuous.

What she found made her heart pound. Two forms locked in a hostile position—a confrontation she had no business observing when it might condemn her. She tried to ease away, but the taller one punched the other so hard she winced in shock. From the attacker's muscular build she gauged him to be a male, but with his hood she couldn't identify a thing. He grabbed his victim by the collar before slamming him into the wall, and finally, the victim's mouth moved to spill whatever information he sought. Her fae hearing might have been able to pick up the exchange if she tuned in her focus, but blood roared in her ears to block out everything except the screaming demand to run.

Yet something kept her eyes glued to the tall male.

Moonlight glinted off the lethally beautiful blade, but that second of distraction was wiped entirely when the steel drowned in the crimson that slicked the victim's neck.

She smothered her cry too late.

Hand clamping her mouth, her horror at the gruesome display stunned her still, though it came second to her dread as his eyes flashed up to meet hers.

Her skin crawled at the notion of being next under his dagger.

Every ounce of her agility rose to the challenge as she sprinted across the rooftops and away. She had no destination in mind, but she couldn't stop even if terror ran her off the edge of the world.

The burn rose through her throat until it numbed. Her arms pushed the speed of her legs, setting a pace that might be as close to flying as she would ever come. The instinct to gain distance canceled out her ability to track if he was following her or how near he was. If he were also fae...

The fact was confirmed when a looming figure dropped down from a taller building. She stumbled to a halt with the force of meeting stone. The exertion slammed into her, tearing apart her lungs and making her muscles throb. Her mind scrambled for an out, but with how easily he'd caught up, the option to flee again seemed futile.

He stalked to her slowly with the ease of a predator. This was the night she would die. She'd always been warned of the dangers outside, and now here she was coming face-to-face with the reason for her confinement.

Instinct wouldn't allow her to stand idle as his prey.

Turning, she lunged only a few strides before a strong arm hooked around her middle, a hand muffling her cry. Completely ensnared, tears pricked her eyes.

He spun her around so fast she choked on her gasp, pressing her back against the tall chimney shaft. His hood shadowed his face, concealing the heartless eyes she expected to find.

Though she tried to tame her breathing, nothing could prepare her for the shudder of her heart when her gaze trailed along the arm pinned to her shoulders and she saw the glint of moonlight off the blade so close to her throat. She'd witnessed how quickly that hand could swipe clean through flesh.

"A-are you going to kill me?" she asked, cursing her stutter.

His assessing silence was a battle of ire and curiosity. She took his moment of distraction to yank down his hood, wanting to see every part of her killer if that were to be her fate.

She didn't expect the stunning silver locks. Cropped to sit above his shoulders, while some strands framed his tanned complexion, two braids on either side held the rest from being a hindrance. Yet the eyes she met forced a few conscious blinks from her own. They reminded her of the night sky to which her thoughts had drifted earlier. His sapphire irises captured the stars, though it was not dreams but nightmares that lay within them. She had to tear herself from their distraction only to map every detail she could about him. His high cheekbones led to a strong jaw that twitched under her assessment. She gauged him to be no older than twenty in human years.

"You shouldn't have done that," he growled.

As he pushed away from her, she was drawn back to his eyes despite the promise of violence ingrained in them. No, that was only a mask. Beneath it, she found notes of hollow sadness, something lost, and she wanted to discover what invoked it.

"You killed that person," she said, sounding braver than she felt. "Am I next?"

"You don't know a thing," he snapped. "And that makes me contemplate it."

Her head spun at the backward remark. "Should you not want me dead for what I *do* know, not what I don't?"

While the skin around his eyes tightened, she took the opportunity to study his attire. All-black form-fitting leathers that highlighted the lethal build she glimpsed under his cloak. An assassin, she thought. That was already obvious, yet something about him didn't settle easily in the monstrous persona. Perhaps he was too young to have become such an entity on his own.

"What is your name?" he asked.

"So I can be another on your kill list?"

"You're making it very hard for me not to give you that wish."

She didn't think that to be true. He could have ended her already, though she wouldn't get too comfortable if she were living on borrowed time. "What does a name change?" she asked quietly.

His dark brows knitted together, a beautiful contrast to his silvery hair. "Everything."

Her heart skipped in her chest at the way his deep blue irises expanded, his frown easing as if he'd forgotten why he'd chased her. What she'd seen. In that moment, maybe she lost sight of it too.

"Then tell me yours."

As he took a step toward her, she couldn't help the flash of fear that compelled her to scan his hands—empty of weapons now. He halted. His fists flexed tight as though disappointed or angry she'd assumed the worst. "It wouldn't be safe for you to know mine," he answered.

Having witnessed the life he'd taken in a heartbeat, and having run from him thinking her fate would meet the same end, the mention of her safety hit like a whip. "I think we're past caring about *safety*."

He assessed her slowly. She didn't move.

"You're not afraid?"

She swallowed hard, and his eyes flashed to her parted mouth, skittering her pulse. This attraction to danger she seemed to harbor surged within, a conflict of thrill and horror. "No." Her answer came sure, though her mind chastised her for the alarm, the *fright*, she'd let slip for the deadly stranger. Unable to fit logic to why, when she looked at him she saw a dagger but felt the embrace of a shield.

"Then why did you run?"

"I thought you would kill me."

"And what makes you sure I won't now?"

Nothing. There was absolutely nothing in his actions nor words that should give her that confidence.

"Take down your hood."

She was in the right mind to deny him, and if she lived beyond being trapped by the alluring killer, she might do well to reprimand herself for listening to her *wrong* mind. Sliding her hands under the material, she didn't break his stare, a current of *something* slowly building between them. Her long lengths of chestnut-brown hair came flowing down her chest.

"Your eyes," he said with a million thoughts behind those words. "I suppose I don't need a name. You're easy enough to find."

That took her by surprise, having never heard such a thing. For all her silent observations of people in the small town of Rhyenelle, she'd always believed she blended in. Then again, she rarely spoke to anyone.

The second thought to register made her blood run hot with adrenaline at first, and then cold with dread. "You're not going to kill me?"

"No."

"Not yet" was what she heard. He'd marked her by her eyes after all. He could find her again.

"I won't say anything."

"I wouldn't care if you did."

"Then you have no need to seek me out."

"What if I want to?"

He approached her again, slowly, but his stalking inspired more amusement than threat, and she had to blink against the change in him.

Too close. *Too close.*

The stone scraped her fingertips as they flexed against it. With no way out, she prayed it would give and swallow her whole. Sense snapped at her to attempt a sideways step, but he planted his hand by her head to stop it.

Their eyes met, the proximity sparking a new intensity that should be *wrong.* Yet she became entranced by the night sky that opened in his irises.

"Are you going to stop me?" he asked tauntingly.

She knew she didn't need to cower at the notion. He wouldn't find her. Not when her days passed inside the same four walls and her nights of freedom were fleeting. And it was likely they would be moving on to another town soon anyway.

"I don't think I could," she admitted.

Then she wanted it.

Wanted him to find her in ways no one ever had.

She offered up the challenge in her naïve desire to find out *why* he'd done what he did tonight. Her mind refused to believe he was capable of raising that same hand to harm her.

Or perhaps she was nothing more than a desperate soul with nothing to lose, so when darkness offered her company, she was all too willing.

His stare roamed every inch of her face, the distance between them gradually disappearing. She'd never known such a closeness, and her body *craved* it. Her long inhale doused her in his scent of leather and spice, and something cold tingled sweetly in her nostrils.

Her breath hitched in her throat when he reached for her hand. Her heart slammed furiously at the contact. Palm to palm, he kept their hands by her head. She wanted his fingers to slip between hers and itched with the desire to know how they'd fit together, but he didn't.

Only after a few seconds did a cool breeze wrap around her finger, alerting her to what he'd stolen. His other hand held up her ring. She lashed out for it until his fingers curled around hers, interlocking their hands. The electrifying sensation shocked her still, warmth racing up her arm to settle in her chest.

If he felt it too, he gave no reaction, admiring the gold ring with careful attention instead. It was embellished with small crystals that glinted in the moonlight: golden butterfly wings and a white opalescent body.

"So you're a murderer and a thief," she said.

The hard snap of his eyes made her wince. He reacted immediately, pushing away, and her hand flexed with the cold absence of his.

"Like I said, you don't know anything," he muttered icily. "Consider this insurance."

"For what?"

"For if you try to run from me again."

"I'm not of any interest to you."

The curl of his mouth made her stomach erupt with a new sensation. "That's not for you to decide now, is it?" he said.

As the stranger pulled up his hood, he left her with one last lingering look. She tracked his graceful movements, but before the night could steal him, he offered four more words. A promise.

"I will find you."

She made it home still in a daze over the night's events. How fast a nightmare situation had turned into a waking fever dream.

If she had any sense, she wouldn't want the dangerous stranger to spare her another thought. Perhaps he'd forget her. He didn't seem the type to pursue someone who offered him nothing. But he'd kept her ring despite her many demands for him to give it back.

Unexpectedly, unexplainably, she smiled to herself.

"There you are."

Her entire body stiffened. This fear consumed her more wholly than her fear of the assassin.

"I didn't expect you to be here," she admitted, the words barely squeezing out through her throat. She twisted to face the owner of the beautiful feminine voice.

Easing out from shadows, those gold eyes pinned her, letting her know she'd been caught. They were golden like her own, yet hers could never match the otherworldly beauty of her mother's.

"I came back early. I returned"—her mother took slow steps, the waves of her impeccable red gown trailing after—"for you."

"Sorry. I-I just needed some air."

"Shh," she soothed. "I cannot blame you, Aesira."

As Aesira accepted the embrace, her mind flashed once again to the stranger who'd so desperately wanted to learn her name.

"But I need you to swear to me you won't go out alone again. The world is full of those who want to do you harm."

If only her mother knew who Aesira had met that night. A killer, yet someone far more than that, whose starry eyes defied her to remain at the forefront of her mind. For now, she could only hold onto her one sure line of safety, riddled with guilt for defying her.

She would never know why her mother didn't want to be called as such. Aesira whispered, "I promise, Marvellas."

PART I
GOLDEN BUTTERFLY

CHAPTER 1

Faythe

DYING? THAT WAS EASY. Painless, emotionless. It was nothing. Perhaps her final breath came so peacefully as a gift for having blessed the world.

But death was not a force to be reckoned with. It took its revenge in the agony that tore through her body. Revenge for the mockery she'd made of the God of Death.

Hours, days, weeks... Faythe couldn't be sure how long the inferno raged while she lay at its mercy. She wished she could explain that this was not her fault. Not some defiant stance. But it was too late.

Her first breath crashed like a wave, dousing the fire in her veins at once, her senses flooding in again in a rush of clarity so pure. The air rushed down her throat, filled her lungs, and awakened her heart with strong, full beats. Through her nose every scent burst to reveal the notes of a dozen more. If she focused on those scents, she could refine and separate each one to discover far more than she'd ever known. Breathing came steady and *new*.

Her lids slid open, the luminance enough to sting her eyes as they adjusted from their slumber. The discomfort subsided quickly.

Her pupils dilated, focused, ready to explore every hidden detail of her surroundings. Everything exposed so *sharply*.

Faythe blinked a few times, overwhelmed but exhilarated.

A shadow was cast over her. Faythe shifted her head, registering the cushion of flesh that cradled her, enveloping her in a scent she'd followed all the way back from the brink of oblivion. Leather, spice, and something as cold as ice.

Reylan looked down at her, his beautiful face distraught. The sight made her chest clench so painfully. She raised a hand to his cheek, and as soon as her skin touched his, Faythe's lips parted at the explosion of sensation. A warm vibration like the one she knew, but somehow deeper. Her thumb brushed the wetness on his battle-worn skin, her eyes fixed on the glistening trails.

"Why are you crying?" she whispered, but even her own hushed words seemed so *loud*.

When her eyes met his, through his irises Reylan connected with her with such a bright flare of awakening Faythe became entranced by them. Sapphire and gold. In his eyes she watched the colors *merging*. Orbiting her to their eternal dance, wrapping around her like a tether that surged through her, tugging at something so bound to the essence of all she was…

The great General of Rhyenelle…is your soul-bonded mate.

That truth didn't settle with the shock it should. It was the faint tugging in her mind, a thread too thin to follow, denying her those crucial fragments of memory that stole her breath. The reality of the present crept back in, snapping Faythe from her dreaming state. Awareness began to suffocate her. She shot up straight, swaying as she tried to adjust to her new fluidity of movement. This body of weightless gravity.

And strength.

And *power*.

Stumbling to her feet, dizzy in her bewilderment, she raised her hands as though expecting to see something alien. She couldn't contain her gasp as she found a single intricate pattern of golden vine trailing past the cuffs of her leathers. She tried to push up her sleeves but couldn't be certain where it ended. Then she found the symbol marking her palm. Horror drenched her.

Aurialis's mark.

It was unmistakable: a hollow circle with three lines scored past its circumference.

Faythe's heart beat erratically. Raising her other trembling hand, she dared to flip it over. A breath of fear left her to find she'd also been branded with Marvellas's mark: a hollow circle with a downward-pointing triangle within it and a single line striking through its circumference.

She'd seen the symbol appear before, when she'd harnessed power from a Temple Ruin. Yet now, Faythe didn't want to believe her skin had been permanently tattooed with the ancient Spirit markings. They glowed in a beautiful gold against her skin, which had caught a tan since coming to Rhyenelle.

You and I will become one, Faythe Ashfyre.

Oh Gods. Her last conversation with Aurialis trickled back in as a haunting note.

A gentle touch grazed her arm, and she whirled in fright. So quickly it shouldn't be possible, Faythe backed herself all the way up to meet hard stone. She winced at the impact, not anticipating her own strength and speed, then raised a shaky hand. Her eyes widened in horror or shock—she couldn't be sure which—when her fingers, which she'd expected to dip over the curve of her ear, instead continued up and over a delicate point.

The final, most physical attribute couldn't be denied.

She was fae.

Her mind flashed to images of what those distinctive pointed ears would look like on her. She shouldn't know. She didn't want to know.

"Make it stop," she breathed in a panic, her eyes clamping shut as though she could cancel out the visuals in her head too.

"Faythe." Reylan's voice cracked, pulling at something soul-deep. "You're going to be okay."

That forced her to see the desolation on his face, the plea, as he took careful, tentative steps toward her. Faythe crumbled. Her knees gave out while her hands rose to cover her face and muffle her sobs. But she didn't take the impact of her harsh fall to the stone; instead, Reylan's arms wrapped around her, lowering them both slowly. Faythe couldn't be sure what she was crying for, only that she was completely lost and overwhelmed. Reylan's warmth grounded her, soothed her. He kept still, allowing her to release the sudden flood of emotion. All Faythe could do was grip him tightly. Out of fear, out of sadness, but most of all, out of gratitude that she could hold him again.

Above everything else she'd come back to face…

She'd come back for him.

Memories of the series of events that led up to here and now barreled into her. Faythe's throat seized tight as the flashbacks raged through her as violently as thrashing waves. She was the boat—too small, too out of her depth, to survive the storm.

It's going to be okay.

Reylan kept repeating his words of comfort until they blurred in her mind. All she could focus on to reel her back to him was the hum of his rough, reassuring voice and the low vibrations from his chest.

Faythe didn't know how much time had passed when her emotions eventually wore her out, tired her tears, and subdued her with a numbness instead. "I died," she whispered. Cheek pressed to Reylan's chest, she treasured every thump of his heart as if it beat for them both. She couldn't let him go.

Reylan stiffened. Faythe studied him taking a few calming breaths. It pained her so deeply to imagine what he'd been through, neither of them knowing for certain they would have this again.

Each other.

"Transitioning" was a generous word for what it took to merge with something all-powerful. Faythe couldn't comprehend that in her new form she harbored Aurialis's power. Didn't yet know what it meant.

"You're right here," he said at last, his voice just as hushed. "You're alive. I'm right here with you, Faythe."

With him. With her mate.

Faythe forced herself to pull back, but his arms stayed around her. She searched those sapphire irises for a long moment, having felt at one with the sky in them since the moment she saw him. She ran her hand through his hair, and when her fingers reached the ends of the short silver strands, she imagined them to continue through the beautiful lengths to his shoulders.

"You once had longer hair," she said vacantly. Faythe had seen it before in Varlas's memory, but the image that focused in her mind right now felt new and personal, so clear her vision blurred.

"A long time ago," he answered.

Faythe wondered if he knew…

Her lips parted, but she couldn't form any of her words into sentences. Faythe leaned out of his embrace to stand. Her mind raced and raced. "Mates," she choked. She couldn't bear to turn around, fearing the impact of his reaction.

Reylan remained silent for an agonizingly long minute. Faythe counted the hard beat of her heart and tried tuning in to his. It stunned her that she was able to hear it from this distance if she focused right. But the two beats pounded to a confusing rhythm.

Finally, his voice cut through her panic, devoid of any happiness. "You don't sound pleased by it."

Her heart could have stopped. Her breath caught. It wasn't elation or liberation that set in as the realization dawned. Her body rippled, so tense and cold. She turned to him slowly, and the chill on her skin might have been from the icy glaze that shielded all emotion from Reylan's eyes as he stared at her. His steel barrier enforced a real wall between them.

"You don't sound surprised by it."

His jaw flexed. More silence. Faythe released a long breath. Her mind scrambled to scan every memory she had with him, yet their battle had been so impossible that all she could do to stay standing was shut it all out.

Her eyes fell and everything around her faded as the world shifted from under her. Faythe's stomach turned. She covered her

mouth at the sight of the crimson stain. So much blood. The scent drifted to her, the copper tang of a life sacrificed.
Her life.
The walls began to close in.
Fast. Too fast.
Her hand lifted to her constricting chest, where the phantom pain from the dagger that had sealed her fate began to tingle, a reminder she shouldn't have lived through such a fatal blow. Yet there was no wound, no lingering tenderness.
Her feet moved before her mind caught up. It seemed as if it wanted to hold her to that cave and make her relive her dying moments. Taunt her with the notion she didn't *deserve* to have this second chance.
Her hair blew behind her. She was running now, faster than what should be possible, desperate to be free of her tomb. Death would forever linger in that cave. The death of the girl who delivered baked goods to keep herself fed, who spent days training with a sword she never believed would see battle. The orphan who wandered, always lost. The Gold-Eyed Shadow who always had something to prove. The human girl who fell in love with a fae guard and succumbed to living the type of mundane existence that had always felt tragic to her.
She had died in that cave. And who would emerge…?
Faythe reached out to the stone wall for stability, her steps so heavy she struggled to put one foot in front of the other. There was no air left in the tunnel. She shouldn't be alive, and it seemed death was desperate to take back the life she stole. She tried to push on, to be free. Darkness peppered her vision.
Then darkness was a helpless fall into a warm and safe embrace.

CHAPTER 2

Zaiana

ZAIANA SILVERFAIR TRACED slow fingers along the frayed edges of the emerald-green banner that hung at an angle. It had managed to hold firm against the unlawful attempt to tear it down. Her gaze cast upward to the obscured stag emblem. She imagined the image would have once appeared mighty, yet now, the side-profiled creature seemed to bow in defeat, conquered.

She wasn't sure why they had come to Fenstead. Being back here brought forth the desolate scenes of carnage she had lived through. She'd led legions for Valgard to claim dominion over the once peaceful land. Every bloom and brightness that once thrived in the kingdom had refused to grow since darkness swept through.

"Dakodas sent me to find you." Maverick's voice crept to her from down the hall.

Her hand dropped as she shifted her cold eyes to him. He strolled over to her, adjusting the cuffs of his jacket nonchalantly.

Zaiana had barely spoken a word to Maverick since they'd left Dakodas's temple. It wasn't because she held any regard for him killing the human. That should have been her act to shoulder.

Perhaps she was simply waiting for repentance while Maverick held out on claiming his praise for completing the quest.

She had felt little at all since. Her mind was reinforced with steel, her chest frozen with ice. She had failed.

Twisting smoothly, she began to walk off without a response.

Maverick's hand hooked around her arm, and the snap of her gaze to him was nothing short of a violent warning. In contrast, foolish concern swirled in his obsidian irises, grating on her irritation.

"You've not been yourself since the temple," he said quietly, as though he didn't want anyone else to catch his arrogant mask faltering.

Zaiana maintained her harsh glare, snatching her arm from his grasp. "You don't have to pretend that you care. That you're *capable* of caring. Dakodas hasn't requested me for anything since we arrived. I'm sure you've had plenty to do." It came out with a sneer, but she didn't care. She couldn't. Harboring no emotion was better than letting in what threatened to destroy everything she had left.

Maverick's jaw flexed. His eyes hardened. He didn't bother to deny it.

Zaiana scoffed, casting her gaze away from him as she began to stalk away.

He'd never caught her off-guard before, so Zaiana could only curse her own pitifully clouded senses for not detecting Maverick's brazen movement before it was too late. He pinned her to the wall, the press of his body holding her still against the flash of rage that jolted through her.

"You're not lamenting because I killed her. You're lamenting over why you couldn't," he whispered as he leaned in. His breath rumbled across her ear, stilling her movements, for the flashback he inspired slipped past the barrier in her mind. Her ire became confused with desire for a moment. "I would do it again. If I have to choose between you or me, I'll step up every time."

For glory. For reward. It had to be. Zaiana's flare of challenge returned.

"Then what are you waiting for?" she hissed. "Why haven't you told her what happened in the temple?"

"Why?" he repeated, war raging in his depthless eyes. The depthless eyes of someone on the verge of slipping. As quickly as it stirred, in his next blink, Maverick's eyes matched her icy glare. "Hate me, Zaiana, by all means, but can't you see this works in our favor? *I'm* their villain. I took their precious princess. They'll be too focused on exacting their revenge on me to see you carrying out Dakodas's work. Isn't that what you wish?"

She gave him nothing while she calculated his words, trying to find an ulterior motive.

"But you'd better get yourself together, delegate, before the truth of how the Transition unfolded is revealed without either of us saying a damn thing."

He didn't back off. Zaiana had no quick retort while her mind processed his words.

"This gains you nothing."

Maverick didn't answer. Those dark, alluring eyes seemed to soften just for a moment as they searched hers. The coiling in her stomach was unwelcome, suffocating. She needed distance.

"Beautifully untamed," he whispered.

The shock of it parted her lips. Her thoughts raced to stop him when one of his hands fell to her waist, drawing her close.

"Perhaps I can put to rest your torment. Just for one more night of *fantasy*."

Zaiana slowly slipped her hand over his chest in the small gap between their bodies. When she reached past his collar, she angled her iron-clad middle and pointer fingers to scrape under his chin, tilting away the warm breath that stirred unwanted flashes of memory as it blew across her lips. Maverick clenched his teeth against the pinch that was just shy of enough pressure to draw blood.

"Never again," she said coldly.

His fingers flexed on her thrillingly. "The thing about a *fantasy*, Zaiana, is that it can begin and end whenever we want." He used her name like a stroke on her senses, but she wouldn't yield any reaction to the prickling of her spine.

Instead, Zaiana summoned her vibrant purple bolts, and his teeth clenched at the mild shock. His hand tightening again on her only drew them closer.

"Keep testing me, Maverick," she said with seductive cruelty. "I dare you."

With a dark chuckle, the bastard angled and dipped his head, not breaking her challenging stare. "Must you tempt me?"

Fingers still poised under his chin, Zaiana wrapped her hand around his throat. The sharp claws of her two iron guards pierced his skin, releasing a stronger current of electricity that made his body tense. She didn't stop until he fell slowly to one knee before her. "You wouldn't still be breathing if I caved to my fantasies about you." She released him with a shove, and Maverick took a few long, hard breaths.

Yet still, his insufferable smirk remained.

Zaiana stepped away, not sparing him another glance as she headed to dine with death.

The castle of Fenstead was ominous in its neglect. When Valgard invaded, it wasn't to any courtly system. Their fae had scattered and occupied rooms without any effective form of leadership. As soon as Dakodas showed up, that changed. A tension lingered in the air, a dark sense of foreboding, as though death whispered around every corner, ready to seize. The essence of the Goddess emanated through the walls.

Zaiana knew where she would be as the Spirit spent her time simply basking in the present, indulging on food and wine, and likely getting her fill of whatever desires she could within a fae body. Zaiana showed no emotion at the knowledge those particular indulgences were likely enjoyed with the dark fae trailing behind her. She didn't care about what Maverick did to be Dakodas's prized pet.

As she glided into the throne room, she noticed the sky through the tall glass windows was eerily overcast. Vines of dead blooms climbed the rows of pillars, and the depictions on the cream stone floor were barely visible through the coating of dust and blood spatters. Upon the throne, which appeared to be crafted entirely of white antlers, Dakodas reclined at a sultry angle, a golden chalice poised beautifully in one hand. She appeared a Goddess in every sense of the word. Shadows surrounded her on the royal seat. Zaiana halted a respectful distance away, bowing low.

"Rise." The Spirit's voice traveled as smooth as ice. As she straightened, Zaiana locked her onyx stare, which gleamed with the confidence of a predator. "You have been very…silent. I should think someone of your reputation wouldn't be so content to be idle after triumphing in such a quest."

Zaiana wasn't sure what response Dakodas was hoping for. She didn't have an answer to justify her pathetic silence. The Goddess expected Zaiana to celebrate their win and seek praise and reward. Instead, she'd kept her distance and allowed Maverick to take what was rightfully his. Yet it was becoming clear he hadn't disclosed the truth to the Great Spirit. The truth that if he hadn't arrived, Dakodas wouldn't be sitting here now in the presence of Zaiana's cowardice.

"I've been awaiting instruction for our next move," Zaiana responded carefully. She should be fearful, or at least hold admiration for the divine being, but she remained impassive.

The curl of Dakodas's black-painted lips was beautifully cruel. "Always looking for the next thrill. I have always greatly admired that about you."

A sense of disturbance unsettled her. How much of her life had been studied by the Spirit while she'd watched over their world? What weaknesses and failures of her long past might Dakodas have seen?

Zaiana assumed she'd find immense pleasure in bringing Dakodas to their realm, the savior of her people, but her quick bout of adoration hadn't lasted long. In her time of reflection, Dakodas had become just another highly regarded fae with immense power. The more accustomed she became to the Spirit's presence, the less Zaiana submitted to the natural order of things. She had no respect for her. But to voice her treasonous thoughts would be a sure death sentence dealt by the embodiment of the dark force herself. So Zaiana would stay silent, obedient, and do whatever it took to win the war now tipped in the dark fae's favor.

Then she would leave it all behind. Everything. Everyone. To claim her freedom.

Dakodas's hair spilled like ink over her back as she tilted her head to sip from her chalice, her eyes fixed on nothing, seemingly lost in her own thoughts. Then she rested her head against the tall side of the throne, her attention settling with a flare of desire on Maverick as though she'd finally remembered he was present. Zaiana's two iron guards cut into her hands, which were clasped tightly behind her back. She didn't want to be around their insufferable flirtation.

"Word has begun to spread. The King of Rhyenelle's lost daughter is dead."

Zaiana yielded no reaction to the news, didn't let her mind linger on the human, for the flashes of her last moments still stung like a chill down to her bones.

"Maverick is of the opinion we should be making plans to strike the mighty kingdom while it is weakened. I would rather like to hear your opinion on how we should react."

"I would have thought we'd be meeting with Marvellas."

The Dark Spirit curved a brow at Zaiana's boldness, but Zaiana had very little to lose. She'd heard so much mention of the Spirit of Souls, the first to ascend and the one who began the war, yet no one had seen her. Marvellas hadn't once visited the mountains in Zaiana's lifetime.

"My sister is rather *preoccupied*. A slight setback in a plan that would have had the heirs of High Farrow, Fenstead, and Olmstone under our control."

Zaiana's interest piqued. She didn't know anything of the movement to take the three kingdoms. From the frustration that creased the Spirit's brow, she concluded they must have come close to achieving their goal, and she was curious to know more. For now, she had more pressing personal matters to focus on.

"I agree with Maverick," she blurted, deliberately not meeting his gaze when it snapped to her. "We should be preparing to attack Rhyenelle, but not without careful consideration."

Dakodas straightened, passing her chalice to a fae whose hands quivered.

Zaiana tried not to cower at the keen attention. "I want to go alone to mark out Rhyenelle's defenses. I can remain hidden and spend some time tracking everything to report back. Reylan Arrowood is Rhyenelle's strongest general. He's one of those who survived us in the mountains to deliver the news of Faythe's death, and since he'll no doubt have told his king all he discovered about us, they'll be preparing for the skies. We need to find out what new defenses they'll put up."

Dakodas displayed the full might of her gifted ability: Shadowporting. Shadows surrounded her like spilled smoke. There were either too many to contain or she simply enjoyed their company. The Spirit's fingers reached idly to play with the living tendrils as she tipped her chin elegantly upward. Zaiana's proposal seemed to please her by the slow half-curl of her mouth.

"I should go with you," Maverick cut in.

Zaiana tightened her hands, but before the protest could spill from her open mouth, Dakodas inserted her own plan.

"There is a different task I require of you, Maverick." Her hand barely extended, but the command was clear.

Zaiana gauged Maverick's hesitation, believing she saw reluctance in his rigid poise as he crossed the distance toward her. When the Spirit's hand curled around his forearm, Zaiana looked away.

"I want the body of Faythe Ashfyre."

Both their gazes locked on the Spirit at the grim request, and a dark chuckle snaked through the hall.

"More specifically, I want her sword. The Riscillius within it."

Zaiana believed she had witnessed the pinnacle of gruesome and disturbing acts in her lifetime, but her flashes of memory from the temple…of watching such ferocity fall to utter misery…the silver-haired warrior who cradled Faythe's body… Those thoughts would haunt her like a ghost.

"And if they've taken her back?" Zaiana asked.

"You will travel to Ellium together. If they've taken her there, then the two of you have the task of seeking out her sword. If not, then you will part so Maverick can find it while you continue to scout the defenses."

It wasn't Zaiana's ideal quest. Mostly due to the company, but she couldn't argue against going with Maverick without rousing the Spirit's suspicions. She kept silent on her real reason for needing to be alone. Tynan and Amaya would still be out there, possibly looking for *her*. She'd left them on the mountain edge with the fae, and the twisting unease that they may not have triumphed against the rest of them in her absence churned her stomach. She even gave a passing thought to Nerida, wondering if the fae had chosen to go against Tynan and Amaya in the presence of her own kind, her Waterwielding ability granting them another powerful ally to stack the odds greatly against her companions.

"I would like to leave tomorrow," Zaiana agreed reluctantly.

Dakodas tipped her head back against the throne. Her hand caressed Maverick's arm. "I am sad we will be parting so soon, but you are right to view this with urgency." She glanced at Maverick, lust swirling through her dark eyes. He slid his hand along the Spirit's shoulder, and as much as Zaiana wanted to tear her attention away, she couldn't help but study his movements. They appeared stiff, unlike his charged touch still imprinted on her skin.

"If that is all, Your Grace," Zaiana bit out, wanting nothing more than to be free of their public affections.

"I have one last request of you."

Something about the sparkle of sin in her black eyes locked Zaiana's spine straight. The following silence coiled like anticipation in her gut as she waited for the command she couldn't escape. Not when it came from Death herself.

"The opportunity presents itself, with him grieving and weakened, to erupt the kingdom into chaos and conquer it once and for all."

"What do you need me to do?" Zaiana's claws pierced her skin in her irritation and dread. She already knew what Dakodas would say but hoped for a different command—*anything* else.

Luck was never in her favor.

Dakodas's smile cut with wickedness. "I want you to kill the King of Rhyenelle."

CHAPTER 3

Faythe

CRACKLING WOOD AWOKE her with a surge of panic. Breath speared her throat as her eyelids snapped open. The darkness Faythe was met with was full of stars, each one emitting a flickering amber hue. The sight soothed her terror, along with the awareness that enveloped her.

Faythe twisted her head, and through the tango of flame she found Reylan sitting on the opposite side of the fire. His hair was long, held back from his face by twin braids. His face had lost years. He seemed so much younger, yet his expression was of one who had been forced to grow up too fast. His hands fiddled with a knife and piece of wood.

But when his eyes met hers…they were still the same starry blue.

She blinked and her vision gave way to the present. Reylan appeared exactly as she expected him to, though she couldn't erase how precisely she knew the intricacies of his younger self. Slowly, Faythe propped herself up, observing him carefully. The conflict of emotion turned her thoughts to loose threads she couldn't connect to understand her true feelings. Reylan had closed himself off.

That wasn't difficult to detect. A clenching pain took over her chest, growing the longer she struggled to decipher what he was thinking. The tension that echoed between them felt...*wrong*.

Faythe was confused. So torn and confused in her heartbreak she didn't know who she was anymore. Would she ever know? This new body and a harrowing destiny. Discovering all this time she had a *mate*. All of it a stark reminder of what she *wasn't* anymore. Human.

Reylan had made their camp on a small, open patch of greenery. He halted his carving while she stared at him, rare conflict set around his eyes. It seemed he was straining to keep his distance from her. Their mutual silence became like a slow suffocation.

Faythe sat up fully and got to her knees, unable to drag her attention from him as her mind raced with questions she already had answers to, but which she needed to hear from him. Questions about what they were to each other.

"How long have you known?" A pain nagged her from within. His, hers—she didn't suppose it mattered. But the moment his lips parted to respond, she echoed the same words with him.

"Since the day I met you."

Faythe shook her head, feeling a fool for not realizing sooner. Reylan's firm expression creased.

"You've told me before," she explained. By the fire in her room in High Farrow. At the time, she thought he meant he knew who her father was, and that was true, but it wasn't the *only* thing he meant. Faythe ran a hand over her face, unable to silence her reeling thoughts. "You thought you had no choice." Her eyes stung, and her emotions rushed to consume her as the pieces slid into place, the sadness so overwhelming it stole her breath.

Nothing made sense before. It didn't make sense for him to want her—to *love* her—in her mortal form, doomed from the very beginning.

"That's not true. Not even for a second," Reylan protested firmly.

When she forced her eyes to meet his again, she found they were *angry*. The fire dancing across his expression added anguish to his sharp features. Though she winced to see the harsh lines on his face, she couldn't deny the part of her that believed, for his sake, it would be better this way. Better for him not to want her.

They stared off for a suspended moment. Faythe couldn't look away. She loved him so fiercely that the best thing would be to set him free against all desire for the opposite. She could reject the bond—

"You know it cannot be undone," Reylan reminded her, detached from emotion.

He read her thoughts so effortlessly. An unexplainable link had always run between them, but now it was like a wide-open channel in its clarity.

Yet a taunting thought surfaced that wasn't entirely true.

Faythe was missing an explanation. A truth. She didn't know what trickled through her mind to convince her not to stop trying to figure it out.

Reylan added in her silence, "But if that's your wish, I will accept it."

Something in her chest, her soul, cried out so sharply it cleaved through her. She recalled Kyleer's words. Their bond wouldn't be complete without the mating.

Reylan's eyes flexed as she contemplated the prospect. He was in pain. Pain she had caused. Though it was nothing compared to what would come if she tore apart their bond. Still, the war was set in motion. Faythe's life was tied to it all. And the thought of bringing him down with her was one she couldn't bear.

"Before you decide, you should know…" He paused, steely features softening a fraction as he searched her eyes and rose carefully from the log he was perched on. Faythe's head angled back to track him as he took a single step toward her. "I've always felt that I was searching for an answer that didn't exist. Every dark path I walked, there was always a light. Every time I knocked on death's door, I was coaxed back before the reaper could answer. Where I expected to see shadows, I saw flickers of gold." He huffed an incredulous laugh with a shake of his head. "I believed then perhaps it was a cruel, twisted joke. This tether that always seemed to stop me from casting myself into the final realm was really held by my eternal tormenter, the one who brought me back because I deserved to suffer. But it was you. It had to have been you. Though I don't expect you to believe me."

He took another step, maybe even two. Faythe's head continued to recline, her gaze captured by him. He was so tall… and broad…and *fierce*. Her need for him grew with every fraction of closed distance.

"One time I even felt you. I was so recklessly drunk and had gotten into a fight with many fae who beat me to near death. I was ready to die then, but as I fell into oblivion, I wasn't only caught by that tether; I was coaxed to reach back and *follow* it. So I did. Toward a light so consuming I thought that was it. The end. And then there you were. I didn't know who you were, but by some miracle you brought me back. My consciousness…entered yours."

Faythe stiffened completely.

"I knew. That night you asked for my help to Nightwalk to Nik, in your gold-and-white mists, I knew I'd been there before. *Felt* you there before. In what I believed to have been a vision in my dying mind. I couldn't see your face since you stood with your back to me, but I answered your call for me to come closer. And when I touched you…when I first felt your skin…the heat of your neck you exposed to me so willingly, it was like…I found my *reason.*"

Reylan halted right in front of her. Faythe tracked him as he slowly crouched down. When he opened his palm, Faythe glanced at the small, delicate carving he held.

A butterfly.

"Tell me it means something to you," he said.

Faythe frowned at the item, her mind racing with the will to give him what he longed for, but she came up blank. Reylan's jaw flexed with disappointment, but he kept on trying.

"I have something I've never been able to let go of. A ring intricately crafted with golden butterfly wings. I don't know where it came from, and I suppose all this time I've rested my mind thinking it was my mother's, but that's not what I truly believe. I sealed it away and tried to forget about it…until what came to me in my dying moment not long ago seemed so familiar I had to follow it. I began to hear thoughts, but not in words. They were echoes of wonder and loneliness and dreams. I don't think I found you, Faythe. At least not at first."

Her heart thrummed so wildly at his soul-searching stare.

He said, "I think you found me."

Faythe remembered. Her head weighed heavy as the memory flooded her. "I see you, and I hear you…" The incredulous words escaped her lips. They weren't just a promise from High Farrow.

Reylan's knees entered her vision, near touching hers. "Look at me, Faythe," he pleaded softly.

She shook her head, unable to comprehend. "I thought it was simply my own childish fantasy. I wasn't accustomed to Nightwalking and Nik was helping me to understand. But I was so lost that night. Without even realizing, I was searching, reaching, for…" The lump in her throat grew painful, but she bravely met his stare. "You were really there, weren't you? You answered me. And I think when you arrived in High Farrow, some part of me *did* recognize you. Enough that I couldn't fear you. It didn't make sense. You were from Rhyenelle, and I'd never left High Farrow. It wasn't possible…"

Reylan didn't move. She couldn't read his blank expression.

"I refused Agalhor's request to attend the kings' meetings. I was set to leave for Salenhaven with no plans to return. So instead, he chose a high fae lord to act in his place and Kyleer to seek out the spy. I packed to leave. I was equipped and minutes away from leaving the castle for good, but I foolishly forgot my sword. I never forget. When I went back to my room to retrieve it, I caught a glimpse of the golden ring I didn't realize had fallen from its box and lay coated with dirt on the floor. It brought me to my knees. I dusted it off and couldn't stop apologizing for neglecting it. I felt as if I'd failed it by giving up. In myself…in my search for this *thing* that didn't exist. Salenhaven was my cowardly plan to run away from it all. Until I saw that ring again and knew I couldn't leave. To regain some sense of purpose, I accepted Agalhor's offer to go to High Farrow, as delirious as it sounded. I knew I could get the main task done the most efficiently. Kill his spymaster. But when we arrived there, when I went before the king, there you were. Your eyes, Faythe. Then, now, perhaps long before, something awakens in me every time. They have become my sun, and should darkness fall for good then so will I."

Then came more internal conflict. *Remember.* But Faythe couldn't, and that desperation almost broke her as much as his tale.

"I heard your voice…and I couldn't understand how I'd heard it before. I didn't want you to ever stop speaking."

Faythe blinked. She couldn't be sure the silver in his eyes was real until the tears spilled and flames flickered in the glistening trail running down his cheek. Reylan had surrendered, his raw emotions open to her, and Faythe's heart seemed to stop. Or shatter.

"It wasn't the discovery of who you were to the king that made the thought of what I'd come to do so unbearable. It was because I fell in love with you slowly. Torturously. I resisted knowing time would divide us, but I couldn't stop. Your strength, your will, your heart, your smile… *Gods*, that smile, Faythe. You captured me completely the moment you showed me it. Because you had been through so much. You had nothing. And when you smiled it was as if life held no burden.

"I'd never before encountered fear like that which I felt in High Farrow's throne room. I felt the power claim you. I felt it clawing to take this bright and precious thing I'd been searching for, and it dawned on me right then, without a doubt, what you were to me. My mate. If there was no fighting, if you wouldn't survive, then neither would I, and so I reached for you. The ruin came so close to taking you, and in that second something so heartbreakingly impossible overcame me. It felt as if we'd been there before, and I was so desperate not to lose you again."

Again.

Faythe took a moment to compose herself against the flashes of images. The throne room. Then a wide-open field. Both scenes screamed in her memory, but only one she grasped with full clarity, and that terror was enough.

"Just know, before you decide what you want, I choose you, Faythe Ashfyre. With or without a bond. As human and fae. I choose you in every life. Your promise to me was that you would always come back to me. And you did. I spent thirteen agonizing minutes believing you never would. Your heart...*stopped.*" The word came out through a pained breath that brought fresh tears to her eyes. It struck with the ghostly truth. "Everything was so still and cold I truly believed mine had stopped too. Thirteen minutes, twenty-nine seconds. You were gone, and I couldn't stop thinking there would be no other salvation. No other search. I would have followed you, but not until I hunted down Maverick and strung out his death for taking you from me. I still plan to hold true to that. But this is my promise to you: no matter what you decide or what may try to separate us, even if you reject the bond, I will always stand by your side."

Nothing else mattered in that moment. Not time or space. War or conflict. The world around them ceased to exist. Faythe was still so riddled with confusion and uncertainty, and Reylan seemed tied to all, but right now, they'd both suffered enough.

She rose to her knees. Her hands met his face, and her thumbs brushed the fallen tears. She'd never seen him look so utterly defeated. She harbored anticipation and fear, but she slowly slid onto his lap, her thighs spreading over his where he kneeled. Her hands moved over his skin, vibrating along his jaw, his neck, until her fingers wove through the silken locks of his silver hair. The sudden urge to find an outlet for her raging emotion was almost too much to bear—especially in this body that could withstand far more than before and took everything to new exhilarating heights.

Reylan's hands carefully grazed her hips, and Faythe lowered until no air could pass between them.

"Why didn't you tell me about the bond before?" she asked, her voice hushed, eyes darting between his. She tuned in to the quickening of his pulse, *scenting* a shift she deciphered as lust. So many new discoveries were expanding her world beyond what her human self imagined. What frightened her was her excitement to experience it all.

Reylan's hand didn't leave her as his fingertips curved up her spine. Her body answered as if she were molding to his every touch. Her mouth parted, and she pressed tighter to him until his palm cupped her nape.

"Out of fear of the very *wrong* reason—which has already crossed your mind—why I'm standing by you. I don't choose you because of some answering bonded power. I choose you because I love every damn reckless, brave, impossible part of you."

His lips crashed to hers, the surprise eliciting a small whimper from her. Their mouths and tongues clashed, every sensation exploding far more than anything she'd experienced before.

"You lied to me," she rasped against his lips, but they didn't break apart. What they shared was an explosion of desperation and anguish, need and heartache. Her hips ground against him, and he groaned.

"You wouldn't have believed me." His arm hooked around her so quickly she barely had time to prepare until her back met the ground. But in this body, the hard terrain didn't register against her strengthened muscle and bone. As fae, Faythe could withstand far more than her feeble human form. She felt…*powerful*. Even if a sting of horror struck her chest each time she became aware of what she was now.

"I deserved to know," Faythe got out.

Reylan's mouth left hers to meet her jaw, and her fingers tightened in his hair. Every press of his lips, every squeeze of his hands, shot electrifying currents through her nerve cells. "You deserve a lot of things, Faythe." The gravel of his voice traveled over her neck, where her veins pulsed with such desire she almost climaxed. "I plan to give you them all."

With enough of her sense and frustration returned, Faythe's leg hooked around his hip, and she pushed up and twisted simultaneously. It shouldn't have been possible, but with her newfound strength and having caught Reylan unawares, her maneuver made him fall to his back, leaving her straddling him. She breathed hard as they shared a bewildered look, long seconds suspended in time. Then the slow curl of his mouth accompanied the hunger in his eyes at what she'd done, and they collided once more.

Faythe's empowering position sparked her pleasure. She couldn't explain her urge. It was something deep and terrifying, arising as though he might vanish in a second and she had to make each one count. Her mind lost control to her new body's demands. Every touch of his fingers on her spine aided the rock of her hips against him. It was all so much *more* than before. Igniting, maddening, every taste of him driving her so far beyond thought or reason she wondered if the need for him could ever be sated.

When her mind took back control, Faythe abruptly pulled away, pressing a hand to his chest to keep him down while she panted to gather breath—and her sanity. "I need time," she breathed. Only a small circle of sapphire broke through the darkness of his claiming gaze. Faythe shook her head to dismiss her words then tried again. "No, thirteen minutes was enough. But I'm so confused, Reylan. I want to know why you kept it from me."

Reylan pushed himself upright. Faythe's fist curled into the material of his leathers as he did, keeping her in his lap. His rugged breaths and the desire glazing his lusty stare fought with restraint, but he held still, allowing her to decide every move.

"It was never my intention to deceive you. But I couldn't stand to think you might believe I was here for any other reason than because...you are everything. And perhaps selfishly, I needed to know you wanted to choose me too. What we have is far more than a bond, and with or without it, I am yours."

Faythe shook her head, and the defeat that flashed in his eyes elicited a sharp twist in her chest. "Nothing would have made me turn from you. But I trusted you. With every darkness, with every impossible truth, I trusted you." Her voice broke as she added, "You didn't trust in *me.*"

"I wanted to confess I suspected the bond the day you surrendered yourself to me behind the waterfall. But I couldn't... I couldn't ignore the fact I would have given my life for you at any moment on this quest, and that it would have been cruel to leave you here with that burden. Knowing I was your mate."

My mate.

Her breath stilled as if she were hearing the declaration for the first time. Because coming from him...nothing ever sounded so joyously possessive. With him she belonged.

Faythe brought her mouth down to his. The pulse to be with him was so strong she couldn't fight it. She remained confused and scared, her thoughts a mess and questions still unanswered, but she *needed* him. Reylan's arm tightened around her, but just before lust clouded her mind once more, he broke away.

Leaning her forehead against his, she asked, "Why do I feel like this? Like I can't get enough of you. I want to shout, cry, but..." Her fingers curled in his hair while her thighs tightened.

"I think you're adjusting," Reylan said.

She peeled away to watch his contemplative face scanning every inch of her. Slowly, his hand came up, brushing a loose strand of hair behind her ear, where his stare lingered. Her *pointed* ear. She couldn't fully decipher his expression. Awe enfolded with a haunting realization, perhaps.

"You are magnificent." Reylan claimed her. "My Phoenix."

Faythe went to speak, but his lips grazing her jaw stole her words.

"We're stronger than mortals. Faster. We have more primal needs and instincts. We feel more deeply." His lips pressed firmly to her throat. "Heartbreak. Anger." Lower, and her breaths quickened. "Lust." A soft sound escaped her as her head tipped back, exposing her neck without thought, *wanting* him to bite. "Perhaps I will." His voice was pure gravel as he answered her loose thought. "But not until you ask. Not until you say you are mine without reservation will I claim you, Faythe."

She fought against every new impulse willing her to surrender.

Reylan pulled away, holding her stare instead. "Every emotion needs constant outlet and balance, or it will consume us."

Us. A simple assurance she was not alone. He was here, and he understood. Yet her panic spiked of its own accord. She looked away from him, mulling over the concept. She had a hard enough time keeping her emotions in check as a human, but as fae… Faythe was already beginning to experience how quickly her feelings turned. How they clouded and consumed.

She thought she heard her name, but a prickling heat began to crawl over her skin, awakening in her palms the most. They slipped from Reylan's silky tresses as her gaze flashed down to the source of the sensation. Faythe wasn't sure there was any breath left in her lungs as the world broke away in fragments. The marks within her palms glowed faintly, along with the vine of finely scribed letters she couldn't decipher that ran past her cuffs. She tumbled back to the present when a cool touch took her hands, inspiring a gentle breeze within. The faint glow winked out, but Faythe couldn't tear her eyes from the Spirit symbols.

"I don't know what I am." She echoed the haunting thought so quietly, trying to process it all.

His fingers curled under her chin, forcing her to look away from her upturned palms to meet his calming sapphire eyes instead. "It doesn't matter what you are. I see you, Faythe." The determination of a warrior, a protector, filled his hard gaze. "I see you as *who* you are. Exactly as I always have." Then a ghostly terror overtook his expression, rattling a chill down every notch of her spine. "I almost lost you." In no more than a breath did he hush the words as though he didn't mean for them to escape. Reylan remained unblinking as though she might vanish now he'd dared to speak them.

The drop in Faythe's stomach was too much to bear. This raw, unprotected version of Reylan had been exposed by her. "I'm here," was all she said, matching his volume. Because the thought of how close they'd come to being parted so finally would forever torment her too. "You brought me back."

His mouth pressed to hers firmly in promise. A soft whimper escaped her, a pain so twisting she thought it might erupt in her chest. A pain of sadness and happiness. Of love and betrayal. So many clashing emotions she didn't know what to do with other than let Reylan help by the only means she knew how.

Right before she gave into the burning need entirely, a spike of awareness stiffened her body. A presence. Not immediately nearby, but somehow she *sensed* the distant approach and couldn't place who the intruder was. Or what. Terror gripped her entirely, threatening to consume her with the flash of fresh memories that rammed into her. Perhaps the dark fae had returned.

And Dakodas.

Oh Gods. In all her bewilderment and world-changing revelations, Faythe hadn't accounted for the biggest event to unfold—the one she'd missed entirely during her own Transition.

The Spirit of Death now walked among them.

A soothing caress stroked her senses, accompanied by Reylan's touch trailing down her spine in reassurance. He must have detected the presence too, but he appeared wholly unconcerned. A flickering of shadows made her jerk away from him, but then a familiar voice carried across the distance.

"Here I thought I'd be arriving onto a far more desolate scene."

Faythe immediately recognized the voice, but her head still whirled in fright. She clutched Reylan a little tighter while she remained straddling his lap.

Kyleer's smile broke in relief as he strolled toward them casually. Then, as his green gaze found her, the curl of his mouth became stolen by wide-eyed vacancy. She saw the moment time stopped for him and struggled to comprehend what he was looking at. His attention seemed fixed on her ears before it shifted to Reylan then back to her. She'd never seen him look so ghostly, nor at such a loss for words.

Despite their newfound company, Reylan's mouth hovered below her ear, his breath causing a shiver as he said quietly, "We are so far from done here."

CHAPTER 4

Zaiana

ZAIANA WAS FASTENING the buckle at her shoulder when an unwanted intrusion made her teeth clench. "What do you want, Maverick?" she ground out, not turning to him as she continued to equip herself for the journey she was to set out on that afternoon.

"What are you up to?"

His suspicion wasn't subtle. Zaiana fitted a blade to her thigh, another to her waist, then strapped her sword belt over her chest, sliding the blade into its sheath on her back.

"I think that's obvious." She finally glanced him, and his flex of ire where he leaned against the doorframe was to her delight.

"You're not some scout to be sent on errands." Straightening, Maverick adjusted the cuffs of his leathers, which she noted were also of combat style, before stalking closer.

"You don't need to concern yourself with what I'm up to. We may be leaving together, but I expect we'll part quickly."

"I'm heading to the city."

"You're to retrieve Faythe's body; you should be heading to the Isles."

Maverick's walk slowed as he assessed her. The bastard was trying to read into any expression that might give away some ulterior motive. "I think we both know I would find nothing there." He smirked at her defiance as Zaiana's features firmed. "There's no way they would have left her there."

She didn't allow her tenseness to ease at his conclusion.

"So, it looks like we'll have the pleasure of each other's company for a while longer. Who knows, maybe you'll come in handy as a distraction while I infiltrate the city and retrieve the dead human's sword? It's all Dakodas wants."

Zaiana couldn't protest his plan. Not without giving away her own. "Just stay out of my way," she warned him, then she headed out to the balcony.

Hoisting herself onto the flat railing, she cast her eyes over the land, imagining it once vibrant and thriving. Yet the greens of the hills were now dull, flat, and yellow, the trees' spindly branches barren, and the fallen leaves dry and black. Not from the shift of autumn, though it felt as though winter were eager to fall this year; what made this land desolate was its reluctance to show its true beauty to the monsters who walked it now.

Zaiana closed her eyes at the sad sight, taking a long, freeing breath of the cool air as she released the glamour on her wings. She rolled her shoulders, feeling their glorious full weight. These wings would carry her to the vast skies.

"You don't plan on saying farewell?" Maverick asked at her back.

"No, I don't." She splayed her wings. "And I'm not waiting around knowing how long yours might take with Dakodas." She stepped off the high ledge, enjoying the embrace of gravity before she defied its laws, shooting skyward, eager to leave the kingdom she'd conquered for Valgard behind.

Heights would always be Zaiana's comfort. Being far above most creatures came with a sense of power. Her mind was eased of its heavy burdens and her demons relented as though their cage had been opened into the endless sky.

She sat dangling a leg over a cliff edge, observing the city of Ellium from such a distance that all she could make out were peppered buildings encompassed by two high circular walls. The construction was smart, she thought. Not a class divider but a brilliant defense.

For anyone without wings, that is.

The crimson-peaked mountains surrounding Ellium also offered protection to the heart of the kingdom. Zaiana was beginning to admire the ancestors of Rhyenelle.

"Five hours, give or take," she said, not turning around when Maverick landed behind her. "I assume Dakodas was far more reluctant to let go of you than me."

"Jealousy doesn't suit you, Zaiana."

She scoffed. "Give me something to be jealous of. I'm sure I could wear it quite well in blood."

His chuckle was smooth as he drew closer. "What's the plan then, delegate?"

The Spirit's order still rang through her mind. A daunting task with the highest prize. It wasn't the act of killing someone that disturbed her; it was *who* wore the target. To be known among her kind as a Kingslayer would no doubt earn her respect like no other, perhaps even put her above the Masters. She might also bear the title of Master now, having won the trial against Maverick before the quest, but Zaiana despised it, feeling it bound her to their wickedness.

She stood. She'd glamoured her wings a while ago and enjoyed the thrill of toeing the fatal height without knowing if she could free her wings in time should she fall. Maverick's boots shuffled through the gravel behind her as she looked down.

"Our destination might be the same for now, but our plans are different," she said.

"If you stopped being stubborn, you'd see our plans could work together."

She turned to him. The wind picked up and she adjusted her footing against its push. Maverick braced, eyeing the ledge while trying to hold her stare. Canting her head, Zaiana shifted back, slipping her heels over the edge.

"What are you doing?"

"I'm going to fly closer to the city."

"Your wings," he bit out as if she weren't aware of her glamour.

Zaiana smirked, sliding back again until only her toes strained to keep her on the ledge. She closed her eyes, enjoying the force of the air that threatened her balance.

Then she was falling.

The air that wrapped around her felt like a pull into another realm—one that both stopped time and made it race. Hair whipped free from her braid. She knew the seconds were zipping by fast and she had to adjust her careless backward fall, yet she didn't want to. To a risky proximity she wanted to test how long she could enjoy the drop into nothingness. A part of her chanted not to twist and release her wings: a small voice full of dark taunts but also the promise of peace and liberation. Just as she was about to succumb to its demands, something wrapped around her, and her eyes flew open. Her breath whooshed at the impact, arms and legs instinctively clamping around the force that stopped gravity's claim.

Maverick's onyx eyes were livid, his brow pinched tight with ire. Zaiana couldn't help herself—amusement broke a grin.

"You really thought I'd fall to my death?" She toyed with his obvious irritation, but when he didn't respond, her smile began to fade. She quickly became aware of the position they were in. A flash of memory, but not with him.

Never with him.

Zaiana's wings expanded and she let go of Maverick, despising the shiver that shook through her at his grip. They stared off in the sky for a moment, but she couldn't decipher the battle between them. Without another word, she shot away. Her wings beat harder. She pushed and pushed, needing the voices to be silenced. Needing the feelings that battered like fists against the locked vault of her mind to stop. She kept flying until the air thinned and an ache formed in her shoulder blades.

 She welcomed the pain. She needed more of it.

CHAPTER 5

Faythe

"Does one of you want to explain what in the Nether happened?"

Kyleer kept advancing, his eyes not leaving hers. He looked, but it was as if he didn't know who he was seeing. A sense of dread pierced Faythe at the thought she might have the same reaction when she finally stood in front of a mirror. She couldn't bear the notion.

She got to her feet, but she didn't know what to say to him to explain the impossible. The truth of how she was still here and alive when she never should have emerged from that cave. Kyleer was right: he should have arrived at a far more desolate scene. One Faythe had witnessed herself, and which would haunt her for eternity. The sight of her pale, still body cradled by the broken warrior beside her.

Reylan's hand on her back reeled her back to present, where she hadn't broken eye contact with Kyleer. Her attention dropped to his shoulder as she recalled the battle.

"You were injured," she got out, but Faythe noticed he appeared in no pain or discomfort. "Badly."

Kyleer shook himself out of his stupor. "As luck would have it, the dark fae had a healer in their company," he explained, still looking at her as if he were interacting with a ghost. A thousand questions swirled in his eyes. "We convinced her to aid me first. Izaiah was wounded worse, and my ability could help to get you to safety if needed. Nerida was tending to him when I left."

Reylan's hand stiffened on her as Faythe's thoughts became riddled with urgency. They had to go to them.

"Does one of you want to tell me what happened here?" Kyleer diverted the topic tentatively. His pointed look wasn't subtle, and Faythe's stomach turned with denial. She couldn't blame him for his reaction, but it served as a reminder that she didn't know who her dearest friends saw when they looked at her now. Didn't know who *she* would see.

"We will. But right now, we should get back." Reylan's words were a command for Kyleer not to press further.

Faythe was grateful, her stiff shoulders easing a fraction as her explanation scrambled in her mind and lodged in her throat. For now, she threw up a barricade against the question, knowing she'd come apart again and again if she were made to relive the raw memories.

Kyleer nodded with an edge of reluctance, but abiding by her wish, he extended a hand. "I'll Shadowport you back. Reylan will borrow enough of my ability to carry himself." His smile turned tender with encouragement as she looked down at his hand, and it soothed her nerves to see he wasn't treating her any differently. She knew that hand all too well, with its slightly crooked fingers and long, raised scar, as it had been her guide in the dark when they'd faced the tunnel collapsing around them.

Faythe took a half-step to reach for him, but a jolt of memory halted her. Her pulse skipped as she straightened, her head whipping back over the mountain edge, past the trees.

"What's wrong?" Reylan reached for his weapons in alarm.

Faythe cast her gaze upward, expecting to find flames far brighter and more alluring in the night sky than those in the small man-made campfire. "Atherius," she mumbled because she couldn't be sure it wasn't all a figment of her imagination. She near swayed with dizzying disbelief as she recalled how she got here.

The Firebird had saved her from her own reckless plummet off the high cliff as she sought to gain its trust. It had brought her here, yet she couldn't be certain what was real since arriving at the Niltain Isles and meeting her end.

"The Phoenix?"

She heard the wariness in Kyleer's tone and nodded. "It was her."

"You consumed a lot of power. Your memories are likely to be gray," Reylan added softly.

They were tiptoeing around calling her delirious and mistaken. While it grated on her nerves, she couldn't deny it until she knew the truth.

"The bird was real," Reylan assured her. "It's impossible this is the exact one you speak of."

Faythe didn't believe anything was impossible. Not anymore. But she was too tired to argue, and it seemed the great Firebird had made itself a whisper of embers once more. She couldn't deny that the thought of never seeing it again dropped with the weight of disappointment in her stomach. Was the bond real, or had she imagined that too—that she could *feel* the Phoenix within her? Perhaps she'd never know.

"Let's just go," she muttered, not wanting to stay on the island a moment longer. She glanced at Kyleer's palm as it once again extended to her in offering. Her stomach was already churning at the notion of Shadowporting. "How long does it take?"

Kyleer smirked. "I think you're the first to ever ask that."

"It will only seem like seconds. Less than a minute," Reylan answered.

Kyleer kept his amusement despite Reylan's sternness, his eyebrow cocked as if in challenge at Faythe's hesitation. "Shall we?"

47

Shadowporting was just as she remembered, except the extended distance made her motion sickness stronger than when Kyleer had traveled with her across the mountain edge to avoid the dark fae's lightning strike. Faythe braced herself, eyes clamped shut as she forced back nausea. But most of all, she fought to suppress the wave of memories from that battle that threatened to undo her. She had so many questions, but right now, she needed to make sure everyone was safe.

Kyleer's hand made her jolt. He winced at her reaction and backed away. Faythe wrinkled her face in apology. She couldn't shake her skittishness at this new ability to detect things it shouldn't be possible to detect. Her senses were held permanently on a razor's edge.

He observed her with a look of caution that only added to her unease.

"I'm fine," she muttered. It was a lie, and he knew it. As they held each other's stares, her brow pinched tightly. Faythe shook her head, her voice barely a whisper. "I'm not fine, Ky."

Kyleer nodded, his arms opening just as she took the step to fall into them. She didn't cry or speak or do anything except embrace him tightly, as if he were a lifeline. A further assurance that this was real and she was here.

"You will be," was all he said, but it meant so much in his understanding tone.

Reylan's presence enveloped her before the shadows cleared to reveal him at Kyleer's back. They released each other, and a muscle in Reylan's jaw flexed as his eyes shifted between him.

"As if he wasn't enough of a possessive bastard before," Kyleer grumbled, but there was a smirk of amusement as he twisted to his brother.

Faythe didn't know what he meant by that.

As Reylan crossed the distance toward them, his expression softened and his gaze didn't leave Faythe for a second, assessing every inch of her face. She forced a weak smile at his obvious concern. It was hard to offer him any reassurance when she had no concept of how to accept herself.

A distant murmur carried on the wind grabbed her focus, and she cast her eyes in the direction of the sound. The longer she homed in on it, the louder it became. But it was overwhelmed by the quiet whistle of the wind, the shuffling of mountain creatures, and the rustling of foliage—things she shouldn't be able to hear with such clarity. Then she distinguished the voices and stumbled back to the present, taking her first steps toward them. The others. Desperation canceled out everything else. She *had* to know everyone had made it.

"Faythe, slow down." Reylan's voice accompanied the gentle pull on her arm.

She slowed to a walk, not realizing she'd broken into a run.

"They'll all be okay," Kyleer assured her. But the implication that some of them could be gravely hurt didn't settle the pain in her gut.

Her pace was quick. She was unable to slow her steps toward the voices that drew her closer until they emerged onto the mountain edge, where she stopped dead in her tracks. Faythe's hand rose to her chest as though Zaiana's lightning had struck her anew. Her body became as heavy as it would if the rain were falling mercilessly even though the night was clear. Her eyes found the spread-out group, but she could only focus her attention on the one thing that breathed life to haunting memories of facing the dark fae in battle.

Wings.

It wasn't only their companions who crouched and stood around the space. Faythe's adrenaline spiked to a frightening high as she noted their company. The kind of terror that gripped her ability to move was the same kind that sealed the fates of those who succumbed to predators rather than fighting back. Despite the power she should harbor and the body that was *stronger,* Faythe had never felt so weak.

A gentle breeze tamed that surge of fear enough to reel her back to the present, where she found everyone's interest had snapped to her. And no one was fighting. Faythe took a second to glance over them, checking for any injuries, surprised that it appeared the dark fae were *helping* them. Reylan stepped up beside her, but she couldn't tear her eyes from everyone to utter her gratitude to him for grounding her. Instead, she walked toward them.

Faythe was too busy analyzing everyone to feel the itch of their stunned attention. Izaiah and Livia had sustained the worst injuries, but it seemed even they were almost fully healed. A stunning blond dark fae straightened from his lax position against a rock, inching closer to a younger one crouching by a fae. The healer, Nerida, Faythe concluded, who looked at her as if she were a ghost. They all did. Faythe slid her attention to Reuben, who locked his gaze on her ears, incredulous as the realization dawned that he was now the only human on the mountain.

Nerida was the first to find a voice among the bewildered faces of friends and foes. "Remarkable," she breathed.

Reylan was so close, near touching Faythe as though ready to shield her from the slightest threat, verbal or otherwise.

"I'm unconscious, aren't I?" Izaiah was unblinking as he rose. A glance at his charred clothing made Faythe wince. "This isn't real."

"It is." Reylan's tone was harsh, and Faythe knew why. She grazed his hand with a need to add something physical to that assurance.

"So you're—"

"Yes," Faythe said, putting all effort into pushing down the panic and nausea that threatened to undo her now she had an audience surrounding her, all on tenterhooks to hear the story of how she came to be.

Reylan's hand took hers fully to halt the rise of anxiety. All she could muster was a weak squeeze in response.

"I'm glad you're all safe," Faythe went on, hoping to divert the topic. She would explain what happened in those caves and how she stood before them now no longer human, but she couldn't let herself believe it changed anything. She had been given an immortal body on mortal time. Nothing was promised.

The shift of a shadow had Faythe's other hand grappling for Lumarias at her side. The tall dark fae inched closer to his companion. "We'll be on our way," he said, but with a sharp edge that implied hostility. It was there in his stance too, the male braced to lunge toward the young dark fae and do whatever necessary to fight them.

"I don't think so, Tynan," Kyleer said, his voice nowhere near Faythe though she could've sworn he was on her other side. From the shadows he emerged behind the dark fae, and Tynan hissed as the point of his Niltain steel blade pressed into his back. "You and Amaya will be coming with us."

Tynan reached for his sword despite the odds.

"We don't want to kill you," Izaiah cut in, but Faythe was sure she heard a softness, a faint plea, in that tone.

"Doubtful," Tynan snarled.

"What are you going to do with them?" Nerida rose from tending to Livia's wound, which seemed on its way to being fully healed. The commander winced as she got to her feet.

"We're taking them back to Ellium," Reylan decided. The command in his voice sent a shiver down Faythe's spine. "They're prisoners of war now. We need to start preparing for a force like we've never known in our lifetime."

Kyleer's eyes trailed the length of Tynan's wings as Reylan spoke, curious and calculating.

"I want to know where they're hiding. What makes them weak. What hurts them. I want to know where Maverick is."

Those threatening notes were chilling from the general. Faythe blinked. Twice. She was sure her eyes hadn't left the dark fae, yet a shimmer briefly rippled over those towering, lethal wings before they…*disappeared*. Tynan's eyes flashed expectantly to Amaya, who read his command, rolling her shoulders before her own wings vanished in the same manner. Now they appeared like any other fae. The fact was both awe-invoking and horrifying.

"Many dark fae harbor the gift of glamouring," Nerida explained to Faythe and her companions. "To tell them apart now would require knowing the shift in scent or how to check their blood."

Faythe studied Tynan's subtle but careful awareness of the

darkling. It was as though he knew that if he attempted his own escape he couldn't guarantee hers. Despite the evil she'd witnessed from the dark fae so far, his protection of Amaya…it was an inkling of humanity Faythe chose to let ease her resentment.

"I hate to be blunt…" Livia's voice was still laced with pain as she leaned against a tall rock. "But what in the Nether happened over on those Isles?"

That spiked Faythe's pulse once more, catching everyone's attention again. Reylan turned stiff beside her, ready to sway conversation, but Faythe knew she couldn't allow her fear to smother the truth from those who deserved to know.

"I guess you could say I died," she said, eyes fixed on the ground because she couldn't bear to see the mix of emotions. Their thoughts and feelings, they swarmed her as if she were a magnet of minds, far easier than before. She blinked hard. Threw up a steel wall to silence some, but it would take practice to master and block them all out. Faythe blew out a breath. "'Transitioned' is what I believe it's called."

"You're dark fae?" Tynan bit out in partial accusation, as though it were her choice.

Reylan's flash of rage was quick and hot, felt through a separate tether that had nothing to do with Faythe's ability, and she was glad to find she could remain open to him but closed off to everyone else. Before he could voice his wrath, she shook her head.

"No, just…" She had to pause. She had to breathe. This reality was far harder to voice and accept. Death was an easier fate to believe.

"Fae," Reylan finished, his words accompanied by the stroke of his thumb on her hand.

Faythe could only muster a nod, biting back any further explanation. Because the truth she hadn't had the chance to confide in Reylan yet was that she was not fae nor dark fae. Not human either. She was something else entirely that remained to be discovered. Her lips pressed shut as her mind rang with Aurialis's reminder to be safe in their present company. The dark fae could still escape, and they couldn't be sure on which side Nerida's loyalty lay.

"I think I've heard of that before," the healer said, fascinated. "Fae being created. But Transitional spells are of the darkest magick. They always require something specific."

"It doesn't matter," Reylan said in a way that ended the conversation about Faythe's *situation*. "What does matter is that Zaiana and Maverick succeeded. Dakodas walks our realm, and they have the Dark Temple Ruin."

"Gods above," Izaiah muttered.

"The Gods won't save us," Livia grumbled.

"No, they won't." Faythe didn't balk at their attention this time. The scale of what they were up against was enough for her to suppress her own troubles for now. She couldn't afford to be weak and selfish. "Nor do I think they ever have. We need to start preparing for the greatest war the realm has seen. A war against the Spirits Marvellas and Dakodas."

"And what of Aurialis? Surely as the last true all-powerful Spirit—"

"She's gone." Faythe cut Nerida off. But as she did, she could have sworn a pulse emitted from her chest. "At least, there's nothing she can do for us now."

The healer was observant; her eyes flashed down to Faythe's other hand by her side, and there was something of question and wonder in them before Faythe clamped her fist around the golden mark. Nerida didn't voice her curiosity.

"You said that you died." Livia retraced her steps carefully.

Faythe slid her attention to the commander and gave a small nod.

"The dark fae and Dakodas—did they see it? Believe it to be true?"

Her stomach hollowed, but she cast her eyes up to Reylan, the only one who could answer. Her knees almost buckled at the quick flex of his expression. Maybe the others wouldn't notice his soul shattering behind his eyes as he remembered that moment, but she did. Faythe squeezed his hand.

"Maverick and Dakodas. I believe they did," he said with a hard edge.

Faythe had never felt more helpless about how to make such a grim, desolate event less traumatic to revisit in memory. She knew no measure of time would lessen its impact.

"Zaiana?"

Reylan's eyes flashed to Tynan, whose posture flared at her mention. "I can't be certain she didn't suspect what was happening to Faythe when she left after the Spirit," Reylan said.

"She would have told Dakodas." Kyleer's statement held a question, followed by the shift of his blade on Tynan.

All eyes pinned the dark fae. His lips pressed together firmly. It was clear he would sooner be cut down than spill a word about his leader.

"I don't think so," a quiet voice said hesitantly. Amaya shrank into herself when the attention shifted to her.

"Say nothing more, Amaya," Tynan warned.

Conflict warred on her delicate face. It was hard to believe the darkling could harbor any of the evil instilled in her kind—or at least the evil they'd been led to believe the dark fae were formed of. Apology was written in her green eyes. She seemed to want to share more about their master.

"Zaiana isn't a mindless follower. She's smart. I don't believe she'd give up such knowledge if she suspected Faythe was still alive, not without biding some time to see if it could benefit her first."

Kyleer huffed a humorless laugh. "Her prize will be in displaying her undying loyalty to the Great Spirit by outing Faythe's Transition."

"You're wrong." The darkling was brave. Despite facing off with powerful fae warriors and the only other of her kind being unable to save her, Amaya didn't appear frightened. "Glory has never been a prize to her. If you can think of nothing else she'd have to gain from delaying such invaluable knowledge from getting to Dakodas, then you're all fools to underestimate her. Zaiana's not afraid to defy orders."

Amaya spoke of Zaiana with such pride it was difficult not to admire her sense of perception. Faythe tried not to think of the bright amethyst eyes that had swept over her along with phantom shudders of lightning.

"We can't trust a word either of you says." Izaiah dismissed her.

"We might have to," Livia countered. She looked to Faythe, who tried not to balk. "We have a chance at gaining the upper hand here. If they think she's dead…so will Marvellas. If she discovers you didn't just live but came back stronger than ever, her hunt for you will take a far more destructive turn. You don't have to share everything you went through with us now, Faythe, but it's hard not to believe it marked a powerful change that could turn the tide of this war. Marvellas and Dakodas would know it too."

"What are you saying?" Reylan asked.

Livia looked between Faythe and Reylan as though she knew her suggestion would immediately be met with protest. "We're not all returning to Ellium," she explained. "Faythe isn't going back."

CHAPTER 6

Faythe

THE GROUP SET up camp in a patch of forest near the mountain edge where they'd battled the dark fae. A whole day passed, and night fell once more. Faythe barely heard the conversations of her fae companions. Their bickering seemed repetitive and offered no solutions. Instead, her mind was preoccupied with silent calculations and wonder. She let the others battle it out without her as though they had the final say on what she chose to do.

Livia's plan was simple: Faythe should avoid returning to anywhere she could be recognized. Not Ellium; not High Farrow. But to what end? This was what the rest of them debated. The key point that struck a nerve with Reylan in particular was that he *would* return to the capital.

To deliver the news of her death.

"You're the strongest of us all. To make this believable, you need to be the one to emerge and tell the story."

"That's a bullshit reason," Reylan growled.

Faythe sat on a log by the fire, letting the ripples of flame calm her mind and soothe her heart from the ache that formed at

Reylan's distress. She fidgeted with the wooden butterfly in her hands, her brow pinching every time her mind wandered to the memory of that night with him in her subconscious.

"You haven't eaten." Kyleer settled down next to her, his voice low as he offered her some stale rations.

"I'm not hungry," she answered, pocketing the wood carving.

"Your body would disagree. I'm surprised you haven't collapsed already. I imagine your fae form is burning nutrients far faster than you're used to."

She couldn't deny her exhaustion. Faythe had barely moved all day since the mere thought was tiring. It made sense that it was due to her new body's needs, and she should have realized it sooner, but there was so much else to deliberate over.

Kyleer nudged the rations wrapped in a bundle of cloth toward her once more. He wasn't going to take no for an answer. Faythe took them, offering a grateful smile as she began to pick at the food, trying to settle the greater twist in her stomach at the mention of her fae form.

"You're the one Agalhor trusts the most. The only one who might get him to listen when all Nether breaks loose at the news. Sending Kyleer and Izaiah on their own with the dark fae won't be convincing enough. I'll be with Faythe. She'll be safe with me." Livia's voice turned soft toward the end.

But it was then that Faythe had enough of being silent. "I'll be safe on my own," she said, drawing the attention of the camp. The dark fae sat together at the opposite end of the fire. Nerida remained near Amaya, while Izaiah watched them carefully should they attempt to flee. "Let them believe their frail human *princess* didn't make it. Because it's the truth. I can't explain what I am now—I'm still figuring that out. But I'm capable of looking out for myself." Faythe shifted her gaze to Reylan, and it was an effort not to plea with him. "Livia is right: you need to be the one to tell him. We owe him that. You won't have my body, and they'll be speculating why that is. Agalhor alone needs to know I'm still alive, and you're the only one he'll listen to long enough to hear it after you announce my death in front of everyone."

Reylan was already shaking his head. "I only just got you back."

Stunned he'd let his vulnerability slip in front of the others, Faythe held his gaze, but it was as if he didn't even remember they were here.

"If something happened while I wasn't there...if they found you—"

"They won't," Faythe interjected, wanting nothing more than to be alone with him. "I know a thing or two about remaining hidden."

"Going alone isn't an option," Livia said. "I don't doubt you, Faythe, but none of us know what you're capable of yet. Right now, you're just as much a danger to yourself as you are to those around you. I'll be coming with you. Let them believe I didn't make it either."

Faythe flexed her fists against the heat that began to form in her palms. She wanted to protest, but as Livia's knowing eyes flashed down to them, she ground her teeth and looked away in defeat, hating that the commander was right.

"We still need to travel out of the mountains together. We'll decide what to do next when we reach open ground." Kyleer stood as the voice of reason, and reluctant grumbles were exchanged before everyone found their own spots around the campsite to settle down for the night.

"I can take first watch," Faythe said, coughing to clear the last bite of dry bread that stuck in her throat.

"I've already got it covered," Kyleer assured her.

She bit her tongue to stop herself from arguing back. Every time she offered to help, one of them jumped in first, and it was grating on her last nerve that they weren't letting her weigh in on anything. Reluctantly, Faythe took her spot beneath the tree trunk and accepted that this was just another thing she'd have to let the others take the lead on.

She hadn't had any real sleep in days. She couldn't as nightmares worse than any she'd ever been plagued with before awaited her in slumber. She was afraid to greet the darkness, having been in the embrace of a darkness so final, and she couldn't shake this new, deep-set terror that it was still beckoning to her.

Hours passed. Faythe sat against the tree trunk wide-awake. The others slept soundly, and in her fatigued state she admitted there was a part of her that envied them. Her head lolled against the wood as she stared through the endless distorted rows of tree trunks, their eerie silhouettes lifting the hairs on her arms. They inspired visions of the dark caves that stole her former life. She couldn't soothe her racing mind.

Reylan lay close by. Faythe guessed he was sleeping. He appeared as still and silent as the others, and as her gaze slipped to him, Faythe found a sight so precious she wanted to capture it. She imagined herself reaching for the strand of silver that was almost touching his eyes. She *felt* herself tuck it back, but it was now too short, and in her frustration she wanted to know exactly when he'd decided to cut it and why. It had happened too long ago for her to believe she already knew.

She studied his face instead. When awake, Reylan's expression was rarely free of creases of horror and concern. Knowing she caused it all was a permanent weight on her chest. He deserved better. He deserved more than to be fated to one so tangled up in darkness and desolation.

Faythe couldn't bear it anymore. With feline stealth she got to her feet and began to distance herself from the camp. She wouldn't go far, but she needed a moment to feel alone. Even though they were all asleep, being around her companions still coated her with unease. She didn't know who she was anymore, and she felt her companions' eyes like a mirror. She'd studied them over the past day, trying to figure out what they saw behind their tentative, wary gazes, but…they looked at her with as much uncertainty as she felt within herself.

She knew where she was headed; she just needed to get out from below the canopy that seemed to compress her tighter. It was as if the trees were wooden bodies huddled together, engulfing her in their masses. While her fae body granted her far more stealth to be silent than her human form, she couldn't stop her clumsy footwork in her rush to get clear of the trees. Claustrophobia gripped her throat and burned in her eyes. She gritted her teeth, hating the weak, irrational, helpless state she'd been reduced to so easily.

She was not underground. Not in the temple of darkness anymore. She was free and alive.

Breaking out past the tree line was how she imagined it would have felt to emerge from that cave, though she hadn't had the chance to do so before losing consciousness. Bracing her hands on her knees now, Faythe breathed and reeled back her adrenaline to prevent the same thing from happening again. Then she walked out until she was toeing the edge of the high mountainside. The cool, unrestricted air eased her panic.

She sat dangling her legs over the edge, not fearing the great height. Memories of her leap off the mountain to gain the Firebird's trust inspired a surge of *strength*. She wanted to feel that kind of high again.

"Mind if I join you?"

Kyleer had been lingering behind her for some time now. She didn't mind it and was glad he'd given her some space to calm down before he finally approached. Faythe only twisted her head in response, giving a small smile, and he read that as acceptance. In truth, she was grateful for his company.

Her thumb idly traced the golden symbol in her palm, unsure of what to make of it.

"It's just power." Kyleer spoke to her thoughts. "It changes nothing about who you are."

She swallowed hard, wanting so desperately to believe it was true. "Power is changing. It's a darkness within us all," she whispered. At the mere thought of the well of magick she was afraid of —lest she find it bottomless—she felt it awaken with a whispering heat. "What happens when one has more than any person should?"

She didn't know what it was about Kyleer that made her so effortlessly bare all to him. She knew he would help or even just *listen* without any judgment, even if he didn't know all the answers.

She didn't need him to say anything, only hear the terrors that kept her from being able to embrace what she was now.

"It's okay to want this," Kyleer said carefully.

Faythe turned to him. It wasn't the reaction she was expecting, but it made her pulse skip a beat.

"I watched you train many times, always pushing as though you could match us when you knew it wasn't possible. Not before. It's okay if you find yourself not entirely horrified to be fae."

A small weight lifted with his words—one she didn't realize had been growing these past few days. But that momentary reprieve was quickly doused by her concern.

"I'm not just fae, Ky. I don't know what I am."

"Do you think that matters?"

"How can it not?"

"Because if you still hold love for those you loved as a human, still treasure the same memories and hope for the future…why should it matter?"

Appreciation for his illuminating advice settled her heart. Faythe nodded, adding a smile to try to convince him of her acceptance. His face gave away a hint of defeat that told her he knew she didn't, not fully, when all this remained to be tested. The situation she'd found herself in was something she had to figure out on her own.

"Reylan isn't the only one with plans to seek vengeance on the ones who did this to you. Maverick and Zaiana best enjoy their days until we catch up to them."

"She let me go," Faythe admitted. "Zaiana. I don't know why. She had me. It should have been her who killed me. But she let me go."

Kyleer was silent for long enough that Faythe had to know what expression he wore. His brows were set in deep thought as though the beautiful dark fae had been consuming his mind long before now.

"Had you met her before?" she asked.

"No," he was quick to say, face smoothing out as if he were banishing her from his thoughts completely. "She's not a face so easily forgotten. Regardless, she harmed you. And everything that happened to you can be traced back to her."

Faythe couldn't disagree. While she'd released her resentment for Zaiana, it wasn't her place to convince Kyleer to let go of his. Awareness tingled at her nape, but Reylan didn't come any closer, instead lingering under the canopy at their backs.

She met eyes with Kyleer, and it warmed her that somewhere along the line of their friendship they'd developed their own unspoken language. His smile as he read her face told her he didn't mind leaving to give her and Reylan some alone time. Kyleer stood and gave her shoulder a gentle squeeze before walking off.

Reylan's advance was slow, careful, as though he could spook her, and she hated it. Not his caution, but that he felt it was necessary. He said nothing as he sat in Kyleer's place. Close, but not close enough when she had such an urge to feel him.

"The nightmares are back," he stated at last, his voice tentative and pained.

Faythe nodded. "I don't think it has anything to do with forgiving myself this time," she admitted. Maybe what caused the nightmares now was something she would never find freedom from. For there was no one else she knew who'd survived the touch of death.

"Maybe not forgiving,"—he aired his thoughts—"but accepting."

"Why does everyone seem to think I haven't accepted what's happened to me?" she snapped—and immediately regretted it. Reylan wasn't deserving of her anger. Faythe bowed her head, tucking her arms a fraction tighter around her knees. She was afraid.

More than anything, she was afraid of herself.

Reylan stayed silent, and she couldn't bear to look at him, knowing she'd come apart the moment she did. She spoke her thoughts aloud instead to the wide-open air that stretched on for miles above treetops and mountains.

"It's as if there's a fire beneath my skin. Shallow, just a hum in response to the thoughts I can't silence, but I think it's a warning.

Of what I am…what I could become. I feel…I feel as if I could burn the world with a thought. I wouldn't mean to, but it's there. Like a tempting trigger. I'm a liability waiting to detonate, and when I do…I can't be certain it'll only be our enemies who catch flame in the fires." She paused, wondering if she should continue voicing all the thoughts that had been tormenting her since she awakened in this new form. "I don't feel good or fearless or powerful. I feel…*dangerous*. The kind that's unpredictable. That won't spare friend or foe. And I'm afraid." Finally, she found the courage to turn to him. It was an effort not to whimper at his glittering blue eyes that reached out for her, pleading to help and not knowing how. Faythe extended her hand, sliding it over his. "Do you feel it?" she whispered desperately. "Tell me you feel it."

The tension in his body spoke of his shock, making her believe he felt that dangerous power too. But she had to hear it from his lips. Had to know she wasn't alone in harboring the entity that was neither good nor evil. It was whatever her heart willed it to be, and that was completely and utterly terrifying.

Reylan shifted closer until their bodies were almost flush, side by side, and his palm met her face. "I feel *you.*"

Her brows knitted together at that.

"I need you to know that before all else, that doesn't change. But I feel the power too. You're not alone. Never again." His hands encased hers and Reylan tentatively flipped her palms upward, holding her stare in case she objected. When she said nothing, his gaze dropped.

Faythe's pulse fluctuated as she followed it.

Reylan's touch was gentle and soothing as he ran his thumb over Aurialis's golden symbol. "We've seen markings in your palms before, but not this one." His wonder seemed like a question.

"And not permanent," Faythe added.

His anger seemed to dance with sadness—no, *disappointment*—as though he blamed himself for what had happened to her. "Faythe…" Her name left his lips in a breath.

She shook her head, averting her gaze, but before he could interpret it as her not wanting to share, Faythe spoke. "I don't know what it means," she tried. Tried to form the answers to her own tormenting questions. Questions the Spirit of Life had left her to discover on her own. There was no contacting her now like before because... "I had to change to come back. Into far more than just fae. Aurialis...I think her power lives on in me now, but I'm not sure what that is. I'm so scared, Reylan. Scared of what I could become and scared there could come a time I don't have any *control* over it." She willed her eyes to gauge his reaction.

Reylan watched her thoughtfully. His furrowed brow made her heart pound. Yet no matter the words he spoke, his calm voice could always soothe her racing pulse. "It's okay to be afraid, Faythe. Fear can be the weapon you need to rise. I've seen you overcome it before; it won't become your weakness now."

He was so sure, so confident. Faythe didn't know what she'd done for him to see such a strength in her. Then another flash of knowledge from Aurialis skipped her pulse as she gazed at his face. He frowned as if he felt her awe.

"You once said you'd only met a handful of others like you before—with your ability."

"I have," he confirmed.

"Mindseers."

Reylan only nodded, his confusion swirling through his eyes. Faythe had to tell him what she knew even if, just like with her own power, she wasn't sure what it meant.

"They can diminish a person's power, sometimes completely. But are you sure you've seen them *use* that power afterward?"

Reylan contemplated this, tearing away from her to stare as vacantly out over the land as she did. "I guess not," he said at last.

Faythe hated the disturbance she felt rising in the pit of her stomach like something bitter. Though it was Reylan's emotion she felt, it was one Faythe was well-acquainted with: the fear of not knowing oneself.

"I don't think I have the only impossible ability to have existed," she admitted carefully. Reylan didn't look at her, too deep in thought, but she watched the moonlight pool over his features. "You're Spirit Blessed by all three of them, able to harness any ability you take. It's something Aurialis believed could be valuable." She could barely whisper her conclusions; it was easier to accept she was the only one in danger. "I can't stand the thought of it, but if Marvellas hasn't already found out about your ability, as soon as she does, she'll want to come after you too."

Their silence became cold and heavy, but Faythe waited patiently for him to judge all she said.

"It changes nothing."

Relief relaxed her shoulders, but her fear remained a taunting force, convincing Faythe he could be taken from her. "Of course not."

He shook his head. "It changes nothing because she's not getting a chance to be near you. None of them are. Despite what use she might think she has for me, I don't care as long as she doesn't get to you."

Faythe opened her mouth to protest his fierce protection, but he continued.

"I'm not being heroic, Faythe, because what I would do to keep you from her goes far beyond any consideration for my life or morality. I won't care what becomes of tomorrow because there wouldn't be another I'd want to see again without you."

He reached a hand to her face. Every touch of his was so gentle, and she couldn't bear it. She needed to take back control of her emotions. And that started with showing Reylan she wasn't about to break with one wrong movement. Faythe shifted, hooking her leg around him so fast it forced him down. She straddled his legs before leaning over him, her chest pressed to his while her hair pooled by his head.

"I'm not made of glass, Reylan," she said, her voice dropping to a breathless plea with the desire that flooded through her body at the feel of him.

Reylan's midnight eyes were ablaze searching hers. His fingers grazed her temple, tucking the loose strands behind her pointed ear, where his marveling gaze stalled.

Then the air whooshed from her, and her eyes flew wide-open as his strong arm encircled her. When they stilled, Faythe was pinned on her back with Reylan hovering above her. The light impression of his hard, toned body ignited something deep within. His hand curled around her throat—not with any pressure, but in an enticing challenge.

"No, you are not." His voice was pure gravel. "My Phoenix."

Their mouths collided, and Faythe's spine curved with the need to be pressed impossibly tight against him. Feeling every glorious contour in this resurrected body of hers was like discovering him anew. Discovering *herself* anew. It was exhilarating. *Gods*, she wanted to explore every new possibility with him right there on the open mountain edge.

Reylan's arm slid under her back, which arched off the ground. Their lips didn't stop moving as he lifted her until her face was angled down while she straddled his lap. Their kiss slowed, heat and passion turning into a soft searching, a longing, as if they were both realizing at once their days were numbered before they would be separated again for another indefinite stretch of time.

They simply held each other. After everything they'd been through, there was never a more treasured moment than this: both of them alone, safe in the knowledge it wasn't the end for them.

"You just told me you feel as if you could burn the world with a thought." Reylan reflected on Faythe's words carefully. His face pulled back from where he'd been resting on her chest while her fingers weaved through his hair. "How am I supposed to leave you and go back to Ellium?"

Faythe huffed a short laugh. "Because I can't have you there to save me all the time. If I have any hope of discovering what I'm capable of, now is the opportunity." Her brow furrowed as she looked over his face, the thought of being parted so soon aching in her chest. "I don't like it either, but this is the best plan we have to find out if the dark fae know about me. One month. I didn't mention it earlier with the others because I've been thinking it over. Livia, Reuben, and I will head to Fenher. It should pass the time enough for you to at least escort Nerida home. If all is still silent, I'll head to High Farrow. Nik will be able to keep me hidden. It seems fitting, really, to go back to where it all began. Go back to my old life."

"You weren't born to remain hidden." Reylan watched her with an air of awe. "You were born to rise. Made to defy. To carry the dreams of those who can't fight for them."

Her brow furrowed tight in thought. "Do you believe in past lives?" she pondered. "Do you think you would remember…if you could come back?"

"You remember all, don't you?"

Faythe shook her head. "That's not what I mean. I— Never mind." How could she explain to him what she couldn't make sense of herself?

"You can tell me anything," Reylan said.

She lay her forehead against his and her eyes slipped closed. Part of Faythe hoped her muddled thoughts could be explained away by the fact her mind was still spinning wild from her rebirth. But in his arms, seeing the reel of images she couldn't ignore, Faythe could only treasure her deeper connection to him. The feeling of having known him for far longer than what they knew to be true.

"Promise me something?"

"Anything." Reylan's lips grazed her jaw, his voice prickling her skin. "Anything at all."

After a few lustful breaths, she said, "Promise me this will never change. That no matter what happens in the war to come, you'll remember that I see you and I hear you. And that I love you, Reylan Arrowood. In every lifetime, I will love you."

Reylan's eyes closed and didn't open again as he leaned forward to press his lips to her chest. Then he locked eyes with her to make his promise. "Before bond, title, or name, despite anything that could try to part us, I love you with everything I am, Faythe Ashfyre." His lips grazed hers. "Until the end of days."

CHAPTER 7

Reylan

REYLAN ARROWOOD SUFFERED through nothing except the chant of the declaration he was being forced to make. Not the wild pounding of the rain that battered him mercilessly, trying to drown him, slow him. Not the thundering of hooves as he rode through the punishing storm. He heard nothing but those words circling in his mind as malicious taunts. Felt only the painful weight of his failure.

He needed to return to Ellium. It was all that mattered.

He drew focus, knowing if he didn't, he risked losing his composure completely. He gambled with the idea of retribution; of damning the world to burn and unleashing his rage on everything in his path.

But that wouldn't help her. Wouldn't save her.

I failed her.

Reylan rode harder, not caring if his company kept pace or stopped. The fury in his bones pulsed so tense and hot he barely registered the noise of their horses' hooves behind him. If he let the anger go, devastation would take its place. He had to remember he still had a duty.

To her.

He couldn't stop recalling the memory that would haunt him for eternity. The failure he deserved to never find freedom from.

The minute the light in her eyes faded out.

The second the last breath left her body.

The suspended moment when his tether to her…*broke*.

He couldn't stop thinking with horror that it wasn't the first time he'd endured such agony. Reylan clenched his teeth. He wouldn't let the merciless beating of the brutal weather win its fight to slow his stride.

Nothing would stop him. He owed her that.

He owed her everything.

The outer wall of Ellium stretched triumphantly over the horizon. He galloped straight for it.

The gates opened swiftly upon his approach. Reylan didn't pause. He charged through the city, the thundering of hooves over stone alerting the sparse pedestrian traffic to move out of his path. The signal of his arrival would have already passed through their swift communication line and Agalhor would know. The cage of Reylan's chest threatened to break against the hard beat of his heart.

Barreling over the courtyard, Reylan tugged on the reins to halt his steed halfway. His breaths blew out hard, spraying the rain that rolled down his face. His cold eyes locked on the portico. On the King of Rhyenelle who stood there expectantly.

Reylan dismounted promptly, each step toward his king weighted as if stones filled his boots. The words he had to speak rose in his throat like burning flame. Behind Agalhor, the court flooded out of the castle, everyone's attention piqued at his obvious urgency in storming through the city. Under the cover of the courtyard bodies scattered and gathered, faces appearing in the windows surrounding them. Reylan held his attention on the king, but it was not returned.

Agalhor scanned the space behind him for far too long as if he'd already concluded what Reylan was to convey. The general stopped advancing, staying at the bottom of the steps.

"We were ambushed in the Fire Mountains by a force too great to defeat. A species thought to be extinct."

Agalhor pinned him with a wide-eyed stare, scarily firm and calculating. Reylan's soul was cleaved, but not for his king.

"The dark fae rise again."

Murmurs scattered—of horror and fear—creating a faint buzz barely audible above the inclement weather. Reylan stood unyielding against it. They had to know. Had to start preparing for a threat none of them could possibly fathom.

Yet it was as if the king hadn't heard his harrowing words.

"Where is she?" Agalhor asked carefully, the calm before an eruption of fury nothing would prepare Reylan for when he got the answer he didn't want.

Hooves clattered over the stone behind him, but Reylan knew as Agalhor noticed the others' approach he wouldn't find who he longed for. His next words sank talons in his chest and caused an unrelenting acidic burn in his throat. Because they were real. That dark acknowledgment slammed into him without warning, striking worse than any physical blow he'd endured and threatening to bring him to his knees. The rain didn't relent, nor did the darkness ease, as Reylan delivered the dire news that would shake the kingdom.

"Faythe Ashfyre is dead."

CHAPTER 8

Faythe

"It's him."

Faythe's voice was low as she kept her hood drawn, face angled down. Through her mask she'd been watching the fae by the corner all night, wondering if he was the crook she'd been on the hunt for; one of the Raiders plaguing the town on the edge of Rhyenelle. The mask that covered half her face was a necessary hindrance. Crafted beautifully to have depthless doll eyes and brows to match, the red was decorated with a pattern of black and gold. It allowed her to see out without anyone glimpsing her golden irises.

Livia set down her cup, not immediately turning to look. "How can you be sure?"

"He's been approached by two separate people this night. Each has been paid. The owners of this *fine* establishment clearly cater to his every need, yet he hasn't produced a single coin for the endless glasses of wine he's consumed. The barmaid—" Faythe halted as the fae raised a lazy hand to summon the beautiful barmaid. She was otherwise confident in her role, smiling as she tended to her other guests—except this fae. Her whole demeanor changed. She braced herself.

She *feared* him.

"Have you tried honing your senses? Extending your hearing to catch his name?" Livia shuffled her cards, in the midst of a game against Nerida and Reuben.

Faythe ground her teeth. She'd tried, yet every time she tuned her newfound fae hearing it overwhelmed her. She'd yet to discover how to block out every irritating noise she didn't want to hear to focus on one thing.

"No," she admitted.

Livia leaned back in her chair. Turning her head brought them face-to-face, and she flinched. "I'm still not used to that thing. It's creepy."

Faythe was caught between a smile and a scoff. "Try wearing it." She subconsciously adjusted the hard mask that had started to slick her skin in the heat.

"You're lucky I have been listening. You're right—one of his *clients* revealed his name earlier. I thought he was going to kill the fae right there. It's Nessair."

"I haven't *not* been listening. I don't know how you do it—separate the sounds, I mean."

"It takes practice. Even young fae need to learn how to master their senses."

"So I'm no better than a faeling?"

"Exactly."

Faythe bit back her disgruntled response. In the near month since they'd parted from the others, Livia had been trying her best to help Faythe with everything new that came with being fae. Every daunting thing that had her feeling out of control, out of touch, with her own body.

"Don't forget how far you've come since everything happened." Nerida was far more encouraging.

Faythe watched the barmaid approach Nessair apprehensively. He'd yet to touch her, but she kept a cautious distance as though anticipating the turn this infamous fae might take. His coarse brown hair needed brushing away from his eyes. He sported three long scars set at different angles over his face. He was the perfect depiction of a composed monster.

Nessair's reputation as the leader of a ruthless band of Raiders had put Faythe on his tracks over a week ago. As they'd set out to Fenher to return Nerida home, Faythe decided to get a head start on eradicating Rhyenelle's Raider problem, which she'd first learned about in Desture. Nessair reminded her—with fresh fuel for her rage and need for revenge—of Rezar, an evil fae whose life she'd taken for the human's he'd ended in her name out of spite.

And she would do it again.

Nerida set down her cards, sliding around the table and tucking herself in beside Faythe. "Look away from him," she instructed. "Sometimes it's easier to take away one sense so you can hone another. He's speaking right now—do you hear him?"

Faythe did as Nerida asked, twisting in her chair but keeping her head dipped. She strained to listen, to reach all the way across the room to where Nessair was occupying a whole booth to himself. His voice she recognized, but it was another murmur that began to throb in her head with everything else she heard.

"Vaguely," she responded.

"Now imagine he's the only person in this room. Just you and him. Close your eyes if it helps. One by one, start to erase the other sounds you don't want to hear as if they're not in the room at all."

She had nothing to lose despite feeling foolish for being unable to grasp the seemingly simple task. Her lids slid closed as she attempted to follow Nerida's instructions. A group of rowdy humans' slurs and loud jeering grated on her senses right away, and her instinct was to retreat. Then there was the barkeep pouring drinks: the clink of tankards, the running slosh of ale. The flipping of cards, the chiming of coins, the scraping of wooden chairs. Laughter. Voices. Laughter. Then…

It wasn't his voice but something else she tuned in to. The high pitch of steel being freed from a sheath.

Faythe's eyes snapped open, sliding back over to Nessair.

"I said I wanted wine, not ale, darling."

Faythe didn't have to try to hear those words as the fae's voice rose with his temper. His knife speared the table in an act of intimidation.

"Don't do anything reckless," Livia warned.

"Maybe you have something far more alluring to offer so we can forgive this mistake…"

The barmaid's shrill cry of protest echoed across the crowded room as Nessair grabbed her by the waist when she made to retreat. Faythe almost broke a smile as Livia swore, slammed down her cards, and disregarded her own command. With one swift throw, her dagger lodged itself into the wood by Nessair's head as she shot from her chair. Faythe followed in no rush, watching the commander handle the situation in awe. More gasps and squeals erupted as people sought distance from the conflict when Livia pounced onto the table, retrieved her blade, and held it to Nessair's throat with a vicious glare.

"Only a pitiful male needs to force a female's affection," she snarled.

To Faythe's displeasure, Nessair's smug lips turned upward in a smirk. "I was wondering what it would take to get you to make your move," he said.

Alarmed, Faythe clutched Lumarias and approached the two slowly. The fae slid his eyes to her then, and she tried not to balk at the attention. It was as though he knew…

Knew who she was.

"You've caused quite the hindrance for me with your antics, *Bloodmasked.*"

Faythe's stiff shoulders fell as he hissed the nickname, and she had to stifle her chuckle. With the crimson red of her mask, she supposed the name fit. Admittedly, she even found it flattering. They'd ended the threat of so many crooks during their stops in Rhyenelle towns that this was clearly the result of those efforts.

"Our antics won't be troubling you anymore," Faythe said. "Once you're dead."

Nessair gave a smooth, arrogant chuckle, but his smile

remained even when Livia pressed her dagger tighter to cut off the sound. Through gritted teeth he said, "There is a handsome prize for your capture." He leaned back as though this were a fight he was watching, not participating in.

Commotion began to rise behind them, and Faythe turned to spy several huge forms filing into the establishment. Nerida stumbled to get some distance from them. As a healer, she wasn't comfortable with violence, but Faythe had witnessed the lethal force she could become with her Waterwielding when it was necessary.

"Many have tried—and failed—to take her down," Livia said.

Nessair's side-smile turned feline. "It is not just her we're after," he said with dark glee. "Evander wants you as well, Livia Arrowood."

Faythe had never seen Livia gawk before. For the first time, a terror so stilling paled the commander's face enough to reveal a rare moment of vulnerability.

It wasn't Nerida's ability or Faythe's steel that was quick enough to stop Nessair's attempt to grab Livia; a full tankard of ale doused him, and everyone's incredulous gazes snapped to the barmaid. Nessair's cry was a higher pitch than Faythe expected.

Then all Nether broke loose.

Her instinct was to spin, immediately clashing swords with one of the others who appeared to have been waiting to advance from outside all this time. She cursed herself for not seeing the trap, but as she ducked under an attempt to swipe for her and picked up a nearby tankard to knock her assailant clean out with it, Faythe quickly decided she was enjoying the dangerous rush of adrenaline.

This wasn't the first group of bandits they'd faced, and it wouldn't be the last. Yet Fenher was only a couple of days' travel away now.

Faythe leaped onto the tables while the inn descended into chaos. Sparing a glance at her friends, she saw Livia had Nessair by his collar, her face heated as she spoke to him. The fae seemed to be mocking her. Meanwhile, Nerida was by the barmaid, the two of them trying to ease out of the fight, but two crooks approached them with sinister smiles. Faythe cursed colorfully, hopping between tables. From behind she jumped onto one of the crooks' shoulders. Hooking her leg under his armpit, she twisted her weight and brought him sprawling to the ground while her knee dug into his chest. He wheezed through his bewilderment, but the pommel of Lumarias connecting with his head knocked him unconscious.

Faythe hadn't avoided injury. She shook off her sword arm, which felt as if it had met with stone. Livia had taught her many maneuvers she'd been able to practice during their time together, ones she never could have attempted against a fae as a human. And while she had a lot to learn still, being free to explore her new strength and agility was the one thing that kept her from spiraling into thoughts of what else had changed within her. The power she had yet to touch. Even the mind ability she had before.

"Faythe!"

Reuben's cry snapped her attention just in time for her to watch him being dragged out by a hooded bandit. White rage stole her vision; instinct drove her movements. Faythe exploded out onto the street. The contrasting silence rang in her ears, and she strained to focus. The tail of a cloak disappeared down a dark alley. She shot toward it.

The stillness was deadly.

Twisting, she raised her sword to block the one that fell. In the same breath, she pushed off it, engaging in a quick sequence of attacks until she realized they were doing nothing but defending themselves and *studying* her.

The person wore a full-black mask like hers, though there was nothing painted on theirs.

"Who are you?" Faythe hissed, shoving off her next attack and taking a few backward strides.

They titled their head as if the question confused them.

Her heart beat against her rib cage as she wondered if this were mere coincidence. Another member of Nessair's gang, yet something about this one seemed more alarming than the crook inside.

"I want to know why you've returned now." The male voice sounded distorted through his mask.

Faythe shivered with a chill when it plucked a string of familiarity, but her mind offered no sure recognition.

The distraction cost her greatly.

She cried out as her arms were grabbed and the string of her mask pulled. She thrashed against the hold, but there were too many, and her cover fell away as they pushed her down to her knees. Breathing hard at the damning position, Faythe kept her head down for as long as she could, praying her companions would find her first. It was all about to be over. Perhaps these fae worked for Dakodas.

The scratch of a blade along her throat made her teeth clench. Faythe defied its sting until she thought they might truly cut her. She cast her eyes up. They'd been looking down on her in silence for so long she didn't know why they were bothering to waste time. The blade trailed along her cheekbone but didn't cut, and all she could do was pour rippling fury into her stare.

"Why give him mercy only to become his downfall once again?"

Nothing he said made sense. It was as though his words were meant for someone else entirely, but there was no hiding her face. Faythe could see no other way out of this, though it terrified her to reach into her newly sensitive well of magick. She didn't have his eyes for easy access, but with her newfound power, she found herself seizing his movements.

The choking sound he emitted surprised the others, who loosened their grip enough for Faythe to give over to the strength of her fae body. Her elbow jammed into one who groaned and released her free arm, allowing Faythe to reach over her thigh for a dagger, which she lodged into the second one's chest as she spun and stood then slipped it back into the holster. As they all rose to advance, so did Faythe's hand, and their splutters sounded out as she seized the four males who'd ambushed her, including their leader.

Her veins pulsed with a sickening heat. It gathered at her nape and ran down her spine. Faythe breathed steady against the dark chant to kill. Sweat slicked her skin, but she sent the three before her into unconsciousness before spinning to the masked male.

The slapping of feet sounded outside the ally, and in her second of distraction fire tore across her thigh. She cried out as she fell.

Faythe pressed a hand over the bleeding wound. Figures surrounded her, and Nerida's floral scent wrapped around her first.

"It's not that deep. I'll heal this in no time," she assured her, already rummaging through her disorganized satchel.

"You shouldn't have come out here alone," Livia scolded.

Faythe straightened on her knees, casting a glance around, but the masked assailant was gone. "Reuben was in trouble," she explained, realizing she hadn't found him. Her spear of panic settled when he came panting down the ally.

"I managed to fend him off," he breathed, examining the blood on his trembling hands, but he had no wounds of his own.

"There was someone," Faythe rasped, but she decided against causing a stir about a person she might never encounter again.

Livia was silent. Curious, Faythe found her staring down the alley, a ghostly *fear* paling her complexion that struck Faythe too.

"What's wrong?"

Accepting Nerida's help to stand, Livia snapped out of her daze. "Royal guards are close by. We should get out of here now," was all she said. She scouted the street from the edge of the ally, and when she deemed it clear they all took off running.

Anytime the group caused a commotion, their intentions were never to kill; only to alert Rhyenelle's swift guards to come detain the crooks as they made themselves scarce. They slowed to a walk when they considered themselves far enough not to be caught. Faythe noted the commander beside her was still quiet.

"What happened back there?" she asked carefully, examining

the disturbance that hadn't left Livia's expression since they came face-to-face with Nessair.

"Who is Evander?" Nerida asked.

The tremble that straightened Livia's back was so subtle Faythe might have missed the movement. It set unease in her stomach to see her so affected.

Livia shook her head. "It can't be the same person."

Faythe heard the commander's pulse drum with fear though she kept her exterior hardened.

"Who?" Nerida tried again.

Livia paused as she marched, and when she spoke again her words were dark and icy. "It's the name of my father. Reylan's uncle." She shook her head with a ghostly vacancy. "The one he killed."

CHAPTER 9

Reylan

THE AIR WAS too thick to breathe. Reylan Arrowood could hardly stand the tension that weighed down the small underground room.

"She's still safe?"

It wasn't the first time Agalhor had asked this, and while Reylan once again gave an affirming nod and relayed more of the truth about their quest, he knew the repetition was more for himself.

It had been several weeks since they parted. Twenty-seven days and sixteen hours, to be exact. As often as they could, the king met with Reylan and Kyleer in the secret underground room they rarely had use for, away from any possible listening ears so they could share updates. Reylan wouldn't admit it soothed his own anxiety to hear it confirmed over and over again that Faythe was safe when Izaiah returned from the skies where he'd been tracking the group's movements. But no measure of time could erase the fear that he could awaken at any moment and be right back in that cave that haunted him, cradling Faythe's lifeless form.

Kyleer stood to the side of the room. Izaiah was absent, posted to watch over their captives in the cells instead.

"They should be nearing Fenher by now, and if all remains silent about Faythe—if the dark fae don't know she's alive—she'll be heading to High Farrow," Kyleer reported.

Every day, every hour, every *minute*, every instinct in his body revolted at his being parted from her. "The dark fae are a force like we've never seen before. They consume human blood. It means they surpass even our best warriors' strength and speed," Reylan went on, sparing a glance at his brother with a wince having heard about his short battle with Maverick. A name that had become the sole trigger to his most murderous thoughts. One he'd marked to end no matter what it took.

"The two captives—have we gained anything more from them?" Agalhor asked.

"Nothing. They will not speak. We'll be moving on to harsher measures soon," Kyleer informed him.

Reylan felt nothing at hearing this. He himself would inflict whatever pain was necessary to get intel on how to combat the dark fae. But on a more personal level, he wouldn't rest until he found Maverick. "Try Tynan first, but he's protective of the darkling. Use her if you need to," he commanded.

Kyleer gave a nod of understanding. A knowing look passed between them, and he gave a second nod to acknowledge it before taking his leave.

Alone with his king, Reylan paced to ease the nerves he was unaccustomed to.

"Something troubles you." Agalhor spoke.

Many things. All of them circling back to her.

He had wanted to confess this for a while, but with everything they'd had to tame and control these past weeks under the guise of Faythe's death, there hadn't been a right moment. Yet Reylan's deception had begun long before this quest. He halted, and it poured out of him. "I need you to know it was never my intention to deceive you. Or her." He'd never felt like such a fumbling fool, childish even. "I also need to make it clear there is nothing I would ever do to harm her, and nothing I wouldn't risk for her. Should all of this have been a horror of reality instead, I would not have returned from such a failure. That is what she means to me."

Agalhor squared his stance. His eyes pinned him with a cool warning that dried out Reylan's throat. There was a chance it wouldn't matter, his confession. That he never had been and never would be worthy regardless of it.

"Faythe is my mate."

No other sequence of words would make that fact any easier to deliver. Though it struck him with pride and fleeting liberation to voice the secret he'd harbored for so long, unwilling, *fearing*, to believe such an impossible dose of magick could be real.

Agalhor's stillness was unreadable, his silence heavy. "She was human. How can you be sure?"

It wasn't acceptance. His tone still held an edge of warning.

"I'm sure."

There wasn't a single doubt in his mind. Their bond—it was unexplainable with words, so he didn't try. Not to anyone except Faythe.

"My daughter will return to us," Agalhor went on tentatively. "She is Rhyenelle's heir." Two titles for her, and he was purposeful in using them. The implication was there. Both wedged a distance between who she was and who Reylan was.

"Yes, she will." He tried to remember who he was speaking to. His king. "And yes, if that is what she wishes to be."

"Who she is will not change."

"You think I don't know that?" Reylan broke down. What Agalhor shed light upon was something he'd kept buried in his torment for so long, since Faythe had decided to come to Rhyenelle and he was torn between his gratitude at having her near and the realization that who she could become here would station her out of his reach.

A princess… He was not an ideal match under the judgment of court. Reylan wanted to believe it didn't matter, but that was a fool's thinking.

Agalhor's posture eased, but only with a pity he couldn't stand.

"I cannot be the one to stand in the way of the heart, but what I will say is that it is not without challenge and opposition for you both. It is not without difficult decision and harsh judgment for *her.*" The king drew near, his hands always clasped behind his back. "Even then, it may not matter what I think. Not as a king when there is a whole council to appease."

It was a dark sorrow to believe he wasn't worth it—what she would have to go through to choose him. And she would. He held no doubt she'd want to choose him, and he wouldn't have the strength to let go.

"Let me ask you this," Agalhor said, his tone dropping to a personal note. "You've stood by my side for a long time, Reylan. Could you bear to stand in my place instead?"

That was never Reylan's goal, but the reality hit him suddenly. He'd never truly considered what being with Faythe could mean one day if they convinced the court of their bond. The responsibility of a crown and kingdom that came hand-in-hand with loving her. It was something he had never desired.

Reylan didn't need time to think it over. "I would do so for her." He couldn't read Agalhor's silence enough to know if he accepted the answer. It didn't matter.

The king took a deep breath, pausing shoulder to shoulder with Reylan as he made to leave. "You've always been like a son to me. I know your father would be proud of what you have achieved, as am I."

Reylan braced to receive what he anticipated would follow. The king spoke as no more than a concerned father about his daughter.

"But make no mistake: she will come first. Her choice will be final, and I will stand by it regarding you or this kingdom. She has been through enough."

His parting words lodged a new dagger in Reylan's chest. He stood still long after Agalhor left, simply staring at the distorted underground walls that flickered with cobalt flame.

Reylan Arrowood had battled many torments since leaving Faythe. He'd never endured such a helpless yearning. It was torture and a pitiful state of mind to exist in. He wanted nothing more than to be by her side, but the lingering taunt remained that they were not promised to each other. Not with the war that threatened, titles that separated, nor names that cursed. She didn't deserve everything she dragged along in her shadow, but no matter what, he couldn't be parted from her again.

CHAPTER 10

Nikalias

NIK WATCHED HIS mate in awe. It was becoming a habit for her to dismiss her handmaiden, but he had no complaints as it meant only he was left to help fasten her gowns. He was only partially dressed in pants when he had to take a moment to watch her. Tauria's leg was propped on the seat by the fireplace as she slowly dragged the material of her stocking up the glorious length. Nik couldn't tear his eyes from every mesmerizing movement she made from where he sat on the edge of the bed.

When she'd finished, the material clinging to her thigh to keep it in place, her gaze slid to him with a knowing smile that stole his breath. Tauria straightened, letting the flowing green material fall. When she picked up the other stocking and strolled over to him, his mind turned wild.

"If you're going to sit there gawking, you can help."

Nik swallowed as she held the stocking out to him, their gazes locked in heated challenge. Only a week since they'd finally arrived back from their trials in Olmstone and he'd hardly been able to leave her be for a moment, in constant awe that this was real and she was his. Every morning he awoke with her in his arms and drew her in a little closer, always bearing the irrational fear she could vanish in a heartbeat.

Nik took the stocking from her. Tauria didn't break her challenging stare as she bundled her dress and lifted her bare leg, placing it on the bed between his. Nik broke, his eyes devouring every inch of her smooth brown skin in a maddening rush of desire while his hand traced her calf.

"You are a wicked thing," he muttered.

Tauria yelped as he pulled her off-balance, his other arm wrapped around her waist. His hand continued higher with her thigh now hooked around him.

"I don't think you need them."

Tauria smiled coyly, her hands sliding through the back of his hair. "The autumn has brought on a chill these days."

Nik's slow ascent didn't stop. He watched her mouth part and listened to her breaths quicken. When his hand curved over her side a low growl left his throat. "And I suppose you're going to tell me the cold doesn't travel up this far."

It wasn't a surprise to find her without undergarments. Knowing she often went without them long before she became his —many, many times in his company—made Nik lose his damn mind. She was beautifully, cunningly sinful.

"I think," he went on huskily, watching in delight as her brow pinched when his fingers dipped through the crease between her thigh and abdomen, heading toward her apex, "you like to know that I could take you anywhere in this castle, at any time, with anyone nearby. And this is your scandalous secret right under the nose of every noble."

A soft moan escaped her as he continued to massage her and trace a featherlight touch up her other thigh. "We have duties to attend to," she breathed, but it lacked any objection. She didn't seem to realize she'd pressed into him tighter.

"Those can wait," he said, not tearing his eyes from the relaxed pleasure on her face. "For you, I'd make the world wait."

A knock interrupted their moment. Tauria let out a small gasp, making as if to pull away, but Nik's hold tightened.

"Should I invite them in?" he asked, hands roaming up her waist to bundle her dress higher. "Would you like them to see what I'm doing to you?"

That made her brow pinch, and her eyes closed. He wanted to reach between her legs and give her exactly what she was silently demanding with the shifts of her body when he pressed his lips to her thigh. He wanted a taste. Just one taste. He couldn't deny his own arousal at knowing his mate's scandalous desires.

"Your Majesties," the fae guard outside the door called, nervousness wavering his tone. There was a good chance he could either scent or hear what was happening. At least enough to paint a picture.

Nik turned his head toward the door when another knock came, but Tauria's hand clamped over his mouth. He chuckled, biting on her fingertips.

"What's the matter, love? I thought you liked the idea of an audience."

"Your Majesties…" the fae cut in again, hesitating before he continued. "There's urgent news from Rhyenelle."

Tauria gasped. The look they shared was one of mutual alarm, overshadowing their lust. Nik let her go, and she righted herself. Neither of them said a word before they were rushing to finish dressing. Because it wasn't the kingdom or Agalhor or anything political that was enough to halt their moment; it was the surge of hope, delivered with a drop of panic since the messenger called it *urgent*, that the news was from Faythe.

Before they headed out, Nik caught Tauria around the waist. "Don't you forget what I owe you."

Nik leaned against the edge of his desk, his chin propped up in one hand in an attempt to smother his restless twitching. Tauria paced the floor in front of him as they awaited Lord Zarrius, who harbored the news they were both on edge for.

"He's making us wait on purpose," Tauria ground out.

At the notes of her distress, Nik reached out, taking her hand to halt her. He knew of no words to console her when his irritation matched hers. Since their return, they'd had very few dealings with the lord, but Nik couldn't help his dangerous protective flair when Zarrius was close to his mate, knowing there was still much to be said of all Nik had planned behind his back. He knew there'd be consequences for his actions, and those repercussions could be delivered at any moment.

Tauria's twisted face smoothed out when their eyes met, but he didn't get the chance to pull her to him as with a short knock the private council room door opened. Nik straightened on instinct—not to formally regard the lord, who stalked in with his usual arrogant poise, but to track his every movement, every flicker of expression, while his hand slid across Tauria's lower back.

"Your Majesties," Zarrius greeted, giving a reluctant, stiff bow.

"We don't appreciate being called for and then kept waiting, Zarrius," Nik responded, his warning clear.

Zarrius's gaze flashed between him and Tauria. Every time it lingered on her, Nik's posture stiffened. It wasn't hard to detect there were many unspoken opinions about their mating, but he didn't care.

"My apologies," Zarrius offered, though it lacked any sincerity. "I don't think I've had the chance to congratulate you. And we're glad to have you back in High Farrow, Tauria Stagknight."

"When we are wed it will be Silverknight," Nik said coolly.

That took the Lord by surprise. Nik deciphered the irritation on his face.

"I think that would be best discussed with your council. I will remember to bring it up in our next meeting."

"No need. It is not something we require counsel on." Nik dropped his hand from Tauria. While it made his skin crawl to put distance between them in company, he knew Tauria had to be seen as a monarch in her own right in High Farrow, not only by his side.

"I must object—"

"The news from Rhyenelle, Zarrius," Tauria cut him off calmly.

Nik almost smiled and went back to leaning against the desk as he watched her with pride. He wanted everyone to know Tauria held just as much authority as he.

Zarrius pinned her with his dark eyes. Nik's hands flexed with the assessing look the lord gave her before he answered.

"Perhaps we should talk in private so that you might decide for yourself how to announce what I have to tell you," Zarrius addressed him.

Nik stayed silent.

Tauria braced herself. "I'll warn you just this once that I expect the same respect as you give to your king. Whatever you have to say regarding this kingdom can be brought to me."

"You are not wed. You are not yet my queen."

His distaste was slipping through, and it took everything in Nik not to break.

"Keep going, Zarrius. You're going to wish I never am."

Seconds of thick tension ticked by, and the lord's face remained firm. Nik planned to keep observing him. Knowing what he did about Zarrius's eye for the throne, it was clear he remained a threat to them both.

It was a relief when he smiled, his opposition lying dormant for now. But when his attention switched to Nik, the condolence on his face doused the king cold.

"I'm afraid the news I bear is not of any hope. Quite the opposite, in fact."

Nik's heart picked up tempo. "Is it regarding Faythe?" He couldn't stop the need to ask despite what it might expose of his care for her.

When Zarrius nodded, Nik stood straight, his pulse skipping a beat. "What happened?" For the first time, he believed the grave look on the lord's face.

Everything quietened. It was as if time slowed. Stopped. For the delivery of the news that felt like a cold lie.

"I'm sorry to be the one to inform you…"

The only explanation was that Nik must still be living in a dark, unforgiving nightmare.

"...that the Heir of Rhyenelle, Faythe Ashfyre, is dead."

Reality lashed him like a harsh whip. Tauria stumbled back, and he instinctively reached out to steady her. She covered her mouth, and Nik's hold tightened as he felt her tremble.

"The news arrived yesterday—"

"Yesterday?" Nik repeated darkly. "You've held onto this since *yesterday?*"

"I wanted to be sure."

Nik stepped away from Tauria, advancing toward Zarrius with a cool loathing that wisely brought fear to his expression. "If you ever get information about any kingdom, you bring it straight to me or Tauria." He halted before the lord, locking eyes with him in a deadly standoff. "If you ever withhold such information again, I don't care what it takes, I'll have you removed from your station, Lord Zarrius."

The adrenaline from the news coursed through him hot and urgent, leaving little room for him to consider the threat he was making to the only one who could rally the power to oppose his reign. He didn't care. He scented Tauria's silent tears at his back and felt her utter heartbreak.

"What happened?" Nik demanded.

"It seems during an expedition the princess did not make the journey back. That is all I know."

The quest to the Niltain Isles.

"And General Reylan?" Anticipation pounded in Nik's chest.

"He was the one to deliver the news to his king."

Nik's mind reeled. The breath whooshed out of him. He had to shift his stance as the room tilted. It didn't make sense. He wouldn't...

"Leave us."

Zarrius clearly wanted to object, perhaps to relish in their distress a little longer, but after scanning Nik's face he backed down. "As you wish." Stepping back, he offered a short bow. "I will allow you to decide how best to release the news to the kingdom. I didn't realize the human had made such an impact on you to invoke personal feelings." His gaze flashed to Tauria behind him with that statement. "But once you are ready, I believe we need to discuss the consequences of your…*mating.*"

That was a conversation Nik wasn't eager to have, but he knew the court would demand answers. Answers to why he never claimed her before and what it would mean for High Farrow. He owed his people that explanation.

"We need time. But I will send for you when we are ready."

The flex of Zarrius's eyes was the only indication of his annoyance.

When the door clicked shut behind the lord, Nik spun to Tauria. She kept her back to him, one hand braced on the table she was leaning against while the other stayed clamped over her mouth.

"Tauria," Nik said softly as he approached her. His hand landed on her back, but she didn't move. "Look at me, love."

Tauria shook her head, and when she turned to him, the desolation in her glittering eyes cleaved through him. "She can't be—"

"She's not."

Tauria's sadness smoothed out to shock at Nik's words. His hand came up to brush away her tears.

"She's not dead."

"How can you say that? Zarrius heard from Rhyenelle…from Agalhor."

"Reylan went back."

Tauria's furrowed brow urged him to elaborate.

"He wouldn't have gone back without her. I believe…" Nik shook his head at his own reeling thoughts, trying to piece together what he already knew to figure out what happened. "I don't know what they're up to, but I know Reylan Arrowood would not be sitting idle in Rhyenelle right now if she were truly gone."

Tauria huffed a laugh that lacked humor as she paced away. "It was clear he held an affection for her, and I know neither of us wants to believe it…but Reylan would have had to return."

"I wouldn't have."

Tauria caught his eye.

"If I didn't have a kingdom depending on me, I wouldn't have returned if something happened to you."

Her expression softened with pain, and it was a fresh slither of cold fear to realize how close they'd come to that harrowing reality of being torn apart in Olmstone.

"This is different, Nik. You and I, we're—"

"Mates."

She nodded, but Nik held her gaze with silence. As if she might draw out his thoughts without him having to speak at all. There was a flex of her brow, then her eyes dropped. She was thinking, calculating.

"That's impossible," she said even though it was clear she was fitting together every puzzle piece.

"Yes, the famous word to describe the existence of Faythe Ashfyre."

A brightness returned to Tauria's eyes, faint, held back with her desire to believe their friend was still alive against the odds.

"I can't be certain, but I've thought it for some time… I believe Faythe and Reylan are mates."

"He's protective—it was clear he cared deeply for her—but that doesn't mean they're mates. She's human."

Nik ran a hand through his hair with a long breath. "A long time ago, when I was helping Faythe with her Nightwalking, there was a time I entered her subconscious while she was active in it." He couldn't believe he was voicing the tiny snippet of information he assumed held no meaning, but perhaps he'd been utterly mistaken. "When I entered, there was another presence already there. It was very faint, and I wouldn't have entered her mind without invitation, but out of fear it could have been another Nightwalker who wanted to harm her, I had no choice."

Nik shook his head, feeling Tauria's approach and her encouragement for him to go on.

"It was Reylan. He had his back to me, but it was more than just his appearance that made me believe it was him. It was so faint, his essence, I thought there might be some mistake. Maybe Faythe had somehow met him before and he was just a vision of her own conjuring. Then he came to High Farrow, and I couldn't believe it. They were acting like perfect strangers, and I knew then Faythe had never met him before. I couldn't shake my suspicions about Reylan."

"You think he knew of her?"

"I think he was just as confused as I was," Nik admitted, trying to recall the general's time in High Farrow last winter. "I don't think he knew her, but I think there was a part of him that *recognized* her."

"As a mate," Tauria breathed incredulously.

Nik nodded. "All the signs were there. It was about far more than wanting to protect her for Agalhor's sake. I'd never seen him so possessive, defensive, of someone he hardly knew. A human. I couldn't allow myself to believe the insanity of my thoughts, but…"

He didn't have a conclusion. His thoughts were impossible but hopeful, and they were all he could offer. Faythe had to be alive.

"I hope you're right," Tauria said quietly, looking out the large window over High Farrow.

Nik walked to her, not hesitating to envelope her from behind. He would never grow tired of the way Tauria fit him so perfectly. His hand locked around hers before he brought them together over her chest. As they watched the glittering city, he knew without saying a word that they were reflecting on the same thing.

"Faythe is alive. I feel it, and I know you do too. But for some reason they want us to make the world believe she isn't, and I don't know for how long. All we can do is play our part until we can get more information."

Tauria exhaled a breath as she relaxed into him completely. "We're masters of pretending, remember?"

Nik chuckled softly, planting a kiss on her head. "Yes, we are, love."

CHAPTER 11

Faythe

LIVIA AND FAYTHE remained awake while Nerida and Reuben slept in the room they'd rented upstairs at the run-down inn. For the past hour they'd sat opposite each other in silence, giving their wine more attention than they'd given each other. It was becoming a habit on their restless nights.

Faythe spared the commander fleeting glances over her cup. Her words from their last escape in the previous town hung somberly in the air between them. Livia refused to speak of Nessair's claim—the *name* he spoke that belonged to Livia's father. It inspired images of Reylan's scars, and she didn't press for answers when her magick pricked her skin at the thought alone.

Then there was the fae in the mask who'd ambushed her. Faythe couldn't shake the feeling the two dark pieces belonged in the same puzzle. He'd spoken to her with words meant for someone else.

Her mind reeled as she fiddled idly with the butterfly carving in her pocket, which she'd hardly let go of since parting with Reylan.

"We should track down Evander," Faythe said boldly, anticipating it would earn the guarded expression Livia wore.

"No, we shouldn't."

"If he's alive, he deserves to suffer for every day past the one in which he should have died by Reylan's hand."

Livia's scowl eased to a small smirk. "While I agree and rather enjoy your vengeful side, if my father is alive and gets to you, there is nothing that could torture Reylan more than that. It's not worth the risk."

"So we just let him live?"

"No, but we can't jump into brash action with someone as malicious and well-connected as him."

Faythe's hand tightened around her cup. She took a long drink to wash down the acidic dread that wouldn't leave her. She thought of the man in the alley as her knee bounced anxiously. Faythe wondered if it could have been Evander, but his words had confused her so much. She didn't mention the encounter to Livia, thinking it would only unsettle her more and tighten a leash if the commander thought there was a threat to Faythe.

"You've barely used your ability," Livia diverted, but her words stiffened Faythe's spine.

Setting down her cup, she countered carefully, "What is your point?"

"We've had many narrow escapes in our *activities*. There's been plenty of opportunity to end it all sooner with what you're capable of, yet not once have you infiltrated a mind. Why?"

They stared off for a few seconds, and it was as if Livia already knew yet wanted to coax it from her anyway.

"What I was capable of before and what I could become now…they're one and the same. Every time I've tried reaching into my power, this new darkness is there, and I'm—"

"Afraid?"

Faythe dropped her eyes. "Yes."

"So you're waiting to be back by Reylan's side? Where he can diminish what you are with a mere touch?" Livia was provoking her. Mocking her.

"No," she ground out. "I just need more time. Space. I don't want to hurt anyone."

"We've camped in lots of open woodland by now."

"I don't want to hurt any of you."

Livia gave a short laugh. "I don't believe that's what you're afraid of."

"I don't know what you're trying to say."

There was a contemplative pause from the commander as she decided whether or not to engage further. Livia slipped a blade free to fidget with as she leaned back against the booth. She guided the tip up to her face, the point resting exactly where her marking began.

"I got this scar the first time I had the courage to fight back." She tilted her head for the candlelight to catch the imperfection. Faythe admired it. With Livia's lax posture, her demeanor, it was hard to imagine the commander before she took on her esteemed position. "It doesn't bother me. In fact, maybe some days I'm even glad for it. For the reminder of the day I finally took back what was mine. My father was despicably cruel, and I was raised to believe I was no better than property. Sometimes just company, but other times…"

"You don't have to tell me," Faythe offered at her pause.

Livia's ice-blue eyes slid to her. "I'm not ashamed of what happened to me. I was for a long time, and I owe a lot of who I emerged as to the three of them, but certain things only to Kyleer. He helped me regain a confidence that was stolen from me without any expectations. It wasn't just sex; it was taking back control. Learning my desires. He understood what I needed and never judged, only accepted my requests with such patience. But it was long before him that I knew my attraction to females outweighed what I could feel for a male emotionally. Or a man—I have been with humans too. But those lovers were typically more…"

"Fragile?" Faythe couldn't help but smirk.

Livia's smile eased the weight of the conversation. "In some ways."

"I don't know why Reylan put up with me before." Faythe huffed a laugh.

"Because he loves you," Livia said plainly. "More than

anything I've seen him dedicate himself to before. Even as a human, knowing the odds that were against you, he believed in you."

"He knew I was his mate. That changes things."

"You're wrong."

Faythe's attention was gripped by the sureness in those words.

"Reylan is many things, but he's never been selfish despite what he might believe. Above all, he's never been one to hold back the truth no matter how hard it is to hear. If he didn't think you could handle the trip to the Isles, he would have challenged you. If he didn't think you could take down Rezar, he would have gone against your wishes and killed him in an instant. If he didn't think you could take care of yourself, *believe* you could master control of yourself, he would be here now. Your being mates has nothing to do with how he sees you, and if that's what you truly think, you don't deserve him."

Her last statement made Faythe's brow arch with its sheer bluntness. "The brutal honesty must be an Arrowood trait," she remarked, but the two shared a smile of agreement.

She thought about Livia's words. Felt them as a warmth in her chest that quickly clenched into an ache. She missed Reylan so awfully. Her nights were long and restless, her days vacant and dull. What hurt the most was that there was no time to measure, no hopeful countdown to when she would see him next.

To test their plan, he couldn't come to them. In case the dark fae were tracking him Reylan had to stay away. The only thing that kept Faythe going was the thought of where she would go after Fenher. If her death was believed by the world and Zaiana truly didn't know of her Transition to share it with her enemies, Faythe would be heading to High Farrow. It was a light in her darkness to get to see her friends, whose absence had left a void in her chest since they were parted.

Jakon, her longest and dearest friend, was the first to cross her mind. How different their lives had become from all they'd childishly imagined together. She wanted desperately to hold him.

Then Marlowe, her beautiful, brilliant friend who'd come into their lives at the perfect moment, the one who made Jakon the happiest she'd ever seen him.

Nik... *Gods,* she missed his jesting, his scolding, his wisdom. She yearned to see him under the crown she knew he'd wear so confidently now he ruled over High Farrow.

As for Tauria, Faythe often found her emotions in turmoil over the Fenstead Queen, hoping she'd made the right choice by going to Olmstone. Hoping she hadn't sacrificed her heart for any call of duty.

The stroke of realization at the thought widened her eyes. Faythe was immortal now, at least in the human sense of the word. Before they'd left for the Isles, she'd accepted the title that would befall her when she returned, but never did she think she would succeed Agalhor. Faythe didn't know when she'd get to return, but it only now dawned on her the prospect of one day wearing the crown for Rhyenelle. An intimidating challenge lay ahead if she wanted to prove herself worthy of being Rhyenelle's heir over Malin, as all she was right now left her no more fit to rule than an untrained, unpredictable *faeling*.

"You need to try." Livia pulled her from her tunneling thoughts.

Faythe nodded in agreement. She didn't want to meet Reylan again as a failure. She knew he believed in her. She just had to try to figure out what lived within her and what she was capable of.

"We should get some rest." Livia cast her a knowing look as she rose.

Faythe swirled her drink. "I'm going to finish this. Hopefully, it'll help me sleep. I'll be up soon."

Fatigue clouded Livia's face, and Faythe was relieved when she nodded, sparing a quick look around the dire inn before she made for the stairwell. Faythe's shoulders relaxed, glad the commander hadn't read any of her eagerness to leave.

Faythe sighed, admittedly jealous of Livia for heading off to get the rest she too needed. Exhaustion weighed down her lids, but she couldn't sleep—not without the tonic that would send her past her gold-and-white mists and straight into darkness.

Because her Nightwalking…it was dangerously tied to her new existence, and Faythe wasn't sure what she was capable of at night. Flashbacks to when she had no control over her Nightwalking set the terror in her that she might be capable of that again.

Of killing.

In each town she had managed to sneak out and obtain the tonic at night by some cautious inquiry. The tonic had run out now, so Faythe was on the lookout for any shop she could try. She'd lasted more than a day without sleep before, but it was not without growing suspicion from her companions.

Faythe blended into the shadows of the night, adjusting her mask and pulling up her hood. The streets were barren. The cold whistled in the wind, and Faythe pulled her cloak tighter around herself. Her steps were heavy with a will to succumb to her tiredness. They were in a very small town, and her hope began to disappear the longer she trailed aimlessly.

Her relaxed posture stiffened at the sight of a silhouette down the path too small to be unaccompanied. Faythe halted, scanning around, but no one came to the child or lingered nearby. As she approached slowly, the hairs rose all over her body. Her hood was drawn and the child's face was buried in her hands.

Then Faythe heard the muffled sobs.

"Hey," she said quietly, so as not to spook her. "You're okay. Where are your parents?" She crouched, and the small shoulders stopped shaking.

"I want to go home." The voice came so soft it tugged deep in her gut. Slowly, the child's hands slipped from their face to slide into their hood.

When the stunning lengths of silver hair spilled out and Faythe saw their eyes…her balance swayed, and she pressed a palm to the ground.

Faythe knew those eyes. Sapphire, but flecked with gold. Utterly entrancing, and her heart took off sprinting at what she saw. In a daze, her hand reached out to cup the girl's cheek, and only then did Faythe notice the small points of her ears. Her eyes pricked at the beauty of the child and the burst of bright hope that erupted within.

"What is your name?" Faythe asked breathlessly.

The child only smiled, her delicate hand touching Faythe's, taking it, and she rose with the gentle tug.

This had to be a dream, but Faythe didn't care. She followed the child as though walking on clouds.

They didn't go far, coming to a halt before a shop. Faythe's shoulders relaxed at the flickering amber in the small frosted window.

"Thank you," Faythe said. The child had led her right to what she'd been searching for.

Her hand became too light, and Faythe gasped as she cast her view down, taking a step back as gold dust flew from her clutches instead. Her pulse skittered as she watched the wind carry away her perfect illusion, and the symbol in her hand winked out its warm glow.

Sadness swept Faythe while her mind clung to the beautiful image of the fae child. She bore so much resemblance to Reylan that it pained Faythe to learn she wasn't real. She wondered why the vision had come tonight. Perhaps she'd gone so long without sleep that her subconscious space where she could conjure the impossible had leaked into her reality.

An eerie creak disturbed the silence, and Faythe whirled in fright toward the opening shop door. No one greeted her, but the flickering candlelight invited her inside.

The shop interior was lined with rows of shelving in a state of disarray. There was no counter with any humble shopkeeper where she could make her quick inquiry and leave. The hairs on her arms rose, but she trailed further inside anyway, swallowing despite her dry throat with every intention of calling out. She lingered to scan the shelves, peering through gaps to find someone. With the rainbow of vials and clutter she wondered how anyone found what they were looking for in this place.

Faythe couldn't help but reach out to an iridescent vial with a shimmering red liquid, entranced by it.

"Do you make a habit of touching what does not belong to you?"

Faythe jerked at the sudden croak of a voice. Her fright knocked her elbow back, and horror struck her at the clamor of some items as they fell. She whirled, catching several easily. Such a reflex never would have been possible in her human form. One vial she was too late to save, and guilt washed through her when it shattered, spilling a green substance down between the aged wooden floorboards.

"I'm so sorry," Faythe managed. As she looked up from the mess, her gaze landed on a hunched-over old woman. Faythe was baffled not to have heard her approach. Her wrinkled face was set in a frown of disapproval, and then accusation, as she eyed the spillage. Faythe scrambled to add to her apology, but she only held coin from one card game earlier that night and still hoped to purchase the tonic, so she simply floundered under the woman's assessment.

"What in the Nether are you looking for, child?"

Faythe's hands bulged holding the various glass vials and brass items she'd saved from falling. She carefully rested them back on the shelves, where they fit in easily among the rest of the clutter.

"I'm not a child," Faythe grumbled.

"Remove that thing, will you? It's rude to enter a person's home with no face." The woman hobbled around Faythe with her cane, which thumped against the wood, and the floorboards creaked in her wake.

Faythe had forgotten about her mask, so accustomed to needing it to hide who she was. Sparing a quick glance around the dainty space, she didn't think she had anything to worry about with one lone human. She untied the ribbon, peeling the shell from her face, and breathed deeply as the air cooled her skin. She headed after the woman as she dipped around the back, out of sight.

"Come, come." Her aged voice was rough and strained.

Faythe walked the narrow hall with tentative steps, until she arrived in a small kitchen where the old woman was fixing tea.

The water was already boiled, and Faythe wondered why she was awake at such a late hour even before her intrusion. She scanned the décor. There were so many odd colors and items, but she supposed they added a warm touch. When her eyes landed on the wall at the far end of the room, Faythe was quick to drop her gaze.

"Why do you avoid the mirror?" the woman croaked.

Faythe wandered over to the table. "I don't."

Her smirk was unexpected. Why was the woman being so inviting to a stranger who had intruded on her home cloaked and masked? Faythe had forgotten for a moment that now she was fae, she wouldn't ever grow old and frail like the human who struggled to sit on the chair she pulled out for herself.

"You're afraid," the woman said, picking up a long, ornate pipe and bringing a candle up to it. "So powerful, yet you hold so much fear. It does not bode well, Faythe Ashfyre."

Smoke puffed into the air, and the woman coughed with such a horrible choking noise that Faythe advanced a step. The woman waved her off, fanning the air to disperse the clouds. The smell wasn't what Faythe expected. Not foul like that which she'd endured from the pipes in the establishments they stopped in; it was soft and floral like lavender, flavorsome like vanilla. She breathed deeply before realization stopped her short.

"How do you know my name?" she asked, her edge of caution sharpening. The woman didn't appear at all a threat, but Faythe knew a blade was nothing against someone with the knowledge of her survival who could spill all and ruin their plan.

Her cackle quickly turned into another round of coughing, and although whatever the woman was smoking didn't seem to be anything harmful, Faythe was sure it wasn't doing her any good. She appeared to be living on borrowed time.

"Aren't you going to sit?" She gestured to the opposite rickety chair.

Faythe wasn't confident it wouldn't tumble to the ground the moment she tested her weight on it.

At her hesitation, the woman huffed. "Not luxurious enough for the Phoenix Queen, I see."

A cold chill swept the room.

"Where did you hear that name?" Faythe should leave, yet she felt compelled to the woman. Her tiredness began to creep up again despite her alarm.

"You have many names. By the humans, by the Gods. In the past and present. What you have never been is one thing, and that is why you cannot find acceptance."

"Tell me who you are," Faythe demanded, her irritation flaring with her alarm. Her hand curled around Lumarias, but not with the firm grip she hoped.

"I have what you seek, true heir of Marvellas."

Faythe's heart was pounding, wanting for answers despite the deeper well of reservation that screamed at her to leave the odd shop.

"Now sit, Faythe."

CHAPTER 12

Reylan

IT WAS AS if the stars had fallen. The tiny flickers of flame were too far and scattered for their amber glow to be visible, but the symbol had glittered through the city all week, and it was breathtaking to realize how much Faythe meant to her people. Each nightfall the city had extended a millennia-old tradition of lighting a single flame in their window in tribute to the fallen royal. Still, it never failed to strike panic in Reylan each time he saw the faint starry lights even though he knew the truth.

Faythe was alive.

"They barely knew her."

The voice that traveled to him grated on his nerves, and Reylan tightened his fist around the hilt of his sword. He didn't turn to Malin Ashfyre. He worked his jaw at his not-so-subtle distaste.

"You don't need to own a diamond to know its worth," he said calmly.

Malin's answering huff made it difficult to refrain from the violence the prince's arrogance regularly stirred. He strolled right up to stand beside Reylan, both of them looking out over the city.

A SWORD FROM THE EMBERS

"Whether here or in the ground, she was a waste of talent."

Reylan's teeth ground so tightly they could break, and his fist trembled at his side. He knew because they were alone, far from any eyes or ears, Malin was testing him. Yet still, he couldn't stand it. "Here or not, she had more talent than you ever will." He turned to Malin, uncaring of the reckless words he spilled. "Your insecurity blares when you speak of her. Even her ghost threatens you."

Malin's hazel irises clouded with hatred. It wasn't the first time Reylan had seen it; it had been there when the prince pushed him to his limit in the past. Yet while Malin was cunning and held favor with the council, he wasn't foolish enough to forget the nobles were only half the running of a kingdom. They couldn't defend themselves without their armies, and Reylan had earned the loyalty of Rhyenelle's warriors and commanders over centuries. Malin needed him.

"Yet there's no body."

The prince's head tilted slightly with the switch of topic, and he observed Reylan for any reaction as he said the words with just enough of a hint of suspicion.

"She was beyond recovery."

A dark and violent smirk pulled at Malin's lips. "Yes, so the great tale goes. A tragic end to a tragic beginning."

"Is there something you want, Malin?"

They were dancing around each other with his careful teasing and Reylan's rising temper.

"It wasn't hard to detect that your devotion to her far surpassed what was appropriate."

"Your accusation is pointless."

The prince's pause skittered over Reylan's skin. He wanted to lay a fist to the gleam in his eye.

"Is it?"

Often, it was as if Malin already believed himself to be king. Thought it so truly that the weight of the crown adjusted his posture, giving him the confidence to speak so brazenly with words always so cunningly crafted.

"I would only be looking out for your station, of course," he went on, his tone switching to sound friendly but deliver a warning. "A general is no match for a princess. As is my understanding, Faythe stood to lay her birth claim to the throne before such...*tragedy* befell the kingdom."

Reylan tried to calculate what Malin hoped to gain from him, the sharp edge of suspicion beginning to slice through his skin.

"Though it may not have been of anyone's concern after all," the prince chirped, "as the lords had plans to challenge her legitimacy. It would have been no small feat for Agalhor to convince them to overlook that crucial fact."

Then it all made sense. Reylan thought Malin must be desperate if he'd come to him to prize out information. Why the prince even cared to investigate set every defense on high alert. He didn't know if Malin knew Faythe was still alive or if all his probing was yet another way to get him to slip up.

"You can relieve your followers of the job of raising such a protest."

The twitch of Malin's jaw made his irritation clear. It was a rare joy to see. The prince glanced from Reylan's boots to his head as he stood a few inches taller. Reylan gave away none of his anger.

"It seems you're a male of routine, Reylan Arrowood." His smile was darkly wicked as he sauntered away. "Letting helpless, weak people die."

Reylan twisted, the flash of rage canceling out all logic as his hand began to draw his sword. A tight grip on his forearm halted him, and his head snapped with wrath to Kyleer, who stood firm against it.

"He's not worth it."

"*She* is," Reylan snarled low. It was as if their short conversation had dissipated to leave only the hateful words Malin spoke of Faythe. And Reylan owed her his fight.

"Yes, and she needs you alive and free, not locked up should you try anything or executed should you succeed."

Reylan pinched his eyes closed, tearing his arm from Kyleer

and turning back to the window. Sliding his eyes open onto the somber sight drenched his anger with coolness all at once. He breathed sure and steady, silent for several minutes before he asked, "Izaiah...?"

"He's still tracking them. We should get an update tomorrow, though I assure you it will be as boring as the last. Antics aside, they're being smart and quiet."

"Her power?"

"Hasn't caused her or anyone any harm. Despite her hopes to try to figure it out, I think she's been holding it all back."

That didn't soothe Reylan. He feared the longer Faythe avoided her power, the bigger its eruption would be. Yet he believed in her, and what he'd guiltily kept from her was that it wouldn't matter if he were by her side this time; he couldn't help her anyway.

"I don't know how much of her magick I can take," he confessed quietly.

"What do you mean?"

"Exactly that. I've taken her whole ability before. It was strong, but it held a form even if it was one I'd never experienced before. Yet now, when she touched me with the intention of trying to show me..." Reylan looked to Kyleer with the fear that had ensnared him the moment he realized. "It's a power like nothing I've felt before. It has no form. No beginning and no end. I can't reach in and diminish it all—no Mindseer could—because she doesn't have magick; she *is* magick. A force that won't be silenced."

"You didn't tell her?"

Reylan shook his head. "She thinks I'll be there to stop it all if she loses control. And I will be there with her, but I can't stop her. I didn't tell her because she'll never try to reach the full extent of her abilities if she doesn't believe there's a fail-safe: me."

Kyleer breathed out deeply with a frown. "It's terrifying for us all. But don't break that trust with her."

Reylan couldn't stand the thought.

"You might not be able to take it all, but I don't believe you're entirely unneeded. It may be on her to stop herself, but she's not alone in harboring her power. Not with you."

Gods, it relieved him to hear it spoken from the outside, but at the same time, it triggered a painful strain within Reylan that she was so far from him. He knew Faythe was powerful and brave and highly capable, but they were stronger together.

Reylan didn't know why he spoke his next words to Kyleer. Perhaps because he was one of the very few who knew his past—every dark and grim detail.

"I feel like I've known her far longer than possible."

"What you feel for each other, even from the outside, there's no denying how deep your bond goes."

Reylan wanted to believe it was as simple as that. He didn't try to explain more when he couldn't be certain of his own thoughts. But since meeting Faythe's eyes for the first time since she awoke from death in his arms…something had been plucking at his strings of memory, inspiring flashes but nothing whole or sure, and he didn't know what it meant.

Though one thing blared with distinct clarity: knowing her showed him there was a door out of his mind of dark torment, and loving her set him free.

CHAPTER 13

Zaiana

THERE WERE FEW things that settled a mind so shrouded in darkness, but open vantage points were Zaiana's safe haven. Ellium was an impressive sight. Far and high enough away, she marveled at how the double-walled city was built as though a star had hurtled through the skies and created the most perfect crater in which to nest the capital. The city was surrounded by tall, crimson-peaked mountains that hugged the city in great waves of stone. It was an impeccable defense Zaiana found intriguing, for it was perhaps not entirely uninfluenced by forces beyond their comprehension. Her eyes cast to the night sky as though those same forces could be watching her now.

A shudder ran through her as she let her gaze drop. It was a ludicrous notion. There was no one left to intervene.

"I don't mean this as an insult…" Maverick's irritating rumble came from behind her, where he'd been lounging while she dangled off the ledge. "But I expected you to have figured out a plan by now. Are you losing your touch, Zaiana?"

Her fists tightened. She had a plan, though what it required was for him to be far away when she decided to act. Tynan and

Amaya were being held prisoner in their castle. That she confirmed after a few days of spying and overhearing the guards' whispers—of fear, in mockery of their capture. It had taken great will not to react, but Zaiana couldn't afford to trigger the slightest alert.

"What is your plan, Maverick?" she drawled as coolly as she could though she itched to hurt him.

They hadn't seen any action in weeks, just endless days of mind-numbing stakeouts. What Maverick didn't know was that she wasn't mapping their defenses or gaining insight into their strategies. That she planned to do from the inside.

The bastard's groan turned her body rigid as it signaled he was moving closer. "The general has been rather…silent."

"He lost someone dear to him."

Maverick scoffed. "Sulking and pining is pitiful."

"What would you expect him to be doing?"

"Strategizing," he said harshly.

Zaiana cast her gaze up to him. It was odd to glimpse his anger.

"He should be coming for me, yet instead he's remained in that damn castle like a pitiful fool."

"He needs time to grieve." Zaiana brushed him off.

"Faythe's body isn't there."

Her jaw locked. She didn't look at him. "No, it isn't."

"Odd, is it not?"

There was a challenge in his tone that grated on her irritation. Zaiana rose. Twisting brought them face-to-face.

"Find Faythe. Find her sword. That is your task, not mine."

The silence between them was charged. Maverick held in a question he would never ask outright, so he tiptoed around it instead.

"I don't suppose you gathered any intel on where I might go looking."

Her eyes narrowed on his. "They're not as foolish as you think," she said carefully. "What I have *gathered* is that Reylan Arrowood is playing the right game. He is in mourning with the city over their lost princess. Though he wasn't the only one who lost her."

Maverick curved a brow for her to go on.

"Kyleer has been wandering the castle and city just as vacantly."

Something in his eyes flared at his mention, yet Zaiana held firm, giving nothing more than fact. "How nice of you to notice and consider him." His tone prodded at a suggestion.

"Yet his brother has not," she bit out. The snap of her tone only made him flinch. Zaiana didn't want to know what he was thinking. She scoffed. "Have you spent these past weeks doing nothing more than indulging on human blood?"

"You wouldn't know a thing about my indulgences." He took a step closer, and she couldn't stand the rise of battle she was all too familiar with. It had always been present between them since he Transitioned and they were pitted against each other, yet since the night they shared…Zaiana could hardly stand to be around him. When tensions rose now, that private battle seemed encased in uncertainty. She damned her own mind, her own body, for dredging the memory every time it seemed their feuds could be resolved by far more pleasurable means.

"You haven't joined me once," he went on, voice dropping to an insufferably low tone. "Tell me, when was the last time you fed?"

The truth was under lock and key.

"That is none of your concern. If you want to test me, Maverick, then do it." Her skin pricked with a steady vibration. She didn't want to fight him. Not now, when she'd been slowly and carefully gathering strength from her well of power for weeks. "The younger brother, Izaiah, hasn't been around them as much. He's a Shapeshifter, and they are far more cunning than you clearly anticipate."

This caught his attention. Maverick folded his arms. "What are you saying?"

"I'm saying birds are sparse around the mountains, yet often does one come and go from the castle. Never the same species—

smart—and yet the flight path stays exactly the same. Sometimes it will dip into the mountains and emerge a different bird. I would commend him for his attempt to throw us off the scent, except he enters through the same window every time."

Maverick's face relaxed in what she dared to think was approval. "You gathered all that?"

Zaiana rolled her eyes. "You might have too if you hadn't spent your time so far as if we're on vacation. As Dakodas's prized pet, I would have thought you'd be far more eager to please."

Though Maverick's posture stiffened, he almost leaned forward as though he wanted to lunge for her. To fight or do something worthy of fighting over afterward she would never know. He took one deep breath before turning away and looking out over the city that glowed red and amber in the night. "You think she made it?" he concluded.

Zaiana had no choice but to share the suspicion she held. "I think they're hiding her and he's the path straight to her."

"Why?"

"Must I do all the thinking, Maverick?"

"I like to hear your thoughts. Your voice…it somewhat soothes me."

He was infuriating.

"Marvellas wants her. If she or Dakodas knew she were still alive, they wouldn't waste a second; they'd be hunting her already. She died in that cave. She should never stand again." A foreign chill swept over her—one of unsettling notions she wasn't accustomed to. "Who knows what she emerged as?"

"I can't wait to reunite," Maverick said sarcastically. "We can track her together, just like old times."

For a few seconds, Zaiana couldn't fathom the twinge in her chest. It was a movement as though she cared for the journey they'd shared, at least before it all turned. The hunt, the calculations… Maybe if she gave more than a few seconds to that unwelcome feeling she'd believe she even *enjoyed* their venture.

"No."

His head snapped to her.

"I still have to scout the defenses," she added quickly. A lie and a truth. It was her task after all. "You were the one tasked with retrieving Faythe's sword. Imagine the glory if you return with the weapon in the hand that wields it." She didn't want to decipher the drop in his expression; the war that flexed his eyes.

"We'll part this night. We can't waste another day." Maverick turned to her fully. She didn't know when he'd closed the distance, leaving only a cool breeze of mountain air between them. She saw the moment he lost his fight.

Zaiana's hand lashed out, connecting with his chest before any more space could be erased. She clutched his leathers tightly while they matched hard stares, always battling. Always conflicted. "Don't," she said as firmly as she could in a whisper. "This stops now. Whatever impulse you feel around me—that look in your eye—you can turn it toward any other." Her chest rose and fell deeply because while she was speaking of his recklessness, she was addressing her own. "This stops now," she repeated, letting him go.

Slowly, his harshness returned to add a darkness to his expression. "You're many things, Zaiana. Many wicked, cruel, and brilliant things." He paced away from her, flexing and expanding his wings. "But you're not so delusional as to stop something that was never there."

The twist in her gut at his words was unpleasant, but she didn't react.

"I guess we'll meet again soon, with your strategy planned and my weapon gained. Just like the honorable servants of the Goddess we are." He angled his head down, looking at the ground, while his brow furrowed. His lips parted as if to speak, but he seemed to think better of it.

Zaiana was glad he didn't see her yearning for those lost final words in the single step she took as he leaned off the mountainside. Maverick disappeared, engulfed by the night entirely. She listened to the beat of his wings for a few seconds before he shot back into her vision, flying high for cover before he began to soar away.

He didn't look back.

She didn't expect him to.

Yet her eyes remained fixed on him until he was a distant spec, and when she blinked, she couldn't distinguish him anymore.

Alone on the mountain, Zaiana was free to feel everything and nothing. She could scream or cry or laugh and no one would ever know. It was both a relief and a despairing thought, so she locked her mind tight against all that threatened to burst free. It was the only way to carry out what she needed to do. They were holding Tynan and Amaya as if it were some great triumph; their first step toward conquering their mighty dark foe. It wasn't out of consideration for their lives Zaiana was doing this. It couldn't be, and they wouldn't expect her help was coming. She was doing this for herself. Her retaliation stewed hot and electrifying under the surface, just waiting to be unleashed.

After all, if they were being mocked, so was she.

CHAPTER 14

Tauria

"No visits, by the king's orders," a guard grumbled. Tauria stood unyielding before two of them in the cells below the castle. She knew it would be an adjustment before they viewed her on the same level as Nik. Without a binding marriage, without the coronation, she was still nothing in law to the people of High Farrow. But she was *his*, and that fact alone was enough to ease the twinge she felt at the look the guards pinned her with now, questioning if she belonged here.

Tauria knew she did. By Nik's side she belonged. Ruling High Farrow and Fenstead together was where she belonged. She could be patient a while longer until the world believed it too.

"Fine. Fetch him. His wrath will not be aimed at me; it will be for you and your insistence to deny his mate." It was a low move, but it was all she had.

The reminder of who she was to Nik cast a growing shadow over her. It made the guards exchange looks, and she hated it, their debate about her authority. It worked though. One made a disgruntled sound and stepped out of her way.

As they shuffled to follow her, Tauria paused. "I don't need protection against a harmless lady," she said over her shoulder. "I will call for you if you're needed."

More hesitation. More debate. The air around the guards stirred, delivering just enough of a warning that she was *not* harmless. When they finally retreated, Tauria pressed on through the cold, dark passageway.

It didn't take long for her to spot the curled-up form in the corner of a faraway cell. She didn't look up, and as Tauria stood before the bars, she couldn't find any pity at the state of her, not knowing what she'd done.

"Hello, Samara." Tauria spoke with ice in her tone.

The tangled mass of blonde hair lifted. Samara's blue eyes were vacant. Tauria couldn't stand it. She didn't want to feel the rise of sympathy. It was hard to hate on someone who'd surrendered.

"Come to gloat?" Her voice was an awful croak, and Tauria winced, feeling her own throat dry up.

"That would imply I had something to lose to you."

Samara huffed a laugh that was cold with resentment. Her head tipped back against the stone. "You think you have it all, but you have nothing."

"I have everything you wanted."

"No."

Tauria's eyes flexed. Her irritation heated her veins, awakening her wind.

Samara went on. "You don't see the cage you're in though it is made of glass."

"I didn't come here to play games with you."

"Then why did you come?"

A darkness rose from such depths that it would be irretrievable if she let it surface completely. Tauria stared and stared, trying to see a naïve person, a foolish heart, but all she knew in that moment was that she was staring at someone who could have taken everything from her.

"You tried to kill my mate," she whispered. Her breathing

hardened and her fists clamped tight to stop herself from doing anything reckless.

"I didn't know you were mated."

"Would it have made a difference?"

Samara looked at her. "Yes."

Tauria's need for revenge ceased. She silenced her wind. "Why did you do it?"

"He promised me everything."

"Zarrius?"

Samara didn't answer, though her eyes flashed toward where Tauria had come from, and she shuddered stiffly before hugging herself tighter. Tauria unclasped her cloak but paused with it in her hands as she realized exactly who she was extending her kindness to. Samara could have killed Nik—had come so close it was unbearable to even look at her knowing that.

She forced her darkness back with a deep breath before slipping a hand through the bars and tossing the material inside. Samara stared at it for a few heartbeats as though it were a trap, but in her bitter-cold state she took the offering eagerly.

Tauria watched her, letting the seconds tick by. She didn't know what she'd hoped to achieve by coming here, only that there was a person living beneath their feet who had tried to harm her mate in the most final way, and perhaps by facing her she would be able to forgive.

She couldn't.

Tauria turned to leave.

"I wanted it," Samara confessed. Tauria halted to listen. "The power he offered."

"A throne is not simply power; it is a world of responsibility."

"Not just the throne." With a wince, Samara adjusted her position, appearing far more comfortable in the new cloak. "He said he could make me something *more*. I've been surrounded by powerful fae my whole life, those with abilities and high status. I wanted it. And Zarrius said on the first full moon after we took the throne that we'd both be granted a higher power. A blessing."

A chill started In Tauria's fingertips, seizing her magick and cooling her blood, and it had nothing to do with the temperature down here. Her mind flashed with memories that caused her heart to beat to an uneven rhythm.

Wings.

Black blood.

Mordecai.

"What they would have done to you would be a curse, not a blessing," she muttered vacantly. Tauria would never forget Samara's betrayal of Nik and how it could have ended. She didn't know if she would ever truly forgive her, yet the Transition that could have befallen her… Tauria wouldn't wish it upon the enemy.

Samara huffed a humorless laugh. "What would you know of being powerless?" she said. "Your ability is fabled; you are a queen. There are those of us who have to walk in the shadows as though having magick is to have worth."

"That has never been a divide."

"Because you are on the side of privilege and do not see it," Samara sneered.

Tauria blinked, taken aback. Though it was not with defense that her heart sank, but at being enlightened to Samara's ignorance. "What do you mean?"

"For too long those with abilities have looked down on us. Even those with mild magick. Zarrius said this was the way to even out the balance of power. The crown would not have granted me magick, but I would have been respected and feared."

Tauria couldn't stand it. The lord had romanticized the notion of becoming a dark fae. She wondered with a cold fear how long he'd been whispering this in the minds of the fae and how many had bought into this grand plan. She didn't realize she'd walked all the way to the bars until her hand reached around the cool metal.

"Your eyes are a beautiful blue. I wonder if they'd be as alluring eclipsed entirely by darkness." Tauria assessed the way Samara's face creased with wariness. Confusion. Tauria shook her head faintly. "I bet he also didn't tell you that your black eyes would match your blood after they Transitioned you. That you would have wings and your memories would be stolen. And the worst part? The one thing you would crave over everything else. More than power or magick or love."

Samara gripped her cloak tighter as Tauria's tale echoed around the cell, as haunting as a ghost story.

"Human blood," she finished.

Samara's doe eyes widened. Good. It was something of a relief to see her horror at what she could have become. That had she known, it wouldn't have been the path she chose.

"Be glad Nik caught you as this cell"—Tauria's eyes skimmed the bleak room—"is a mercy." She dropped her hand. Samara was simply a young, naïve fae, and though her crimes lit a match to Tauria's anger, she now thought with time she would learn to forgive her.

Though she would never forget.

"It's not just me," Samara confessed quietly, but not without a fearful scan around as though she believed the stone were listening. "If what you say is true, he has been working for some time to convince people of his plan. I didn't know the sacrifices, and he didn't tell us. Tauria…" A violent tremor swept over Samara's huddled form and her voice dropped even further. "You could have an army gathering within these very walls. Some may have already…*changed*. I cannot be certain, but Zarrius…his arrogance has to come from a place of knowing he has some great weapon should you try to oppose him. Should you try to take him down first."

Tauria blanched with horror, but adrenaline kept her focused, calculating, absorbing every detail she could so she'd know how to silently turn the odds. Because if Zarrius found out they knew, he could strike with a force no wall could defend them against.

They were already surrounded.

CHAPTER 15

Faythe

FAYTHE HADN'T TOUCHED the tea she was offered. In her exhaustion she was tempted by its soothing warmth, but the woman was more focused on her pipe to drink, and so Faythe didn't either.

"Who are you?" Faythe tried again.

"I am but a simple shopkeeper. I hold many treasures in these walls."

Faythe had observed that, and she wondered how the woman had come to possess such an assortment of items and elixirs. "You said you had what I was looking for," Faythe prompted her, growing irritable since this was more conversation than she'd hoped for tonight.

So tired…

The woman puffed another cloud straight across the table at her. Faythe coughed, rising to her feet but bracing herself with a hand on the table at the wave of fatigue that swayed her vision.

"I do."

Something slid across the table toward her, and Faythe blinked to focus on the item. Blinked again when she couldn't make out if what she was seeing was real. She hadn't brought it with her. She retrieved the object, holding it up to examine it. From the front it looked identical, but when she flipped it over…

"Where did you get this?" Faythe breathed.

Her mother's pocket watch. What Faythe held could only be described as its twin, for on the back was Marvellas's symbol, and yet Faythe's was adorned with Aurialis's mark. To be certain it wasn't the same watch, Faythe flipped her palm, eyes darting between the golden lines she wore and the identical drawing on the brass as a cold fear grew.

"You discovered where the Ruins are. But you will need the aid of someone long detached from our realm to get to them."

"That's what's inside?" Faythe asked, incredulous, recalling the time Marlowe discovered the information locked in her mother's pocket watch all that time ago: the locations of the Spirit Temples.

"How would I know?" the woman drawled. Her frail hand held the table, trembling, and protruding veins appeared under paper-thin skin as she strained to stand.

"This isn't what I came for."

"Your sleep tonic. You'll find that somewhere out front. But come with me."

Faythe didn't want to go after her; all she wanted was to sleep. Yet her steps moved to follow the intermittent thump of the woman's cane, her shuffling steps. The longer she listened the sounds became less present, more of a distant echo coming from no sure direction. Candlelight became fleeting as they trailed down another dark hall, creating an eerie darkness. The woman's silhouette was engulfed by shadow, but Faythe couldn't hurry fast enough to keep up. Her feet weighed heavier, her eyelids drooped, the hall narrowed and tilted, but she remained upright, only following the alluring scent of the woman's pipe.

She didn't think the small shop could extend back this far. From outside it seemed no bigger than their hut back in Farrowhold. At the end of the passage was a door. Out of it streamed light she wasn't really yearning for with the darkness being so welcoming in her fatigued state. Faythe took a couple of steps inside, but horror doused her, snapping her awake, as she spun to turn back.

The door was gone.

There was no way out.

Faythe clamped her eyes shut, adjusting her footing when she swayed. She couldn't even bear to look for the woman, for where Faythe stood now was in a room of mirrors.

She knew this room.

"I'm scared."

A small voice sent chills racing down her spine, forcing her gaze to open, but she couldn't turn around to face the reflection she'd avoided for weeks.

"I want to go home."

But Faythe knew that voice was too young to hold such terror. Against all that skipped her pulse and churned her stomach, she twisted around.

Dark forestland surrounded them. Charcoal timber, a misty ground. Though there were infinite trees, Faythe knew these ones —she'd stood between them before. On this night she couldn't comprehend how she'd become trapped in her memory of the Westland Forest. The child from before stood there, and Faythe wished she were anywhere else. She wanted to run to her, protect her with everything she was.

"Mother said I wasn't supposed to go into the woods." Tears fell from those golden-flecked sapphire eyes.

Faythe's pulse picked up in trepidation. She was feeling what the girl felt, her hurt and terror and loneliness. "You're not real," she whispered, though she wanted this to be—if only so she could hold the small child in her arms.

Her palms heated, prickling with senses that were dulled but fought to keep her aware that none of this was real.

A hall of mirrors…

Faythe shook her head, trying desperately to grasp at the loose threads of reality to stop herself from being ensnared entirely by this cruel mind game.

"You're a Dresair."

"Oh my," it drawled, stepping to the edge of the mirror. It appeared in the next large shard.

Faythe whimpered at its new form.

Her mother.

"You have wasted too much time running."

"I don't want anything from you," Faythe choked out. She was suddenly back in High Farrow, haunted by the knowledge that had taken a dear friend. Caius. His innocent face, robbed of the life he deserved to live. Faythe hadn't forgotten for a single day.

"I think you have something for me," it cooed. Its eyes fell pointedly, and Faythe dipped into her pocket to retrieve the brass watch. It was the first time she'd noticed the hands were not ordinary. This watch was not a time-teller; it appeared more like a compass. Its hand flickered, becoming more frantic, and Faythe wasn't sure why her pulse raced with the desire to be rid of it.

"I will take it off your hands," the Dresair probed again.

"I don't want anything in return," Faythe said warily.

Its grin sliced too high to be natural, striking Faythe with such terror that without thought she tossed the watch toward the mirror. She winced, expecting it to shatter, but her awe replaced her fear when the solid item passed through the glass as if the pane were made of water, rippling the image of her mother, who didn't move.

When it stilled, the watch was gone.

"I will not burden you with knowledge. Rather, I will give some back to you."

Faythe braced herself.

Though the Dresair didn't speak again. A tiny phoenix flew against the grim illusion of the woods, so vibrant and mesmerizing. Faythe watched in fascination as it broke off and dispersed as glittering embers. It formed into letters, then words, until four lines were structured clearly.

Come the return of the lost first son,
The end will fall at last.
For only if the heirs unite,
Can they right the wrong of the past.

Faythe read it several times before the embers dulled and faded away. She reeled over the beautiful delivery of the message by the phoenix illusion and stored away the words she knew to be important, slowly unlocking something in her mind.

"I think you owe me for this favor."

"It's not a favor if you request something in return."

"What if—"

"No."

Her eyes squeezed shut. She couldn't bear to look at her mother's face.

"My Phoenix."

A choked sob left her. "Please stop."

"I will." It soothed her in Reylan's voice. "If you free me."

The surprise of that request forced her to look. Reylan stood there, and her mind battled her body with the need to run to him. *Gods*, she missed him so much. From her thoughts the creature formed him in every perfect detail.

"Not him," she begged.

It ignored her. "Marvellas did not plan for you to rise, Faythe. You were in the past, and in your return, only a means to an end for her to reunite with her sister at last. But if it will bring you comfort, she did once care for you, and that sentiment may be the thing to end her still."

Faythe tried to decipher the meaning, but the Dresair's words overwhelmed her.

"Should Marvellas succeed in conquering you, the one true heir of Marvellas, she will end the Mortal Gods once and for all. This realm will no longer be accessed by its creators."

"I'm not the only true heir," Faythe said. It was the only thing that rang with familiarity within her. "There was another before me. Do you know what happened? How did they not succeed?"

Laughter scattered around the space, yet Faythe couldn't pin its source. It itched over her skin, and her hands rose to her ears, only halting when the Dresair eased its amusement enough to speak again.

"Oh, dear child," it drawled. Faythe saw it had taken her own face. "It is almost time for you to remember. We have all been waiting. Marvellas achieved her goal after all with you, but what she could not anticipate was the last sister's interference turning the end into fresh hope. You have been a pawn for too many lifetimes. Now, Faythe Ashfyre, you must become her doom."

Dreaded images that didn't make sense tried to enter her mind, but Faythe clamped her eyes shut and cast it all away. She saw flaming red hair and eyes golden like her own, but these ones with an added ethereal fire. So much terror filled her, and she couldn't breathe, couldn't think. She wanted to run from her own mind so as not to see the visions that tried to push through.

"I've given you a lot. More than perhaps I should. But I have spent far too long in this forsaken place."

Faythe had never been more glad for the wicked voice for it dragged her from the spiral in her head. She found the will to face the Dresair again. But who she found nearly buckled her.

Agalhor and Reylan stood side by side. A creeping dread coated Faythe's body. Her adrenaline spiked to protect them, though all they did was stand and stare.

"I wonder who you would choose," the Dresair taunted.

She blinked and they were on their knees.

"Stop," she breathed, fearing so truly for them.

"Your father, a powerful ruler with the heart of the people. He could be an invaluable influence in this war to come."

Two figures eased out from the trees like shadows, a glint of steel catching her eye through the dark.

"Or your mate. Your bond, which has defied what no other has before. The one who, without memory or reason, never truly forgot."

Her breaths were suddenly short and hard. Words clawed in her throat but couldn't escape.

"Maybe you will be too late to save either one."

The black wraiths raised their swords, and all Faythe could do was scream. A surge of heat shot to her palms as she slammed them to the ground. A gold essence dispersed along with a blast of pure power, and she had to clamp her eyes shut. Glass shattered all around her with an ear-splitting crash. Her arms rose on instinct, but none of the raining shards hit her. When the shattering stopped, her ears were filled with a high-pitched ringing that matched the thrum of her heart.

Until a crack sounded behind her.

Faythe clumsily got to her feet. Her vision came and went as she tried to focus on the silhouette stalking toward her. Sluggishly, she freed Lumarias, but she barely had the strength to lift the blade.

"I knew you held the power to do it." A serpentine voice snaked toward her. "Shatter all the mirrors at once and seal their end with what lives under your skin. You are unmatched indeed. Though only if you find the will to use your power before it uses you."

"What are you?" Faythe rasped, fighting for consciousness.

"Out here, I am whoever I want to be."

Her eyes focused enough to catch onto the figure. Horror-struck, Faythe stumbled back, glimpsing the creature with gray skin and depthless holes for eyes. The Dresair's true form was a thing of nightmares.

And she had unleashed it.

"I could be you. So much power it is tempting…" It took seductive steps forward, and Faythe tried to gain distance. "I give this knowledge as a gift, not a curse, Faythe Ashfyre. This sweeping winter shall be the longest the land has seen. When snow falls, it will not end until the war is won. There will come a time when you will lose all. Lose yourself. What you have broken today will be your only way back. Or you will choose to seek a new unknown."

Faythe swallowed hard. Her mouth parted with questions, but

the Dresair lunged for her, and she cried out. Her eyes clamped shut as she stumbled back. Then her ankle twisted on something, and she was falling.

And falling.

And falling…into darkness.

CHAPTER 16

Zaiana

TWICE NOW HER subconscious had made her heart lurch on account of Maverick. Not out of consideration for his well-being, but in anticipation of his arrogant input. She feared his opinions about her spying would give them away at some point.

Just as quickly as she jerked, Zaiana remembered she was alone. It had only been two days. She shook her head as she pressed her back to the stone wall and stared out into the night. Her toes strained awkwardly to remain on the ridiculously narrow ledge.

She was simply awaiting the next guard rotation before she swooped down. It didn't really matter as she was sure she wouldn't make it to her destination without some fae dying in her wake. Though she wanted to reduce the exertion as much as possible.

Call it resourceful.

Her wings were glamoured. For what she planned to do they only served as a weakness; a vulnerability that made her shudder with the torture she knew could be inflicted on them. She wished for anything else. Her taunting mind raced with the thought they could be inflicting such barbaric pain on Tynan and Amaya, using them to figure out the dark fae's weaknesses. They would know to use their glamour ability for safety, but the right kind of pain could force that protection to drop.

Zaiana often enjoyed climbing across architecture instead of taking to the skies. It offered more of a challenge and honed her focus. She leaped, arms reaching to catch onto a balcony. Swinging, she landed on the railing below with feline stealth, only pausing for a second to extend her senses and determine if the room was occupied. Her time and energy were worth far more than useless killings. She'd rather not deal with any unwanted occupants tonight.

It hadn't been easy to get this close to the castle. If she were anyone else, Zaiana didn't doubt she would have been shot down or captured by now. Archers patrolled both city walls, and from her observations over the weeks, never did they lose focus. It was easy to see why the kingdom was so difficult to conquer when they never once wavered in their protection of the capital, always braced for a war they knew could arrive at any moment, just as it had in Dalrune and Fenstead.

It was admirable, she had to admit.

Zaiana was nothing more than a lone stroke of shadow as she carefully navigated her way through the cracks in their defenses. The opportunities were slim and didn't appear often, and she'd be an arrogant fool not to believe that at any given moment she could be captured. She wanted to get as close as she could to the castle with the least amount of fighting.

She was almost there. Hauling herself back up to the rooftops, Zaiana marveled at the grand courtyard below. Their mighty Phoenix emblem on the ground glittered under the moonlight and the amber glow of the torches, creating the illusion that the still image was alive.

He came out of nowhere, eluding her senses like no one had before. Her first sign of him was when he rested a cool blade against her throat. She caught a glimpse of dispersing shadows that piqued her intrigue.

Zaiana held still, though she did not fear.

"I have to say, I'm disappointed." His voice rippled a vibration low on her back, creating an unexpected shiver beneath her leathers. "I believed you to be far more cunning."

In a kingdom known for the legendary material, Zaiana's first question was why the steel at her throat was ordinary when Niltain steel would have harmed her far more. "It's good to see you again…" she drawled nonchalantly, aware their position could be mistaken for some twisted romantic embrace. "Kyleer."

"I can't say the same." His tone was laced with something familiar. A wicked thrill. "But this night just got far more interesting."

He spun her around in one swift motion, the point of his blade grazing up the column of her neck until he was using it to tilt her chin. Their eyes met, his an odd mix of brown and green set into his tanned complexion. His hatred toward her added a sharpness to his features, which were already cut. She couldn't deny she found him beautiful, but more so intriguing. There was something rogue beneath such a hard exterior, just waiting to be unleashed. Through lust or combat—perhaps both. A few tresses of his wavy deep brown hair framed the curve of his brows, adding a disheveled look of danger and hidden passion.

"Zaiana."

Her name in his low, rough voice touched the tip of her spine. She gave him her best sultry smile. "I wonder, Commander,"—Zaiana raised her hand, gritting her teeth as Kyleer pressed the sharp point tighter, almost drawing blood. She traced a slow finger along the blade, unfazed—"if you will deign to chase me this time."

Quick as a flash, Zaiana summoned her lightning, gripping the blade fully. It cut into her palm, but it was worth the pain to watch Kyleer spasm with her shocks, his groan deeply satisfying. Sheer adrenaline had her sprinting away rather than staying to enjoy it for longer.

She darted stealthily over the rooftops, not faltering a single step or pausing for calculation. Zaiana let her senses guide her, confident she could navigate even without sight as she'd been so ruthlessly trained before, her senses reduced one at a time as she was forced into trials that would test each one.

Never give them a weakness.

To her glee, Kyleer did chase her. He closed in impressively fast, albeit by cheating. His shadows were mesmerizing as they circled and answered to him. He emerged from a thick cloud into her path.

"Is that all you can do with them?" She paused to inquire, watching the smoke as it dissipated in the mild wind. "Jump from one place to another?"

"Why don't you come closer and find out?"

He riled something in her. Unexpected, but not entirely unwelcome. He offered a challenge. Perhaps he'd even be a worthy match.

"You'd like that," she said, adding a sensuous note.

"What I would like is to kill you on this rooftop. But why let your foolish decision to walk right into the heart of your enemy go to waste?"

Zaiana freed a blade, flipping it nonchalantly. "Use me and kill me. You have no idea how often those threats come hand in hand."

"Yet still you live."

The curl of Zaiana's mouth spoke of pride and triumph. "People don't get close enough to achieve either feat." She sent the blade hurtling for him, merely a distraction as she began her descent. Zaiana leaped and swung, skidding down slanted roofs and hopping over balconies. She remained at too risky a height to attempt a leap, but when she felt his increasingly pissed-off presence creeping in again, she cursed, having to use a kernel of her gathered magick to unglamour her wings just long enough to step off the ledge and glide down.

What followed turned fae warriors into frightened children. Landing in the center courtyard wasn't Zaiana's ideal plan. She knew how many guards were circling the perimeter. Twenty. But she'd faced worse odds before.

The guard she locked eyes with first stepped into a quick

fighting stance, but not before his terror-filled gaze trailed up the length of her lethal taloned wings. She smiled at him and relished in watching the bob of his throat.

Though Zaiana enjoyed the horror her dark fae heritage instilled in the guards, there were too many archers, and here she risked her wings being nothing more than ample targets. A familiar tingle rippled through them before the weight of her glamour, like an extra layer of armor, settled on her shoulders. Her displeasure came from watching their tension ease with her wings gone, as though they believed her to be an easy prisoner without them.

Their lack of urgency was insulting.

"I wish to speak with your king," she announced to the courtyard, taking casual steps forward.

None of them spoke back, which ground her irritation. Patience had never been Zaiana's strong suit. As she heard the pull of strings, several guards nocking arrows at once, she decided to demonstrate why she didn't make demands twice.

Zaiana took one breath to tunnel away from the confines of humanity.

They have Tynan and Amaya inside.

Her magick hummed, rejoicing at her will.

They made a mockery of me in capturing them.

Her lightning was charged, but she planned to rain down on them with a show of steel and agility first.

Releasing that breath, Zaiana didn't falter. Freeing a dagger from her thigh, she shifted left, braced firm, and sent it with deadly accuracy through the throat of a guard who took one step closer than the others. Over his splutter she heard the faint whistle she anticipated. Before his body fell, Zaiana pivoted on the spot, catching the arrow that would have pierced her back in flight. Twirling it around in her fingers, her next move was to brace for velocity as she conjured enough magick in her arm to send the arrow straight through the chest of the second guard who darted for her.

He would probably live, unlike his companion.

Zaiana didn't waste a second.

Sprinting, she ducked around the next guard's sword and kicked the backs of his knees. He went down with a cry, which was quickly smothered by her hand plunging through his back and tearing out his heart.

She didn't bother to free her sword.

Twisting again, she caught the next guard's wrist, bending it until his shrill cry drowned out the snap of bone. Zaiana caught his blade, and without turning she plunged it backward and felt some resistance before submerging it in flesh. The guard fell to his knees behind her.

"This could have ended with far less blood if you had listened," she mumbled to the fae who pleaded for his pathetic life in her clutches. She let go of his broken wrist. He stumbled back, and to be sure he wouldn't immediately follow in the others' footsteps, she kicked his chest and sent him flying backward until his head cracked on the stone.

Zaiana made it to the doors, slipping inside the castle as if she lived there. All her senses were on high alert, and while she found it odd the remaining guards hadn't rushed in after her, she didn't suppose it mattered. Through the halls lined in brilliant crimson the emblem of the Phoenix featured proudly. Zaiana didn't drop her focus, but the memory of the beast on the mountain inspired her awe and curiosity to learn more.

The next set of guards who rushed around the corner disturbed her moment of peace. They halted abruptly, and she grew irritable, trapped in the endless maze. Their sights were focused on her hand, and wisely, none advanced.

"The king," she uttered with cold intent. She made a show of admiring the red blood that stained her pale skin. "I assume he sent you to retrieve me."

Zaiana enjoyed the intoxicating scent of their fear, but she didn't dare breathe too deeply for the sweet tang of blood tightened her throat with thirst.

The guards turned back the way they came, and Zaiana stalked them. Their occasional glances were met with her sinister smile.

Upon entering the absurdly large room, she spied her target easily. His poise was unmistakable; he radiated an energy of authority and power. The king stood a tall, broad figure at the head of the table as Zaiana sauntered in with unfaltering confidence. From his lack of shock, she surmised he'd been waiting for her. More guards than were stationed in the courtyard surrounded the hall. She deemed the room far too grand and pristine to be sullied by her presence, all white marble and glittering crystal. The council table appeared to be crafted from the stone of their mountains, only this surface was polished, the dark stone broken by beautiful crimson.

Zaiana strolled lazily into the space, unfazed by the many threats that targeted her. She cast her gaze around to marvel at the intricate stained glass and its beautiful depictions of the Firebird that inspired a heat of remembrance. Then she drew a long breath as her attention settled on the King of Rhyenelle. His shoulders were angled and broad, his height and stature dominating, but it was his cool demeanor and assessing look that made him the mighty leader he was.

Despite Zaiana wearing the blood of his guards, the king didn't react with the outrage she hoped for.

Zaiana examined her hand. "I did ask politely to see you, Your Majesty. It was their own stupidity that killed them." Dropping her arm, she braced her stance, folding her hands behind her back. She wasn't willing to make him an exception to her thinning patience. "I believe you have something of mine," she said with enough threat to leave weaker males quivering. "I want it back."

From the opposite end of the room, one figure in particular stole her attention as he stalked in with a rippling fury so tangible and familiar—one that slithered along her spine with a darkness akin to her own. There was no saying what he might be capable of if that fury were unleashed.

Reylan Arrowood radiated the power she knew him to be capable of, and though she would never admit it, he was perhaps the only male in that room who yielded a fraction of respect. Even when her gaze flicked to Kyleer. His anger hit her differently, and she wondered why he'd sought out the general when he could have chased her a second time. *Disappointing.* Zaiana's mouth curled so faintly for him. No one would notice the flare of hatred in the flex of his jaw.

When Reylan came to a stop near his king, it was as if *he* were the ruler. With a quick glance around the room, every guard's attention was fixed on him, waiting for any slight signal.

Zaiana didn't balk.

"Allow me to offer my condolences, General," she said in greeting. They held eyes in challenge, and she saw his acknowledgment in the faint narrowing of his. "Did I miss the funeral?"

Reylan's hand tightening around the hilt of his sheathed sword was a delight to see. "Careful," he said, his voice dangerously low as though they were alone.

Against him…the battle would be intriguing to say the least.

"A great loss," she went on regardless, enjoying straining his tethers of control. It was marvelous to watch his strategy overpower his reckless rage.

"Why did you come?" Agalhor Ashfyre had a voice of authority. His lack of reaction to anything was unnerving.

"I thought I made that clear."

"You thought you could storm my castle, kill innocent soldiers, and seek your prize alone."

"You haven't seen me *storm* anything," she warned. Her fingers flexed, drawing their attention to the small purple bolts she played with. "I can guarantee the death of everyone in this room in seconds should you provoke me to unleash such a mood."

"Perhaps. Though you would not make it out of this castle alive. That I can guarantee you." Agalhor matched her standoff. "Powerful as you may be, I don't believe even in your arrogance you would argue otherwise. So I ask again, why do you come?"

Her proposition was laughable even to herself. Yet this was the only way. "You think you hold anything of value in two powerless dark fae? They answer to me. They know nothing like what I know." She had his attention, yet she couldn't believe how pitiful her next words had to sound. "I am the sixth master of the dark fae, delegate of the Silverfair bloodline."

"Yet you walk right in here like their cattle," the general said.

She took a calming breath at the insult before cutting Reylan a look. Kyleer shifted at the threat she pinned on him. Zaiana could fight toe to toe with Reylan without an ounce of exertion. She spoke to the king but didn't remove her daring stare from the general. "At least they would not allow failures to stand by their side. I do not know how you still live letting the Heir of Rhyenelle die. Letting Faythe—"

A slam ricocheted off her mental barrier, so strong she took a step back, wincing at the force. Reylan attempted to seize her power, and for a second she feared he could with the sheer fury and will that erupted in him.

The hall remained still in their silent battle, but the wrath that emanated from Reylan alerted Kyleer enough to draw his sword. Reylan retreated, but his cut features were frightening.

"Don't. Speak. Her. Name."

Zaiana contemplated pushing further, wanting to know if he would give in to his desire to kill her against his king's orders. It would be reckless, foolish, yet Zaiana had a bigger plan. "As I was saying," she drawled, sliding her eyes to the king, knowing her casual brush-off would rile the general further. "I hold far more value than those you have locked in your cells."

"Are you offering yourself in their place?"

Hearing it aloud sounded even more despairing. "I am."

"I could hold you all."

"You could *try*," she amended. Like a whip, her lighting struck the marble floor with the quick motion of her hand. Everyone winced at the thunder that resonated through the hall. She'd hurt no one.

Yet.

Summoning with her other hand, she held the reins of control on her magick. "Or we could agree it's not worth the countless lives I could take and substantial damage I could wreak on this castle before you stop me."

The king knew it too. He wasn't an impulsive male, and she was quickly coming to appreciate that about him. Agalhor deliberated, as she expected. After all, what she offered seemed to come with a catch. Except there was none, and she couldn't be certain her plan *wasn't* completely futile. It would surely rage with the promise of death if the masters or Mordecai found out.

"I want to watch them be freed. Only then will you have my complete surrender. You have my word I will not fight."

"You word means little," Reylan snarled.

It was becoming difficult to keep from engaging the general in combat; from doing something impulsive. Her iron-clad fingers dug into her palms. She wouldn't give him the satisfaction of a look.

For the first time, Zaiana didn't have a secure plan. Her ideas over the past weeks relied upon her making it up along the way. She hoped to discover something in her imprisonment that she could offer to the masters to quell their wrath when they learned she'd been plotting all along to turn herself in like a coward for her kin.

Tynan and Amaya were as disposable as any foot soldier to them.

"I'm losing patience, Your Majesty." Zaiana locked eyes with the legendary ruler. Her confidence wavered faintly as she noticed which parts of him Faythe resembled and how she'd almost been the one to take a daughter from a father.

If they were sending the Shapeshifter to track Faythe wherever they were hiding her…the king had to be a part of the ruse.

A ruse that would be all for nothing if Maverick caught her.

"Fight me or accept my surrender," Zaiana said. "Either way I will achieve what I came for. It is your choice."

CHAPTER 17

Tauria

"Tauria Stagknight, I was not expecting you." Zarrius straightened from where he leaned in deep thought as Tauria glided into the games room. She kept the twitch of irritation from her face at believing his use of her last name was deliberate. He was testing her reaction to it, which spoke of his refusal to embrace the joining of her name with Nik's.

"I wanted to come to you myself," she started, her posture tall so as not to give away her unease at being around the lord. Tauria looked expectantly at the male engaged in a game of chess with the lord.

As if asking for permission, he looked to Zarrius, who gave a short nod. Her teeth clamped at the subtle brush-off of her authority.

She slid into the vacated seat, not asking before she began to reset the ornate wooden pieces. "We haven't always seen eye to eye. I've often wondered why it is you hate me so." She watched his reaction as she slipped the last of her pieces back to their opening positions. Holding his stare, she placed her queen. "You start," she said when the white pieces were lined up on his side of the board.

Zarrius obliged after a short hesitation. His pawn opened the game. "Hate is a strong word, princess. I apologize if that is how you interpret my having the interests of this kingdom at heart."

Tauria mirrored his pawn, as expected. He drew out his bishop, and once again she countered with the exact same move.

"Might I ask what it is about me that isn't in High Farrow's interests?"

They exchanged more moves. He claimed her pawn, she took his bishop, and though they chatted Tauria studied the game, wondering how often he sat before these wooden figures and considered their moves as real strategies.

"If you want my true counsel, I believe your mating to be brash and heedless."

"Oh?"

"This kingdom relies on more than just monarchs. You have upset the lords in your failure to consult them on a matter that affects us all."

"Two monarchs are stronger than one. We have bound two great kingdoms."

His gaze slipped from the pieces to her, bearing a judgment that made her skin crawl. "I mean no offense as I say this, Your Highness—"

"Twice now you have failed to address me by proper title," she cut in with a warning. It was dangerous to fan the flames of a fire as unpredictable as Zarrius, yet she would not bow to his attempt to overpower her.

"In law, that is not true. You have no kingdom, Tauria Stagknight. No true crown. In binding yourself to our king you have brought a burden to this kingdom we are not strong enough to defend ourselves against. Not alone. We needed an alliance that would *gain* strength for High Farrow in the face of what's to come, not a drain on our resources."

His statements stung, each cut like small daggers she'd felt before. The wounds hurt, but then they'd scab and heal completely, ready for the next person to attempt to bleed her dry. Tauria wasn't here to vouch for herself. She wasn't here to waste a second of breath convincing the prickly lord she was *worthy* of his pitiful approval.

"Leave us."

Tauria didn't glance up as she echoed the command that made the guards shuffle from the room. She made her counter move on the board, stealing another pawn. She was picking them off one by one.

She didn't dare continue to talk until they were entirely alone.

"You are right," she said finally, catching the hook of his brow as she moved her knight to lock his rook. "I became Nikalias's spy in Olmstone. The bond kept us able to communicate, and it was smart. I thought I could see a happy life by his side, yet being back here only reminds me every day of the idle title I wore for decades. No one knew how much I despised being Orlon's ward, and Nikalias was no different to his father."

"Do you think me a fool to believe anything you say is true with the bond that ties you?"

"No." She shrugged, claiming his rook and attacking his king. "But I have a feeling you can help me, and Nikalias cannot find out."

"Be careful, princess."

Tauria looked him dead in the eye as she took his king. "I can't stop thinking of two things I learned in Olmstone. One, an offer that could benefit us all. Two, a way to sever the bond."

The silence dropped heavy. Zarrius's surprise was not to hers.

"You wouldn't want either of those things. Nikalias would not allow it." He tried to play his moves nonchalantly, but Tauria had stolen his intrigue.

She smiled darkly. "Mordecai offered me everything I have wanted for over a century."

"He is the one who took it from you."

"Wrong. It is Marvellas who leads this war."

"Yet she would be the one to sever your bond. You need her."

Tauria didn't let her triumph show. Zarrius knew everything.

"I wouldn't enter into this if I didn't have anything to gain. I love my friends, and I will always love Nikalias. Marvellas remains a threat to them, and Mordecai can help me end her in exchange for my hand, which is not yet bound."

The wheels in his mind were turning. Tauria had sunk her claws and had him contemplating.

"Nikalias could be listening right now through your *mind*, Your Highness. What you speak of is treason against my king and kingdom."

Of course he'd remain on the edge of protecting Nik, though Tauria knew Zarrius would sooner let him die if it meant he could take his place.

"He could be. Like this game, you have to see many moves ahead or you've already lost." Tauria claimed another knight but sacrificed her bishop to do so. "You have to decide which players are worth keeping to lead the fight,"—a pawn gain to her; a rook gain to him—"forfeiting small to win big because they didn't see it coming."

Zarrius thought he'd been winning for some time now. Until he realized he'd lost.

"Give them security so they won't see their downfall."

Checkmate.

"You can't possibly expect me to believe you would wish to see the ruin of your mate."

"Of course not. Nikalias is my mate in power, but there's always been something missing between us to keep us from being romantic over the many decades we shared." It was a plausible explanation—one she watched Zarrius absorb slowly. "If only there were a way for me to speak with Mordecai at the utmost discretion." She planted the seed and then stood, smiling at the game he'd played right into. "To win wars, you need to join the fight. Sometimes you triumph not by force, but by strategy. You of all people should know that."

CHAPTER 18

Faythe

FAYTHE AWOKE WITH a gasp from the rough, disorienting pull at the front of her jacket. She blinked a few times, dangling in their grasp until she made out the pissed-off face of Livia Arrowood.

"What in the Nether were you thinking?" Livia seethed.

Faythe planted her hands behind her, and Livia let go. As she scanned the room, dregs of memory started to trickle back in with a rattling horror.

Surrounded by glass, the Dresair…

Was all that real?

There was no evidence of any slain creature Livia might have battled to save her; no trace of the hideous *thing* she couldn't be confident was ever here.

"There was a woman…" Faythe thought back. The old woman who had led her back here.

"There's no one here, Faythe." Livia was exasperated. Her boots crunched over the shards of the mirror as she paced. "Gods, I thought maybe—"

"I'm sorry," Faythe got out, still blinking with bewilderment as she swayed to her feet.

"What were you doing?"

"I—um, was looking for…" Faythe stumbled over her words, scrambling for an answer while trying to reorient herself. "What time is it?"

Livia halted her steps, pinning her with ire, and Faythe winced. "Sunrise. When we didn't find you in any of the rooms or downstairs for breakfast, we split off to find you. I picked up on your scent and feared what you might be doing in a long-abandoned store."

Abandoned?

Faythe shook her head, ignoring Livia as she stormed back to the shopfront. In the small kitchen everything was bleak, no hint of the vibrant array of colors or the woman's clutter. Her teacup was dried out, a cobweb across the top of it. Faythe's chest constricted, and nausea burned in her gut. Rushing out to the front, she skidded to a halt. A lot of the shelves were bare, though still in a state of disarray, items and vials all over the place. Faythe was hardly present as she walked down the row of shelves, taking in the neglected sight, noting everything was old, discolored, and coated in a thick layer of dust.

In her rising panic she needed air. She burst out the door that barely hung on its hinges and gulped greedily, taking a few seconds to piece together everything…except nothing made sense in the reality she was living.

The sound of shuffling dragged her attention to a passing human. Faythe hurried down to them. The woman seemed startled as Faythe intercepted her path, pulling the small child to her side. A dizzy wave struck her. A flash of silver hair, sapphire golden-flecked eyes, and the most breathtaking fae features. Yet who she stared at was simply a frightened human.

"Did an old woman live there?" Faythe asked breathlessly, guilty for her frantic intrusion.

Casting a glance at where Faythe pointed, the woman's face fell with sorrow. "A little over ten years ago, yes. No family, so no one to take over the business. It was steadily stolen from until all that remained was of no value."

"Faythe." Livia called her name like a warning.

She would have reacted to her reprimanding tone, but as Livia held her mask, Faythe realized her error. Though she didn't believe this human and her child to be a threat, they weren't what Faythe was afraid of. Anyone who might possibly know who she was could be a target.

"I'm sorry," Faythe muttered to them, stumbling away with guilt. She took the mask quickly from Livia, despising the hollowness in her stomach as she fixed it to her face. It was a familiar feeling to hide, to pretend to be someone else, but it was never something she enjoyed.

"Here," Livia said softly.

Faythe looked down at what she held out and tension lifted from her shoulders. She swiped the vial, not having the energy to wonder how Livia knew.

"We have to get control of your magick," Livia went on carefully. "If it's affecting your Nightwalking, we need to go back to before you even knew how to use that."

Faythe appreciated her choice of words. *We.* Without realizing, she'd been falling back into old habits that were hard to break, such as carrying every burden on her own shoulders. It was within her to figure it out, but without help she feared she'd never have the courage to control it.

When they spied Nerida and Reuben down the path, their faces relaxed with relief.

Faythe took a deep breath. "You're right. I'm ready to try."

"There's no one around for miles," Livia groaned.

Faythe stood flexing her trembling fingers. "You're not helping," she grumbled back under her breath.

The commander would hear her despite being several meters away by a stream with Nerida and Reuben. The location was deliberate: a large body of water for Nerida to wield in defense should Faythe do something out of her control. What that might be…well, they'd been out here in the thick of the woods for hours now, and she'd yet to surface even a trickle of magick so they could find out. Nerida had been encouraging Faythe with soothing words and gentle exercises. Livia had stayed silent, but her thinning patience was becoming tangible.

Faythe thought of the abandoned shop. The room full of mirrors. It was hard to grapple with those feelings when she wasn't certain what was real or a dream. The glass was shattered. Maybe it had been all along and there was no Dresair. Yet the pulse of magick that coursed through her as she'd watched Reylan and Agalhor's lives hang in the balance…

A familiar heat gathered in her palms. Faythe slid her eyes closed to quell her fear of it and tried to focus on finding the reins of control should she surface more. The heat grew, trailing slowly up her arms like lines of shallow fire. It crawled over her shoulder blades until the two lines met in the middle and a pulse began in the tip of her spine.

Faythe gasped, her breathing labored in her panic.

"You're doing great." Nerida edged forward carefully, but she was too close.

Faythe shook her head, ready to retreat from the energy as it continued to build, shaking in her grasp. "Get away from me, Nerida," she said.

"What does it feel like?"

Faythe's brow furrowed at the question, though she tried to answer it. "It's warm—almost hot. It's not as sure as a vibration but like a low tingling."

"Where do you feel it?"

"In my palms at first. But it's in my chest too, like it could stop my breathing. It's in my mind, like it could change my thoughts and make me want to hurt you instead."

"Where is it coming from?"

"Me."

"I don't think so." Nerida's gentle pondering offered a question. "We have a well of power that restricts what we can wield, but it is not the only, nor the original, source of magick. It's all around us. Try feeling it in the earth; as an essence in the air. Perhaps you feel it so recklessly because without realizing you're absorbing it all."

That was terrifying. Like a trigger Faythe felt her control slipping, an urgent need to let go. Snapping her eyes open, she glanced at her palms first. They were glowing brighter than she'd ever seen them before. As if sensing it, she heard the flow of water as Nerida took a few backward steps and stood with a moving wave suspended above her head.

It didn't help. Staring at that mesmerizing veil of water flared Faythe's magick with the desire to take Nerida's.

She wanted to know what it felt like.

Take it.

The chant angled her body toward them. Faythe reached out a glowing hand for them...

Water shot for her so quickly she didn't register it until her back slammed against something solid and she was drenched completely. Faythe fell to her hands and knees, panting hard.

"You were going to attack us!" Livia shouted as they ran over.

Faythe leaned back on her knees, gathering breath. "I told you I didn't want to do this around you." She scanned their wide-eyed faces, but she couldn't even surface guilt, only ire at their incredulity when she had been warning them during their weeks together. "This was pointless," she grumbled, rising. As she wrung out her hair, her irritation grew. Her drenched clothing weighed heavy.

"Sorry," Nerida said sheepishly. "You told me not to take a chance if there was a moment of doubt."

Doubt that Faythe couldn't control herself enough not to harm them. The shame that overcame her made her unable to stand to look at any of them. Yet as Faythe paced to the stream, she reflected on what had just happened.

It wasn't anger or darkness she'd felt in those seconds; it was magick. A raw calling of magick. She hadn't wanted to strike, only take…

Cracking branches far away pricked her hearing. Livia was the first to react, drawing her twin swords. Reuben scanned the woods in a delayed reaction, but he was becoming attuned to their fae signals and retrieved a long dagger. Nerida braced but didn't otherwise move.

Most likely, they were simple passersby. She couldn't detect if they were humans or fae yet. Livia looked to her expectantly, and she refrained from any sourness as she retrieved her mask. Faythe inhaled deeply as she raised it to her face, but she paused.

She listened.

For the first time, it was effortless as the voices reached her in her desperation.

Unbelievable.

It didn't make sense.

The voices grew slowly. Two of them.

Faythe's eyes moved to where she tracked the sound. She only saw woodland, but she took off running. She faintly heard the hiss of her name and knew Livia was chasing her. She didn't care. Faythe had to know if her senses—or her mind in its delirium—were playing cruel tricks.

Her vision began to blur with the clench in her chest. A sob escaped her at the realization of her disappointment should she be wrong, or her utter elation should the faces in her mind turn out to be real in seconds.

Faythe halted abruptly. The world slipped away to reveal only one thing.

Them.

They were laughing and looked so wonderfully carefree, having not spotted her yet. Wetness trailed her cheeks, and she didn't move, wanting to treasure the beautiful sight, but with a fear that she could blink and they would vanish.

Then he looked at her and a shuddering sound escaped Faythe's lips. He pulled his horse to a stop, dismounting. He only tore his sights from her for a moment because he wasn't alone.

Faythe couldn't advance for them as one hard reality stopped her in her tracks.

What would he think of her now?

"Who are they?" Livia asked, keeping her caution, but her voice was soft.

Faythe's lips parted. She tracked every flicker of their expressions with rising nerves until they were close enough to see what she was now: fae. Her voice was strained with emotion as she finally answered Livia.

"Jakon and Marlowe."

CHAPTER 19

Zaiana

ZAIANA STOOD IN a room casting her gaze over the intriguing sight of the bustling city. Five guards accompanied her, but she gave them her back with deliberate arrogance as if to say she would not be threatened by them even if they decided to ambush her at once. Occasionally, her gaze slipped to Kyleer, who stood the closest. Sometimes she lost the fight of keeping her mouth from curling, enjoying the flex of ire it provoked on his face.

"Why didn't you chase me a second time?" she pondered out of nothing more than boredom while they retrieved Tynan and Amaya.

"Because you would have liked it."

Zaiana smiled cruelly, raising her chin while admiring how the crimson-peaked mountains glittered in the sunrise. "So might you."

The door behind them swung open, and Zaiana twisted to it smoothly, firming her stance at the thought of how she might find her companions.

They were being roughly handled—two guards on Amaya and three on Tynan. Zaiana clasped her hands behind her back to keep from letting slip the rage that itched under her skin, especially when her eyes fell to their red, torn wrists. She knew immediately why their shackles had caused such damage.

"Remove those," she warned with slow words coated with ice. She might not have felt such rippling fury over the restraints if they hadn't been crafted of Niltain steel.

Amaya's eyes dropped, lethargic but shocked as she stared at her. Tynan didn't appear as affected by the material, but Zaiana knew it would be drastically reducing his strength.

None of the Rhyenelle soldiers moved at her command. Though Zaiana was unfamiliar with the lack of response, she wasn't such a fool to think the guards would answer to her. It was the commander she aimed her wrath at as she turned to him.

Steel sang at her movement, but Kyleer lazily met her pointed look.

"Now."

"No."

Zaiana's vision flashed as she stepped up to him. Weapons rang out again, waiting for his signal. Kyleer wore a cool arrogance, arms folded, face bored. He didn't fear her opposition in the slightest, and it grated on her irritation.

"You have five minutes with them," he said, daring her to unleash her anger on him. "Then the only shackles you'll have to concern yourself with will be your own."

Kyleer was asking for death by her hand. She put effort into stifling her lightning as her fingers flexed in habit. He noticed without glancing down and the bastard huffed a barely-there laugh.

She wanted to hurt him. Badly.

He didn't have to speak before the guards were filing out. Kyleer made for the door, but he shot her one last look as if to provoke her further.

Zaiana didn't get a second to feel her wrath toward the commander before Tynan hissed, "What in the Nether do you think you're doing?"

She didn't appreciate his tone. "Fixing what you gods-damn messed up."

"Expect our lives to be forfeited if we're caught." His fury was palpable as he recited what she'd warned them all many times. "That has always been the order. There's no damn way they're having you surrender to free us."

Tynan's will to protect her was understandable. It was his duty. Yet she wouldn't stand for her judgment call to be challenged. Even in its insanity.

She ignored his pitiful heroism. "You'll stick together. Don't go back to the mountain—they can't know. Find Maverick. He'll know how to keep the masters from finding out about this."

"No way in—"

"I made myself clear, Tynan," Zaiana cut in, her voice hardening with an authority she rarely had to use against her companions. "Don't question me. This is an order."

"Thank you." Amaya's quiet voice snapped both of their attention. "For coming."

Zaiana's teeth ground at the pang in her chest—or to refrain from snapping at her weak words. She simply looked away from the desolate state of her. Paler than usual, hollow eyes as if she were braced for death any day. Amaya wanted to *live*. It was a rare sight among their kind—at least in the bright and hopeful sense the darkling clung to like a child. Something about that fact tore through Zaiana's stomach, but it solidified her decision.

"What happened to the healer?" she asked, keeping from using her name in case it spoke of more attachment than she was willing to admit to.

"Faythe and two others decided to escort her back to Fenher. They're keeping her hidden in an attempt to figure out if you've told Dakodas she's still alive."

Zaiana pondered their thinking, part of her calculating why they believed she'd remain silent despite all she'd done to Faythe. "Maverick knows," she admitted. "It was the only way to distract him from me." She looked to neither of them as she turned back to the window. Her voice dropped low to elude the guards outside.

"This isn't surrender." Zaiana stood in the heart of the city teeming with life, vibrancy, power, and joy. The kingdom that had never fallen. "You've never doubted me before, Tynan. Don't start now. But I need you to listen to me so you know exactly what's going to happen the moment you fly out of my sight."

Within the inner-city wall the buildings were more pristine, but they still varied in size and structure. Zaiana noticed the paths were mapped out like a maze, strategic in the event of an invasion. Several led into what could be considered a trap to an enemy group, but in everyday life they were merely cul-de-sacs where children played and fae gathered to socialize. Many high walls ran throughout the city, patrolled by archers who were always ready. Ellium was unlike anywhere she had ever encountered before.

Though it had never fallen, Zaiana didn't consider the city unbreakable.

She hadn't moved a fraction since Tynan and Amaya were taken away. She did have a view of the courtyard, and she watched as their shackles were removed and they unglamoured their wings. Tynan spared her a glance, but she felt nothing, fixing her eyes on her companions until a glare of sun stole their silhouettes. Then she stood alone for some time. She didn't think of fighting. Didn't want to make the king out to be a fool as she attempted her great escape. Perhaps she could be stealthy and ruthless enough to succeed, but it wasn't her plan to risk her life over something so stupid.

Kyleer was the first to return. She felt him before she heard him, his presence like a dark and dominating caress.

Zaiana kept her hands clasped behind her, knowing what came next anyway. The commander stepped right up to her, but she yielded nothing except a flinch of her eyes, which he couldn't see, when ice battled fire against her wrists. The Niltain steel shackles were heavy and tore through her with such pain she had to focus on taking long, deep breaths.

Kyleer's hand wrapped around her upper arm and his tall form stepped closer than necessary as his breath whispered across her ear. "Let's go."

Zaiana ignored the ripple down her neck as he tugged on her arm, pulling her with him. "I can walk just fine," she grumbled.

Kyleer didn't answer. His grip was firm, his pace marching, and she struggled to keep up. They wound their way through many halls. Too many, Zaiana thought. She knew then that they were trying to disorient her to prevent her from mapping the castle. Zaiana suppressed her smirk at the amateur measure.

"Magnificent, wasn't it?" she drawled, eyeing the tapestries. "The Firebird."

Kyleer maintained his silence. She cast her gaze to his stern commander's face though he refused to engage.

"She put up a valiant fight, I'll admit," she went on anyway. This seemed to provoke the twitch of his jaw. "Tragic the beloved princess didn't make it—" Zaiana winced as she was slammed against the wall, the impact made worse by the awkward twist of her arms that crushed her bound hands.

"If you want to live beyond a day you won't speak of her like that again," Kyleer seethed in her face.

Zaiana matched his icy glare. His hand curled around her neck, but not with any choking force. Gentle, like hands she'd felt before.

"You're not worthy enough to think of her." Those green eyes flicked between hers, and for a moment she wondered if he was searching for even a kernel of something to contradict his next words. "You're not worthy of anything."

He pushed off her, but she didn't move. They stared off for a long, tense second, and she couldn't decipher why his eyes flexed as he watched her. She deserved his words, though she couldn't stand the faint disruption in her gut. She'd heard far worse before. *Thought* far worse of herself before.

"If you want to hurt me, you're going to have to do so with a blade." She brushed him off icily.

Kyleer was fighting within himself. His fists clenched as though he were holding back from launching to clamp them around her throat again. "Take her to a cell far on the east block." He didn't remove his eyes from her while he gave the command, his tone so beautifully sharp it had the guards moving instantly.

Zaiana was held by that dark stare of threat and anger, but it was born of Kyleer's passion to protect and defend. She stored away anything she could figure out about the commander. She would find his weakness.

He turned abruptly and stormed away. Zaiana didn't realize how rigid he'd made her in their standoff until she was watching his back, his march that was so livid and such a thrill to witness.

The guards approached her, and Zaiana snapped back into herself. Unlike Kyleer, the step she took toward them caused a flash of wariness, and they hesitated in reaching for her.

Zaiana pinned them with warning. "I said I can walk."

CHAPTER 20

Faythe

H ER HEART RACED as though she were standing before the judgment of strangers, and it was gut-wrenching to feel such a way in the presence of her two dearest friends.

Faythe couldn't go to them out of fear they might reject her in horror if she did, so she waited for them to approach. All it would take was one of those quick, assessing looks she was all too familiar with from Jakon and she'd be instantly detected.

Though Marlowe tucked herself into his side, Faythe couldn't shift her eyes from Jakon, waiting on a razor's edge for his reaction, the moment he saw she was now one of the beings they'd been raised to fear. One of those they'd spent endless days mocking on patrol through the streets of Farrowhold, believing they were all arrogant and power-hungry, and that what little she and Jakon had was better than ever desiring the same comforts as the fae beyond the wall. It was all a twisted memory now, but she couldn't shake that it had formed a large portion of their lives.

Jakon stopped a few feet away. He knew. He had to have noticed already. Yet his face—*Gods,* he hadn't changed a bit—bore nothing but yearning, a sadness, and that was when she broke.

They moved at the same time, colliding like stars who'd been separated for far too long, their constellation exploding in reunion. Faythe shook with sobs, arms clamped around his neck, flooded with such overwhelming relief when he held her tightly back without hesitation. Minutes could have passed for all she knew. Faythe breathed in his scent, which was so familiar it wrapped her in a contentment she didn't realize she so desperately needed. With her fae senses it was all-consuming. Notes of Marlowe encased him, his cinnamon and woodsmoke scent touched by lavender and rose.

They finally released their hold on one another. As she stared into those brown eyes Faythe had to blink back her tears. Jakon's smile bore equal parts love and pain. His hand rose to her cheek, drawing his focus to her ears, and she held her breath, anticipating the shift to horror.

It never came.

"This is certainly the twist of the century," he mused.

Faythe chuckled. Laughed. Cried. It rammed into her all at once until her emotions weighed her head so heavy she had to rest her forehead on his chest while he simply held her. No one interrupted them, and she didn't know how much time passed before she calmed. Jakon smoothed down her hair, letting her release it all as he'd done so many times before.

"I missed you so much," Faythe whispered.

"Me too." His lips pressed to her head. "Me too, Faythe."

"I want to tell you everything."

"You will. When you're ready."

With a deep breath she found the will to step back fully, but she barely had a second to gather herself before her gaze switched to Marlowe, who was waiting patiently, and she fell apart all over again. Their embrace was crushing. The two shared giggles of joy and sadness and nothing at all.

Their time apart wasn't all they had to talk about. So much had changed. Who Faythe was now…she was still discovering for herself, never mind trying to explain what had happened to Jakon and Marlowe.

Amid all their heightened emotions, the most confusing part of it all returned to Faythe as she remembered where they were. "What in the Nether are you both doing all the way out here?"

Jakon drew Marlowe close to him—a natural gravitation he didn't even notice anymore. "We have a lot to catch up on," he said. Then, for the first time, Jakon's gaze found Reuben. His eyes widened and a laugh of disbelief left him. "By the Gods, a lot to catch up on indeed."

They found an inn as twilight began to set in. Faythe sat across from her three human friends while Nerida and Livia sat on either side of her.

"Where's Reylan?" Jakon asked carefully, eyeing Livia, who leaned in, twisting a dagger point-down into the table. The commander didn't try to be intimidating, but though her features were soft, she was always carefully calculating her surroundings and company.

"He has to stay away for now." Her chest tightened and she dropped her eyes. "In case the dark fae have eyes on him." Faythe quickly averted her gaze from catching her reflection in the ale in her cup. When she opened her mouth, her words floundered as though speaking about what she was made the reality dawn all over again. "You don't seem shocked," Faythe tried, flicking her attention to Jakon. "About my, um—"

He chuckled lightly. The sound relaxed her tense shoulders and gave her the courage to face the topic with a smile.

"I had my suspicions," Marlowe chimed in.

Faythe huffed sheepishly. "A little warning would have been appreciated." She meant for it to be a lighthearted comment, but Marlowe's expression fell.

"It wasn't as clear as knowing you would Transition. I knew you'd come to great power and that there wasn't much hope for you to harbor it in your human form. Then, after the solstice—" She paused, and something changed in the atmosphere between

Jakon and Marlowe. It was there in the look they shared and the comfort he offered her.

"What happened?" Faythe pressed. She battled with her own rising pulse at the recollection. The solstice. The solar eclipse. Her dying day, but also the moment she came to be all that she was now.

It was Marlowe who pinned her with a look of wonder she'd strangely missed. "It was the day you Transitioned, wasn't it?" It was like watching a light switch on in her brilliant mind, revealing the final piece of a puzzle she'd been searching for. Her eyes trailed over Jakon then back to her.

Jakon's arm went around her, his face assessing as he watched her carefully. "I think we felt you. But Jak…"

"Felt me?" Faythe cut in with horror.

Marlowe only nodded, still calculating. "I'm not certain what it means, but I think we're all connected somehow. But with you and Jak…there's something else."

Faythe shuddered with a wave of uncertainty. She met eyes with her dearest friend, and for the first time she was struck hard with a flash of memory, perhaps lifted from his mind to hers. They had many of them, but in this memory he looked younger, and with him…

"You never met her," Faythe breathed. Shaking her head, she expelled the twisted image.

"Who?"

"My mother." Faythe frowned at him. "You never met her."

Jakon wasn't quick to agree. He was thinking. It was as though he'd been wondering the same before. "I didn't think I had. Yet I've been seeing things: you, someone older. Me, right there with you both. It's all in pieces and I'm not sure what to make of it."

Faythe held no thought or answer either, shaken as she was with unease, but it was becoming a familiar sensation. To halt her spiral, she asked, "How are Nik and Tauria?" The thought of their bright smiles smoothed out her expression with hopeful anticipation.

"Mated," Jakon answered proudly.

Faythe's mouth fell open as countless emotions and questions barreled into her, along with a twisting ache. She wanted to see and hear it from them. Above all, so much joy burst in her chest for them.

For the next few hours, the group exchanged stories, their meet-up lasting long into the unsociable hours of the night, until the establishment was left bare. There was too much to delve into in a single night, but everything Faythe absorbed and what she managed to explain ran her emotions dry.

"You're heading for High Farrow?" Jakon doubled back.

Faythe nodded. "I should be able to remain hidden there."

"To what end?"

She wasn't sure. What her life had become was a pool of uncertainty.

"I need to learn this new power I have," she offered.

That piqued Marlowe's interest. Her curiosity landed on Faythe's hands. Growing accustomed to the golden symbols, Faythe was no longer shy to let go of the cup she was clasping to flip her palms up. She figured if anything, her brilliant friend might connect something from a book or a foresight of her own to shed some light on what they meant.

"They're beautiful," Marlowe said, reaching to take one of Faythe's hands.

Faythe thought so too now the horror had subsided. There seemed to be no way of getting rid of them, so she allowed herself to find some consolation in their appearance. Simply touching her magick essence was enough to add a faint glow to the tattoos, but it was only brief before she retreated, sealing the symbols out of reach once more.

"It's astounding," Nerida said, and it was only then, at hearing her tone of voice, Faythe was struck with the reason why she'd felt such a natural ease with the healer. Her gaze flashed between Nerida and Marlowe, and when she found their wondrous natures aligned Faythe broke into a smile.

"It's infuriating, that's what it is," she grumbled.

"Only because you're so reluctant to figure it out," Livia cut in.

"I'm not reluctant."

"Stubborn. Afraid. Does it really matter what we call it?"

Their challenging glare was never malicious, but Faythe was coming to her wit's end. Because Livia was often right.

"Are there any libraries nearby?" Marlowe wondered. "That might be a good place to start."

"The Livre des Verres would be a great place. Perhaps the only place that could hold such obscure knowledge. There's one book in particular I'd love to seek out," Nerida answered.

"That's in Olmstone," Livia added as though it were not an option.

From all they'd heard of the kingdom from Jakon and Marlowe and what happened after Nik and Tauria made their narrow escape, it didn't seem safe to venture there when it could be overrun by Valgard.

"She was really there?" Faythe whispered in fear.

Jakon knew who she meant. His expression creased with protection but an edge of wariness. "Yes. Marvellas was there. Perhaps she still is. None of us were certain how long Marlowe's enchantment would hold."

It was so much to take in, what her friend had discovered she was capable of. Faythe stole glances at Marlowe and all she could see was their days of careless laughter in the blacksmith's workshop before either of them dipped their toes into the impossibility of what they were. Marlowe still looked the same. She still sounded the same. Faythe clung to hope that no matter what, nothing would change between them.

"Where's Reuben?" Jakon asked, alerting everyone to his absence. Faythe had forgotten about him in the midst of all they had to talk about.

"He had too much to drink. He headed for bed about an hour ago," Livia informed them.

Faythe winced sheepishly. She hadn't noticed to bid him good night.

"We didn't get the chance to hear of his great return," Jakon mused with a chuckle, taking a long drink. As he did, Faythe's attention caught on a glint from his finger. Her brow pinched, struck hard with such a flood of emotion her eyes pricked with tears. "What's wrong?" he asked in alarm.

"You're married," she whispered, then she dragged her eyes to his before they fell to confirm a matching band adorned Marlowe's finger.

Their gold rings met when Jakon reached over and took her hand. Faythe quickly swiped at her face.

"We didn't want to wait, but we were hopeful one day we could celebrate with everyone. With the war coming, it felt right," he explained softly.

Faythe was happy for them, so consumed by joy, but that wasn't all. The reality flushed through her unexpectedly. Of how time had become so precious and she'd missed so much of it with them. Just as they'd missed out on her coming to terms with being Rhyenelle's heir, she hadn't even been able to tell them about her bond with Agalhor or how deeply she'd fallen in love with Reylan. Faythe's hands rose to cover her face. It wasn't long before she was enveloped in Jakon's warmth.

"You're still you, Faythe," he said quietly. "That doesn't change. Not ever. Pointy ears or not."

Her choked sob turned to a laugh as she lowered her hands. "I'm so glad you're here, Jak. It's not been the same without you."

"We're two sides of the same desolate coin, remember? We'll always find each other."

Her burden felt instantly lighter. What she had to face within herself…it didn't seem all that terrifying anymore.

CHAPTER 21

Tauria

"Are you sure you know what you're doing?" Lycus's concern was understandable, but she'd chosen to let him in on her plan, and his reaction felt justified. It could be considered dangerous, or in his words "insane," yet Tauria wasn't going back on it. They walked the halls of High Farrow's castle, no particular destination in mind.

"I only told you because I need your help."

"If he agrees to risk himself to come here," Lycus pointed out.

Tauria knew what the plan rested on, but it wasn't Zarrius she was hoping to convince, and she'd grabbed Mordecai's interest once before when he decided to hear her out. "It may be a long shot, but I have to try."

"And Nik?"

"He doesn't like it, of course. But he knows everything."

Lycus ran a hand over his face. "I don't like this."

"I only need you to trust me."

"I'm *trying*," he drawled.

Tauria's spine straightened as Zarrius rounded the corner and started walking toward them.

"Ah, princess, I was hoping to catch you."

Her heart skipped, and when they came to a halt where their paths met, the Lord cast an expectant look at her general.

"I'll call for you soon, Lycus."

She could tell he was fighting his reluctance in the firming of his brow. His dark skin flexed as he pinned the lord, but he gave her a small nod before he left them.

"Has there been news regarding my request?" she asked discreetly.

He motioned for her to continue walking with him. "I cannot cater to your request as I have no correlation with dark forces intent on taking down our kingdom," he began.

Tauria's heart lurched at the opening, and she braced, realizing she'd need to switch tactics to defend her inquiry if he turned on her now.

"But to protect this kingdom, I have my sources, and they are keeping an eye on such threats. I may have been able to get an anonymous message out that has indeed sparked a certain High Lord's interest."

Tauria kept her expression neutral, though a conflict of nausea and rising triumph unsettled her gut at the thought he might agree to see her.

"The king requests a gathering," a guard announced behind them.

Lord Zarrius smiled—the kind of smile that held a knowing gleam—but if she took this, she would go down on her own with nothing to incriminate him for being involved with the dark fae. He held out his arm, offering to escort her, and while it sickened her, she looped her hand through it. Zarrius tucked his other hand over hers, making her strain with the need to seek distance from him even more, until she felt something small slide into her possession.

"I hope you know what game you are playing, princess."

In the throne room, they found Nik standing by the dais with the court gathered around him. Tauria broke from Zarrius, meeting Nik's warm smile. Three thrones were still present as it hadn't been on either of their minds to update the arrangement. Tauria by routine was about to take up her usual place, which had been to Orlon's right, but Nik held out a hand.

"*Hello, love.*"

She shivered with his accompanying caress on her senses. "*You've been busy,*" she sent back.

Nik led her over—not to her usual place, but right before High Farrow's single ancient throne. Her gaze snapped to him with hesitation, nerves bundling to know the whole court was watching and this was not simply a seat; it was a statement. Nik's only answer was a warm smile and a dip of his head, so Tauria took his confidence, turned, and sat while all eyes tracked her. Some wide, some turned away from her to whisper to their neighbor. She tried not to read into any of it, owning her right to be there.

Letting go of her hand, Nik leaned against the tall back of the throne instead. "I summoned you all here to watch justice be served." He addressed the suspense at last. "It is no secret we held a traitor in our midst—one who not so long ago made an attempt on my life."

Just then, sobs echoed throughout the hall, the sound accompanied by steps and shuffling as guards escorted Samara into the room. Despite the rage that would always live on in her for what she attempted, Tauria was not so heartless as to be numb to Samara's vulnerable state. She took no pleasure in the fae's humiliation, but for the severity of her crime, her sentencing had to be public.

Samara was pushed to her knees before them. Tauria gave no outward sign of her sympathy.

"This is your last chance to confess anything that could affect your punishment," Nik said, dangling a lifeline.

If she confessed to being a pawn, it would be open for investigation and might even spare her life if her claims could be proven. Tauria did not hold out hope for her.

"No," she whimpered quietly.

"Speak up."

"I acted of my own free will," she snapped.

Tauria felt Nik's rippling resentment as he pushed off the throne. "Why?" she demanded. "What could you have had to gain from an attack on your king?"

"He is not my king."

Gasps broke out among the crowd.

"And you are not my queen."

"You make it easy, Samara," Nik drawled, unfazed by her words. "I gather all these people for a trial, expecting you to plead for your life, but here we are. Left with only one measure. Wouldn't you agree, love?"

Tauria spared one look at Zarrius out of mere curiosity, to see if he would offer any protest, any emotion, to show he'd ever cared for her life like she cared for his. She found nothing but a cold and cruel look of triumph. He was watching Nik carry out exactly the end he'd hoped for by manipulating her to kill him.

"Your attempt on my life is treason of the highest form, and there can be no more just punishment than to take yours. Samara Calltegan, our sentencing is death."

"You cannot do this!" a male voice boomed out from the crowd.

"Father," Samara whimpered, turning to see him, but guards grabbed her shoulders to pin her forward.

Tauria knew the political stir this would cause. The Calltegans were a family who brought great wealth into the kingdom with their trades. Just as they'd hoped, Zarrius moved through the crowd to the distressed lord. As much as Nik despised the fact, Zarrius was the only one he thought capable of keeping peace with the family, however much he had to manipulate them.

Samara's death was Zarrius's gain.

"I will grant you a choice, however," Nik went on when the disruption eased. "Out of respect to your family, your death will not be made public. You will be comfortable, and you may choose how it happens."

Her crying turned silent. She stared at the ground but gave a small nod in acceptance of her fate.

"Take her back," Nik ordered.

Tauria looked away while Samara was hauled off. Someone who was once a fae of high respect and great prospects had been used and discarded, and Tauria had never resented Lord Zarrius more. Her nails dug painfully into the arm of her chair until Nik's hand enclosed it, and she dragged her attention up to find his knowing expression also held rage and disturbance.

"You look beautiful," he said to her mind.

Tauria cracked a smile despite everything, and as if he didn't care about the room full of spectators, Nik's fingers grazed her chin.

"And powerful. And like you were meant to be mine for how perfectly you occupy this throne. I'm glad the whole court is getting the first glimpse of your long reign here, Tauria Silverknight."

CHAPTER 22

Zaiana

Her cell wasn't all that bad. No bed, but a decent provision of hay. It even had a small window through which she'd watched the day pass into night three times now. Zaiana had been confined under far worse conditions for far longer. She didn't mind their idea of imprisonment. Even the food was generous for a dangerous captive. Considering she'd killed within their walls, she wondered why they were bothering to feed her anything more than enough to keep her barely alive.

The silence kept her company like an old friend. Zaiana spent her days training her mind to detach from everything as she had before. It was easy when her desires rarely knew the light of day anyway. How to cope with nothing? Easy when she knew the bed of stone far too well.

She was not afraid of what they would do to her for whatever information they sought to gain. They would be fools not to try. All she could do was relish how they tried to break someone who'd been fractured too many times to yield to physical torture.

They'd taken her sword, plus the many daggers she wore. They'd taken the pins from her hair, leaving her braid annoyingly loose, thick tendrils around her face. They'd taken her cloak and removed any clothing adorned with metal buckles, leaving her in a fitted black undershirt and pants. They could have left her to shiver during the nights, yet a guard had unshackled one wrist long enough for her to throw on an oversize black sweater.

At the sound of someone's approach, Zaiana halted her calculated pacing.

"To what do I owe the pleasure, General?" she drawled, lazily dropping her eyes from the stars she counted through the window.

Reylan was alone. Extending her senses, she could tell he'd dismissed the guards in the hall too. Zaiana leaned back against the far wall, watching him silently debate his words.

"When you left the temple..." Reylan trailed off, leaving a pause. The look they shared aligned a thought but raised a defiance. When she looked at him, all Zaiana could hear was his chilling promise to end her for harming Faythe. A fraction of that death stare remained, making him a volatile and real threat.

The iron bars between them were as good as glass.

"You said—"

"I know what I said," she cut in.

"What did you mean?"

Zaiana straightened her head and crooked an eyebrow. She didn't believe for one second Reylan didn't know. He wanted her to admit she did too. Zaiana held one thing against him, and she would be damned if she let it go.

"You tell me."

His hand came up to curl around the bar, his piercing blue eyes growing with fresh wrath under his careful control. "Where is Maverick?"

Those three words sent a chill down every notch of her spine before scattering across her skin, each one delivered with revenge. For what Maverick had done, and for Reylan having to witness the most unforgivable crime. The general harbored something that could only ever be settled with one thing.

Death.

"I am not his keeper."

Zaiana shouldn't care about the dark bastard. Yet the thought of him crossing the general's path tightened her stomach.

"It sure seemed like it," Reylan growled. "Did you tell him to come to the temple? Was it on your command that he—?"

"No." She didn't owe him anything, but she wanted to survive. Her silence on Maverick's actions could unleash the darkness she didn't want to test within the general. It was rare that she remained so uncertain of what someone could be capable of. "I did not expect him to follow me."

"You would have spared her." Reylan was trying to calculate why she'd waste such an opportunity.

Zaiana stayed silent, still in turmoil over her own stupidity in that moment.

"Why?"

"It changes nothing, General. She is dead."

Reylan wouldn't know her harsh statement was a question. One he'd revealed the answer to instantly, exactly as she'd hoped.

Faythe was alive, and they were all part of the ruse.

He stood firm, staring her down with hard breaths of anguish, not the deep grief she expected.

"I was hoping for a better interrogation from you," she said to sway the conversation away from the matter before he could attempt to probe her further. All Zaiana had was time. She wanted to figure out what their plan was with the rise of their princess. What Faythe was, what she was capable of, or if nothing had changed at all in the one touched by death.

His fist clenched with restraint around the bar.

A shuffling sounded from down the block, soon joined by the ripples of a presence that could offer even more entertainment.

"Agalhor is looking for you," Kyleer mumbled low as if she wouldn't hear it.

Zaiana slid down the wall until she was sitting, growing deliriously bored while they exchanged more words of little interest. She examined her raw wrists, which had become numb to the pain of the Niltain steel.

Reylan left, but Kyleer stayed. Zaiana's tipped-back head

straightened like a dead weight while he stood awkwardly still, watching her.

"Are you waiting for a show, Commander?"

His cut features had eased of some of the rage he wore when she last saw him. He still looked particularly pissed off to be around her, but she gauged he was feeling less murderous.

"Are you offering?"

Zaiana tracked him as he walked a few paces. Reaching for a chair, he dragged it right in front of her cell. Her irritation flared when he sat on it.

"I question your skills if they've reduced you to playing babysitter," she ground out, hoping this were a test. He wasn't really going to sit there for any considerable amount of time...was he?

His casual recline spoke the opposite. Kyleer gave an overexaggerated sigh as he folded his arms. "Why is your chest still?" he pondered curiously.

"How often have you been fixated on my chest?"

Kyleer flashed a hint of a smile. What was more jarring was that it caused a shudder over her body. "Why did you give yourself up?"

Zaiana huffed a dry laugh. "Do you treat all your hostages so warmly and expect them to offer up everything?"

"Oh no, we haven't started with you yet. Consider this my own curiosity."

"It's pathetic."

"Look at where you are, Zai."

"Don't call me that."

She realized too late the error in her words. She'd given him something to spark that insufferable delight in his eye. Her mind dangled an image she'd buried. A face. A name.

Zaiana twisted her head to cool down, taking a second to compose herself while keeping it all from being deciphered by the bastard who would use the weakness. It was a battle against the first real emotion she'd felt in so long.

She wanted to hear it again. Yet she didn't.

She didn't.

"What was his name?"

Kyleer's question was all it took for her to embrace a cold detachment. She didn't look at him. She gave him nothing. If she were free and found a blade within easy reach, her instinct would be to answer with violence.

Instead, she had nothing but her silence.

Kyleer stood, making as if to leave, but she didn't care. Her eyes slipped closed, her mind tunneling away from hurtful thoughts. Just as she was embracing the stillness once more, he returned. Zaiana didn't plan on giving him any more attention, but an alerting high-pitched sound made her eyes snap to him.

It wasn't in fear of the blade he held.

It was *her* sword.

Her fists balled to know he could mock her by merely having possession of it. There was a pride in one's sword.

"Name?"

Her eyes narrowed on him while he watched her expectantly. His expression grew bored with her lack of engagement. Kyleer set the scabbard aside, examining the craftsmanship of the sword, trailing his eyes over the length of steel that glittered with notes of Magestone. He flashed her a knowing look, to which she responded with a cruel curl of her mouth. He was careful to avoid touching the length. The hilt and cross guard were stark black but intricately woven, and as his fingers grazed the lone strip of aged material there, she clenched her teeth so hard she thought they might break.

Zaiana waited for the probing or mocking or taunting over what it was.

Yet Kyleer said nothing.

She slid her eyes back to him just in time to see a small, thoughtful frown vanish as he continued his examination. Just below the cross guard he squinted.

"*Nilhlir,*" he recited. "It's not of the Old Language." He didn't ask her again. He twisted his wrist once, though the sword was not at all of a comparable size to what he should wield. "Impressive blade," he admired all the same.

"Why are you here, Kyleer?"

He tilted his head. "I'm trying to figure you out."

She didn't expect his honesty. Her head fell back against the stone. "When you do, enlighten me."

His smooth chuckle drew out a shiver.

Kyleer dipped into his pocket, and what he produced inspired a flash of white rage she had to suppress. He held up the iron guards—the two for her right hand, as far as she could tell. Her hands had felt so light and bare these past few days.

"Can you conjure lightning without them?" he asked, giving them the same expert attention he'd given her sword.

"Unchain me and find out."

Kyleer glanced over her through long, narrowed lashes. Something in his look darkened—not with threat. What spilled through that long pause sparked a tension she wanted to ignore.

"I quite like you in chains." He dropped his tone low, taking a single step closer.

"There are a million ways I could still kill you in them."

"I could make that the last thing on your mind."

Zaiana had played this game before. Many times. It was disappointing to know how easily the commander fell into the trap. She eased herself up. They'd bound her hands in front of her now, and she curled them around the bars, peering up at him with her best look of seduction that made men drop to their knees. She knew how to make her voice a caress to entrance him. Parting her lips, grazing her teeth along the bottom to draw his eyes to them…

Kyleer did as expected. Yet for the first time, a quick flutter pulsed in Zaiana's stomach.

"Then open the door."

Kyleer's look eased with a desire she was familiar with. He pocketed her jewelry, then his hand slipped though the bars, taking her chin. His rough, calloused fingers angled her head. With their new proximity, she didn't know why she cared to notice the hazel flecks through his green irises. They reminded her of moss, earthy and calming. There would have been an air of freedom in those beautiful eyes were it not for the shield of something dark and broken. Zaiana didn't know when she'd pressed herself tighter, feeling the hard impression of iron against her ribs.

Then, like the flick of a switch, his cold glare returned. His mouth firmed tightly, eyes flinching in what Zaiana registered as *disappointment*.

"You're not that special, Zai." He released her, stepping away, and Zaiana had never been so dumbfounded. It was an art to lure men into her web. She'd done it countless times, yet never had she risked becoming tangled in her own spool.

Her embarrassment raged, flushing her skin and making her gaze burn. Her words would form the daggers they took from her. "Look at where they've stationed you, babysitting a single prisoner. I watched you for some time, you know. Out on that quest. I watched how easily Izaiah and Livia bonded, how *in love* Reylan and Faythe were." Zaiana let out a bitter laugh. "They even gave the pitiful human more attention than you. You mean the least to all of them, and you always will."

She took a large step back. Her throat...why did it tighten?

The stillness of the commander was unexpected, but he swallowed any words of disagreement. "I guess we just found some common ground," he muttered vacantly, already taking steps away. "If you want to hurt me, you'll have to do so with a blade."

CHAPTER 23

Reylan

REYLAN'S FINGERS WERE poised over the piano keys as he wondered where to place them next. He tried one sequence. Shaking his head, he thought it over again.

He didn't care what it made him to be up in Faythe's rooms finding distraction in the instrument. It was all he could do to keep her close. Though he didn't enter through the door for anyone to see; a kernel of Izaiah's Shapeshifting ability hummed in him.

Contemplative notes filled the silence, resting his torment for a while. He repeated them, rearranged them, until the music felt right. He couldn't stop picturing her seated beside him that first time he played for her. How beautifully thoughtful she'd looked though she didn't know how much he ached to confess everything he felt for her.

Reylan closed the lid of the piano when he detected a nearby presence. The falcon swooped to the balcony before a flash of white light revealed Izaiah.

"You know, I always feel like you dampen my flight speed with the time you take," he commented, sauntering through the open balcony door.

Reylan ignored him as he stood. "How is she?"

"The journey was fine, by the way. I'm only a little worn out from the flat-out round trip, but—"

"Izaiah."

He smirked, but Reylan didn't have room for amusement. "She's still well. They all are. They should be in Fenher by week's end."

"You're still keeping an eye on their surroundings too? No one seems to be suspicious or following them?"

"No. Though their antics are both hilarious and admirable."

He'd first heard of the disruptions weeks ago. Reylan himself had dispatched several patrols to the outer towns where Raiders were being conveniently outed, though none of his soldiers had been able to find out how.

Until Izaiah witnessed who was behind it all.

Reylan had been filled with pride but also riddled with anxiety that they weren't entirely sticking to the plan. Faythe was masked. Smart. But he couldn't rest easy knowing she was deliberately getting in harm's way. Though he couldn't blame her for needing some excitement.

"Do you really just sulk in her rooms every night?" Izaiah strolled around the games room, peering into the bedroom that remained untouched.

Reylan felt the rippling essence of magick before the shadows dispersed.

"He does. It's unnerving," Kyleer chimed in.

While his irritation flared, Reylan knew better than to react to their jests. "Did you find out anything else from the prisoner?" He could hardly stand to say the dark fae's name. Seeing her chained and at his mercy, it had taken all his willpower not to damn everything and end her. All he could picture when he looked at her was the blade she'd held to Faythe's throat.

"Not yet."

"Don't waste time," Reylan warned.

It didn't sit well with Kyleer, whose stance shifted to him, and Reylan flared with the challenge.

"I told you I was handling her. And I am. You can't be trusted."

As though anticipating his next step, Izaiah shifted casually between them. This tension was wrong. Everything was wrong, and he despised his own willingness to spiral.

"Perhaps 'trusted' is the wrong word, brother." Izaiah hedged his bets cautiously. Twisting smoothly, his upbeat attitude was a grinding contrast against the tension. "Though you would be volatile to kill her without thinking, she's not shy to provoke it. Zaiana is cunning, and she would not entice you to strike without a plan none of us would see coming." Then he threw over his shoulder to Kyleer, "And we can't allow her to get between us without having to utter a word."

Reylan knew he was right and only hated that it should have been him to voice the strategy. He paced away from them both, staring directly at the bed in the next room that flashed far more peaceful, yearning memories.

Kyleer lay a hand on his shoulder. "She'll come home. Soon."

CHAPTER 24

Faythe

FENHER WAS BUSTLING with people, both humans and fae. The atmosphere lifted the spirits, and Faythe gawked from all angles as she walked through the streets. It was nothing like what she was expecting, having only heard of the large town from desolate memories. She often forgot how long ago that battle was since the story was so new to her. She couldn't bask in the pleasant nature completely when notes of sorrow tightened her brow with the thought of what this town meant to Reylan. Days of slaughter and desolation she couldn't fathom.

They decided to try to enjoy the day, breaking off to sample what the town had to offer. Livia disappeared on her own endeavor while Jakon, Marlowe, Nerida, and Reuben headed toward a packed market square. Faythe joined them for a while, but she had something else weighing on her mind.

Her mask was growing unbearable in the crowd of people. She had to constantly adjust it when it stuck to her skin and almost damned the disguise to feel the cool air. It didn't help that when she tried to stop the occasional person to ask for directions, she received many startled shrieks and a reluctance to engage at all.

She couldn't blame the strangers. Aside from her unnerving doll-like appearance, they no doubt wondered what need she had to wear it.

A couple of fae offered her brief directions, but she still managed to get lost multiple times in the maze of streets. As her irritation grew toward giving up, she finally reached her destination.

The open field of grass spanned far and wide. Faythe halted the moment she stepped onto it, so much emotion barreling into her she couldn't organize it. Sorrow. So much sorrow lined the field. She took slow, vacant steps, finally coming to stand before the first tower of gray stone.

There were so many names. Three columns, each at least one hundred names high. Faythe was horrified because when her eyes fell back down, there were so many stones just like this one. Thousands—tens of thousands of names. She blinked back her wave of dizziness, made all the worse in her heavy cloak and mask, and she wanted to take both off and fall to her knees. Hearing about the Battle of Fenher was one thing, but standing in the face of the colossal loss from those dark days was an immeasurably desolate feeling.

So. Many. Lives.

What she struggled to believe was that they could come to face it all again. Faythe couldn't stop seeing every person walking through the field of tribute as one who could meet the same fate. She had never felt so helpless to stop it, but with a rising, *burning* need to do all she could regardless.

A hand on her shoulder made her jolt. As she spun around, Nerida winced at her reaction.

"Do you need help looking for someone?" she asked softly.

Faythe's eyes burned. At Nerida's kindness; at other people's lifetimes of grief she stood among. "All I know is that her name was Farrah," she confessed.

She had debated whether it would be appropriate to seek out her grave without Reylan here, but knowing it was within reach,

Faythe wanted to pay her respects to someone who meant so much to him.

Nerida blew out a breath. "We could be here some time. But at least they're organized alphabetically. Do you know her family name?"

Faythe dropped her head with guilt. "Could we try Arrowood?" Her stomach twisted to say it, but though Reylan had never told her they'd been married, she figured it was worth a try.

Nerida's expression creased with realization. Faythe couldn't bear it. Twisting, she decided to begin with the first stone.

As they walked the field, a coating of despair weaved through the stones. Faythe glanced down the rows with a churning gut, spiraling at the image of the grass soaked in crimson, innocents fleeing, and steel singing. Had Reylan stood on this very field to fight? Was this where he watched the one he loved get slaughtered right in front of him?

"He's your mate." Nerida's voice pulled her from her tunneling, desolate thoughts. "Reylan Arrowood."

"Yes," Faythe answered, grateful for the distraction that made warmth burst in her chest instead.

"Yet you loved him before you knew?"

The way she asked was inquisitive, and after giving a nod, Faythe realized there was something she was trying to figure out.

"Have you met your mate?" Faythe toyed with anticipation, figuring Nerida would have spoken of her mate by now or gone straight to them if they were in Fenher.

"No. But it almost didn't matter when I would have married."

Faythe blinked with surprise but stayed silent. Nerida's face was thoughtful but disturbed as she stared ahead.

"I fled from that arrangement."

Faythe winced. "Was he not…good?" She didn't know how else to word it, but she wouldn't pry should Nerida choose not to share more.

"It's complicated," she offered with a pained smile before tracking her footsteps.

Faythe's chest twisted for the gentle healer. She was everything that was right in the world, pure and kind, and Faythe admired her immensely, having been the one to keep their spirits high with her permanently positive outlook since they'd left Reylan and the others. Though now it was clear she had not been spared from life's twisted cruelties.

"I think you could love someone just as much with or without a bond," Faythe offered, knowing now why she asked. "I don't believe it has anything to do with how much I feel for him. The feeling can't be tied to something so explainable."

Nerida's expression brightened. Faythe thought that telling her about Reylan would give her hope to find love regardless if it was with a mate. Whatever Nerida's reasons, Faythe felt a sense of pride toward the healer who'd had the courage to walk away.

"No Arrowood," she said.

Faythe followed her line of sight, scanning the names where his would have been engraved. Her brow pinched hard, and she swallowed through the tightening in her throat. She didn't know what she felt.

"You won't find her here."

Livia's voice had them twisting to find her strolling toward them. A mournfulness weighed on her poise. Faythe had never seen the commander so down.

"Reylan chose his own resting place for her, along with Greia."

Of course he did. *Of course he did.* Gods, her pain at what he'd endured was like an unrelenting twist in her gut.

"I would like to see."

Faythe halted on the hill, knowing what she'd find if she kept climbing. She'd come alone after Livia told her where to go, yet she stilled in wondering if she was doing the right thing—if it was right for her to be here without him.

Removing her mask, she pressed on, feeling compelled to visit the grave. As she reached the crest, what struck her first was the magnificent willow tree that stood proud and alone. Faythe's head tilted back in awe as she wondered the age of the biggest tree she'd ever seen. But when her eyes fell, so did the cold embrace of sorrow over what stood protected by the beautiful nature.

Two headstones.

Her walk was slow and thoughtful as she made her way over. Her mind drew a blank, not knowing what she wanted to say or what she'd hoped for by visiting. She just knew she couldn't pass by Fenher without showing her gratitude to one who had meant so much to her mate.

Standing here now staring at the ending of Reylan's tragic tale of his past, it sank deep all at once, and she lowered to one knee. Faythe stared and stared at Farrah's name, wondering what she looked like, what she would have been like. But Faythe knew then why she'd come.

"Thank you for loving him," she whispered. Because Farrah had once been a light to guide Reylan through all he'd faced. He was a warrior who never knew love nor nurture, not from such a wicked upbringing with his uncle. "He's safe with me." She crouched and reached out a hand.

The moment she touched the stone, her lips parted for the shock of energy that pulsed through her. It warmed her chest and tingled in her palms.

"He always has been."

Faythe gasped, falling back on her hands at the feminine voice. The fae's blue eyes sparkled with her smile. Her ethereal blonde hair blew softly in the wind, along with flowing lengths of white gown. Faythe thought she must be cold. Her arms were bare, and she had no shoes…

"How is this possible?" Faythe shook her head in denial that who she was looking at was real. Though her face rang so familiar it made her heart gallop.

Farrah.

"We would have fought with you. He would have wanted to remember you, but I'm sorry you had to face it alone, and I wish… I only wish I could fight it with you this time. But you found him,

Faythe. You will always have him." Her melodic voice arrived like an echo.

Faythe shook her head. "I don't know what you're talking about."

"I hope you will someday, but right now you need to run, Faythe."

Her lips parted, but her words floundered. The hairs on her arms pricked as she rose slowly, scanning the open space.

"Run!"

Faythe snapped her head around, but Farrah was gone. She didn't get a moment to contemplate if she'd ever been there at all when a shadow was cast over the sun.

Her attention landed on the silhouette as it fell. As it struck the earth, the vibrations gripped Faythe through her toes, ensnaring her in a web of trepidation. She didn't have the courage to turn.

"Like the Phoenix, an heir comes to rise once again."

That voice… She would never forget it. For it was the one to utter the final words she heard before it took her life.

That voice was her death.

"Maverick," she whispered.

CHAPTER 25

Faythe

TIME WAS IMPERCEPTIBLE. Faythe hoped to be wrong, but as she turned back, gravity didn't weigh her down anymore.

There he was: a dark, towering silhouette against the blazing sunlight. A form she would never forget. Those tall, taloned wings froze her completely. Flashes of haunting memory stole her bravery. The sight captured her will to run…or fight…or do anything but succumb to the terror of being back on that mountain edge in battle—or worse, back in the Temple of Darkness that was her tomb.

Before Faythe stood her killer.

Night had switched to daylight in this spinning reel of memory. Stone to grass. Rain to sun. Death to life. It swayed her vision, and Faythe blinked hard to land on the present. Breathed consciously to stay grounded.

"I killed you," Maverick drawled, stalking toward her while he adjusted his cuffs. "Yet here you stand. I'll admit I'm impressed." He was so lax, unfazed, as though they were old friends catching up after running into each other. "Chilling" was too tame a word to describe the sting of ice that climbed from the tips of Faythe's toes up her legs, threatening to hold her helpless at his mercy. "What are you now, exactly?"

She snapped back into herself with the *heat* in her palms that contrasted the cold. She had the power; she wouldn't allow him to triumph against her again. "Strong enough to defeat you," Faythe said, quelling enough of her fear to turn to him fully. She cursed the wobble of her hand as it reached for her sword.

When Maverick was close enough, the sun's glare didn't shadow his wicked glee. "You've come back with fire. I like that," he said.

"You have no idea what you created, Maverick."

Amusement and delight twinkled in those onyx eyes. "I plan to find out. This will be far more entertaining than I hoped. I was worried it was going to be as easy as the first time."

"I question your skills if killing someone weak on their knees is a win to you."

His chuckle was dark, rich, and it trembled down every notch of her spine. "Then let's have the fight we missed out on, shall we?"

Faythe freed her blade, but Maverick simply watched her, waiting. Her grip was painful to offset her tremor. Then Faythe heard shuffling from behind her, and as she spared a glance, she didn't think the world could tunnel away from her farther. It was simply unbelievable that the fates could condemn her like this time and time again.

"You make it too easy, Faythe," Maverick taunted. "Don't you know capturing leaders only leaves behind vengeful followers?"

She looked out over the bodies climbing up the hill. So many fae. Some she recognized, and with Maverick's words she concluded who they were.

Raiders.

All with a wrath to exact on her.

The dark fae sang, "The time for hiding is over, *Bloodmasked.*"

A heat gathered in her palms, prickling in her fingertips. All this time she'd feared her power, yet now she had to believe in herself enough to be able to wield it then control it. Every lesson she'd attempted with the others she had to recall here, with her survival on the line.

"What will you do without your Mindseer by your side? We all know how reckless you became last time."

"You wouldn't have survived through your first words if he were here," Faythe spat.

"Do you need him to fight your battles?"

"Do you need Zaiana to fight yours?"

That made his smile drop. Faythe's head tilted to watch his reaction. Flickers of cobalt caught in her vision, drawing her attention to his hand as it lifted, growing an alluring flame under his touch.

"There's no leap to take here, Faythe Ashfyre. No Phoenix to save you."

Faythe had begun to reach into her power. It was of light and danger, raw and uncertain. "Keep saying my name," she said, extending the ability she knew, feeling the pulse of minds beckoning to be seized. "And remember I am the Phoenix you created."

Twisting, she avoided Maverick's first dart of flame as it blasted with a cry into a fae behind her. Her hand raised, gathering the essence of three minds. Her darkness chanted to shatter them, but Faythe fought against herself, silencing the crooks to unconsciousness instead. It was a push and pull she had to learn within herself, and right now her only alternative was hope.

Faythe had no choice but to take her eyes from Maverick as the bandits at her back closed in. She turned in time to clash swords with one. Then the world blurred. Her sword met steel and leather and flesh. Killing wasn't her goal, but some wounds she had to inflict, and she couldn't be certain they weren't fatal. She fell them with her ability and her sword. She was wind and ice and fire, owning the new body she'd paid the ultimate price for, drawing upon every ounce of heightened speed and agility and channeling it into the battle moves she could carry out blindfolded. Faster, with a laser focus that canceled out the world, answering to a mind that once spoke to death and promised not to meet him again. Not anytime soon. Not until she had *lived*.

The attack ceased all at once.

The bodies began to back away from her, and Faythe breathed heavily, twisting her blade. "Is that all the effort you'll put into seeking revenge for your captive leaders?" she goaded at the ghostly looks on their faces.

Eyes of hatred and uncertainty bore into her in reply.

"Impressive," Maverick commented. "I just wanted to make sure you could deliver a worthwhile fight."

Faythe heard his advance through his mind right before he threw up a firm barrier against her. But she turned, locking blades with one charged with a mesmerizing cobalt blue. Maverick pushed into her, and he was stronger, there was no doubt. Yet he didn't make any further move to strike as she glimpsed his smirk of triumph through the flickers of flame.

Then his smirk slowly began to fall, mixing with confusion as he looked over her. Maverick glanced at her palms clamped around the hilt of Lumarias, but she didn't waste time pondering why he'd paused. Faythe slid her blade against his, emitting a sharp note. Twisting, she kicked the backs of his knees. He hissed as he went down, but she wasn't fast enough to pin her blade to his back when he reached behind her and gripped her leg. He pulled, and then she was falling.

Faythe's head hit the ground hard, sparks peppering her vision. A sharp pain in her skull disoriented her, and she blinked at the blue sky, watched the rolling clouds for a moment of peace. Against the bright daylight, a dot of darkness blocked the sun's glare. It burst out from the fleeting clouds with purpose, growing larger and larger.

It was falling—no, *diving*—for them.

"I killed you once," Maverick said as he got to his feet. "Don't make the mistake of thinking I can be merciful."

Faythe kept her eyes on the dark bird, her heart stopping still. Not out of fear, but pure, exhilarating relief. Then her eyes closed against the glare of light as it struck the earth. This was no creature; it was a brilliant warrior she'd missed so much.

Izaiah straightened, so elegant and nonchalant. "Sorry I took so long. I thought bringing backup would be useful."

Just then, loud male cries erupted with the clang of steel. Faythe lifted her head just in time to catch Jakon firing his next arrow and Livia cutting through the fae like timber with her twin blades.

She didn't waste the opportunity.

Kicking Maverick's legs out from under him, she watched as the dark fae fell. But his blade clanged against Faythe's once more as she rolled and straddled him, and she was stunned by his swiftness.

"One-on-one you cannot defeat me in battle," he said with a confidence she knew he'd earned every right to. With his diet of human blood, he outmatched her in strength and agility alone.

Faythe tested his mind for entry. It was firm, near impenetrable, and she wondered if his heritage had any influence on that too. He was a Transitioned, as was she. Aurialis's power was different from what she'd inherited from Marvellas.

Maverick sparked a new flame along his blade, and Faythe felt a prickling sensation. Not heat, but something inviting. While she lost focus to admire it, Maverick growled in frustration, bafflement returning in the knit of his brow.

"How does it not burn you?"

Though chaos ensued behind them, it became distant to Faythe as she reached back to the unexplainably enticing vibration, figuring she had nothing to lose. Their blades were still locked, but any second now Maverick could switch his tactic and overpower her. Faythe let go of her reservations and embraced her magick, testing what it wanted to do.

She couldn't believe what began to happen.

Maverick's eyes widened, just as stunned as she was, and both of them forgot their fight for those few seconds as they held their stares on their steel and watched Maverick's flames slowly dim. As his eyes darted along the length of the blade, his bewilderment confirmed it wasn't happening by his command. And when the cobalt winked out completely, Faythe pushed off him, stumbling back as she stood.

She breathed hard. She trembled with control. A vibration hummed in her blood, heating and pulsing. Maverick rolled over and rose, eyes downcast to his ordinary blade. On her exhale, Faythe looked down at her tight grip on Lumarias.

From her fingertips, waves of cobalt burned down the Niltain steel length. She watched—she *felt*—the fire as it was released from her hold.

Without realizing what she was doing…

She'd absorbed Maverick's conjured flames.

And she could feel it. Her other fist was clamped tight, but as she raised it and slid her palm open, she found a blue flame had ignited within it.

"Impossible," Maverick sneered.

Faythe admired the dancing flame. It felt like danger and intrigue. It tasted like ash and salt. "Sometimes you have to fight fire with fire," she mumbled to herself in awe.

Maverick sheathed his sword. He watched his hand as he sparked his flames anew. "How are you doing that? When I don't feel I've lost even a kernel of power."

Then his fascination seemed to drop faster than Faythe could react. She was still scrambling to figure out what her magick was doing when her flame winked out as Maverick's struck her chest, sending her soaring backward. She collided with something solid and unforgiving.

As gravity pulled her to the ground, she drilled all her focus into not losing consciousness. Lumarias lay too far out of reach, and it too had lost its fiery glow. She couldn't make sense of what had happened. Faythe tried to feel for that foreign magick she'd harnessed just a moment ago, the unique essence of fire, but adrenaline made her too clumsy to focus. She had to wonder, in her exertion, if she'd imagined the obscure sensation.

Faythe leaned back on her knees as Maverick advanced toward her. She was so exhausted, battling with her magick, taking the brutal beatings Maverick didn't hold back. All she could be grateful for was that her friends had arrived and seemed to be triumphing against the Raiders, sparing her at least from that fight.

Sparking a new flame, the dark fae stalked up to her slowly, arrogantly. The smooth twist of his wrist sent that ball of flame hurtling for her without hesitation. Faythe winced and her eyes clamped shut. There was no escape from its precision strike. Her hands rose, and then...

A pulse tingled in her palms, but not with the scorching blast she'd felt from Maverick's fire darts before. Sliding her lids open, Faythe could do nothing but succumb to her disbelief at the lethal glow that hovered just shy of touching her palms. There it was: the return of her magick. Without sparing a second to wonder how, Faythe pushed back with everything she had, crying out as she sent that ball of flame hurtling back toward its maker.

Maverick didn't see it coming. It struck him hard, sending him flying back, and Faythe scrambled to her feet, about to advance, when a cry too young to belong on a battlefield caught her attention.

Her head snapped to the source, and she found a fae male overwhelmed. In his youth, his striking will to defend reminded her of Caius, but something else about him was familiar. The world drifted away from Faythe until it was only them.

The grassy hills turned to stone, and she coughed as smoke and dust clogged her lungs. The young fae fought valiantly until Faythe saw one of the enemy racing for him from behind.

Horror struck her to act.

I can't lose him.

That urgent plea rang out on repeat.

Faythe moved as if she already knew the sequence of events to come. With no sword, she raced for the bow discarded on the ground, snatched up an arrow, and before she'd registered any of it, held her trembling aim on the foe.

If she missed...

The enemy ran so fast, and time seemed nonexistent. He would die. Faythe didn't know how she knew him, but he *couldn't die.*

Too many seconds she let slip, but she couldn't stifle her trembling as she choked on a whimper. She knew this weapon; had struck true with it many times.

She blinked hard.

No. She'd been afraid of it.

So why did it feel so sure in her grip?

Her arrow soared as the enemy raised his sword above the fae's head. Faythe screamed his name when it rushed to her suddenly, but she already knew she'd failed him. Terror, guilt—nothing was enough as she watched her arrow *miss.*

Their eyes locked, his so wide, sealed with glassy fear for all eternity as the blade swiped clean through his neck. Faythe's bow dropped from her hands.

She missed.

Her body fell as his did.

She could have saved him, and she *missed* when it mattered the most.

As her eyes closed, a cool breath of metal met her throat to snap them back open like a jolt of lightning. Her breathing speared her chest. The setting changed. Bright daylight opened up in place of the dark, overcast sky, and her eyes stung, mind scrambling to restructure reality. Faythe's fingertips grazed the strands of grass to be sure it was real.

"We have Zaiana!"

Izaiah's voice thundered over to them with a rage she'd never heard from him before. This was real. The bow she'd held didn't exist when she scanned the ground, but her missed shot haunted so truly she still trembled. Her stomach turned and turned, spinning like the world around her, and she grappled with consciousness.

The fae...

His name was Kerim.

"I'll give you one chance to think of a better lie to spare her."

Maverick's snarl lifted her back to the present, but Faythe was too exhausted to fight. Sorrow and agony for a loss she couldn't fully remember encouraged tears from her eyes, and she bowed her head. Her mind couldn't stop chanting her apology to such an extent she almost spilled it aloud.

"She offered herself up," Izaiah taunted.

Maverick scoffed. "Now I know you're lying."

"She walked right into our throne room and gave herself up for the release of Tynan and Amaya." Izaiah threw something onto the grass before them.

Maverick's eyes locked onto it for a few long seconds before the blade at Faythe's neck disappeared and her palms splayed on the grass. She caught a flicker of what Izaiah had tossed right before Maverick snatched the objects up.

"A trick," he hissed, but he continued to examine the jewelry closely, clearly trying to decipher if the two metal guards were Zaiana's.

"Harm anyone here and we'll take you in to watch as we kill her," Izaiah threatened, cold and calculating. It was rare for Faythe to see this side to the commander.

"Where are Tynan and Amaya?" Maverick's fury pulsed so tangibly Faythe turned nauseous.

Izaiah merely shrugged, not deigning to respond.

Jakon kneeled by her, but she couldn't look at him. Her head pounded, her heart fractured with it, and she couldn't move. The scene of Kerim's death replayed in her mind over and over, and Faythe sobbed.

"You're okay," Jakon said softly.

Maverick spoke some more to Izaiah, but Faythe could hardly catch their words. She was traveling elsewhere, unable to be anchored by time.

Izaiah crouched beside them, his voice a new tether to the present. "Can you stand?"

Faythe shook her head. She'd rather the ground open up to

claim her and free her of this misery. She let Izaiah scoop her into his arms as the battle and her emotions dwindled, and a new sense of detachment coated her senses.

"He died because of me," she whispered to no one at all.

"We're all alive, Faythe," Izaiah said. "No one died."

Her brow crumpled. She couldn't make sense of how she knew him or why she'd seen his death, but Kerim deserved to be remembered…and somehow, she'd failed him in that too.

CHAPTER 26

Zaiana

"Sorrow."

Zaiana stifled a groan where she lay. She'd been enjoying the peaceful chirp of birds before the vibration of Kyleer's voice crawled across her skin.

He diverted from his initial topic to say, "That's a perfectly good cushion of hay you've completely disregarded."

Her head lolled lazily toward him. "You're welcome to come in and test just how comfortable it is. You'll find both to be of equal *firmness*, yet down here, one has the advantage of not being spiked by straw with every slight movement."

He huffed nonchalantly. "The horses appreciate it far more. I'll make sure they don't waste any more provisions on you."

"Are you likening me to a horse?"

"Never." He leaned against the bars, and Zaiana's gaze trailed the length of her blade, which he spun casually against the ground. "Their company's far more tolerable."

He was insufferable.

"You'll dull the point," Zaiana grumbled, ignoring his gibe to push herself upright.

Kyleer raised her sword to eye level, scrutinizing it just as he had before. She held back from giving him the satisfaction of letting it rile her.

"*Nilhlir,*" he recited. "It means sorrow."

"It wouldn't have been easy for you to find that out."

"It wasn't. I was out of my depth among the books, I'll admit. It's never been my point of interest."

"Clearly."

"Are you calling me dim?"

"Something like that."

He broke a smile—the kind that made it clear he relished their banter even if it grated on her nerves. Perhaps *because* it grated on her nerves. "Battle plans, weapons, strategy—hand me scripts on those and I'll happily lose hours to reading them. They're practical."

"And language is not?"

"When it predates even the oldest living king, I believe not."

Zaiana didn't want to entertain him, but he was becoming like an itch. Annoying, but irresistible nonetheless. Besides, learning everything she could about one of Rhyenelle's leading warriors would only serve to her advantage. So she humored him.

Rising carefully, Zaiana drawled, "I can assure you"—she stalked toward him, her chains clanking—"that word does not predate the oldest living king." Smiling cruelly, she paced her cell while she let the statement linger.

"Mordecai is not a king. Not anymore."

She was glad it didn't take him long to catch onto her meaning. "He is the greatest dark fae king to have ever lived." It wasn't what she believed, only what she recited from the teachings that had been drilled into her.

"Can he even be considered alive?"

Zaiana gave him her attention, holding his eye for long enough to make it clear she was being serious. "You would be right to fear anyone who has touched death and still walks. Not a simple graze, not with a dangerously slowed heart—I mean true death." In the look they shared, perhaps they both thought of the same face. Not the face of a dark fae, but one of beauty and strength. Zaiana didn't allow the thought of Faythe to linger. "But one who has slumbered with death for centuries? Who knows what they could be capable of?"

"Not much if he's been hiding all this time."

Zaiana couldn't stop the huff that escaped her. It was almost a laugh.

"You know she's alive," Kyleer accused, his voice dropping low.

Taking a long breath, she cast bored eyes around the cell. "You'll have to be more specific in your interrogations, Commander. Gentle doesn't suit you."

"You'd like me to be rough with you," he said, and she almost shivered at the gravel in his tone. "And that time will come." Kyleer slipped his hand through the bars, propping up her sword and not breaking eye contact. Maybe she could be quick enough to swipe it from him while his green eyes twinkled and goaded, but she didn't move, keeping her expression bored as she leaned back against the wall.

"Why sorrow?"

"Why do you care?"

"I'm interested. A sword's name says a lot about its owner."

"Maybe I'm not the original wielder."

"It's crafted perfectly for your body."

"What would you know of my body?"

"Not nearly as much as I'd like."

He was provoking her to lash out, wanting her to break her composure. Zaiana was almost insulted that he believed even for a second she might unravel to any attempt at seduction or praise. She would not break. She invited the shift to physical torture lest she suffer through any more of his poor attempts at flirtation.

Kyleer reached to his side, pulling free a mighty blade. He retracted his arm to stand the swords side by side, and while Zaiana was proud of her blade, she couldn't deny his made a powerful companion.

"Knightswood," he said.

"I didn't ask."

He shrugged, admiring the two blades and their similarities, such as the leather binding around the hilt for better grip and the way the rain guard came to a point over the steel. "I was given this sword by Agalhor when I became commander nearly two centuries ago."

"I didn't ask," she repeated through clenched teeth. Zaiana needed to figure out his strengths and weaknesses, yet he was swaying her off course with tales she held no use for. It made her fists clench because regardless, she found herself wanting to listen. Wanting to coax him to tell her more even if the useless trivia offered no advantage and was only a distraction she could not afford.

Kyleer paused, but after a slow study of her, he chose to go on regardless of her outward disinterest. "He said it belonged to the famous General Fredrick Salver. Have you heard of him?"

Giving up since he wasn't going to quit, Zaiana shook her head. "Would it not better serve his own esteemed General Reylan Arrowood?"

A spark twinkled in his eye at her engagement, but it seemed foolish for him to care. "I wondered the same myself. But Reylan declined the sword. He didn't think it should belong to him."

"How noble."

"Not exactly. Believe what you want about him—it makes no difference, and he will not care. Though I don't believe his reasons were selfless or because he didn't feel worthy."

Zaiana had many thoughts about the general, some she might even compare to admiration. She couldn't figure him out, but she wasn't sure she wanted to. "I'm sure your general would not approve of your methods with me so far."

"You're right. If he had his way, you wouldn't even be breathing."

"Lucky me that the king sent you instead."

"You'll be glad to know I volunteered."

Zaiana gave a mocking laugh. "And why would I be glad of that?"

Kyleer sheathed his sword. "Don't get too comfortable, Zaiana. I still plan to make you scream."

She ground her teeth.

"The servants will draw you a bath. You'll be closely guarded and still bound, but this is not an act of kindness—"

"A *bath?*"

"Never heard of one?" Kyleer was pulling tighter and tighter on her tether of control, and she was doing a commendable job of not allowing it to snap.

"No." The word cut like a cold warning.

"Tub of hot water, naked skin, soap—"

"Your disgusting fantasy would only happen against my will." Fear trickled through her defenses as she wondered to what lengths he might go with his torture and if she'd just exposed a great weakness. The mere thought roused a dangerous fighting instinct in her.

She watched his jaw lock as if he wanted to counter but decided against it. Then her breath left her easily when he turned and walked away without another word.

CHAPTER 27

Zaiana

A NEW VISITOR offered a welcome distraction from her painstakingly dull days. Zaiana almost wished they'd begin interrogations so she'd at least have *something* to pass the slow hours. She twisted from watching the clouds roll through the boxy window and pining to soar between them. Who she found waiting at the bars of her cell certainly drew her interest.

"Now what is such a pretty face doing down here in these grim depths?" she mocked the visitor. He was nothing of importance to her, but she chose the angle deliberately to gauge if his stunning but feeble exterior was just a guise.

"I would watch your tone with me, darkling."

His voice wasn't what she expected, though it rang of his distant eyes. Zaiana peeled herself from the wall. Her shackles clinked, but her mind had long since detached from their constant bite.

"And why should I?" she challenged.

"Because I may the one person who can help you."

Zaiana lifted a brow, sparing a glance down the dark hall, and he read her wariness.

"If you help me," he added.

Her expression fell. She even rolled her eyes in disappointment as she began to pace. "I hoped for a second you wouldn't be so highly predictable."

"It is a great risk, my being here at all. Wouldn't you like to hear what I have to say?"

"Why would you trust me not to speak of your visit if it could grant me favor with the court?"

"No one would believe you."

Zaiana pondered this for a second, concluding it wouldn't matter; the seed would be planted by a prisoner with seemingly nothing to lose. Fear seemed to surface in him when she curled a cruel smile, not having to say a word.

He added with a note of hatred, "And because I have something you want."

"I don't make deals."

"Oh, this isn't anything like that. I wouldn't trust you for a second. Consider this more like…an understanding."

Zaiana gave him her back—a movement she knew he wouldn't be used to and one that would rile him further. It was becoming the height of her entertainment. She was almost glad for his decision to bother her. "You wasted a trip. Now leave."

"I know why your heart is still."

Her fists clenched. "You cannot trick me."

"You don't believe you were born with it—not truly."

She turned back to him with nothing short of a threat, pinning him with dead eyes to make sure he knew no one ever fooled her and lived to tell the tale. "Be careful of what card you play. Now what is it that you so desperately want from me to be ballsy enough to risk my wrath?"

She could hardly stand the kernel of regained confidence that made him roll back his shoulders. "I won't be visiting you again anytime soon. You know my offer, and I know yours."

Zaiana flared at his arrogance, but he was already making steps away as he voiced his next thought.

"You'll bring down the inner-city wall."

CHAPTER 28

Faythe

FAYTHE HADN'T SPOKEN since the battle with Maverick. She sat with her knees tucked up tight, leaning into the corner of the booth.

They'd found a small inn for the night. The establishment was bustling with so much sound it upset her senses when her mind sought calm. But they'd wanted somewhere with enough bodies that they'd blend into the crowd.

Every movement turned Faythe rigid. She kept glancing at the door as if Maverick would storm through it any second to finish what he'd started. Her leg bounced. The lute player and singer at the back of the inn played wonderful songs, but Faythe only begged for silence.

"What happened back there?" Izaiah startled her he was so close.

"Besides facing the dark fae who killed me once and tried again?"

His mouth curled in amusement, enjoying her sarcasm. "You still have your spirit. I was becoming worried."

Faythe appreciated his easy company. "You said you had Zaiana. How?"

"She came to us." Izaiah shrugged, sipping his drink.

"Why would she do that?"

"We had two of her companions. She made a rather epic display of infiltrating our defenses, all to surrender herself for their release."

It didn't make sense that one who embodied her wickedness would be so...*caring*.

"Simply to spare their lives?" Faythe quizzed, trying to figure it out, but with Izaiah's shrug it seemed they were content to accept her reasons.

"We have her locked away, bound in Niltain steel. She is powerless."

Faythe didn't believe that for a second. It would be wrong to underestimate Zaiana when she'd felt and seen her ruthlessness. But her mind raced with thoughts of what they could find out from her, though she didn't believe it would be extracted by any easy means.

"You deflected his fire back there."

Faythe jerked with Marlowe's change of topic.

Her delicate face was thoughtful. "Have you ever tried to conjure it?"

Faythe huffed a laugh. "I am not a Firewielder."

"I don't think you are any one thing, Faythe. You never have been." Marlowe slipped from the bench abruptly. Jakon moved as if to go after her, but she didn't go far, returning quickly with an ordinary glass of water.

"Can I have that?" Reuben asked with a partial slur. Faythe had to admit she was becoming concerned with his growing appreciation for wine.

"No." Marlowe set the cup on the table. Sitting, she clasped her hands, and Faythe curved a brow at her odd behavior. "Just hear me out, okay?" she said in a way that held reprimand. "Try to move the water with your magick."

"You can't be serious."

"Just try to move the water."

Faythe cast a wary look at her companions. Reuben was near falling asleep; Jakon nodded in encouragement; Nerida waited in fascination; but Livia and Izaiah tried and failed to hide their amusement. "No." She crossed her arms, perhaps childishly, as she anticipated the fae's playful mocking.

Izaiah's laughter rumbled. "Oh, come on. Don't lose out at our expense. We're merely excited to discover your talents."

"You two are insufferable," she grumbled.

"It can't hurt to try," Livia said.

"If either of you makes one comment… I don't need magick to throw that glass of water over you."

Faythe gave no one any attention as she stared at the cup of water. She took a long, deep breath to shut them out, feeling a fool for what she was about to attempt. She tried to feel for her magick, imagining what it would be like to move the water, but she had nothing to grasp. No sense of what it felt like. Flame was made of ash and salt. It inspired danger and passion.

Faythe raised a hand, trying to silence the buzz of the establishment and the gentle song weaving through it. The thought of alluring cobalt called to her. Her palm tingled, and when she opened her eyes, everyone's attention was fixed on her hand with complete fascination. She tried not to immediately balk at the shallow flame she held.

"What does it mean?" she breathed. Her panic threatened to rise with her uncertainty, and her fist clamped tight to wink out the fire.

For a split second, a surge of terror had her scanning the establishment. Faythe extended her senses as far as they could go. Relief washed through her when she couldn't detect Maverick. But it only brought up more confusion about how she could conjure the flame.

"It's like what I said in the woods: I don't think you take your power from others," Nerida assessed. "Perhaps once you've sampled an ability, it's as if it unlocks within you. To master it, that's on you."

"Aurialis is the original source of elemental magick. It might be wise to assume that's where you'll be strongest. But your mind ability will remain from Marvellas's bloodline," Marlowe added.

Faythe tried to absorb the information that seemed too much to process all at once.

"Nerida, would you?" Marlowe instructed.

The healer hesitated, only as she tried to figure out Marlowe's thoughts like the rest of them. When she reached up a hand, it was mesmerizing to watch the water in the cup lap around lazily before rising like a gravity-defying stream out of the top of the glass. Everyone leaned in to watch the suspended rippling water with awe.

"It's beautiful," Marlowe breathed. "Now try to move the water, Faythe."

Faythe met eyes with her over the water, expecting laughter, but she was serious.

"I know we've all had an eventful day, but I don't feel like being the source of everyone's entertainment," she said bitterly.

"You're not," Jakon said softly. "We need to rule out things one by one. Trust us." He was the only one who nodded his encouragement while the rest became giddy at the thrill of watching Nerida's magick.

Faythe huffed a harsh breath and copied Nerida.

"Don't focus on the water itself; feel for the magick coursing through it," Marlowe said.

"Explain it to me," Nerida prompted.

Faythe felt for it like she did with fire, but the contrast was stark since it was difficult to touch the essence of water. "It's calm," she tried. "Cold and soothing and healing." A new energy vibrated in her palm this time. Her heartbeat quickened, but not out of fear. Faythe focused, and what she felt was wonderful. Water… It tasted sweet and airy. Refreshing. But that wasn't to overshadow the lethal force it could become.

"By the Gods," Izaiah muttered. His awe sounded genuine, though she'd expected another gibe. It drew her attention to him, but he was looking at Nerida.

Faythe followed his gaze to find Nerida's hands in her lap, the water still levitating in the air, the glow of her palm reflecting off it.

In her shock she let it go all at once.

The water splashed onto the table, and everyone jerked as it spilled over the sides, yet their concern quickly faded when all eyes pinned her.

"She can take people's power…like Reylan," Livia pondered, a small glimpse of triumph shining through.

It was then Faythe realized all this time the commander had been just as on edge trying to figure out what to do with her magick as she, equally at a loss for what to suggest while she kept her distance after all Faythe had been through. Faythe's gratitude couldn't be voiced in that moment, but she made a mental note to thank Livia for enduring this with her these past weeks.

"Faythe's power is raw," Marlowe said. "She doesn't need a vessel. She draws from the source of magick before us and can turn it into whatever she wants if it's an ability she's experienced."

"I wonder if I can help," Nerida interrupted. "Now that Faythe is known to be alive, I assume you'll all be heading back to Ellium. I can head north to Olmstone and pay a visit to the Livre des Verres. I'll report back with anything I find as soon as I can."

"We don't know how safe Olmstone is after everything that happened," Jakon said apprehensively. "I wouldn't risk it to find out if Marvellas is still there or the dark fae have taken over. We left it in the hands of Chief Zainaid and the Stone Men to fight for the kingdom. I don't know what happened to King Varlas after everything, but Tarly, the prince, has gone missing. Tauria tried to find him before we fled."

"Tauria Stagknight?" Nerida interjected, but she quickly subdued her interest when all eyes fell to her.

Jakon nodded. "The Fenstead and High Farrow queen, yes."

A warmth erupted in Faythe's chest at hearing Jakon title her as such. It was so fitting and triumphant for Tauria, and the image of her and Nik ruling their kingdoms side by side was one she swore to see. It added fresh flame to her drive to fight.

"You'll want to be careful about flaunting that kind of magick."

The new voice made her jump, and everyone moved to draw their weapons.

Faythe's eyes landed on a tall man who pulled down the hood of his long leather coat to reveal shaggy, unkempt brown hair as he approached. Yet his attention only lingered on her for a moment before it slid to Nerida.

"One with such a rare talent can fetch pretty coin on the mainland, Waterwielder. Bonus for the unique beauty of you too."

Faythe's protective side flared, but Izaiah spoke up first.

"Unless you're making a threat, you'd best leave, pirate."

The man's smooth chuckle flexed the unruly scar on his lips. "I just thought you might appreciate the warning not to go wandering alone."

"She's not alone," Faythe cut in.

The man's dark eyes slid to her, twinkling in delight. "I don't know what *you* are, but the same could be said for whatever lingers under your skin."

"What do you gain from approaching us?" Livia asked, jamming her dagger into the table.

He gave a nonchalant shrug. "Consider it an act of kindness to repent for some of my sins."

No one matched his devilish grin.

He rolled his eyes. "Maybe I believed you lot might offer some entertainment for the night, though it seems the drunken states in the corner would offer better company."

"What is your name?" Faythe tried.

His smile turned sly. "I'll tell you mine if you tell me yours." He studied her as if she were a trophy. "What a peculiar—"

"Set of eyes. I know."

"Spirit," he corrected her.

Faythe's breath caught in their stare-off. She'd slipped up, and she cursed her own childish error in alerting him to something that would now stick in his mind. Her fists tightened so as not to give away their faint glow.

"I think you'd better leave," Jakon said, rising.

The man held up his hands. "As you wish."

Something about him didn't feel right, yet Faythe couldn't place it. She didn't realize she'd shifted forward. His eyes lingered on Nerida as he backed away, and the healer's soft hand took hers. As Faythe's eyes snapped down to it, she was whipped into an entirely different mood at the flash of memory. While her skin had gained a tan during her time in Rhyenelle, Nerida's warm brown tone against hers brought forth joyful but yearning images of Tauria.

"I think we should all get some rest," she said softly. Their eyes met, and Nerida's hazel gaze was appreciative, though Faythe wasn't sure what for.

Rest would at least pass another night and welcome a new day. One closer to their heading back the city. One closer to home.

One closer to *him*.

Faythe finished the last scoop of her breakfast the following morning and set down her spoon to tune in to the melodic singer wandering around the tables performing quietly. Her volume was far more bearable in the daytime. Marlowe and Nerida sat with her while they waited on the others, who were outside securing two horses.

"I guess this is where we say goodbye," Nerida said in a sad tone.

It only now dawned on Faythe that the healer was at home in Fenher and would not be coming with them to the city. "Are you sure we can't convince you to come to Ellium?" she asked. "Your skills would be invaluable, and you would be housed and paid well." Faythe had already extended the offer, and she knew Nerida had made her choice to stay.

"Thank you, but my attention is needed here for now," she said, but at the drop of Faythe's enthusiasm, she added, "But I will not forget. Perhaps our paths will cross again sooner than we know."

They hadn't known each other long, but something about the healer drew Faythe to her with ease. She trusted Nerida. Her nature was inviting, hopeful, and almost familiar, especially her hazel eyes.

"Thank you, Nerida, for all you've helped me with."

"Don't be afraid of what you're capable of." Her golden-brown hand met Faythe's over the table. "I have something I've been waiting to give you." Dipping into her satchel, she produced a small item wrapped in parchment.

Faythe frowned at the item, taking it warily.

"I never told you all about my time under the mountain with the dark fae. It was short, but to get me out I believe Zaiana used a path that goes far deeper than any of them typically venture. On that path we discovered a woman. She was old, barely clinging onto life, and I…I had to deliver her the only mercy I could." Nerida fidgeted with the item, the memory making her hands shake, and Faythe reached out to encase them.

"You helped her. There would have been nothing of kindness to greet her at the end without you." It was all Faythe could say to ease the guilt that surfaced in the healer.

She gave a grateful nod. "She didn't give a name, but her eyes…they were like yours—or at least, they might have been once."

Faythe straightened at the fact, her heart tumbling out of her chest. "Eyes like mine," she breathed. Shaking her head, she had to step back to breathe air. It didn't come easy.

No, Nerida couldn't have met the only person who surfaced in Faythe's mind at the news.

She couldn't have met her mother.

"She would have given a name," Faythe thought out loud. "But then who?"

"She told me to only give it to you. She used your first and last name, Faythe. She knew who you were."

Faythe fixed her eyes on what Nerida held, realization dawning that the answer she'd been searching for could be right in front of her. "You never opened it?"

Nerida shook her head, extending the gift once more. "It was not intended for me."

It was Faythe's grasp that shook now. The item that slid into her possession was heavy, but not in weight. She didn't know why, but her gaze slid to Marlowe, and for a second they were back in the humble blacksmiths in Farrrowhold, discovering the ancient note hidden within her mother's pocket watch.

Her friend gave a knowing smile, advancing forward. "Do you want me to?" she asked quietly.

Faythe could only nod while her ears filled with the hammering of her pulse. She felt the others nearby, attentive but keeping their distance as she began to pace, restless. She blinked hard a few times as she heard the paper unravel, chewing at her fingertips as she waited, and from Marlowe's pause Faythe decided there indeed must be something written on the underside of the parchment.

"Is it my...?" Marlowe couldn't bring herself to finish. The faint shake of her head accompanied a wary frown. "Not your mother," she confirmed, passing her the crumpled parchment.

It read:

> *She taunted me with your name. She knows who you are but tells me you do not. It is part of her plan to keep you forgetting, only to have you remember the parts she wants. You have to remember it all.*
>
> *I don't know how this will ever find you. Perhaps it never will. I couldn't achieve what you asked, and trying to led to my capture.*
>
> *Should you remember, know my fate was not your fault.*

"This was wrapped in it," Marlowe said. "Just like the one you own." She slid a brass pocket watch across the table.

Faythe was beginning to hate the sight of the thing that didn't seem to stop duplicating. "Dakodas's mark is on the back," she stated without knowing.

Marlowe flipped it over, confirming the etching of the circular symbol with a crescent moon, two lines striking its circumference. "I wonder what could be inside," she marveled.

Faythe wasn't so keen to know and slid it into her pocket, where it became a new weight of anticipation.

The singer's words filled her ears as they fell into silence. Faythe tuned in to her subconsciously as she took a swig of water and they all stood to leave. Then her steps halted abruptly with the next verse of the song. She was suddenly hit with why it sounded so familiar...

The heir of souls will rise again,
Their fate lies in her palms.
With rings of gold and will of mind,
She'll save the lives of men.

She'd heard it before.

Faythe whirled around. Not knowing why, she leaned her hands on the table the singer was wiping clean. "What is that song?"

The woman startled back at Faythe's abruptness, but her adrenaline couldn't force an apology through her tight lips.

"It's a very old and common song. I did not mean to offend."

"Where is it from?"

The woman shrugged. "I heard once that it was part of an epic that some musicians turned into song."

"Poems?"

The singer nodded, backing away as though Faythe could be dangerous.

"Time to go!" Izaiah called out.

But it didn't sit right with Faythe that this was all they were. With her time up, she couldn't risk it becoming something she forgot. She turned and met eyes with Nerida.

"Are you still planning to head to the library?" Faythe asked quietly.

Nerida spared a glance around as though one of the others would come barging over to scold her. Then she nodded. While Faythe's unease rose in concern for her venture, no part of this war would be won without risks.

"Do you think you could look for something for me? I think I've heard that song before, a poem. It might not be anything, but maybe—"

"I'll try to find out what I can," Nerida said gently, squeezing Faythe's arm to defuse her guilt for asking. "I didn't think this would be the end of each other's company," Nerida went on. Her smile could disperse any cloud of negativity in the room. "Until we meet again, Faythe Ashfyre."

CHAPTER 29

Faythe

AFTER ANOTHER WEEK the group stopped in a small town called Gasvern. They passed the days with casual conversation. Faythe heard more about Jakon and Marlowe's time in High Farrow since she'd left, but she feared for Nik and Tauria as they told her about the threats to their reign. Faythe told them about their quest, not leaving anything out as time was too precious for half-truths. She wanted to share every harrowing tale, but also every wondrous thing.

Now, she was so tired from her travels with a yearning to be home that time began to mock her with its slowness. They made camp in a forest, everyone in low spirits as they'd run out of food and coin a day ago.

"We'll need more wood if we're to keep the fire going all night," Livia said, poking at the dwindling flames.

It was twilight. The darkness would cloak them soon, and Faythe shuddered at the thought of its embrace. She pushed up from the log she was perched on.

"I'll go," she offered.

"I'll come with you," Jakon said, but he was cut off by Izaiah.

"She'll be fine. There should be some close by, and I can gather more on my watch later."

It wasn't like Izaiah to let any of them go off on their own, but Faythe wasn't going to point that out when she desired the solitude.

Her friend's brow knitted in protest, but Izaiah held his eye, and whatever Jakon read in his had him backing down. Marlowe offered some comfort, placing her hand over his thigh. The movement seemed so loving and carefree, and Faythe hated that their affections twisted in her chest. Her own hand subconsciously dipped into her pocket to clutch the wooden butterfly as the reminder of Reylan's face, his hold, made her body cry out in longing.

Faythe said nothing, not looking to anyone as she turned and began stalking through the trees. She didn't look for wood for a good measure of distance, needing to simply walk and clear her mind for a few minutes to ease the prickling in her eyes.

She skulked through the woods, eyes tracking the brown foliage scattered across the ground. Her feet kicked at useless branches while she began to stack logs in her arms big enough to create a fire. Twilight was fleeting, and she had no desire to be so far from the group when darkness fell.

Faythe was about to turn back when the shuffling of foliage spiked her alarm. Her heart stilled. There was a beast near the stream ahead, but thick trunks restricted her from seeing exactly what it was. Lowering her pile of wood, Faythe curled her hand around Lumarias at her side as she approached with feline stealth. If it was something she could take down on her own, Faythe figured the beast could be traded in for coin they could use for their journey or at least a hearty meal.

The creature huffed loud enough that she immediately doubted her choices. It had to be large. Its dark coat eased out from the trees a little more. Then, when its head dipped to feed off the frosted patch of grass, Faythe stopped in her tracks.

This wasn't real. It couldn't be.

She closed her eyes tightly, yet when her lids opened, the horse remained exactly where it was. When its head straightened and turned to her, the world around her stopped. Vacant steps closed the distance between them. Faythe's fear was nonexistent, but her furiously pounding heart warred with her mind, not letting her believe this could all be a dream.

She stopped right before the obsidian horse. Its head lowered to meet her hand as she stared into those glacier-blue eyes, and familiarity struck her chest with a joy so overwhelming her eyes began to blur.

"Where is he?" she whispered to Kali.

She was answered by an awareness that raced along her spine before scattering over every inch of her skin. Faythe barely heard the crack of branches at her back, but the world silenced at the presence.

"I'm right here, Faythe."

Her breath shuddered in an exhale. She delayed turning around with the emotions that barreled into her all at once at hearing the voice she'd missed so much.

Faythe's hand dropped from Kali as she twisted.

There he stood.

She choked out, "Reylan."

The general nodded.

This is real.

Then she was running. In only a few quick strides they collided, and the completeness of that embrace broke her down. Her arms clamped around his neck, straining from his height as he straightened. Her legs wrapped his waist, and he held her tight. Reylan buried his face in her neck, breathing in her scent, and she didn't care how much time passed in this moment she wanted to treasure forever.

Faythe started trembling with quiet sobs mixed with euphoric laughter. She didn't want to let go, but she had to look at him. She pulled back just enough to take his beautiful face in her hands. The connection in their stare spoke of a mutual impulse as her mouth angled down to meet his. Their kiss exploded within her. Their time apart drew out a feverish urgency, and Faythe didn't register any other movement until her back was pressed against something solid. His body molded to hers, wrapping her entirely with a warmth, safety, and contentment she only ever felt with him. One hand gripped her thigh and his other hugged her waist tightly as she clung to him, wondering how she'd survived weeks without this, realizing just how hollow she'd become in his absence now her chest, her mind, pulsed so bright and strong with him nearby.

Their kiss began to slow, turning to a soft yearning, and her fingers weaved through his silver locks. They broke free, foreheads resting together while they caught their breath.

"I haven't felt a moment of peace in forty-six days," he rasped. When he pulled back, the tree kept her still while she leaned into the palm that encased her cheek. "Not for one damn second—until right now."

Her brow pinched, and she nodded in agreement. "Why are you here?" She couldn't be more glad for it, but they were heading to Ellium anyway.

A dark shift filtered across his eyes as they scanned every inch of her face. "Izaiah got word back to us about what happened. I wasn't going to stay away a second longer." His breaths turned hard, deep, as though he were trying to suffocate his rising wrath as he fixed his stare on the ground. "Maverick was here. He could have—"

"He got nothing," Faythe cut in, unable to bear his turmoil. Her hand gripped his chin, forcing him to look at her.

Those sapphire eyes snapped open. The anger in them she'd only seen once before, and Faythe fought against the sickening shudder to be back in the temple. Then, slowly, as they shared a deep look, it was as if they both realized at once what mattered. Here and now. Being safe and together.

"I'm not leaving your side again," Reylan promised.

Faythe nodded. "Good."

He leaned down to kiss her again, instantly pulsing a desire so strong she pressed herself to him, *moved* against him, without conscious thought. Their scents shifted and mingled to bring them back to the time before they were parted. Lust. Against her core she felt his arousal, dipping her hand before she knew what she was doing.

Reylan groaned against her mouth with her first firm stroke.

Faythe didn't care where they were, calculating she'd traveled far enough from the group that they could have this private moment. Her need had been building since the Fire Mountains.

He pulled back, holding her face in his hands, searching her stare with wild, blazing eyes.

"I need you," she whispered.

He didn't stop the heel of her palm from dragging down again, and he gritted his teeth with a hiss that sparked through her. *"Gods,* I missed you," he said, colliding with her, and she moaned as their tongues clashed with a wild urgency.

Faythe had felt a burning lust for him before, but now, in this fae body, it was inexplicably maddening. Every touch ignited, every instinct turned raw and primal, and a part of her raced with the thrill that what she'd experienced with him before would be nothing compared to what they could share together now, as equals.

Faythe worked him again and again, her core tightening each time he thrust into her hand, driving her toward the brink of climax. His mouth left hers only to trail kisses across her jaw and down her neck as if he might devour her. Faythe clutched him tight, her thoughts scattered as she roamed over his chest, imagining his skin rather than the textured leathers. The scrape of his teeth drew her gasp.

"I'm seconds from taking you against this damn tree," he growled.

"I want it, Reylan," she panted, tipping her head back, wondering if he was aware of his own shallow movements against her core from their position. "I want all of you."

The friction was torture. More so, the pants she still wore.

Reylan swore, pushing off the tree. He only walked a few paces before Faythe gasped as he lifted her higher, and spying Kali, her leg hooked around him on instinct. Faythe glanced back as Reylan braced.

"We should tell the others—"

Reylan hauled himself up in one smooth glide, slipping in warmly behind her, and she could have melted into him.

"If Izaiah let you go off on your own without knowing I was here, it might have been enough to distract me from you to strangle him."

Faythe smirked, relaxing into him.

"Where are we going?"

"Only a bit farther away. There's a small running lake." His lips pressed to her head, then down to her ear, and she shivered. "I want this one night with you without the possibility of hearing about it from them by morning."

A blush crept along her cheeks. Her thighs tightened.

In a few minutes, Reylan pulled them to a stop, and her heart fluttered when he dismounted and poised to aid her. Bracing on his shoulders, she eased down, but instead of planting her feet on the ground, Reylan's hold slipped around her waist and her legs wrapped around him. The twinkle of desire in his eyes resurfaced her lust.

As he carried her, Faythe's head angled up and her lips pressed to the soft spot below his ear. His body turned taut, hands clenching her upper thighs, and she smiled, traveling lower over his neck.

But something overcame her in that second—a desire so frightening and new...

Bite.

Her gums ached, but the ache was dulled by the new feverish impulse that doused her with panic. Her tongue traced her top teeth and she gasped at their sharpness.

Reylan lowered with her. The cool grass against her back didn't register as her eyes widened and her hand darted to her mouth. Reylan's attention fell there in confusion, then realization. Tentatively, he pulled her fingers away and his thumb brushed her bottom lip. All she could do was watch the awe swirling wide in his midnight irises as his breathing became delightfully rugged.

"Beautiful," he admired, fixating on her elongated canines. "You have no idea how *insane* it drives me to see this."

It was the first time she'd felt them. There were new discoveries around every turn, it seemed, and having Reylan here meant the fear that threatened to rise turned instantly into confidence as he coated her in pride.

"They kind of hurt."

He gave a side-smile. "They won't after a while."

"Why didn't they come out when I was in danger?"

Reylan looked puzzled.

Faythe clarified. "The fae use them as a threat."

His smile bloomed, wide enough in rare amusement that it showed his own sharp teeth. "I don't know who told you we bite to attack," he teased.

Her cheeks flushed.

"The dark fae, perhaps, with their taste for human blood. Fae don't bite fae for any reason other than pleasure."

Faythe couldn't remember where she'd heard the obscure fact, though now she felt like a foolish child to learn her insight was nothing but a wicked bedtime story.

Reylan hovered above her, and a few silver strands fell over his dark brow. Faythe reached up to comb her fingers through them.

"I'm glad you came," she whispered, choking up. "It was all for nothing."

He shook his head. "If there was even a chance we could have kept you hidden and safe, we had to try it. Nothing about the plan was a waste, but I resent them for driving us apart, even if it was only for a short time in the forever I promised you."

That beautiful ache in her chest grew so strong she had to act. With her hand on his chest and her legs hooked around him, Reylan read her gentle push and gripped her hips, switching their position. A new hunger flared in his eyes.

"I'm beginning to really love this position," he ground out.

"You are?"

"Yes. Sinful thoughts aside, your confidence is growing. You're taking what you want. If it has to start with me—with us—take it all."

Faythe yelped as without warning he hooked an arm around her and twisted. His hand pinned her wrists, a few loose curls near touching his passionate eyes.

"And I'll challenge you every damn time until you know you can take control when you need to and it is nothing to be fearful of."

Her brow pinched with that because he wasn't just speaking about their lust in that moment. Not submitting but encouraging her to rise. To fight. It struck a chord in her to have him shed light on what she assumed she was failing at.

"Push back," he dared.

Faythe strained once before slumping back down.

He gave a soft smirk. "You're not even trying."

"How would you know?"

He leaned in close, warm breath across her collar. "I know *you*."

"Are you sure?"

She felt the near touch of his lips on her throat, and in his distraction, Faythe's knee tucked up between them, about to jab into his abdomen. Reylan was quick, however, and he shifted back, one hand grabbing her calf and pulling. He held it around himself instead, bring their bodies flush together. His mouth barely moved from her skin.

"Yes," he purred.

Faythe arched into him to give the impression she was falling for his seduction. But her competitive side still hummed through, and Reylan reacted exactly as she'd hoped.

Hands freed, Faythe's thighs clamped tight around him, and she reached to his side, using all her strength against his to make them tumble once more. When they stilled, chest to chest, her sly smile reflected on the blade angled against his throat.

Reylan's bewilderment quickly eased to a clouded lust. His hands trailed up her thighs and squeezed.

"Is it bad that I found that highly arousing?"

He spoke to her in her mind, the stroke on her senses somewhat more intimate than his external touch.

"You still have a lot to figure out, and I'm with you every step of the way. But I see you, Faythe—the progress you're making—even if it doesn't feel like you're moving anywhere fast."

She didn't realize how much she needed someone to see what she couldn't. And coming from him, those words of encouragement gave her a strength like no one else could. Faythe had no words; could only bring her mouth to his to express her gratitude, her love, to the one who had never once dropped an ounce of his belief in her.

She pulled back, eyes instinctively falling to his neck. "Pleasure," she whispered—more as an escaped thought that raged through her. "If I bit you, would it…?"

"No," he answered. "It wouldn't complete the true mating bond without a declaration from each side. It's a law that protects against forced matings."

The fact drummed hard in her chest and tingled heat straight to her core. "Would you enjoy it?" she asked, but she already knew his answer by the desire clouding his irises.

"Very much so."

"Would I?"

"Yes."

It was a surge of something primal she wasn't used to. It terrified her and raced a thrill that canceled all thought and reason.

"I want to," she breathed.

A wildness flared in his expression at her words. Faythe braced, but she didn't know what for—only that she wanted him wholly unleashed. Then a softness replaced their moment of passion and his hand curled around her nape, guiding her head down to meet him in one firm kiss.

"I know," he mumbled. Carefully, he sat up until she straddled him, propped up on one hand while the other stroked between her shoulder blades. "But it's intense, biting. It could overwhelm you right now."

When his words started to dispel her reckless lust, Faythe knew he was right. She was grateful he had a handle on restraint while she was still figuring out her impulses.

She eyed the water and her thoughts drifted to how everything was still so new to her—even her power. With Reylan here what crossed her mind didn't seem so frightening. And he didn't know what they might have discovered about her magick.

"I want to try something," she said, not taking her eyes off the flowing water as she slipped from his lap and kneeled by the stream.

Reylan wordlessly shifted behind her.

"I need you to be ready, and to take it all from me if I can't let it go." Her hand trembled as she dipped it into the water, the bite from the icy-cold stream jolting through her.

"I'm right here," was all he said, his warmth a welcome contrast as he tucked himself in close.

Faythe took a long, deep breath. She wasn't sure if she could do it, but if what Marlowe said was true…

She closed her eyes to focus. Though her mind sparked with terror, she tried to erase Maverick's face from her memories so she'd only focus on his ability. Fire. The heat it brought to her chest, the vibration of its essence in her palm, the taste of ash and salt…

Slowly, it became tangible, and she retracted her hand with the need to see it. Her eyes slid open, and she grappled with the tethers of her panic at seeing the shallow cobalt flame dancing over her palm—not touching it, but its blue light shone over the gold symbol that lived there, which awakened with the use of her magick.

"This is an interesting development," he said quietly, but the awe in his voice quelled her fear. Reylan's hand eased under hers, and they marveled over it together. His sharp intake of breath spiked her alarm. "I can feel it," he said, stirring Faythe's confusion, until he slipped his hand from under hers, and with the movement, the flame diminished from her palm only to reignite in his. "I can take it."

"You have always been able to do that," Faythe pointed out, but she furrowed her brow at the shake of his head.

Reylan manipulated the flame, growing it, weakening it. He broke it in two, holding the fire in both hands. "I haven't been entirely truthful with you. When you asked if I could feel your magick I never lied, but I discovered that I was unable to reach it—to take any of it—because there was no one thing to take and use. Not like when you only had your mind ability."

Faythe's mind blanked as she tried to make sense of what he was saying.

"When you translate it to something, this raw well of power you harbor...*Gods*, is it a relief to feel your magick. To know I can still help you, though it will take us time to figure it out."

Emotion lapped over her as she watched him marvel at the flame. The small smile he wore lit a warmth in her chest.

"Can you still conjure your flame?" he asked.

With a deep breath, Faythe thought of the essence. Each time it sparked to life it came a little easier, though it was a mere matchstick flame compared to what chanted darkly within her each time to push and push and *push*. Faythe didn't know how destructive she could become.

"Good," Reylan said, winking out his own fire. "At least you got something back from that bastard."

At his enthusiasm, Faythe allowed herself to smile. To see the power she harbored as something other than an entity that could harm and consume and destroy. Even if it were just a kernel she'd surfaced, her power could be beautiful, and maybe one day controlled.

Her next breath eased out of her much lighter, then she lowered her hand to the water again. The flame fizzled out, but Faythe focused on the harsh contrast of the bitter water that wanted to silence her Firewielding ability. She willed the heat to stay, felt it tingling through her veins right to her fingertips, until it escaped into the water. She kept going, thinking she could keep her control on this small change, but it began to grow. From the heat in her palms, she knew the line of script was slowly lighting up over her arms. She could feel the familiar burn and knew it would end between her shoulder blades, but by then it would be too much.

"Reylan," she rasped, beginning to tremble with her reluctance to know what would happen if she kept going.

"You're doing great." He didn't touch her again.

"You said—" Yet her words halted because he'd made no promise to stop her.

"Breathe. You are the master of yourself—don't let your magick take away your control."

Faythe shuddered, her eyes scrunching shut as she exhaled. She wanted to believe him just as fiercely as he believed in her. The water became hot—soon too hot, hissing over the surface. Faythe felt no end; no burnout. Steam began to moisten her face, and her eyes snapped open.

"I could dry up the entire lake! You have to stop me," she rushed out, pulse racing. She couldn't move her hand, fearing if she did, without the water as an obstacle, the fire could erupt from her and harm Reylan.

"I'm right here," was all he repeated, hand slipping around her waist.

For a moment she felt no change, but then she thought of how beautiful the water looked with its misty veil across the surface and how she'd warmed it and not caused any destruction. Slowly, she drew away from her magick. As if it were cast out on a line, she reeled it in slowly. Faythe lifted her hand out of the water, watching the symbols' glow wink out before she clamped her fist. She balled them on her knees, panting lightly, silencing the last vibration of magick completely.

Then she grinned.

She chuckled, shaking her head, but her brow pinched tight against the sting in her nose. "Thank you," she said.

"I didn't do anything," Reylan answered softly.

Her head tried to twist to him, but he shifted behind her instead. His hands came around her shoulders, and her back curved into him with a thrill when his fingers began to undo the buckles of her leathers.

"You didn't...?"

Soft lips grazed the tip of her ear. "It was all you." His whisper shivered down her neck, making her eyes flutter. "We can't let the heat you made go to waste."

As she caught onto his plan, a giddy knot tightened her stomach. Faythe's hands rose to aid him, but he took her wrists instead.

"You consume my every thought, Faythe," he murmured huskily. "Everything we've done, but more so, everything yet promised." His hands dipped to the buttons of her pants, and she inhaled. "Up on your knees," he commanded.

Faythe obliged, easing into his body as he rose too, and when he undid the last button, her head tipped back and his hand curved down. His groan rippled over her collar when his fingers trailed through her slickness.

"Tell me how often you thought of me doing this to you while we were apart."

Faythe's hips ground into his hand while blood roared in her ears, the pleasure he ignited so familiar yet so *different*. As fae, she felt his touch as if he were setting every nerve alight one by one. "Often," she breathed. "So often I think it's been the cause of my irrational frustration and lack of productivity."

Reylan's light chuckle was entrancing. "We can't have that." He removed his hand, and Faythe couldn't bite back her whimper quickly enough. "If this is what it takes to ease your *frustrations*, I'll oblige every time." He began to peel away her jacket.

The crisp air tensed her muscles, and she shuddered until the steam from the water drifted over her bare skin. Reylan took one breast in his hand, massaging slowly while the other hand traveled low again.

"Do you know, there is not a surface I can look at now without picturing how beautiful you would look splayed upon it for me?"

Faythe swallowed hard. "The thoughts I've had..." She moaned without restraint when a finger curved into her, beginning a slow stroke.

"Tell me."

"Are thoughts I've never had for anyone before."

"Like what?" He added a second finger, and her grip tightened on his forearm. She found it highly arousing that she could feel every flex of his muscles as he worked her.

"The first was what you said about the piano," she confessed, feeling his smile against her throat.

"I'm glad that caught your attention."

"But I don't think there's an end—no boundary I wouldn't push with you."

Reylan groaned. It was a needy, satisfied sound that stroked at her new dominance. "You doubt yourself, but I have never—not for a second." He kissed the edge of her jaw. "This world is far from done hurting you, but know that I hurt with you. I fight with you." His arm hooked around her ribs, and she gripped his forearm tightly, submitting to his pleasure.

Some primal noise of approval sounded from him, palpable in the speed of his fingers. Faythe's vision began to pepper, and she had to close her eyes, feeling a high she'd never experienced while she rocked her hips against the hardness of him behind her. She wanted *more* of him inside her, and she couldn't stop. Or speak. Or beg. She could only *chase*.

"If you don't stop that—"

His words were muffled as her thighs slipped farther apart so she could ride his hand unashamedly, unable to keep her need for release in check. His tight grip was necessary when bliss shattered through her—waves and waves of trembling pleasure. It felt endless, otherworldly. Her tremors subsided slowly, stretching out into a climax that lasted so long it took a moment for reality to reform.

Faythe slumped against him in breathless bewilderment.

Reylan's fingers easing out of her drew forth a coolness that made her shudder. He was panting hard, and she hadn't even noticed his own state of arousal while he'd been gripping her hip tightly, his forehead pressed into the crook of her neck. It dawned on her instantly with his final shudder.

"Gods above. This was supposed to be about you," he mumbled hoarsely, coming down from his own release. His teeth nicked at her collar, and she gasped. "Just wait until I can have you in a far more comfortable setting. I'm going to explore every inch of this new body and bow to your every desire." His arm around her pulled them both to their feet as his words brought color to Faythe's cheeks. "It's just as well you heated the water."

CHAPTER 30

Faythe

THEY DIDN'T RETURN to the others until morning, choosing instead to build their own fire—which Faythe lit with great triumph—and spend the night they deserved alone with each other.

Faythe heard Izaiah before she saw him as they trudged back to camp. She tucked herself in close to Reylan as they walked, needing every second of normality she could steal since they were about to head back to the city to face the storm they'd conjured.

"Ah, not eaten by a bear," Izaiah drawled, spotting them as he looked up from his puny meal. His gaze moved over her from head to toe and his mouth curled. "But a lion."

Faythe gaped, finding his shameless joke astounding. Livia covered her mouth as she choked on her food. Marlowe and Jakon wore looks of confusion, much to her relief, and as Faythe's eyes drifted, she was glad for the opportunity to change the subject.

"Where's Reuben?"

"He went to scout the nearby town for horses," Jakon answered.

Faythe's concern spiked. "Alone?"

"He's a grown man—he can take care of himself."

She wanted to agree, yet with the threats that lingered and the possibility that those who were after her could bump into him, she was riddled with dread at the thought of any of them going anywhere alone in public.

"You know, I just had a thought." Izaiah perked up, rising to his feet. He pointed between her and Reylan. "If Marlowe's theory is true, Faythe is kind of like your upgrade, Reylan."

"We already knew that," Livia chuckled. "But your abilities could be *similar* now."

Faythe glanced up at the general and found him looking back with nothing but warm assurance. They would share their discoveries eventually, but right now, Faythe treasured what they were slowly figuring out together.

The distant rush of footsteps snapping branches set all of them on high alert. As Reuben stumbled toward them, Faythe's feet moved to match his urgency.

He halted, panting, completely out of breath. "You might want to come deal with this."

The screams hit her first. Faythe ran, closely accompanied by Reylan, Izaiah, and Livia. They made it to the nearby town in no time with their fae speed, the only thing obstructing their pace worse than the staggered trees being the frantic crowd of pedestrians.

Faythe paused to stretch out her hearing, but mainly she followed her instincts, racing in the direction the crowd seemed to be fleeing from. Though they staggered and stumbled, she tried not to let her bravery slip at the many blanched faces making their retreat.

What she eventually saw made her falter. The ghastly sight split her attention between two places, starting at the creature whose teeth sucked the life from a human man in front of her, and ending back under the castle in High Farrow, where she'd been filled with the same type of all-consuming dread at the sight of a force so utterly horrific.

"Dark fae," Faythe muttered.

Livia stopped behind her with a gasp. "What happened to make him look so—"

"Hideous?" Izaiah supplied.

Faythe shook her head, trying to subdue her horror to make room for calculation. This dark fae was not like Zaiana and Maverick; his flesh was torn, blackened like poison, and the way he drank was characteristic of a starved animal. Her hand subconsciously rose to her neck as she wondered if the puncture wounds were still there from her ordeal or if they'd been erased on her fae form.

A new scream pierced the air from another direction, then another, as bodies pushed past them, and Faythe didn't know how to react. Fortunately, she didn't have to as Reylan took command.

"Izaiah, you should shift and take the east town. Livia, you go south. If you find yourselves too greatly outnumbered, draw them back to where we can take them on together. Faythe and I will handle this one. Go." His words were unwavering, owing to his status as general.

Izaiah and Livia didn't argue, both giving a firm nod before taking off.

Before they turned to the threat, Reylan blocked Faythe's view of the creature, his hand on her waist as if to make sure she was still grounded enough to help. "Are you all right?" he asked.

Faythe nodded, beginning to draw her blade, but Reylan's hand eased around hers to halt her. When she met his sapphire gaze, his eyes sparkled with challenge.

"Want to lend me some of that fire, Phoenix?"

Her pulse skipped, but she wasn't sure if it was with a thrill or wariness. "Are you sure this is a good idea?" she mumbled, but her raised palm spoke of her willingness to try.

"Not at all. But why not test yourself when with these enemies there's only one option: to kill?" He watched her palm as Faythe ignited the cobalt flame. His smile curved wider, and he raised his own palm to display a twin flame. "I can diminish your fire if you lose control, but I'd be lying if I said the thought of watching you come unleashed doesn't excite me." His squeeze of her waist drew out a short gasp that made her flame flicker. "Keep your focus," he warned, but his gravelly tone inspired the opposite.

Only a guttural moan snapped her attention from him. While they'd been speaking, the dark fae had drained the man dry. Faythe's gut twisted with sorrow for the loss of life, but as Reylan moved aside and the creature stepped into her path, her desire for revenge grew as hot as the flames she sent soaring toward him.

Her first blast struck; her second he pivoted around with impossible speed, but Reylan advanced from the side, catching him off-guard. Together they exchanged blows, but it was as if the dark fae didn't feel anything at all beyond the impact that made him shuffle back a step.

"Niltain steel is the only thing that will kill him."

Faythe sent the reminder to Reylan.

She got back: *"But this is fun, isn't it?"*

If she wasn't so focused on the dark fae's advance toward her, she would have shot him an incredulous look.

"Hardly my idea of fun."

Faythe drew more fire darts, but in her inexperience they were sloppy, sometimes missing him entirely, and her inadequacy began to grind her irritation.

The creature let out a loud growl of annoyance, close enough now that Faythe's fire winked out in her panic to reach for her sword. She drew Lumarias halfway before the jab of a blade through the dark fae's chest elicited the most earth-shattering screech.

When the body fell, Reylan's blade dripped with the foul stench of black blood.

"And what is your idea of *fun?*"

Faythe's mouth snapped shut, but she fought a smile at his playful jest. He was trying to lift the mood to offset the chaos erupting around them.

"I enjoy cards," she offered, gathering breath after the spike of adrenaline.

Reylan stalked toward her with an enticing hum.

"Sometimes chess. And surprisingly, I think I enjoy horse riding."

"Anything else?" Now right in front of her, his fingers tilted her chin up.

"Cake, if we're talking food," she said. "You know, I never got to taste a morsel of the one you pulled me from in High Farrow."

Surprise lifted his brow. "I left you as you requested."

"No, you didn't," she whispered.

From the moment they'd met he hadn't left her thoughts at all. He wasn't always at the forefront of her mind, but Reylan had slowly entangled himself in every fiber of her existence.

His mouth pressed to hers firmly, and Faythe arched into the kiss. It was short and needy, but he drew back since they couldn't be sure another dark fae wasn't lurking, ready to attack.

"Then I won't forget that I owe you," he said against her lips.

A shiver raced along her spine, but she didn't get long to enjoy their intimacy as awareness drew them apart.

"I hate to break up a moment, but we have company," Izaiah called out.

Faythe had already ignited a flame for Reylan as they turned to him. She momentarily gawked, not anticipating the half-dozen creatures of torn flesh and black blood that raced for them.

"This way too!" Livia called from behind, baiting another four to join them in the open space.

Freeing Lumarias, Faythe exchanged a look with Reylan, sealed with a nod, for their plan didn't require words. In a flare of white light, Izaiah shifted into a huge black panther.

Then they attacked.

Livia took on one, and Faythe twisted to begin striking through those who were advancing from the opposite side. Meanwhile, Reylan held the others back with fire, and Izaiah covered Livia, preventing her from becoming overwhelmed.

Honing her battle skills against the dark fae, Faythe's blade slicked through flesh, black blood poured, and the creatures fell one by one. She was coming to her last dark fae when an invasion in her mind made her gasp aloud. It happened so suddenly and with such ease Faythe didn't know how it was possible. She lost focus on all else. The sounds of the fighting, the screams, drifted away as she searched frantically for the source.

"*Faythe,*" the voice drawled like an omnipresent echo. "*What a delight it is to finally see what you came back capable of, even if this is only a glimpse.*"

Feminine, otherworldly. *Familiar.*

Terror gripped her still as she pictured a face of striking beauty. She knew every detail of the red hair tone and bright eyes even though she shouldn't. Faythe scanned frantically for the vision to become real flesh.

"Marvellas," she whispered aloud. Or at least she thought she did, though it felt as if the Spirit had taken her away and planted them both in their own still dimension.

"*I can't wait for us to be together, Faythe. This next chance we've been gifted.*"

"Then face me," Faythe said, her hand trembling with an iron grip on her sword.

A dark but entrancing chuckle vibrated through her, setting every hair on edge.

"*Time and order, my child. We will be together so very soon. I only had to see you, to know what power you have come into since Transitioning. Since coming back to me.*"

"Everything I have become is for the purpose of defeating you."

"*There are two ends to our story, Faythe. I have every intention for us not to repeat history. The desired end will keep us together and create a world I know you will come to see is right.*"

"You're afraid," Faythe said, reading between her words, "that my will for the opposite ending will triumph yours."

"*Fool yourself once, and a second chance is granted. Fool yourself twice, and there will not come another.*"

All at once Faythe was catapulted back into the realm that

raced at full speed. Her hands lashed out to grapple with something that would ground her. Her fingers curled into leather and her tipped-back head straightened.

"There you are," Reylan breathed.

She trailed her hands along his forearms to his wrists in bewilderment as he held her face.

"What in the Nether happened?"

Faythe blinked at her surroundings, finding Izaiah and Livia staring down at her with concern, and she wondered when she'd fallen to her knees with Reylan. Black blood flooded the gray stone, but she could no longer hear the screaming or detect any more dark fae. "Marvellas," was the only word she could surface, trying to figure out what it meant. Why she would be here, and why she would unleash this attack. "She was here."

With an arm hooked around her, Reylan pulled them both to their feet. Everyone braced in alarm, scanning around them as though the Great Spirit would step out any moment.

"I think she's gone now," Faythe tried to explain.

"What did she want?" Livia asked.

Faythe had no sure answer. Pressing tighter to Reylan, she wondered with a sweeping chill why the Spirit hadn't taken the opportunity to seize her. That she hadn't even tried rattled a fear far worse than if she had.

PART II
PHOENIXFYRE

CHAPTER 31

Tarly

BEING NO ONE was peaceful, existing only to enjoy the simple pleasures in life. No crown sat on his head for Tarly Wolverlon was the name he carried no longer, not since the moment he'd stepped over the border into Rhyenelle territory days ago. Yet Tarly wasn't in entirely new land. The woods he camped in were familiar, sitting at the edge of Fenher, a place he knew from times of battle over a century ago. Still, he felt…free.

Cracking branches and a steady pant signaled Katori's return. Every time she left, he wondered with a hollow loneliness if it would be for good. But so far, she'd always returned, this time clutching two limp rabbits in her powerful jaw.

Tarly huffed a laugh—one of pride and relief that they would both be well-fed tonight and he wouldn't have to go hunting. He'd done so plenty of times, but that evening he'd put all his efforts into a fire instead. Twilight was drawing in.

He was finishing up the tie on a new set of arrows when someone's approach tingled in his ears. It was distant, but he grabbed his bow anyway, deciding to duck under cover until he could be sure it was only a harmless traveler. Tarly couldn't let his guard down, not while he was still so close to Olmstone's border and he wasn't certain there was no active search for him.

He tucked himself behind a large tree trunk, and like always, Katori read his signal and instinctively made herself scarce. He kept still, extending his senses to gauge all he could. Their steps were light, and the scent that drifted to him was floral, like rose mixed with a note of cinnamon. If that wasn't confirmation enough of the female presence, her gentle humming eased his caution completely.

Until…

Tarly tensed again when he picked up on the others approaching. Many of them, and all male judging by their musky scents of ale and sea. He couldn't stop his compulsion to peek out and match a face to the delicate humming voice, overcome with dread for the stranger's safety should the others turn out to be malicious.

His sights fell on her instantly, and though she stood with her back to him, staring through the trees as she halted in alert, her brilliant silvery hair against her warm brown skin mesmerized him. The light penetrating the canopy highlighted her like a Goddess, an angel, and he had to wonder what she could possibly be doing alone in the thick of these woods.

It was a relief to see she'd picked up on the possible threat too. Tarly nocked an arrow but made no move to expose himself unless absolutely necessary. He hoped the males would pass and the beautiful fae would be on her way, singing happily once more.

He should have known that in this cruel world, that outcome was the stuff of dreams.

"Don't be afraid, little one," one male drawled. The belittling tone alone already marked him as Tarly's first target.

Still, he waited, needing to figure out how many could be easing in around her.

"I never said I was," she said with admirable confidence.

Four males, Tarly detected. Not such outstanding odds even if he were quick with his shots.

"You look it," another taunted.

His teeth ground with a flash of rage. Tarly didn't know her, but he didn't need to. His disgust at them for cornering a lone female triggered his violence. He peeked back around, finding them starting to close in on her from different sides, *herding* her as if she were a feeble lamb and they a pack of lions.

"I tried to warn you," a new voice sang.

Tarly's eyes were drawn to a tall form. His long leather coat seemed like the wears of a pirate. There were five of them now.

"Yet you flaunted your tricks and cast my help away."

"You weren't helping," she snapped. "You were marking."

"Smart you are," he said in a way that reduced her to the opposite. "But you forget I did in fact tell you not to go wandering on your own. You can't blame me for seizing an opportunity when you are so willing to be caught."

She remained so calm considering her odds. Tarly couldn't imagine what the males wanted with her. He didn't want to know despite their conversation indicating they'd all crossed paths before.

"I wouldn't say willing. But I don't want to hurt any of you."

Four of the males exchanged mocking laughter, but not their leader, though he flashed a yellowing grin.

"You have but a flask of water," he pointed out.

"It's more than what I'd need to hurt you." She spoke as if it pained her to admit it. "All of you," she added.

Leaves shuffled and more bodies started to ease out from behind the trees. Tarly's pulse quickened at the perilous odds, having to suddenly reassess how to get both of them out of these woods alive. He couldn't fathom what they wanted with her, though he had no doubt it was evil in nature. Twelve against one... His fist tightened around his bow at the spineless brutes.

When a branch snapped as one stepped closer to her, Tarly moved without sane thought. Ducking out of cover, he made a show of slowing his pace as all eyes targeted him.

"There you are, angel," he rushed out through a breath of

forced exertion. He came right up to her, not hesitating to reach out an arm, but he didn't touch her, and when her surprised features twisted up to him, time halted, for he was looking at the most stunning fae he'd ever seen. Tarly wondered for a heartbeat if she were truly real in her unique beauty. "When you didn't make it to our meeting place, I got worried." He continued his impromptu story.

Warm hazel eyes enraptured him, striking a familiarity that made the *stranger* feel less daunting. Her silvery hair falling around her brown skin made him wonder so many things about her—such as where she came from and what she was doing here. It was a difficult notion to want to know so much about her when his plan had only been to aid in her escape and then the two would part ways.

"I-I…yes, I got caught up," she said, finally dropping her gaze back to her assailant.

Tarly's tense shoulders eased to know she was playing along. He took a deep breath of false confidence. "As you can see, she is not alone. We'll be on our way."

Though he wasn't such a fool to believe that was all it would take when his first step to steer her away with him was answered by shuffling on all sides.

"I don't think so," the tall man said. They were all human, yet against so many, Tarly's odds were still damned. "Quite the prize you have. She would fetch handsome coin."

"You won't see the flash of gold again if you don't watch how you speak of her."

The man chuckled. "You fae are so foolishly emotional over your mates."

At hearing the last word, the stranger stiffened beside him completely, near shifting to step away as though he'd triggered a flight response. Tarly dropped his arm from her, and the wince she gave him tore at his heart.

The pop of the cork on her water bottle drew his attention, yet she didn't take her eyes from the men. He wasn't sure what she was doing, but Tarly somehow knew to brace. Marking his first target, he waited.

"If you know how to use that bow, do it now," she said under her breath.

Tarly almost smirked, but he didn't need a second to protest. He had his first arrow nocked and soaring in the space of a breath. The man's knees had barely met the ground before his second arrow was striking through the chest of his companion. Steel sang and a commotion began to erupt at his attack.

Tarly twisted to finish watching his shot pierce the man's shoulder before an iridescent sheen made him halt in disbelief. It rippled through the air, passing over his head, and his sights whipped to the fae beside him. Her hands were poised elegantly, a frown of focused anger etched into her smooth features. With one quick movement the water dropped. Not much of it doused the men for it was all she had in her bottle.

The leader shook his head, droplets scattering from his unkempt brown lengths. Dark amusement curved his mouth as he examined his damp clothing. "At least we know you can make it rain," he mocked.

Her eyes flexed with an ire Tarly couldn't believe such an angelic face was capable of displaying. Hand still raised, she closed her fist, and with the movement cries echoed throughout the space. Tarly glanced over at the men in shock, seeing them all tense as the water froze to ice in her grip.

"Run," was all she said, already sprinting away.

Tarly chased her, not entirely conscious of his effort, as the thought of letting her drift out of sight drummed an urgency in his chest. Not out of fear of her—or for her—but because she'd sparked his intrigue in a way he wasn't accustomed to. Her attack plus their speed gave them a high chance of eluding the bandits, but he didn't believe she was entirely free of danger.

"That was impressive," he commented while they ran through the staggered rows of trees.

"Hardly," she answered, not meeting his eye. "I didn't need your help."

"Clearly."

"So why did you bother?"

"How was I to know what ability you possessed?"

She didn't answer for a long moment while they kept running. Without faltering, she bundled the skirts of her blue-and-white cotton gown—hardly the right attire for the activity.

Tarly spotted the tree line only because it opened up onto the biggest lake he'd ever seen. They halted on its rocky bank, and he gawked at the massive body of crystal-clear water in the most spectacular glade enclosed by small mountains and trees. The place was so bright and ethereal, and the fleeting sunlight exposed tiny glowing creatures in the pool that began to glitter with starlight.

"Stenna's Fall," the fae said, and he found her studying his admiration of the place. "You've never been here before?"

The name rang with familiarity, and his memory lit up like a beacon when an old reading came to mind. The lake was famously named after a water nymph who in lore had reigned over the waters below. "Some say Stenna ruled from this lake, but not in the traditional sense." He recited what he could. "She was once considered the High Queen of Ungardia for her channels of water connected all the kingdoms. Though the kingdoms each had their own reigning monarchs, she kept the peace between them all."

The silence that settled had him glancing for her reaction. The girl's expression wandered curiously over him.

"Who are you?" she asked.

That was when it all came crashing back. From the moment he'd lain eyes on her he felt as if he were living inside a dream, but now reality lassoed around him and tugged hard. Tarly's guard was rising. He couldn't stop it, the wall that defended what little remained of himself with its harsh exterior. She didn't know who he was, and giving her his name seemed too much of a risk.

Her features smoothed out before he could respond. She seemed to read all without him having to say a word, her eyes scanning every inch of him. He tensed as though if she looked long enough she'd see his broken crown of failure, the kingdom he'd abandoned, and the name he was undeserving of because of that.

Instead, her attention fell behind him. "You're from Olmstone," she observed.

Katori's fur skimmed his hand as she passed him, walking right up to the fae. The beast took one cautious sniff before nuzzling into her. Tarly was about to apologize, but the fae's soft giggle made him halt. Made time halt. He watched her for a few prolonged seconds…and smiled faintly at the sight.

"She's beautiful." The fae's hazel gaze flashed up to him. "I'm Nerida," she offered.

The name echoed in his mind and fluttered like warmth in Tarly's chest, but he tried his hardest to cast it away. He didn't want to know this personal piece of information. It only brought him one step closer to her when he needed to take two steps back.

"I didn't ask."

The wince his rejection gained from her sank in his gut. "My mistake," she muttered. "Thanks for your help back there. I can protect myself from here."

Nerida turned, and Tarly stood rooted to the spot watching her back. He counted one, two, three steps before he called on impulse, "Wait."

He cursed himself repeatedly when she stopped, yet he couldn't stand the thought of her facing another band of crooks alone.

"They could catch up with you, or there could be far worse people wanting to do you harm."

Nerida turned, mildly incredulous before her features firmed. Then she lifted her hand and the water from the lake answered. He watched in fascination as with a few swirls of her hand the water morphed…into a wolf. It stood right beside her.

Katori dropped into a crouch with a snarl.

With a flick of Nerida's wrist, the water beast lunged for Tarly. He was about to brace when midair it lost its form, raining down before his feet as her magick left it.

"I think I'll be fine," she said flatly, not waiting for his reaction before spinning on her heel again.

"Where are you headed?"

She didn't answer, and she was gaining enough distance from him that his whole body turned rigid against the unexplainable pull he fought so hard to resist. "Shit," he swore under his breath eventually, giving in to the instinct to follow.

CHAPTER 32

Faythe

"We're almost there, but if you keep shifting like that, the others will reach the city gates long before us."

Reylan's quiet rumbled words scattered down Faythe's neck as he leaned his mouth down to her ear from behind. She couldn't help that her hand reached back to his thigh in response. The constant dip and shift of Kali's walk had been driving her to distraction all week.

"We could have stopped to acquire another horse," she said.

Reylan chuckled lightly. "It was because of your protest that we didn't."

Faythe suppressed a coy smile. She didn't want to delay the group, but more importantly, she wanted to be close to Reylan for every second she could steal. Being wrapped in his warmth took away the burden of what they were to face in a few short hours.

Her return.

He'd spent the journey comforting her of the nerves she didn't often realize were the cause of her restlessness. Words weren't always needed; he consoled her with gentle touches, a light kiss. He'd distract her with tales of the towns they passed through, and she absorbed everything, lost in his storytelling as he spoke so entrancingly.

"I can't wait to see the famous city," Marlowe said from beside them.

Faythe flashed her a smile that resonated in her chest with pride. Her friend rode with Jakon, and it dawned on Faythe how close they were and how she could show them everything that had left her yearning for them before she left on the quest.

"I couldn't have done it justice in a letter or with any words. It's truly magnificent," Faythe answered, leaning further into Reylan as this was something they shared.

Their home.

The climb over the next hill brought her vision to life, stealing Faythe's breath as if it was the first time she were seeing it. Her heart lurched to know she'd left this city as a completely different person from the one who'd be returning, both inside and out. She knew she'd face her father here, and what often consumed her with nerves to the point of sickness was that they'd be facing each other as strangers all over again. And she had failed in her quest.

The drum of her pulse filled her ears, and her breath came short. She didn't realize Reylan had halted Kali until her eyes caught onto their friends making paces away from them. Reylan said nothing for a long moment, but a gentle caress lapped at her within.

"What are you afraid of?" he asked gently.

Faythe didn't know how to answer. So many things rushed to the surface that none came coherent.

"What if I'm not *me* anymore...?" she trailed, knowing it shouldn't make sense, but Reylan knew. "What if everything is different?"

"Do you want it to be different?"

She thought on his question—one she'd asked herself before. "People have always underestimated me," she said. "I don't want the reason they start believing in me to be because I'm not human anymore. Because I am... Human and fae and possibly something else."

"Then you'll make them believe in *who* you are, not what you are. You've done it before, with me and many others." His lips brushed the tip of her ear. "I see you and I hear you...and it's about time the world did too."

Faythe nodded, hoping he could feel her gratitude. She expected him to press Kali on, but Reylan hesitated, and Faythe twisted as best as she could to catch a glimpse of his face. His expression seemed sad as his hand rose to encase her cheek.

"You are my heart, Faythe. That doesn't change, no matter what. Tell me you'll remember that."

Her brow pinched as she wondered what could have caused the insecurity. "Always," she promised, but she couldn't ignore the twist in her gut that he felt it necessary.

He smiled, but it was barely-there. She wanted to ask what brought the question forth, but he scattered her thoughts with a kiss. Short, firm, but necessary.

Then Reylan snapped the reins as he said, "I'm not the only one who's been anticipating your return."

As they passed under the wall, Faythe held her breath. They rode slowly through the city, and she sat so stiffly it was near painful. She didn't fail to notice Reylan had shifted back a fraction, their position no longer so intimate. Faythe almost questioned it, but as soon as the murmurs of the people started up, she could focus on nothing else. They gasped and ran to each other, everything becoming such a buzz that she only caught a few loose words.

"She's alive."

"Faythe Ashfyre."

"It was a lie."

"The princess has returned."

The weight of their attention hummed in every nerve cell. Faythe and the others passed into the inner ring, and while the voices in here weren't as loud, their disbelieving stares were just as piercing.

"She's fae."

"Impossible."

"A miracle."

"An impostor."

She took deep, steadying breaths. They had every right to their thoughts and suspicions; to wonder how their heir could die and rise again. They were right and wrong, and Faythe wondered if the world would ever truly believe her story.

Then the castle gates came into view, and her heart pounded against her rib cage. She could see him. Agalhor stood with a few others atop the portico, and she couldn't tear her eyes from him as they emerged onto the expansive courtyard. Everything was deathly quiet, save for the horses' hooves against the stone.

More bodies poured out—flecks of movement and color Faythe couldn't pay attention to as she tried to gauge the king's every reaction.

Their horses stopped, and Reylan dismounted swiftly. Faythe tore her eyes from Agalhor, who had yet to move an inch, only to glance down and see Reylan poised to help her.

"You're doing great."

Bracing on his shoulders, Faythe landed on the ground weightlessly. His hands didn't linger for a second, and it pinched her chest when he took a step back. Reylan's smile spoke to her protest until he turned to the royals awaiting him. It was then she noticed Malin near the king, his expression as cold as always, but those eyes were attentive.

Faythe straightened her shoulders as she released another deep breath and turned to begin her walk toward the King of Rhyenelle. Agalhor's formal stance unnerved her, creating the fear that who he saw was no longer his daughter. Just as quickly as the panic rushed in, it eased all at once when he broke position. Faythe's nose stung, eyes blurring, as he descended the stairs, dropping the firmness of a king to let the concern of a father flood in.

There was no pause, no hesitation, when his large arms opened and Faythe fell into them, uncaring of what was proper or who was watching. All she needed was that embrace that lifted away the burdens of the world.

His acceptance.

"I failed." She whispered the haunting truth.

His large hand held the back of her head as he peeled her away, studying every inch of her face, his gaze lingering with concern and awe on her ears. "Not at all, my dear." His fingers tilted her chin. "The fact you stand here as you are—it's a defiance that can win this war once and for all."

"I'm just glad to be home." She barely got the words out through the tightness in her throat. Faythe had never called the city that out loud before. She looked over her people, stunned by the masses who had crowded in to look upon her not with distaste, but relief. Faythe might never have gotten the chance to embrace them all as *home*.

Her gaze caught on her cousin, and the warmth in her chest froze over at his piercing assessment. In her next blink it was gone, and he plastered on a false smile as they headed toward the castle.

"A masterful plan you kept up this past month," Malin commented. "I am glad the harrowing news of your passing turned out to be a ruse."

Faythe read the undertone to his words: they were far from the truth.

They headed inside, Reylan trailing behind them, and though it didn't sit right with her, she didn't look back.

"We have much to prepare for," she said as confidently as she could.

"Indeed. I look forward to discussing it all, hearing of your tales and what your...*change* might mean for the kingdom." Malin's tone was laced with cunning—something she hadn't missed nor forgotten about. "A council meeting should be called immediately. The lords have been restless since the news of your impending return."

"In due time," Agalhor inserted calmly.

Faythe's pulse skipped with the notion. Even before leaving, she knew this time would come—that she'd have to integrate into an active court role if she were ever to claim permanent status here in Rhyenelle.

"I'm afraid it cannot wait long. With the new threats, as you said, the kingdom is weak while the matter remains unresolved," Malin insisted.

Walking the familiar halls eased Faythe's tensions and filled her with gratitude that she'd lived to do so. Though every time her eye caught on the Firebird emblem, a creeping heat swept her skin as flashbacks stole her attention.

"Wouldn't you agree, Faythe?" Malin asked, and she snapped her head to him.

Her cheeks flushed. She blinked a few times with the rush of overwhelming words, feelings, and thoughts, realizing she'd missed what he said.

"I think we should wait..." Agalhor started.

"I'm ready as soon as the council will have me," Faythe cut in. She wasn't sure what Malin believed was so urgent, but Faythe had matters of her own that couldn't wait in the wake of the looming threats.

"You can take time to rest."

Reylan spoke to her mind, but she didn't look to where he lingered a few paces away when they all stopped in the hall.

"I've taken enough time."

She kept her eyes only on Malin, riddled with wonder at what the gleam of his delight at her willingness meant. She didn't have room to decipher it right now.

"I'll have it set up for week's end." Malin gave a nod of his head, flashing a quick look at Agalhor before he left them.

As soon as he was out of sight the tension of his presence lifted. Faythe rubbed her temple where a dull ache began.

"Do not push yourself too soon," Agalhor told her softly, resting a hand on her shoulder.

"I'm not. But I meant what I said: we need to prepare. And I need to tell my story."

Pride danced in his hazel eyes, and she allowed herself to accept it.

"I want more time with you, my dear, but you must be in need of rest. I will see you very soon." His hand gave hers a light squeeze, and she smiled gratefully as he glanced cautiously at Reylan before turning away.

Guards still lingered, but finally, Reylan came to stand beside her, saying nothing as she led the way to her rooms. At whom they saw around the next corner, Faythe lit up running.

As she collided with Kyleer, the two of them rumbled with joyous laughter. When he set her back down, he looked over her brightly.

"You're collecting a fine list of names, *Bloodmasked.*" Kyleer chuckled when her mouth popped open.

She flashed Reylan an accusatory look. He hadn't mentioned he knew of the nickname.

"You were spying on us the whole time?" She'd suspected they were since Izaiah knew when she was in danger, but she hadn't realized for how long.

Reylan gave way to amusement. "It was getting dull around here without your antics. We had to be kept in the know to pass the time."

Faythe huffed a laugh, but then she remembered. "You have Zaiana."

Kyleer's expression switched so quickly she couldn't read what else firmed his features at hearing her name. "We do. I've been overseeing her detainment." His attention flashed briefly to Reylan, and Faythe felt something between them in that exchange she wasn't used to. It felt as though she'd stirred some disagreement.

"Have you found out anything yet?" she asked.

"Not much, but we haven't moved onto more…*forcible* methods yet."

Faythe didn't want to know what that would entail. She'd been itching to speak with the dark fae as soon as she heard of where she was. As much as it haunted her to think of facing her again, she had so many unanswered questions, and Zaiana was perhaps the only one who held the answers to them. Though she knew it would be difficult to draw them out of her.

"I want to see her," Faythe blurted. "Alone."

"Soon—"

"Now." She met Reylan's stare firmly, hating the tension she locked on him, but she didn't need permission.

"It could overwhelm you, facing her."

"It could, but I won't know until I do." Her expression softened, and she took a step toward him, though Reylan glanced away as she did, surveying who could be near. "Is there something you're not telling me?" she accused, hating how he'd been acting cautious since they arrived.

"Things are changing right now. More than ever our actions are being watched."

"What does that mean?"

"We need to know where you stand, Faythe," Kyleer cut in gently, voice dropping low as he came closer. "Until you speak with the council, we can't give anyone the impression something's going on between you two. It would only give them further reason to discredit you."

The weight of the revelation sent her a step away from Reylan, her incredulous look sliding between them. "*Further* reason?" she breathed, suddenly feeling the meaning behind Malin's eager gleam.

"Don't worry about it right now. It's just a precaution."

Denying what lay between her and Reylan as a *precaution* made a sickness roll through her. It felt wrong.

"Why didn't you tell me?"

"I didn't want to dampen what little time we had," Reylan said guiltily.

Her anger quickly dissipated to a drop of sorrow. As much as she longed to be back, if staying cautious around him in the public eye was what it cost, she'd rather be anywhere else.

"I'll see you later," Faythe said, trying to hold back her disappointment. She didn't know if Reylan would even risk coming by her rooms, and the thought of nights without him didn't settle well. She turned to Kyleer. "Take me to her."

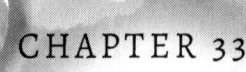

CHAPTER 33

Tarly

"You've been following me for nearly an hour and you've said nothing."

Tarly came to a stop. The snap of Nerida's voice was a shock though he had in fact been trailing her from a distance for a countless stretch of time. "Maybe I happened to be going this way anyway," he countered. She'd kept to the lake's edge, though he didn't have a map to guess where she could be headed.

A loud splash caught their attention, but it quickly fell when Tarly beheld Katori wrestling a large fish in her jaw.

"You have your company. You have your meal. Leave me alone," she grumbled, turning to continue her walk.

"You can't expect me to leave you wandering alone at night."

"Like I said, I don't need your protection."

"Seems like you did," he muttered under his breath.

She whirled to him again. "Your name," she demanded.

Tarly blinked, stunned to learn that was what was keeping her hostile. When he didn't answer, her huff was adorable.

"That's Katori," he offered eventually, casting a hand toward where she padded over to them, the fish now limp.

Her mouth parted, and he resisted an amused smile. "You need a haircut," she commented.

Tarly ran his hand though his disheveled blond locks. Before he could utter a word, she studied him with her gaze.

"Your clothes could use replacing too. You're alone with a wolf for company, camping in the woodland. You're hiding."

He didn't appreciate the assessment, nor could he stand the clamp in his gut that encouraged him to give up caring about what might become of her if he let her walk away for good. "Once we reach a town," he said, "you won't have to worry about me following you for another step."

Unhooking the bow from his back, Tarly set it down, and he didn't bother to look up again as he paced to the tree line, where he began to gather sticks for a fire since a chill was starting to seep through his clothes as night fell in. He was using rocks to form sparks over sheddings of Katori's fur when Nerida approached, setting down the small pack she carried and taking a seat opposite him.

"I know what it's like, not wanting people to know who you are," she said quietly.

Tarly's hands slipped, but it was with the right amount of force as the embers finally caught on the lint. He flashed her a look as he shuffled the wood, watching the amber flicker over her thoughtful face while she stared at his hands.

"Because of what you are?" he asked. He'd thought he was content with silence, that he'd accepted his bottled feelings and terrorizing thoughts, if only so he could be spared from the cruelty of the outside world. Yet her voice made him want to break free. "You're from Lakelaria, aren't you?"

He couldn't help that it slipped from his mouth. He was making the assumption based on her ability and the mesmerizing tone of her hair. Perhaps he'd refused to acknowledge it was a magnet for his intrigue since any such reminder of the great island brought forth memories of his mother's love for it.

"I guess you could say that."

He didn't know what she meant by that, but it would be hypocritical of him to push for more information considering he was withholding the most basic of knowledge: his name. He feared it was the key to a door that would blast right open and expose everything he wanted to forget he once was.

Nerida shuffled closer to the fire, raising her hands to warm them. "I'm heading to the Livre des Verres."

Tarly's head snapped up. "You can't."

She said nothing at first. The narrowing of her eyes he explained away as outrage, but it also offered a challenge.

"I mean, it's not safe to go there."

"Alone, you mean?"

"At all." He matched her tone.

They stared off.

"Are you in the habit of telling those you've just met what they can and can't do? Where is and isn't safe?"

"You know I've come from Olmstone."

"I don't know how long ago."

"Weeks," he snapped. "I was there just weeks ago, and I guess you haven't heard, but that kingdom has all but fallen."

Her hard expression eased, yet he couldn't stand it that her realization fell to sympathy. He saw the benefit of giving her the knowledge—it let her believe he was simply a citizen fleeing from a besieged kingdom without a monarch.

"What happened?"

"Valgard," he said, and that seemed to be enough. He took no feeling from the horror that passed over her face. It shrouded them with a heavy silence, and Tarly used that time to skewer the fish and set it over the fire, delighting in the scent as his stomach had been twisting with hunger all day.

"Then that's all the more reason I need to get there."

This fae was unbelievable. He looked at her like she couldn't be serious, but Nerida only stared out over the huge lake, lost in a pool of her own thoughts while she hugged her knees. The image of her stole everything for a second. She looked so ethereal with the fire and moonlight painting her warm brown skin and making her hair twinkle.

Tarly shook the admiration as quickly as it came.

"I can assure you there's nothing in that library worth risking your life for."

"I appreciate the warning, but I'll know to be vigilant."

"Nerida…" He paused, letting it sink in how much he enjoyed the feel of her name on his tongue. But he ground his teeth with the unwanted thought. "There are plenty of other libraries."

"Not like this one. Livre Des Verres is the most guarded library in all of history. They don't make copies of books often. It holds knowledge you can't get anywhere else."

Tarly knew this and likely far more interesting facts about the library than she did. Not that he could say much without risking exposing himself.

"Dare I ask what you seek to find that is so important?"

It was in that moment he realized the common ground they stood on. Nerida was being careful of how much she shared with him not because she was a stranger, but out of a habit he knew all too well.

"I'm helping a friend," she said.

"Must be someone great to be so worthy of you making such a long trip even despite being enlightened to the dangers."

She gave a smile, and he had to drop his gaze out of fear of how much he enjoyed it. "It's a bit more complicated than that. She's…special."

Tarly tried to read between her words but decided it wasn't for him to press the matter. He reached for the cold end of the stick when he gauged the fish to be cooked. Then he extended it to her.

Nerida shook her head. "Thank you," she said quickly, "but I don't eat meat."

Tarly blinked at the fish, feeling guilty for the kill he never even made. "Uh…no, I'm sorry, I don't have anything else." He fumbled like a fool.

"I have some provisions. Please, don't enjoy the fish any less on my account."

Nerida rustled through her pack as Tarly picked at the fish. She produced a small bundle of cheese and crackers before extending it to him. He was shocked at her kindness, unsure of what to do with it.

"All yours." He shook his head. "Thank you."

She gave one of those smiles of pure innocence, the kind that lit like treasure in their harsh world.

"How long have you not eaten meat?" He tried to start a conversation, feeling awkward that he wasn't sure how to be...*interesting*.

"My whole life. I, um..."

Again, her pause to deliberate whether she should share the information or not he could only sympathize with. Tarly kept quiet.

Nerida spared a glance around as though extending her senses before she went on. "I'm a healer too. I enjoy helping people, and I guess the thought of harming another creature has just never felt in my nature."

Tarly was stunned into silence that she would share this piece of herself with him, a perfect stranger, without knowing that it touched upon such a deeply rooted memory. His mother, who'd held a weak essence of the same ability Nerida harbored. In that moment he wanted to give a piece of himself right back to her, but the words stuck in his throat. He swallowed hard, so overcome with grief and longing that his appetite left him completely. Tarly threw the fish over to where Katori lay, and she wasted no time in devouring it.

"Did I say something wrong?" Nerida's soft voice only tugged at his despair.

"No," was all he could reply, unable to meet those hazel eyes he was sure would bore through him with sadness. "I'm just tired. It's been an eventful night. We should both get some rest." He shuffled down, facing away from her. All he had to do to rest his mind was see her to the nearest town, where she'd be surrounded by people, and if she were smart, she wouldn't wander through any more woodland alone.

He listened to her fold away her food without eating much either and his eyes tightened shut against the hatred he felt toward himself. She didn't deserve his lousy company, yet he was forcing it upon her because of his own damn restless mind. He couldn't let her go off alone despite her impressive water defense display.

"Are you always this sullen?"

Her question was more of a demand. Surprised to hear her voice again, Tarly rolled to glance over his shoulder. She was lying down but had propped herself up with a hand to call him out.

"Probably," he answered.

Her lips pursed, and when she huffed back down and out of sight behind the flames, Tarly let go of the small smile that twitched at his mouth.

"If you're not going to give me a name, then I've found one for you. Sully."

Tarly couldn't stop the huff of a laugh that escaped him. It was a foreign sound and a light feeling he cut off quickly, but it eased the tension he'd dropped on the night.

"Very well, Nerida."

And though it was utterly ridiculous and somewhat insulting, he embraced the fact she even cared to give him a name at all.

CHAPTER 34

Faythe

FAYTHE WRUNG HER hands the whole way to the cells. They passed the guards at the end of the hall, but before they went through the next door Kyleer caught her elbow.

"Are you sure you're up for this?" he asked quietly.

Her mind couldn't stop racing. She wanted to say no. Wanted to confess her bravery had left her completely with the flashbacks that slicked her skin with sweat as she pictured those amethyst-cored eyes. The absolutely lethal beauty of them she'd battled through the heavy rainfall, Zaiana coming close to ending her life. But she could not cower. Not now. She'd failed in letting Dakodas ascend and could only listen to her urgency that she needed to be stopped along with Marvellas.

"I can handle it," she said weakly, and Kyleer sensed her fear.

"She's chained and has no magick or wings. She can't hurt you. She's just another fae."

Faythe breathed in relief at one fact: no wings. Perhaps without them her mind could ease off seeing Zaiana as the deadly creature she was.

Just another fae...

Focusing on taming her pulse, Faythe counted her steps until she spotted the form sitting against the back wall. Time slowed when she was standing right outside, and those eyes that haunted her awake drifted lazily down from staring out the small window to lock directly on her. Then Zaiana's mouth curled slowly, so familiar in its cruel amusement.

"Hello, Faythe."

Those two words were all it took for the bars to be removed, leaving them face-to-face on that mountain edge once again, the shadow of high taloned wings casting over them. Faythe's head snapped to Kyleer. Eyes darting to his shoulder, she expected to find him bleeding, but he was still. She met his eyes with horror, trying to blink hard to stay present.

"This was a mistake," he said.

"I don't think so," Zaiana sang.

Again, those words she'd heard before projected her back to the past, sounding out over the rain while she held Zaiana under her sword. The clang of chains made her jolt, and she snapped her attention to the dark fae as she stood.

"How do you expect to overcome a fear if you run from it?" Zaiana drawled, taking up a casual lean against the back wall. "I can assure you it will only chase you until the end of your days."

Just another fae. That was all she was, and with the acknowledgment Zaiana was right, all that threatened to consume Faythe started to ease.

"I'll be fine," she said to Kyleer.

He stayed reluctant, and Faythe observed the tilt of Zaiana's head that accompanied something like a challenge directed at Kyleer.

"I'll be right outside this door," he muttered to Faythe, but he didn't take his stare from Zaiana.

When he left, the groan of steel over stone echoed a ripple of awareness. Faythe breathed steadily.

"So,"—Zaiana broke their silence—"you've come back as an

ordinary fae. I did wonder if we'd be able to take our fight to the skies sometime. Disappointing really."

Faythe stiffened against a shudder at the possibility that hadn't crossed her mind.

She could've returned as dark fae.

Zaiana chuckled at her reaction. "You don't know what you're missing out on."

Faythe couldn't be sure what she expected from the dark fae without the fuel of battle, the pump of rage, and the focus on the task of capturing her. The Zaiana who stood before her now embodied someone else entirely, and Faythe couldn't decide if the cold-hearted ruthlessness that dwelled within was even more terrifying now it was encased in such a normal exterior.

"You knew I was alive the entire time." Faythe spoke at last.

"Does it matter?"

"You told Maverick where I was."

Zaiana's smile fell instantly. Faythe planted her feet against the sudden sweep of darkness shadowing the surface of her striking purple irises.

"You mean he found you?"

Faythe's eyes narrowed, trying to assess if the reaction was genuine. "He tried to kill me," she confirmed. "I wonder how he's coping with the impact of a second failure."

Zaiana pushed off the wall, causing a jolt in Faythe's chest. "How did you escape him?" she asked with a cold, dead calm.

Deciding to test Zaiana's temper, Faythe shrugged casually. "It's becoming something of a talent of mine."

Zaiana's jaw locked as she took a step closer, and though the heat of her skin betrayed her nerves, Faythe held firm against the advance. "Was Reylan there?"

"What if he was?"

Zaiana's thinning patience became palpable. Faythe remembered the chains, the bars, the Niltain steel. Repeated that she was safe on this side.

"You want to know if he's still alive." She voiced the question she knew Zaiana would never speak out loud.

"I've wanted to kill that bastard for longer than you've lived, Faythe. Don't goad me with pitiful notions as if I care for him."

Faythe only gave her a look, but Zaiana took another step forward in warning, so close now she could reach out and touch if it weren't for the cage. "Did you only come to rest your terrors? To see your monster caged and convince yourself you'll finally be able to sleep well at night?"

"You didn't kill me when you had the chance."

"A fatal mistake on my part. One I won't make again."

Faythe shook her head. "You think you won the battle, but you only started the war." She raised a hand, focusing to conjure a familiar heat before it sparked as a shallow blue flame over her fingertips.

Zaiana straightened, eyes wide as she focused on it too. "How?"

"I have Maverick to thank really. For forcing me to feel what it was to hold fire, to tame it…play with it."

"Did you kill him for it?"

Though she tried to hide it, Faythe felt the echoes of Zaiana's trepidation as she waited for the answer. She could torment the dark fae by not replying or delight in watching the mask obliterate if she lied. Yet glancing at her stunned face, all Faythe could think about was how Reylan would have felt in those moments he believed her to be gone.

"No," she said, winking out the flame with a closed fist.

The relief that fell on Zaiana's face was so faint she could have missed it. "What are you?" she asked, and Faythe thought it was more to divert from her almost spilling her care for Maverick.

She held no answer. Instead, she said, "There will come a time to choose sides. You'll either be a part of what I am or feel the force of what I will become."

As they held each other's eye, Faythe chose to believe it would invoke the dark fae's consideration. Though she'd never admit her true reason for coming here was that she had to see for herself if the one who'd spared her life was genuine or if she'd merely sacrificed one gain to await another. The rise of her chin was all Faythe needed to walk away.

"Your name," she said, nearly at the door when she clarified. "Your name was all it took for him to stop his attack. That was how I escaped."

CHAPTER 35

Zaiana

Z AIANA THOUGHT OVER Faythe's quick visit days ago. She analyzed every word and flicker of expression on the face that looked so familiar yet embodied something horrifying, her thoughts reeling back through the visit over and over again. When her silence was disrupted, it was by more than one set of boots. Zaiana didn't balk at the figures who stormed down the passage. She sat bored, knees bent with her arms draped over them, meeting their seething stares with impassiveness.

Four males she'd never seen before stopped abruptly. They hesitated, staring her down as if the force of their anger could inflict pain alone. When none of them moved, Zaiana smiled sweetly.

That seemed to snap the tether of the one closest to the door. The rattle of keys echoed through the space before the cell door swung open.

"Am I getting a tour?" Zaiana drawled.

"Shut up," one snarled.

She didn't give him the satisfaction when his grip lashed

around her arm, hauling her up with brute force. At least he thought so. It was somewhat gentle to her.

"You're brave," she mocked darkly. Another grabbed her other side, pulling her with such unnecessary power it was beginning to shake her composure. "All of you."

One scoffed. "You're powerless. Nothing more than a worthless mutation."

Zaiana was many things. Dark, wicked, cruel. Many unforgivable and heinous things.

But never powerless.

Even bound in Niltain steel, she was confident she could end them all. She wouldn't, of course. Zaiana had a bigger game to play and wouldn't let their misplaced arrogance be their end.

"Does your commander not like to get his hands dirty?"

One of the fae who wasn't holding her veered into her path. Zaiana heard the second he flipped, caught his shuffle out of the line, and braced with clenched teeth long before the hard strike across her face. The sting pulsed in her jaw. She took two seconds to breathe, blowing her loose hair harshly to reel back her instinct to rip off his head with her chains alone.

She said nothing. When her eyes opened and her head straightened, Zaiana poured death into her stare. Unblinking, she held him, marking him with it. And she saw the message was received in the way he balked, the movement so small maybe the others wouldn't notice his slip of bravado. Then she turned to each of them, remembering their faces, and made sure they too knew their lives had been placed on borrowed time.

Zaiana spat the blood that pooled in her mouth, a shining silver against the dull gray of the ground.

The fae's expression twisted in disgust. "I'm going to enjoy spilling more of your foul blood," he sneered.

"No more than I'm going to enjoy spilling yours."

That earned her a decent punch to her abdomen. She tensed in time for that too, knowing how many breaths it would take for the crushing pain to subside enough for her to straighten as though her insides didn't feel ruptured. They weren't. Zaiana had sustained far worse injuries and she didn't fear what they'd do to her. Her entire existence had trained her for this moment. Capture, torture. She would give them nothing.

They led her through a series of underground passages. She mapped each one. These idiots didn't even try to make sure she wouldn't know her exact route out should she escape. It had her wondering about Kyleer's judgment if these were the best guards he could send to kick off interrogations. In fact, what she'd witnessed so far spoke nothing of the stories she'd read of the mighty kingdom.

The room they arrived into was empty, no windows. Two guards placed their torches in holders, and Zaiana spied the two metal rings with long chains hanging parallel on each wall. She knew what was coming. Focusing her mind, she began to tunnel away from who she was, where she was.

A hard hand clamped her shoulder, forcing her to her knees, which cracked off the unforgiving ground. One wrist was freed only to be hastily shoved into a new restraint, then the other, until she was splayed there on her knees, the chains only just long enough so her arms stretched wide.

Zaiana knew this position all too well. It had been a long time, but she focused everything she had into not projecting back there. These grim walls beckoned her mind back to the black warped stone under the mountain.

"That's better," one fae mocked.

They circled her, feasting on her pitiful state, enjoying every second they held their dark sister species at their mercy. They goaded her, hoping she'd give way to an ounce of rage, but Zaiana stayed silent, tunneling and tunneling until she reached the well of detachment that would numb the world just enough that she could endure what was to come next.

But not forget.

She would always remember this.

Zaiana wished for anything else in place of the long leather whip that lapped across the floor in one snap. This method of punishment was the most recurring demon from her past: stripped top-bare, braced against the masters' long stone bench while they each took their fill.

The leather snake approached. Zaiana couldn't waive her steel composure before they even got past one round of torture. She closed her eyes. Every muscle in her body locked as she felt the presence close in behind her.

"You are a stunning little monster," one of the guards cooed. His foul hot breath against her ear pinned him as the first on her list to die.

Picturing how she would end each of them was all she could do to keep from breaking.

"We'll save that pretty face of yours until last if we can."

Her whole body gave off a stiff tremble when the sound of clothing being ripped rang through the room, projecting her back to the masters' *private* chamber with a flash as cruel as the whip.

Breathe. Control. Breathe.

One lash tore through her sweater, but as she expected of any beast who favored this punishment, one wasn't enough. The second tear was the cropped undergarment she wore, though the long black sleeves kept her front from full exposure.

For now.

Laughter broke out. Tears pricked her closed eyes, and she despised it. The hatred burned agonizingly in her throat.

She wasn't under the mountain.

These were not the masters.

These beasts she would kill the second she got the chance.

"Looks like many have had their fun with you before us," they mocked.

Her hands twisted around the chains, fisting them tightly. Her hot rage had no outlet. She hoped the loose hair from her braid was shielding her clenched eyes as she tuned out their degrading words because she could track nothing but leather grating over stone, the guard circling her, preparing to strike.

One leaned in close to whisper, "Count for us, darkling."

Zaiana knew the suspended seconds before the crack of a

whip. At the first strike, her body lurched forward against the searing burn, wrists straining in their steel hold.

Why don't you count for us, Zaiana?

It was Master Koy's voice that replaced the Rhyenelle guard. He liked to watch, not inflict.

"This can end in twenty lashes," another taunted from across the room.

It only starts when you begin counting, Zephra would say.

"Otherwise each before then is just more fun," a guard sang.

Zaiana retained her silence. She would not break.

The whip cracked again, scoring her flesh.

"Or this can end one other way."

She would not break.

Leather against stone, a whistle through air.

Strike.

"Show us your mighty wings, *darkling.*"

She would not break.

"I think they'd make great trophies for our halls."

Within, she *was* counting, only to know how many cuts to inflict on each of them when she had her revenge. If there was one thing she would take from the masters, it was that the fae and humans…they would never relent to her kind. Never see anything past the monsters they were, and yet it was all in aid of taking back what was stolen from them. Freedom, power. They thought they'd rid the world of the dark fae, and Zaiana basked in the knowledge she would have her victory.

While they had their fun, she separated mind from body. Her training had been ruthless and unforgiving, but it had made her a master of endurance. Soon she would feel nothing, hear nothing, and after their sick joy had been satisfied, she wouldn't remember the pain—only her wrath.

Zaiana's palms clenched tightly for the next strike. Her teeth slammed together, shoulder blades locked…

The whip fell, but her flesh didn't take the impact. Her eyes snapped open, landing on a pair of boots that seemed familiar. She trailed her tired gaze up from them, and the sight of Kyleer coated the room in ice. Not only his presence, but the livid, frightening fury that didn't just cut through his features but emanated throughout the room like an energy. Jarring, confusing, as he intercepted the fall of the whip that wrapped around his leather-clad arm before it could strike Zaiana. And that rage…

It was directed at his own soldiers.

His voice was a cold sweep of shadow as he said, "What do you think you're doing?"

"We planned to get information on—"

Kyleer pulled the whip from the fae, and it clattered to the ground where he tossed it. Sparing a glance, Zaiana found the others gaping at Kyleer.

"On whose orders?"

The silence was deadly.

He moved lightning-fast, pinning the fae who'd inflicted her lashes to the wall with such an impact it made Zaiana wince. "On whose *gods-damned* orders?"

Zaiana hung her head. The whip wasn't what exhausted her, though her back stung and throbbed; it was the mental toll it took to tighten her mind against all that threatened to reduce her to a frightened, pleading victim.

"Our own." The guard's tone was stripped back to a quiver.

"How many lashes?"

His pause earned him another hard slam into the wall.

"Twelve," Zaiana answered for them. Her body shuddered though she didn't look up.

"Get. Out," Kyleer commanded, his tone so dark her bones rattled with it.

The four fae shuffled, leaving her and Kyleer in a silence she couldn't place, nor really care about. What she didn't expect was for him to drop to one knee before her, taking her chin with a gentler hold than she anticipated. His glare of rage and hatred was the only strangely normal thing.

"Don't pretend like you're not enjoying this," she got out.

A muscle flexed in his jaw as he searched her eyes. Then he let go of her abruptly to stand. Kyleer moved around her, and she stiffened completely once more, knowing what caused his stillness. He was staring at the map of scars on her exposed back, and she couldn't bear it. She wondered why it made shame and embarrassment rush in to have the commander see them. A building, twisting sickness. Zaiana barely took in his movements until after her wrists were back in her old chains, bound in front of her.

"What a pathetic mode of torture," she said, her words weighted with fatigue. "They didn't even ask about my *still chest,* yet it was the first thing you were interested in."

Something heavy fell on her shoulders. It wrapped her in his scent, and she should have had the mind to shrug it straight off. Yet she couldn't. Zaiana took steady breaths. Having her back covered was a relief, but that *scent*... A secret she would take to her grave was that she found comfort in it. She felt as if she didn't have to fight so hard to protect herself when it was near.

The thoughts were unbearable, traitorous. She emptied them from her mind.

"You need to pick better guards if you want any hope of extracting information," she said.

"They weren't looking for information." Kyleer helped her stand. She didn't see any reason to expend more energy fighting him. "They're afraid and used you to prove to themselves they have nothing to fear."

Her gut twisted. "I suppose they got what they wanted."

"No," he growled. "You gave them the opposite."

Her eyes widened, unable to react as she normally would when Kyleer leaned down and swept her feet out from under her. "I can walk," she snapped.

"I know."

He marched out of the room, carrying her wrapped in his crimson cloak, and though in her tiredness she accepted it, everything else screaming at Zaiana from within did not.

"Put me down," she warned. It was so wrong. *So* wrong. No one had ever held her this way before, and she didn't want to pay mind to the thoughts that clung to the tenderness of his grip. Kyleer didn't speak, wouldn't even look at her, so all she could do was study his hard face. He was silently warring with himself, and she knew that look—had worn it herself many times.

"Am I hurting you?" He broke the silence, but his question was reluctant. Kyleer's arm was already high enough not to rub the material against her raw skin.

"No."

More silence.

"Tomorrow, servants will draw you that bath—"

"No."

The thrill that raced down her spine was unwelcome under his darkening stare. The challenge and passion in his eyes seized her. He stopped walking, and she thought he was about to drop her. There would be no graceful way to catch herself. Yet he simply stared her down as though wanting to go to war against her...or *with* her. She couldn't be sure.

"Your stubbornness is remarkable," he grumbled, pressing on.

"Why did you stop them?" The question tumbled from her mouth, and pathetic anticipation coiled in her stomach as she waited for his answer.

"They were acting against a direct order."

"What order?"

They reached her cell, where he placed her down. His gentleness with her was driving her insane. She couldn't bear it.

"No one touches you."

Zaiana breathed through the spike of intensity shooting through those green irises while he crouched before her.

"Except you."

He stood, sealing her cell door as he left it. "Except me."

Those two words sparked something in her dead chest, only because they were accompanied by a look that captured her for a second. A look that devoured.

"Kyleer," she called to halt him as he walked away. "You forgot something." She clenched her teeth, making as if to shrug out of his cloak.

"Keep it," was all he said, not giving her the chance to object before he disappeared completely.

CHAPTER 36

Tarly

TARLY AWOKE DOUSED in alarm. He pushed up, glancing sideward, then remembered who he expected to find.

Nerida was gone.

Scrambling to his feet, he snatched his bow, scanning the lakeshore for Katori but not finding the beast. The snap of a branch had him whirling, bow poised and arrow knocked.

A familiar beauty that stunned him all over again started back with a gasp as she beheld his arrow. Tarly dropped his aim immediately, eyes flashing to Katori, who was wandering along beside her, head lowered as though braced to lunge but relaxing along with him.

"I didn't mean to frighten you," she said carefully, edging closer warily.

Tarly ran a hand through his hair. "I'm sorry." It didn't feel enough for the target he'd made of her, and he couldn't erase the flash of terror that he might have struck her. She didn't know him. She shouldn't trust him. No one usually did, and Tarly had accepted that their time together would be short anyway. "We should get going," he grumbled, fixing the bow to his back.

"I picked some berries for breakfast," she said, holding out a cloth stained with pinks and purples. "Katori and I ate plenty while you slept. These ones in particular will help with energy, and these—"

Tarly watched her while she went on about the other fruits she held along with some nuts. While he absorbed her knowledge, what fascinated him was the passion she spoke with—her true healer's nature coming into play.

When her hazel gaze flashed up to him, she halted abruptly, and so he wouldn't seem like he'd been gawking like a fool, he dropped his eyes to the offering and took it with a quick thanks.

They walked for some time in silence. Tarly enjoyed the berries and wanted to tell her, but the spark of conversation died every time he looked upon her face. She seemed to be soaking in the sights of the grand lake peacefully, and he decided his voice was nothing more than an unwanted distraction.

"We should come to a small town by nightfall. The path I plan to take to Olmstone by then is fairly open—no depthless woodland," she said at last.

That was all he needed to know. She could take care of herself. So why wouldn't the twist in his stomach unravel? Tarly only gave a short nod when she turned to him.

"Sullen and somber. Your solitude is making more sense."

"I figured you were enjoying the silence," he said.

"If that ever becomes the case, I'll tell you to shut up."

Tarly's brow lifted, yielding to the curl of his mouth. He didn't doubt she'd speak her mind. "How did you come to be on the mainland?" he tried.

Nerida pulled away at the question, and he cursed himself, knowing it was better to keep to himself in his dampened mood. "I came here around three centuries ago. I was fairly young."

Every piece of her he gained he found himself storing away. They were small pieces of a grander puzzle he didn't know how long it would take him to complete, but he knew the picture would be worth waiting a lifetime.

He pondered what she told him, not wanting to press, so

instead he felt compelled to give something back. "I lost my parents during the Great Battles," he said calmly, and it was the truth. Tarly didn't linger on the fact he wasn't sure what had become of his father once he fled. He was a pitiful son, but he had long mourned Varlas as a parent.

"Much was lost then. I'm sorry."

"It wasn't your fault."

"No, but every life lost before its time is a tragedy. I mourn that our world has come to this. Fighting each other."

"The war is simply a larger-scale representation, an enlightening visual, of a darkness that has always been present."

Nerida's stillness grated on his nerves. He wanted to take back his words like an inhale, but he knew they were caught in the wind.

"You're rather thoughtful, you know."

It wasn't the response he expected. His fists flexed against the heat that skittered over him. "I'm just making conversation."

"I didn't mean to sound condescending."

"You didn't. Just—forget it."

"Sullen," she muttered. "Oh!"

Tarly jerked in alert at her sudden shout. Scanning her over, he could see nothing wrong save for a confusing brightness. He followed her line of sight and spied a small hut upon a grassy hill overlooking the lake. "What interests you about an old hut?" he grumbled, irked by the unnecessary fright.

"I know the fae who dwells there—I should pay her a visit. She likes her solitude too. You two might make great acquaintances."

Tarly bit back his retort. "Then I'm sure she would appreciate not being disturbed."

"She doesn't hate all company. She simply found that out here she doesn't have to pretend to be someone she isn't."

"You said the town was near." He tried to divert the topic.

"I also said you don't have to follow me."

Instead of heading through the tree line like he hoped, Nerida steered the opposite way. He internally groaned, watching her begin the incline that gradually steepened to reach the small home with smoke puffing through its chimney.

Tarly feared time. Time with her. Every minute added to his reluctance to watch Nerida in all her silver-haired fascination drift away from him for good. All things worth keeping had a habit of slipping through his fingers—not without suffering the damage of his hopeful longing first.

His steps pressed on toward her as darkness began to fall. Tarly's eyes drifted to the overcast sky that promised an angry storm, and perhaps it was a blessing that it might break just as they reached the quaint home they could stay dry within.

A few hours. He could spare a few more hours of keeping Nerida at arm's length, only to see her to the town when the rain passed.

At the crest of the hill Nerida didn't pause for a second, marching straight for the hut. Tarly heard the faint knock, and she waited. More seconds than expected had passed by the time he stood by her.

"Erilla, it's me, Nerida." She tried calling through the wood. With only silence for an answer, she knocked again, louder. "She must be home—the fire is burning."

Tarly took it upon himself to circle around to the window, wiping it with his sleeve to clear the layers of dirt so he could peer inside. The fire *was* burning, but it was also the only living thing he beheld. Eyes darting around the space, what he caught at the edge of the doorway jump-started his pulse.

"What's wrong?" Nerida asked, reading his face when he came back to the front.

He wasn't thinking as he took hold of her shoulders. "You might want to stay here."

Her brow pinched in confusion but quickly lifted, along with her hand to her mouth. Tarly's lips firmed against the shock and panic on her delicate face. He let her go, taking a deep breath before bracing and eying the door. Then his shoulder rammed into it.

Tarly knew his error the moment he felt the impact. He

should've taken it easily, but instead blackness crossed his vision and fell him to one knee. Pain erupted across his chest and down his arm, stunning him still—not with fire, but a pain that pulsed and froze. It began to feel like endless needles piercing his skin.

He should have remembered the bite wound that was often numb with the salve he was running dangerously low on. The thought had even crossed his mind that the town in which he would part with Nerida might offer a place to purchase more. Yet as his dominant right arm, he'd used it out of habit.

"Sully?" Nerida's voice came into clarity repeating the ridiculous name. "Are you all right?"

"I'm fine," he rasped, knowing later she'd believe him to be so weak as to be brought to his knees by a door. "You should wait outside—"

Her smothered cry cut him off. Tarly squeezed his eyes, knowing she would have discovered exactly what he thought he'd seen.

Rising, he dared a look at her first. Her wide-eyed horror while both hands clasped her mouth struck through him more powerfully than he anticipated. He stepped toward her, but Nerida rushed past him, and he spun just in time to see her crashing to her knees beside the fallen fae. His urgency to follow spiked at one crucial thing: she was still breathing. But the wood beneath her was stained dark. The coppery tang stung his nostrils.

Too much blood.

Nerida didn't waste a second, tipping her satchel to scatter its contents, which she quickly rummaged through. Tarly jumped into action, reading her movements and scooping what he could into her peripheral as things rolled away. Her hands were shaking, and her sniff drew his eyes to hers as she tried to blink away her tears. He wasn't thinking when he took her wrists.

"What do you need?" he said calmly.

That forced her eyes to his. "I-it has a green hue. Mistleweed. It'll numb her pain." The steadiness returned to her voice.

Tarly nodded, and she went back to examining the fae while he picked up and examined the tiny bottles.

"We need to get you some kind of pouch to organize these," he said, more as a distraction from their panic, but he didn't slow his search.

"That would be...nice," she answered, and it was a relief to hear her calm voice.

The name lit up like a blazing beacon when he found it. Tarly popped the cork as he spun to her, but then he halted in utter fascination when he beheld the purple glow emitting from her palms. It covered the gruesome sight of the deep wound on the collapsed fae's abdomen. He couldn't fathom Nerida's pain for her friend.

Tarly didn't need her to ask; he leaned over, holding the fae's forehead and slowly pouring the liquid into her mouth. Nerida's hands began to tremble, and he thought it was the return of her anxiety, perhaps even just adrenaline, but then he beheld the sheen on her forehead.

"You're trying to heal too fast. You're using too much," he said.

"She's bleeding out rapidly—if I don't stop it, she'll die in minutes."

"If you don't stop *you* could die."

"I've done this many times, Sully."

"Or *I* very well might die if I have to hear that name again," he grumbled.

She huffed a laugh, a fleeting assurance she was fully present and not falling victim to the magick she pushed.

Tarly continued to watch the shimmering glow of her magick, entranced by it. The longer he stared, the more he felt a pull to it —a compulsion to reach out and know what it would feel like. It formed whispers, and though he couldn't decipher the words, a warmth emanated through him in small caresses, lavender and honey notes touching his tongue. He didn't realize he'd reached out his hand. Vibrations shot up his arm as it hovered over hers.

"What are you doing?"

Her voice snapped him out of his trance, and he pulled back all at once, rising to his feet with the need to seek distance from the pull of her energy. "How much longer?" He diverted the topic.

A long breath stuttered out of her as she removed one hand to wipe her brow. "The bleeding has slowed, but it feels like something important has ruptured. I believe it may have pierced her lung. I can't let go until that's sealed and I clear the internal bleeding."

It sounded like complicated work, but she brushed it off simply to curb the severity of what it would take from her. Tiredness already swept her face. Tarly was about to voice his concern, but in his distraction he didn't detect that they were no longer alone.

His bow was off his back, arrow nocked and released in a breath. The archer in the front doorway choked as he fell to his knees, but Tarly's horror settled when he gleaned the assailant's bow was also empty.

There was no explaining the flash of dread that sank him far from reality in the second that slowed as he turned back to Nerida. She wasn't hovering over the fae's body anymore, having fallen back, but her hands caught her fall. The assailant's arrow was protruding from the neck of the fae she'd tried to save, but Tarly couldn't give way to anything but relief that it wasn't Nerida instead.

"Get up," he barked, retrieving another arrow, when a footstep creaked the floorboard behind them. Nerida remained still in her horror, and he cursed, whirling to soar his second arrow without hesitation—but it was not a lone man this time. He fell one, only to narrowly escape the fatal blow of the other's sword, which slashed across his arm like fire. Tarly hissed, gripping the man's wrist and snapping it with a sickening crack muffled by his cry. The sword clanged to the ground, but instead of killing the man like his rage pulsed for, Tarly gripped his head, slamming it against the wall and knocking him unconscious.

"Nerida," Tarly panted. Whirling, he found she'd scrambled to her feet, but her wide eyes were fixed mournfully on her friend. "I'm sorry," he rasped, clutching his injured arm as he strode for her. His boots shattered small bottles, the only thing that snapped her attention. "But we need to go."

Nerida didn't speak, and he turned cold with her detached

shock as she dropped to her knees as though trying to salvage the remaining tonics. Tarly gripped her arms against it.

"We need to go," he repeated as softly as he could when in his urgency he wanted to haul her out of there, unsure of how many more bandits could be nearby.

She nodded, but it was shallow, vacant. Nerida's gaze was about to fall back to her friend, but Tarly caught her chin.

"You eased her pain. She's not suffering anymore."

Her eyes creased, but before his chest could cleave at that look, his arm around her forced her out of the hut. He was halfway to pulling up her cloak hood for the rain when her hands grazed his.

"I'm fine," she said quietly, but with enough emotion he believed she was returning to herself as she fixed the hood into place. The light fall promised a looming downpour.

"You're hurt," she said.

"It's nothing."

"Let me see—"

"As easy as attracting a moth to a flame."

Both their heads snapped up. Tarly moved subconsciously to shield her from behind, scanning the crowd of men—over a dozen this time, led by the same tall leader who'd ambushed Nerida in the woods. He approached arrogantly with a predator's gleam.

"I didn't appreciate you killing two of my men back there—four now—but I'm willing to let bygones be bygones for a reasonable price." Those wicked eyes flicked over his shoulder.

"If you want her," Tarly said calmly, realizing the odds—but his mind was calculating what weapons he had, analyzing the weakest in order, and preparing for the right moment to strike—"I dare you to try taking her."

"I'm guessing you have no other talents," the leader went on, brushing off Tarly's threat. "Though they are always looking for new bodies to mine the camps. You could fetch a decent price too. But *her*—she's exactly what they're looking for to gain access to Hyla's Cave."

Tarly didn't let the knowledge falter his focus, but he stored every piece of information that spilled from the man's foolish, arrogant mouth.

"What's in Hyla's cave?" Nerida stepped around him, drawing down her hood despite the rain that lashed down heavier now.

Tarly slicked back the lengths of his hair, watching her, watching them, with a laser focus. He couldn't believe her inquisitive side was coming out now.

"You do not know the tales? Surely, as a Waterwielder, your kind know all about the treasures on the opposite side of this lake."

"It's a myth as old and fictitious as the merfolk."

"Someone doesn't seem to think so."

Tarly unsheathed two daggers as the man braved a few steps toward her.

"Someone who has passed on through generations the instructions to locate it."

"Then they will know the merfolk were not fabled to be humanlike or merciful. That they were creatures of nightmares who lured victims to their waters with a glamour, only to drown them, consume their flesh, and steal their riches."

"And so *you* will know one of those very riches is foretold to be Seanna's Song."

Nerida huffed a laugh, but he thought it was laced with wariness. "Only a fool would risk their lives in the hope of finding such a thing."

Of all the books Tarly had absorbed, nothing of what the group spoke of rang with familiarity. He knew of histories and stories, though myths were not his favorite.

The man canted his head. "Which is why he enlists the likes of your kind to go looking for him."

With the next step he took Tarly braced, ready to fight—

A loud wail over a vicious snarl attracted everyone's alarm, and Tarly twisted just in time to watch Katori rip out the throat of her first victim. The men started scattering, but she was upon another.

Tarly didn't waste the mercy of her perfect timing. His first dagger went through the throat of one man, and as the second lunged for him, Tarly twisted around, plunging his second blade into his back. He took no pleasure in the killings—would have avoided them if he saw any other method—but with his adrenaline he was too aware of his new companion to leave room for second-guessing.

With the thought of her, he whirled to find Nerida hadn't moved an inch; had only braced her legs, arms poised as though she held an invisible force and was trembling with it. He followed her line of sight, in awe while he watched the suspended lasso of water surrounding the leader.

"She did nothing," Nerida croaked. *"Why?"*

The pain that came from her echoed through him. He knew she'd get an answer that would only further her guilt for her lost friend.

"Call it a test. To know if you were more than simply a Water-wielder—and you are...so much more." He was as fascinated as if he beheld a jewel before him, not a person.

With a cry, Nerida tightened her lasso, forming a sphere that encased his head from his neck up. The man clawed at his throat while she drowned him slowly. Tarly studied her face, pinched tight while rainwater rolled down her skin. He couldn't distinguish her tears, but her eyes held so much pain it stole his breath. Her braided curly hair was limp, a sad gray with the rain and overcast sky.

"You don't have to do this," Tarly called to her.

It struck something in her, and all at once she let go. She wasn't a killer, but it was as if it rattled her with guilt *not* to be.

The man fell to his knees, gasping for breath.

"You kill me, this won't be the end. I have already sent word about you. Kill me, and your capture will be far worse than what I could offer you."

"We'll take our chances," Tarly said and let go of his arrow, which he'd nocked in his rage at the threat toward her.

Her nature couldn't carry out her revenge, but he could.

They were left only with the growing patter of rainfall against stone and grass. Tarly spared a look around the ghastly sight of fallen bodies, most of them mauled by Katori, whose white fur was stained crimson and weighted with water, turning her into a frightening wild beast.

"Why did you do that?" Nerida's quiet voice cut through the eerie stillness. He found her eyes still fixed on the leader who'd fallen onto the arrow through his chest.

"He didn't deserve to live after what he did. Then what he planned to do. He would have come for you time and time again. A man with such ambition wouldn't stop."

"I didn't ask you to do that," she snapped.

Tarly was taken aback at the harsh look she pinned him with. His own flare of anger flashed across his vision. "Most people would say thank you," he bit back. "So, you're welcome."

Nerida held him with that intense look, and for a second he almost feared she'd surface her magick against him. Instead, she stormed to him, then right past him, knocking into the arm he clutched, enough for him to let out a hiss. He turned to her, expecting to find her marching away, but she'd halted a mere pace behind him, fists trembling at her sides as though she were battling mind with body.

She whirled around so suddenly Tarly's only instinct was to believe she would strike, and he winced. "Let me see your wound," she demanded, but her expression eased carefully at whatever she read on his. "Did you think I would attack you?"

Tarly swallowed any response, his guard rising, defense firming. He turned for the cottage. "Stay here."

Inside, he numbed himself to the lost life he stepped around. He found a broom and thrust it into the fire until it caught. He made his way around, letting the flame loose so it would catch and lick all perishable things. It blazed and grew, and when he was satisfied it had been freed enough to devour the entire house even against the storm, Tarly left. He didn't look at the healer as he passed her.

"Let's just get to that damn town."

CHAPTER 37

Faythe

FAYTHE MADE IT to her rooms unescorted, needing the time alone to gather her reeling thoughts after parting with Kyleer from their trip to the cells. Her first step inside hit her all at once. She halted just past the threshold with a burst of emotion she hadn't anticipated at seeing the bed in which she'd shared many treasured nights with Reylan, as a human. The walls she'd claimed as a human. The room in which she'd slowly come to feel like she belonged as a human. With vacant steps she surveyed the room as though it were new all over again.

A wonderful scent drifted to her, and a presence registered in her senses as she whirled to the dining area in fright. At the fleeting glimpses she got before the person detected her quiet entrance, Faythe's vision blurred. She stood in the doorway and watched her assembling the table.

Gresla startled upon seeing Faythe, and she couldn't help her smile. "I suppose I'll have to get used to your new light footing," she commented.

Emotion choked Faythe's response at hearing the first notes of her voice.

Gresla looked over the assortment she'd laid out. "Stew and bread, just as I promised."

Faythe let go of a sob then, and Gresla's old face pinched knowingly as she rushed over to embrace her.

"I can't begin to imagine all you've been through, Lady Faythe. But remember you are here, you have returned, just as I knew you would no matter what changed."

It was all she needed to hear. Faythe was almost able to let go of the fears that kept her from embracing what she was now with complete acceptance.

"I'll leave you to eat and rest, dear." Gresla smiled up at her. "Welcome home."

So few words spoken with such great impact. When Gresla left, Faythe was one burden lighter. Her stomach twisted at the scent of food in her hunger, and she eyed the second place that had been laid at the table just as awareness stroked her spine.

"How are you feeling?" Reylan asked quietly.

She twisted to him, but he made no move to come closer, and the distance felt wrong. "It's been a long day," she said, unable to hide her drop of disappointment as she sat before her meal.

Only then did he come to take the place opposite her. Faythe could hardly look at him.

"It's best if my scent doesn't linger on you more than what people might expect from me being your guard."

"My *guard?*" Faythe was incredulous.

He winced at her reaction. "It's the only way I have reason to be close to you often."

Her hand tightened around her fork. "Who knows you're my mate?"

"Only your father. And those you're already aware of."

"So it means nothing to the council," she ground out.

"We don't know yet. But it's best kept secret for now."

"I hope it doesn't, because it means nothing to me. Not if this is the price to pay." Faythe rose from the table with her declaration. "I can't use it as an excuse for my feelings for you, nor will it make it easier for others to understand what you mean to me and that you deserve to rule this kingdom."

"It's not as easy as that."

"Nothing in my life has ever been *easy.*" Her voice broke.

Reylan rose, face pinching with conflict.

"Except loving you, which comes as easy as breathing. I have this one sure, *easy* thing, and they can build as many obstacles around it as they want, but I'll knock each one down one by one."

He came around the table, wordlessly taking her face in his hands, and her body relaxed in relief. "Together," he said. "We'll knock them down together."

Faythe gave a soft whimper when he sealed that vow with a kiss.

"Now eat, please. Your bath will be getting cold."

Faythe stood in a short silk robe, breathing in the delicious scent of orange and something like spice and florals. The water wasn't visible through the biggest mound of bubbles she'd ever seen. She twisted her head but quickly snapped it back on habit before she caught a glimpse of her reflection.

"Have you looked at yourself at all?"

Reylan's interruption shivered over her skin. Faythe dipped her hand to scoop up some bubbles as a distraction.

"No," she said honestly, blowing them from the tips of her fingers.

Reylan leaned in closer. Reaching his hands up, he grazed her skin with his fingertips, hooking them into her robe. Faythe answered by untying it and letting him peel the thin material away with deliberate slowness.

"What are you afraid of?"

His voice was thick, and while she couldn't see him, the impression of his eyes over her naked body made her lids flutter. Then his lips pressed lightly to her shoulder.

"I thought you said you shouldn't touch," Faythe breathed,

raising her hand behind her with a need to tangle it in his hair, but he stepped back before she could.

"I won't push it, hence the bath."

Faythe eyed the inviting tub with a new reluctance. It flared something ugly to think its purpose was to erase his scent as much as possible. "This isn't right."

"Trust me," he groaned, once again hovering the words over the skin of her back. "I want nothing more than take you right now, so much it's driving me insane, and I should not be standing here—not with every inch of you on display. It's taking everything in me not to imprint my scent all over you, and inside of you, until the whole damn world can make no mistake in knowing you are mine."

Her core tightened with an impulsive lust.

"But the world can be cruel, and I need you to help me help you. At least until we know how this might be received. I can't be responsible for jeopardizing the future of this kingdom, *your* future, because of my selfishness. One obstacle at a time."

Faythe's gut twisted with the plea in his tone. She let go of all her protests, knowing she was only making it harder on them both. She sighed instead, dipping into the water and easing back with the heat that coated her skin and relaxed her muscles. This was her first hot bath in what felt like forever.

"I didn't take you for one to enjoy a bubble bath," she commented. She hadn't bathed with such luxurious soaps before.

"I'm not the one in the bath."

Faythe inhaled sharply when cool hands settled on her shoulders. She bit back her moan of pleasure as Reylan began a slow massage, lathering a honey-scented liquid over her.

"Though I'd very much like to be. And I would endure the bubbles for you."

Faythe giggled at the image, knowing one day she'd force him to join her in the most ridiculously extravagant bubble bath she could create. Then, through their pause of peaceful silence, something nagged on her mind.

"Have you ever wondered…why us?"

Reylan's breath was long and affirming. "I have." His hands didn't stop tracing her shoulders, sensuously smooth on her wet skin, adding just the right pressure to her tight muscles. Her tension eased and her eyes fluttered as she listened to his voice. "I believe we come into this world when we're needed. For others, to do things we probably don't even realize make such an impact."

"Do you believe…?" Her mind stumbled over the ridiculous thought, but Reylan gave her shoulders a reassuring squeeze. "Do you believe we could live more than one lifetime? Do you think you'd remember?"

"I don't know," he answered honestly. "But if so and I didn't remember, I would still find you."

Her eyes pricked with tears, and she closed them to stop her emotion from spilling.

"I've witnessed platonic mates. I've seen hostility between them. Some pairings never meet at all. Magick is its own force; the heart can have other plans. Falling in love…" His hand curled around her throat, then up her jaw, and he twisted her face to look at him "That was our choice. Do you believe that?"

"Yes."

He smiled softly, letting her go to resume his work easing her arms, her chest. "I'll never forgive what happened to you. I'll never rest until I find all those who wronged you. I would have loved you until the end as a human. Maybe this makes me selfish, but Faythe, you being fae…is it wrong of me to find joy and relief in that?"

Faythe wanted to give him the answer he hoped for, but it came with a story, a confession, she finally had to set free. She watched the water ripple around her fingers as she traced the surface. "For the longest part of my life I was taught the fae were ruthless and cruel. I suppose in High Farrow, under Orlon's twisted reign, it was somewhat true. Yet my mother never once tried to say otherwise. She loved my father. I can't stop thinking about how the whole time she was alive but far from him, she loved him still. She knew how kind and compassionate the fae could be, just like the humans. We're not so different."

Faythe paused. Her stomach dropped as she realized she didn't know which side she was on now: human or fae… She drifted with hopelessness for a second, feeling tied to neither. "I've tried to ignore it, but I resent her for it. She kept me in the dark about many things I forgive her for, but I can't find a reason for her sheltering me from the world beyond Farrowhold. There's so much to discover, so many walks of life, and maybe if she'd helped me to prepare for it sooner it wouldn't overwhelm me as it does now. Despite all I've seen, there's still a part of my child self that feels I should be horrified at what I've become. Fae. There was a time when I would have wished for death before I became like the cold, heartless beings I thought you all to be."

Faythe counted his breaths.

"And now?"

She twisted in the bath to look at him. His brow furrowed, disturbed by her thoughts and longing to hear a counter side. The air caught on her wet skin, and the bubbles that clung to her and concealed her naked upper half began to dissipate slowly. She shuddered.

"Now I'm so gods-damned relieved, Reylan." She let go of the confession she'd harbored deep since she Transitioned out of fear it was a betrayal to everything she'd been before. Reylan's face smoothed out; his stiff shoulders loosened. "Before, something always felt just out of reach, yet I couldn't figure out what it was. I think a part of me has always known, but *hope* and *impossibility* clashed only to leave me forever reaching for something that can never exist. I didn't think I'd ever be whole." She shook her head, weightless in the embrace of her new reality. "I died…yet I've never felt more alive."

Reylan slipped off the stool and onto his knees, bringing their faces level as he shifted around to the side of the bath. His hand reached for her face, his eyes soul-searching. "You are exquisite, my Phoenix." His lips pressed to hers, and Faythe's mouth opened to deepen the kiss. She savored it as each one they shared was now forbidden and secret.

Reylan's hand dipped into the water and trailed along her thigh. Faythe fisted his hair, begging for more now the bath's heat came second to her hot need for him. He teased her deliberately, never reaching her core as he explored the length of her leg.

"You're making this impossible," he groaned against her lips.

Faythe undid the top tie of his shirt. "You started it."

His low chuckle vibrated along her jaw as he said huskily, "Hardly."

"Get in the bath, Reylan."

"Is that an order, princess?"

Faythe bit her lip, but the hook of her teeth released with a small gasp when he held the side of her face with rough passion.

"You're becoming rather demanding," he said thickly.

"Is that so?"

"It drives me wild for you—more than I thought possible."

Faythe couldn't take the searing gaze that touched her in a blaze like his words. She pulled his face to hers and their kiss turned drunk with fervor. On her knees, the water lapped low on her waist, and Reylan's hand reached beneath the surface.

She moaned as his fingers worked between her legs and their kiss deepened, tongues clashing with a demand that rocked her hips.

She needed more.

So much more.

"I can't join you this time," he rasped, hooking two fingers into her, and Faythe cried out, her head tipping back. "But I can give you this. Gods, if I had any decency, any sense of duty, I wouldn't. But with you right here at my mercy, I really don't give a fuck about anything except the pleasure you ask for."

His mouth closed over her peaked breast, and Faythe chased the release building in her lower stomach. She clutched him tightly, nails scraping down his back, which only seemed to drive his pace harder. Reylan's other hand glided over her wet body, worshipping every inch as if it were the last time, and she wouldn't have that, no matter what it took.

Faythe was teetering on the edge and Reylan felt her, letting go of her breast to peer up at her.

"Eyes on me, Phoenix."

Locked onto those icy sapphires Faythe came apart. Her brow furrowed tightly as her thighs slipped farther open, her body trembling helplessly with waves of all-consuming bliss. He devoured her every reaction, slowly reeling in his feverish pace. When he removed himself from her, Faythe slumped down in the water.

Reylan leaned in to kiss her once. "This is going to be a torturous few weeks."

CHAPTER 38

Faythe

IT HAD BEEN so long since Faythe last stood in the familiar comforts of her white-and-gold mist. She'd been here for some time since drifting off alone with an ache carrying through her that Reylan wasn't here beside her.

Faythe hadn't told him she'd been stifling her ability out of fear of touching her magick. She didn't know what harm it might do if she lost control and Nightwalked unintentionally. Now, with her slow discoveries, Faythe was braving the one thing she'd been yearning to do for so long. There was one last set of people who had yet to be faced with her new twist of fate.

Clutching Nik's star pendant around her neck, she paced with nerves. Last time, it took merging with Reylan, but now she was stronger and more confident she'd make the leap. That wasn't what caused her hesitation though. She was fearful of what her magick could do to Nik if it began to consume her.

Fear was a permanent shadow, and with a stomp of defiance and irritation Faythe stopped her pacing and began to focus. She felt herself project though time and space, her body utterly weightless as she traveled to her destination. When she was finally standing outside the barrier of Nik's mind it didn't feel so indestructible, though it was solid. Faythe waited, fighting the dark chant to take her own entry with her magick.

The resistance lifted and Faythe stopped moving, slowly peeling open her eyes. She could have dropped to her knees at the familiar whorls of black-and-gray smoke; the distant memory it sparked to be back here.

From the shadows a figure emerged, and as the first flicker of emerald broke the darkness her eyes blurred the image of him. She couldn't move or speak; could only stand trembling, stifling her sobs, at the sight.

Nik stalked toward her slowly, deliberately, hands in his pockets and wearing a soft smile that held pain. He was beautiful and elegant and somehow far more befitting of his title as king, yet not a part of him appeared different.

He halted when they were near shoulder to shoulder, and her first tear fell. A hand reached up, tracing delicately over the tip of her pointed ear. *"Not* human," he mused in a whisper.

Faythe released a sharp sob then, and their arms opened for each other when she twisted to him.

"I knew you had to be alive. You're far too stubborn," he mumbled into her hair.

Faythe was crying. Laughing while she cried. Clinging to him like a lifeline, but too soon he peeled away to look over her face, brushing her wet cheek.

"And brave and strong and so gods-damned remarkable."

"Nik," she whimpered, her forehead falling to his chest. The one who was first to know her differences and had never judged her, only guided. "I don't know what I am."

He squeezed her upper arms. "Just Faythe and the fae guard in the woods, remember?"

Her brow crumpled. "I wish you were really here."

There would always be something different about him. A tether of absolute understanding bound them both.

"Right now, we just have to make do with how we can see each other," he consoled her.

Faythe nodded, and when her tears blinked back, she took a moment to scan every piece of him. A smile of pride and joy bloomed on her cheeks, widening to a grin.

"You and Tauria…Jakon told me everything."

Nik breathed, slumping in relief. "They made it to you. I can't tell you how much of a gift it is to hear that. Jakon and Marlowe, we owe them a lot for their help with the conflicts in High Farrow, then for their aid in freeing Tauria in Olmstone."

"Are you both safe now?"

"There's still the threat of Zarrius, but we're being vigilant. Don't worry about us—you have much to figure out for yourself." His hands took hers, and he examined the symbols within them then glanced again at her ears. "Is it wrong of me to say I think you look radiant, Faythe? That looking at you now…I have to wonder how you were born human when fae suits you so."

"I'm still figuring it out," she muttered.

"You might prove an equal match in combat now."

Faythe chuckled. "What I wouldn't give to have just one rematch in those woods."

"We will."

Their eyes met, and a promise fused between them.

The magick within Faythe had been humming, beginning to grow, but Faythe was desperate to hold onto as many precious minutes as she could.

"Don't worry about us here. We're figuring out how the dark fae may have infiltrated our defenses, but you need to be preparing on your end. The only way we can fight them is together."

"We are," Faythe confirmed. "We have a captive and we're learning what we can, but it's slow-going. I fear they could strike any moment."

"What's the plan now?"

Faythe had been thinking that over. "We lost the Dark Temple Ruin. Dakodas has it now, and we need to find out a way to retrieve it."

Nik must have felt the panic her words roused from the way he gave an assuring caress to ground her. "Do you know where?"

She shook her head. "I hope we can find out from our captive. Then there's still Marvellas's to retrieve. We need them all."

His palm cupped her nape, his expression firming with determination. "You're not doing this alone. Not for a second longer now this is our war too. We trapped Marvellas and Mordecai in Olmstone's castle, but I'm not certain how long they've been free. Leave Dakodas's ruin to us."

"No. You don't know what she's capable of, nor where it could be."

"You have to trust us. We might have a good lead on where to start looking."

Faythe wanted to protest, could hardly stand to look at him as her head bowed in his hold with the thought of them risking themselves.

"You've given your all to this, Faythe. More than any of us could, and I know you'll continue to. It *kills* me, despite how triumphant and brilliant you are, what you had to give up and what you had to go through for it. But you can't be the only one to sacrifice yourself time and time again. Let us help."

Faythe had no choice. This was not her war; it was all of theirs. She told him everything she could, not leaving out a single detail about what had unfolded. It rushed out of her, and her pulse became rapid, her head throbbed faintly, and she was all too aware of her magick continuing to rise.

"The dark fae who tracked you…can you show me?"

The only way to show him would be to unfold the scene around them. To relive what had kept her from sleep many nights and transported her right back to that moment at the most unexpected of triggers.

He must have seen the blanching of her skin. "You don't have to—"

"I will," Faythe rushed out before she could succumb to her panic. She had to. Maverick and Zaiana were two of their leaders —enemies she couldn't withhold from Nik should they make an attack on High Farrow too.

Faythe stepped away from him and began to tunnel for the

memory. She walked but kept her eyes closed. The damp heat of the ash-clogged air and rain came first. Then the scent of smoke, which circled in her lungs. Bright—it was so blazing bright, and before her the great Firebird heaved its powerful wings.

"Gods above…" Nik's whisper was faint against the roar of Phoenixfyre.

Faythe still didn't open her eyes though she knew she'd be standing there all over again. Without looking, she cast out her hand, remembering exactly where everyone had taken refuge. "That's Zaiana. We have her in our cells."

Nik didn't speak. He didn't have to.

Faythe pointed again across the mountain edge. "That's Maverick."

Something struck her so powerfully it forced her eyes to snap open. Not her own stab of shock, but Nik's. Yet the image around her halted her before she could turn to him. She wasn't prepared though she knew Atherius would be standing before her.

Time slowed in her vision. Faythe's heart pounded in her ears to a mighty drum, but the blazing red fire flickered with tranquility. The rise of its wings and the flick of its flaming mane happened so slowly she almost fell to her knees in awe. Yet she knew what the Firebird was bracing for. She felt a breeze lick up the sweat that trickled down her nape, over her forehead, and knew she was seconds from being devoured by Phoenixfyre.

On instinct she glanced at her wrist.

"Faythe, remember, it's not real."

She heard Nik's words, but they didn't echo with the same clarity as the cry that pierced the night from Atherius. She was confusing memory with reality.

Her wrist was bare where she expected to find the amulet that would give her a fighting chance. A panic so gripping took hold of her every muscle, stopping her still, until a form appeared in front of her as if to shield her from the fire—though it would only kill them both. Her eyes flicked up to warn them, but those emerald irises connected with hers like lightning, drawing out a gasp that tightened her lungs.

Nik couldn't be here. He was never here.

Hands took her face. "Listen to me, Faythe. This is *your* mind. You have control." His voice was strained, and the fragmented truth of the present began to form back together.

The ground beneath them vibrated. The mountains broke off and boulders crashed as the fire blazed higher. Faythe searched frantically for the others, but they were gone.

Atherius was gone.

"You're hurting me, Faythe," Nik said, his voice far clearer, and his pain pounded in her mind.

"I can't stop it," she breathed in horror. Her palms glowed so brightly with the magick that had erupted from her. She tried to hold Nik's gaze, but the edges of her vision glittered in gold too, close to consuming her.

"Yes, you can."

She could kill him. Kill them both. It had been a mistake to believe she held enough control to Nightwalk to him, to use the technique she already knew, because the essence that lived within her now was not content to be separated or lie dormant. It laughed at her lack of ability to wield it.

"I need you to know something before you pull back. If he comes for you again, you need to know." Nik's teeth clenched, and her forehead creased as he fought the magick within her that would take him down too. He leaned his forehead to hers, echoing a few words in her mind that stopped the world. They echoed over and over in her disbelief that he might have rejected the knowledge. But his tone was urgent.

Then a flare of gold erupted around them, and Nik was stolen from her completely.

Faythe's eyes snapped open, but all she was met with was gold. Shimmering, brilliant gold that felt trapped in her lungs as she drew breath as if air didn't exist. Her eyes scanned frantically from side to side as objects started to take form—though still gilded, glittering with that rippling amber power.

"*Faythe.*"

Relief whooshed from her all at once at the echo in her mind. She reached up a hand up to confirm he was real.

Reylan was straddling her lightly, pushing the sweat-slicked hair from her face. He breathed a long sigh before his lips pressed to her forehead. "You scared the damn Nether out of me."

Exhaustion caught up to her all at once as she glanced over the swirls of white and gold around them, the colors drifting through the air as if she'd expelled a translucent form of her subconscious into their realm. "Do you see it?" she whispered.

Reylan eased off her, shuffling back on his knees as Faythe propped herself up. "Yes."

"What is it?"

He studied her with confusion pinching his brow. "Your raw power. At least I think so. I couldn't… Gods above, Faythe, I almost couldn't get through to you. I couldn't take it or stop you."

Faythe couldn't stand his turmoil. "You still felt me." Rising to her knees, she carefully shuffled over in case he would retreat with the caution that had kept him from sleeping next to her. "You still came."

When his arms encircled her waist, she breathed in relief. His head rested on her chest, and they held each other.

"If you destroy yourself then take me too. If you destroy the world, I'll be right there beside you."

Her fingers curled into his silver locks. "Does that make us villains?"

Reylan pulled back, looking up at her with sparkling sapphires of determination. "Yes," he said, studying how she'd react, but Faythe felt…liberated. "We're the villains in someone's plan, someone else's ideals, their wants and desires. Here's a promise to you, Faythe Ashfyre: I'm damn well honored to be a villain *with* you. And for you. To whoever stands in the way of you fulfilling your dream of a better world."

Faythe angled her head to kiss him fiercely. "Stay with me tonight," she said against his lips.

Reylan answered by hooking an arm around her. She felt weightless as he drew her back to lie down. He hovered over her, and Faythe's hands couldn't fight the impulse to run up his bare torso, eliciting a groan from him as he kissed her jaw, her neck. She curved into him as if her body were molding to his every touch. His rough fingers trailed up her thigh, fully exposed as they lifted her short silk nightgown. Just as he reached the hem he halted, planting a firm kiss to her chest.

"Best not to push it," he rasped, fighting restraint.

Her protest was strong, but her will to protect him was stronger. "Best not," she agreed, though she was just as needy.

Reylan lay on his side, tucking up behind her and pulling her in close as she faced away. All that mattered was that he was here. Faythe watched the last fleeting notes of her power wink out slowly like dying embers. Then, in the silence, only Nik's last words replayed again and again, knowledge that changed everything and nothing.

She didn't know what she would do with it.

CHAPTER 39

Nikalias

"N*ik!*"

The urgency of his name sounding out through his mind snapped him awake. His hands gripped the form that straddled him, gaze flicking up to find Tauria's horrified expression drop with relief all at once. Her weight slumped though her hands remained braced on his bare chest.

"Thank the Gods," she panted.

Nik blinked while his consciousness splintered back. He started to remember the clutches of Faythe's power within his mind that had rendered him helpless. He'd been trapped and held in his own subconsciousness. It was like nothing he'd come close to experiencing before.

"What happened?" he asked, wondering what she would have felt from it.

"You tell me." Tauria leaned back so Nik could prop himself against the headboard. His hands hooked around her thighs when she tried to back away. Despite his sweat-slicked skin, he needed her close. The feel of her skin as he ran his hands up and down her legs grounded him while he reeled back from the ordeal.

"I saw Faythe," he explained.

Tauria's fingers wove through his hair. "I want to be thrilled, but I'm wondering what could have happened that meant I couldn't reach you. Your pulse was too fast, your skin was hot… I feared the worst, that another Nightwalker had gotten to you, and that's the one place I can't help, and I—"

Nik cut her off with a tender kiss. "I'm sorry it frightened you, but did you really doubt me against another Nightwalker?"

Tauria's smile stretched to a teasing grin. "Not until now."

He gave a soft chuckle. Then a frown formed with all he had to explain to his mate about their friend. What Faythe had become. It should have shocked him, stunned him, but all he saw was…clarity, as if Faythe had removed a cloak of pretense and now stood in her true, perfect form.

"Faythe is not just another Nightwalker," he began.

Tauria only nodded in agreement.

"She's not…human anymore either." He watched her carefully.

The flex of her eyes was calculating. "Not human?"

"And somehow, I think…not just fae. She tried to explain what she could, but I don't think she realized it didn't all make sense in her rush. But the Firebirds, they're real. I guess we knew that from the Phoenix Blood potions, but Faythe showed me the one they faced. They still live." Nik listened to the drum of Tauria's heart, tucking her loose hair behind her ear while she took in his words and tried to grasp them as true.

"She's fae?" She shook her head vacantly, and then her frown eased. She smiled, grinned, and Nik's own mouth tipped up with hers until they shared a laugh—one of absolute incredulity over the impossible that finally felt *right*.

"She is something," Tauria mused with a hint of sadness. "I wish I could see her. She needs her friends now more than ever."

"Jakon and Marlowe made it to her."

Tauria's face lit up with joy and her small gasp turned to a partial cry as her eyes closed. Nik understood the feeling of that weight being lifted. Wondering if the humans were safe in

Rhyenelle had been a constant itch in the back of his mind, and Tauria cared just as deeply.

"There's something else," he said. He had to take a pause before telling her about the unfathomable task, but he knew Tauria would do it, and what they would need to give seemed far less than Faythe's sacrifice. "I love you, Tauria. I have always and will always love you no matter what."

Tauria seemed to know where his thoughts had drifted. She nodded softly. "Always," she whispered, kissing him firmly. "That never changes. No matter what. I love you, Nikalias." She squealed as Nik flipped them, leaning over her.

With the scare and every darkness they'd decided to face, Nik would treasure every second they still had. He kissed her mouth, her jaw, her chest. His teeth grazed over her skin and pinched her peaked breast through the thin silk nightgown. Tauria arched beautifully into his every touch. He continued lower, enjoying her soft breaths, sliding the silk high to expose her. Tauria was needy in her desire, waiting for him to go further.

"What do you want, love?"

He knew it would earn him a moan of frustration, and he smiled, slipping a hand through her slickness, fingers curving inside of her. He watched the perfect angle of her body bowing on the sheets, clutching them tightly.

Nik would go slow. Torturously slowly was what he felt like tonight, so he could stretch out the hours since his mind was so far from being able to rest.

Not that he needed any excuse to worship every inch of Tauria, time and time again.

CHAPTER 40

Zaiana

THE ICE THAT doused her was real, and a damn rude awakening.

Zaiana gasped, jerking back completely disoriented, wincing when she hit solid stone. The freezing water drenched her heavy and left her panting. The shock that struck her chest was almost enough to jump-start her dead heart.

"Since you're adamant in your defiance," Kyleer's insufferable voice sang, "I thought I'd bring the bath to you."

Zaiana glared but blinked with bewilderment as she processed his words. How he had managed to make it all the way up to her cell without waking her up puzzled her. Glancing down at the now soaked cloak weighing her down, she realized just how deeply she must have fallen asleep wrapped up in it.

She shuddered violently, teeth clamping together to keep from chattering. "You're tempting death, Commander."

His chuckle was smooth, lighter than usual, but she still itched with a desire to claw it from his throat. "I think we're past that."

On her knees, the cold air reacted to her wet clothes. Her fists balled, and she tensed not to give away how frigid she was, thinking of a distraction instead. "I completed a method of training once," she rasped, keeping her eyes on the ground. "I was made to walk across a mile-long mountain ledge in the dead of winter. Repeatedly. Each time, they would take something from me—my cloak, then my shoes, then my top layers—until on my final walk I didn't know if I would survive. I could hardly move from the freezing grip of the cold. The ground wasn't quite layered with snow—it was frost and ice, tearing the skin off my feet as I walked, but if I didn't make it to the end, I would have been left out there for the night. The walk was brutal, but no one would have survived a full night out there."

Kyleer processed her tale before he asked, "What was the lesson in that?"

She huffed a laugh. "They praised it as endurance, but I think it was a lot of their own twisted boredom. It's instinct to look at someone and see a breakable thing. It's down to us to take the glass we were born of and turn it into steel." Zaiana flexed her fingers to keep from turning numb. She barely raised her head but slid her eyes to the door when she heard the keys. "Can't you just Shadowport?"

"It's as if you can read my mind." Kyleer was in front of her before she could blink. His shadows surrounded her, caressing her in a way that parted her lips and drew out a gasp. An alluring darkness wrapped around her—*his* darkness, but not the evil kind she was akin to; this one was of awe and starlight. Her gaze snapped to his, and for a few seconds it was just the two of them in a beautiful void of shimmering shadow. A dark galaxy where the stars whorled around them so mesmerizingly she wanted to suspend time and stay there for any precious seconds longer than what she was granted. This place he traveled through…it was time and space and infinity, untouchable by their cruel world. A place she wanted to venture through without ever letting go of the large hands she gripped so tightly in her shock.

Then everything stilled. Too soon.

Kyleer's shadows dispersed though her mind, and she tried to cling to their beauty with unblinking eyes. Then, when the grim walls of a tragically familiar realm returned, her gaze dropped to his. She fixed him with wonder as the owner of such a gift she hadn't known to appreciate in the slightest until now.

Her crash back to reality was a familiar cold drop.

Zaiana's chains rattled as she pulled her hands from his. She scanned their new surroundings. This place didn't look much better than her cell with its bare stone walls, but when she eyed the bathtub, she instantly shot him a glare.

"I said no."

"You'll freeze."

"Did you not hear a word of what I told you? You'll have to try a different method."

"This is not a punishment."

"It should be," she snarled. "Does Reylan know how *gentle* you've been with Rhyenelle's most prized captive? I know things that could be of great use to you, things that could perhaps tip the scales of the war after your epic failure in letting Dakodas ascend. Yet all this time you've been toying with me, offering me a *bath*, rescuing me from your own soldiers who've clearly had enough of your weakness and just want to do what needs to be done."

"You want me to hurt you?"

Yes. She did. Because that was better than the repulsive awakening of something far worse. Feelings she'd buried long ago because they only served to get one killed.

"I expected better of you," she spat.

"Then I guess we're both disappointed."

She didn't know what he meant by that. Her muscles were so painful in their tenseness, but the worse of it would pass soon. Gods, she was so damn cold.

"What do you want from me, Kyleer?"

He didn't respond at first even though words seemed to fight to break through in the flex of his jaw. He stood, pulling a short dagger free to fidget with as he leaned against the back wall. "I'll take you back when the water is cold," he said blankly.

Zaiana heaved a long sigh. She had endured many trials and tortures in her life, yet never before had one person exhausted her so much with such little effort. In her shivering state, all she could think about were the minutes draining the heat from the water just a few feet away. For a second, imagining those waters called forth a face in her mind, and she snapped her eyes open against the flashes of memory. It wasn't often she bathed in the luxury of hot water—that had always been a product of Maverick's Firewielding—and though she would claim to despise it since it came hand-in-hand with suffering his company, she would never admit the sense of comfort it provided.

She wondered what he would be doing right now. With a miserable twinge she realized she might even be pining for his company, if only for the familiarity. Until she remembered their parting stare and how dejected she'd felt when he first left.

Those thoughts were banished quickly when a beautiful dark fae Spirit flashed to mind.

Zaiana rose to her feet, her clanking chains the only sound that resonated through the room. She paused, grinding her teeth with the dregs of her defiance, but ultimately…she gave in. "I can't undress with these on," she muttered.

Kyleer slid his eyes to her, trailing her from head to toe, and she hated that her body shivered in reaction to it. He pushed off the wall, and her regret grew thick as she watched him stalk toward her. Zaiana had avoided the bath specifically so he wouldn't see how punishment had marked her skin, but it didn't matter now. Nor would it when he saw it again—every time she'd been helpless enough to allow those scars.

"I can't take them off," he said, and she might have believed the note of disturbance in his tone as he glanced at her raw wrists.

"Then I guess you'll have to help me."

There was a shift in his scent. *Her* scent. She tried to ignore both, but she couldn't take her eyes from his.

Kyleer stepped up to her, their bodies near grazing, and carefully slipped the heavy, wet cloak from her shoulders. It fell with a slop to the ground. A jolt like lightning shot through her, making her squeeze her eyes shut and bow her head against the air that breezed over her exposed back from the torn clothing. Kyleer's hands gripped her upper arms as though she would collapse. After a shuddering exhale, and when the tight coiling in her abdomen had loosened, she forced her attention back to him.

His rough fingers trailed over her shoulders, and her brow flinched. He halted. "I will stop when you say," he said with a quietness she'd never heard from him. "I promise you that."

"It's fine."

"Zai."

She assessed that faint plea in the way he said her name and wondered what it meant. *"I'm* fine," she amended.

He gave a barely-there nod then began to peel away the cold material that clung to her. Slowly, never breaking eye contact. It was dangerous how easily she escaped in those green irises.

Zaiana stood bare-chested. She wasn't shy of her nakedness, only protective of what she'd endured in the skin that saw her still alive today. She didn't flinch when he tore the sleeves off one at a time until she was free of the shredded sweater.

"Aren't you going to look?" she tempted.

His features eased a little to give way to a partial smirk. "You don't have anything I haven't seen before."

Zaiana let go of a near smile, glad for the lifted tension since she could hardly stand it. But when his face fell with a thoughtful frown, so did the upturn of her mouth.

He stepped back. "I'm sure you can handle the rest." Kyleer turned around, and with his back to her, relief weighed her truly.

She hastily peeled off her boots and pants, heading to the water to find it a milky white that would conceal her body once she was inside. As she dipped her toes in, the stark contrast of heat against her frozen skin shot sparks of pain through every nerve. Despite wanting to throw herself in all at once, she took it slow. Inch by inch she submerged herself, biting her lip, until her eyes fluttered closed with the most consuming pleasure she'd felt in so long.

Zaiana lay with her head propped over the edge and forgot Kyleer's presence altogether while she took that moment for herself without apology. "You got what you wanted," she drawled over to him. "Now will you tell me about your fascination with the bath?"

"Not the bath. Your scent."

"You could have just insulted me until I caved."

"Allow me to amend—" He moved, but she didn't twist her head. Kyleer held something out to her. Soap. "Not your scent. *His.*"

Zaiana stilled with the loathing he poured into that single word, knowing exactly who he meant.

"You're lucky it's faint. I had to interrupt Reylan's visit to you, or he would have killed you without thinking straight if he detected Maverick on you. Or perhaps he would have used you far more ruthlessly to force him here, because what lingers on you is something closer, more intimate."

"You're wrong."

Kyleer dropped to a crouch, bringing them eye-level. "I could hardly stand it myself. Being near you fueled my own need to kill you. It was as if he were right there."

Her chains lifted out of the water as Zaiana reached for the white soap bar, but it slipped from his hand just before she could take it.

Deliberately.

She should have predicted the game when she noticed his sleeves were rolled up to his elbows, showing off beautiful black markings that caught her intrigue. But not enough to drag out a conversation. Kyleer beat her to the soap as his hand dipped into the water, and she inhaled sharply at the first graze of his knuckles against her thigh.

"Who hurt you, Zai? You talk of the masters…"

Was this the start of his attempt to draw out information? Seduction rather than torture. "Many people hurt me," she got out while tracking the tingling graze of his fingers near her leg. "So many it would make your nightmares seem trivial. But it's just flesh. It means nothing."

"It means—"

Zaiana nearly tipped her head back when his hand met her

calf. It was a bold move, daring, yet she couldn't stop him. Didn't *want* to stop him. The odd sensation of the round soap bar coupled with the light graze of his fingertips deepened her breaths.

"It did not break you." He watched her intently for every reaction to his touch.

She wanted to have the strength to shake his confidence. Refuse his closeness. React far more menacingly than submitting to the desire that flushed her skin beyond the bath's heat. The smooth glide of his hand holding the soap grew an ache between her legs. He continued up, curving over her bent knee, inching a fraction along her inner thigh. Reason scattered, protest dissolved, and her lips parted while they held each other's eyes with an attention she'd never felt before. Soul-searching. As though his fingers were merely a distraction while he surged deep into the essence of who she was; *what* she was. She wondered if he had answers to the questions she wanted to know about herself since the world had left her lost and wandering.

His hand left her abruptly, and Spirits be *damned* did it make disappointment drop through her. Kyleer held up the soap again, but his hand twisted to show his knuckles instead. For the first time her attention caught on the long, raised scar across his hand and two crooked fingers. Whatever torture he'd endured—his hand had been crushed was her guess—she knew it must have been strung-out and repeated over and over to have left such permanent damage on a fae.

"Who hurt *you?*" she asked, surprised by her own darkness rising. Imagining him in pain, *agony*, inspired something grim and unforgiving. But Zaiana couldn't care about him. When she got her chance to escape, the monster that lived within her would kill Kyleer if that was what it took.

"Someone who never got the satisfaction of breaking me either."

Zaiana didn't know how she'd allowed this to happen. Here she stood on common ground with the commander. It was a trap —it had to be. They had to have known physical torture would be wasted energy on such a soulless being who'd endured it all before.

"Would you sit forward for me?" he asked with a gentleness she didn't know how to react to. It wasn't seductive or taunting or anything of ridicule.

Her hands gripped the edge of the bath before she could listen to the protests in her mind out of a curiosity to know what his tender expression would do if she gave herself to it. Kyleer moved to sit on something behind him, and Zaiana curled her knees to her chest, fighting against the urge to lash out, fearing her anger would chase him away.

"Can I touch you?"

"You didn't ask just seconds ago."

"Can I touch your scars, Zai?"

Her shoulder blades locked and her breaths came hard. She had such a strong urge to say no, but it battled with a strange desire to say…

"Yes." It was barely a whisper, as if she hoped he wouldn't hear her.

He did, of course. With every inch closer he came her chest rose faster and her throat tightened. The vibration of his fingers lingered over her back…

"Wait," she rushed out. She wasn't sure why, or what she was thinking. "Wait." Only that a panic so foreign and sudden had gripped her entirely and she didn't know how else to respond. "Why are you doing this?" That ugly barrier of self-preservation pinned him as a target; saw cunning in his kindness.

"It needs tending to—what those bastards did to you."

"It's nothing compared to what you *should* be doing to me."

"And nothing compared to what I *want* to be doing with you."

She shot him an incredulous look over her shoulder. His mouth only curled in amusement, and she couldn't stand the fluttering in her stomach; the fact her mind paid attention to the slick, long waves of hair that met his jaw. "Take me back."

"Your wounds will scar if you don't let me help you. You're healing at the pace of a human with the Niltain Steel."

"I said take me back," she snapped. "I can't stand to be near you. I'm understanding more why they cast you aside so easily. You're overbearing, suffocating. Their slowest method of torture was assigning you to me."

Her hearing reached out for his heartbeat when she couldn't see his face. It pounded hard, strong, but there was always a faint stutter that echoed with hollowness. Zaiana had read many books on how the heart was nothing more than an organ to push blood around the body, but she studied it with a precision no one else did. Each person's heart spoke more to her than any outward expression, and with the disruption in Kyleer's chest, she wanted to steal the words back. She wouldn't, as to do so would give him a weapon. Because maybe she was slipping from her own steel composure. Maybe…

She cared.

CHAPTER 41

Tarly

TARLY ENJOYED THE cold—the kind that formed crystal ice and glittering snow. The kind he could wrap up warm in but still enjoy the bite against his cheeks. But being drenched with rain while he trudged over a mile in the oncoming winter was a miserable kind of cold.

They made haste into a small inn. Nerida folded her arms around herself, lips faintly blue and teeth chattering. He figured her small form took the impact of the weather harder.

"Did you enjoy the climate of Lakelaria?" Tarly asked curiously as they made their way to the desk.

"Very much so. But I would be far better equipped for the temperatures over there."

He smiled faintly. "Agreed."

Behind the reception desk a man reclined lazily, flipping through a book.

"How much for two rooms?" Tarly began fishing through his pockets, though he already knew his coin was sparse.

The man gave them a quick assessment, as though their appearance deemed the price. "Two silvers a room," he grumbled.

Opening his palm, Tarly cursed internally at the six coppers that equaled one silver to add to the other he held. Anything Nerida might have carried, including coin, would be long perished in the cottage fire.

"We'll take one room," she said.

Tarly laid out the change on the desk. The man gave it a suspicious once-over, grunted, then went to find a key.

"You can stay here. I have a few coppers to get a drink while you dry off, then—"

Swiping the key, Nerida pushed him. "Room seventeen."

Too stunned to do anything but move to her demand, Tarly led the way up the stairs. The door he stood outside was small, and when Nerida jammed the key and opened it, Tarly ducked a little to fit through.

"I mean it, I can—"

"We're both too cold for this debate, Sully. And at risk of catching fever or worse if we don't dry off and get warm. Trust me, I've seen what becomes of those too stubborn to take care of themselves."

He watched her unfasten her cloak, which she slung over the small desk chair she dragged over to the dark fireplace.

"You're far more clued up on fire-starting than me."

Tarly relieved himself of the weight of his own cloak before wordlessly wandering over, crouching and reaching for the logs, which he began to pile into the grate. "If only you were a Firewielder," he mused when the silence began to make him shiver more than the wet clothes.

Nerida huffed. "Don't we all wish for our ability to manifest as what best suits the moment?"

"Those with magick, I suppose."

"You speak as if you don't have any."

As the first sparks caught on the timber and began a blaze, Tarly cast her a dead look over his shoulder. Or he intended to, but when he spied her in nothing more than her undergarments, he whipped his head back around.

"It's just skin," she teased. He could almost hear the laughter in her voice.

She was *not* just skin. His mind had captured the enchanting image, though he tried to expel it out of decency for her.

"I'm not trying to scandalize you." She was *enjoying* this. "It's safe to turn around now."

Tarly stood slowly, turning with rigidity to find her clutching a blanket around herself. It wasn't much better when he knew what was just shy of being released by that hand.

"You need to do the same, I'm afraid." The golden glow of the fire danced off her features. Nerida took two cushions from the bed and walked past him. They fell to the floor and then she with them, cozying up by the fire.

Tarly wanted desperately to strip from the uncomfortably sodden clothes and join her where she looked so warm and peaceful, her head tipped back while the heat caressed her skin. He hesitated, knowing the wound he wouldn't be able to hide from her if he did, and not needing the sympathy and bafflement of another healer when she realized there was nothing that could be done.

"The longer you stay in those clothes, the higher your chances of losing functionality of your toes," Nerida reprimanded. "I won't look—you have my word."

"I'm not shy of you looking," he grumbled.

"Finally, you speak."

"I'm going downstairs—"

"Sully." The smack of her hand against the wood floor shocked through him. "I can guarantee you will be suffering by morning if you don't do as I say. If it bothers you so much to be close to me I'll sleep right here. Just strip and get in the bed."

Tarly blinked at her. Then he couldn't help it when, at the same time, their mouths pulled up and they chuckled. Laughed. He didn't know why exactly, only that their situation seemed unbelievable, and maybe they were delirious from the events that had led up to now. Nerida's chuckling eased into a sorrowful frown, and she looked away from him and into the fires.

"I'm sorry about your friend," he said gently.

"Me too."

Nerida cared deeply about everything. His chest clenched for her pain, and he decided his refusal only added to her concern. Her healer's nature would not let him suffer.

Tarly took a deep breath then began to undress. He laid out his clothes, and, true to her word, Nerida never once tore her attention from the fire. Hugging her knees, she appeared beautiful, lost in thought. He joined her slowly, dressed only in his undergarments, and his awareness started to ease with the enveloping warmth that chased away his somber thoughts of the day and what they'd faced.

"Where were you headed to, Sully, had you not found your hero complex in thinking I needed saving?"

Tarly watched her—he couldn't help himself. "Nowhere," he responded. "And everywhere."

Nerida nodded. "I traveled for a long time too. When I came to the mainland, I thought I'd head straight to Fenstead. Maybe it was cowardice that caused me to wander before I finally settled in a town on the outskirts."

"Why Fenstead?"

Her lips pursed with a contemplative pause. "It sounded wonderful."

"Is it part of your heritage?" Something about her seemed familiar, and he was only just realizing this could be why.

She barely shook her head, not offering more.

"The only time I ever got to travel was during the Great Battles, though I didn't venture far," Tarly confessed.

Her gaze slid to him, and he stiffened completely, but her sparkling irises held only sadness and question. Then he tensed when her eyes fell and her mouth opened on a shallow gasp. As though forgetting how little clothing she wore, Nerida shuffled over on her knees.

Without the blanket.

"You should, um—"

"You were seriously content to suffer rather than say anything to me?"

Tarly couldn't respond when all he could think of was her

proximity in the thin cotton corset and short underwear that hardly covered much.

"I've never met someone so stubborn it would literally be the death of them," she continued. High on her knees, Nerida assessed his shoulder. The humming warmth of her body intoxicated him, her skin so smooth it took a lot of resistance for him not to give in to his impulse to feel her. He turned his head, occupying his thoughts by studying the old chips along the floor instead.

Tarly gritted his teeth at the first touch. Not in pain, but at the foreign feeling. He couldn't associate her with the old fae healer who'd tended to him before, not when Nerida was all but naked and her touch far more desirable. What arose in him was terrifying. His fist clamped tight against the instinct to push her away, already seeing the hurt it would cause on her innocent face.

"I've never seen anything like this before," she muttered vacantly. "What bit you?"

"You wouldn't believe me."

"Try me," she mused.

"I don't want to frighten you."

Nerida took his chin. The boldness of the move stunned him, and he peered up into her twinkling gaze. "You can't scare me, Sully. I've experienced plenty of nightmarish things and read far more." She let him go, and a faint purple glow caught his eye, the small essence of magick so soothing he hadn't felt it.

"You read?"

"Don't most people?"

"Not really. Not beyond what's needed to see them through a decent education."

"I enjoy reading for pleasure, yes."

Then suddenly he wanted nothing more than for them to reach the Livre des Verres. To know what books would draw her attention, to see how she looked while engrossed in a story. A flash of *desire* he'd long forgotten; a hopeful pulse. Tarly shook the thought as quickly as it came.

"What are you doing?" he mumbled instead, eager for sleep to mark the passing of another night, another day closer to parting ways with her.

"I'm trying to feel for what's happening beneath to offer some kind of diagnosis or treatment. Though it would help if you told me what bit you."

"It was...a creature."

"Hmm...unhelpful."

Tarly stifled his grumble. "Have you heard of the dark fae?"

Nerida's hands left him, her shock retreat making him guilty. Fear crossed her expression. "A dark fae did that to you?"

"So you have heard of them."

She shook her head, and he was about to explain when she said, "I've met them."

He listened to the increased tempo of her heart. "What do you mean you've *met them?*" Tarly battled with flashbacks of Lennox. He'd appeared ordinary, kind, and had lured Tauria right into trusting him, only to turn into a savage monster like the flip of a switch. A savage monster that knew only killing; had nearly killed him and might still have that last victory as his wound had been slowly worsening. The gray color had spread to his collarbone and down half his bicep. Darker veins protruded, the sight stomach-churning. One thought had crossed Tarly's mind to explain what could be happening—one he hadn't faced until now.

"You don't think I could be...*Transitioning*, do you?"

That seemed to snap her from her trance. She reached up once more to continue searching through her magick. "It was a Transitioned that bit you?"

"Yes. He pretended to be a friend for a long time. We had no idea."

"We?"

Tarly couldn't tell Nerida about Tauria. How could he explain his closeness to the Queen of Fenstead? "A friend."

They met eyes, understanding written in hers.

"I know what it's like to want to remain hidden," she said softly, as if it were a slipped confession.

Nerida was a wonder he hadn't expected. This bright, caring, wondrous thing that should never have crossed his dark and hateful path. Though maybe he could be different. Maybe he could be better.

"You were running from something," Tarly observed. "Someone." He knew the moment he'd stepped over a boundary he had no right to intrude upon. The walls that formed clouded the cheer from Nerida's expression and made her flinch.

"It's spreading like poison." Nerida diverted the topic, and Tarly couldn't be disappointed. She owed him nothing of her past. He silently reprimanded himself.

"I figured—" He hissed at the sharp pain. It felt like dragging tiny needles through his blood.

"Sorry. I wanted to see if it was something I could attempt to extract, but it's…it's merging with you. Not just in your blood but your skin."

"So I could be—?"

"No, not like that. It's not changing your matter; it's killing it."

Tarly huffed a laugh. He only found her look of bewilderment even more amusing. "How long then?"

"Why do you do that?" Nerida sat down on her knees, her brow pinched as she tried to read him, but Tarly knew he was a scrambled mess of a being. "Why do you make it seem like it would not matter if it were a day or a decade?"

Her concern warmed his chest. She was so filled with love and care for others and the world. Which meant she was everything he wasn't. He asked again, softly, "How long do I have, Nerida?"

"I don't know." Her voice took on a harsh edge. "It should be spreading a lot quicker. Maybe you should be on the brink of death by now, yet it seems you get an extended pass of time. Though it's clear you don't want it thanks to the small essence of healer's magick in you."

Tarly's brow furrowed. "I don't have magick."

Nerida scowled, shifting away from him and snatching her blanket. "I was wondering when you'd open up to me about it, but Gods forbid we actually have something in common—that would be torturous." She stood abruptly. "We should get some proper rest while we can."

Nerida took her pillows, arranging them on the bed before she lay down. Tarly didn't move, eyeing the cushions he had left and figuring the fire would keep him warm enough without a blanket down here. He shifted to get comfortable. Many times since he was limited to one side, but even on his good shoulder he could last no longer than a few minutes pressed against the hard floor.

"Neither of us is going to get any sleep with you creaking the floorboards," Nerida scolded.

He lay on his back, still and silent, trying to send his mind elsewhere as a distraction.

Nerida gave a huff, drawing his eyes up to where she sat, a frown etching her skin that he found both amusing and adorable. "You are terrible at reading anything unless it's spelled out for you."

He propped himself up on his hands. "I don't know what you mean."

"There's a perfectly good bed to fit two people, and it's still rather cold over here."

Tarly blinked at her, a childish heat rushing over him. "You want me to sleep with you?"

"Must you make it sound so scandalous?"

His mouth twitched, but he didn't give way to the grin he fought.

"Though what I will never live down is if you make me insist."

She had a point. It was just sleep. Though while she claimed the bed fit two people, as he stood, he knew with his size there wouldn't be much room at all left between them. Nerida held the blanket to her chest, their stares never breaking as he made his way over. The withering thing in his chest skipped at her look, yet he couldn't be certain what it was. There was a change in the atmosphere between them, a flutter he almost missed, but he could have sworn she was refraining from looking any lower than his face.

Tarly sat with his back to her, taking a few steady breaths to calm his instinct to retreat. He needed to expel these long-dormant feelings that were stirring before they boiled into a resentment he'd ultimately turn on her.

"Are you sure?" he asked. One last chance that begged her to say no while he longed to hear—

"Yes."

Tarly barely nodded, closing his eyes for a long second. His body relaxed, and he eased back until he was lying down, trying not to glance her way. To make his presence smaller, he rolled onto his side away from her.

Nerida was right: the fire had yet to adequately warm the room, and he tensed against the creeping cold until part of a blanket already warmed and coated in a floral scent was draped over him.

"The night would pass faster if we...if we, um—"

For the first time he heard a shyness and turned to find her curled into her own body heat. He realized what she meant then. *Gods above.* He had to take a second to gather his sanity and calm the rage of something so long forgotten at the idea of her body pressed against his. He wanted to know if her golden skin felt as soft as it looked. He wanted to hear the sound she would make as he touched her. Though the dark thoughts convinced him she would turn away from him. That any touch of his had always been fleeting. Forgotten. Never treasured.

Tarly nodded. He couldn't leave her to shiver.

Nerida shuffled closer slowly, as though any movement could spook him. He thought she'd feel warm, but her hands were cold, and he clenched his teeth. She inched closer again, pressing her skin flush to his, and her feet against his legs were ice.

"Is this okay?" she whispered, perhaps feeling his tenseness.

"Is this supposed to benefit us both? You're damn freezing."

She giggled softly, the sound easing the awkwardness as she shifted a little closer into him once more. Tarly closed his eyes at the contentment he'd done nothing to deserve, yet it came so easily he allowed himself not to feel guilty for it for one night. Her form was small against his back, tucked in so perfectly, but something about the position wouldn't settle in his mind. He felt it was like a rejection to her.

"We should switch," he blurted before he could stop himself. "It'll give you more heat," he tried to justify pathetically.

"You can't lie on your other shoulder," she mumbled sleepily. "I'm not done figuring out what it is and how to treat it, by the way."

His chest clenched with an unfamiliar feeling. He pushed it aside. Taking one deep breath to drown out his hesitation, Tarly shifted onto his back, and Nerida propped herself up in question. Their stare communicated his suggestion, and he thought he caught the rosy flush of her cheeks. But she hooked one leg over him, and Spirits be *damned,* she only straddled him for a second, but his hands reached out on instinct to aid her, fitting so effortlessly on her waist that they ignited something that tingled from his fingertips to his chest. Then she was off him, shuffling down on his other side when he shifted back.

Tarly took a second, fascinated by the spilling of her silver-white hair, before tucking up behind her. She gave a soft sound of sleepy contentment, and he replayed it many times before his own mind started to drift. Her skin against his… He wanted to run his hands along her thigh, her hips, her waist, but he simply draped his arm around her carefully, no more than a position of comfort.

He knew she'd fallen asleep by her deep, even breaths. Tarly closed his eyes, but one thing tormented him, so he whispered knowing she wouldn't hear: "You were right. I don't want it. Time." He paused, nearly swallowing the final confession until it slipped free. "But maybe I could."

CHAPTER 42

Faythe

FAYTHE AWOKE TO an ache swelling her abdomen. She groaned, curling into herself with the intensifying pain. Terrible cramps were usually something she could handle, yet these were particularly punishing. She had to wonder if, with all the strengths of becoming fae, this was a particular downside.

When the sharpness dulled, she finally rolled onto her back. Tipping her head, she found a glass of water on the nightstand, but it was the sweet scent drifting across that had her propping herself up. Her eyes widened at the chocolate chip cookies, and she beamed. There was a note under the glass, which she read as she drank.

Take two drops of the tonic. Then if you awake and the bath has chilled, I'm sure you can handle heating it back up with your newfound talent.

I will find you later.

Faythe smiled, enjoying the eruption of butterflies instead of the torturous cramps of her cycle. She wondered how Reylan had known of it when Faythe had been so caught up she hadn't kept track of the last one. One thing was certain: she had skipped months.

As the next painful wave subsided, Faythe could think of nothing more inviting than a bath. In the washroom, lavender and honey filled her nostrils. The air embraced her with humidity, and a mound of bubbles floated atop the water. Dipping her hand in, she surfaced a little heat with her Firewielding to bring it from warm to hot. Stripping down, she noticed Reylan had also left fresh linens for her. Faythe's face crumpled, perhaps emotionally heightened today, at the gentle gestures he'd made.

After what felt like the longest bath she'd taken in a long time, the tonic seemed to have dulled the ache of her cramps enough that she could face the day. Fresh and surprisingly upbeat, she headed out to find Reylan, intending to thank him. It didn't take long. Maybe there was some subconscious force of gravity pulling her toward him that made it too easy.

He was in conversation with another commander, the two of them walking toward her, but his blue irises slipped to her, never failing to skip a beat of her heart. When their paths crossed, Reylan spoke his final words before the other commander nodded, pausing to bow his head to her, and then left them.

"How are you feeling?" Reylan asked immediately.

A blush crept along her cheeks. "My insides don't feel like they want to erupt anymore," she said. He winced. "Thank you for everything, by the way. How did you know?"

Reylan scratched the back of his neck. "It's, uh...there's been a shift in your scent for days. I was wondering when you would tell me about it. You *can* talk to me about anything—you know that, right?"

She had never seen him flustered like this, and Faythe bit her lip. Reylan drew a breath watching her mouth. He spared a look around before his thumb reached to unhook her teeth.

"I know," she answered quietly, overcome with the rush of lust that small act invoked, though it switched to irritation when he let go of her quickly. She took a deep breath to collect herself. "Truthfully, I didn't realize. Is there a difference in how often and intense a cycle comes? With me being fae now, I mean."

Reylan's nervous edge returned, and Faythe couldn't help her smile.

"You don't know a thing about human cycles, do you?" Faythe assumed.

He shrugged. "I haven't exactly had a reason to. But with the fae—"

"I can take it from here, big cousin," Livia cooed at Reylan as she approached, patting his arm as his face dropped to a light scowl.

She cast him a dashing grin over her shoulder as she passed and hooked her arm around Faythe's.

Faythe's mouth opened to protest, having only just met with Reylan, but his expression softened with a small nod of promise he'd see her later before Livia spun her away.

"Let me guess: you woke up feeling as if someone was practicing tying knots with your intestines."

"That's one way of putting it," Faythe sighed.

Livia didn't unhook her arm, and though it was somewhat jarring from the commander, Faythe found it comforting.

"Yes, the pain is more intense for the fae. But only because our cycles are mercifully less often. Four times a year for three to five days."

Faythe could live with that and made a mental note of when next to expect hers.

Livia pulled Faythe to a stop, sparing a glance back as if to check Reylan hadn't followed them. It pulsed trepidation in Faythe.

"I've been looking for Evander," Livia said.

Faythe's eyes widened. "On your own?"

"Yes. And I'm only telling you because I can't forget the glimpse of a figure I saw when we found you in that alley. I thought it was just another crook you hadn't gotten to before he could escape, but you spared him for a reason, didn't you?"

"Livia, I—"

"Please, Faythe." Something about the note of fear in Livia's voice rang with great urgency.

"I don't know who it was," she admitted. "But he spoke as if he knew me. More than that…it was as if I should know *him.*"

That seemed to relax her, but Faythe couldn't ease her own worry for a second.

"He's never met you." Livia seemed to air her thoughts as she folded her arms.

"Could you show me a memory?" Faythe asked.

Livia shook her head. "Don't ask me to think of him."

"You're already thinking of him," she tried again softly.

Vulnerability was not an emotion Livia yielded easily. At watching it strip back her fierce exterior, Faythe's heart clenched.

Then Livia reached out a hand, and though both of them knew it wasn't needed for Faythe to glimpse her mind, Faythe gave Livia's palm a reassuring squeeze.

"I just need to hear his voice," Faythe said, tunnelling away as if she were in two places at once staring into the blue of Livia's eyes.

The commander clutched her tighter with the first echo, but it was distorted as though underwater. All Faythe would need was one clear line to confirm or ease both of their fears.

Two voices were in the scene that was nothing more than a blur of colors. They were shouting, and she could recognize one of them with any barrier in the way.

Reylan.

Livia's grip turned painful, subconsciously blocking the memory, but Faythe fought the resistance.

"You're doing great," Faythe said aloud. She didn't hear and wouldn't catch the commander's response as the scene grew louder.

Almost there…

Then she saw them. Evander and Reylan. Faythe observed them with a bit of distance from a window, but she strained her fae hearing, honed her vision, and saw everything in the home clearly.

Reylan's silver hair was cropped to his shoulders, two braids on either side, and Faythe almost lost focus and retreated from Livia's mind completely at the confusingly familiar sight of both males. Evander had darker hair and blue eyes, attractive with a vicious edge that erased anything worth admiring. Just as her silver-haired warrior slammed his uncle into the wall with a threatening snarl, Faythe was overcome with waves and waves of terror.

Livia's terror.

Evander said, "You will regret this, son."

Faythe caught a flicker of movement at the edge of the window and found Livia advancing toward them. She was sobbing hard, and Faythe's eyes burned to take away her fear, her pain. There was so much of it coursing through the stunning auburn-haired commander. Yet that wasn't who Faythe saw. This was long before she'd claimed that title.

Livia's red dress was torn and crumpled.

"Please stop, both of you!" she cried.

Faythe understood her heartbreak. Despite what Evander might have done, a part of Livia would always ache to see her father harmed.

A new heat over Faythe's skin started to quell all else. This time, it was her own emotions taking over. Her breath caught with the realization of something crucial: she was observing the scene from a particular vantage point. A tree. Somehow, Faythe knew exactly where she was in this scene, and panic began to creep over her. Her ability threatened recklessness in its confusion, becoming an entanglement of two minds recalling different angles of the same memory.

Faythe tried to pull herself free, but she was locked in, not feeling Livia anymore when all she knew was herself. Trickles of how she got there; impossible visions of what she would do next.

"Faythe!"

Drawing a deep breath, Faythe felt as if she were being dragged through a long void of time. She was on her knees. Planting a hand on the cool marble confirmed she was back in the present.

"What happened?" Livia pressed when Faythe couldn't speak.

Her eyes traced the same pattern on the marble only as a way to focus while she replayed the scene again and again, finding new pieces of memory that fit before or after, though none of it made full sense.

"I don't know," she answered vacantly.

Livia's terror had been so raw and real that it snapped Faythe back. Their eyes met, and the open vulnerability in the commander broke something in her.

"You're incredible," Faythe said, though it wasn't enough. Nothing ever would be for how much Livia had endured and how bravely she had risen from it all.

Livia's brow pinched together as if she wouldn't allow herself to truly hear it. They rose together. Faythe didn't think she would get this moment, relieved when Livia made the first move to embrace

her. She savored it, closing her eyes. Livia could be tough with her love, and while Faythe bickered back, she loved every moment they got to spend together.

Livia pulled back, swiping away an escaped tear. Then, in one deep inhale, the commander slipped back into her armor.

"Did you hear him?"

Faythe nodded, and maybe her expression alone spoke everything as Livia paled, looking away and out of the long window.

"He is really out there," Livia said.

"What are you going to do?"

"Find him."

Faythe admired the bravery and sureness in that tone despite Livia declaring a hunt for her longest nightmare.

"And kill him."

"I want to help," Faythe said.

Livia shook her head. "You have so much to do here. It might take some time to track him down if he's remained hidden all this time anyway."

"Will you tell Reylan?"

"Yes. He deserves to know. He won't like it, but he can't stop me."

"Promise me you'll come to us if you find him."

Livia eased a hollow smile but gave a nod. "I will."

Faythe could hardly retain any focus, and even in training she barely found the energy to lift a blade as the dull aches returned in waves. She'd come back to bed. The cramps were tolerable enough, but she couldn't drift off.

Her mind hadn't let go of the image of Evander. Thoughts of him in the vision, then the confrontation she was certain was with him in the alley, kept her wide-awake trying to solve the puzzle of events.

A soft knock sounded, and though she hadn't detected him sooner, she knew it belonged to Reylan even before his head of silver hair eased through the door. With her back to him, Faythe cast him a weak look over her shoulder as he came around the bed.

"This is bold," Faythe murmured. "Wouldn't want people to think you're scandalizing me."

"You're in pain. This is an exception."

Reylan sat, leaning down to untie his boots, and Faythe yearned for him.

"Pity exceptions," she mused. "I'll take it."

He huffed, the corner of his mouth tugging as he climbed over, still dressed and above the covers. She wasn't about to argue. Instead, she tested her limits and scooted closer until her head rested in his lap while he sat against the headboard.

Reylan's hand trailed over her arm, dipping to her waist, and Faythe's breath caught when his palm flattened over her abdomen. She thought nothing of the touch until a warmth grew there, traveling deeper as if her skin were absorbing it, encasing every twinge of the clenching ache until it was numbed altogether.

Faythe couldn't help her moan, fully relaxed with his help as she nestled closer to him.

"I wish you'd come sooner," she sighed contentedly.

"I thought you would have taken another dose of the tonic."

"It makes me nauseous—more so than the cramps."

"I should have sent a healer," he said, brushing strands of her hair behind her ear.

The gentle vibration of magick over her stomach along with his touch invoked such bliss she was torn between sleep and basking in the moment far longer.

"Instead you stole their ability," Faythe said, peeking up at him.

His smile down on her burst in her chest.

"I'm merely taking advantage of the opportunity."

"I'm glad you're here," Faythe whispered.

Reylan's fingers began an idle caress her eyes fluttered to.

"Did you get what you needed from Livia?"

Faythe was clouded by the more sinister point of their conversation with the question. She wondered if the commander had told him yet.

"Yes," Faythe answered. She was about to leave it there but knew the question would burn in her mind until she knew. "Did Livia tell you about—?"

"Evander. Yes."

He spoke so calmly that anyone else might believe it didn't faze him. Faythe's hand curled around his thigh as she detected the simmering heat of anger.

"You didn't kill him."

"It seems not."

Then she felt the echoes of his disappointment as if he'd failed.

"You've both had all this time to live in peace from him thinking he was dead. That's got to count for something," Faythe said.

He continued combing his fingers through her hair, lost in his own battle of thoughts she wished she could ease.

"It does," he said after a thoughtful pause. "But now neither of us will rest until he truly is."

Faythe's retribution sharpened to a dangerous edge with the face that taunted at the forefront of her thoughts. She'd killed before, but there were very few she'd reserved as targets in her mind, unable to rest until they were shot down.

"We'll take care of it," Reylan said gently, as though he could sense her spike of adrenaline. "We always do."

Faythe nodded, not pressing the topic further. Right now, she would give herself over to the safety and bliss of this moment with Reylan, but she was far from being rested from the growing need to exact her revenge on Evander.

CHAPTER 43

Faythe

FAYTHE WATCHED THE tiny hairs move as if each were a thread of flame. If she took a step back, it appeared nothing more than a large, still feather. She'd been studying it, a book full of intrigue and wonderous legends of the Firebird splayed over her hands.

"She's real," Faythe said, thumping the book shut as she felt Agalhor's tentative approach. "She's alive."

"You're discovering your senses admirably fast," he commented.

Faythe tore her eyes away to track him as he stepped up to her side. "I've always had a challenge hearing things—too many things. In my mind or otherwise."

"I can't pretend like I know what you're going through, but your will to adapt is strong."

"How can you know that?" It came from her lips like a plea.

His brow furrowed knowingly. "Because we have all seen it. It's easy to forget the leaps we've taken when the steps forward become so small. But never forget you are still moving. You are challenging yourself with every day you decide to face your reality."

Faythe was overcome by how much those words resonated within. She captured them, storing them where all the treasured wisdom from her father stayed, never forgotten as if his words held magick. No matter how much time passed, those notes of encouragement would echo again when they were needed most.

"I don't know where Atherius went or why she left after saving me."

"It's a remarkable tale. Albeit very familiar."

They exchanged a knowing smile.

"There was little left to lose on that mountain. I wasn't sure she'd detect the bloodline so far back, but I can't explain the language I heard seconds before making my decision to take that leap."

"I envy you, Faythe. There is nothing I wouldn't give to have seen her. Perhaps I would have heard her too. Though I know I should not envy the position you were in."

Faythe couldn't help her huffed laugh. "No. Though if it weren't for the dark fae, I would have more awe than fear of that night."

His deep inhale was contemplative. "The one we hold below will be dealt with for what she did to you."

"She let me go." Faythe didn't take her sights from the feather though she had all of his attention. "Zaiana…she's powerful. I fought her, and I know her intentions were to capture me then kill me, but something changed her mind."

"Something you believe to be salvation."

"I don't know," Faythe answered honestly. "What I do believe is that the world is taunting and cruel. There are those who bend to the mold of their upbringing, and those whose will is to break it."

Quiet chatter disrupted their moment, and Faythe's gaze flicked up to see Jakon and Marlowe returning from their wander around the library. Marlowe held a book splayed over her hands, engrossed in it, while Jakon's arm around her seemed to be subtly steering her on the right path. When she caught sight of who Faythe was standing beside, Marlowe thumped her book shut, and both of them offered a short bow to the king, tense with nerves.

"I've heard much about you, Jakon and Marlowe Kilnight." Agalhor greeted them warmly.

"As have we about you, Your Majesty," Jakon replied.

"Rhyenelle is remarkable." Marlowe's gaze drifted with wonder, marveling over the long feather. "I'm sure you're aware of what this can do."

Faythe realized she was speaking to Agalhor.

"I am aware that in our history they have been used to enhance magick."

Marlowe nodded. "I, uh, I…" She seemed to stumble over what she wanted to add to the conversation, apparently thinking twice about it at the last second. She and Jakon exchanged a look, and somehow, Faythe read into it with a flash of memory.

"Nik's feather?"

Marlowe's attention snapped to her, her ocean orbs flicking between Faythe and Agalhor as though wondering if her knowledge would be safe. "It was outlawed many millennia ago," she explained, willing to stop there should the king show any outrage.

"Phoenix Blood," Agalhor offered like a token of reassurance that she could speak freely of it.

Faythe's intrigue was sparked when Marlowe nodded.

"He owned a much smaller feather, but it was real."

"Was?" Faythe probed.

"Yes. I harbor some essence of magick and was able to create the potions. It's true, everything that they say it can do, and this…" Her hand traced along the glass case. "It feels powerful. I can only imagine the power it would grant if used in such a way considering what it did for Nik."

"What did it do?" Faythe asked.

"His Nightwalking. He gained a conscious ability similar to yours. When we left him, he still had that advantage, and there's no telling when it will wear off."

Agalhor cut in. "The strength of the potion is not determined by the size of the feather but the bird it came from. You may feel the one here is more powerful, but if both feathers come from the same bird, the only difference lies in how many vials you can produce."

Faythe's pulse galloped with wonder and awe at the facts, flashing images of Atherius in her blazing glory that no longer struck her with fear but pride. And longing, she realized, deep and fiery in her chest. She wanted so much to see the great Firebird again.

"This knowledge cannot leave us," Agalhor said, his tone coated in command. "No one must find out what this feather can do. In the wrong hands, it is a weapon beyond our imagination."

Faythe swallowed hard, instinctively extending her senses with the unexplainable urge to protect the feather. When she confirmed it was only the four of them standing in the library, her tension eased. Jakon and Marlowe nodded their agreement before offering to escort Faythe back to her rooms, but she wanted to stay a while longer and knew Reylan would come for her soon.

Alone again with Agalhor, Faythe's insecurities began to rush to the surface. She was all too aware of the impending council meeting mere days away.

"What will they think of me?" she asked, not really expecting an answer to soothe her worries, but in need of any small comfort that could come from a father, not a king.

"Whatever you make them believe."

One sentence, and it was enough.

"What do you believe?"

"Exactly what I always have. That your worth is not measured by the body you inhabit."

She heard him turn to her, but in her cowardice she couldn't move; could only bow her head in thought.

"My dear Faythe, there is no person who can say they understand you, for what you have been through is your own. No matter their opinion of how resilient you are, how you embrace this new fate with such awe strikes me. You do not have to be grateful to have a life that was forced upon you simply because you *live*. You do not have to part with what you were to embrace what you are becoming."

Her tear fell straight to the ground, one of pure gratitude and liberation.

A large, calloused hand pulled up her chin, and she met eyes with a father's warmth. "You care deeply about this, what the council will make of your right to reign. It shows how much you want this, my dear. It fills me with a pride I never thought I would have in this life."

"What if I didn't want this?" she whispered.

His smile only widened. "No matter what you choose, you'll fly with those wings that have been caged for far too long."

CHAPTER 44

Zaiana

THEY DIDN'T HAVE to do anything further for Zaiana to be suffering in the aftermath of their lashings. Her back stung to no end, but worst of all, it was itchy beyond belief, and she commended the humans a little more for their endurance while healing.

With nothing to distract herself from clawing at where she could reach, she tucked her knees up tight and buried her face into her crossed arms. The darkness was taunting, an illusion of freedom for the dreams she could conjure within its depths, living through mind rather than body. It worked for a time to take her out of that cell, out of her miserable existence altogether. She passed the time through many lives, wondering who she could have been in an alternate world. Yet nothing she thought of seemed particularly alluring. She didn't want Nephra's life or Mordecai's or Dakodas's. On her opposing side, she didn't want Faythe's life or Kyleer's.

She didn't want her own either. At least not with these phantom chains anchoring her as someone's servant.

In her tiredness and delirium, Zaiana couldn't fight the

thoughts of Maverick. She wondered again where he was, if he knew of her capture yet, and what he would do with that knowledge. Trust was not something she extended often, but she realized in that moment she'd given a lot of it to him. Zaiana trusted him not to tell the masters when he knew the punishment it would condemn her to.

Her chest squeezed and her nails dug into her flesh to counter the *yearning* that slipped through her weak defenses. For Maverick's familiarity. For the part of her that missed his insufferable pestering. For his touch…

"Go away, Kyleer," she groaned, not lifting her head, irritated he'd timed his intrusion just as she was finally drifting off for a moment of peace.

"Are you going to let me help you now?"

Zaiana was beyond caring. *So damn tired.* And cold, she realized with a painful shudder. Yet her skin was slick as if she'd been running through hot summer fields. She swallowed, but her throat was like sandpaper.

"You haven't eaten or drunk anything."

She heard Kyleer's voice as distant, underwater. Zaiana lifted her head, snapping it to him with the intention of a scowl, but the world tilted rapidly. Bliss and misery weighted her fall. She faintly heard a curse and caught the blurry sight of smoke and stars before her head met something soft and her surroundings faded away.

Zaiana awoke with a gasp. Panic ensnared her, and a cry was smothered by her clenched teeth as her wrists met the ends of their restraints. Her vision wouldn't focus for long, but as she propped herself up from where she'd lain on her side, her fingers flexed with the surprise of meeting soft sheets instead of stone.

While trying to orient herself she breathed long and deep. The scent that coated her called for her to lie back down and feel safe in sleep, but the face that flashed to mind made her blink her lids, searching and glancing sideward.

There he was.

Kyleer sat on the edge of the bed with his back to her. He stared silently into amber flames across the room, but he had to have detected that she was awake. Zaiana scanned her new surroundings. Instinct had her mapping a way out, but her curiosity caught on anything that would confirm where she thought she was.

Kyleer's sword was unmistakable on one side of the room beside many other weapons. Including her own, Nilhlir. She didn't have it in her to care that he'd kept possession of it. Clothing lay discarded over an armchair, a single book sprawled on a table with a piece of parchment as though he'd been studying it. The room echoed with a humble warmth, nothing lavish or grand, though she believed his position to be high enough that he could request any luxury.

"I shouldn't be here." Her voice came out in an awful croak, and she coughed.

"No, you shouldn't be," he answered, detached from any emotion.

"Then why am I?"

A hand dove through his wavy brown hair. He didn't look at her, as though her presence in his room could still be denied. "What was I to do when you're so damn stubborn you'd rather die than admit you need help?"

"I don't need anything from you."

He huffed a laugh so far from humorous. His light shirt exposed every impressive contour of his back, defined shoulder blades shifting. Kyleer was the most impressively built of any guard she'd seen. "You're burning up. I managed to force you to drink a tonic that will subdue the fever for now, but it will come back if you don't get those wounds seen to—the wounds you've been reopening and inviting infection into."

Gods, she cursed the Niltain steel.

"You haven't—" She couldn't bear to ask, though she noted

her black sweater was still on, along with her pants. No boots, strangely, allowing her toes to curl in comfort against the material.

"Touched you? No."

"How did I get here?"

"It wasn't easy. And if they discover you're gone then pray to the Spirits for both of us."

A dark dread started to rise in her stomach. She couldn't be here. He couldn't be known to have brought her here. She was already set for punishment, but him…

"Take me back."

"You won't last another week down there unless you get the aid you need," he gritted.

"Whether I live or die shouldn't be of your concern," she bit back.

His head whirled to her, and she recoiled at the fire blazing in his mossy irises. "You're right." Kyleer's knee on the bed made her breath hitch. "You shouldn't be my concern." Not removing that smoldering gaze, he crossed the short distance. Zaiana wasn't fully aware of how to respond when he planted his hand by her head, and as he coaxed her to lie down his other dipped behind her, right between her shoulder blades, igniting sparks where no wounds were and stopping her back from hitting flush against the sheets.

Some strands of his hair fell as he hovered above her. His jaw lined in shadow made him all the more firm and alluring. But it was those eyes of passion that pierced through her like always, allowing him to get too close before any rational thought could push through.

"You are a fool for bringing me here." He didn't even know the danger he'd unleashed. From here she could easily escape.

"Yes, I am."

"You should have left me to suffer."

"I should have."

Zaiana ground her teeth against all his agreements. She had to whip sense into the commander. Her legs hooked around him, and her knees clamped tight. Kyleer reacted faster than she anticipated, or she slower than she usually would in her miserable state.

He gripped her chains, pulling her hands above her head. To keep her from flipping them over, he pressed his hard body into her.

The gasp he pulled out of her stopped her urge to fight. The warmth of him, the awareness that to move would be to move against him, froze her still. Another traitorous thought flashed so quickly—until she incinerated it in her mind. The bout of desire that *wanted* it. Him. Wanted to know what every inch of that broad and powerful form would feel like, skin to skin against hers.

"Do what you have to, Kyleer," she hissed.

"You're a wild, obstinate creature."

"If you don't get off me, I'll scream and alert every guard within earshot."

He flinched, but his words were almost a dare. "Turn around."

The low gravel skittered over her skin. When he eased back, letting go of her wrists, in her fatigue she gave over to his command. She tucked her hands to her chest as she lay on her stomach, the bed sinking down to ease the digging of her shackles.

"You could just remove these and save us both the hassle," she said, staring into the tango of fire.

"I'm a fool for bringing you here, but not *that* much of a fool."

Zaiana would have laughed in mockery of his obliviousness. She could show him, yet that fight in her dwindled further in his presence when intrigue had her forgetting, just for a moment, how quickly she could kill him.

"I'm going to tear this," he warned, pausing until he got her response.

Zaiana only nodded, and despite the notice, her body turned to stone at the rip of fabric. The breeze rippled across her bare back, causing a shiver. The tonic he'd given her—or maybe it was the fever—had her eyelids fluttering against drowsiness. The soft sheets she lay on were like clouds, but most of all, the scent of pine coaxed her mind to find peace.

She strained her hearing to decipher what Kyleer was doing. The scrape of wood signaled a stool being pulled over. He set something on the nightstand, and from the faint splash she knew it was a basin of water. He dunked something into it, occupying the stool.

Then stillness.

"This will hurt," he said, his voice surprisingly tender.

"You can't hurt me, Kyleer."

She didn't know why she said that. Her physical pain meant nothing; it was but a fleeting sensation that would cool and heal. It could mark her appearance, but the wounds that told of far more eventual stories lived deep within.

Zaiana braced at the heat closing in against her skin. Her teeth clamped tight against the superficial sting, but it was his hands she had to focus her whole mind on to be sure they weren't hands to hurt, but hands to heal.

She didn't realize he'd paused, the cloth under his palm still, his fingertips tingling where they touched.

"I'm fine," she whispered, wondering if that was what he was waiting for.

He moved with the warm, damp cloth, and awareness snapped her wide-awake. She needed a distraction. *Anything.*

"You have a brother," she stated more than asked.

"I have two," he answered. "One just happens to look far more like me."

Zaiana thought on his words. "Why do you regard the general as a brother if he is not your blood?"

"Blood doesn't make family."

Zaiana's brow knitted. She had a mind to disagree, but she longed to hear more of his strange reasons. "What does?"

His hands left her, dipping back into the water, and she looked up on instinct. Kyleer waited again, and only when her shoulders relaxed did he continue his gentle strokes.

"Those who stand by you no matter what. Those you would do anything, *give* anything, for. When you've been through the Nether with someone and they've seen the worst parts of you yet choose to stay, how could they be anything less than family?"

Zaiana gave over to the romantic, albeit damning, notion. To care, to love—they were open weaknesses for any enemy to enjoy.

"Do you have family, Zai?"

The switch of topic to herself raised her defenses. She didn't answer for a stretch of silence while the nip of her wounds started to fade to a craving for his touch.

"We're taken from our parents the moment we're born. I do not know who mine are or if they had other children. I assume not, as it's rare for any couple to yearn to go back to each other. Darklings are given to the masters, where we train to fight for our species one day."

Kyleer hummed thoughtfully. "Any family not of blood?"

Her instinct was to ridicule the notion. Yet her mind flashed images she sifted through one by one. Tynan, Kellias, Acelin, Drya, Selain, and Amaya. They were her soldiers, her close circle of trust and loyalty. She thought they might be the closest thing to what his kind would call the word she feared.

Family.

"No," she answered.

Kyleer reached up—no cloth, only flesh—and when this featherlight touch trailed between her shoulders her hands fisted the sheets tightly. "This is where your wings would be," he said with an air of wonder. He didn't know what he was doing to her, but if he didn't stop, he was sure to scent it.

"Yes," she managed to breathe, trying to ignore the pleasure that relaxed her body, unable to tell him to stop.

"How do you hide them?"

"With a glamour."

"What does it feel like?" He traced the other side, and she bit her bottom lip to stifle the moan that caressed her throat.

"It's like a weight on my shoulders and an itch that grows the longer it's held." Talking was becoming difficult when all she could track were his fingers.

"Explains why the wounds affect you to the point of having to claw at them endlessly."

"I suppose."

"Explains why you're enjoying this so much." He applied pressure as though he knew exactly where they would expand.

Dark Spirits be *damned*, she couldn't stop the tensing of her muscles, the parting of her mouth, nor the pinching of her brow. "Don't flatter yourself."

He chuckled. Low and genuine, but with a dark tease that had her swallowing hard. "Are they sensitive when your wings are exposed?"

Zaiana had nothing to lose by obliging. "No. The glamour isn't exactly pleasant. Your hands…" She took a second to breathe through the blissful torture he was beginning to grasp he could inflict, and she realized then her error in answering his questions. "It eases the pressure. It's—"

"Pleasurable?"

Zaiana clamped her mouth against confirming that, but she could feel his smile.

"Your blood is…"

"Wrong?"

"Beautiful."

Zaiana blinked at the fire. "You're the first to have called it that."

"It is."

"You're supposed to find me monstrous."

"I do." A dark change entered his voice.

Zaiana listened to the cloth being returned to the basin, but he didn't pull it back out and wring it again. The bed behind her dipped, a large hand curled over her arm, and Zaiana knew she should push him away, but instead she rolled to his silent demand, her whole body flush against his. He encased her with such protection.

"I find you utterly wicked, stunning…"—with each word the low vibrations inched closer to her neck—"and *monstrous*." His hand slipped over her bare waist.

Zaiana blamed the tonic, her illness, her wounds—she blamed anything she could for the responses she gave him that felt so wrong but *so* right. She pressed into him tighter when that strong, calloused hand lightly trailed over her abdomen.

"Why do I hate you yet cannot resist you?" he groaned into her hair.

Her hands clutched awkwardly at the blankets in their restraints. His fingertips traced her skin torturously, causing her to occasionally shift against him.

"I've heard that before."

Kyleer stopped moving. She could have bit out a protest, but he reached to sweep the loose hair from her face, his nose grazing her ear, and her lips parted with a shiver.

"I could do very bad things that would mean you'd never compare me to anyone else who came before me again. And I will, if that's what it takes."

"Not a comparison," she defended breathlessly. "An observation."

Kyleer chuckled darkly. "Don't mistake me for mindless pleasures that were never enough to make you remember a face or name."

She couldn't deny she found his confidence highly alluring. His words were spoken like a promise, not with the same empty arrogance she'd heard before. "You don't know that—"

Kyleer's other arm dipped under her, giving her a few seconds to object before he took hold of her breast. Zaiana made a gasping sound, arching into his play.

"Just as I thought," he said, lazily swirling his fingers over her abdomen. "You fit me so well."

Her hips undulated in a silent demand. Her brow pinched and her eyes closed at the tension he built within her—utterly maddening, though this torture she wanted to prolong. It numbed everything, an ounce of pleasure in so much bleakness.

"We shouldn't be doing this," she said with no real protest.

"It torments you to want this." He undid the buttons of her pants and a flutter erupted in her stomach. "I know because *nothing* has tormented me like you." Kyleer hugged her tight.

Overcome with momentary lust and tenderness, Zaiana wanted to succumb to it all before it was too late.

"Say you want this," he growled, shooting sparks down her spine and making her spill the response without hesitation.

"I want this."

"Thank fuck."

Kyleer's hand dipped under her waistband. Her soft moan mixed with his groan when he found her slick with the need he'd caused between her legs.

"You feel better than I could have imagined," he said sinfully.

"You've thought of me." Zaiana enjoyed his words, feeling them fueling her lust as much as his hands.

"Too damn often. I've wanted you since the moment I saw you, but it's more than that. *You* are far more than that." A long finger curved into her, and Zaiana cried out for him. "I could listen to you for hours, days," he encouraged, drawing unchecked sounds from her as he slipped in and out of her slowly before adding a second finger. "How long have you imagined this? My hands driving your pleasure."

She wanted to clamp her lips tight against giving him what he wanted, but it spilled from her mouth as if she were unraveling at his every command.

"For a while," she confessed. It was all she would give him. She wouldn't allow him to know that perhaps a scandalous thought or two had crossed her mind long before she arrived at the castle. While she'd watched him over many weeks on his journey to the Niltain Isles and punished her mind for thinking anything past wanting to kill him.

"Please." The word tasted foreign, yet it was all she could say for the teasing pace that wasn't nearly enough. Not nearly what either of them craved.

"You don't have to beg for this, Zai. Though it sounds fucking beautiful when you do."

Zaiana shifted her legs to give a better angle and her hips met his every stroke. Kyleer adjusted his position, massaging her breast, pumping into her hard, and working his thumb over her apex to send her chasing an end that was so close, and yet she didn't want to reach it. Didn't want this moment of utter bliss to end and reality to ruin it all.

But she couldn't stop the unstoppable.

"Ky!" She cried the name on the tip of her tongue.

Then Zaiana came completely undone.

Held tight in the arms of her enemy, she shattered. Pieces of her scattered far and fast, only to snap back together but reformed in a way that liberated her of any burden, though short-lived just like the bright pulse in her dead chest. For a second, she thought her heart might be beating. No—not beating, for it was not whole and strong like Kyleer's, which thumped beautifully, *wildly*, against her back. The movement in her chest was something like a skitter, but still a treasure she wanted to believe.

Kyleer removed himself from her, his breathing rugged as he blew into her hair, and she shivered. Drowsiness lapped at her, and in the arms of one so strong and brave and warm she didn't fight it, though she should.

She didn't regret it though it was wrong.

He let her go, but Zaiana held his forearm clutched over her chest, her brow knitted as she nestled her face into the perfect space as though she could hide there and forget the world. But she knew the pain of her reality would crash back in soon.

For now, she didn't want to leave this net that had become something she'd never felt before so wholly and unquestionably: *safe.*

CHAPTER 45

Samara

SHE WORE A different face walking through the Westland Forest. For her crimes she had become the bait. It seemed fair for the price of her life, yet the terror of who she'd fallen prey to consumed her.

So still, so silent.

Her predator could be watching her at this very moment.

He will find you.

The instruction was clear, easy. Yet there was nothing clear or easy about living out the terrifying plan.

"You came."

The dark voice stroked her nape from behind, standing every hair on end and making her step falter, cracking on a branch. He sounded pleased, and as she braved the will to turn to him, every muscle in her body locked stiff in anticipation of him seeing right through the trick.

No description, no preparation or warning, could have been enough to ease the shock of seeing the high lord in the flesh. Power radiated from him, yet she couldn't tell why. He stood so tall, and by the *Gods*, he was stunning in a roguish, dangerous kind of way.

An older fae, yet in some ways still youthful, his ink-black hair disheveled around his angular features. A shadow lined his jaw, and eyes of onyx bore into her with delight and promise. He had no wings, however, and she was surprised by her own disappointment that he'd kept them glamoured.

"Tauria Stagknight."

She swallowed hard. Though it was confirmation of who he saw, she couldn't shake the feelings that arrived so unexpectedly. She wanted him to see the truth.

No. That would earn her a fate far worse than the one she'd already condemned herself to.

Why did she make such foolish choices? Damn her. Damn them.

"I'm glad you accepted my request to see you." She spoke confidently, like a queen. Like the one he expected her to be.

Her chin she held high as he took slow, deliberate steps closer to her. A thrill raced through her blood, spiking her pulse. Her terror fizzed to want; her shyness quelled to confidence. *Too easy.* It was too easy to fall into the trap of his dark allurement.

"I must say, I was surprised to hear of your proposal after all you did." His anger seeped through, and that was the first crack in the enchantment that had started to wash over her.

"I did what I had to. Becoming dark fae was never part of the deal, nor would I have agreed to the slaughter of a child."

"You mistake everything," he said calmly, with a dark wrath.

He stopped right before her, their proximity drawing hard breaths she had to steady. She had to keep her composure and refrain from looking away.

"I'm here to make it right," she said, matching his standoff.

A dark brow curved, and she was drawn to it. To his face—so close she wanted to reach up and touch. She shouldn't. He was the enemy. *The enemy.* But perhaps he could save her.

If she told him, maybe he could *want* her.

"Do explain, princess."

It was then she snapped back. He didn't see her. He saw a

different face entirely, and that hurt. She hadn't expected it to hurt when they told her this fae was a monster.

"My offer still stands." Her throat was so dry. She wanted to tell him, to be seen. But they were counting on her to open this ruse. To test what he was capable of.

They didn't care about her life. No one did.

"I am still unwed," she went on, still playing their side though the darkness was tempting.

"You are mated," he countered with no small amount of disgust.

"A necessary measure to overthrow Varlas." She spoke evenly. "I needed communications in High Farrow. Nikalias trusts me. You must see the advantage in this."

His hand came up, slipping calloused fingers under her chin, and her lips parted. "I don't like to share, Tauria."

"You wouldn't have to."

Not with her. The *real* her. She didn't say it, but it taunted her. It wouldn't stop taunting her.

"He could be listening, *watching*, right now."

Every word of his raced up her spine. "I want to go with you," she said. The shock that widened his eyes a fraction he couldn't have felt often, she surmised. "Soon. I can't leave so abruptly, but when I've found out all I can about High Farrow defenses it will be time." Samara spoke her rehearsed lines, trying to match the tone, the poise—everything he expected of the face he saw on her. "Nikalias will have no choice but to bow to us."

"There is only one way I can trust in your word right now." His voice dropped low with a vibration that coiled in her stomach. His fingers on her chin traced down her neck, cupping her nape, and she soared with an awakening. She allowed him to decide. She put up no fight against the space between them that shortened and shortened but not quickly enough. He watched her every flicker of expression to detect a lie, a hesitation, and this part she knew she could play expertly.

She wanted this. Wanted to feel those lips that promised a

passion she was sure would explode with something dark and twisted but all-consuming.

When their mouths met softly her eyes slipped closed. Then, without thinking, she gave over to impulse, hands slipping up his chest, grasping his exquisite jacket, and she pressed into him with the arm he drew around her waist.

Gods, this was wrong. They wouldn't know how much she enjoyed it. Though they watched, they'd think it was for show, that she was doing this for them, yet this was for *herself.* She didn't want it to stop, so when he pulled away abruptly she couldn't bite back her whimper.

His eyes bore into her with feral surprise. They searched hers, and she wished he saw blue instead of hazel; wished he saw blonde instead of dark hair.

Wished he saw *her.*

Her lips parted, but the words wouldn't form. Not when the shadowy passion in his eyes could cut to betrayal and humiliation so fast if he knew the truth. The trick.

All she would ever be was someone's ghost.

Their pawn.

Their plaything.

"You have my attention, princess," he said, his voice delightfully rugged from her kiss. *Her kiss.* It couldn't be denied, and she chose to believe the feelings she'd stirred in him weren't solely for the beautiful princess he saw.

Her hand reached up, fingertips brushing over the rough surface of his jaw, and she gave him her best eyes of seduction. "You would do anything for me?"

These were her words, not words they'd put in her mouth.

His hand tightening on her erupted a flutter in her stomach. "If you were mine, there would be no limit to what I would do for you."

Delight shot through her until she remembered they were planning to use her only this once. He would never know of her existence; never know she could have been good for him. The real her, but she could still tell him

She could tell him.

Shaking her head against the taunting voice in her mind, she stepped away. The distance felt cold, lonely, compared to his darkness. "How can I reach you again?" she asked.

"You cannot," he answered, eyes fixed on hers with such admiration she wanted it to be real.

She could tell him.

"I have one question for you, Tauria Stagknight." Then he was flush against her body again, his lips leaning down but only grazing hers to ask, "Would you do anything for me?"

Her heart beat wildly and she was sure he could hear it, *feel it,* pressed against him. It was a given response, yet also her own. Her answer came from the minds of two people but spilled from only one set of lips.

"Yes."

CHAPTER 46

Tauria

Tauria stood deathly still high up a tree, overseeing Samara's interaction with Mordecai. "*It's working,*" she said through the bond.

Nik pressed up against her back where they were balanced precariously on the same thick branch. He continued teasing her dangerously, his fingers circling her bodice or slipping into the cut of her gown. Never too far, but enough to distract her with a gathering need.

"*Too well,*" he replied, his tone far from pleased, and as though he had to be sure she was really within his arms and not Mordecai's below, he pressed his lips to her neck.

"*Keep your focus, or this will be over before we achieve anything,*" she scolded, though her body didn't want him to stop.

Nik still harbored his heightened Nightwalking ability from the Phoenix Blood potion, and it had been a highly dangerous and reckless plan to test it on Mordecai. Tauria didn't want to care for Samara's life, but Lycus stood by ready to act should things take a turn for the worse.

So far, the high lord was calling her by name, and when he

advanced Tauria detected no suspicion. He stopped near touching her, and though it was Samara he unknowingly looked down upon, Tauria's stomach churned with the thought of how easy it would be to grab his attention if she were willing to be his.

When Samara and Mordecai kissed, Nik went utterly taut behind her. His lips paused on her shoulder, and a possessive anger pricked her skin.

It took her a moment to realize why.

Mordecai believed in every way that it was Tauria he'd kissed, that she'd willingly kissed him back with such passion, and the thought was nauseous. Nik had manipulated Mordecai's mind to see her, smell her, possibly even taste her. No one could know the intricacies of a kiss with Tauria better than Nik.

Her fingers interlaced with Nik's over her hip, and she leaned into him a little tighter while they continued to watch Samara and Mordecai. Heat flushed her cheeks at the intimacy, and she wanted to look away, but they couldn't risk missing something. They didn't need for her to go this far, but Samara was convincing in her desire for him.

They broke apart, uttering a few more words to each other before Mordecai walked off. Tauria and Nik stayed still for a while longer as part of the plan, not wanting to give away their position even to Samara. Lycus approached cautiously as instructed, and when they were sure the high lord was long gone, he escorted Samara back to the castle through the secret tunnels.

To the people, she'd been killed for treason. To them, it was all a part of their plan when they needed a decoy. Samara had been almost eager to accept their bargain for her life to be spared, not seeming to care for the danger that would come in place of her end.

Nik began to climb down, stopping on each branch to aid Tauria, and while she found his concern endearing, she was at one with the height. Adjusting her footing, she leaped when he scaled down again, close enough to the ground already that she didn't cause too much of a disruption as she conjured a gust of her wind to break the fall. She reached out her arms, gathering the element before pushing down with enough force to land weightlessly.

Tauria stood, straightening her clothing as she extended her senses and scanned around. All clear. Nik thumped down behind her.

"Must you show off, love?" he said, his words gravelly before his warmth enveloped her from behind.

"Always," she replied, a smile curling her lips.

Nik groaned in pleasure. His hands on her waist twisted her, and before she could breathe she was pinned to the tree they'd been spying from. A primal shadow swallowed the emerald of his eyes as he planted his palm by her head and brought his body flush against her.

"He thought it was you," he mumbled darkly.

"That was the plan," she muttered.

His look held her, *claimed her.* "He thought he had his hands on you," he growled, fingers finding the slit in her dress without breaking eye contact. "He thought he was kissing *you.*"

Nik's mouth came down on hers hard. His palm curved over her backside and squeezed before sliding back down to hook her thigh around him. Tauria moaned softly as he pressed himself against her core. All that separated their skin was the material of his pants, and the buttons hitting her apex shot sparks of pleasure that had her unashamedly grinding against him. His tongue clashed with hers, a feverish demand. She kept her leg around him when his hand slipped between their bodies instead, knowing she was bare underneath. The first pass of his fingers through her slickness tipped her head back.

"You are mine," he groaned against her throat. "If anyone dared to lay a hand on you, I would kill them."

"I'm yours, Nik," she panted, aching with emptiness while he teased her, almost punishing her. "Always yours, and only yours."

The scrape of his sharp teeth pulled a gasp from her. His tongue traced his mark, and her knees became weak.

"I need you."

"I want to taste you here," he purred, planting his lips where she wanted him to bite. "But first..." Nik dropped to one knee, adjusting her leg over his shoulder, and she near climaxed at the sight of him below her. "Here."

Tauria bit down on her lip hard to suppress the moan that caressed her throat when his lips, his tongue, his fingers, devoured her. As her hands slid through his hair, she couldn't stop her hips from undulating in response to the assault, chasing and racing and skipping toward a pleasure so all-consuming. The wholly inappropriate location fueled an impulsive lust. They were perhaps safe in the dead hour, but this was still a public place, and there was no telling what human could decide to pass through the Westland Forest.

"Does this excite you, love?" Nik pulled away only to sink a finger into her as he climbed back up her body, planting kisses along her thigh, over her hip, until he stood working two fingers in and out of her at a slow, torturous pace. "Imagine the shock of our kingdom finding their king and queen in such a scandalous, sinful position so openly." His words vibrated along her jaw, his hand stroking and stroking, and Tauria was so close but just out of reach, and he knew it. She felt his smile along her neck. "But you enjoy that. In fact, I bet you wish someone were watching right now. Watching what I'm doing to you. You taste incredible, and you feel"—Nik groaned, curving in deeper, his other hand cupping her breast, which she wished were bare—"fucking perfect."

Tauria couldn't take it anymore. Her hands slipped from their tight grip in his hair, finding the buttons of his pants, which she fumbled with clumsily to undo. His hips jerked into her touch when she palmed the length of his hard arousal.

Nik's fingers retreated from her, and she moaned, needing more. Needing this wild urgency unleashed between them. Hooking his hands around her thighs, she wrapped her legs around his waist. Her hold on him lined him at her entrance, but he didn't move. His lips trailed over her chest, her collar, teasing her to madness over his mark.

"Nik, please," she breathed.

His hips slammed forward suddenly, and that pain shot to pleasure so fast she had to clutch him tightly with a cry when he stilled within her.

"I'm going to take you hard and fast right here," he growled.

Tauria could barely muster a nod, wanting it so badly with the fullness he created. "I want it," she rasped, kissing him once, twice. Trying to wriggle for some *friction*, but when his hold tightened, she whimpered. "I want you. I will always want you."

"With and without a bond," he said against her lips, a quiet note of pain slipping through that caused a sharp stab in her chest.

Tauria nodded. "With or without a bond, I choose you."

Nik began a slow thrust, and her brow pinched tightly. "If we do this…" he whispered, but he stopped himself.

She kissed him firmly, pouring the absolute ache of her devotion into it. "I love you," she said, pressing her lips to his jaw. "I love you." Down his neck and his pace picked up. "As eternal as the moon I love you, Nikalias."

Tauria's teeth sank into his skin, and Nik slammed into her. The taste of his blood flowed down her throat, and she was euphoric, greedy for it, the sensation mingling to shatter the stars within her body one by one, and she didn't ever want to stop detonating.

She pulled her mouth away and soared so far with him, the essence of what they were entangling her completely. Her head tipped back in utter bliss, eyes tightly closed as she climbed and climbed toward the peak of a shattering end with his hard, unrelenting thrusts, not feeling the roughness of the tree he pinned her against nor caring where they were, *who* they were.

"*Gods*, you are incredible," he rasped, the vibrations tingling over his mark, and she teetered right on the precipice of what he was about to do. "My queen, my mate. Mine." His teeth sinking into her skin made her clamp her legs around him tightly. His hands squeezed her thighs as he barreled into his own end. He didn't stop. Nik pounded into her at a furious pace that stretched their climax long and far. She trembled helplessly, her heart racing with adrenaline, every nerve cell touched by his pleasure, and the slow comedown was otherworldly.

Nik gave one final thrust before he stilled within her. His teeth left her, tongue lapping the raw wound tenderly. They panted in each other's arms, neither speaking for a suspended moment of ecstasy.

"You are my whole damn world, Tauria Silverknight."

She shuddered as he slipped from her, not breaking apart when her feet touched the ground. Nik fastened his pants, but she didn't want to go back just yet.

"I feel like I should be scared of what we're setting out to do," she said quietly, tracing thoughtful fingers over his jaw, his lips. "But I'm not afraid when I'm with you, even in the face of our worst enemies."

He took her hand, kissed her palm, and held her with sparkling emeralds that took her *home*. "As long as you are with me, I am at peace."

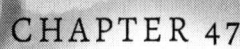

CHAPTER 47

Tarly

TARLY MARCHED THROUGH woodland, not registering the snag of branches that clawed at his ankles. He'd left Nerida four hours ago, and though he shouldn't be counting, he couldn't stop. He'd slipped out before the sun dawned and she awoke. She was safe in that town, could earn provisions by offering quick work—or be cunning enough to steal. He shook his head instantly. Her heart wouldn't allow her to steal, and the fact he felt confident of that only powered his steps harder. He already knew too much, felt too much, and couldn't afford to care for someone who could walk out of his life as quickly as she came into it.

Just as he was now.

"*Shit.*" Tarly paced the same spot as if it would untangle his thoughts. Or ease the tension of the pull to go back.

He was a pitiful, spineless coward. Katori whined as if in agreement.

"Don't you start," he grumbled.

He ran his hand through the lengths of his dark blond hair, in desperate need of a cut, like Nerida had said.

"*Dammit.*"

He marched back the way he came, and Katori took off running. He watched her until she disappeared out of sight and then earshot, not knowing if she were heading the same way or had simply ventured off for a while…or for good.

By the time he made it back to the town it was near twilight again. Tarly made a mental note to somehow acquire a horse. He rushed into the same inn, passing the desk and ignoring the man shouting after him as he leaped up the steps. Tarly burst into the room they'd occupied, knowing it was a long shot but clinging to the chance she'd still be there.

She wasn't. The bed they'd lain in together was empty, no trace they were ever there now everything had been rearranged for new guests. Tarly stumbled out of the room, taking a second to picture her face and how mesmerizing the golden glow of her brown skin was against the flames. He thought of his skin against hers, and how perfectly she'd fallen asleep against him. It was all real.

At the desk the man was seething, but Tarly ignored him. "The fae I was with—did she say where she was going?"

"You'd best leave and not come back," the man grumbled.

Tarly flexed his fist. "I don't want to threaten you, but I'm running low on patience."

The man took a second to assess if he were any real threat. Tarly was seconds from drawing a knife to emphasize his urgency.

"A man was in there having a drink, seemed to recognize her, and she left with him."

Tarly's heart lurched. "Willingly?"

He shrugged. "I guess so."

He did draw his dagger then, spearing it into the wood. "The scconds of mine you waste are seconds added if she's in danger," he snarled.

The man's throat bobbed, the first sign of fear quivering his expression. "They were chatting about a farmhouse, I believe. Someone ill."

It wasn't much to go on, but if she hadn't been hauled out kicking and screaming, Tarly clung to the hope she hadn't been found by the thugs who were after her. Still, the man's words enlightened him to the fact people recognized her here, some of whom even knew of her ability, and he was wrong: she was not safe in this town.

Tarly jogged onto the street and tried to catch a scent, but there were too many. He tried to ask around about a farmhouse, but the reception wasn't friendly or helpful. He didn't stop trying, looking down streets, pushing through crowds. He didn't think it could be hard to locate a farm, though there were several in this town, and he was beginning to itch with urgency.

Until he spotted something that stopped him in his tracks. Katori sat patiently in the distance by a narrow street as though waiting for him to catch up to her. Tarly huffed a laugh as he jogged her way, running a hand down her neck and allowing her to lead.

The end of the path opened up to an unmistakably large off-white building, surrounded by a field only occupied by a couple of grazing cows. Tarly breathed in the hope that she could be here and hadn't left this place too with how long he'd taken to come back.

He waited after knocking, anxiously flexing his fingers until the door swung open and a tall man answered with a far from warm welcome.

"I'm looking for a fae who might have come here with you," he began.

The man instantly shook his head. "No one here."

Tarly slammed his hand against the door he tried to close, and to the human's credit, he didn't balk, only made his frame taller in opposition. "I'm a friend," he ground out, though the dominant side to him sneered at the threat.

"I said there's no fae here."

"Sully?"

Gods, he'd never been so damn glad to hear that stupid name.

He gave the man a dead look. "Really?"

The human's jaw locked.

Only when he caught sight of her white locks did Tarly's

posture relax from the painful stiffness it had been locked in since early that morning.

"I thought you left," she said sheepishly. "I waited—"

"I did leave." The way she shrank back was a fist to his gut. "But I came back."

"Unnecessary of you." He deserved her cold tone, but damn, if it wasn't another gut punch. "You can drop the savior status for someone who needs it—someone like you. I'm perfectly fine."

"Do you want me to get rid of him?" the human asked her.

"I would invite you to try," Tarly snapped.

Nerida shot him a warning glare. "No, Derren, this won't take long," she assured him, resting a hand on his arm and stepping around him.

Tarly didn't like the bitter thoughts that stirred within him at Derren.

"Go be by your wife's side."

That seemed to switch something, and Derren nodded, but not without casting Tarly one final threatening look that flared his irritation.

Alone, she stood cross-armed as though waiting for him to explain, yet all words abandoned him. He didn't know what he would say to her when he caught back up.

"Are you still planning to head to Olmstone?" he tried lamely.

"You know I am."

He swallowed hard. "Short detour?" He gestured to the house behind them, only making her narrow her eyes.

"He happened to catch me as I was leaving the inn. His wife is very ill."

"Will she live?"

"Now she will, yes."

"That's goo—"

"I waited for hours," she cut in, the note of hurt stabbing his chest. "I thought maybe you went hunting, or to find more provisions, or that you were an early riser and wanted to enjoy the morning. I should have known right away you'd simply left since it was your first desire before we got here. Why pretend any differently?"

"I'm sorry." It was a pitiful response, but he meant it all the same.

"I don't need you to come with m—"

"I *want* to come with you." He spilled the confession even to himself. There was something about her that plagued his thoughts. That someone with the cure for sickness had somehow become his... He felt the slow spread of something terrifying, but he craved it. "People who get close to me…they have a habit of disappearing," he said. Nerida's face fell, but before she could voice the sympathy he couldn't bear, he rushed out, "But I realized I don't need that from you—for you to stick around. I just so happen to be a great tour guide for your destination."

Nerida surveyed the area in thought, an adorable sternness creasing her skin. "Dammit, Sully." Opening the door, she stepped aside, twisting to invite him in. "I just need to finish up here."

He wandered around, not dropping his edge of caution when she clearly felt at ease here. Tarly followed her upstairs, where they entered into a large, sparse room, but his attention was only drawn to the sickly woman in the bed, Derren sitting by her side with his hands clasping hers. The man didn't appear best pleased to see him, but his attention was stolen by Nerida, who was tending to his wife.

"We have very little coin to pay you," Derren admitted guilty.

Nerida only smiled. "I do not expect payment."

Tarly wanted to argue that her time and skills were worth something, the internal debate brought on mostly by the fact they were in desperate need for their journey. "We'd take a horse," he interjected before he could stop himself.

Nerida shot him daggers he expected, but if she wasn't willing to take the credit, he would.

"We only have one. She is all we have to travel and sell goods."

"And we have no desire to take that from you," Nerida said—more to Tarly than Derren.

Tarly gave a disgruntled head shake, leaning against the

window frame. "I just need to fetch some water to cool her down with. When the fever is tame, your wife will recover slowly after a few more days' bed rest."

Nerida shot him a warning look. He said nothing but peered out over the grounds while she slipped out.

Tarly observed the lack of cattle. "Rough season?" He attempted conversation.

"Nothing that the likes of you are familiar with," Derren grumbled.

He tried to keep his cool. "You don't know a thing about me."

"You think a few weeks overdue a haircut and some unwashed clothes can hide where you come from?"

Every muscle of Tarly's locked in defense. There was no way this man could possibly know.

"Although your arrows are made by an unskilled hand, your bow could fetch a handsome price. You can't afford craftsmanship and material like that unless you're someone with expendable coin."

It was clear Derren held something of a sour note for the fact, and Tarly wondered how impoverished they were. He decided not to engage further with someone who clearly held no interest. It was fine by him—Tarly preferred his company to be silent if he was forced to endure it anyway.

He scanned the field. Down the long path, movement caught his attention, and Tarly straightened with alarm.

"Who knows she's here?" he asked without taking his eyes off the approaching humans. Many of them.

"No one. Not that I know," Derren muttered, but something off about his tone attracted Tarly's hard look. The human didn't meet his gaze.

Could it be possible there was already a price on her head? Money was a temptress, a betrayer, and the existence of it he knew could turn friend to foe in desperate times.

"You have three seconds to tell me," Tarly snarled.

"I have no idea—"

"Two. You won't like the alternative if you don't."

"I-I didn't think she wouldn't ask for coin. And we…we need—"

Tarly swore. Already in front of the man, he grabbed him by the collar. The man's terror-filled eyes pinned him as though he thought his life would end in Tarly's hands.

"I won't say a word to her because it would break her heart to hear someone she thought she knew well enough to extend her kindness to would sell her out." He shoved the man, who stumbled into the bedpost. "But we're taking the damn horse."

He was downstairs in a few heartbeats, tracking her to outside, where she'd just finished filling a bucket from the well. They didn't have time for him to explain as the clamor of hooves grew louder. Tarly grabbed her hand, pulling her along, and the urgency made the bucket slip. He cursed as it ricocheted off the ground and sloshed water under their feet.

"What do you think you're—?"

In the barn, Tarly pushed her against the wall, clamping a hand over her mouth. Then he hissed, snatching his arm back.

"Did you just *bite* me?" Tarly stared down at the two puncture wounds that were already healing in surprise. His wholly inappropriate thoughts dispersed as he closed his fist, but the lick of her lips and her vacant look didn't help them stay away.

"I suppose I did," she muttered as if shocked by her own actions.

The horses outside shuffled to a stop, and Tarly took her hand again, pressing a finger to his lips as they crouched. They slowly made their way along the empty stalls until they reached the only one occupied. Tarly flicked the lock.

"I said we are not—"

"You seriously have no read on signals, dammit. Keep your voice down," Tarly whispered.

She seemed to read his concern and dipped low, eyes casting cautiously over the stall while Tarly tentatively grabbed the saddle and slipped it over the brown horse.

"Who is out there?"

"Friends of ours," he said sarcastically, swiftly equipping for a ride.

"We share friends now? Great."

Tarly's mouth curled as he braced his hands on her waist. Her palms went over his as if to protest.

"We can't take their only means of transport."

"He offered when he saw the incoming threat." Tarly shrugged. As far as he was concerned, it was the least Derren could offer after what he'd done.

Nerida threw suspicion over her shoulder, but he didn't have time to persuade her.

"Jump," he instructed.

Mercifully, she did as he asked, and with his aid she effortlessly swung her leg around to sit on top. "I can mount on my own just fine," she sniped.

Thrusting one foot in the stirrup, Tarly hoisted himself to slide snugly behind her. "I don't doubt it," he said with a hint of suggestiveness that surprised even him.

It was like he could feel her blush. Nerida shifted on the saddle but immediately seemed to realize that any movement she made was against *him*. He internally groaned. He should wish there had been another horse, yet with how warm and safe she felt against him, he was shamelessly relieved there *wasn't*.

Tarly guided the horse from the stall, knowing they'd alert the band of crooks the moment they took off.

"This seems ridiculous. How could they possibly know? It's likely just some acquaintances of—"

With a jerk of his heels, Tarly sent the horse into a canter out of the barn, taking the back exit that would lead into the woods instead of back through town.

"Over there!"

He heard the distant call and pushed the horse faster, knowing those on horseback would be quick on their trail. At this speed they could cross over into Olmstone within a day. That fact riddled him with dread and a want to turn away, but somehow Nerida's safety had become more important. Even Nether-bent on visiting the damn library, he couldn't abandon her now.

"I think they'll tire soon once they realize I'm not that special," Nerida said, breathless with adrenaline.

Tarly had many protests for that. "I think you underestimate your value. Whatever they want, they've decided you're the best way to get it."

"We know what they want, but there are other Waterwielders. This seems rather obsessive for one person." Something in her tone wavered with fear. A fear of being caught—but he didn't think it was about her physical being. He shook the thought to come back to the imminent threat.

"Perhaps. But I assume this trove is somewhere deep for them not to have found it already. They'll capture as many as it takes to find one with the power to reach it."

In his peripheral, he knew Katori was keeping up with their pace. The crooks were gaining on them, and Tarly swore. Up ahead he spied a cliff and couldn't be certain of the jumping distance to the other side.

"You need to slow, or the horse won't have time to stop," Nerida said, fear spiking in her voice.

Tarly ignored her. Leaning forward, he pressed them tighter together as he pushed the beast faster.

"You don't know this horse—it might not make that jump!" she called, anticipating his intention. "Katori won't make it!"

"She will," Tarly responded, confident in the wolf far more than the horse they'd stolen.

His plan wasn't so much a plan as it was a complete leap of faith.

He caught the sound of running water faintly over the pounding of hooves on the woodland terrain and the adrenaline pulsing in his ears. It confirmed a ravine below, but not one he thought to be deep enough to save them should the horse miss the gap.

Nerida swore this time, colorfully and repeatedly, adjusting herself as if she'd decided to brace for his reckless suggestion. Not that he'd given her much choice. "I'm trusting you won't let me fall," she grumbled.

He wasn't sure what she meant, didn't have a second to ask, when they approached the ledge, bracing for the leap that rose a quick dose of fear as he saw how large the gap was. He calculated, but it was too late. The horse didn't hesitate, to his immense relief, but those seconds in the air drummed with uncertainty. Until they landed, just barely, the horse's back feet catching on the ledge spiking his pulse.

He didn't have a second to breathe his relief when Nerida pushed up on the saddle, bracing one knee as she twisted around. In his utter shock, instinct hooked his arm around her waist. A loud crash of water roared behind them. Tarly spared one glance back, stunned by the mesmerizing wall of water she'd erected, and through that rippling veil, the men on horseback halted, calling out their curses.

Tarly looked up at Nerida in complete awe, unaware he'd pulled them to a stop. "Nice trick," he said.

Nerida huffed a laugh, though exertion began to tremble through her braced arms. Tarly didn't let her go as the horse pressed on, and she didn't let that barricade fall until they'd disappeared from out of the bandits' sights.

CHAPTER 48

Faythe

FAYTHE DIDN'T GLANCE in the mirror, but the outfit she wore exuded confidence. Fiery and bold, the asymmetrical crimson gown embellished with ornate gold detail squared her shoulders, and in true Rhyenelle style, her legs in black pants and knee-high boots had freedom of movement from the lengths behind her. Faythe sat quiet while Gresla braided and pinned her hair in an elegant fashion. She caught glints of more gold embellishments before they were slipped behind her head to adorn her pointed ears. The way they drew attention to them might have been intentional, but Faythe said nothing. She imagined it all to be beautiful, but more importantly, powerful.

When she opened her door, the sight of Reylan posted outside sank in her stomach. It never got easier to see him there like he had been all week, waiting to escort her as a mere guard. It churned a sickness she'd been battling, but now the meeting was here she had a chance to end the ridiculous *formality*.

"I wish you wouldn't demote yourself for me," Faythe said quietly as they walked to the grand council room.

"It's not like that—"

"You're Rhyenelle's leading general. You shouldn't be made a mockery of with babysitting duties." Her tone wasn't directed at him; these were remnants of the words she'd lost a lot of sleep over trying to figure out how this meeting would go, yet she knew nothing could prepare her. Key words scrambled around in her mind, but no sentences formed articulately enough. Faythe had been in a mental tug-of-war knowing no amount of finery would cover up the street garb she grew up in. No amount of time in fae court would fix her lack of elaborate schooling. Everything she presented herself as was a lie, and her mind taunted her with the knowledge over and over.

Reylan hooked her elbow, and as they met eyes, he seemed to read everything that stormed her mind. "I want to be here. By your side, in whatever way I can be." He drifted his senses down the hall, and Faythe tried not to let her ire rise. Then, gently, his knuckles tingled featherlight over her cheek. Though the touch was barely-there, it soothed her tenseness. "You have no idea how utterly stunning and daringly bold you look, Faythe." His hand dropped, but the confidence he instilled she grasped with everything she was. "I don't know how this will go, but I'll be right here when it's over."

"You won't be inside?"

He shook his head. "You're meeting with the highest nobles in the country. It is no place for me. No guards will be inside."

It was as much a place for him as it was for her. She couldn't possibly be the only one to see it.

"No matter what happens," he said, but he seemed to think better of believing his words were safe. He sent the rest to her thoughts instead. *"I love you."*

Gods, she wanted to embrace him so badly in that second she almost broke.

"They're waiting for you," a guard called from down the hall.

Her pulse jumped, then scattered, then scrambled to a rhythm she couldn't tame. But she nodded, raised her chin, and walked.

With one deep breath for composure, Faythe rounded into the hall without a glance back at her silver-haired warrior. Eyes...so many eyes fell on her in the chamber that was far bigger than High Farrow's. This wasn't the small council; this was the *whole* council of Rhyenelle, dozens of fae tracking her every movement. They studied her closely for the first time since hearing of her existence as a whisper.

Rhyenelle's lost heir, flesh and bone before them.

Agalhor sat at the head, watching her and offering comfort in his small smile. Sliding her sights to Malin was a mistake; the curve of his mouth tinged it all with unease in a second. The silence blared with judgment. Only the faint click of her shoes disturbed the hush they'd all fallen to the moment she glided through the doors. The path to the vacant seat on Agalhor's right seemed to stretch farther and farther ahead no matter how many steps she took. Her pulse drifted until it was no more than a faint reminder to keep breathing. Gravity anchored her—a new gravity that threatened to sink her deep into the earth, taunting at her that she was unworthy of walking this land in the crown she sought to wear.

The scrape of a chair rang through Faythe's racing thoughts. A human stood for her to take a seat, and when she did, it took everything in Faythe not to slump with relief that she'd made it. She smiled gratefully to make it believable that she belonged there.

Agalhor reached over the table, and though it stiffened every muscle to know all eyes were on them, Faythe lifted her own hand, sliding it into his upturned palm. He gave a faint squeeze, eyes communicating just what she needed to hear.

You belong here.

"I'm glad you all could join us today on such short notice, as I'm sure there are many questions regarding the fate of the kingdom and the threat of the war rising once again." Agalhor spoke so compellingly, with such certainty, every piece the leader he embodied. He let go of Faythe's hand and continued to list matters of concern that would be open for deeper discussion should anyone speak out.

Faythe absorbed every word, studying how he moved, how he pulled all attention to him so effortlessly, and occasionally she would steal glances down the table to see that while he spoke, everyone listened. Not simply because they had to; their faces were etched with admiration, attentive. She had stood watch over many council meetings in High Farrow, and the difference here was blaring. Despite all that came with her spymaster position from Orlon, Faythe was beginning to own every piece of her experiences, good or evil. Everything came with a lesson, and she was slowly escaping her cage to embrace it all, use it all, to hopefully one day become a worthy ruler like her father.

A lord halfway down the table became the first to speak after the king. "Your Majesty, I bring forth a concern that has been circling the kingdom for some time. The moment the princess was announced to be the princess. You can imagine our shock."

Faythe knew this was coming, knew the majority of the meeting would be a blanket of attention on her since she hadn't faced their questions before leaving on the quest.

"And now," the lord continued, "as fate will have it, upon her return she has become even more of a... *liability*."

The word locked Faythe's spine.

Agalhor spoke coolly. "Speak with explanation, Veseron."

Faythe forced her eyes to the lord, finding him nervously shifting his gaze from her as she met it. The quick glance he spared Malin put his next words into clarity.

"There are many who are concerned about who will be Rhyenelle's heir."

Malin's fingers traced the etchings of his goblet nonchalantly, but a barely-there curl twitched one corner of his mouth.

"Yes, I'm sure you have all been wondering if the line of succession has changed. I can assure you, it has not."

Faythe's heart tumbled from her chest, her skin slick with humiliation. She had been wrong in his belief in her. But Agalhor continued before she could spiral too deep.

"As tradition goes, the crown shall be passed on to the first born. For some time, we were led to believe that may never happen. Then we were blessed with a miracle that returned to us not once, but twice. To challenge that right would be foolish."

Just like that, panic switched to pride so fast she fought to keep her firm composure.

"Faythe."

Her name was a bell, a symphony, blaring out for all to hear. The king believed in her without question. Her head tilted, and she looked down the table at the many wary faces. They didn't know who she was or what she was, and it was on her to make them believe she had every right to her seat.

Faythe swallowed, subtly wet her lips, and took a deep breath to straighten. "I was sheltered from Rhyenelle for most of my life, but no more. I came here knowing the name that was attached to mine, but not with the expectation to have you bow before me because of it. I was but a stranger in your halls, a human with no experience of what it means to sit here today." She took a pause to remember her voice didn't have to be quiet. "There is something coming that is bigger than all of us. Some months ago, I left on a quest to stop it."

"And you did not succeed," Malin cut in smoothly.

"I did." Her face twitched in ire, but she would not let him win. "Or I would not be sitting here today."

"Your power is volatile," he went on anyway. "We have all heard of your personal execution of a fae in the town of Desture during your quest."

"That fae took a human life."

"And it was not on your judgment to end his. That is not how it is done."

Faythe's palms tingled with heat, her damned anger slipping as she fell for his goading. "I did not execute him without fair trial. I fought him in combat and won."

"Using mind tricks is not fair trial."

"As a human against a fae, I would argue it was more than fair."

"You acted on reckless impulse, and you cannot stand to admit it." Malin sat straight, speaking down the table to humiliate her further. "This is not the kind of heir we can entrust with the safety of the kingdom in light of what we face. She is impulsive and reckless with a power she cannot control."

A rumble vibrated over the table, and Faythe didn't realize she was the cause of it until she glanced at her hand resting upon the dark gray and crimson stone, beholding the glow between her fingers.

Malin only smirked. "You see? There is no telling what she's capable of at the slightest provocation. It would be madness to place the fate of the kingdom in her uncontrolled grip."

A new voice interjected. "All have been our concerns also."

Faythe's cheeks flushed. She knew it would be no easy task to sit under scrutiny today and was prepared to face objection, though the images in her mind of what could be said and how her character could be tested were nothing compared to sitting in the spotlight of it all. From more angles than she could count she beheld their nods of agreement.

"There is also the concern of Faythe's legitimacy," another added.

"Allow me to rest that concern." Agalhor had taken on a dark edge, and this was the first time she'd heard him invoke a challenge. His hand extended, and a young man eagerly brought over a document. Faythe knew what it was. "There is no one here who does not remember Lilianna Aklinsera. But what you do not know is that she was my wife. Her leaving did not break that." Agalhor rested the document on the table, inviting anyone to take it, but no one moved. "Faythe Ashfyre is our legitimate heir by blood and birthright."

"In our history, the line of succession has always fallen to the first *male* heir," a lord down the table said.

Faythe wondered how many people Malin had convinced to sway the vote in his favor. So far, this was by far the worst remark to surge her anger and determination and *need* to let him watch her rise.

"Let me add, she is my heir by *choice.*" It was bold of Agalhor to declare such a thing, deigning Faythe more fit to rule than Malin in front of the entire council. It may take their agreement to see her into power, but they trusted their king, respected him, and his judgment bore the respect of centuries of fair rule and strong leadership.

The flash that darkened Malin's hazel eyes spun a dizziness over her. He pinned her with a quick look of loathing in his embarrassment. "I agree," he said. Two words that were so far from liberating when they pierced Faythe with such purpose and precision. All she could do was prepare for the twist of the blade. "Faythe in power *could* be advantageous, as she grants us a hand to tie that could greatly strengthen the kingdom."

There it was: her worst dread coming to pass. She'd been a hopeful fool to believe it was a leash he wouldn't jump to so quickly. Malin had thought of every turn this meeting could take and come up with a solution to triumph every time.

"I need no tie to strengthen this kingdom." She spoke calmly, though in her rising anger she wanted to lash out. There was a time when instinct would have come too fast for her to see the mistake and stop it. Yet she was all too aware of the magick that rejoiced at those impulses. Her rage, her grief, her irritation—they were fuel that could erupt if she fed them too much.

"This opportunity could present itself perfectly," Malin went on regardless. "I'm sure you know of Lord Zarrius in High Farrow. He expressed his interest some time ago in an alliance, and he would make a highly advantageous match considering his influence in the king's council and his wealthy ties to precious trade." Malin recited it like a speech, and Faythe knew then this plan had been lingering for some time.

Malin knew. Knew how much Reylan meant to her—possibly what bond tied them. This was his most expertly crafted punishment.

"Our alliance with High Farrow is as good as forged," Faythe said, not backing down.

"As good as? These are not words you can run a kingdom with."

"King Nikalias is a dear friend."

"Again, we cannot trust your word from your time playing

spymaster for his father. Legitimacy means nothing without credibility."

"And what would make me credible? Being a son, not a daughter?"

"If your intentions were solely fixed on the good of the kingdom, you would see the prospect of this union could be of great benefit."

Faythe's hand flattened on the table—not with great force, but enough to communicate that she would not balk at his intimidation. "You have not seen what I have seen. You have not faced the dark fae. You have not faced *death*. I have, but not alone. This kingdom doesn't need forced alliances that offer nothing beyond appearance. It needs real strength in those who have fought with steel and will do so again, on the battlefield, for these people. Those who will stand for what is fair and right, and who always have and always will put the kingdom first." She wanted to speak his name but forced her mind to filter it out, knowing once she did there'd be no taking back the implication of what was between her and Reylan, and then they could remove him from his station.

"It is only forced if you resist," Malin said, disregarding all else to continue adding weight to the marriage proposal he'd anchored her to. "Lord Zarrius will be attending the Comet Ball next month. It would be my counsel that the princess at least entertain him, and should he come to offer what could strengthen us in this war, then you have my vote as Rhyenelle's heir."

His vote. Her stomach churned with sickness, more and more as she gleaned so many faces nodding in approval. She wanted to look at Agalhor—to beg, to plea, to know if there was a way for him to intervene as the thought of her *courting* someone else, never mind the infamous lord, crawled her skin like a violent betrayal.

He would have heard it all. Knowing Reylan stood right outside those doors dropped that guilt further. And Malin knew it too—she could tell by the wicked gleam twinkling in his eyes as he drank slowly.

"Very well," Faythe said, silencing the outbreak of murmurs.

"Your Majesty, if I may say one last thing?" Faythe didn't tear her gaze from Malin to make the request.

"Freely," Agalhor granted.

She took one deep inhale to find her courage. Bracing her hands on the table, Faythe stood. Then she trailed her eyes over each and every council member. "What you think you fear is a woman with power, but what you truly fear is the acknowledgment that our power already surrounds you. I may be the only woman at this table, but need I remind you, one of the most resilient monarchs of our time is Tauria Stagknight? One of the greatest minds is Marlowe Kilnight. One of our most esteemed commanders is Livia Arrowood. And one of our most powerful enemies is Zaiana, whom we keep well-guarded beneath our very feet." Faythe paused, letting her message sink into the small minds of those who sided with her cousin. "I will entertain Lord Zarrius by my will, my way. It will be with the interests of the kingdom in mind, to find someone who can bring strength and unity, not a spectacle. And should I see neither of those traits in Lord Zarrius, rest assured my mission to find it won't change."

Silence grew thick for seconds that dragged like minutes. Faythe didn't move, and neither did a single soul, but she dared to gauge their expressions. While none offered warmth or assurance, she also detected little objection or wariness.

"Agreed." Agalhor was first to break the silence. "I think that means we are done here for now. The matter of this…alliance can be discussed further privately, unless there is reason to inform the council."

When no one spoke out again, the king's nod had chairs scraping back, and the lords started to leave as the main doors were hauled open. Faythe couldn't stop her eyes from darting through the heads to spot his silvery hair, but Reylan wasn't outside. Her head felt weighed down.

"We will want to make an impression with the High Farrow lord," Malin sang, watching the backs of the last fleeting bodies.

Faythe's graze snapped up to him then with the might of her rage.

"It will not be a great start if he believes your reputation to be…compromised."

"That's not what this is about, and I couldn't give a damn about *that* reputation." She spoke quietly, aware the doors were open though the last of the council had gone.

"If I may cut in," Agalhor said calmly over their feud. "What Malin suggests is a smart political maneuver."

Her gaze snapped to him, and the faint rise of his brow was a reprimand to listen before she spoke.

"But Faythe is right. This kingdom has always been led by those able to see strength in the unlikeliest of places. This will be Faythe's judgment and choice. No marriage has ever been forced in this name, nor will her claim to the throne depend on it."

Faythe could have sagged with relief, but not fully. Though she had the king's assurance her hand could not be sold, it didn't erase the fact marrying her off was a favorable option to the nobles vouching for Malin's every word.

She wondered with a heavy heart upon leaving the council room if the other half of her soul would be the price to pay for the crown with two hands reaching for it.

CHAPTER 49

Tauria

TAURIA COULDN'T TEAR her eyes from the note she held. The fire she stood before beckoned to claim it.

"Nik," she breathed.

He pressed into her from behind, planting soft lips to her shoulder. "Love."

"He wants me by week's end, or it's over."

Nik stiffened, his hands on her waist circling around her tightly. "We knew this was coming," he said, but the calmness of his voice released a shadowy threat.

She did, though it did nothing for the panic that tried to seize her. It tightened in her throat, convincing her she couldn't go through with it, couldn't lose…

He spun her around, palm slipping across her cheek to steady her rapid breaths. "We make sacrifices in order to advance. Lead him into the gambit we set. But no matter what he believes, you are mine, love." Nik kissed her firmly, passionately.

Tauria gripped him, pulled him, gave him everything she was now their days were numbered. It terrified her what could change. That *they* could change.

A knock on the door of the underground room drew them apart. Despite expecting them, it was an instant relief when Lycus slipped inside escorting Samara.

Tauria eyed Samara with an edge of caution. She couldn't quite figure out the complexity of the former lady's mind. She didn't trust her fully, but she was their only hope. "How are you?" she forced herself to ask, unable to let go of the small kernel of sympathy she held for Samara over her resentment.

"I'm well, Your Majesty." Samara shifted, casting her eyes to Lycus as if he were the only one she trusted.

"You put on an excellent performance last week," Tauria commended, watching her every flicker of emotion. "You know the kiss was not necessary, don't you?"

"Yes."

"Yet that part you played excellently, I must say."

"I-I did what I thought would get his attention."

"It worked," Tauria announced, holding up the small parchment. "We leave in a few days."

"Are you sure you want to go through with this?" Lycus interjected.

Tauria slipped a look to Nik, whose eyes were saddened in agreement.

"It's the only way to gain his trust and get him to take us right to the ruin," Nik said.

"And if he doesn't? What if he takes her somewhere else entirely?"

Tauria answered. "Then we'd better hope Samara continues to be an excellent actress to coax the information from him."

Samara stood a little straighter as though the prospect excited her. Tauria couldn't comprehend it when she'd fully expected to feel regret for using her.

"You two are willing to go into this no matter what could happen?" Lycus looked between her and Nik, who gravitated toward her.

"We don't need to be reminded," Nik warned, his hand slipping around Tauria's waist as if he wasn't even aware of it.

"I'm coming with you."

"I won't stop you."

The two of them shared a nod of respect, though Tauria was riddled with unease to have them both in potential danger.

"Zarrius is heading for Rhyenelle. The timing is exactly in our favor, and they don't even know it."

"Where are you hoping he'll lead you?"

"To wherever they're holding the ruin," Nik said. "To Dakodas if need be."

CHAPTER 50

Faythe

REYLAN HAD LIED.
He wasn't waiting for her when she left the meeting. He wasn't at her rooms. He didn't meet her for supper. Faythe was overcome with a restlessness like she'd never felt before. A piece of her felt disconnected from the rest, and she couldn't focus.

"I'm sure he has good reason." Marlowe's words weren't a comfort, but Faythe appreciated her friends' company, or she'd be driving herself to madness with the ugly thoughts that stirred at Reylan's absence and what it meant.

"Likely called to whatever general duties he gets up to," Jakon offered.

Faythe stood by the window watching the sunset burst across the sky with fiery colors. Her foot tapped, and she bit at her fingernails.

"This Comet Ball, is it a Rhyenelle tradition?"

She knew Jakon was only trying to distract her, and she obliged because she needed it. She twisted to where her friends sat across from each other in the small games room, each holding a fan of cards.

"They call it Matheus's Comet. It appears every seventy-five years."

Faythe couldn't sit still, so she'd opted out of the game, but she floated around to Marlowe's side in her curiosity.

"I for one am very excited to see it. It's a chance in a lifetime for us." Marlowe's chipper voice was a short-lived brightness, as though she realized the moment it left her lips the tone was out of place.

Faythe flicked her brief attention to Jakon, heart cracking at the quick flinch of his brow as he reorganized his cards. None of them knew what kind of lifespan Marlowe would have, though Faythe intended to find out. She could only guess the age of Augustine, who'd appeared around forty—

Faythe drew a shallow breath. She was stolen away from the world around her by a memory. Something that opened answers too incredible to believe. He was the only one who could confirm the impossible truth, and Faythe blanched with it. She had to seek him out.

Phoenixfyre. That was what Gus had said when she asked how to find him again. But how…

"Everything good?" Jakon's voice tugged on her tether to the present. Her mind reeled, but to divert, she glanced over at Marlowe's cards.

"Knight diamond."

"Hey, no cheating," Jakon scolded.

The laugh that escaped Faythe settled a longing in her chest when the echo died. Things that were once as carefree as their joy now felt like tokens to be savored.

"I don't have to cheat to best you at cards." She brushed him off.

He grumbled, choosing his counter move. Marlowe's soft giggle fluttered throughout the room. They swapped turns, Faythe the player and Marlowe obliging her every decision. They laughed, and it was a sound that defused all burden, leaving them fully in the moment. To remember, just for a little while, that despite so much change this was who they would always be. At their core, they were three friends who meant the absolute world to one another.

Marlowe set her cards down with the last vibrations of her chuckle when Jakon folded out. Then reality creeped back so fast it threatened to snatch the warmth they'd expelled from the room through their games and jokes.

"I made something I hope can help you," Marlowe said, standing.

Faythe followed Marlowe's hand as it dipped into the pocket of her dress. She produced two bracelets, one a little thicker, both adorned with a stone that seemed to trap shadows within it.

"It worked for Nik and Tauria—the concealment magick I put in them. But there was little physical touch that needed to be hidden with them. It was the bond between them that was successfully cloaked, but they had to be cautious."

Faythe blinked at the silver bands. "You mean…they won't detect Reylan's scent on me?" Hope gave life to her withering heart in its pitiful state.

Marlowe's face was both uncertain and hopeful. "That's the idea. But like with Nik and Tauria, I would limit how much you share. My magick isn't all that powerful. I'm still figuring it out, but—"

Faythe's hands closed over hers. "It will be enough, and I can't thank you enough, truly. You're utterly brilliant."

The flush of Marlowe's cheeks at the compliment was a familiarity Faythe didn't realize she'd missed so much. She pulled her friend in for an embrace. She couldn't be more grateful to have them both here. After everything she'd been through, and to find out all they'd faced in their time apart…

There was no greater gift than right here and right now.

Night cloaked the sky and the stars had awoken by the time Faythe tore away from her friends, reluctant to be trailing the halls toward a lonely destination. Her rooms she could hardly stand to sleep in without him there.

Closing her door behind her, Faythe halted, struck utterly still at the tall figure leaning over her balcony railing. The sight of Reylan raged conflicting emotions: a pain that swelled and swelled from missing him; an ugly wrath that felt *wrong* aimed at him; and the exhaustion of her ache for him. She unlocked the balcony doors, yet he didn't turn to her when she stepped out. Her jaw locked in disappointment.

"Is that it then?" She broke the silence at last, watching the muscles in his shoulders lock. "Someone threats to stand in our way and you just bow down."

Reylan straightened, and her breathing came hard, trembling her body with how foreign her nerves were around him. When he turned, his features cut hard, but they also weighed heavy as if he'd come from battle. She couldn't bear his silence. Faythe continued the outpouring of emotion.

"You would really let me go so easily? What about—?"

"No," he said before she could even finish. "I'm doing something wrong if you haven't gathered that I *can't* let you go. Not for a damned minute."

"Then where have you been? You promised…" Her voice wobbled and she cut off her words, swallowing the growing lump in her throat that seemed selfish.

"Faythe," he breathed her name. The defeat in that tone made her heart stumble.

"You heard it all, didn't you?"

He didn't need to confirm when the glittering misery in his sapphire irises ripped through her. Faythe looked over every inch of him. There was nothing formal in his attire; he only wore a loose shirt and black pants, and paired with the roughness of his hair she wondered what outlet he'd turned to with the emotions she could feel the remnants of beating within him.

"It means nothing," she whispered, broken by the turmoil she'd caused him. "Entertaining the lord. It's just politics."

"Just politics." His bitter laugh stung. "Your hand is not a chess piece."

"Nor will it ever be. You have to trust me."

"I do. I trust you more than I've allowed myself to trust anyone in my miserable lifetime, Faythe."

"Don't talk like that."

"Like what? Without the pretense to cloud over what neither of us wants to see?" He drove his hand through his silver hair before he gestured at her. "Look at you, Faythe. I almost went to my knees the moment I saw you today. So fucking perfect I couldn't believe I ever thought I could stand by your side and call myself your equal."

Faythe's chest rose and fell deeply. No sorrow or pain; only anger and incredulity, so she couldn't take any of it as a compliment. "Don't do that," she said through gritted teeth. "Don't discredit yourself on words of bullshit. You are my equal, like it or not, Reylan Arrowood. The fates have damned you to be."

"Damned me?" His sapphire eyes were ablaze, the smile he wore dark. "Gods, I want to fight with you until it drives me to madness. I want to love you until it kills me."

"Then don't *run*."

They stared off, building a charge between them, matching breaths of anguish in a battle of hearts.

"I knew the consequences of falling in love with you as a human, but I couldn't stop. I knew the opposition that would stand in our way if I were in love with the daughter of a king. Fate is twisted and cruel, pairing us together with so much to separate us. But I wouldn't change it. Not for anything. I don't want anything as much as I want you. Even if it means I have to stand by your side and watch you with another, because I can't leave you, no matter what it means for me."

Faythe crossed the few steps to him, trying not to hesitate when he almost retreated. Reylan opened his mouth to protest, but Faythe took his hand after dipping hers into her pocket and slipped the metal band around his wrist.

His eyes met hers with question.

"I hate everything about it. But now, will you kiss me like neither of us gives a damn about *title*? Like we both remember I too came from nothing, and I was yours long before I was dedicated to this kingdom. Kiss me like we can stand against it all when the time is right. Like this is what you want. Loving me is not without challenge, nor question, nor a whole lot of mess, but Reylan, I choose you, and if you still choose me, then to the Nether with anyone who opposes that."

Reylan's hand curled around her nape, his jaw locked with anguish and heartache. His fingers wove through her hair and fisted, drawing out a gasp as he angled her head to lock with his irises of icy flame. He shook his head in disbelief. "So fucking perfect."

His mouth crashed to hers with a force that exploded every pent-up emotion. Not just from that day—maybe it had been building since they acknowledged this fight would come. Their defiance ignited, fusing a silent promise until the end of days.

Reylan's hands squeezed at her waist, crawled up her spine, and roamed her body with such reverence she almost lost her mind. Yet Marlowe's warning still rang through, and all she could think of then was protecting him.

Faythe broke their kiss, panting in his tight hold that brought their bodies flush.

"We don't yet know how strong the enchantment is with physical touch," she breathed. "Best not test its boundaries too quickly."

Reylan's groan pricked her skin, his mouth lingering over her throat to say, "Best not." He trailed his breath around her until they'd switched sides, and Faythe's eyes fluttered. "As much as I wish to worship you right here, outside, in every scandalous way, before your kingdom."

"*Our* kingdom," she corrected, and the notion flared something powerful and defiant in her chest.

Reylan released her lust, turning it into something far more tender when he cupped her cheek. "You make me *want*, Faythe.

Want things I never have before. To be with you. To be *worthy* of ruling by your side."

"There's nothing I could want more than you, Reylan."

His forehead rested against hers, his troubles far from eased. His demons far from chased. "You handled yourself incredibly in there," he said quietly. "Like a true leader."

"I didn't think you stayed."

"Until the very end. You should know that I had every intention of waiting for you despite how dangerous I felt being mere feet away while Malin tested you time and time again. I can't deny I didn't already know his proposition was a possibility—only, I didn't think it would come so soon. That he would try to scare you from the throne by tying your hand by obligation."

"I only said what I had to. I have no plans to truly entertain Zarrius. There's more to him you should know, but…" Faythe searched the conflict in his eyes, her chest aching. "Why did you leave if not from what you heard?"

Reylan shook his head. "It doesn't matter right now. I'm only sorry I wasn't there for you."

Faythe's arms wrapped around him, her cheek pressed to his chest, and she soothed all the aches of the day with his steady heartbeat.

"You're here now."

CHAPTER 51

Tarly

THEY TRAVELED FOR days, stopping only when necessary to catch some rest, not that it was of any great comfort, nor did it offer any substantial hours of sleep in his state of alert. They ate whatever berries Nerida found and deemed safe, but Katori was lacking in her hunting skills, and his hunger started to grate on his mood.

That, and Tarly knew he stood on his homeland territory. He couldn't help always looking over his shoulder or studying Nerida as if the traitor he was to Olmstone were branded all over him. He'd abandoned the kingdom when the worst time had come. He'd run, and with that choice he no longer deserved the crown he once wore.

When Nerida slipped one foot into the stirrup, Tarly by default went to aid her.

"I don't need you to help me do everything."

The surprised of her words made his hands drop, but his low energy left him no room to argue. Nerida mounted, and Tarly chose to take the reins and walk for a while.

"Your display with the ravine has likely only fueled their hunt.

It's no small feat to be able to do that," he all but grumbled.

"What happened to 'nice trick'?"

It was beginning to show he wasn't the only one feeling the effects of very little food and rest. He didn't deign to respond.

"You know, if this is becoming too much for you—"

"I'm not leaving you."

A pause of silence.

"Get on the horse, Sully."

"That's not my name."

"You've still to give me one. Until you do, it stays."

He took a deep breath to keep from spilling his irrational irritation. Not toward her—not really. If only they could find a way to get some damn coin for a decent meal...

"You're so Nether-bent on staying with me, yet I hardly know who you are. How do I know you're not like them? Luring me to sell me," she wondered, though without an ounce of real concern.

"It does sound tempting right now," he grumbled.

"You're even worse company when you're hungry," she muttered back.

"We're coming to a small town called Vansire," Tarly diverted. "You might not like the idea of theft, but it may be all we have to gain something of sustenance."

Nerida hummed. "Don't do anything rash. I've been collecting herbs and plants I can make into remedies if I find an apothecary that will lend me a station for an hour and some minor ingredients in exchange for a cut of the profits."

In his current state, Tarly didn't voice that kind of patience might not sustain him.

"Are we far from Vesmire?"

The name rang through him, jolting his heart with dread. "No." Not far at all. They could be there in a day by foot, then another to the library he could barely think of without flashes of horrific memory that roused a panic he tried to ignore. His shoulder subconsciously hitched, the screech of Lennox as a dark fae echoing in his ears, then a flame that seemed to come straight from the Nether erupted through his body when Lennox's teeth pierced his flesh.

"Are you all right?"

Nerida's voice lashed him back to the present. He didn't realize he'd stopped walking, and with his hold on the horse, so did she. Tarly shook his head to dispel the trickle of that haunting memory. Straight ahead down the hill, the quaint town came into view.

Tarly still walked beside Nerida on the horse down the stone path that led into Vansire. Twilight fell, and the streets were lit with an amber glow.

"We should split, just while you hopefully find your herbal place."

Nerida swung her leg around the horse, bracing on his shoulders only lightly, always aware of his injury, and something about that never failed to warm him. He guided her down.

"Apothecary," Nerida corrected.

"Right," he muttered. "I'll find you in an hour. If anything happens, this town is small and quiet enough that I should hear if you make a loud enough commotion." Tarly began to walk away with the horse.

"I'm glad you're here."

His whole body stiffened with her jarring words. Twisting his head back to be sure she'd spoken them, he found Nerida fidgeting with her fingers.

"I'm glad not to be alone, I mean."

Of course, it wasn't his company in particular that was desirable, but it didn't matter. A warmth fluttered through his chest, though all he could give was a nod and a barely-there smile.

"One hour," she repeated, twisting and quickly making off as if nerves had overcome her.

Tarly watched after her for a few seconds until she disappeared around a stone corner. He blinked away the flash of desire to follow her, immediately feeling like a pining dog.

Tarly had his own reasons for needing away, and he led the horse to find it.

He scanned various streets in search of Nerida. It was a little short of an hour since they'd parted, but he hadn't been able to shift the itch since she left. His concern for her became a new consuming thought, keeping him on edge and unable to settle unless she were right by him.

He laughed at himself. It wasn't as though he'd offered her any substantial protection considering all that she was capable of. It didn't matter. Without realizing, Tarly had promised her every arrow in his quiver, every punch he could throw—at least until they made it to the library and he could escort her somewhere he knew she'd be away from potential danger and out of sight of those who sought her.

It kept him...*wanting*. To do something other than watch the sun turn to the moon without much care about what happened on the land around him.

He managed to ask around enough to find what they deemed a close enough version of an *apothecary*. Nerida wasn't there. He became antsy in his search. Katori whined, taking off, and his hope sparked as the wolf had led him directly to her once before. Yet the person Tarly caught a flickering glimpse of instead as she stepped into an establishment...

Stopped time.

He halted abruptly, blinking once, twice. Even though she dipped out of view, his mind captured that image, tormenting him that he was wrong, or worse...*right*.

He strained in a physical and mental tug-of-war, his heart pounding, splitting open a wound that hadn't fully healed. Tarly stood outside the inn, wondering what outcome he was hoping for by storming inside, but one thing was certain.

He had to know.

Tarly scanned the occupants furiously, diving deep into his consciousness that would never erase her scent even after all this time. The sting of alcohol and the musk of men and fae made that difficult, but he could find her in any crowd. The edges of her beauty were blurred, but he would never forget.

When he landed on familiar golden locks from behind, his pulse stuttered, and the ground was nearly pulled from under him. *It didn't make sense.* He marched for her, ignoring the disgruntled protests as he pushed through the crowd waiting to be served a drink. He didn't think about what he was doing when he hooked her elbow, spinning her around. Tarly had never tunneled so far from reality than in that second. He locked onto those eyes, certain he had to be dreaming when the pull into the green of them stabbed him with a relief so overwhelming it almost brought him to his knees.

"Isabelle," he muttered, blinking many times as though the fae's features would change. As if he could be wholly mistaken. So quickly, relief became dread. Dread became a battering of questions he was certain to crumble under. But he had to know. "How is this possible?"

Only at seeing the recognition flash in her wide eyes and blanched skin did the weight of the truth crush him. It was her.

His mate.

"Tarly," she muttered as though seeing a ghost, though it was she who was supposed to be dead. She glanced over him slowly, and he could do nothing but release her as if the sound of her voice were a trick. "What happened to you?"

Disappointment flooded over him at hearing her first reaction. Not joy or relief or longing. Not the reunion he'd dreamed of endlessly, a fool's fairy tale that he could defy death to see her again. The one wish he held over all had been answered before him but only impacted him like the day he found her body.

Thought he found her body.

"What happened to *me?*" he breathed, incredulous. Anger—no, *rage*—started to cloud over him while he tried to make sense of it all. He shook his head. "I organized your funeral," he said darkly. His eyes pinched closed as he stumbled a step back, praying in that moment this were a nightmare because it was *wrong.* Something was horribly wrong, and the anticipation of her explanation coiled so tightly in his gut.

"What's going on?"

Tarly's gaze snapped to the voice that joined them. He didn't think he could be smacked harder with the unfathomable truth. He recognized the fae as a guard who'd been close to his father until he deserted his role. Pieces slid together so fast Tarly couldn't stop them despite the ribbons that sliced apart his soul.

The fae's hand slipped around Isabelle's waist, and then it all became clear. It slammed into him so hard that what little he grappled of his heart obliterated.

"You," Tarly growled, the flash of rage overtaking his vision, and before he could calculate his actions he'd pinned the bastard to the wall. His fists connected with his face over and over, unable to stop the unleashing of an agony so deep it felt like it would kill him if he didn't release it.

People were shouting, a clamor ensued, and a few people tried to grab him, but Tarly didn't register any of it except his target…until his vision blurred, his chest heaved, and it took three fae to haul him away from the ex-guard who lay slumped in a bloodied heap.

Tarly started to come back into himself, realizing the physical beating he'd delivered, unlike anything that had ever come from him before. A violence that wasn't him. But he was hurting so badly he couldn't even feel disgust or shame. He caught his breath, turning his utter heartbreak toward the one who caused it all.

Isabelle clamped a hand over her mouth, eyes wet with tears, but they meant nothing to him. She looked to him as if he were a stranger—a monstrous one. She looked to him as if he'd shown her every reason why she'd done what she did to him, and that understanding cleaved through him, turning his pain to numbness. A painless, worthless, numbness.

"Was a life with me truly so awful to imagine?" he rasped. Dipping into his pocket, he produced his mother's necklace. "So awful that the only way you thought to get away was by faking your death." He could hardly stand the sight of the necklace. All it reminded him of now was the day he picked it up from the burned remains of an unknown he'd believed to be his mate.

For a second, she showed remorse. But it quickly fell to a *pity* he despised more than anything. It risked raising his anger.

"I didn't want that life…"

"I would have let you go." His voice rose again. He shook his head vacantly before defeat weighed him quiet. "As much as it would have torn me apart, if that was your wish, I would have let you go."

"I tried to tell you I wouldn't fit that role, that royalty was never what I wanted, but you didn't listen. You told me we would work it out and the court would understand, but they would not, Tarly. I was low in station; you didn't know what it was like to be the laughingstock of court."

"I never forgave myself, thinking you'd taken your life because of me."

"I'm sorry—"

"The exile?"

She flinched, and Tarly wanted to walk away in fear the dagger lodged in his heart wasn't done being twisted. "I went to Keira—"

Tarly raised a hand, slowly clenching it into a fist he dug into his forehead with his eyes clamped shut. That was all he needed to hear to figure out the rest on his own.

"I don't doubt you loved me, Tarly, but you can't deny I was also a defiance in the eyes of your father," she accused.

Tarly's jaw locked, wanting to shout and rage, but as he breathed deep, he became aware that the entire establishment had hushed at their display. A few tended to the groaning fae who was slipping in and out of consciousness from Tarly's brutality. A few looked at him in fear, awe, and he realized all at once their conversation had enlightened everyone there to who he was, shining a spotlight on their *prince* in a volatile, disgraceful state.

"Is it true what they say…?" One brave voice spoke up. "Has the capital fallen? Are we under the rule of Valgard now?"

Tarly had no answers for their wariness. He stood before them as their deserted prince, and he couldn't bear it. A flicker at the window caught his eye, and the silvery wisps of hair sent his heart tumbling from his chest. Immediately, he spun for the door to catch Nerida, hoping she hadn't heard too much, but he was halted by Isabelle's call.

"It's time, Tarly," she said quietly.

He didn't turn around, but he couldn't move, hearing only echoes of her words as if they were underwater and he was drifting. His soul cried out, scorched with an immeasurable pain, and while it immobilized him, he accepted it. The scent of her blood drifted to him as the final *snap* of their mating bond. His rejection of it singed like flame, cleaving him in half, and a ringing filled his ears. He tried to stay composed, tried to coat himself with numbness instead as he took one step forward, but he stumbled. He couldn't turn back to see if she was suffering the same. It felt as if a knife had been lodged in his gut and the pain was spreading like a rapid fever. He took another step, needing air…needing away.

Rejected.

It settled easier than he thought, though he supposed it was a concept he'd come to be acquainted with long before now. Yet the physical effects were punishing.

Outside, he gulped the air greedily. It had started to rain, a misty kind that made visibility foggy, and dampness coated him fast. He had to find Nerida. Above his exhaustion from such a life-changing severance, he needed to know what had caused her retreat. He needed to know she was safe.

Clenching his teeth, he pushed through the weight of feverous magick and took off running.

CHAPTER 52

Tauria

Her heart had never weighed so heavy, but it was time. Tauria had made peace with the many ways this first meeting could unfold. At least, she thought knowing, preparing, could make it easier.

She had lied to herself all week, holding Nik tighter, using their bond in every way to leave nothing of it untouched, unexplored.

The horse she rode cracked the branches scattered across the Dark Woods of Galmire. Mordecai's instruction was clear: enter the woods and he would seek her out. Every hair rose as her eyes darted over the misty floor, squinting through the darkness. Everything was so deathly still she couldn't fathom passing through here unless absolutely necessary. The sound of her pounding heart canceled out anything else, but she didn't think anything pleasant would echo chirps or song through these woods anyway.

"There you are," he said, voice distant like a stroke of shadow. "My princess." Closer now, and Tauria's next exhale shuddered from her.

"Did you doubt I would come?" Tauria answered, not allowing her eyes to seek him first as the horse pulled to a stop.

A rumble of dark humor drifted over her. "You think me a fool to trust you so easily after all you did?"

She couldn't give in to the snare of fear.

To be safe, Nik couldn't help her even through the bond. This part she had to face entirely alone. To keep her calm, Tauria replayed that morning over and over. Remembered every treasured feel of her mate and the hours they'd lost to each other. The promises they'd sealed for each other.

Movement caught in her vision, and every muscle locked stiff.

Sharp talons raced her pulse, almost eye level with her atop the horse. She'd hoped he would have had them glamoured. The texture up close reminded her of leather. Thick over the cartilage but with a transparency to their span, which tucked in tightly.

"Are you afraid, princess?"

His question snapped her gaze down to his for the first time. Stark onyx with a predator's gleam she would never forget.

"Intrigued," she all but whispered.

The curl of his mouth dried out her throat. Then his hands came up, poised to assist her down from the horse, and she couldn't refuse.

Having to lay her hands on him twisted her stomach, and she checked again and again that her connection to Nik remained impenetrable. Mordecai took her waist, guiding her down with surprising tenderness, and when her feet planted on the ground… he didn't step back.

She knew the twinkle in his black irises. It was one of prize and admiration, and she could hardly tame the beast in her chest. Maybe he stepped closer. Maybe he leaned down a fraction when she wished he wouldn't. She'd hoped Samara hadn't left *that* much of a lasting impression with her kiss that he'd immediately crave it again.

No. No, no, no.

It could ruin everything if she couldn't go through with it.

"You're really in this with me? There is no going back," he said with a gravel that grated her skin with its wrongness.

"I'm here, aren't I?" she whispered, playing along. Always with a mask to wear.

His knuckles grazed along her cheek, and she turned to stone. She stopped breathing. "I confess, Tauria Stagknight, I haven't quite figured out what it is about you, but I haven't been able to get you off my mind. Our reign...would be most legendary."

Breathe. Just breathe. She couldn't allow her empowering vision of standing by Nik's side to be tainted by the high lord's twisted fantasy. "Why do you think I risked all this?"

That earned her a smile of pride and conquer. Mordecai was winding to her every word, and she should have been relieved, but all that trembled beneath the surface was hot and cold dread, so all-consuming the only thing she could do was hope he couldn't detect it.

His fingers angled her chin, and she could do nothing but answer to his touch, or everything would crumble in a second. His lips inched closer, and *Gods*, she wanted the world to open up beneath her to spare her from such betrayal. *Wrong.* It was so, so wrong, and tears pricked her eyes as she tried to numb herself to the waves of grief that lapped at her.

"I have many important things to do, Mordecai."

Tauria gasped at the sensuous voice that had plagued her nightmares. The shortness of her breath to keep from inhaling the high lord's scent didn't match the skips of her heart. Her balance swayed. Twisting, the face she expected came into full, fiery clarity against the stark backdrop of the woods.

"Marvellas," Tauria choked. "Why is she here?"

She knew. *Gods*, she knew, yet Tauria wished she didn't. She prayed to every damn entity that could hear her that she was wrong and the Spirit's presence had been lured in for some other purpose.

Mordecai's hand on Tauria steered her toward the Great Spirit, who stood there assessing her, not hiding her boredom. Mordecai's touch repulsed Tauria, though she decided she feared Marvellas far more than the high lord whose direction she wanted to protest.

"You'll understand, princess," he said calmly, but with enough of a warning that she heard the test, "why this is necessary. You said you would do anything for me."

She knew he'd never trust her without this, but she'd spent weeks that had gone too fast in turmoil, begging everything, *anything*, that would listen, but knowing there was no way out of this.

He locked eyes with her when they stopped before Marvellas, and the chill that seeped into her bones she welcomed, hoping it would numb the soul-deep agony that was to come. "I don't like to share, Tauria. Especially not when it comes to you. So tell me,"—a long, drawn-out pause stretched between them—"are you willing to sever your bond for me?"

There it was.

Having recited the million ways this condition would be delivered, Tauria realized now it didn't make the blow hit her any less. She couldn't breathe—wasn't sure gravity still held her when a weightless *nothing* took over. This Netherworld she was living didn't seem real. The sacrifice she'd have to make to advance was second only to her own life.

A life.

Faythe had given hers, and at the thought of her undying bravery, Tauria found solace in the belief that what they would gain was worth far more. She planned to still have her future with Nik. As long as they lived, that would never change.

"Yes." The word slipped from her lips, but she didn't hear it. Didn't feel it. It went against every instinct screaming and clawing to fight. "Though are you sure this is what you want?" Her question was delivered with futile, fleeting hope, but she had to try. "You know it was vital in my communications with Nik in Olmstone. It could benefit us to have that insight with this new path."

"Forgive me, Tauria, but I do not trust that to be true. That Nikalias would stand by and allow this to happen, and frankly,"—his hold on her tightened, and a slipped flash of anger lodged a cry in her throat—"I don't like to be thought of as a damned *fool.*"

"As entertaining as this is," Marvellas drawled, "I don't have much patience for your lovers' spat." She stalked a little closer, eyes trailing over Tauria, but her attention was fixed on Mordecai. "I hope you know what you're doing," she continued, and it was then Tauria caught a glimpse of the dark fae hierarchy. While Mordecai was once a king—and even now radiated authority and dominance—Marvellas stood above him. In every way, she outranked him. "Should this turn and you were wrong…" Marvellas's head tilted so beautifully, but the threat she delivered in those molten eyes struck like flame. "You wouldn't like to feel my wrath."

"Do it," Tauria interjected.

The Spirit's golden eyes would never fail to rattle her with the images of her dear friend. Faythe. Tauria straightened with will and confidence. She had cherished and lost before, had come back from the worst devastations, and she would survive this. The world was but a cruel map dotted with monsters ready to attack. Tauria filled her mind with the treasured memories of her mate instead. What their bond had brought into their lives…it was enough. Because what they had forged between them before knowing of the bond, Tauria knew that was truly unbreakable.

"Very well," the Spirit sang, the curve of her perfect brow matching her rouge-painted lips. Her hand rose, and Tauria braced. "I admire your willingness to part with this, Tauria Stagknight."

Her eyes burned and she didn't fight it. A dark touch entered her mind, stroked a taunting and cruelly painful finger down the tether that ran within her, and she knew Nik would feel it. However far he stood by…this was it. Tauria had felt this invasion before, on her knees, clutching Nik tight. She could have whimpered knowing what Marvellas stood to break.

With the first sharp tug she did cry out. Mordecai kept her upright through her need to sink into the earth and have it swallow her whole. She tried to be brave, but she shattered. Fire tore through her, and the woods around them tilted. Another tug, and she wondered if the Spirit were drawing out her torture as a means to get back at her for the mockery she'd made of them in Olmstone.

Yet what Marvellas was taking, Tauria planned to get back with a vengeance so strong it began to quell the scores of pain through her body.

She plucked and stroked and relished in Tauria's cries.

She pulled and pulled and pulled at this precious, living thing within her, until…

The bond *snapped*.

A high-pitched ringing filled Tauria's ears, and her vision exploded into stars then engulfed her in complete darkness. There were no words to describe the all-consuming agony that scattered over her skin, scorched fire through her body, and shattered in her mind.

She came to slowly. So slowly she couldn't be certain this wasn't death instead.

Her body trembled, but she couldn't feel it. Exhaustion swept over her, and there passed a yearning for the forever embrace of it to take her from this living nightmare.

It was gone.

Tauria searched, but she was hollow. So empty and hollow where there was once this bright, affirming line of safety and warmth.

No matter how lost or far…

Gone.

Her tears flowed, but she wasn't sobbing.

"It may take time for her to adjust." Marvellas's voice sounded different. It seemed so faraway, yet the tone held a note of sympathy.

"She will be fine," Mordecai assured her.

Tauria tuned out of the rest. She would have sunk to her knees were it not for the high lord's hold, but she didn't have the emotion or strength to shrug away. It worked better for the guise this way anyway.

Gods, she didn't want to think of how Nik was coping. It brought on a fresh round of silent tears.

She heard shuffling but didn't look up.

"I imagine I'll be seeing you again soon, Mordecai. I expect great progress."

Marvellas left. Tauria didn't care either way.

"I think it will be best if we fly—"

"No." She found her voice, snapping back into herself enough to remember the plan. "I need a moment. A day, at least, to rest before you take me anywhere new. Please." Tauria was playing on the effects of the severed bond, hoping there was enough of a shred of humanity within the high lord that he would grant her this.

To her immense relief, she caught his nod. Staring at him now, she couldn't believe the shift from darkness that almost made him look...*concerned*. From all she'd known of him, seen of him, it felt jarring.

"Very well. We can spend a night in the town if that is your wish." His voice became softer, and though it did nothing to ease her hatred for him, for what he'd taken from her, it placed him in a fleeting new light. "Though you should know we are not heading anywhere new," he added as Tauria slipped her foot into the stirrup and his hands caught her waist. "I plan to oversee how Olmstone fares. I thought you might like to revisit."

She couldn't hide the surprise she bore down on him from atop the horse. Balancing between a numb confusion and trying to stay present in the aftermath of what still tore through her, she tried to remember she had to find out all she could.

"When you left there..." Her breaths became short. "Did you meet with Dakodas? I'm sure that triumph must have compensated for Marvellas's loss in Olmstone."

He walked casually beside her, heading back toward the town. "We did. The Spirit of Death is rather...unpredictable."

"You have two ruins then. A great advantage."

"One ruin," he corrected easily. She wanted to be thrilled with the knowledge, but her obliterated heart could do nothing but store it indifferently.

"Has Marvellas not retrieved hers?" Tauria tested.

"Why would she? It is safely guarded in her temple."

"What does she plan to do with them?"

"Destroy one and perhaps find a way to weaponize the others."

"Destroy?" Tauria's mind rang with alarm for the fact she didn't expect.

"I assume the heir hopes to collect them to open the Spirit portal and send her creator back." His dark eyes shifted to her, apparently disappointed she hadn't already concluded this. "Break one, break that ever being a possibility."

Dear Gods.

"Marvellas can't be killed by mortal means," Tauria thought out loud, sliding the horrifying pieces together.

There would be no way to stop her.

"This is her realm," Mordecai said coolly. "It has been for some time."

"Are you happy to be a pawn in it?"

His laugh became genuine. Tauria didn't want to keep seeing these notes of him, of a real person, when he was nothing more than a monster. "When Marvellas brought me back, I thought I'd have my chance at revenge. Tell me, Tauria, do you know much of the history of the Dark Age?"

A fever swept her skin, but the chill to her bones only came from the reminder of who Mordecai was. An evil force from another time. Resurrected when she couldn't be sure what that meant and if it changed anything of the dark fae he was before.

"You sought to overthrow the fae rulers when they took a stand against your desire to have the dark fae granted the law to feed on human blood," she said carefully.

"If only it were that simple," he mused. "I suppose they would have erased from history the fact that humans *came* to us. *Wanted* us to feed. You see, there's a certain pleasure to it, though I will admit it had the effect in some to inspire a dangerous craving, and that was what sparked the war. At that time, the Transitioned did not exist. We never had a desire to dabble in such dark, forbidden magick. That was all Marvellas, yet I was the key. My blood."

Kill Mordecai, stop the Transitions.

Tauria could have gasped with the enlightenment, but she kept her face neutral. It was all becoming too much with the storm that raged within her. She needed rest. She needed Nik. Tauria grappled to hold on.

"I fought for the dark fae, for their right not to be seen as monsters when it was the humans who were weak. I will admit, things spiraled into far more than we could have prepared for. I stood against the fae rulers, yes, only because they never saw us as like them. My people were evil, heartless beings. They refused to accept us on the mainland. They cut off trades."

"You proved them right." Tauria let the accusation slip, unable to stand the thought of the carnage that unfolded.

"I proved to them," he said sharply, "that if you're going to paint by your own assumptions, you'd best be prepared to face the monster you created."

His narrative did something. Lit a match to show a new side to the painting the world had so far only perceived in one way.

"Now," she dared to ask, "what do you fight for?"

"The same," he answered simply. "Though something unexpected happened. *Someone.*"

From his tone, the way his words drifted afar, Tauria knew he was picturing them. "A former lover?" she tried.

"Not quite."

She was glad her sacrifice seemed to have staked in him enough trust to open up a fraction. She'd stolen everything to wield as a weapon, unable to forgive what she'd lost.

"Though one might say the product of such a…*relation.*"

It hit so overwhelmingly that her grip tightened on the reins. One palm splayed against the horse when the dip of its walk added to the sway of knowledge. She couldn't believe it.

"You have a child."

CHAPTER 53

Zaiana

Zaiana awoke against the familiar firmness of stone, though he wasn't gone completely. She didn't move. Curled on the ground, her lids slid open to meet bleak gray. She lay still, breathing in both torture and longing with Kyleer's scent on the fabric wrapped around her. A simple black cloak, but she knew it to be his.

Her back felt soothed and dressed, but that wasn't what kept her down. Zaiana was drowning. Just for a moment she suffocated slowly in the aftermath of him. In a few seconds she would entomb it all. Last night, what he did, what she wanted more of. Even now. Something she'd never been prepared for…was stumbling in her own plan. Harboring a growing fondness for the mark she'd set out to kill.

Gods, if any of her kin could glimpse her traitorous mind, she would deserve the punishment for her weakness.

"Do you regret it?"

The quietness of Kyleer's voice was so unlike him it created a sharpness in her gut. Zaiana had trained all her life to lure victims to her web, to kill and not to feel, to hurt and not to think.

Emotions in others were a weapon for her to use, and her own a weakness.

"I could have killed you," she said finally, embracing the ice that froze over whatever he'd thawed.

"No, you couldn't have."

Zaiana chuckled, a breathy sound lacking any humor. She pushed herself up. "They'll punish you if they find out."

"Is that your concern?"

"No. To be honest, I rather hope they do."

"Do you regret it, Zai?"

"Yes," she snapped. The wince it earned from him struck like a knife. Just as well she'd learned to endure deep wounds as a sting. "As should you."

"I can't."

"Remember what I am, what I've done. Hate me like you should, Kyleer."

"I do. I hate you so damn much for making me want you. You're in my head too often. It's infuriating."

"Then stop."

"I. Can't."

Zaiana stepped up close to the bars, charging the anguish that radiated between them. "I'll make it easy for you, Kyleer. This can never happen. I've killed many people. I am not *good* like you or them. I never will be."

"I don't believe you."

"I don't care—"

"I don't believe you because you let her go."

Zaiana's breath drew short. "I would have killed Faythe—"

"Not her."

A twist tightened in her abdomen. She shook her head. "I don't know what you're talking about."

Kyleer stepped closer too. His hands curled around the bar, looking down at her as though his answer were written over every inch of her. Like he could see things no one ever had before without even trying. "I wonder if you will chase this time..." He recited her words from the rooftop. "Because I didn't the first time we came face-to-face, and you darted away before we had the chance to cross swords."

She gave him nothing.

"It was your scent at first, but maybe something more. I recognized it even before you intercepted us on the mountains. Yet it was your eyes that made me realize right then why you were familiar." Kyleer reached a hand through the iron bars that separated them. His fingers hesitated, but when she didn't move, they curled under her chin.

She'd never been held, entranced, by such a stare, and she wanted to slap sense into herself for allowing his touch.

"That day in Fenstead, I saw Tauria Stagknight and her guards head down an alley. I cut through the battlefield just to be sure she'd escaped as that was the only thing that mattered when it became clear the kingdom was all but taken. When I ran into that street and saw the guards were dead, I was ready to fight you, whatever it took. Then you turned to me, yet you didn't attack. I might not have been able to identify you from that day, except in your curiosity you tilted your head just enough for me to glimpse the most magnificent irises I'd ever seen."

He searched her eyes for a long moment, but she couldn't decipher his torment.

"I hadn't forgotten them for a damn day since, and then there you were. Those eyes. Pupils eclipsing blazing amethyst suns. A vibrant core of purple striking enough to hypnotize long enough for such a beautiful creature to kill if glimpsed without caution."

No one had ever paid such deep attention to her. What stole her breath completely was how long he'd held onto that note of her without ever knowing who she was. It was unfamiliar, this *feeling*. Like someone was carving out the dead weight in her chest. Like air would only come easily if she allowed herself to surrender to his romantic words.

He could not become her weakness.

"Did you remember me when we came face-to-face on that mountain edge?"

There was something odd in his tone, as if disappointment

would follow with the wrong answer. It was also *his* eyes...the reason why she'd never been able to let go of a yearning for forests, an inclination to lay down her weapons and surrender to their peaceful nature. Those features, that body—they radiated with a protective pull that was hard to resist.

"No," she breathed. It wasn't a lie. Though he would never know familiarity drew her to him like a moth resisting a flame. His eyes flexed with a rejection she braced for, but in the way it flashed by and his expression firmed, being a ghost, forgettable—it was not an unfamiliar concept to him. For a second she wanted to take it back, if only to see what light would flare at hearing the words...

I remember you.

Zaiana's senses snapped back to her all at once, the brutality of her past sealing her lips against any flicker of kindness that had condemned her before. She took a step forward until their bodies were almost flush, only the thick iron between them. "No one will believe you."

Kyleer chuckled. Dark and smooth, and she hated it. *Hated it.* Because it had become a sound she craved.

"I have no one I wish to convince of it."

"Because it doesn't matter."

He dragged his hand up her nape before fisting her hair. The surprise of it parted her lips, which were angled so perfectly to his she felt the end of his harsh breaths. His green eyes were livid but filled with a wild passion, and she wanted to feel the snap of the control he held onto.

"Because frankly, I don't give a damn about what they would think of this."

Her breath had never stuttered so hard to a racing, building thrill. It was ludicrous given where they were and *who* they were. Zaiana had seduced males before—she could allure them with little effort—but this...it felt different. It was both a terrible, terrible ache and a raw fury waiting to erupt, near maddening to think of what could be unleashed between them. So wrong, but that only built on the desire.

Against all that screamed for her to tear out his heart before it could awaken something in her cold, dark chest, Zaiana spilled her reckless words. "About what?"

The spark in his eye was a hunger that struck. Hard. Kyleer's mouth crashed to hers and she answered to it, damning to the Nether the bars that kept them from colliding in a way that would have been angry and ugly but blissful all the same.

There was little way they could move to the demands of their bodies. Kyleer's hand around her waist crushed her against the metal poles just as he pressed himself to them. His tongue slid into her mouth, and she moaned, the flame igniting raw and furiously. It sparked in her chest to make her feel alive, shooting a vibrant light in her mind against a permanent shroud of bleakness, lifting every burden and transgression just for a single moment in time she simply…forgot. She craved more. *Needed* more. Zaiana wondered why he didn't Shadowport to put them both out of their misery.

When Kyleer pulled away abruptly, her mind whirled in a daze, scrambling to try to piece back together who she was. "I should have done that last night," he said thickly.

Then he released her, and all she could do was curl her fingers tighter around the iron, gathering her breath with bewilderment. He walked away, and her forehead met the cold metal, her eyes slipping closed. She tried to expel him from her thoughts, but all they replayed was that kiss. The taste of him…smoky and earthy. It wasn't enough. Not nearly enough. Yet the conflict began that she couldn't have this; couldn't want this.

Because if she did…she was sure to fall.

CHAPTER 54

Faythe

"Dancing."

Faythe's voice echoed spectacularly through the ballroom so huge she felt no more than a speck on the intricate pattern painted on the marble. And the magnificent paintings and sculptures. Even the piano and small ensemble of instruments on a dais seemed so far away.

"I didn't want to stir your nerves until it was absolutely necessary," Reylan said beside her.

Faythe looked up at him with question, but another voice bounded through the space.

"Our princess will be opening the ball with a dance, and I truly can't wait for that entertainment." Izaiah beamed wide as he strolled into the hall, Kyleer close behind him.

When his words registered, her head snapped back to Reylan. "No, I'm not," she rushed out.

He winced at her reaction. "I could try to get you out of it, but there would be speculation. It would have been Malin, but since you're to be Rhyenelle's heir…I can't deny it would be advantageous exposure."

Faythe mulled over the concept. It made sense, and at the thought of giving her cousin what was clearly supposed to be an *honor*, she wiped her protest.

The only thing was…Faythe was a horrible dancer.

"Hence the lessons," Reylan teased, reading the slipped thought, or maybe the daunting notion was written all over her face with the thought of so many eyes on her, being unable to rely on guidance over a missed step.

"You're going to teach me?"

His small smile fluttered in her chest. "Would you want me to?"

Yes. Without hesitation she wanted that. The memory of their dance in High Farrow became preciously guarded in her mind. Faythe didn't have much experience with fae dancing. The grandeur of their parties, the way they moved and feasted and enjoyed the night to a scale that was overwhelming to her simple human mind.

A hand grabbed hers, and Faythe yelped in surprise when she was spun then pulled into a tall, slender body. Blinking, she stared into Izaiah's eyes, which sparkled with mischief. "I think you'll find me more favorable than these two brutes in this particular skill," he said.

"You enjoy it," Faythe observed. Izaiah's enthusiasm was a natural balm to her erratic nerves.

"So might you if you learn to see you're already great at it. Just let go of the sword."

She had never thought of it that way, but reflecting on the routines Reylan had shown her many times, the poise Kyleer had instilled in from her archery, removing the weapons started to give it all a new meaning. A boost of confidence that she wasn't a complete novice if she could simply translate the movements she knew already.

"Dancing is lighter, however." His arm around her waist turned them both then tightened as he dipped low with her. In fright, Faythe lashed out, thinking she would fall. "Let go of the defense that's keeping you stiff. You're not fighting *against* someone; think of this like fighting *with* them instead. Trust, don't oppose."

Light piano music began to weave through the hall. Faythe's attention traveled—and Izaiah straightened with her—to find Reylan watching them both while he played softly.

"You don't take your eyes off your partner." Izaiah didn't allow her a moment to bask in the beautiful sight of the general, sending her twirling with a hand above her head once again. As he brought her flush to him Faythe stumbled off-balance.

"This is going to take some work," he mused.

"You said I should already be good at it," she grumbled, pushing away from him.

His chuckle pulled at her own mouth.

"Tuning your movements to be eloquent enough that you're not looking like a stiff board out there will take some work," he amended.

"Thanks for the confidence boost."

The playing stopped, and Faythe caught the hum of words being exchanged to find a young fae had approached Reylan. The general's gaze flashed up, looking past Faythe, who felt compelled to follow it. Livia stood by the doors dressed in her combat suit, which hugged every beautiful curve, though Faythe couldn't admire her for long when something about her poise and the restlessness of her hands over her buckles gave off an unusual anxiety. Faythe fought the urge to find out if she'd gathered any leads on Evander, but it was Reylan she sought alone.

Reylan passed her, and Faythe called with a surge of panic he left without a word, "Is everything okay?"

He paused as if only just remembering the rest of them. His hard features smoothed out as he twisted back to her. A mask, she thought. "I'll find you later," he promised.

Her gut churned, twisting to pain when she realized for the first time she couldn't trust those words. Or at least, her "later" had become a far smaller measure of time than his. It had become clear how differently they lived their lives within the castle walls, and Faythe often wished to be back out on their wandering days. To continue to pretend that she wasn't preparing to see an end.

"To let you both know," Izaiah cut in before Reylan could leave, "your scent is still on her, but it's faint. I think as long as you continue to be cautious, no one will suspect anything more than what would linger from your position as her guard."

Her guard. She couldn't accept that no matter how many times she heard it. Faythe studied the ground, and though she felt his hesitation, Reylan's steps away sank her mood. She caught him chatting to Livia quietly before they both disappeared without so much as a glance back.

"Now, we have much to teach you and only a month, give or take, in which to do so." Izaiah perked up, trying to erase the somber drop in mood. Faythe appreciated the effort, but her anchor was cast for that day.

She met eyes with Kyleer, who stood cross-armed with a knowing smile.

"I have to leave you as well, I'm afraid," he announced.

That piqued her attention. "Have you found out anything more with Zaiana?"

He looked between her and Izaiah, his gaze so fleeting she wondered what it meant.

"Nothing of importance—right, brother?" Izaiah said.

Faythe couldn't decipher his tone, but Kyleer's eyes turned to daggers at Izaiah, who merely scoffed.

Kyleer had kept his distance since entering the hall. Faythe hadn't questioned why until she began to feel a deeper kind of separation. A defense, perhaps, although she didn't know why, and with everything that swirled her mind with her new status and what it meant, she wondered…did Kyleer feel his relationship with her had become too personal to be appropriate?

"Some rogue soldiers tried to extract information without authority," he informed her. "It's set us back. She's healing from the wounds, but at the pace of a mortal."

"How do you plan to get her to talk?"

"He has his ways, it seems," Izaiah commented.

Kyleer shot him a warning look. "We're still figuring her out. Physical torture won't work on her."

"It might if—"

"She's been through it all."

Faythe recoiled at the bite in his tone. Kyleer seemed to register his error as his arms dropped when Izaiah took a step closer to her.

"Careful where you entangle yourself when it affects us all."

Kyleer's jaw flexed as though he wanted to argue with his brother, but ultimately, his gaze softened as it fell back to Faythe. "I only mean she has felt torture not even our methods have inflicted. She's been raised by it. Physical harm will not get her to talk, and our soldiers only made us look pathetic to her and proved what she's been led to believe: that we hate her kind for their blood and heritage, nothing more."

Faythe thought for a moment. As much as it roused a fear to pull up the memory, she thought of their wings, their silver blood, and even the black blood she had seen spilled. Faythe thought of how they'd only managed to capture Zaiana because of her sacrifice for her companions. She even thought of Maverick, how everything he did was wicked and merciless, and how he would kill Faythe again if given the chance, but…it was for her. For Zaiana. She couldn't help but draw the conclusion.

The dark fae were taught to be monsters, but they were not entirely *monstrous*.

"We need to switch tactics," she thought out loud.

"I'm trying to learn what I ca—"

"Right down to anatomy," Izaiah interjected.

"But it's taking time," Kyleer finished, ignoring his brother.

Faythe shook her head to focus since she couldn't juggle their tension. "We don't have time. We have no idea when they plan to strike, and who knows what Marvellas is planning now?" Faythe wasn't in the mood for dancing but would trudge through this lesson. Everything had to form a part of a bigger plan, and the wheels of her mind were turning. Too much time had passed, and her fear grew with each passing day they made no advancement.

"I'll speak with her soon," she said. Zaiana was the only lead they had, and the task was either to outsmart—something she held little confidence in—or gain the trust of their deadliest foe.

After her dance lesson, Faythe couldn't face her lonely rooms. She found Jakon and Marlowe but didn't want to interrupt their peaceful walk through the gardens. So she wandered with no destination in mind until what she found had her staring at the most triumphant sight. Her awe planted her before the stairs that led to the biggest throne she'd ever seen. The dais stretched to nearly the full width of the great hall, many dark stone steps leading up to what she knew to be a throne, but not in the traditional sense she imagined. This one appeared to grow from the ground beneath it. Dark stone, except the seat held a familiar crimson sheen.

Fyrestone.

"Daunting, isn't it?"

Malin's voice appeared behind her like a snake. It slivered up her spine to lock in her shoulders.

"Not my description, no," she answered calmly.

It wasn't a lie. Faythe had been marveling at its power and beauty, playing with the thought of not staring at it, but *from* it. She had thought that would flood her with insecurity, but Faythe found the notion surprisingly exciting.

Malin entered her peripheral, stopping so close it rattled her nerves. "I didn't expect to find you wandering alone. Without one of your dogs at least."

"Do you call all your respected commanders that?"

"Only those who turn weak in the presence of a pretty face."

Faythe couldn't stop her huffed laugh.

"Amusing, is it?"

"Yes," she said, still not engaging eye contact. "You continue to underestimate me, Malin."

"Your confidence has grown. I like that."

"Is there a reason you sought me out? Other than your insecurity." Faythe breathed through the quick flash that rippled over her. Malin's rage she could feel without even a glance, as hot as it was icy. Maybe it wasn't wise to rile him, yet she was beyond being silent when she knew how cunning he was willing to be for the throne.

"The confidence I admire. The arrogance...it doesn't suit you, Faythe."

She didn't believe for a second there was anything he *admired* about her. "You say that as if I could give a damn about what you think."

His chuckle vibrated, darkly smooth. "You want the throne? Go ahead. Take it."

Faythe studied how the stone had been carved into a Phoenix's head at the top; how the craftsmanship was both harsh and soft, curling stone feathers embracing the illusion of wings around the back. Her feet moved while her mind drifted, forgetting her cousin, forgetting the room, as she simply marveled at the power that called to her.

As she ascended the steps her heartbeat slowed until she was standing right before the mighty Fyrestone Throne. She didn't stop, drifting around the chair to discover what she'd believed to find from the jagged sculpture she glimpsed below. The back of the carved-out chair brought the entire image of the Firebird to life. Not smoothly carved; this was harsh and angular, adding a lethal edge to the depiction. Sharp rock spilled out from behind like the unraveling of its tail feathers Faythe had seen before in real, fiery life.

Finishing a full lap, she reached out a hand. The stone emitted a faint warmth while the daylight glittered its crimson hue. Then she spoke to Malin, who still watched her from below, answering his attempt to shake her nerve.

"I already have."

They locked eyes. A challenge. A defiance. A fight that was far from over.

"I trust you two are getting along."

Agalhor's interruption drew both of their attention, dispersing the tension as if it were their secret battle.

"Of course," Malin said sweetly, hands clasped behind his back. "We were just discussing the history of Rhyenelle's legendary throne. It seems our princess has much to learn. We should see to it that daily lessons are put in place. Along with etiquette that could use some work for the upcoming celebrations."

Faythe only heard each suggestion as more opportunity to overwhelm her, and more time spent apart from Reylan. But she could do nothing but agree with him if she were to ever live up to the standards of fae royalty.

"It could be advantageous for you, Faythe. Should you so desire."

Agalhor stopped below the steps, and Faythe's palms clammed up as she realized she stood above him. She wondered if he thought anything of it.

"I had similar thoughts myself," she agreed.

She hadn't, and she cursed herself for it.

Agalhor reached out a hand to Malin's shoulder. Nothing but a father's love warmed his face, but Faythe jolted at the touch, assessing if it was just her opposition toward her cousin that made her see Malin's smile as hiding a cool hatred. "She could learn a lot from you, son. You should tell her of your time spent in Lakelaria in your second century. It is a magnificent great island indeed, and we were once close allies before the tragedy that befell the queen."

His mention of the kingdom sparked a distant memory. Of the child the queen had lost, whom Nik had once told her about. Malin's jaw twitched. His shoulders moved like his fists, which flexed behind his back, and she could only pin it down to his lack of desire for the *bonding* time her father encouraged. Faythe couldn't stand the hope he expressed, knowing it would never be true. Even if she were to rule and Malin stayed in council, she didn't believe her cousin would ever let go of his resentment enough to find love for her.

"I look forward to teaching her all I know," Malin responded tightly. Agalhor didn't feel the lie, but Faythe turned cold with it. "I have things I must see to," he announced, offering a small dip of his head in farewell before flashing Faythe a final daring look before he left.

Only then did Agalhor climb the steps to stand level with her, assessing the grand throne. "I'll admit I haven't sat in it much. It's horribly uncomfortable."

Faythe gave a soft laugh. "It's beautiful."

"It was crafted by Matheus with the help of Atherius."

Faythe's head snapped to him, heart skipping a beat at the mention. "Atherius was in this hall?"

The vibrations of the king's chuckles tingled through her fingertips. "You have seen her—how do you suppose she would have roamed our halls with her size?"

Faythe's cheeks flushed, but her mouth curved with the tease.

The singing of steel echoed, drawing her eyes to the most magnificent blade. The cross guard fanned like two golden wings, and its pommel shone with a brilliant eye-shaped ruby. He held it out to her, and Faythe gawked at him in surprise.

"The Ember Sword belonged to Matheus," he explained.

Faythe's palms went slick at the thought of holding such an ancient sword, but at the king's eager look, she reached out a shaky hand. Testing the weight, she found it was heavier than her own. Faythe ran her attention along the metal—no ordinary steel, nor Niltain. "Fyrestone?" she pondered, admiring the catch of crimson against the dark metal.

"Yes, but there's something you should know about how Phoenixes use their fire." Agalhor paused, and Faythe read that he was extending his senses to be sure no ears picked up on their conversation. "The mountains that surround us are indeed torched crimson from the Phoenixes that flew across them for centuries. But those bonded with a Phoenix shared more than a telepathic connection. It is said that the fae were able to manipulate Phoenix-fyre, but only if it was willingly lent by their bonded, making them lethal partners in any attack. But there was one way to permanently brand something with the power of a Phoenix." His shoulders squared, attention flicking between her and the sword. "What you hold is a sword from the embers of Phoenixfyre. Not just touched to give it color like this throne; it is a weapon said to be able to defeat any foe."

Her mouth fell open in astonishment as she realized she could be holding the single most valuable weapon on the continent. But when Faythe looked down she drew out a gasp, stumbling back and almost dropping the sword. Her wrist tingled, warmth expelling from the bright flame on her amulet over each finger, bringing to life again the stone in the sword.

"A Phoenix has two eyes," Agalhor said, entranced.

"Did you know this whole time?" Faythe breathed, unable to tear her gaze from the twin flares.

"Yes. The Eyes of the Phoenix will always find each other."

Faythe's face crumpled she was so overcome with that measure of safety he'd placed on her if she were ever lost.

"You used it, didn't you? On your quest…there was a moment the stone in the sword flared to life. Gods above, I almost sent warriors after you in my fear for what it could mean. At first it echoed like fear, hot and blazing, but then it reduced, and while this may sound like madness to anyone else, I can't explain how I knew your fear had switched to *acceptance*. That you no longer used the eye as a defense but as a *merging.*"

Agalhor was right. To explain all he eerily knew through the twin eye would seem impossible.

"I'm glad," Faythe choked. She had nothing more to explain how grateful she was. Her nose stung with the realization he'd been there with her to face the Firebird. That in some ways he had taken that leap too, and maybe the echo of his belief had come through enough to give her that bravery in that moment.

"I haven't told anyone this, Faythe." Agalhor's voice dropped quiet with an emotion she couldn't place. "Having you here put so many things into perspective for me. You have liberated me, so to speak. It is my hope to step out of power as soon as you are ready. Maybe in a few decades, maybe in a century. It will seem long to you at first, but not with the many years you have ahead of you now, and I want to be able to watch you grow. To see you sit upon this throne."

Faythe blinked to push back the prickling in her eyes. The notion daunted her, but the pride he coated her with made it insignificant. Her acceptance left her parted lips so quietly but surely.

"I want that too."

CHAPTER 55

Tauria

IT TOOK SOME persuading, but Mordecai agreed to give her the night alone. She couldn't be certain if he were occupying another room or standing by somewhere close to ensure she didn't have any alternate plan despite sacrificing her bond.

She had barely moved in hours. She sat on the edge of the feeble bed at the inn until the hour she was to slip out. Tauria didn't feel anything. Her body became vacant. Everything was too quiet, yet some part of her mind clung to the denial. She kept searching for him within, waiting for the pull that she would answer to, waiting to hear the song of his voice to soothe the terror.

Too quiet.

Tauria bounced to her feet. It was a little earlier than they had planned, but she couldn't wait here any longer, or she was sure to succumb to her anxiety and implode. She had to see him. Feel him. Smell him. When all that assurance had been robbed from her, she *had* to hear from him that it would all be okay.

Slipping cautiously from the room, she knew the hallway was abandoned from extending her senses. She hoped they were already at their meeting point, and maybe there would be some part of her mate that would detect her sooner than expected. Her eyes burned, air restricted.

Tauria pulled up her hood as she exited the inn and took off in a hurry while keeping to the shadows. Her adrenaline pushed her forward—perhaps not as stealthy and aware in her desperation. Past the tree line she dipped into the woods. Trees surrounded her, and she searched between them frantically. Her senses felt filled with cotton. She couldn't feel him, couldn't reach him, and the world was spinning and spinning, and she almost collapsed in defeat, until…

She stumbled to a halt when she saw him right ahead. Her chest rose and fell deeply with her inability to know what he felt, what he thought. Lycus stood nearby with Samara, but she barely registered their presence.

Tauria broke first, tripping over branches, and she came apart the moment his arms wrapped around her. She shook with sobs, struggling to breathe his scent but needing it so badly. Her hands fisted his cloak, his jacket, while one arm hugged her around the waist and other hand cupped her nape.

"I've got you, love," he mumbled softly. "I've always got you."

"Did you feel it?" Tauria whispered against him.

He turned stiff beneath her as his hand stroked her hair. "I feel you," he said. "It changes nothing."

"It's gone," she whimpered, suddenly wondering if it had been worth it. What had they been thinking?

Nik pulled her back just enough to search her eyes. "I need to go place the compulsion in Mordecai's mind," he said, and she knew this. "We need to leave you here for a moment. Will you be okay, love?"

Tauria wanted to clutch him tighter, wanted to say no, but she couldn't. She simply nodded, swallowing the lump of grief that threatened to consume her.

Nik led her over to a large tree, one that created a cozy alcove with the thick base of its roots. His hands didn't leave her for a second as he helped her down. He unclasped his cloak although she already had one and draped it around her shoulders, and it was only then Tauria realized she was shivering.

His palm cupped her cheek, and despite everything Nik smiled softly, planting a tender kiss to her lips that erupted the first warmth in her chest since the bond was broken.

"I'll be right back. But call and I will hear you still. I will come."

All she could muster was a nod while inside she begged him to stay, but Nik stood.

Then he was gone.

Minutes tormented her as hours. Or days. Or weeks. Tauria sat huddled against the tree, not feeling present at all anymore. She hugged Nik's cloak tight, breathing the scent of him deeply to at least remember she was alive.

They had been preparing for this for weeks, had come to peace in knowing they could offer this sacrifice to gain an advantage in the war. They all had a role to play, and this was bigger than them.

It didn't make the void feel any less like it had cleaved from her very being, a piece of her forever lost.

Tauria felt him first. *Gods*, she was so glad to be able to detect his essence from a small distance as if their bond were now an echo. Still, she couldn't move.

Nik sat beside her. He wordlessly drew an arm around her, and she shuffled until he cradled her to his chest. She tuned in to the strong, hard beat of his heart, taking this moment of bliss when her troubles seemed insignificant in his arms.

"I love you," he said quietly.

Three words that shattered and reformed her world as if she were hearing them for the first time. She buried her face into his chest; he pressed his lips to her head.

"And I choose you, Tauria. I chose you long before we ever got to claim the bond. It changes nothing, not a single thing, about my feelings. You know that, right?"

Tauria did. Because she'd always known what lived in her heart, and his heart was one and the same. For each other, for the world they wanted to build around them, there had never been a doubt about what they shared.

"Yes," she whispered. "I'm glad you found me on the rooftop the night we met. I don't think I've ever told you...I planned to evade as much of the Solstice Ball as possible. I was up there because people kept escorting me back to the ballroom when I stepped out to find a moment. Then I saw you, and after that short encounter I hoped you'd find me inside. I wanted to annoy the Nether out of you because I hated that you made me *want* to be there." Her head tilted back, meeting emeralds that sparkled against the tendrils of moonlight filtering through the canopy. Her hand slipped up his chest, and her exhale stuttered. She still felt the electrifying sensation brushing the skin of his neck. "You left the next day, and you took a piece of me with you. The jeweled comb, yes, but also something deeper that you haven't let go of since. I never want it back. It's yours. I am eternally yours."

Nik leaned his mouth to hers. Sparks ignited with that kiss. Everything she knew, but more. A promise forged between them that they were an unstoppable team and this could not destroy what was bonded to them truer than magick.

Her fingers grazed his collar, a sudden anticipation making her shift onto his lap. A pulse of fear drummed in her chest as she pulled back the material. Breath whooshed from her. She hadn't thought to check herself, but Tauria's mating mark still remained on his skin.

"How?" she wondered out loud, brow pinching now it blared before her with defiance. She was so damn happy to see it, even if it could fade with time, that a huff of laughter escaped her. Nik smiled at the sound, and she couldn't stop. Her laughter soon turned to a wave of exhaustion, and he cupped her cheek.

"Because what we have is something even Marvellas can't

break." As if he wanted to be sure, Nik's touch shivered along her skin, drawing back the folds of the cloaks to see his mark there.

Tauria grinned, and with it, she broke from the cloud of sorrow. They were going to be okay.

"Did everything work with the compulsion and Lycus's story?" she asked.

Nik idly combed through the lengths of her deep brown hair. "I believe so. He seemed hesitant with Lycus joining us, but Samara is quite persuasive in this role. I can't decide if that's a relief or a concern."

"Concern?"

"That her allegiance could be swayed. I spent a lot of time with her. She has a very troubled mind from Zarrius's manipulation of her, and I can't deny I played a secondary role in it."

"You did what you had to. And she tried to kill you."

"Maybe I deserved it," he chuckled.

Tauria shot him a flat look.

"Having Lycus now means they'll travel by land. I worried we'd need to exert ourselves to keep up if he chose to fly with Samara. I can't say how long the compulsion will hold, so it's best to keep a check on it daily in case his mind starts to rebel."

"Did you bring the other Phoenix Blood potion?" She had to check as this would all be over if he lost the ability to infiltrate Mordecai's mind.

He nodded. "I'm surprised it's held for this long, but while it was heavy and confusing at first, I quite like it."

Then he was within her mind, and she almost whimpered.

"It can be as if we never lost anything."

Tauria hadn't thought of that. While it wasn't as personal and sure as their bond, he could still speak with her in her mind.

"Can you hear me?"

"Yes, love. Always."

He tucked a strand of hair behind her ear, his knuckles grazing her cheek. "I promise you, the bond that matters most, the one that was threaded the moment I found you and has been sewn into every piece of what I am since…it is *unbreakable.*"

CHAPTER 56

Zaiana

KYLEER DIDN'T SPEAK a word when he came to her cell. Neither did she. As they walked the grim cellblock passageways she couldn't untangle the knot in her stomach. No guards were around; he'd come alone. He held her arm to guide her. Zaiana's mind raced with multiple possibilities of where he could be leading her that required he give the guards leave, though his march expelled anything of pleasant nature.

They came to a door she recognized, and while she was used to being routinely dragged to far more torturous places, it seemed her vulnerability had begun to slip in front of the commander. She hesitated with her footing but tried to keep walking in the hope he wouldn't notice, although Kyleer pulled her to a stop with him.

For the first time, an emotion flexed on his firm features. Disturbance. Maybe even understanding. "They're not going to hurt you," he said, voice so low she almost missed it. A muscle in his jaw flexed. "Especially not like that again."

"I don't care."

He gave a short nod as though hearing something else entirely. Then he opened the door, and who greeted them within was far from whom she'd been expecting. The click of the door sealed them in. Zaiana couldn't help it: through the awkward stillness, she chuckled.

Reylan stood, hand poised on his blade, close to Faythe by a bench on the other side of the small room. Izaiah lingered against a wall, but out of them all, he pinned Zaiana with the coldest eyes. Then she noticed two humans she'd never seen before. The man folded the blonde woman into him a fraction tighter as Zaiana's fleeting attention passed over them.

Amusing.

"You really must be running out of options to have come here yourself," Zaiana taunted Faythe.

"We've barely started with you," Izaiah uttered darkly.

"You shouldn't have come," Kyleer said to him.

Izaiah huffed a laugh, pushing off the wall. "I had to see the witch for myself."

Zaiana's fingertips pricked with the insult. "You've seen me. Now what, would you like a show?"

He stalked toward her with an aggression she thought looked misplaced on his tall, impeccable frame. Out of all of them, Izaiah was the least fitting in this grim setting. "You're good at those, aren't you?"

It all made sense then. Zaiana found herself sparing a glance at Reylan, confirming what she believed since she was still breathing. Izaiah knew about Kyleer's transgressions with her, and while Reylan looked to be puzzling over their tension, she knew it was only a matter of time before he understood too.

"Unchain me and find out."

His smile only grew, and she cursed that it caused Kyleer to step closer to her. "I think the chains are part of the appeal—right, brother?"

They stared off, the heat in the room rising, or perhaps it was just her skin that flushed with Izaiah's boldness.

"Leave," Kyleer said. One word delivered so icily she knew it was over. There would be no end to Reylan's speculation now that they were done here.

Zaiana blinked at her wave of dizziness as Izaiah smirked, flashing her his attention for a fleeting moment—a warning—before he left. She shouldn't care about the petty arguments they might have had or what the repercussions would be for Kyleer. Yet her throat began to tighten as something twisting and nauseous filled her stomach. A hand grazed her back, but Zaiana jerked away from it. It was as if a jolt of her lightning had snapped all sense back into her at once.

"Why am I here?" she demanded.

Faythe and Reylan were still confused over Kyleer, but her voice seemed to draw them out of their thoughts too. Wood scraped across wood, and what Zaiana beheld on the table straightened her posture with disbelief. She found herself unable to tear away as she muttered, "You are all damn fools for flaunting that in front of me."

Faythe only shrugged, taking up a lean against the bench, fingers idly tracing the ancient markings. "I want to know how you can wield it."

"You're wasting your time."

"I have plenty."

"No, you don't. You're desperate, and this is your last resort." Zaiana looked over them as though waiting for the punchline. They remained firm-faced, and she huffed a laugh with the shake of her head. "Best get me into those bonds again, Commander."

Zaiana didn't look to the wall the shackles hung from. Didn't drop her gaze to the spot on the floor where she'd hung at the soldiers' mercy. Didn't glance at Kyleer for his reaction.

"We're not going to waste energy on that," Reylan said.

"Then why are we all here? Should I expect a damn tea party?"

Faythe ignored her. "Dakodas can't wield her ruin. Neither can Marvellas. So they trained you to do it… How many others?"

"Aren't you powerful enough on your own now?"

Her silence grew Zaiana's smile.

"You can't even control that, can you? Yourself."

Faythe reached out a hand, and the cobalt flame from the

torch against the wall snuffed out, cloaking them all in darkness before it reignited in her palm.

"Nice trick."

"I'm not one thing. But slowly, I will control it all."

"Perhaps..." Zaiana watched Faythe return the fire, trying not to give feeling to the thoughts of a certain dark fae the blue flame stirred. "But like I said, you don't have time."

"Is that a threat?"

"A warning."

"So you know what Dakodas and Marvellas are planning."

"Do you really think I would tell you?"

Their standoff was somewhat thrilling. Zaiana couldn't deny that remembering her fight with Faythe made her want a rematch now to test what she might be capable of.

"Zai."

Her stomach sank with the soft tone in which he spoke her name in front of the others. She swallowed hard, trying to salvage what she could to convince them the complete opposite of all he was exposing.

He added first, "You don't want her to get the information the other way."

It dawned on her then. Zaiana hadn't prepared for *this*. Through her reckless planning Faythe hadn't been here, with no sure timeline for when or if she would return. The one with the greatest weapon in the whole damned castle, and Zaiana couldn't be sure of the strength of her powers now.

"You'll do it anyway," she accused, a fear rising that she wasn't accustomed to. Didn't know a way out from.

"It is not my desire to infiltrate your mind," Faythe said. "But I will."

Zaiana's mind had been well-guarded over centuries, but she knew her weaknesses. The Niltain Steel could have an effect on her mental barriers, and she wasn't sure of Faythe's strength. If it wasn't enough... A stiff chill rattled her bones at the thought of the Temple Ruin, which remained concealed for now.

"It took me centuries to wield the ruin, and it was not without a suffering you couldn't imagine," Zaiana bit out. "There were many times I nearly didn't survive. They wouldn't have cared. It's as if it sets you on fire from the inside out, but worst of all, it is a fire of your own making. Fire you should be able to control, yet it devours you instead. It is the worst torture, and if you want my advice, I'd learn to win this war without it."

"That's not an option if they have others who can wield the ruins they have—"

"There's only me. Many tried and their lives were forfeited on as little as the first attempt. Some made it close to being able to master it, but ultimately, magick won."

"So what makes you different?"

Zaiana breathed a long sigh. "I guess you could say the Gods are having a wicked time with my eternal torment."

"Where is Marvellas keeping hers?" Faythe diverted the topic.

"I do not know."

Her eyes flexed with impatience. "Where is Marvellas?"

"You'll have to be more specific with your questions, *Your Highness*. She is but a fable to me."

"You expect me to believe she's controlled the dark fae and never shown herself?"

"How do you think she managed to reduce her existence to a fairy tale?" Zaiana shook her head at their lack of common sense. "One with that much determination doesn't go making herself known even to her allies. Until the time is right."

"Now." The blonde human spoke, her voice too soft, too delicate, for their hostile company, though she wore her confidence well. "Marvellas is making herself known now. She openly exposed herself to us, and to Nik and Tauria."

"It seems your hourglass is running out of sand. She'll be coming for you with more determination than ever, Faythe Ashfyre."

"Where's Maverick?"

The death promise in those two words dropped all warmth out of the room. Zaiana dared to give the general her attention, refraining from reacting.

"I would not know."

He ground his teeth, and Zaiana braced herself. "You know more than you're letting on."

"You're not asking the right questions," she sang.

"Faythe." Reylan's fists trembled with restraint.

Faythe deliberated the question in his tone while Zaiana assessed the exchange.

"You can't take her power to enter my mind," she concluded, skipping with triumph that she was learning more of them than they were of her.

That lethal stare from the general eased all at once when it slid down to Faythe. "I'll do it—I just need you to give me it."

"I've answered all your questions," Zaiana defended, a cruel slither of fear taking over.

Though it was not enough. Of course they would never trust her.

"I can't take that chance," Faythe said, and she felt her test the barrier of her mind. "As you said, we don't have time."

The pressure increased, and Zaiana knew then that while she could hold it off, in her weakened state Faythe would break through with enough force. Panic wasn't an emotion she juggled well. She didn't feel it often enough to know how to manage it. Or at least she hadn't in a long time.

Zaiana stumbled back, caught by a firm force. "I'll tell you what you want to know," she breathed.

Faythe couldn't get inside. It was the one torture she could not stand, the invasion of everything dark and ugly and unforgivable. Zaiana wasn't afraid to admit those things, wasn't even scared of Faythe seeing what made her a dark force. It was her memories, those locked away even from herself, that Zaiana was terrified for her to be able to unlock. Maybe she wouldn't even realize—not until it was too late and they were both standing there in the face of all she *couldn't* be seen to be.

"Stop," she tried. Her eyes clamped shut as she focused everything she had left to keep that barrier firm, but Faythe's power pushed stronger, more than any other she'd felt before. *"Stop."*

429

"Faythe, she said she'd tell you." Kyleer's voice became distant, but it vibrated at her back.

"Stay out of this, Ky," Reylan commanded.

Breathing came in short gasps. An arm folded around her as she doubled over, dizzy with the mental toll it took to keep that block firm.

"I'll only see what I need to."

Faythe's voice in her mind only signaled she was winning. Zaiana couldn't bite back the single breathy whimper that escaped her lips. She didn't care how feeble she would seem to them, only that the one place she had left was about to be infiltrated and there would be nowhere left to go. No place safe for her childish thoughts, her dark thoughts, her lonely, pitiful thoughts. Her mind was a cage, as cruel as it was kind, but it was *safe*. The only part of her left untouched, unmoved, uninfluenced.

Voices chatted, maybe shouted. Zaiana wasn't wholly present in the room anymore as Faythe finally cracked through the barrier of her mind. Instead, she was falling. She wanted to be anywhere but here, in her own mind. Zaiana wanted out of there if she was to be forced to endure another mind combing through the wickedness of all she was inside.

All at once the pressure eased, just before Faythe took her opening. Zaiana breathed hard, slammed her walls back up, and slowly came around to her surroundings. Kyleer was holding her tightly, but they'd both fallen to their knees.

No one spoke for a long moment while her dazed mind cleared. Her eyelids stung from tiredness and weakness and the realization of all she'd let slip before the enemy she couldn't bring herself to look at. She focused only on the cracked gray stone, feeling at one with it. Broken, only an illusion of strength, when all it would take was one strike for her to never be the same again.

Footsteps shuffled then halted.

"I said we'll find it another way." Faythe's command was firm.

Kyleer should have let her go. Zaiana should have shrugged him off. Yet she could do nothing but succumb to her weakness in that moment. It wasn't a lack of physical strength that kept her from killing them all right now; it was that her mind embraced a numbness that made her forget about her will to escape. She closed her eyes, listening to the sounds of their boots against stone, the creak of the door hinges, and then silence.

"What happened?" Kyleer asked softly. She couldn't bear his tenderness—not when she knew he would suffer for it later.

Her dry lips cracked open. "Take me back."

CHAPTER 57

Tarly

H IS BOOTS FELT as if they were filled with stones. His breaths were restricted in his tight throat. Not even the chill of the misty rain could cool the heat of his skin. Footsteps—no, too many, too light. *Paws* caught up to him. Katori ran ahead, and he followed the beast, trusting this time it would be Nerida. He pushed the confrontation behind him while all he could focus on was finding her, at least to simply explain.

Tarly could have collapsed when he spied her hair through the staggered trees. The silvery sight of it had become a beacon of relief. He called her name, but she didn't falter her hurried pace. In his weakened state and with a drumming filling his ears, he couldn't be certain it left his lips with the velocity he intended. He recited it in his mind as though it would build enough tension to push past his choking airways.

"*Nerida!*"

She had to have heard him. He blinked the mist from his eyes, catching her pace as it slowed, and only with reluctance did she stop to let Katori catch up to her first. Tarly came to a stop a few paces away, bracing on his knees for stability. Nerida whirled to him. Her face seemed momentarily blank, but it morphed to surprise and then concern as she saw the state of him, but she stayed back.

"Tarly," she uttered, and despite everything, he enjoyed the sound of his real name coming from her lips. "Tarly Wolverlon, I presume. That's why you wouldn't tell me."

He knew she would guess. If she hadn't heard Isabelle, Nerida was too smart and well-read not to put the pieces together at hearing such a well-known name.

"I can explain," he rasped.

She shook her head, and urgency caused him to straighten. "I don't need you to. But I think it's best we go our separate ways. The library isn't far from here."

His brow furrowed as he contemplated her response. She didn't display the anger or outrage or disgust he thought she would. Nerida seemed…wary.

"It means nothing," he tried. "I'm not that person anymore. I turned my back on them like a coward, and I've accepted I have no right to that name anymore."

"I wish it were that easy."

"What does that mean?" He took a step toward her, but she retreated a step in response, angling her body as if she would take off any second. "Please." The plea slipped from his mouth before he could swallow it.

Her features creased, and he couldn't bear the conflict. Tarly realized his error. Like a rough dislodging of the dagger Isabelle had submerged into him and twisted, he understood.

He couldn't make that mistake again.

"Go," he said.

Nerida didn't move. It was in her nature to care, but he wouldn't allow another person to feel trapped with him.

"Be safe, Nerida."

Tarly turned away, shuffling his steps and feeling as if he were trudging through a sinking swamp. He listened to her stillness for minutes until she turned too, and the realization they would be going their separate ways made him tunnel into despair.

He didn't care anymore. Didn't care if the darkness that called to him now was final, when existing had become too much for him to bear.

He remembered finding a shallow cave for shelter. Remembered his fire dying out but being unable, uncaring enough, to find the strength to ignite it again. He remembered instead curling into himself against the chill, deciding this pitiful end seemed fitting for the little he had lived.

In reflection, Tarly could think of nothing he had left to make him want to keep suffering for. He hadn't had anything for some time, yet he kept on waking to the demand of dawn that urged him to *keep trying.* But trying had become exhausting. Trying had become wandering. Trying became never achieving but never failing either.

Trying was just...existing.

Tarly thought of Opal, his sister, who was a bright light he vowed to keep from the plague of his gray cloud whatever it took. He feared it was a force that, once touched, seized, controlled, and doused the world bleak. Opal saw in color and vibrancy, and it was for her he kept answering the sunrise. Yet now she was safe and away from him. At least, that was all he could tell himself to keep from being consumed by the guilt he'd had to leave her with Keira and hope they made it to the farmhouse he'd sent them to.

Warmth slowly returned to him. Tarly no longer shivered; he lay back, feeling slightly more comfortable. He wasn't sure how much time passed. Hours, likely days. Possibly weeks. His consciousness drifted in and out endlessly.

When a loud crack jolted him awake, he drew a long breath that felt as if it had sat in his throat for too long. Clarity came to him enough that he was able to distinguish the flickering amber flame against stone. Something was cushioned under his head, which lolled to find the fire blazing.

"Don't move too fast—"

The voice alerting him to another presence made him wince, contrary to the command. Tarly blinked a few times, his vision tilted, and all he could think upon witnessing the silvery locks and glowing skin was *angel*.

She came fully into focus, and he stared long enough to believe she was real...

Nerida was here.

"You left," he said, scrambling to remember something he might have missed.

"So did you," she answered, tending to something on her knees. "I guess we're even."

Tarly pushed up, wincing. Nerida paused her work, her expression concerned, fearful, hesitant to speak, but he waited patiently.

"I need you to know I understand what it's like to want to remain hidden. To be someone else. It's not your secrecy that made me try to walk away, Tarly."

"I don't understand."

"That's the problem," she confessed, brow creasing with a sadness so disturbing to him. "I've wandered many places for many years on my own. I've made friends, but they can never stay. I've lived in houses, but never a home."

Tarly started to realize what she was trying to explain. "Nerida isn't your real name," he said carefully.

The confirmation came in the way she fidgeted with her fingers in her lap. "It's one of them."

Tarly was overcome with an unexpected pride that she found she could trust him enough to share something so closely guarded. He wondered how many others, if any, knew.

"But if you need to know more, I can't stay."

"I don't," he said quickly. Against all that felt heavy and aching still, he sat up, a hand propping him up from behind. "I don't need to know anything. I'm not leaving you. But if you must leave me, I won't stop you."

Nerida smiled, but it was barely-there. She finished with what she was working on.

"Remove your shirt," she instructed quietly, looking away for him to do so.

He had questions, but he was too tired to ask them. Tarly turned toward the fire, teeth clenching against stiff, sore muscles as he folded out of his shirt, realizing Nerida had somehow managed to remove his cloak and he'd been lying on it.

"What happened back there?" She closed in, the echo of her presence tingling over him. "Your fever came out of nowhere. You've been in and out of consciousness for days."

Tarly turned hollow with the fresh memory she inspired. He thought he'd feel a deeper heartache or longing, but all he embraced was *closure*. He wasn't wanted by his mate—a fact he could do nothing but accept when it would not change. As much as he loved her and believed a part of her loved him back, it was not enough.

"You didn't hear it all?" he asked.

Soft hands touched his shoulder, making his breath hitch with the coolness she spread there. "I was too afraid after hearing your name. I-I left as soon as I concluded the family name that went with it."

"She was my mate."

Nerida halted spreading the salve she'd made. "Was?"

It was a careful question, one she wouldn't press to know the answer to, but Tarly didn't have anything to hide.

"She rejected the bond right there, but she decided I wasn't her life match long ago. I didn't believe she was still alive."

"I'm sorry," she said sincerely. "Magick doesn't always think of the heart in its will to find a comparable match. It can overlook many things."

"Have you met—" Tarly halted, thinking better of the personal question he had no right to ask. He heard her nervous swallow and accepted it wasn't a topic she wished to discuss. Though it riddled him with a desire to know…

"I didn't realize the effects of a rejected bond," she diverted sadly.

Tarly glanced vacantly into the fire. Hearing the confirmation that Nerida hadn't experienced it before was a relief, for it was misery he'd suffered, and he'd never wish the same on her. Though it inspired a selfish, entitled thought.

He huffed a dry laugh. "Imagine being punished for not being wanted." Tarly pulled his mother's necklace from his pocket. "She faked her death to escape me and left this on the remains of someone I'll never know."

He thought he felt ripples of anger and sorrow, but that didn't seem right coming from her.

"That's cruel and wrong, and you did not deserve that."

It wasn't the response he expected. Tarly could hardly stand the sight of the pendant dangling in his grasp, only seeing rejection reflecting over it. In an impulsive rage he went to toss it into the fire, but Nerida's small hand wrapped around his wrist. Their eyes met, so close as she leaned over that they shared breath.

Until she tore her gaze from him to fix it on the necklace.

"A healer's charm. You can only get these from the academy on Lakelaria's capital, Alandra. The color of the stone changes depending on what stage of training has been completed. Amethyst is the first."

While Nerida admired the pendant, Tarly admired her. The way she spoke like a song, the wonder smooth on her features. He was so grateful for the small tale he'd never heard before.

"It's beautiful."

"It was my mother's," he admitted. "It feels tainted now. She told me to give it to someone who would protect it. I failed her by giving it to someone who disregarded it to trick me."

Nerida didn't speak. He watched her pinched face, thoughtful as she stared at the dangling pendant. Tarly's anger fell. He retracted his arm, and she let go of her soft grip on him.

"Do you have one?" he asked.

Nerida shuffled back. "I did."

"What happened to it?"

"It was taken from me before my final exam. Broken in front of me. And that night I left."

Tarly felt an unexplainable wash of dread, a creeping heat of rage. "Who did that to you?"

Nerida shook her head. "It doesn't matter."

"You matter," he said before he could stop himself.

Large hazel eyes glittered with an ache he knew, a longing he felt. It was so brief he didn't know if it came from his own feelings or if he drew them from hers.

"Here." He extended the charm to her.

Nerida shook her head sharply. "I can't possibly take that."

"I want you to." It was all he could do when he could think of no one else deserving of it. His only regret…was that he hadn't met Nerida *first*. He couldn't stop the flashes of what could have been had they known each other long ago. It hit him so surely, so heartbreakingly, with guilt to think she'd made more of an imprint on him in their short time than Isabelle had in centuries.

Tarly dropped his graze with self-resentment. It didn't matter. He wasn't worthy of either. He lowered his hand, but a softness encased it.

"Are you sure?" she asked quietly.

He nodded without hesitation.

A faint spark lit in his stomach when she took it from him. He watched in utter fascination as the amethyst color began to swirl, changing, until it stilled to a beautiful emerald green.

"I didn't think it would do that considering my abandonment of the academy."

"Maybe it knows you did what you had to do."

Tarly was slowly beginning to read between the lines of her story, but he would be patient. "Would you?"

Nerida extended it back to him, and he read the signal, but his pulse skittered. She turned, holding the clasp to him behind her nape, and he took it slowly. Maybe purposefully.

Shifting until he felt her warmth, he secured the necklace, but his fingers lingered desirous at the feel of her bare skin. Tarly subconsciously swept the few strands of hair she'd missed. He wanted to lay his lips on her back, her shoulder, her *neck*… *Gods,* he'd never wanted to know what a person would feel like, taste like, so badly. It was all that clouded his senses.

Her head turned, breathing shallow. She said softly, "You didn't deserve that torment."

Tarly eased away from her.

When she turned and he saw the pendant resting against her smooth brown skin, liberation overcame him. He didn't deserve to think it, *feel it,* as he'd given the necklace away before, but in Nerida's possession…it lifted a burden to know it was unquestionably *safe* with her.

"You don't know me. What court is like—"

"I know escaping by whatever means can seem like the only option," she cut in firmly. "I don't believe for a second you would have forced her to stay had she spoken her mind."

"Maybe not with chains and threats—"

Nerida's wince halted him as if he'd slammed into stone.

He couldn't resist. "Has someone—?"

"We should go back for the horse. We could be at the library before evening tomorrow." She cut him off, taking a deep breath and busying herself with the few items she had.

Something dangerous stirred within him. Her flinch replayed in his mind, over and over, and he wanted to know. *Who, when, where?* He wanted to see if they'd left marks on her wrists he hadn't noticed before. He should have paid her more attention, as she deserved.

He realized it wasn't a story to drag from her, and though it took effort to cool his wrath and he was far from letting it go, he could wait to hear what had caused that disturbance. Then he'd make sure it could never draw terror from her again.

"I sold the horse," he said, needing a distraction.

"If you'd found me first, I could have told you I got decent coin in exchange for my skills."

"I didn't trade for coin." Tarly's nerves made him shift before he could meet her question. Momentarily, he sank in thinking he'd lost what he was looking for. Until he found the small satchel next to where he lay. "You didn't look inside?"

"It's not mine."

Anxiously, he reached for it, scratching the back of his neck as he passed it to her. "It is."

Tarly had to turn from her, focusing on the heat from the fire, which he raised his palms to, itching to take it back when he couldn't be sure why. Only that he felt foolish. He listened to her open it, finding out what was within, and wordlessly she examined it. Tarly's tense muscles only tightened more without knowing what she made of it. If it was even close to what she needed.

"You didn't have to," she said quietly, the emotion in her voice aching in him.

"They seemed important," he muttered. "The ones you lost." He didn't turn back, knowing she was examining the pouch of small bottles, each with their own slot so she could see them all clearly.

A scent drifted to him that straightened his spine. He inhaled again to be sure. Salt. Her tears… He didn't know what to do, what could have inspired them, and suddenly an awful twisting clenched his gut and he had to look at her.

"I didn't mean to remind you of—"

"It's not that," she said quickly, wiping her face and plastering on a new expression. "It doesn't matter."

Of course it matters, he wanted to say. Yet Nerida didn't seem willing to talk. Her fingers lingered over a pair of silver scissors, and the upturning of her mouth eased his quick drop of heaviness.

"We can cut that hair of yours before people think this cave is your dwelling place."

Tarly couldn't help but match her teasing and surrendered to her, allowing her to do what she wanted. He couldn't deny the length now touching his shoulders had become burdensome to maintain. "As you wish," he grumbled, but in truth he was grateful. More for the spark of excitement it brought out in her as she slid the scissors free and reached for a waterskin she must have picked up in town.

"Tip your head back," she instructed.

The cool water running over his hair made him shudder with a chill. He straightened again, and the first feel of her fingers combing over his scalp was bliss. Her hands anywhere always seemed to relax him, but *this*... She massaged from his roots to his ends several times, and the sensation quickened his breathing, feeling like something intimate. Then she began to cut.

"You don't have to answer," she began, searching for something to fill the silence, "but what happened to bring you out here? I heard your father was ruling well. Olmstone has stood for some time with the help of its allies in Rhyenelle."

Tarly thought about whether he should share what he knew with her. Not out of fear of her knowing his past, his family, but because of something far worse. He couldn't stand the thought of any tie to him putting her in danger.

"Nothing is always as it seems," he offered. "My father was a broken male. He had been for some time after losing my mother. He lost his way long ago and became easy to manipulate. Nerida—"

She paused at hearing her name, and what rose within him was desperation.

"After the library, after we part, you should deny you ever met me. I don't know what is left of the court since Nik and Tauria left. I abandoned them all like a coward only to see my sister to safety. I can't be sure if they're seeking me still, and it's safer if you forget me."

Nerida didn't answer for a long time. Didn't resume her cutting. "Tauria Stagknight?"

He almost twisted to see if the disbelief in her tone was reflected on her face, but she reached for his hair as if to distract him from the fact she'd backtracked to the name at all.

"You did what you had to do," she said. "Is your sister safe?"

The question made his thoughts drift to her. Knowing he couldn't give a sure answer rained down on him like failure. "I hope so," he said, more to himself, with a note of yearning. If Nerida wasn't going to double back to the one who'd caught her intrigue, Tarly was. "You said you lived in Fenstead for some time—did you meet Tauria?"

She seemed to debate her answer. Shuffling around him, cutting hair that fell around his face. He only held faith she knew what she was doing. "Of course not," she settled on. "I glimpsed her a few times from afar like everyone else, I'm sure."

The brush-off felt deliberate. She was withholding something.

"Did you…have something with her?" Nerida hedged.

"Yes. Though not really in the way you're thinking."

"How do you know what I'm thinking?" Nerida came to his side, fingers working delicately through his hair. Tarly managed to steal a few glances, only struck now with clarity about why she'd never felt like a perfect stranger.

"You remind me of her," he said thoughtfully, hoping she wouldn't take it the wrong way.

"I can't see why," Nerida huffed, shuffling a little away from him.

"I think it was your eyes at first," he went on.

"They're a common color."

He wanted to object that they were the exact same hue of hazel, darker than his, but with warm tendrils when they caught the light. Like now. He couldn't help but fixate on them as she circled him to stop right in front of him, high on her knees, assessing and combing and cutting his hair, which felt so much lighter and tamer already.

"Then it was your determination and bravery. You two could storm together, wind and water."

Nerida pretended not to take his words too seriously, but faint flickers around her eyes and the quirk of her mouth told him she enjoyed the thought. "Did you have feelings for her?"

"I wanted to," he confessed, earning a pinch of her brow. "Her heart always belonged to another, and mine… I could never have loved her like she deserved."

Nerida's hands combed through his hair slowly, admiring her work before her gaze dropped to his.

"Why do you think that?"

He could hardly breathe with her position. "I don't have that kind of love to give. Not anymore."

Nerida lowered, her fingers still lingering at the back of his head, and his pulse beat hard. "I don't believe that," she said, hushed and wondering.

The impulse to touch her flexed his fingers against the stone, a rush of desire to draw his arm around her and pull her so close it frightened him.

"Why?" The question slipped out as barely a breath. Perhaps he wondered what she saw that he couldn't feel within.

"Because that's too easy," she said, her gaze holding him still. "That allows the ones who've hurt us to win. I can't accept that. Time won't forget—or heal. We have to do that for ourselves. It may be the hardest thing we have to face, but if you still have a will to try…it's not the end for you."

A will to try.

Tarly's chest gave a full beat, a thump of warm enlightenment that lingered in his pulse, fleeting but there.

A will.

He did touch her then—*had to*—slowly, from her waist, and when her lips parted but she didn't retreat, he curved his hand around her. Their faces inched closer, and he held his breath. It wasn't the first time he'd wondered about the feel of her lips, and fear erased in at the closeness of her. He felt the tightening of her fingers in his hair, the way she seemed to give over to the gravity that pulled them together in that moment…

Until it stopped as if a wall had slammed between them. Nerida turned rigid the moment his arm curled all the way around her, and he was so close to bringing their bodies flush together and surrendering to the unexplainable current that grew.

"I can't," she said with a note of pain like she was denying herself what she wanted. Nerida pulled away, and the fire couldn't replace the loss of her warmth that ran far below the surface.

Tarly threw his guard up, realizing his foolishness to make an advance on someone he couldn't get attached to anyway. He shuffled away to seek more distance, overcome with suffocation and a need to be alone.

"I'm—"

"I don't need your pity, Nerida. I don't need you to try to replace something I just lost," he said darkly. The words burned like acid, and he knew she didn't deserve them, but he had no other way to set the boundary that would keep them from feelings that could break them both.

CHAPTER 58

Reylan

REYLAN MARCHED THE halls after leaving the cells, barely able to muster a response after escorting Faythe to her rooms with a promise he wouldn't be long. He had one thing on his reeling mind that wouldn't settle after the confrontation below.

Kyleer came into view down the next hall, and Reylan's eyes flashed at the sight of him. This was after all who he'd been on the hunt for. His brother seemed to brace for his wrath, flinching when Reylan took him by the jacket and slammed him to the wall.

"I thought I could trust you," he snarled low.

Kyleer pushed him away. "What's that supposed to mean?"

"Your games with her end now. This *infatuation* ends now."

"You have no idea what you're talking about." Kyleer matched his dominance with a dangerous, palpable energy, and there was no telling what they would do. Reylan had fought him before, not always in training. They were brothers in all ways except by blood, and that came with challenging each other when it was called for. It could get messy and ugly, and the victor usually depended on who was more pissed off.

"After all she did, all Maverick did, how could you betray Faythe like that?"

"Zaiana isn't Maverick."

Reylan laughed, the sound cold and dark, as he dove a hand through his hair. He could barely stand to look Kyleer. "They are dark fae. The enemy who seeks to destroy us all and is preparing to strike this very moment. I didn't believe you'd ever let beauty cloud your judgment. A prisoner is still a prisoner."

"You're wrong. I'm getting through to her more than those damn soldiers could by whipping her—more than you could by forcing yourselves into her mind."

"There is no mercy for those like her."

"You're only proving her right in painting her a monster just by her blood."

Reylan's fist slammed into the wall, splitting the stone. "There is *no* mercy because she harmed Faythe," he seethed. "She would have killed her, and you're a damn fool if you think she wouldn't try again given the chance. And let me be clear to you, Kyleer: she will *not* get the chance to be free around her."

"I would have thought you of all people should believe in second chances. The will to change, *brother.*"

Reylan's breathing came hard. He had to close his eyes to block out his implication. He battled memories that flooded to the surface at those words, unable to silence them now Kyleer had pinned him with the dark notes of his past.

"You would liken me to her?" he asked with a chilling calm. "To *them?*" He couldn't help it. There was no looking at Zaiana without seeing Maverick, and it took physical restraint every day not to do something impulsive with her in reach. To draw Maverick here in the hopes she was important enough to him, or perhaps his torment would relent enough if he only killed her for now.

"You know I would never betray Faythe," Kyleer said carefully. "I need you to trust me. Please."

Reylan's eyes scrunched with a plea so rare it struck him to realize how deeply Kyleer felt about this. "You care for her."

"I can't explain it," he confessed. "But I would never trust her if I believed she was capable of killing Faythe."

"She is more than capable."

"Willing then. I cannot convince you with mere words; I only beg for time. Let me try to get through to her. Think about it, Reylan. With Zaiana on our side…it would change the tide of this battle completely. Think about what she knows, who might answer a call to join her. Those leading the dark fae…I *believe* to be her enemies too. She's smart. Too smart—"

"Yet you cannot see her playing you right into a game you will *lose*, Ky."

"You're hardly the one to preach on this," he snapped.

Reylan was so damn close to losing his temper, and his fist trembled at Kyleer's tone.

"Let me continue to handle this. That's all I ask."

Reylan couldn't stand his hopeful words, his hidden message that the king could not know since his wrath could be far worse than Reylan's.

Izaiah interrupted with a slow approach. "So we all stand by on the sidelines and watch you court the prisoner in the hopes you can make a dead heart beat?"

Kyleer's fists tightened, and while Reylan took no pleasure in having Izaiah side with him, it was a relief to know he wasn't totally biased in his opinions where Faythe was concerned.

"It's not like that," Kyleer growled.

"Oh?" Izaiah strolled nonchalantly, hands in his pockets. "She's all over you, brother. You couldn't hide that kind of entangled scent even by rolling in the stables." Then Izaiah's expression released its accusation. "Tell me it's just lust. That I could understand. Tell me you don't truly *feel* for her."

"You think I didn't notice how often you visited the cells before we had her? Even now, your absence hasn't gone unnoticed," Kyleer snapped.

Reylan studied the tightening of his lips, the trembling of his poise. It was so unlike Kyleer to lash out at his younger brother that he braced to step between them.

"If you're going to accuse me of something, say it outright, Ky," Izaiah challenged.

"Let's just say you checked up far less on the darkling."

"She was hardly a threat."

"You mean she hardly held the appeal of Tynan."

Izaiah stepped up to Kyleer, and while Reylan was ready to grapple with them both if needed, he stayed back.

"At least I knew where to draw the line and not fall for a pretty face."

"Stop this," Reylan cut in, his mind finally clearing to see the wrongness of the tension between the three of them and where it had come from. "If we let this continue then they win without having to do a damn thing," he hissed. He ran a hand over his face in exasperation. "We need to know more about the ruin, how it can be wielded. Faythe seems to think we need all of them to send Marvellas back to wherever in the Netherworld she came from. Faythe fears them because they speak to her, and reaching for their power could destroy the damn world if she doesn't know how to control them first."

He couldn't believe he was about to turn his back on the trap he feared his brother was falling into. Agalhor couldn't find out, or Reylan knew the punishment that might befall him would be out of his hands completely.

"You have to be discreet with however you go about it. I don't like it, I don't agree with it, and we are running out of time. If you can't get anything of use from her in a week, we do this my way," Reylan decided. Then, when his anger cooled, all he could surface was his concern. "But you need to be careful. She's cunning, smart. She lures people in to get what she wants, and I can't stand by and watch you fall victim too."

"I'm not a victim," Kyleer defended. "I don't care for your opinion of her. She spared Faythe's life—don't forget that."

Reylan risked unleashing his barrel of rage upon Kyleer. Anger that had built from the moment he returned with Faythe. Resentment and anguish and a pitiful yearning. For everything she was—stunning, powerful, royal; everything he couldn't consider himself worthy of matching. He'd heard the council all but agree she was a prize too high for someone like him. She deserved a lord or a prince, or anyone of wealth and status. He had nothing. Nothing to offer her but his heart, which he feared wasn't enough.

"One week," he uttered, and he couldn't look at Kyleer again before storming away.

Reylan hesitated outside Faythe's room, battling the sense to stay away from intimate contact but raging with the *need* to see her. Bracing a hand on the frame, he lost his fight and knocked.

Barely a heartbeat passed before the door swung open. Her lips parted to speak, but Reylan broke. His mouth claimed hers, and the soft noise of surprise only caused him to hook his hands under her thighs and find the nearest wall, where he pressed into her, unable to get close enough, taste enough, feel enough. It was inexplicably maddening. The eternal flame he held for her blazed into an untamed inferno.

It took everything in him to pull away before he snapped and buried his scent into her. He leaned his forehead into her collar while both their chests heaved with his unexpected assault. Her fingers relaxed their tight grip in his hair.

"What was that for?" she asked through a delightful breathlessness.

"For everything, Faythe," he answered quietly. "For existing."

Her huffed laugh didn't just flutter his chest; it fucking ached. He didn't want it to ever stop hurting, this reminder of how alive he felt with her.

"I should exist more often."

His mouth curled faintly before his brow pinched and he squeezed her thighs. "I want to sink my teeth into this pretty throat of yours so badly it's torture."

Her legs clamped around him tighter, and he groaned. "I want that too."

"Why did you stop? In the cells, after all she did to you…why offer her mercy?" Reylan searched those glittering amber eyes as he made it to the bed and sat, keeping her straddling his lap. He couldn't ease this tightening in his gut and wanted to know how she had it in her to be merciful even to those who'd wronged her and would do so again.

"You didn't feel her terror," Faythe tried to explain.

"She didn't care for yours. Or for any of your weaknesses on that battlefield when she hurt you over and over as a dark fae against a human." And he hadn't been there. His eyes pinched closed but opened to her palm sliding along his jaw.

"We can't pass judgment based on a past that has wronged us. We judge the now based on what we see and what we can change for the future."

Gods, she was brilliant. And fair and kind and strong. Not afraid of darkness, but never consumed by it. He loved her so fiercely he was terrified she might be a dream he would awaken from.

"Zaiana spared my life, and I have to believe it was from some part of her that *cared*. She can't see it, or maybe she does and that was what caused her fear of me being in her mind. She's of a different world that has taught her empathy is wrong, that her life depends on conformity and terror, so it is what she embodies."

Reylan stroked her thighs, peering up with awe as she spoke, choosing to see deeper into a person, not judge from the surface. It made him recall his own liberation with her patience and love.

"Her thoughts, infiltrating her mind, it felt as cold and full of fear as death."

"You are too good for this world, Faythe Ashfyre. Certainly too good for me."

"That's not true. Not even for a second."

"I would have done it," he confessed. "Despite her fear, even if she'd begged, I would have infiltrated her mind." Shame wrecked him to know it went against her compassion. His heart could never match his mate's—an incompatibility that terrified him.

"I wouldn't have blamed you for it," she said at last.

"Don't bend your morals for me. I can't bear it."

"I wouldn't have blamed you because if she'd harmed *you*, nearly killed *you*... I'm not as good as you think I am, Reylan."

Then it became as clear as if the world had opened before him. Faythe was his balance and his light, and in that moment, he chose to believe, *accept*...that she was his equal.

CHAPTER 59

Tarly

THE INN THEY stopped at to get a hot meal and bed for the night was hardly luxurious. The front room was filled mostly with men and fae males. Tarly couldn't tear his eyes from them all. His fists flexed as he stood awaiting drinks at the bar while Nerida sat oblivious to their attention. He swiped the tankards with little more than a grumble of thanks and slapped down a copper.

Tarly set one of the drinks down in front of Nerida before sliding in opposite her, trying to keep from shooting a warning look at the group eyeing them the most. He took big gulps in silence, not meeting Nerida's gaze either. They'd engaged in very little conversation since the cave.

"So sullen," she muttered under her breath.

Tarly's jaw worked. He slid his gaze to her for the first time but knew she was preoccupied with the small bottles in her pouch.

"You picked a good selection, by the way."

"It was the shopkeeper."

"Except many of them are exactly what I had before."

"Happy coincidence."

Her shoulders slouched with the glare she cast him. "Do you ever accept thanks?"

"You didn't say thanks."

"Credit then."

"They're bottles of herbs and tonics. Hardly a diamond necklace."

"They mean more to me than that."

They stared off, their conversation ridiculous even for children, never mind full-grown fae.

"You're welcome," he grumbled reluctantly.

Her response was only to roll her eyes. A couple of times now he'd noticed her gaze wandering to a group of fae males in the corner, and it stirred his ire every time though he had no right to feel it.

Their meals were brought to them. Two vegetable broths.

"You can eat meat in front of me," she commented, stirring her bowl.

"I know."

They ate in silence. The warmth that filled his insides was bliss compared to the bitter night they'd come in here to escape. Between mouthfuls, Nerida's attention kept wandering.

"Do they interest you?" Tarly snapped before he could stop himself. "If you desire company in your bed tonight, I won't stop you."

Nerida set down her bread harshly. "Is *that* what's been making you so grumpy?"

"I am not."

Nerida leaned over the table to hiss, "Do you really think so lowly of me?"

His jaw flexed, then he dropped his gaze to his empty bowl. "No," he admitted.

"You haven't been listening to their conversation. They've been talking of Hyla's Cave."

Tarly was instantly alert. "Then we should get the Nether out of here lest they happen to be thugs who'd hand you over for coin should they put two and two together and realize what you are."

Nerida scowled, standing abruptly. "I just want to find out what they know of it."

His hand lashed out to hers as she moved away. "Are you out of your damned mind?"

She twitched under his hold, but something stopped her from ripping it away. She leaned down close—too close. Tarly almost leaned back. "Unless you want them to believe I'm very much *available*, be nice."

Tarly swallowed hard from her low tone, caught completely off-guard. "Why does it matter about the cave?"

Nerida leaned back. "I'm curious." She brushed him off.

Tarly wanted to press, believing she was withholding something, but she pushed away from the table and made her way over. He swore under his breath, going after her in a heartbeat, and he flared at the many sets of eyes that pinned her as she approached.

"What can we do for a pretty thing like you?" one male drawled.

Tarly became tense in his efforts not to lash out.

"I heard you talking about Hyla's Cave. It grabbed my interest. Mind if we join you?"

The male with rugged brown hair took a long inhale from a pipe. Smoke billowed around his assessing gaze, which landed on Tarly, itching every inch of his skin.

"You, we wouldn't mind. He, on the other hand, is killing the atmosphere with his presence." He leaned his forearms on the table. "What is your name?"

"Anna," Nerida answered without missing a beat. "You'll have to excuse my husband's temperament."

Tarly could have choked. Her hand curled around his forearm, and the unexpected lie stunned him for a moment. The males set suspicious eyes on him, expectant.

Meeting Nerida's gaze, he read the prompt and reluctantly cleared his throat. "Sully," he offered, and he swore he felt Nerida's amusement.

With a single nod, the other three males shuffled to make room for them.

"The name's Yakquard," the male said, leaning back casually. "And what is it about the cave that interests you, if I may ask, milady?"

"I am no lady," Nerida said humbly. "I wondered what you knew of it. We had an unfortunate run-in with some human sailors who were not so...*kind* on the matter. They seek it out."

His dark brow curved. "Ah yes, so I've heard. It is what we were discussing."

"For Seanna's Song."

Tarly eyed Nerida carefully, wanting to ask what caught her intrigue now when she'd been so convincing in her belief it was merely a fable.

"That is what they say."

"It's a dangerous weapon in the wrong hands."

This caught Yakquard's attention. He bore intense eyes on her, suspicious. "What do you know of it?"

Tarly had to admit he wondered this too.

"How did people learn of the song?"

"You didn't answer my question, princess."

Nerida startled at the title, seeming to level Yakquard with her own caution. "Never mind," she said and rose from her chair.

"You're from Lakelaria." Yakquard reeled her attention back.

It worked to snap her gaze to him, and Tarly stood too with a protective flare. "Keep your voice down," he warned.

It earned him a goading smile. "Why so secretive? You came over to me, remember."

"I'm not from anywhere," Nerida defended.

"Let's go." Tarly went to steer her away from them.

"Not even the best Waterwielder could reach that cave. They are fools to try."

Tarly swore internally as they gripped Nerida's curiosity once again. Yet she didn't engage; she only pondered the information before she walked away. He swept one last look over the small gathering, assessing if they were a threat should they decide to come after Nerida, who was making herself an intriguing target.

He caught up to her, hooking his arm through hers before she made for the stairs. She yelped in protest as he led them outside instead.

"We paid for a night," she objected when they emerged onto the street.

Tarly reached for her hood, but Nerida snatched it from him to fix it herself. He pulled up his own just as Katori came pattering up beside them. "Not anymore," he grumbled. "I won't risk them cornering you wanting to find out more."

"They seemed harmless."

"So is a knife for as long as it's sheathed."

They marched in silence for a long stretch before breaking through the tree line of a small woods. He only hoped it wouldn't be long before they found an adequate shelter or softer ground to rest upon.

"Why the interest in Hyla's Cave?" Tarly demanded. "Since you're set on nearly outing yourself over it."

"The song—it's too great a weapon if it falls into the wrong hands. They gave me what I needed. It must be deep enough to be safe for good."

"What kind of weapon?"

"Do you know nothing of the sirens? They are not a myth, Tarly. Many millennia ago, they were powerful creatures of the sea with the Shapeshifting ability to walk on land. But it's said their bloodline can be found in some fae from when they used their song to lure in lovers—some with solely wicked intent, to feed and drown and take their riches. As a result, there became a race once known as hybrid sirens."

Tarly became surprisingly enraptured in the tale. "What happened to them?"

"The War of the Black Sea. Sailors fought back for the many lives they'd lost. And in truth, no one really knows. Perhaps they do still exist somewhere no one can reach. All that's left to our knowledge is that most diluted bloodlines reside in Lakelaria. As for the song, it's a weapon of persuasion. The beholder need only speak and their enchantment washes over a person. There's no trace, no magick to burn out. You wouldn't feel it like an attack."

The thought shook him to his core. "Just as well it's within untouchable depths then." When she didn't respond, he cast her a look. "It is beyond reach like they said, isn't it?"

"Unless they find someone who can breathe underwater."

Tarly blanched, and Nerida huffed a laugh.

"I'm fairly certain there's no one alive with enough siren blood to have that ability."

She didn't meet his eye again as she trudged forward. He watched her for a few seconds, until her face lit up and he followed her gaze to a shallow cave beside a running stream. As she rushed ahead, Tarly slowed his pace, bending to retrieve what logs he could for a fire to last the night. Katori chased after her, and he watched with utter fascination as she played with the stream as though it relaxed her to use the ability that lived within.

Nerida's soft laughter fluttered through the night while Katori leaped to catch her floating water. Tarly didn't realize he'd stopped looking for wood. Stopped walking. Stopped thinking of anything but how innocent and perfect she appeared in the moonlight.

He didn't want this. Someone to care for who would leave a new permanent scar when she left. They always left. Tarly wasn't certain how much more he could suffer, and he wondered with a despairing thought what would end him first.

The poison that placed his life on borrowed time, or the impact from the fall he could not stop.

CHAPTER 60

Faythe

"I SAID THREE steps left, not two."

Izaiah's exasperated command echoed through the ballroom, cutting through Faythe and Reylan's chuckles. She'd miscounted, stepped on his foot, and would have gone tumbling were it not for his save.

"Seriously, a whole week and you're still like a newborn lamb."

Reylan's eyes only sparkled with amusement, and she was glad for his being there when duty usually pulled him away.

"General Reylan."

The smooth, irritating voice stood the hairs on her arms. Malin strolled into the room with a cool arrogance and glee, causing Reylan to release her, his whole body going taut.

"I didn't expect you to be one to offer yourself up for a dance so eagerly," he commented, his accusation lingering: Malin knew he was only doing so for Faythe's sake.

"I have to observe what I need to correct," Izaiah said with enough of a challenge that Faythe tensed. "It took some forcing, but since he's here as her guard anyway."

"About that," Malin sang. "I came to inform you of a post needing your attention for the next few weeks."

Reylan crossed his arms. "There are plenty of commanders to oversee postings."

"Yes, but there has been a particular setback in one of the outskirt towns. The leading commander there demands you attend, and as you're our top general, I think our king would agree."

Faythe watched Reylan's jaw flex. He wanted to protest but knew it would be wasted breath. Faythe knew it wasn't a coincidence. This was her cousin's newest wedge between them.

"I will speak with him," Reylan responded coldly.

"It is rather urgent, especially with the impending threats. We cannot afford for weaknesses not to be dealt with."

Reylan's fists tightened, and she sent her assurance to him silently within. It eased her own discomfort to watch it deflate the rigid posture he'd adopted since Malin set foot in the hall. He met her eye, and Faythe offered a small smile of understanding with her nod. Then he was following her cousin from the ballroom.

"I can't stand him," Izaiah muttered under his breath.

"I never would have guessed," Faythe grumbled.

He took her hand, giving no warning before he twirled her and pulled her to him. "Let's get you moving before that sulk sets in."

"I don't sulk."

Izaiah chuckled. "It's like being around a puppy-dog."

Faythe gaped at him then snapped her mouth shut at the amusement lighting up his face. "Just teach me more of the damn dance."

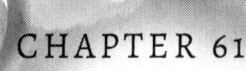

CHAPTER 61

Tarly

T HE GREAT LIBRARY Livre des Verres remained closed off.
Nerida didn't question Tarly's hesitation. Maybe she hadn't picked up on his anxiety at all as they stood in a dark alleyway spying on the patrols keeping anyone from gaining access. There were fae...and dark fae. Tarly was riddled with memories from the last time he saw them, attendees of both his wedding and funeral, which he and Tauria had narrowly escaped.

The city seemed functional at least. Less bustling, though he supposed the new invading force kept the people in hiding. But he was more than relieved to see the city full mostly of Olmstone citizens, that they hadn't all been slaughtered or forced out by the dark fae.

Nerida pulled down her hood, looking over herself and adjusting her clothing.

"What are you doing?" he questioned.

"I'm going to distract them while you find a way in," she said simply.

Her flat tone didn't sit well with him, along with the way she could barely hold his eye. They'd traveled for the past day in near silence, but part of him believed it was better this way.

"That's not happening," he said firmly.

She cut him a look that said, "Try to stop me." His only response was to hook his arm around her waist on impulse when she almost stepped out from their cover. Her gaze snapped to his, and she glared up at him. It was hard to fight his smile.

"How exactly do you plan to do that?"

"Charm," she bit out. "Something you clearly lack, so no, our roles cannot switch."

Tarly scoffed. "I can be charming."

"To anything other than people, perhaps."

His eyes rolled as he released her. "Then how do you plan to get inside?"

"You'll have to trust me on that one."

"Not good enough."

"I wasn't *asking.*"

The tension between them pulsed with frustration and anguish—so much that he risked breaking. He only sighed, crossing his arms and leaning back against the wall.

"Besides, we can't take our chances with you being noticed, or they'll come for you."

"If anything goes wrong, if anyone lays a hand on you, call out immediately." He cast his gaze down into the darkness.

Nerida hesitated only for a moment, but then he listened to her leave without another word. As soon as he lost the sound of her steps, he took off to find her. He watched as she pulled down the bodice of her dress once more, and though he had no right to the emotion, knowing how she planned to *charm* the male guards angered him enough to clench his fists and jaw, and he had to refrain from going against her plan.

Every nerve strained when their eyes landed on her. She appeared lost. Innocent but *flirtatious.* Her fingers ran through her silvery tresses, and he wanted it to be him. His hand; his attention. The guards were drawn to her like moths to a flame. She was exquisite. Her brown skin glowed in the sunlight, her hair shimmered, and he imagined her large doe eyes would be working wonders on the males who forgot their duties to admire her.

Tarly scowled, cursing as he couldn't waste her efforts, much as he wanted to turn their attention to anything but her. He dipped out of cover and darted across the street in the shade, scaling the rooftops and spying an open window. It had been shattered. Phantom pain pulsed in his shoulder while he crouched, and he tried hard not to let his mind go back to the consuming terror of hearing the library shatter knowing he'd left Tauria there.

Shaking his head, he slipped inside.

He couldn't believe what had become of the legendary space as he wandered through it slowly. The library had always been quiet, but this silence was one of desolation and lost hope. What was once a sanctuary of safety had now been defiled. His quiver of arrows and the few daggers weighed him down like rocks, and he muttered a silent prayer to be forgiven for bringing the weapons here.

At the balcony, he glanced down at the glass sundial glittering mesmerizingly in the light, then he cast his eyes up to see the true sky beaming down.

The creak of a large door snapped his attention. Tarly reached for a knife, but the flicker of white made him sag with relief.

"They let you walk right in?" he grumbled incredulously.

Nerida shrugged. "They seemed nice."

"I'm sure they did."

"Which is more than I can say about you."

Tarly clenched his jaw, but Nerida was already walking away, brushing him off as if she couldn't get rid of him soon enough.

"I told them I knew what I was looking for and wouldn't be long," she said over her shoulder, marching through the aisles.

Nerida must not have noticed the missing dome roof from outside. Her steps halted abruptly at a large serration of glass lying in her path, and she immediately looked up to find where it came from. "What happened here?" she breathed, a hand reaching to her chest with true heartache.

Tarly wasn't sure how to explain it all. "Tauria's a Windbreaker," he stated, thinking that was ample enough information to explain *how*.

Nerida snapped her gaze to his. The knowledge didn't seem new to her. Her expression flexed with awe and fear, maybe *concern*. "Why would she do this?"

"She was under attack." He hitched his shoulder subconsciously. "By the same dark fae who condemned me."

Her attention fell briefly to his wound with a pinched brow. "She was not bitten?"

Tarly found her worry for Tauria endearing. "She is well."

That eased her soft face, but her attention lingered on him as though she wanted to speak but held her breath.

Tarly saved her from trying, diverting the topic with, "What *are* you hoping to find here?"

Nerida gave a thoughtful scan of the library. "I'm looking for a particular book, but now I need another as well." She took off again, and Tarly followed. "We're going to find a cure for you."

He huffed a short laugh. "Don't waste your time. Get what you came for. I'll be okay."

"You won't."

"It's not your concern—"

"You are," she snapped.

Tarly halted, but she kept going. Pain stilled his steps as he wondered why. What he'd done to have her still wanting to help him. Wanting to save what didn't want to be saved. At least…he hadn't wanted to be saved before.

"Did you come here often?" she called, snapping him from his moment of tunneling thought. Her voice traveled distant all the way across the balcony.

"Yes," he admitted.

She met his eye across the long expanse, leaning her hands on the railing. "What kind of books do you like to read, Tarly Wolverlon?"

The way she used his full name, the slight tilt of her head— Nerida's curiosity about him was something he wasn't used to. He scratched the back of his neck, heat flushing in as he wondered if there was a wrong answer. One she might mock or disagree with, likely not on purpose, but he couldn't help his anxiety for her opinion.

His reservation got the better of him, and he said instead, "Medicine and Healing is this way."

After climbing two staircases, Tarly halted and muttered a curse.

"Tauria?" Nerida concluded as she crept up behind him. "Must have been some fight."

Of course she would have collapsed the entire row they needed.

"You might want to inform your guard *friends* you could be a while longer," he grumbled, walking over to the nearest fallen bookcase.

"Are you jealous?" she said, skipping around to his other side as Tarly braced to push the heavy shelving back upright.

"Of what?"

"That I find five minutes of their company more pleasant than an hour of yours."

He sliced her with a look, and her only response was to settle into a firm crouch. Without a word, they erected the bookcase with great difficulty, and it gave a resounding thump as it found its balance.

"Then perhaps you should invite them to search with you." Tarly began snatching books, placing them in no particular order back onto the shelves but checking each one first to decide if it could be of use to her.

"Of course, you can't be jealous," she quipped, shelving books in the same manner. "When you make it your mission to have everyone dislike you, and you them."

He paused to glance her way, thinking over her words, which he knew to be true. Yet he couldn't imagine any other place he'd rather be in that moment. Even the solitude he often sought because nothing could hurt him there.

Before Nerida could catch him staring, he busied himself in the mountain of books. "You're right," he said. "This has been a rather torturous expedition, having enjoyed my weeks spent gaining distance only to end up right back here."

"I insisted time and time again, yet you still followed."

"What else was I to do?"

"Let me go."

Tarly didn't let her see the breath he didn't fully inhale. "We'll be relieved of each other soon," he muttered, not lingering on the feeling that twisted within him at that realization.

Nerida didn't speak again, though he itched for it. They lost themselves in placing back books and scanning titles, and maybe he didn't particularly rush the task, knowing it would only make the moments in her company speed by faster.

Near an hour into their silent sorting, the main library door groaned. Tarly straightened in defense, shifting in front of Nerida. Her hand curled around his bicep. Meeting eyes with him, she pressed a finger to her lips and pushed him sideward.

"It's the guard from outside," she whispered. "Don't let him sense you."

Protest rooted him, but with her second shove of urgency, and detecting the presence inching closer, he made himself scarce.

"Ah, there you are," the male chirped.

Tarly shook his head with an inward groan at his overly bright tone. Two balconies up seemed sufficient enough distance for the guard to be too enthralled by Nerida to notice him spying on them.

"I've been trying to find my books, but as it seems, the section I need faced the worst damage," she explained sweetly.

"I can help you," he offered.

Tarly's fingers flexed with ire. He wondered how long he'd have to stay here and witness this.

"No, that's all right. I should be done in another hour if you can allow me the time."

He didn't expect her to refuse the company she claimed to be better than his. He'd been prepared to get comfortable and tolerate them from afar.

"A pretty thing like you shouldn't be alone. It's criminal."

"I quite like being alone." She brushed him off, trying to busy herself sifting through fallen piles. "It leaves room for thought."

"Indeed. I was left alone on patrol for ten minutes on my own, and all I could think about was you."

Nerida laughed, and Tarly's ire dissipated entirely. He watched how her laughter lit such brightness on her face. She showed teeth with a full grin. He studied how she tucked a front curl behind her ear that never belonged in her braids.

"You needn't flatter me," she said, rose coloring her brown skin.

"It's just my truth."

Tarly wanted to take his insufferable words and shove them back down the guard's throat. Closing his eyes, he shook his head against the petty violence he wasn't so accustomed to. Not for this. Nerida had every reason to entertain the guard's advances, and it was not for Tarly to intervene. He tried to engross himself in a book—a romance he hadn't intended to pick up, but it was the first he happened to reach for. It was the last thing he wanted to read about.

They continued chatting below, and at last the guard toned down his poetry. Every smile he drew from her, every flutter of laughter, hollowed Tarly's chest. As Nerida stood, the guard stepped close to her, and it had Tarly closing the book he'd been using as a prop and straightening up. She took a step back, but he followed it. Tarly's fists clenched. And when the guard raised a hand, he didn't watch it meet her waist because he was already moving.

Damning the secret.

Damning the world.

Damning himself for *caring*.

"I think her signal to keep your distance was pretty clear." Tarly didn't recognize his own tone as he approached.

The guard shifted in defense, but Tarly was already upon him, grabbing his collar and slamming him into the bookcase that threatened to topple again.

"Allow me to add to it."

"Sully," Nerida warned.

That name fluttered a beat of his heart in the way one could hate something but still find an odd comfort in its familiar touch.

"Y-you're not supposed to be in here," the guard stuttered. He seemed completely harmless, yet it didn't lessen Tarly's distaste.

"Only *pretty things*, isn't that right?" he snarled.

"I'm sorry. I-I didn't know she was taken—"

"I'm not," Nerida interjected firmly, but her hard gaze was fixed on Tarly.

He released the guard, driving a hand through his hair as they stared off.

"Do I know you?"

Tarly's jaw worked at the question. "Doubtful," he answered. Yet he slid his attention to gauge if the guard believed him. He swore under his breath at the widening eyes of recognition as the guard pieced together who he was.

"Y-Your Highness, we thought you were dead."

Tarly took no pleasure in what he had to do. He didn't waste a second debating the move when the guard could go scuttling off to warn the new leaders. His fist connected with the guard's face.

Nerida gasped. "You didn't have to do that!" She rushed over to the fallen fae, immediately flipping open her satchel to retrieve her pouch.

Tarly watched him as a new shame rose, his irrational irritation calming when he realized she was right. He thought if the guard were to warn the others to seek him out, it could put Nerida in danger too. Yet she was safe here from his threats…as long as she wasn't with him.

Taking a few paces back, he fell into a numb detachment as he muttered that he'd find her outside. He needed air. To figure out the mess of his head, which had become so wild and tangled he didn't know what had come over him. Why he felt this way.

Night had fallen, and he pulled up the hood of his cloak for more cover and bowed his head. A familiar whine followed by the pattering of paws drew his gaze up enough to find Katori. A relief since he'd wondered where she'd run off to.

As he reached down to run a hand over her fur, something cold and harsh lashed around his wrist. The assailants who caught him off-guard had completely managed to clamp his other wrist before he could strike, and then they were bound behind him.

Magestone.

His strength and speed were diminished in an instant. Adrenaline pumped through his veins with an urge to fight—not for himself when all he could think of was what would happen if they went for Nerida too.

As the world faded to black when something was thrown over his head, his chest ached that should he not return, it would be easy for her to believe he'd left her for good this time.

CHAPTER 62

Faythe

FAYTHE GLIDED THROUGH the halls next to Izaiah after yet another long, tedious dance lesson. She'd almost learned all the steps, but putting them into practice was a whole other learning curve.

Their idle chatter was interrupted when she picked up on murmuring voices. They exchanged a look, brows furrowing at the odd sound of a gathering. At the couple of small gasps, her heart picked up, along with their pace to find the source. Faythe listened to their tones—mostly whispers, but they were of shock, concern, and they had her jogging in anticipation of where they led.

By the time Faythe spied the cluster of bodies all the way down the hallway of Phoenix paintings, her pulse was filling her ears. Part of her wanted to run the opposite way with the fear coursing through her body. She had to see it, thinking the gathering of horror was far too excessive for what she anticipated to find as the source of the scandal.

She was about to start pushing through when a loud order from Izaiah had the people glancing back, and they began to ease away with small bows as she passed. Faythe couldn't pay them any attention. They parted too slowly, but when the bodies were no longer in the way she saw it.

Faythe stumbled to a halt in the great library, eyes fixed, knowing Agalhor stood by, but she couldn't look away from the glass case.

Empty. Her stomach knotted in guilt.

Though the shattered glass case and stolen feather wasn't what crawled time.

It was the scent that caught her senses, licking a cold dread down her spine. The metallic tang of blood tainted the air, and it was only then she noticed the splattering on the marble around the pedestal, and her eyes dropped to find the body.

The white robes of the library scholar stained the marble a ghastly crimson as if the banner of Rhyenelle slung around his waist had bled all over him.

He wasn't the only one.

Faythe's eyes darted around the space on their own search, finding another, then another, then she stopped counting in her shock. She didn't hear sound but felt strong hands grip her arms, a tall force stepping into view to prevent her from seeing more.

"You should not see this." Her father spoke with concern. "Take her away."

She recognized Izaiah responding, but she planted her feet against his hand as it hooked around her elbow. "What happened?" she asked in a ghostly whisper. She met his hazel eyes and saw the cut of rage and calculation before it eased just enough to express sympathy at whatever he read on her expression.

"We will find out. Don't fear, Faythe. There will be no measure of protection spared for you and your friends until I find the monster who did this."

Faythe's balance threatened to fail her. Izaiah might have anticipated it; his arm circled around her waist, and she didn't fight his gentle pull this time as he tore her away from the massacre.

In her dread and horror she spiraled fast. Her skin flushed hot, sending sparks across her arms. Denial for what she saw only churned her sickness.

Then a spear of panic.

"No leads?"

Faythe paced the floor of the games room, finding it had become a regular hangout spot for them to find a distraction. Yet Faythe could never concentrate on the games they played.

"Nothing," Faythe muttered to Jakon.

It had been a couple of days, and she'd hardly been able to sit still—or eat or dance or anything. It wasn't just the rippling dark aftermath of the library horror; Reylan had been absent, still away on post.

"He should return tonight, but I have a feeling it's just to check back in before he'll be called out again." Izaiah seemed to read her thoughts.

She couldn't feel pitiful in her pining when she yearned for him now more than ever. Antsy with a confession that threatened to crumble her, and he was the only one she wanted to confide in. Faythe only gave Izaiah a grateful nod.

"Check," Izaiah said with triumph.

Faythe's attention fell to the chessboard between him and Reuben.

"You've been absent too," Faythe muttered carefully to her friend.

Reuben flashed her an empty look and shrugged. "I've been admiring the human towns, actually. They remind me of home."

That made her stomach clench, but she forced a smile.

Jakon squeezed her arm. "Is there anything we can do?"

Faythe blew out a breath. "Stay safe and alert. We have no idea if they could strike again, or if they're long gone if that's all they came for."

"Why kill all those scholars?"

"It would have been no easy feat to steal it," Izaiah answered. "The scholars swore an oath to that library to protect everything within it. Maybe they fought, or maybe the murderer only thought to leave no possible witness."

The unsettling feeling in her stomach rose. She swallowed the rising burn in her tight throat.

"They had to have had inside help," Jakon pondered.

"It would seem so," Izaiah said.

The fact lingered in the air like a chilling embrace. They were wandering the halls not knowing whose hands wore the blood of the massacre. She looked down at her own before clamping her fists tight and pacing over to the window.

Marlowe sat silently on the window seat looking outside. She had yet to offer any smile or words and had been quiet all week.

"We will find them," Faythe said as she approached.

Marlowe jerked from her thoughts when Faythe touched her shoulder.

"You are safe here."

Marlowe offered a hollow smile. "I know."

Yet Faythe wasn't convinced. Marlowe's complexion had always been like smooth porcelain, yet the paleness accompanied dark circles around her eyes now, making her appear sickly. "You haven't…*seen* anything?" she asked tentatively. She didn't want to believe her friend was capable of withholding anything that could help them catch the traitors, yet she hated the kernel of doubt.

Marlowe fidgeted with her skirts. Faythe's pulse skipped, and she held her breath, until Marlowe shook her head and the anticipation fell to…disappointment. Perhaps it was only her fear and desperation that roused an ugly accusation, making her want to ask again and give her another chance if she were withholding something. As her mouth opened, Jakon sat, taking Marlowe's hands.

"She's just not been feeling well," he insisted, reading her intentions.

Faythe nodded and in her concern lay a hand on her friend's shoulder. "You should see a healer."

Marlowe only nodded with a forced smile.

"Reylan should be here." She echoed her frustrations out loud to divert the topic. "With this type of threat, should he not?" Her gaze pinned Izaiah as the one who likely knew most about his *situation*. The most convenient of timing to keep him away from her—and away from the crime scene. She eyed the pieces on the chessboard, watching Izaiah take Reuben's knight and in turn lose a pawn. Then another. The whole time, Izaiah strategically maneuvered his players around the king, and Reuben came to the mercy of Izaiah's bishop, which had slipped through his defenses in his distraction.

Then something in Faythe snapped like an icicle.

"Where are you going?" Izaiah demanded, chair scraping back.

She didn't answer, storming from the room. Her mind raged, collecting a storm of feelings that mixed with her perhaps outlandish thoughts, but they all circled back to one person. One who wanted power—who wanted her gone—and there was no telling what he would do, or who he would use, to achieve it.

A form closed around her to block her path. There was no kindness in her eyes as they pinned Izaiah.

"Get out of my way," she demanded as calmly as she could.

"I know what you're thinking, and let me tell you, there is no taking back such an accusation to someone so powerful."

"He's nothing but a coward," she hissed as though her mind had already pegged him as the culprit.

Izaiah surveyed the hall. Pulling on the handle behind her, he pushed Faythe into the small room without leaving her time to utter a protest. "Listen to me, Faythe. You don't know what game you're playing if you go toe to toe with Malin Ashfyre. You think you know him, you think you've seen what influence he holds, but you have not. If you accuse him of this, you'll start a fire that only sets you aflame. I hate to say this, but you are still being tested. You haven't been here long, and if it becomes your words against his, I promise you right now, you will lose."

Faythe closed her eyes, pacing away from him with the sting of the truth. It didn't matter what she thought, and perhaps she was being quick to accuse with her personal feelings, though she couldn't shake the feeling he was the one with most to gain.

"Kyleer is taking over the investigation. You're right, Reylan would be useful here, but we also can't afford to have weaknesses anywhere with what could be coming."

They shared a look, a cold sense of foreboding echoing between them, and Faythe shuddered. She didn't know what was coming, only that it was dark and deadly.

And they were not ready.

CHAPTER 63

Zaiana

Only at night did her mind feel peace. She wasn't sure what it was that itched her skin about the daytime, as though it were a spotlight to all she should be doing, and the night eased the guilt with the promise a new day would come to try again.

But now, even the night didn't feel safe. Zaiana couldn't settle her unease that to sleep was to risk her mind falling prey to the Nightwalkers. What roused her resentment was that she couldn't be sure if they'd already tried and left her forever unknowing.

"I killed my own father."

Zaiana wondered when Kyleer would speak, but his first words were wholly unexpected since he'd halted outside her cell minutes ago. She didn't drop her eyes from where she'd been mapping constellations with her back to him.

"Is that supposed to scare me?"

"He's not the only one I've killed. Not even close. Nor will he be the last."

Her curiosity got the better of her. She turned to try to get a better understanding of why he thought to share the grim revelation.

"If you want to trade body counts, just say so."

His seriousness eased just a little.

"I'll have you beat," she added.

Shadows surrounded her, phantom hands taking her shackled wrists and pinning them above her head. Kyleer forced her back to meet the wall. He stood right in front of her, peering down with moss-green irises slowly devoured by black.

"You once asked if I could do anything else with my *shadows*." His voice lowered to a seductive murmur. Real skin grazed her chin to tilt back her head, but an arm of featherlight darkness coiled around her thigh. "Many things that would have you forgetting any count but one. How many times I could make you call out for me."

She fell for it—only for a fleeting second before she yanked her hands down, free from the shadows that yielded easily. "What is this?" she hissed, pushing his chest when she couldn't stand the stab of *hurt*. "They know what we've done and still they send you here. Use that against me—is that what this is? It meant nothing to me, Kyleer. *You* mean nothing to me."

He planted his hand by her head. "The night my mother disappeared my father needed someone to blame, and believed I knew where she had gone, that I had somehow helped her. Three fae held me down while he crushed my hand repeatedly, letting me heal enough before he did again for my *confession*."

Zaiana twisted her head, knowing it would be that hand by her —the one with a deep scar and two crooked fingers.

"I think he started to believe I had no idea where she went, yet he laughed at my pain. They all laughed every time Izaiah begged them to stop, and I think they kept going for their own sadistic pleasure."

"Why are you telling me this?"

"Because this world *is* full of monsters. In the fae, in the humans, and in the dark fae. You—" He shook his head, pushing off the wall and stepping back. "You're using it as a mask."

Zaiana smiled cruelly. "Only a mad fae would wake up in a nightmare and see a dream."

"You're not a dream, Zai," he said, his expression falling, just for a second. "You're my beautiful nightmare."

"I'm not your anything."

"My most recurring, taunting, *punishing*—" With each word Kyleer's face inched closer. Her back curved when his hand trailed around her, never breaking that searing gaze. "Beautiful nightmare." His fingers stroked down the right path where her wing would be, offering enough pressure her lips parted and the sensation weakened her knees.

"Why don't you stop wasting both our time and ask what you came here to find out?" she demanded, cursing her breathlessness from his seductive distraction.

Kyleer took a long breath before he backed away, and she shuddered in the absence of his warmth. "Dakodas has her ruin, but what about Marvellas?"

"Did you not hear when I said? The Great Spirit did not make her appearance known to us."

"I did. But surely to learn to wield one they would school you about all three—what they could do and where they are."

"I assume your Phoenix Queen already knows where her ancestor's temple lies. Get better with your questions, Ky. Boredom has a habit of raising my reluctance to talk."

Something caused a tug of his mouth, which he quickly fought as he paced the floor.

"What?" she ground out.

"I like it when you call me that."

"Think nothing of it."

He continued to push back a smirk, though, telling her he was thinking *too* much of it, and she cursed herself for the slipup.

"Did you know Aurialis's was missing?"

Zaiana's lips firmed. She wondered how much information she could share with him to make them believe she was being cooperative, but never enough to give them any kind of advantage. "I knew the twisted King of High Farrow was looking for it, yes. He had the help of dark fae soldiers with the ability to glamour."

"Does Marvellas know we have it?"

"Anyone with a connection to that damn thing knows that now."

Maybe she'd slipped up too much, but she was incredulous to hear how completely oblivious they were in this war.

"What do you mean?"

"When the ruins are used, anyone who has wielded them before or has a Spiritual bloodline connection to them can feel their power. Maybe only a distant echo that would be hard to pinpoint. For me, I could have come for your precious queen that day in High Farrow. The surge of power she awoke from that thing… I didn't know it was her, of course. I figured they'd found it and Marvellas had some other poor soul trained to wield them since she cannot do so herself. You can imagine my surprise to learn of the impossible human heir, and my absolute thrill to be placed on her trail."

"Was she there?" Kyleer's note of fear was unexpected. "On the mountain edge, you used the ruin. Was Marvellas watching the whole time?"

Zaiana hadn't considered this, and his enlightenment to the possibility furrowed her brow. "Would it matter if she were?"

"Yes. It's an unfair advantage to learn an opponent's style before a fight."

Zaiana shook her head with a smile that lacked any humor. "This is no fight, Kyleer. You have no idea what you stand against."

"I think she fears more now what could stand against her."

She didn't know why she was rooting for their victory. She admired those who stood brave enough to fight for what they believed in, and she supposed Faythe had become a new threat. Who was Zaiana to know if her powers could match the Great Spirit she descended from?

"I don't know if Marvellas has others who can wield the ruin, but I know it was important to her. Assuming the masters are her puppets, as they so kindly volunteered to exact the brutal lessons."

"So *you're* important to her."

Zaiana shrugged. "She could train another. Believe me, there is no sentiment, no special *chosen one*. There is no one coming for me if you think you can use me."

"I wouldn't want you going anywhere near those bastards again."

"Don't do that." The words slipped through her lips without thought.

"Do what?"

"*Care.*"

"Because it frightens you?"

"Hardly."

"It frightens you to feel anything with warmth," he continued anyway. "When it can touch the scars no one sees."

"I feel nothing for you, Kyleer."

"Maybe you need a reminder of just how you felt me the other night."

"Lust is a natural craving; it meant nothing."

He flinched, and maybe for a split second she wanted to take her words back. She wouldn't, not when it was already a weapon being wielded against her.

She never should have let him touch her.

"If you think you can hurt me with that, you can't. You're a wicked, cold thing. I haven't made the mistake of feeling anything of value for you either."

Never before had words pierced her like a blade. She remained outwardly like stone, but within…those words stung, triggering a violent defense she risked unleashing on him. "I don't come from your romantic world of lovestruck mates and happy endings," she spat.

That seemed to strike something within him, tensing his broad shoulders and clenching his fists.

"Neither do I."

"Must be hard," she went on despite the voice that rebelled against her ugly words that tasted like acid. She knew they would hurt him. "Watching those around you fall in love, devoted to one another in their perfect mating. I pity the one who's bonded to you."

"She's dead."

Just like that, Zaiana was overcome with a new darkness she'd never felt before. It clouded her like sorrow, thick in her lungs, and she wished it were enough to stop the next words she knew would seal his hatred of her. "Seems to me she's free."

Kyleer's lips thinned. She wanted him to shout at her, lash out, do *something* other than stare at her with eyes of hurt that blinked to nothing.

Absolutely nothing.

"You can't hurt me with that either," Kyleer said without an ounce of emotion, though she knew it was a lie. "She didn't choose me. She never would have even if she lived."

"I thought fae mates always chose each other."

"You thought wrong."

Kyleer turned to leave, and something like regret made her stumble a step after him.

"Did you choose her?"

He Shadowported through the bars. "I never got the time to decide that. Maybe I would have, or maybe I would have set her free from such a torturous existence to be *bound* by my side." He walked away, and the call came quicker than she could stop it.

"Ky."

He didn't turn to her.

Zaiana breathed hard, warring with herself, not knowing what she wanted to say—only that she didn't want him to leave. Not really. Not with what she said to him as the last thing he heard.

I didn't mean it. It was there—*right there*—yet four words became gripped by one: *weak*. The pulse of it was so strong and tormenting it formed shadows to tighten her throat against setting her regret free. The chant of her mind overpowered her will to take back her hateful remarks. She wasn't worth his feelings. So Zaiana only closed her eyes, shrinking back into the wall as she listened to his footsteps echoing away until silence swept in once more.

CHAPTER 64

Nikalias

TWO WEEKS OF travel had turned out to be something of a holiday for Nik and Tauria. He watched her with a smile of awe as she packed away their supplies once again while he tended to their horse. Despite what they'd had to give up to fool Mordecai, the time they got to spend away from court together to simply *be* had become a treasure. They'd laughed. *Gods,* he couldn't remember the last time they'd laughed so much. Finding streams to bathe in and fooling around like childhood days. The nights they stayed up mapping stars together when sleep didn't feel necessary.

"We should be stepping onto Olmstone territory in a few days." Tauria's voice echoed over to him, a hint of sadness in it.

"What concerns you?"

Her hazel eyes flicked to his, and when she noticed he'd been standing by admiring her, her adorable scowl made his lips tug upward. She stormed over, shoving the pack into his arms, and Nik chuckled as he secured it to the horse.

"I hope Tarly made it out," she admitted quietly.

Nik finished securing the last buckle, and what he wouldn't

admit was that for everything he'd done for Tauria, and how they'd bonded, he hoped the bastard lived.

"We have to keep believing he fled with his sister, and that he took her to safety and stayed there too."

Tauria nodded, but it was hollow.

Nik pulled her to him. "It's time to catch up with them again," he mumbled, kissing her forehead.

They stayed as far away as they could, but it was essential for them to catch up every day so Nik could keep checking the mind compulsion was holding. He aided Tauria atop the horse before sliding in behind her. He had no complaints that it was logical to only acquire one horse so they'd have less to hide and would make the least amount of noise. In fact, their hours on horseback tucked tightly together had also become a comfort, and often arousing.

"Samara and I will have to switch back in Olmstone," Tauria said, and every muscle in Nik's body tensed. "You can't fool that many minds, and we can't be certain Varlas isn't still a puppet king."

He kissed her shoulder, her neck, breathing in her scent with the protective, primal need that coursed through him. "I don't like it," he murmured against her skin. "If he lays a hand on you, I can't promise I won't kill him."

"He won't hurt me," she assured him.

"Any hand, Tauria," Nik clarified, his own slipping around her waist.

"Seems a little dramatic."

"I think it's reasonable."

Nik's teeth scraped along her neck.

"Don't," she breathed, the scent of her lust filling his nostrils, contrary to her word. "We won't catch up to them in any good time if you do that."

He wanted to bite with such a feverish desire, but instead he grinned at her scolding, pressing his lips to her one last time before easing away. After a few beats of silence, he said, "You really think Mordecai has a child?" He couldn't picture him as a doting father figure. And if Tauria was right, Nik almost pitied the poor soul.

"He wouldn't confirm with words, but I swear the answer was there. There's no telling if it's a son or a daughter, or if they plan to fight this war with him, or if he's protecting them."

Nik mulled over the concept. "We need to learn more about him. His history, who he was before. It might give us some clues."

"Perhaps. We need to know if whatever happened to him to make him *come back* could have transferred to his offspring."

"So far, he seems perfectly ordinary. Powerless, even, to what you and I can do."

"He's Marvellas's puppet. Just like her, he plans to have all of us. She can't rule a whole continent herself; she wants us to keep our thrones, but by her lead as high queen. It was once a known concept, only the seven rulers were in agreement."

Nik listened in awe while Tauria explained from her readings about Stenna's Fall and the siren ruler. The history was remarkable, and he found himself wondering what changed: where she had gone, or did she perhaps simply have no heir to succeed her? Not a high queen to overrule, but one to keep the peace and maintain communications throughout all kingdoms.

He didn't believe for a second that Marvellas planned to rule so fair and merciful.

"It's a weakness, and we need to find it."

"We're talking about another person, Nik, not a *thing* to exploit."

"If they're anything like their father, I'm not pinning them as human."

"If we were all judged by our parents' actions, the cycle would never break."

Nik drew in a deep breath, his fingers trailing up and down her arm not of conscious effort. He adored Tauria for her fair judgment, for being his better half in every way.

"You're right, love," he mumbled, squeezing her waist. "You're always right."

Nik leaned cautiously against a tree trunk, keeping far enough away to evade fae detection, but close enough he could slip into the high lord's mind. He couldn't deny the thrill of the ability, and while thinking of Faythe's absence made his fists clench, he found himself projecting back into their early days of discovering what impossibility lay within her.

Using what he believed was a close match to her conscious ability, he relived the guidance he'd tried to project to her, now translating it for himself, and those memories were a bright joy to reflect on. *Gods*, he missed her. He didn't expect to, not so deeply, yet he couldn't shake the fear he was missing out on so much his dear friend had been through. In some ways, he'd abandoned her when he'd once been her first call for help.

Hands slipped around him from behind, and Tauria's enveloping warmth, her scent, relaxed his tense poise completely.

"Everything okay?"

He caught the projection of her thought, not daring to speak aloud with their proximity to Mordecai.

Nik observed the three of them. Lycus was helping Samara pack up their few belongings. Mordecai wasn't paying them any attention at all, his back turned to them to gaze through the trees. He only slipped into the high lord's mind to write the compulsion. Nik wasn't confident enough in his ability to shift Mordecai's thoughts without detection, and now was far from the time to test it out.

The idea became a dark temptation. He wondered if he could get the answers to his lingering questions if he only dared *reach*. A part of him was horrified at his desire to peer into private thoughts, and it became a new twist of guilt to think Faythe harbored a far purer conscience than him.

"He doesn't seem suspicious. I believe the compulsion is still working," Nik answered, trying to keep his focus when Tauria's cheek pressed to his and her hands caressed his front.

Dipping into Lycus's mind, Nik checked in with him.

"How are you holding up?" he teased, already feeling the ripples of his displeasure.

The general gave a quick glance in no particular direction when he couldn't see Nik's position. *"If you want to compel him to see me and take my place instead, I won't object."*

Nik suppressed a smirk. *"He doesn't look to be that intrusive,"* he observed.

Mordecai hadn't moved a fraction.

"I can't decide if that's a concern or a relief," Lycus admitted. *"He's been...kind to her. It's unnerving."*

Nik's fingers laced through Tauria's subconsciously. He cooled his wrath to ask, *"How is Samara holding up? Has he been physical with her?"*

"She's well. Surprisingly at ease. Though Mordecai hasn't interacted with her through much more than courtesy. Perhaps it's my being here that has him holding back. He has even less interest in engaging with me."

Mordecai didn't care to expend the energy to get to know Tauria's closest general. Nik supposed he didn't have to when his method of leadership was to inspire fear, not love.

"Tauria will be taking her place in a few days when we reach Olmstone borders."

Lycus's protective flare didn't need to be spoken. Nik felt it too, and his thumb brushed her soft skin. He was barely able to think of her being within the monster's reach.

"With my life, she'll be safe," the general promised.

Nik hadn't had the luxury of time to get to know Lycus, but his fierce loyalty and friendship with Tauria he didn't doubt for a second. There was no one else he trusted more to protect her.

She hugged him tighter, sending her thoughts to him. *"I can't bear the silence,"* she admitted quietly.

Nik's chest fucking ached. Hands joined with hers, he kissed her palm. He felt the same when their severed line of communication left a separation within. Though it wasn't needed, they had grown to cherish the luxury, and it would take time to adjust.

He turned to her, hand cupping her nape. *"I'm right here, love,"* he said to her mind. *"All seems well. Let's enjoy the next few days together. Just you and me."*

CHAPTER 65

Tarly

THE BAG OVER his head seemed wholly unnecessary when he knew exactly which route they'd taken to lead him to the castle. Though he was confused as to why his assailants used the hidden passageway through the stables.

He stayed silent. There was no point in trying to fight them with his senses dulled, though he calculated there were only four of them. They spoke nothing of another captive, and no one had intercepted them.

All Tarly could do was pray they hadn't seen Nerida with him.

They were trailing toward the castle now, but still he could tell they were taking the least used hallways, pausing and checking as if all five of them were sneaking around. They entered a small council chamber, and without warning, the bag was pulled from his head roughly.

Tarly blinked to adjust to the luminance, and as he was about to glare at his assailant, a flicker of movement caught his eye. He was stunned into place by the person he saw looking out the window, giving Tarly his back. Though the sight of his wears, and the colorful beads woven into his hair to match…

"So you triumphed," Tarly commented. His wrists were unbound, and he hissed, rubbing the red abrasions the Magestone had caused.

Panting caught his attention, and he caught Katori's—

No, it wasn't her. The spot of brown in one eye told him the wolf must be Asari.

"Not quite," Chief Zainaid said, his voice as calm and powerful as Tarly remembered. "A strategic compromise, for now, to have them believe we are on their side."

By "them," Tarly concluded he meant the dark fae who had destroyed his kingdom, killed his mother, and likely his father.

"You're a traitor."

"I am not your enemy, Tarly Wolverlon. Apologies for the method of bringing you here, but there is a lot you are to catch up on before you lay your accusations."

"So are you the king now?"

"No," he said simply, hands clasped behind his back as he came around the desk. "You are."

That froze him. He wanted to shake his head, but the outright denial he feared in front of the Stone Men. "I turned my back on them." Tarly eased his protest another way. His cowardice would be nothing when he would become no one once again.

"Yet here you are," Zainaid said calmly.

"Not by choice."

"Then why did you return?"

His question relieved one concern that had been crawling under his skin. They couldn't know about Nerida or they would have asked about her.

"What happened to my father?" Tarly asked instead. He wasn't sure he wanted to know the exact details. He had mourned his death long ago, yet the confirmation that he no longer lived as a tormented mind residing in a hollow title, that he was finally at peace, felt like closure.

What he wasn't prepared for was the confirmation he still lived.

"He is detained in the cells far below."

Tarly snapped a dark look at Zainaid. "You sold him out to take your place here—is that it?"

"I did what I had to." The chief's voice rose for the first time, making Tarly back down as he saw the difficult choice he'd had to make. "The dark fae have numbers we can't comprehend. If we had fought them that day you fled, we would have lost. They would have wrecked the city, killing every innocent just as a punishment."

"So instead you chose to side with them."

"Varlas is a broken male. He has been for a long time—I think you know this." He took Tarly's silence and the guilt that weighted his posture as confirmation. "In Marvellas's eyes he failed her. She was supposed to have all four of you in her dark fae army. You, Nikalias, Tauria, and even your sister. You would have kept your kingdoms but been entirely at her command, and there's something powerful about royal blood that makes the strongest of dark fae, or so she claims. Varlas was detained by her command, and by our negotiation he is never to be freed."

"Why are you telling me all this if you risk her wrath?"

"I tell you because despite all we yield to her outwardly, we are still working against her in this war. What she sees is necessary for a *fair* and *strong* continent...it is unfathomable."

Tarly had never thought to wonder what the Spirit hoped to achieve in her reign. What change she deemed necessary. He became riddled with foreboding, needing to know but not believing he was prepared to. "What does she want?"

"To eradicate weakness."

He tried to work the cogs of his brain to conclude what that meant. The answer was too many things. From what little he knew of the Spirit, one thing was clear, and that was the value she placed on abilities and power.

"I might be on her list to eradicate then," he pondered. There was nothing about him that could be of use to her.

"I don't entirely doubt that, but I believe you would be another stage in her plans." Zainaid began a thoughtful pace to a bookcase. "The thing about ambition, it is never-ending. You reach one goal, there will always be another. Something bigger, better. Every triumph becomes a stepping stone to an infinity of dreams and desires. Ambition can create the greatest leaders, both good and evil."

"How do I know you're not working for her now, bringing me here in the hopes I'll sit upon that throne as her unwitting puppet?"

"You will not sit upon that throne, for you are right: that is exactly what you would become. If she knew I had you, believe me, your days as fae would be numbered. A full moon *is* approaching."

Tarly was about to ask how he'd known where he was, but his answer came padding into the room. Brilliant white fur and pure silver eyes. He could hardly contain his glare.

"I will admit I never held the greatest respect for Varlas. He ignored many of my urgent requests to negotiate the matter that sees both of us short. There is a great mass of land that remains neutral territory, and I wished to come to some agreement we could use." When Zainaid turned to face him, Tarly subconsciously straightened. "But we are not our ancestors. What I saw in you that day we lost I believe could be a worthy ruler. It is not my desire to sit on Olmstone's throne."

"I ran," Tarly admitted, unable to accept the notion.

"You saved Tauria in your own ways. Then you left to save your sister, did you not?"

He gritted his teeth. He didn't need praise, nor for his cowardly actions to be warped into heroism. He decided right then what he needed to do.

"Opal is safe, and should I find your men to be trustworthy and your loyalty true, then I will tell you of her location so you might send protection. She is the one who needs to be guarded. Opal Wolverlon, when the time is right and she is of age, should be the one to rule Olmstone." It filled his chest with pride to imagine it. Her big heart and bright nature would make this kingdom flourish, restoring its values better than he ever could.

"You would relinquish your claim?" Zainaid asked carefully.

"Yes," he said with confidence. "I will work with you to keep this kingdom from collapse, even if it means I am not *here*. This war and its threats are far bigger than a single kingdom, and it is time we start seeking alliances and information to strike in the way she will least expect. Opal will be kept safe and away until Marvellas is defeated."

Chief Zainaid wore an expression that caused a pinch in his chest. Human, yet it was with a father's pride that he looked upon Tarly now. He had so long forgotten the feeling of that look.

"I knew I was right in what I saw," he muttered, more to himself than to anyone. "Our visions for this kingdom align, Tarly. In the meantime, what will you do that could help if you're not here?"

Tarly took a deep breath. His mind rose with a dormant sense of determination and something he had let go of ever having again. *Purpose*. He thought of Nerida and how her path had crossed with his on her way to aid the one with the best chance of taking down Marvellas.

Her heir.

Tarly struggled to picture the human girl he'd barely taken note of other than finding her integration into Orlon's court at the king's meetings bizarre. He couldn't comprehend she was the one who'd been sitting there with the most power all along. But he believed in Nerida, who'd risked the journey here to find information for her, and for that reason, Tarly knew what he had to do and where they would be heading.

"The Heir of Marvellas lives," he explained vacantly, trying to fit together what pieces he could. "I think my path leads to her, and she's the key to ending it all."

"I have heard of such fable, though I did not know a true heir lives again."

"Again?"

Zainaid nodded. "There was one other long ago, back when the conflicts started, but though a true heir, they were not the one the prophets spoke off. They disappeared without a trace."

In that moment Tarly felt sorrow for the human woman with

the fate of the world on her shoulders. Yet she wouldn't do it alone—that he was sure of.

"Stay the night. It is dark, and rainfall has begun. I will advise you not to leave your rooms when you're escorted to them. Some dark fae reside in the castle, and if news of you gets to Marvellas, your plan is over before it can begin."

Tarly wanted to argue, but as he stared at the darkening sky and the first droplets hitting the window, he knew he wouldn't find Nerida until morning. She had some coin, and he could only hope she hadn't ventured too far away yet thinking he'd abandoned her. Though Tarly knew he wouldn't achieve much rest that night.

CHAPTER 66

Faythe

Two candles were all that illuminated the parchments spread around the table. The exact table her mother had stood at countless times trying to figure out how to break the time curse and be with her father. Faythe had spent a long night pacing with a stormy mind, ignoring the churn of her stomach at the thought of visiting the library and eluding the guards posted outside her room. She'd had to influence their thoughts to wander elsewhere while she studied.

Faythe couldn't shake the feeling she was missing something. She pulled out the note from her mother's pocket watch, along with one she had yet to open, and laid them on the table.

"Three watches," she pondered out loud.

Suddenly, Faythe was awash with dread at the trickle of memory she had recklessly given one away. She'd watched it ripple into the mirror, and there was no telling where she'd sent it. What realm or time.

What if she had given away a key piece of information they needed?

There was no use in pondering that now. She shook her head

against the self-doubt. Faythe had no blacksmithing tools to unscrew the backs. Perhaps she could wait until morning and ask Marlowe... But in her frustration, she cared too little to preserve them.

Picking up both watches, the force of her anger surfaced to her palms, and the glass cracked and shattered, cutting her hand, but she kept squeezing until the metal bent and distorted. Her hand trembled and her eyes burned hot, for her mother's watch had been destroyed by her touch. It was all she had left of her, but it no longer felt like a sentiment, only a curse.

Her hands glowed brighter, and Faythe closed her eyes. Tears fell. Her palms burned hot, a mix of the blood trickling through the gaps of her fingers and her magick, which tingled with a familiar sweet essence. The solid objects she gripped slowly turned to dust, and she looked down to watch the last of them disperse as glittering particles.

Then she drew her magick back all at once, not moving with fear she was right. But she was too exhausted by all the heavy emotions that had been relentless since her return to Rhyenelle to muster any excitement or relief when all that remained in her possession was one folded parchment.

She set it on the table to prevent it from becoming any more bloodsoaked. Faythe examined her injuries, finding the symbols in bloodied stripes, and part of her yearned for them to heal.

Her eyes were closed with the pain that was a fuel for her frustration when his voice interrupted through the dark.

"It's past midnight."

Faythe didn't look at Reylan as he strolled into the library.

"I waited for you this evening when they said you would be back tonight," she muttered, flipping a page of her book.

"I only just arrived."

All she could muster was a nod, hardly able to look at him, though it was tearing her apart.

"You shouldn't be wandering the castle alone right now, especially not in the dead of night."

"You heard what happened then."

"The same day, yes."

"So it was not of your concern then; it should not be now."

Reylan's hand planted firmly on the pages before she could turn another. "You think I've rested a damn second since I heard of it? Knowing how far away I was and that I couldn't leave without exposing my only reason was you. You were safe within more than capable hands in their eyes." His hand took her chin, forcing her to look at him, and she broke.

"I hate this," she whispered. Her lips tightened, disappointed in herself that she was crumbling. "I hate that you have to be some forbidden secret. I needed you all this time. I don't blame you, never, but I can't stop wondering if this is all too much. That I was a fool to believe I could return and wear this mask of bravery when I don't know what I'm doing, only trying to lead with what is expected of me. I thought I could be strong, but it *hurts*, Reylan."

His expression eased from firm, cut lines to share her grief in an instant. He caught her hands, upturning them to find the cuts had healed and the blood had dried. He pressed his lips to one before drawing her arms around his neck. Faythe pushed up on her toes for that embrace, burying her face into his neck, and just like that, the weight of the world lifted for however short a time before she crashed back to a cruel reality.

Yet she knew these moments could carry her through.

"I hurt with you," he mumbled into her.

Gods, she knew he did. Knowing she was powerless to end it for them both had wrecked her for weeks, and if it were as easy as breaking the bond, perhaps she would have let him go. But Reylan was entangled so deeply it was its own bond—not one of magick, but heart.

He let her go too soon. Always too soon.

"What did you hope to find here tonight?" he asked, not dropping his arm from around her as he leaned into the desk with the other.

The small comfort burst in her chest, giving her the motivation to face what she'd set out to discover. "When we were in one of the towns, I came across an abandoned shop." Faythe skipped past the scene that played out with perfect haunting clarity since she couldn't be certain it wasn't all a hallucination. "I found a watch identical to my mother's, but with Marvellas's mark on the back. I...I gave it away. But then Nerida gave me the final watch with Dakodas's mark."

"And where is it now?"

Faythe winced, and Reylan read her answer in the subconscious flex of her hands. Unexpectedly, he huffed a laugh, leaning in to drop a kiss on her shoulder.

"You're becoming rather destructive, you know."

"That amuses you?"

"It thrills me."

"Should I be concerned?"

"Not when I'm thinking of other ways that destructive, wild, beautiful anger could be unleashed."

Desire crept with heat along her collar at the low gravel tone he spoke in. To distract herself from his enticement, she held up the folded parchment. "This was inside, just like in my mother's."

He took it tentatively, and Faythe laid out the translated version of Marlowe's. "You have the temple locations... What are you expecting to be within this?"

"I'm not sure, but we likely won't be able to read it right now anyway. It took Marlowe weeks to translate the first."

"I'm beginning to think all bad things come in threes," Reylan muttered.

Faythe watched him begin to carefully unfold the parchment. Her pulse drummed, fingers trembling to get it over with and discover what was within. She breathed hard when it was fully open, and she watched his confusion before he laid it down.

"An image," Faythe pondered, squinting at the lines.

What he presented before her was a puzzle complete, yet her mind scattered with its pieces, struggling to know why it looked familiar but different. The lines crossed over each other in a beautiful symbol, three striking through the emblem and circumference by a shape with seven sides that had words of another language down each one. Then she doubled back.

Symbols...

All three of them overlapped.

"The Spirit Symbols," Reylan concluded at the same time as she did.

Faythe nodded vacantly. "What does it mean?" she wondered aloud. Faythe had seen them many times. She *wore* them. Yet she had never seen this merged version.

Reylan's hand smoothed down her nape, but before he could respond he stepped away from her completely. Faythe felt it then, the distant approach of someone, and she would never get used to the hollowing of her stomach as if their closeness were a scandal.

Kyleer jogged into the library, his expression horror-struck, but his shoulders slumped with relief when he caught sight of her.

"What's wrong?" Reylan marched to him, slipping into honed focus at Kyleer's alarm.

"Gods above, when I saw—" He shook his head, his breathing labored.

Faythe's skin crawled with a thousand needles. She'd never seen him look so ghostly.

"Your room, Faythe. When I found it wrecked I feared the worst. And your handmaiden. The guard has been alerted, and the castle's being put under lockdown."

Faythe swayed a step back before a strong arm hooked around her. "Gresla?" Her thoughts flashed from one conclusion to another. Why would she have been there so late?

Kyleer's silence dragged her eyes to him in the hope his mouth would spill the assurance she needed. He said nothing. He didn't need to when his eyes communicated her worst fear.

"No..."

Faythe took off running.

Voices called after her, but the pounding in her ears, the whip of the air, drowned them out. She sprinted through the halls as if she could reverse the past, refusing to believe the nightmare Kyleer had painted.

Until it came alive right in front of her.

Faythe didn't feel tethered to her own body. She blinked hard, but when the scene didn't change she closed her eyes, searching desperately for her Nightwalking ability because this was sure to be a terror of her own wicked mind.

But the body was real.

Her lids sliding open released her tears freely. Gresla's form lay deathly still, facedown, without care. Crimson pooled from beneath her. All at once, the reality lashed her without mercy.

Faythe would never see those motherly eyes again. Never feel the warm embrace or hear her tender laughter, and Faythe sobbed. Never again would she call her by title, and all those times she'd cringed she wished she could take back now and tell Gresla how much it meant to her that she believed Faythe deserved to be here.

Gresla was gone.

"Come with me, Faythe." Reylan's gentle coaxing sounded out as if he were above water. She didn't know when she'd doubled over until all that held her from falling were his arms.

The room had been wrecked, and Faythe saw the box she'd kept it in sprawled on the bed.

They'd found it.

"It's my fault," she croaked.

Reylan twisted her, holding her tightly against his chest while she thrashed to unleash the retribution that bubbled dangerously inside. "It's not."

Faythe stopped struggling, clutching his clothing desperately instead as her grief switched her emotions so fast she began to feel lightheaded. "I didn't mean for any of them to get hurt. I didn't hurt them."

Reylan took some of her pain. And while she deserved to feel every ounce as though it could kill her, Faythe accepted the assistance of his calming presence to speak.

"It was me," she confessed. "I stole the Phoenix feather. And what was left of it…that is what they came for tonight. I didn't hurt anyone in the library, only sent them to unconsciousness… I didn't—" She choked.

Reylan took her face, his eyes calculating but remaining soft to her.

It didn't matter that Faythe wasn't the one to wield the knife; every death since she stole the feather was on her shoulders.

"Listen to me," Reylan said firmly, his thumbs brushing her tears. "If that's what they came for, they would have gotten it in the library first, and they would have killed for it anyway."

It didn't ease her shame, but her heart hollowed, unable to argue.

"I need you to tell me why."

She owed him that, but she needed to be anywhere but in this room. With her cleaved heart she was seconds away from turning around and falling by Gresla's side.

"I heard the commotion."

That voice flipped something in her. Her vision was stolen by a flare of white in an instant. A need for revenge surged her movements, and she felt for the hilt of the dagger at her thigh. The slam of the wall rippled faintly through the heat that pumped her blood fast. Only when her arm was pinned across Malin's chest and the tip of her blade was touching his throat did she realize what she'd done.

"What did you do with it?"

"I could put you on trial for this."

"Go ahead," she dared, past any logical reason.

"Faythe, this isn't the way," Reylan said calmly.

"This is *my* way."

"No, it's not."

She didn't want to direct her reckless anger at him, but she couldn't help his intervention feeling like a betrayal.

"You should listen to him." The slight curl of her cousin's mouth triggered her need for violence.

Reylan and Kyleer shifted when her blade moved, resting now along his skin.

"This does nothing but condemn you," Kyleer reasoned.

Her teeth gritted so hard they could break, her tight fist trembling as she battled with the strong desire to end her cousin right now. She had no proof of his responsibility, but she couldn't unsee him as the culprit. Perhaps in her own hatred she needed to pin the blame.

With a cry of anguish, Faythe's blade nicked his throat as she backed away. Malin's smirk fell to darkness as he raised a hand to the mild cut.

"How can you expect to run a kingdom with such unhinged emotions and brash reactions?" he sneered.

Faythe didn't care. She could hardly stand to look at him while the blade still dangled in her grasp. Reylan's hand went over it gently, and Faythe didn't protest as he led her from the room.

Out in the hall, her adrenaline slowly dwindled. Her steps moved her vacant body, but the reality of her situation anchored her as heartache made her numb.

Her emotions had exhausted her completely. She lay tucked up in the corner of the library on one of the plush seats. They'd come back here because Faythe knew sleep wouldn't call to her for the rest of the night.

"I needed it to send a message. From the knowledge I found in some texts, I thought if it truly was from Atherius I could use it with my bond to her." Faythe held no emotion as she recited the truth.

"We can discuss this tomorrow," Reylan offered for the second time.

She only shook her head.

"Why didn't you ask Agalhor for it?" Kyleer spoke.

"He wouldn't have simply given it to me. Something so ancient and guarded doesn't belong in the hands of someone barely making herself worthy here," Faythe said. "Maybe he would have believed me, but I knew with what I needed I couldn't return it—not all of it. I thought one day I'd be able to tell him, maybe replace it with a new one. I don't know." She buried her face into her hands at hearing her selfishness aloud. No matter how important she thought it was, too many lives had been taken since the act.

Reylan halted his worried pacing. He strode for her, crouching, and took her tilted chin, which weighed so heavy she could hardly look up. "I need you to stop these harmful thoughts. No death is on your conscience."

Faythe didn't bother to argue. His jaw worked knowing he couldn't persuade her.

"There was an attempt on the feather before you," Kyleer said. "Just tell her." He directed the last part to Reylan.

Faythe broke from her slump, finding strength in her limp bones. Reylan's look confirmed the news, but her adrenaline spiked to hear it.

"They killed two of the library masters weeks ago but didn't get further before the alarm was raised and guards swarmed. It's the closest anyone has ever come to infiltrating the library, whether for the feather or some other valuable things that are kept here. This library is well-guarded and has a strong defense protocol. I'm sorry I kept it from you. It didn't feel worth your worry as they didn't succeed." He took her hand. His thumb tracing her skin brought warmth to their chill. "So you see they would have killed them all to get to it regardless. I assume now that when they discovered someone had beaten them to it...well, they're savage beasts anyway."

"I left them vulnerable," Faythe muttered. "I left them unconscious."

Reylan sat beside her, and she couldn't reject his comfort when he pulled her into his side. "What did you achieve with it?" he asked—an attempt to sway the conversation, but it only swept her with more shame. His hand ran over her arm as though he could feel it too.

"I was testing if I could extract the Phoenixfyre from it."

"And did you?"

"Yes." Though she begged for him not to ask more. "All that was left was half the feather. In the wrong hands..."

"We're straining every resource to track them down," Kyleer assured her.

Faythe was so tired she let her head fall, resting it contentedly between Reylan's neck and shoulder. His scent soothed her enough to find just a moment of peace from her aching heart. His fingers weaving through her hair and stroking along her nape offered the final push for her to give herself over to mournful exhaustion.

CHAPTER 67

Tauria

THE TIME HAD come for the switch.

Tauria's fear coursed cold through her body. She was unable to be still. For a fleeting moment she was glad Nik couldn't sense her distress so easily, until she remembered the permanence of that severed connection.

"You don't have to do this, love." His gentle voice pulled her from her reeling thoughts. Her gaze shifted to him, emeralds sparking with ache and concern. "We can find another way."

Tauria knew that despite the danger, the fight that would erupt if she succumbed to her cowardice, Nik would face it all gladly if that were her choice.

It wasn't. It couldn't be. Even within Olmstone's castle she still had vengeance left unsettled. She wondered if Varlas was still alive, and worse, what she would do to him should she discover he still ruled with cruelty by Marvellas's will.

"I can do this," she told him, stepping up to savor every second she could be wrapped up in his safety,

"I know you can," he said, kissing her firmly.

Twilight fell around them, and by nightfall Samara would slip away and Tauria would truly be the one in the high lord's company.

Nik's hand took her wrist, and Tauria felt the weight of the silver band before he slipped it on. She stared down at the familiar concealment bracelet, hating the very sight of it while the feel of it itched her skin.

"Me too." Nik agreed with her thoughts. His fingers tipped her chin up. "The show goes on. But no matter what, you are mine, and I am yours."

"Yes," she breathed, and she fell into him completely, needing nothing more than to be held by him right until the very last moment.

Parting with Nik was never going to be easy. Even without a mating bond, still something strained inside with every measure of distance. She saw Lycus sitting up by a tree and headed straight for him, yet a shadow caught in her eye just as the general rose.

"When we arrive in Olmstone city, I trust you'll have many questions about how it came to be after you made your grand exit."

Tauria shivered at the dark, bitter notes of the high lord's voice. "Is Valgard in power?" she asked confidently, as if to portray she would be glad if it were true.

"Valgard," he mused, and she caught the silhouette of him easing out from the tree he'd been leaning against. The firelight and sin contoured his expression. "Tell me, do the people fear less to name a kingdom as the villain?"

"It was they who invaded. Wearing *your* crest."

"Yet now you know better. You know things aren't always what they seem." He stalked to her, hands clasped behind his back, making him taller and all the more intimidating. "Have you ever been across the sea, Tauria?"

He knew she hadn't, so she didn't respond.

"What if I told you to kill your enemy *Valgard* would be to slaughter darklings? Mothers, siblings, those who work and live in peace. You might find"—he halted close to her, and Lycus shifted with the proximity, but Mordecai paid him no attention—"our species aren't all that different."

Tauria's pulse thrummed, praying he wouldn't touch her. Hoping this wouldn't be the time he decided to reveal his affection for her in front of Lycus.

"You have a son," Tauria blurted as the first thing to rush to mind, desperate to disperse the tension that radiated from him.

Mordecai's eyes narrowed, and she thought her rib cage might break from the beast within that struck hard between his longing and threatening looks. His emotions could switch so fast she teetered on a knife's edge with anticipation.

"Why so certain a son?"

She wasn't, but he'd fueled her suspicions.

"Do you protect them?" she asked.

"They are perfectly capable of protecting themselves." His head canted in curiosity. "You need not worry about it. I can assure you they are certainly old enough not to need my attention. Not that I gave them any throughout their upbringing."

"You didn't raise them," she probed, testing dangerous waters —but while he was willing, she had to try.

"I almost killed them."

Her heart finally stilled.

Mordecai studied her reaction, and something made him decide to continue. "I had no desire or sentiment for a child. When the dark fae I had relations with came to me with the claim the child was mine, I killed her. The notion was ludicrous, and I don't like to be made a fool of. I could have simply given the child to the masters to be like all other darklings, passed over to be raised as soldiers for this war, but I was enraged at the mockery. I shouldn't be able to produce an heir."

"Because of what you are?"

"What am I?"

It was a test. Or a longing for the answer. Tauria wasn't sure what she read in his dark eyes that seemed to hope she knew… because he didn't.

"Your heir…you let them live," she sidetracked again, not knowing when she became enraptured enough by the tale to forget about Lycus's presence completely. "Why?"

"It all changed when they looked at me. I didn't see the eyes of a darkling with no telling what could become of them. I saw what could only be an interference from the Gods themselves. I knew then I wasn't brought back simply for Marvellas's bidding; I had created a legacy for the realm."

Tauria couldn't imagine the poor child…

She shook the thought. No, Mordecai had confirmed they were not young, though she could only guess what that meant to him. The way the high lord spoke of them offered nothing of a father's love, and she pitied the soul. Yet more so, Tauria feared what this meant. If they were powerful and could prove to be a great weapon against them in the way he described with admiration…

Her racing thoughts held her in such a tight grip she didn't realize Mordecai had stepped closer and reached his hand up, slowly cupping her cheek. He angled his head to her, and before she knew what she was doing, her palm was pressed to his chest. Tauria breathed hard through the flash of darkness at her rejection, scrambling to recover.

"I can't yet," she rushed out. "I need time to recover. I can't explain how it feels…the severed bond. I want you, but I'm confused, and I can't—"

He cut off her ramblings by taking her chin instead with a gentle hold she didn't expect. "I can wait," he said, and she believed him.

Until something snapped in him. So suddenly Tauria choked on a gasp, hands gripping the one he lashed around her throat.

Steel sang as Lycus armed himself. "Release her," he warned with a snarl.

Mordecai didn't flinch, holding her with emotionless eyes and a silence that pierced her. He searched as if the betrayal she harbored would speak to him against her will.

"He has three seconds to let you go before I damn the plan to the Nether and rip out his throat."

Nik's threat didn't help. She'd hoped he would have backtracked with Samara to a safe distance by now. She should have known he wouldn't have left her with the high lord so soon.

"Two."

"If I find out you have tricked me, princess," Mordecai finally said, "don't make the mistake of believing I won't end you and your mate and lay to waste both your kingdoms."

"One."

The high lord let go, stepping away, and she doubled over. Immediately, Lycus's arms were around her and she leaned into his safety.

Tauria found the rage to shoot a glare at Mordecai and realized she'd almost listened to the small voice in her heart that wanted to see better in him. Some shred of humanity.

She should have known no tale or time could erase blood from the hands that bathed in it.

CHAPTER 68

Faythe

DEATH NEVER BECAME easier to welcome. The names of her losses tethered themselves to her soul, never to be forgotten.

Gresla's funeral blurred past three days after her death. That morning, Faythe wasn't able to pay any attention to the young handmaiden who arrived at her new rooms ready to take her place.

What did change was the aftermath of grief. With her mother's death, her child-self had become broken and hollow, wandering and lost, even when she was found. With Caius, she'd been vacant for weeks, showing up for the people around her and acting as if life were okay when she would have sacrificed hers for the guard to live. With Gresla, Faythe became detached in her denial, but acceptance was beginning to creep in much faster.

There were no safe corners in this war, no exceptions. All Faythe could do now was grieve and use her vengeance to drive her forward.

She didn't change out of her black gown. Reylan hadn't left her side, and for once she hadn't sought solitude. They'd wasted too much time. He spoke over their measures of defense with

Kyleer while Faythe lost herself in thoughts of the parchments they hadn't been able to examine for long when Gresla was first discovered.

In her curiosity, she touched her fingers to two pieces of parchment: the untranslated text from her mother's watch, and the new piece. Her palm tingled, trickling a warmth right to her fingertips. She watched in awe as a gold dust dispersed, shooting along the broken line. She no longer feared the small doses of magick she tested. A few heartbeats passed and her fingers lifted. The light died out, and the paper became whole again.

"How did you do that?" Kyleer asked through a breath of wonder, lifting the parchment.

Reylan's hand slipped across her back, his eyes speaking of pride and joy. The soft curl of his mouth fluttered her stomach.

"I'm trying to use small amounts of this…*other* magick as and when I can. I'll need it to fight Marvellas, I believe."

"One day at a time," Reylan assured her, his thumb brushing over the symbol in her palm. "It's beautiful."

"Can I take this?" Kyleer interrupted, frowning at his hands.

"I was going to ask Marlowe to translate the new words."

"I think we have someone who can do that far faster." Kyleer passed a look between her and Reylan, and Faythe concluded his meaning before he explained himself. "I recognize some of these markings from trying to decipher a particular word from a particularly stubborn dark fae."

Zaiana's expression twinkled with glee when they all came to stand outside her cell. Even Reuben had insisted on visiting the dark fae, and Faythe figured the more allies who heard the information she sought to gain, the more successful they'd be.

"I'm flattered you all thought to check in," Zaiana drawled.

"Does this mean anything to you?" Faythe held the parchment through the bars, not in the mood to dance around what she wanted.

Zaiana sat casually against the back wall, her legs crossed, arms limp. She didn't appear frightening at all, yet Faythe wouldn't let her guard down for a second. The dark fae's head tipped back, brow curving in amusement, but Faythe saw it: the recognition that sparked like a candle in her chest.

"So you've come for bedtime stories."

"We'll get comfortable," Izaiah chimed in, leaning cross-armed against the bars. "Start talking."

When ire flexed around Zaiana's eyes, Faythe wondered if it was a bad idea to allow Izaiah to come given their obvious hostility for each other.

"Why would I do that?" Zaiana challenged him.

"Because you want to live."

"Your words, not mine."

"Izaiah," Kyleer cut in hard.

"Fill me in later." Izaiah pushed upright, not looking at any of them as he left the cells.

Faythe shook her head at the conflict, needing to let it lie for now though it stirred questions. They had a task to do.

Kyleer took a nervous breath. *Nervous.* Faythe watched him carefully as he approached the cell and his gaze eased to something softer than his brother had offered—something far more...*personal.* On instinct, Faythe flashed a look up to Reylan, and though he didn't move an inch, her confirmation was there.

"We don't need your help," Kyleer said. "Marlowe has translated this ancient language before, and she could do it again. But you know this language, don't you?"

Faythe passed the paper into his outstretched hand, observing how differently Zaiana bore her attention on him. She was still reserved, always aware of the many others lingering around, but to him, her mask slipped just enough to rest the games and let them see she was deliberating his every word.

"Nilhlir." Kyleer spoke quietly. "It comes from this tongue."

"So you're not dim-witted."

"I'm insulted you ever thought I was."

The shadow of a smile appeared—not on her mouth, but in

her eyes—before Zaiana glanced over at the rest of them. Faythe stiffened, thinking the reminder of their presence would seal her lips.

Zaiana assessed Reuben and Marlowe, and perhaps Jakon by her side. "Are you sure you have the right company for this?"

Something eerie crawled up Faythe's nape as she read the warning, but she wasn't sure what it meant. She extended her senses for a quiet minute to be certain there were no guards within the block and no bodies lingering within earshot outside the dainty window.

"I'm sure," Faythe said, though the words tasted like the opposite.

Zaiana didn't voice the rest of her accusation, simply giving a shrug and shuffling awkwardly with her hands bound to her knees. "Does anyone have chalk? Or a willingness to lend their blood. The medium is not important."

Kyleer muttered that he would fetch it, not leaving them a second to respond before he disappeared in shadow. His ability would never cease to amaze Faythe.

"You said it took you over a century to master the ruin." Faythe filled the silence. She didn't hope to interrogate Zaiana, nor was she holding out hope for an answer. Only out of fear did she speak to the one person she knew had experience with what lay ahead. "What if I don't have that time? Not even close."

"You won't like my answer." It was a small relief that Zaiana had deigned to answer at all, but her tone held an apology, whether the dark fae realized it or not.

"I wasn't expecting to," Faythe mused.

A rare line of connection ran between them, fast, and then it dispersed like a falling ember.

"I don't know what kind of power you harbor now, Faythe Ashfyre. Maybe you have it in you to wield the ruins; maybe you could join the ruins…but you will not survive it."

Reylan's hand on her waist didn't ease the stiffening of her body. It was a natural response, though her mind stilled with the answer that on some level she had known. Had even come to terms with. Zaiana's confirmation didn't raise dread or fear or doom. Faythe knew her second chance hadn't been granted in aid of a happy ending; it was a weapon to free many others.

Zaiana's attention fell to Reylan's hand, and she gave him a look Faythe couldn't decipher before her attention drifted to nothing. "Perhaps between you there could be a chance, or maybe it will kill you both."

Her gut twisted to pain, in protest of something not yet in motion. It rocked through her hard, but the appearance of starry shadows within the cell snapped her mouth shut.

Kyleer came into full form, crouched low and close, holding out the shard of white chalk to Zaiana. Though he had watched over her as their captive for months, Faythe tensed at their proximity, not believing for a second Zaiana was incapable of harming him greatly even with the restraints.

The dark fae took the offering, quickly dropping eye contact with a deep breath. Kyleer didn't retreat from the cell.

"I'm surprised none of you could identify the Mark of the Seven Gods," she sighed as though schooling them like children who should know better. Her amethyst gaze flashed up to Marlowe in particular, but her friend yielded no reaction.

Her firm expression was unlike her, but given their company, Faythe understood.

Zaiana tried to suppress a smile. "Where do you think the Spirits came from?" she went on, leaning forward to begin her drawing. Faythe almost felt bad for her momentarily, wincing as she maneuvered within her restraints. Zaiana drew a circle. "Aurialis." Then a downward pointing triangle within it. "Marvellas." Over that, her semicircle created a fallen crescent moon. "Dakodas." Zaiana struck three lines through the combined symbol. "Three Spirits to balance the realm." She huffed a mocking laugh. "Or so they thought."

She didn't stop there, marking side after side around the circle, and Faythe glanced down at the parchment in her hands to find the dark fae was drawing the same symbol without reference. It rattled a chill to wonder how many steps they still had to take to catch up to their enemy's knowledge, and what else they could still be in the dark about.

"Seven sides, seven Gods," Zaiana said, leaning back on her knees to admire her handiwork.

Jakon spoke up. "Where are they now? If what you say is true, they created the Spirits to protect us. Why not step in when they've gone against them?"

"The Gods have many realms. Or perhaps they are aware but have been blocked from their own creations. You would be wise not to underestimate what Marvellas is capable of in her desire to claim this one as her own. Do you even know what that means? You seek to stop a foe whose end game you do not understand."

"And I suppose you do," Reylan said irritably.

A gleam flashed in her eyes with the hint of a goading smile, and Faythe figured Zaiana found entertainment in riling Reylan up. "I might."

Reylan cast his gaze to the cell roof as if to yell at those very Gods and ask, "Why me?" Faythe tried to suppress her own amusement, sending him a piece of her within to soothe his sharp ire.

"She wants to rule the seven kingdoms," Kyleer tried.

Zaiana almost seemed disappointed by his conclusion. "Nothing is ever as simple as that. Even if that were true, for what means? By what cause? You are all content to see a villain because it opposes your *order.*"

"She wanted to turn Nik and Tauria into dark fae—is that her goal? To have the world Transitioned?" Jakon asked.

Zaiana's chuckles vibrated chillingly through the space. "A very flawed assumption if that any of you have the wits about you to think logically," she bit out, growing impatient.

"The Transitioned dark fae are volatile, bloodthirsty…" Reylan was calculating, sifting his thoughts down to Faythe. "The creature in High Farrow's underground and those we faced in the town."

Faythe nodded at the grim memory, airing her conclusion to Zaiana. "Some can be Transitioned beyond being anything of humanity."

"Yes," Zaiana confirmed. "There are many who lose their minds during it. It's obvious, and they're separated from those who still have the wits to be trained. But the others…they're kept alive, and it's a slow deterioration from there. They don't feel pain, they don't die easily, and they don't have any thoughts but one: their thirst for blood."

The air pricked with ice. Flashbacks to being hunted by one of those beasts, their short battle against a dozen, and what Zaiana described made Faythe's pulse quicken at the idea of a whole battlefield full of them.

"Are there many?" she dared to ask.

A long, frightening pause came.

"Yes."

Faythe swayed a little, forgetting Reylan's touch until the squeeze of his hand on her waist dragged her back to the present.

"The Seven Gods." Marlowe uttered her first words. "Tell them."

Zaiana hooked a brow at Faythe's friend while Faythe tried not to pay attention to the sickness rising in her gut at what Marlowe could have already known. She tried to understand that with her gift she couldn't always tell them, yet it stabbed like betrayal.

"It can't be easy knowing your friend could hold the answers that made you desperate enough to come to me instead," Zaiana taunted.

That only twisted her gut tighter with the need to defend. But Faythe couldn't deny she'd thought the same, even if fleeting, in her will to believe Marlowe wouldn't put any of them in danger regardless of the *balance* and *order* she held a duty to keep.

"I don't know everything," Marlowe was quick to say. "Only pieces. The Gods created the Spirits, yes, but they didn't entirely abandon the realm when in their image they created the Mortal Gods. Things don't come to me as clearly as that. I piece them together as I learn new things, so consider this my reaching the end of your explanations just a little quicker than the rest."

Relief and pride lifted Faythe's unease all at once with Marlowe's confident explanation. To her surprise, Zaiana grinned, showing those pointed canines Faythe had seen before, and considering they used those canines to feed off humans, she wondered if Zaiana couldn't retract them or simply didn't want to. She shuddered at the reminder, but it also offered her the realization Zaiana didn't depend on feeding off humans to exist. She'd seemed perfectly healthy in the months she'd been without human blood.

Faythe was...*hopeful.*

"This is where the story gets long. You might want to get comfortable." Zaiana paused, contemplated, then said, "I want cake."

Everyone was stunned by the request. Faythe wasn't sure if it was because it was so completely random or the fact it painted the dark fae in a normality that felt jarring.

"Why is that so surprising?" she asked, offended, glancing at everyone's bewildered looks. "The food is rather bland, and I've been stuck down here for an ungodly amount of time."

Reylan crossed his arms as he said, "I'm waiting for you to request it's frosted with the chef's blood."

Zaiana shot him a flat look. "Chocolate will suffice."

"It's yours," Kyleer responded, fighting a smile. "Anything else?"

Their gazes met, and along with their proximity, for a split second Faythe fought the urge to look away. It clicked then with blazing clarity as she stared at them, skipping a beat of her heart and canceling out any kindness she might have felt toward the dark fae. Her need to protect Kyleer pulsed so strongly her fists flexed.

"Don't do anything reckless," Reylan said gently to her mind.

"You knew?" she accused.

It was so obvious she wanted to slap herself. Kyleer's odd behavior; Izaiah's hostility. Faythe cursed herself repeatedly for being so distracted not to have seen it sooner. The feelings he had grown for the enemy.

"Not for long, but it is not for us to stop."

"She's using him."

Faythe had to focus not to let her anger show, or it would start as a blaring beacon in her palms. Reylan's caress stroked her senses. It helped, but a new wall of suspicion had built when she might have been softening to Zaiana.

The scraping against stone distracted her from that surge of emotion. Faythe watched as Zaiana translated the first word, again without needing to refer to the parchment. Along the first slanted side of the polygon she wrote: "Strength."

"When the Gods made this realm, there was no reason for them to stay, and they quickly grew bored. It took all seven of them to create the Spirits to balance the species and guard the realm, or so they thought. But Gods are fickle beings, always believing they can trump each other, so the Spirits were not enough. They agreed that while the Spirits would remain as guardians of the world, they would each create their own being to roam the lands in flesh. Demetris, the God of Strength, believed the world could be saved through honor and sacrifice. He created the first Mortal God in his image, a fae he named after himself, as did they all in their arrogance."

She swirled the letters of the next word down the vertical edge: "Wisdom."

"Erosen was next, the God of Wisdom. He believed the world could be balanced with patience and forward thinking. Again, his creation was fae."

Faythe became wholly entranced by the tale, feeling it sink deeper than her own understanding of history, trying to open a door she didn't hold the key to.

"Iyana, the Goddess of Knowledge"—Zaiana scribed the word —"was the first to choose a human creation. She believed in fairness and that power was not in the body but the mind. The God of Courage, Helios, was said to have had a certain adoration for Iyana's ways, and so he too chose a human form to embody him, believing bravery and willpower no matter the odds were what the land needed, and that their humans would prove that."

With three sides left, no one else uttered a word, all eyes transfixed on Zaiana's drawing, hypnotized by the way she spoke.

"Fedara, the Goddess of Resilience, is a personal favorite." Zaiana mused at the word. "They often overlooked her values.

Maybe some thought them weak. Though the lands would not be as vibrant and full of life as they continue to be without her vision that peace and forgiveness would settle the lands. It was her fae creation that began the order that would make peace flow between the kingdoms."

Faythe listened to every word about the Gods feeling like she knew them, or like they had always been a part of her.

"Kitana, the Goddess of Darkness and Light, was the only one to go against the others, creating her image as dark fae. She was considered an untrustworthy God—only to the others who misunderstood one with a will to do whatever was necessary, even if morally gray. Her love could be harsh, but she believed in the will to bend—to use darkness if needed—but she was not cruel."

Faythe found herself *agreeing* with Zaiana though she wouldn't speak it. She allowed her to finish her final word.

"At the top of the pinwheel we circle back to Lasenna, the Goddess of Power. The Gods might like to pretend they are equal, but I believe even they knew Lasenna had more power than them. They respected her because she did not abuse that fact, though she could have. It was within her capabilities to go against them all if she wished. But she believed in selflessness to balance the power she had, and she might have chosen a human image were it able to contain what she gave them. But power is often angry and dangerous and unpredictable."

Her silence vibrated, forming many strings of thought from everything Zaiana shared, but Faythe couldn't focus. Didn't yet know what it all meant and how the new knowledge could help them.

"What happened to the Mortal Gods?" Kyleer asked at last.

Zaiana gave a shrug that said her next words were guesswork. "This was the Dawn of Ungardia. My guess? They lived and died in any regular fae and human lifespan."

"Their descendants…could they hold the same power still?" Reylan quizzed.

"Doubtful through such a diluted bloodline. We're talking many millennia."

"Unless the True Gods have found a way to intervene again." Marlowe's voice held a familiar hopeful note as though she'd found another piece to the endless unformed puzzles of her mind. "There's a prophesy, isn't there? One Marvellas knows about, and which mentions the Seven Mortal Gods. I think I've seen pieces of it." Her expression pinched in confusion as she tried to scramble for answers she only harbored in halves.

"I don't know of the prophesy," Zaiana admitted, and Faythe believed her words to be genuine. "But I know *you're* important to her, Faythe. I thought that was only because you were her heir." Zaiana dropped her chalk, sitting back against the wall. "Perhaps you have a bigger advantage than you know. One that Marvellas may discover first and eradicate if you're not smart enough. From today's observations, I can't say I'm hopeful for you."

Faythe would have rolled her eyes at the gibe, but Zaiana was right: they were thinking of battle and war and weapons when they could be overlooking something crucial, only to be found in books, not steel. "The last line," she said, examining the four words left underneath the image.

"*Fesia omarte, Fesia lasera.*" Zaiana recited them with a beautiful eloquence.

But it was Kyleer who translated the message. "Fall one, fall all."

CHAPTER 69

Faythe

FAYTHE HAD ALTERED many minds this night to slip out of the city. While she was becoming surer of taking short-term memory, she quickened Kali's pace out of fear any one of them could slip through and alert the others to her absence

She had no choice but to risk it.

They rode hard, slowing to a walk as they came to the closest small town just outside the capital city. Faythe wasted no time in securing Kali and heading into the quaint inn. There was no guarantee her plan had worked, nor that her message had been received. It had been a desperate shot in the dark, and her heart pounded furiously that it could have been for nothing and it was all her fault what happened to the masters of the library.

Her pulse stuck in her throat when she entered and paused in the archway leading into the main room.

There he was.

And from the full tankard and neatly placed fan of cards, it seemed he had been waiting for her just as she hoped.

She slid onto the bench. He kept his hat tilted down, attention only on his ale and preparing the game. She breathed heavily, everything she wanted to confront him with crashing to surface.

Faythe began with, "How old are you?"

That earned a deep inhale from him, right before his head straightened, and Faythe was met with familiar ocean eyes around the sailor's aged skin. "I think the question is, how old are *you*, Faythe Ashfyre?"

Augustine opened with tricks. She knew he would, yet it ground her irritation.

"Twenty," she said through gritted teeth.

"What is a physical body…to a soul?" His gaze fell pointedly to the hand of cards she hadn't touched.

"I didn't come here to play."

"I'm impressed you figured out how to send a Fyre Message for us to be here at all."

It was all she'd stolen the feather for. She'd discovered she could harness the small embers and write her words with their flame before they took the form of a small Phoenix and soared from her window. Yet her awe and triumph at the revelation had long since turned to a nightmare of gut-wrenching guilt.

"When you live within the castle of the Phoenix kingdom, there's bound to be text on the Firebirds not found elsewhere."

"Indeed, and you took my hint to call to me. I am flattered."

"Gus." Her palm met the table, allowing her emotions to slip around her magick. The cards caught in a shallow flame until they disappeared as nothing more than gold dust.

He observed her spectacle with wonder. "Fascinating, all you have become. Perhaps your fate is more kind than cruel after all."

Her fist balled. "You knew." It came out as a whisper as the pain that shot through her stole all else.

Only then did he set down his hand, and his look fell with sympathy.

"Why didn't you tell me then?"

"What would I have said? What could I have possibly told you that would have been believable? No. It was not for me to speak. Nor did I truly believe we would be able to now, but I am glad."

Her eyes stung, threatening to blur her vision. "All this time. How could I not have known?" Piece by piece she was breaking down, and she had no one to turn to.

"You have gained far more than you lost. Her means will be to your ultimate advantage. The companions you have this time, the power you wield… I do make light of all you have been through, but I trust in the order of events that have led us here. You must too."

Faythe shook her head, not having full clarity about what he meant. It was becoming an eternal headache. "I don't know what to do," she confessed. "I don't know everything. I can't be certain I ever will."

"You have to," he said. His voice was firm, but his heart opened up to her, and that…the familiarity of it, made her bury her face in her hands. Gus was not one to offer comfort in an embrace. "You have been through a lot. So much more than any soul should. I don't hold the answers you seek, though I truly wish I did. But the very fact you're here gives me hope you will figure it out. All I do know is there will come a time that will test your *will* to remember."

Faythe had never thought of it that way. Did she want it? Or would the truth expose her to merciless wounds that would never heal for all she'd done? All she'd failed.

"Marvellas had a son. Do you know if the message was received?"

A son.

The knowledge didn't slam into her like it should. Instead, it tempted her to a void in her mind Faythe feared more than anything, for it attacked her with words, images, and impossible truths. She avoided touching that part of herself all together. But this…

"No," she said, placing deep attention on the chipped wooden table as she thought. Taken right back to the abandoned shop and the Dresair she faced. "But perhaps it will be now."

Gus raised his tankard a fraction before taking a long drink. "Let us hope you are heard."

She hadn't recognized the item then, but now it flared a new beacon of hope from long ago. Faythe's leg bounced along with her mind, which reeled over a war that was not new, only a continuation. Not lost, only dormant.

"He does not know?"

Gus wasn't really asking. Knowing who he meant in the switch of conversation, Faythe turned rigid. Her pulse pounded furiously, and her throat tightened with so much grief and guilt that breathing became difficult.

"No."

"Why not?"

"Because what do I have but broken fragments of an unfathomable truth?" She took a long, shuddering breath. The most prominent reason squeezed her chest so tight her heart verged on eruption. "And because I'm afraid he will never forgive me."

She felt the silence like judgment.

"After all this time, perhaps he already has."

He said it to ease her burden, but Faythe's sorrow only weighed heavier. Gus had all but answered her question on his lifespan by being here at all, bringing to mind another reason she sought the knowledge, and she looked up. There was no easy way to say it, but Faythe couldn't harbor this secret she owed them both.

"You have a daughter."

Gus flinched, taken aback as he leaned away. "You are confused."

"I'm not. Her name is Marlowe Kilnight and she's an oracle."

His eyes closed as if it would stop him from hearing anything more. Faythe's gut twisted.

"That's not possible."

"The woman who abandoned you in Farrowhold—she didn't do so because she fell out of love. She was protecting her child."

"From me?"

His anger made her flinch, unused to seeing it on his usual jester's face. "From a life of uncertainty at sea," she explained calmly. "She's the smartest person I know. Kind and brilliant, and she looks—"

"Stop."

Faythe frowned. "You should meet her."

"I won't." He met eyes with her then, delivering a warning in his cold stare. "Have you told her?" he asked in a warning tone.

"No."

"Don't."

"She deserves to know."

"What good will it do her?"

Faythe realized then. "You don't want to know her?"

He didn't answer, which flared Faythe's anger in defense of Marlowe. Her friend deserved so much better.

She rose, staring down at Gus as she tried to surface her thoughts. "I won't say anything, for it is not my place, but I think it would be cruel to rob her of the truth. She is kind and gentle and sees only the good in people. She believes herself to be an orphan. Not long ago did the man she thought to be her father die, and he was *good*. But you are her father, another oracle, and she has been so lost trying to find her own way with her power."

His expression became hard to read. The peppering of hair along his jaw shifted, his ocean eyes conflicted, but he didn't yield. "She would be better off without me."

"So her mother thought. I guess she was right."

That earned her a look of resentment. Though Faythe didn't balk as he rose, the wooden thump of his missing leg ringing like a bell through her.

She blurted her sudden thought. "You were there. You lost your leg fighting."

"Why did you come, Faythe?"

"To know that I'm not losing my *damn* mind."

The tension that had risen between them eased all at once. Faythe's face crumpled when his expression switched to one of mutual longing. She moved before she could stop herself, knowing his embrace would be stiff and feeble but needing to feel it anyway.

He wrapped one of his arms around her.

"She deserves to know," Faythe whispered against him. "It's never too late."

It would offer Marlowe nothing but confusion and heartache if Faythe told her about her birth father knowing he held no desire to meet her. She left the decision with Gus and prayed his heart could open for a daughter. Faythe knew from finding her own father that lost time didn't matter so much as what could be gained.

"She is your friend?"

Faythe moved with the rumble of his chest, and the fact he'd asked anything about Marlowe gave her small hope. Stepping away, she nodded. "Yes."

"Then she is in good company." Those words dropped her spirit, but Gus's lips tugged upward with a small, fatherly smile. "My promise to you remains unbroken. I will always answer your call. I hope you find yourself as who you want to be above all else."

PART III
PHOENIX QUEEN

CHAPTER 70

Reylan

THE MOMENT HE knew where she'd gone he was sprinting. The people around him became blurs of color, their terrified cries drowned out by the pulse in his ears. She'd lied. His soul cried out with peril. He wouldn't survive it. Without her, he didn't want another breath in this world.

In the Nether in which he was living he couldn't push his legs fast enough through the winding streets. The chaos around him obstructed his path to her, creating a surge of rage. He could destroy the world in his wrath.

When the horizon broke, he was forced to halt, breath heaving from him as he scanned the masses of allies and foes on the battlefield.

The name he wanted to scream became entangled with another. He clamped his eyes shut to block out the movement of bodies. Confusion rocked him; he should know which name to call. He searched for her another way, hoping there'd be something within that he could still follow to get to her.

Reylan freed his blade, knowing he'd torn flesh in his determination, but he couldn't feel it. He didn't stop. Cutting through enemies as if every one of them sought to stop him from reaching her, unable to falter for a second when he felt her.

So close. He was so damn close to her.

Fire tore from his chest, and in that second, he felt what it was truly like to have the world around him stop. He saw her as she stumbled back. Two arrows were protruding from her abdomen, and he raced for her. One arm caught her fall while the other lashed out for the third arrow about to strike her. Reylan snapped it in his palm, finding the archer, and with an agonizing battle cry, he reached into their mind and commanded a sharp twist to snap their neck.

It did nothing to alleviate the freezing grip of something more consuming than terror, more frightening than any living person should ever experience. Reylan lowered to the ground with her slowly, cradling her while he assessed her wounds.

"You're okay," he said vacantly, sheer panic erasing the fighting around him and stealing time, gravity, and all things as he accepted reality. "I'm here. You're okay." He smoothed back the sweat-slicked lengths of her chestnut-brown hair.

"You're not supposed to—" Her breath caught, golden eyes casting to the stars, and the agony in them tightened his arms around her. "You weren't supposed to be here."

"That's a ridiculous notion," he brushed off. He felt every second of her faltering and begged each one to slow. Her eyes slipped to his, filled with pain and fatigue.

"Don't you dare," he breathed.

"Lie with me, please."

He fought her. Gods, he fought that hold with everything he was. His vision blurred her beautiful face, battleworn and tired but still so damn perfect. He wanted to map every inch like he'd done so a thousand times; like he planned to a thousand more.

"All I want…is for you to lie with me."

Reylan shot upright, registering the pressure straddling him but somehow knowing it was salvation, not a threat. His breathing came hard and fast, but he clutched Faythe tight, filling his senses with her scent while their hearts pounded against each other. Her arm encircled his shoulders, and the slow stroke of her fingers through his hair slowly brought him back from the terror from which he'd emerged.

"It was just a dream," she soothed.

Reylan's hands slipped up her back, over the silk of her nightgown, to feel her skin while his forehead remained against her neck. "It didn't feel like a dream," he whispered. He couldn't explain it any further. How could he when what he witnessed didn't make sense? It was too sure, the soul-tearing feelings too raw, to be a vision, though he wished he could stop the shattering in his chest with the belief that was all it was when it haunted him like a memory. Like those he had of Farrah.

"I'm sorry if I woke you." He found the will to pull back just enough to see her face, but those glittering amber eyes flashed with the horror of his nightmare. He cupped her cheek, blinking it away to remember she was safe in his hold.

"I felt you," she said, brow pinching in disturbance. "You can tell me about it."

He shook his head, coaxing her mouth down to his with a surge of need. The softness of her lips, the taste of her, wrapped him in a blissful reality he calmed to. With an arm around her, he guided her down until she was lying beneath him. They broke apart, and while the moon flooded over her features he mapped every part of her, still battling the rise of panic from his dream.

"It seems neither of us sleep well when we're apart," she said, tracing idle fingers over his chest.

He took her hand, planting a kiss within her palm before lying next to her. "It seems so."

Faythe wiggled in close. The warmth, the beat of her heart—everything about her fucking ached, and he needed the pain of it.

"Promise me something, Faythe," he blurted.

"Of course."

"I don't ever want to forget."

She angled her head back, and he almost missed the quickened tempo of her pulse. "Why would you say that?"

"Because I know you could do it—take my memory far more effectively with the full power you have now. And that terrifies me more than following you to death."

Faythe shuffled away from him, and he propped himself up when she slipped out of bed. "I should go back to my room." She twisted her bracelet. "We shouldn't push it, remember."

"Don't leave."

"I'm sorry." She took a few backward steps as if she might change her mind. Then the shake of her head sank his gut before she turned and slipped out of the room.

Reylan stood watching after the ghost of her presence, resisting the urge to go after her. He ran a hand through his hair, knowing his hours of rest were over for the night.

CHAPTER 71

Faythe

FAYTHE WAS ENDURING her most tedious time in Rhyenelle so far: a week that stretched like a month with its endless classes. In the mornings she'd be chauffeured by Izaiah to his dance class, which was becoming more like a military drill, and later the same day she'd suffer through teachings on the royal lineage and Rhyenelle's traditions. The times she was passed off to a new tutor for etiquette lessons tugged on the grief in her heart for Gresla. The same happened when the new young handmaiden tended to her daily instead of Gresla with her bright warmth. A day didn't pass without her guilt slicing deeper.

Reylan was often called away by Livia—something she yearned to ask about while her concern for Livia tracking Evander grew. If it wasn't his cousin absorbing his attention, apparently what carried him away for days at a time was the civil unrest in the outposts. She only caught short moments with him which meant they'd hardly spoken since her guilty exit from his room, and she didn't know what to say to him.

Faythe was heading to meet Izaiah first thing that morning. Two guards trailed her at all times, and though she felt it excessive, she hadn't fought her father's concern, knowing the threat could still be lingering. As they passed a slightly ajar door, her attention was drawn to the voices within, but she intended to pass by...until a familiar blond head caught her eye. What rang alarm bells more was his company.

Whatever reason Malin Ashfyre had for cornering Reuben could not be good.

"I hope you know exactly what you're do—"

Faythe burst through the doors, and her friend jumped back in fright. "What do you think you're doing?" She directed her hostility at her cousin. Sparing Reuben a quick assessment, she found no evidence of physical harm, only blanched skin. Faythe could almost see him trembling. Her rage pulsed as she wondered what Malin could have said to him.

"Just chatting. Right, Reu?" Malin chirped.

Before his hand could land on her friend's shoulder, Faythe reacted. Her hand rose as though her grip were real, and Malin's teeth gritted with the circle of blue flame that wrapped around his wrist. "Touch him and I make it burn."

"It's fine, Faythe. We just happened to run into each other," Reuben said calmly.

Her eyes narrowed at the switch from frightened to looking at her as if this were a common occurrence.

"I heard of your little fire tricks," Malin chided, admiring the cobalt flame.

Faythe wondered where or how he'd heard of them considering she'd only shown very few. She stalked toward him, and it was as if all she could feel were the words she never got to say to him after witnessing the library scene. Looking at him, she saw someone capable of it all. Perhaps not the murders, but the orchestration.

"Go, Reuben," she said without taking her eyes from Malin.

He hesitated as though looking for some other signal but left before she had to ask again.

Faythe's fire extinguished as she came to stand before her cousin.

"Something on your mind, princess?" he asked with smooth enticement.

"Where were you during the library killings?"

A calm darkness passed over his face. "Are you sure you want to go there?"

Faythe retreated when he stepped closer, the challenge so palpable she choked under it.

"Where were *you*, Faythe?"

She swallowed hard. "With Izaiah."

"What a scare you must have had to find your rooms destroyed and your handmaiden slain. Nothing missing?"

Faythe's back met the wall, but her vision flashed with the sinister prod. "If I find out you had anything to do with it—"

"You'll what, Faythe? You threatened me once without merit—do it again and you'll find games with me become snares, and you—"

Faythe batted his hand away before it could graze her chin, throwing the heat of her fury into their stare down.

"You make it so easy to set them I'm almost becoming bored."

"Why do you hate me so?"

The skin around his eyes flexed. "Wouldn't anyone hate a stone in their shoe, a weed on their path, a thorn in their side? You are nothing more than a court jester with eyes on a crown that will crush you. Might you see I'm saving you from your own over-ambition?"

She couldn't deny she fought the stumble of her mind as it tried to agree with a voice that had shrunk but would never fully leave her.

"Ah, there you are."

Izaiah had perfect timing; Faythe was close to allowing her razor-sharp emotions to win. He stood in the doorway, beckoning with a hand.

"Come, both of you."

"Both?" they said simultaneously.

Izaiah shifted a look between them, and Faythe bit down on her cheek.

"Yes, both. We're taking classes in the training room today."

Faythe perked up at that, even enjoying the passing thought of getting to unleash her aggravation for her cousin through a blade.

"I'm afraid I won't be of much aid in that respect," Malin declined.

"Oh, I only need something to piss Faythe off," Izaiah chuckled, eyes twinkling with mischief. "Your face on the sidelines will do the trick."

Izaiah was right.

Every time she heard an insufferable comment from her cousin or even glanced his way, it was an effort to stifle her magick and only focus on combat. Kyleer joined them and became her sparring partner while Izaiah observed and directed, though she was yet to see how this translated to her dance.

"It's not too late to hand over the duty of opening the Comet Ball to me, you know," Malin offered, horribly sweet. "Exerting all this effort for a mere dance is laughable."

Faythe twisted around Kyleer's vertical swipe. "The only thing that'll be laughable is when I trip you from across the hall." With magick, she was confident she could figure it out.

Malin tsked. "Childish antics."

Lumarias clanked with Kyleer's mighty blade, crying a high-pitched noise as it slid off it, and she ducked to avoid his next attack.

"You bring out the best in me."

"Keep focus on him, Faythe," Izaiah chimed in. "Dance *with* his movements, not in fear of them."

"That makes no sense," Faythe panted, but she didn't stop.

"Swords down," Izaiah instructed. "That was just to let out your frustrations; now we channel them. Dancing is just like swordplay. That adrenaline you feel, you need it for this dance. It's not slow. You can't rely on the lord to guide you. In fact, it's more of a female lead."

That only rattled her nerves. Malin smirked as she passed over her blade.

"Do you remember the steps to *Kallsan Seven?*" Kyleer asked.

"Of course she does."

Faythe gasped with a thrill at Reylan's voice behind her, but she fought the impulse to meet him. He seemed to notice her hesitation, and she traced the symbol in her palm instead.

"No swords. Let's see the routine then." Izaiah's instruction saved the tense silence. "General, want to have a try?"

Faythe's pulse jumped, both glad and nervous when Reylan accepted the offer, removing his jacket and rolling up his sleeves. He sent to her mind, *Do you really remember this routine, or did I give you too much credit?*

She met his sapphire stare, and so easily the tension between them dissolved. She almost shook her head for the anxiety she'd succumbed to more and more with each passing day. *"I guess we'll see."*

"I won't go easy."

"I'd be insulted if you did."

Their eyes spoke to one another, and it was a delight to watch the sparkle in his.

"You've never done this without your sword," he pointed out.

"I'm particularly looking forward to it."

He caught her meaning. *"You are a taunting, beautiful thing."*

"I've missed you." It slipped out, and she only wished they were alone for her to express how much.

"Stances," Kyleer cut in.

Faythe saw the look he spared Malin. How reckless they were to be speaking in their minds around him, knowing it could give away too much. She tried not to let it dull her mood, taking up a stance that felt both odd but weightlessly pleasing without her sword. She admired how Reylan appeared poised to ask her to dance, and it almost made her falter to wonder if they would get that chance. If it would ever be *appropriate.*

She was beginning to despise that word.

Reylan moved first, and Faythe answered to it. He went slowly so they could adjust to each other without a blade, and though she were a leaf and he the wind that guided her, they danced. Faythe lunged softly under his arm, twisting around, and their backs grazed. Her hands still moved, and her phantom steel sang the melody she timed her steps to.

"*You are mesmerizing,*" Reylan said in her mind.

She ducked, she spun, she stepped, and soon they picked up pace, Faythe dancing on a slow crescendo that harmonized with him. At the speed of combat the room faded to a blur, leaving nothing but him and her and this passion that ignited between them. Her only wish was that it was a dance floor; the only thing she yearned for was his touch.

They stopped moving and Faythe gathered breath. Her brow pinched with the desire to embrace him.

The slow clap that came from one side pricked Faythe's skin with hot annoyance. Malin didn't smile with his applause, and she read it more as a warning. His eyes said, "I'm onto you."

"Just like that, the duckling becomes a swan," Izaiah fawned.

"I thought I was a lamb on ice," Faythe grumbled.

Izaiah only waved her off. "That right there is exactly the kind of balance and passion you need for the Comet Dance. Bravo for pulling it out of her, General. Nice try, Kyleer."

Faythe chuckled at his brother's disgruntled sound, glad for the lift in mood, and most of all grateful for the vote of confidence that she was getting somewhere.

"It's a shame you might miss it," Malin drawled, sauntering over with a hand stuffed in his pocket.

Faythe frowned, looking around to see which of them he meant, but one glance at Reylan's hard expression outed him. "You said you'd be there." Her voice fell from an accusation to a plea.

"I'm only back for two nights. Then I'll be overseeing the final adjustment to a new defense in the outskirt post," he explained. "I hope to make it back in time."

"But we know the journey itself is long, and in the past, this would have been the perfect excuse for you to avoid such a party,

General." Malin's lingering accusation wasn't subtle as he went to leave. "How times have changed... Oh, I almost forgot." As he spun back on his heel, Malin's smile made Faythe's skin crawl. "Lord Zarrius should be arriving tomorrow. You'll be glad for the chance to practice with your true partner before you're performing before hundreds come the end of the week."

Faythe had never felt such a desire to attack someone with their back turned. But all those motions soon fell away when a hand snaked around her abdomen as soon as he was out of sight, and she sank blissfully into the force that enveloped her from behind. Reylan's lips touched her head.

"He's not worth your energy," he said softly.

"I've never liked him," Kyleer said, staring vacantly after her cousin's ghost. "But I can't shake the feeling something is off about his arrogance."

"It's rising because he thinks he can scare Faythe from the throne," Izaiah commented.

"That's always been true. I can't put my finger on it, but this lord...you have to be cautious with," Kyleer said.

"I've heard a lot about him from Jakon and Marlowe. His allegiance is to himself," Faythe grumbled.

"And that is the kind who will switch sides depending on whose ship is sinking fastest," Kyleer added.

"Which can change in a heartbeat," Reylan said. "We need to learn him before he learns you."

"I only remember him briefly from High Farrow. His mind I was ordered not to search. Orlon said he was one of the very few he trusted completely, and I wasn't going to argue with having one less head to infiltrate when I could hardly stand what I was doing."

Reylan's arm tightened around her a fraction at hearing of her past though he already knew it all. He said to her thoughts, *"Never again will you be used by anyone. Your power, your choice. On my life, you will always be free."*

CHAPTER 72

Tarly

His hand reached out, finding the softest skin that ignited strange new feelings in his chest. His fingers slipped through hers, not caring how she'd found him or why she was lying with him, only that she was here, and he could rest easy now. She shuffled closer, diffusing a scent of cinnamon and lilies, which he breathed in deeply.

"Why did you leave me?" she whispered.

"I didn't mean to."

Tarly's lids slipped open to a breeze of cold reality. He lay alone in his dark room, seeming to have drifted into near sleep, but the thoughts of Nerida, where she was and if she was safe, kept him awake.

Turning out of bed, he threw on a shirt, some pants, and his boots. Katori whined in protest, but he didn't listen. One thing was tormenting him beyond reason, and he couldn't leave without facing his demon. His mind would never relent with the lingering unknown.

Stealthily as a ghost, Tarly took every hidden passageway and dark spot he knew to move around the castle. In his lonely days, all he'd had was time to map and explore and wonder if the structure would ever offer anything new no matter how many times he ventured it. Two guards were posted at the cell entrance. Dark fae. He should have known it wouldn't be so simple to get through here. He knew of another entrance—one he'd used to keep check on Lycus while he was imprisoned.

Slipping through the narrow stone passageway, he came out on the other side. It was only a short walk before Tarly saw him.

He hadn't known what he'd feel upon seeing his father, yet the male who was curled into himself in the far corner didn't inspire any emotion other than the same pity Tarly would feel for a stranger.

"Hello, Father." He barely got the words out through his bone-dry throat.

Varlas lifted his head, and those hazel eyes he thought he knew were already dead. The torture his father had to endure now was simply to live—something Tarly didn't expect to resonate so deeply.

"Why did you come here?" His father's voice was distorted, a lifeless croak. "To bask in my conquer?"

"This was never what I wanted," Tarly defended.

Varlas gave a cruel chuckle. "Go now. Be king, my son."

His mocking tone didn't heat Tarly with rage; it stabbed mercilessly as if he'd had the confirmation he anticipated already. A harsh closure that he was not loved nor wanted by Varlas. Not anymore.

"Did you ever care for me…after she was gone?"

With the cold and heavy silence that followed, Tarly braced himself thinking he'd never get his answer. But then Varlas spoke, head resting against the abrasive stone. He could hardly stand to look at him.

"I tried," he said, so distant like a ghost, "but I could not. You look just like her. Your face, your eyes. Even in your spirit you always took after her more. Every time I looked at you, all I could see was my failure in letting her die. She would never return to me, and I didn't deserve to have you as a gift, so you became my punishment. This is not what you want to hear, but it is my truth and all I can give you."

"I was your *son.*" Tarly broke, squeezing the word through clenched teeth. His eyes burned, but he forced the threatening tears back. "You knew Isabelle wanted to flee. You *helped* her and watched me believe she was dead. How could you? Knowing what the loss of a mate meant, how *could* you?" A cold tremble shook through him. His throat constricted tightly.

"Things changed when Marvellas came to me. She offered something she now denies me: a chance to forget. I wasn't opposed to the idea of becoming dark fae when she made it sound like a new beginning. I wouldn't remember your mother; I wouldn't remember my torn soul. And perhaps you and I would have bonded anew. I might have been able to give Keira more affection, and Opal. It was for you all that I did this."

"None of us would have wanted that. To become monsters."

"I didn't see it that way, nor do I now."

"You're a spineless coward," Tarly seethed, though it tore agony through him.

"Perhaps. But son, I have no regrets."

He couldn't bear it. "I'm not your son. Not anymore. You are nothing to me, and my one wish…" His chest rose and fell deeply, but he was unable to stop the horrific words when he'd felt them for so long. "I wish it were you who died, not her."

Tarly's violent tremors knew no outlet as he stormed from the cells, not knowing how to cope, nor having anyone to hold him in his anguish. He thought this time the internal gray cloud might kill him.

The last splinter to break him down came from his father's final whisper.

"So do I."

The rain answered his anguish. It suffocated his cries, which had been unlocked from a tomb he permanently strained against. His loss, his grief, everything he was and wasn't—it all came pouring out of him as aggressively as the hard pelt of water.

Tarly Wolverlon hadn't cried in so long he didn't know how to stop. He perched on the familiar rooftop he'd sat on with Tauria before, his knees tucked up and his head buried in his hands, while a tempest more violent than the weather unleashed from him. He cried in mourning for his mother all over again. He apologized for failing her and for allowing himself to succumb to this numb existence with a father who didn't want him, knowing she would have encouraged his heart to love, and for him to follow his desires wherever they led him. Since her death he had become the opposite. The hurt in his chest hadn't stopped expanding until he'd learned to live on shallow breaths. A bleak cloud of misery followed him, and every time it released its rain he wondered if this was the moment he would finally drown.

Tarly didn't feel the punishing rainfall drenching his feeble clothing, nor the bitter whistle of the wintry wind. No pain was sharp enough to counter what cleaved within. Old wounds tore open, and he bled freely.

He'd thought he wanted to remain up high and alone, releasing it all in solitude with the taunt there was only one way to end the pain. He rocked against the whispers, not knowing why he even held a protest to them when he had nothing to want from this cruel, lonely world.

Until now.

He thought he felt her, though his mind taunted she wasn't real, merely another mode of torment to shackle him to this hollow existence. Tarly shook his head, his hands fisting tighter in his hair. "You're not here," he whispered to himself.

The echoes of her eased in closer, and Tarly squeezed his eyes shut. She would leave as soon as she saw him. The real him. This pitiful, worthless state. To love him would be like stepping under his blanket of misery.

He couldn't stop shaking. Not when she came so close it

would've been foolish to deny her. He didn't know how or why, but acknowledging her presence broke some other wall, this time one of relief and gratitude, so fleeting and easily devoured by his agony. Tarly didn't want her to see him like this. He couldn't look at her and didn't have the strength to cast her away and save her from the entanglement of his messed-up existence.

Nerida's hands touched him, shooting warmth through his cold detachment. Perhaps she was just another figment of his desperate loneliness. He'd fallen from a height this time and none of this was real. Still, he clung to the hope of her and didn't protest when her palm slipped through his hair, grazing his tightly fisted fingers. Her other hand curled around his knee, and she tucked him in close. So close it obliterated his chest. Nerida slipped through the numbness that coated his body, this real, sure, *beautiful* thing, and he didn't know why or what he'd done to deserve her. But this token of salvation…

He craved it with every fiber of his being.

"It's okay," she said, her voice breaking. "I'm here, Tarly. I'm here, and you're not alone anymore."

Then he shattered from the inside out, releasing his tight grip on his hair only to wrap his arms around her waist where she kneeled beside him. He half-expected to meet air, so when she pressed into him like solid assurance, it was all he could do from holding her securely as if she'd vanish any second.

Tarly had long succumbed to being a prisoner of his mind, but she'd crafted a door and become the key. Maybe it was selfish of him to want her guidance as he took those first steps out to discover what lay beyond, but his hand climbed her back, his forehead pressed to her chest, and all she did was hold him back. No one had held him at all in so long he'd forgotten the feeling of peace, and Nerida…she was more than that.

She was absolution.

He didn't know how she'd gotten here or why she'd sought him out on the rooftop in such dangerous weather, but he was grateful for her. *Gods*, to have had someone so angelic come into his life and turn his greatest fear on its head…he was lucky.

Because now what he feared the most was that she too would leave him too.

But here she was.

And with Nerida at his side, the darkness of his eternal cloud began to lighten. Just enough for him to remember he was still alive, and he *wanted* to be.

CHAPTER 73

Zaiana

"Everything is in place."

Zaiana was beginning to despise the cool arrogance of the voice. She didn't turn toward it, staring at the crystal-blue sky instead. Her time here was nearly up, and while that should be a relief and triumph, the creeping countdown that would split open an event for history lingered cold death. This wasn't her plan, and she never could have predicted her perfect opening would come from the inside.

"Be ready. And don't lose focus or gain mercy for them now."

Zaiana flexed her fists to stop the prickling of her fingers at the subtle insult. She wanted to kill him. Despite being an ally, she wouldn't trust someone so slimy for a second. "Remember who you're speaking to," she warned him calmly. "You're not exactly the exception for *mercy*."

"Don't threaten the one who got you an out."

Zaiana's laughter was a wicked, haughty sound. "Your arrogance will be the death of you. I would delight in it myself, but I have a feeling it will come about in a far more entertaining way."

"You're a fickle witch."

She leaned her head against the stone with a smile. "Your fear cloaks you thicker with each visit."

"Remember our deal, Zaiana. You are to kill him first. Then, when you have your freedom, take to the rooftops."

When he left, her false smile fell and her forced confidence dissipated. Zaiana dug her forehead into the gritty stone, her fingers biting into it too, eyes scrunching against the sting, but it was not enough.

Not enough to quell the sickness. Not enough to silence her thoughts. Not enough pain to counter what tore and scratched and clawed in protest at words that would not stop repeating. A simple command that was once easy to fulfill, sometimes a dark pleasure. She didn't know how she'd allowed this one time to become a countdown she dreaded seeing the end of. An hourglass, and she wanted to shovel the sand back until she ached, if only to prolong the inevitable.

You are to kill him.

CHAPTER 74

Reylan

REYLAN LINGERED BY the side of the room, on a razor's edge with anticipation. The King of Rhyenelle stood unyielding and with a nerve-wrecking palpable energy. When Kyleer arrived, Reylan could barely look at him knowing what was coming.

"What's going on?" he asked, flashing a look at Reylan for an answer, but he didn't give any hint.

"Kyleer Galentithe, you've been one of my most trusted commanders for a long time. You have always served me well and with great loyalty."

The churning in Reylan's gut wouldn't stop knowing the accusation that was about to come Kyleer's way from his brother, though Reylan was not responsible for the king's intel this time.

"What is this about?" Kyleer's frown was etched with defensiveness.

"I didn't task you with the role of overseeing the prisoner; you volunteered. I thought nothing of it. After all, an esteemed commander such as yourself would know enough about the importance of his station never to risk it."

"Of course," Kyleer edged cautiously.

"Yet someone cares for her enough to have supplied her with a tonic that would prevent me from Nightwalking through her."

Reylan pinched his eyes closed, having not figured out himself how Agalhor knew when it should have been obvious. Yet he didn't think Kyleer would be so careless.

"We're finding out things from her—it is not necessary," Kyleer defended.

Never before had Reylan wanted to shrink so far from confrontation he was merely spectating. Agalhor had come to him to question, and Reylan was still suffering with the guilt of being torn between them.

"That is not a judgment for you to pass." Agalhor kept a cold, calm tone that was more terrifying than a rise in volume.

"Have you spoken to Faythe? She agreed—"

Agalhor broke composure then, his large hand slamming onto the table beside him. Even Reylan flared at her mention. "You do not bring her into this!" Agalhor shifted his warning to both of them. "She does not hear of it. Nor when that tonic running through the captive's system leaves and I do Nightwalk to find out what she knows."

"You don't have to do that." Kyleer danced on the edge of punishment.

"Ky, we can't take any chances," Reylan tried, though the commander's glare only darkened on him. Reylan had to remember Kyleer's feelings had driven him to this recklessness, but his dominant side crawled with an itch to respond, not back down.

"She will tell you anything if infiltrating her mind is the alternative. Just ask her," Kyleer pleaded.

"As Reylan said, it is not a chance I am willing to take. Let me warn you, if this were anyone else, they would have been exiled for treason."

That lingering threat seemed to dawn on Kyleer only for a second before his defiance returned, and Reylan prayed to the damned Spirits at seeing his look.

"I offer you this pass and ask that this stays between us, but make no mistake, Kyleer: I will not forget this lapse of judgment.

You are not permitted to see her again, and depending on what I find, she may be out of your sight and mind soon."

"You can't do this," Kyleer protested.

Reylan didn't have a second to brace for the fury when the king moved, pinning Kyleer to the wall with a physical anger he so rarely saw.

"You put this kingdom at risk—the Heir of Rhyenelle at risk. Your leniency with the dark fae affects us all, and this ends now. I'm going to choose to believe she is nothing more than a masterful seductress to have blinded you to turn your back on the good of this kingdom. Or tell me now that is not true, but be prepared to face the full weight of my punishment."

They stared off, the dominance and anger and even heartbreak so thick Reylan wished to be anywhere else. He felt for his brother, but more so, he couldn't help but side with the king's logic when there was no telling what the dark fae's true intentions could be. He expected better from Kyleer.

To Reylan's immense relief, despite the anguish contorting his expression, Kyleer seemed to find a shred of sense and didn't respond.

Agalhor released him. "Faythe doesn't hear about this." He repeated his last warning to them both before he made to leave.

"We've always valued fair trial and interrogation," Kyleer called out. Reylan could have strangled him to keep his mouth shut.

"She harmed my daughter, Kyleer. She threatens this kingdom as a leader to one of the biggest threats the continent has ever seen. Sometimes our values must bend no matter how harsh. For the safety of my people, I will not apologize."

As the king left, Reylan braced for the redirection of Kyleer's unsated rage.

"You told him?" Kyleer seethed.

"No," he ground out. "It's not hard to fit the pieces together, Ky. I didn't know he even attempted the Nightwalking, but I can't say I'm not glad for it."

Kyleer advanced forward a step. Reylan didn't take kindly to the threat.

"Do we need to take this to the training room?"

Kyleer's jaw worked. "That might not be a bad idea."

It had been too long since he'd challenged his brother at full force in a sparring session. With Kyleer's added anger, Reylan's determination not to be bested brought out a laser focus.

"You've lost your touch," Reylan chanted, knowing Kyleer was far from releasing even half the pent-up aggression he needed to calm.

"You're asking for injury," Kyleer bit back.

They removed their sweat-drenched shirts, but the air offered little breeze over their tattooed skin in their blurred movements. Reylan chuckled, knowing the heat would be a violent trigger to amplify the ferocity of Kyleer's attacks.

Izaiah's low whistle sounded behind them. Kyleer lost focus for a split second, and Reylan took the opening to land a punch to his gut, throwing out a hand to connect his palm to his shoulder, which twisted him off-balance enough for Reylan to hook his leg and send him crashing to his back. Reylan gave a slow grin at the victory, having felt Faythe's presence approaching minutes ago. He twisted to her and Izaiah and cursed his error. He should have known Kyleer's dirty tactics would come out in his anger.

Reylan's feet were kicked out from under him, slamming him down beside Kyleer, where his groan of pain turned to laughter. Kyleer straddled him, landing a decent punch to his jaw before Reylan raised his arms, letting him hit out some frustration before his own fist connected with Kyleer's face, then his abdomen, forcing him off.

"Are they always this violent?"

Reylan heard Faythe's question and switched positions. His knee dug between Kyleer's shoulder blades, and he took a second to confirm his victory before pushing off him.

"Hmm," Izaiah assessed. "I would say yes, though I detect some heightened aggression here."

Kyleer rolled onto his back. Reylan extended a hand in offering, but he only batted it away, staying down to gather breath.

"I don't think I've ever seen you so exerted," Faythe commented.

"That sounds like a hint, General," Izaiah added, mischief lifting the corner of his mouth.

Reylan swiped up his shirt, using it to wipe his face. As he ran a hand through his slick hair, Faythe's gaze traveling over him riled up some primal satisfaction.

"If you don't stop looking at me like that, this is nothing compared to the energy I'll exert with you."

Gold eyes flicked to his. *"I hope that's a promise."*

Reylan almost groaned. Five words, and they were utter torture.

"Someone want to tell me what's got Ky so worked up?" Izaiah crossed his arms. "Or shall I go with my best assumption that it has striking purple eyes and little bat wings?"

"They're not little," Faythe interjected. "In fact, they're quite impressive."

Reylan would always admire Faythe for her ability to see the good in a situation; her *will* to see the best in people. Izaiah simply waved her off, keeping his distaste, which Reylan could relate to, only out of protection for their brother. Kyleer had been through too much. The loss of a mate was unfathomable to Reylan, though the thought of losing Faythe was a fear worse than death. Their circumstances may be different, but he would be damned if he stood by and watched Kyleer's fractured heart get shattered in the clutches of a dark fae who only sought personal gain from it.

"We hate to bring somewhat begrudging news…" Jakon's voice came as a surprise. He wandered into the space with Marlowe. "We picked up on the murmurs Lord Zarrius has arrived."

Reylan flared with resentment at the mention. He didn't remember the lord from during his time in High Farrow, but he didn't need the image of his face for violent thoughts to stir about the purpose of his visit. His attention landed immediately on Faythe, and he sank at the tenseness of her poise knowing there was no way he could help her.

"I suppose the king will be hosting a supper for him," Izaiah grumbled.

"Yes," Faythe confirmed. It was the first Reylan had heard of it, but not a surprise. "I believe it's a small gathering, just as a welcome." Her hesitant attention switched to him. "You don't have to be there."

Because there was no place at the table for him, he knew. Faythe couldn't hold his eye through her discomfort at the situation.

"I want to be," he assured her, though it did nothing to lift her spirits.

It wasn't a lie. If he had the chance to even ease her nerves a little, he would suffer through the lord's attention on her enough to listen to their proposals regarding her hand in marriage. It twisted his gut to no end, but for her, he would endure it.

CHAPTER 75

Faythe

FAYTHE WAS THE last to arrive at the dining hall. Reylan moved away from her the moment they came into view, and Faythe's attention pinned Zarrius like a target on instinct. She wanted to feel like the predator, but the closer she got, the more his smile edged on glee, making her shrink as his prey.

"We were waiting for you, my dear." Agalhor spoke warmly.

She could only muster a smile, finding all words she'd tried to recite to make her appear confident or *changed* were lodged in her tightening airway. Sinking into her seat, she felt the eyes of two vultures opposite her.

Malin and Zarrius.

Seeing the lord threatened to strip all she'd built within herself and take her right back to being the helpless, terrified human moved by the hands of an evil king. Zarrius was no different as one of Orlon's most trusted advisors.

"It's a pleasure to see you again, Faythe Ashfyre." His voice grated through her, the sensation offset by Reylan's presence behind her, and she couldn't be more glad for his being here. "I must say, this change you've adopted as fae…you are most exquisite. And quite an extraordinary thing." He was almost off to a good start, until he'd wrecked it all by exposing that he thought of her as a prize rather than a person.

"You'll forgive me—I can't say I remember much of you," Faythe said, innocent and sweet.

Malin sliced her with a warning look. She paid him no attention. Though what she couldn't shake was her realization that the two males before her were eerily similar. Not in appearance, but with their matching cunning auras. Their expressions, mannerisms... Faythe didn't trust the lord for a second. But she would play along, give them what they wanted, then find her own way to turn down everything they thought was *best* for the kingdom with her as their pawn.

"I was Orlon's—"

"Yes, I remember," she cut in, feeling the snap of eyes and the rising tension. "Orlon was very specific about which minds I should leave unchecked. He trusted you greatly."

That seemed to recover his ego, and he curled a smile that was all satisfaction. "As Nikalias does now."

Faythe could have choked on the wine she brought to her lips. It was astonishing how believable he thought that to be. Maybe he was more of a fool than Faythe thought, having bought into Nik's ploy to subdue him.

Last night, she'd Nightwalked to him once again. Only for a short time so as not to risk losing control again, but it was enough time to confirm Lord Zarrius had limited days from his attempts on Nik's life and the threat on Tauria's. It made sense he would seek a crown this way after the spectacular collapse of his plans this past summer.

"This could be a great binding of two kingdoms," Malin said.

With barely any conversation had, Faythe was ready to retire from the guise of their supper. "Zarrius, you will know of my close relationship with King Nikalias," she tested.

"Yes, I do believe he mentioned you two bonded during your time in High Farrow."

Faythe didn't pour triumph into her smile, but her gaze slid to Malin, who knew what she was onto.

"A friendship is not a binding alliance," her cousin said with an irritation only heard by her.

"It is of my understanding that some of the truest alliances of our history lived long and prospered on nothing more than friendship and trust. Was it not out of friendship with the King of Fenstead that you opened the borders to and housed their citizens, Your Majesty?"

"I was close with him, yes," Agalhor confirmed, slipping a hint of approval.

"With no written treaty or agreement that forced your hand?"

"No. The King of Fenstead was a great ally I never once questioned. He is still tragically missed to this day."

"And if Tauria Stagknight should ask for aid in reclaiming Fenstead?" Faythe's chest was pounding, feeling this move on her chessboard would be the one to trigger the hatred Malin tried to keep from his exterior.

"If the plan for such a movement had promising odds, I would answer her call."

That was all Faythe needed to hear.

"Before I am even in power, I have an established relationship of this kind with both the King of High Farrow and the Queen of Fenstead. If you do not believe me, I invite you to ask them yourself." Faythe turned her attention to the lord, momentarily chilled that once again it was like staring into the same detached eyes, only these ones with a different color: a bleak gray. "I appreciate you coming all this way, Lord Zarrius, and I assure you it is not in vain. I only point out that marriage isn't the only way to secure prospects, and one might argue I have earned my right to choose."

"You have always been free to choose, Faythe." Malin's tone took on a cheerful note that always hid a sly plan. "But who you do choose reflects on us all."

"And what about a mate?"

The room stilled all at once. She couldn't see him, but she felt the ripples of Reylan's unease. Yet Faythe couldn't get one hopeful thing Nik had enlightened her to out of her mind.

She added, "Ungardian law states there is no better ruler to succeed a fallen monarch than a mate."

"Something you wish to share, Faythe?" Malin challenged.

Her eyes narrowed, but she couldn't implicate Reylan in this mess until she was certain it wouldn't backfire on them both.

"She is right," Agalhor interrupted casually.

"You still have a duty to this kingdom as its heir," Malin said. "To marry below station could create discourse."

Faythe ground her teeth. "Station shouldn't matter more than the will to protect this kingdom."

"Placing a commoner by your side would tarnish the Ashfyre name," her cousin insisted.

"More than I already have?"

"No one has claimed you have."

Except you, she thought, not forgetting how clearly he'd made his feelings known in that carriage ride many months ago. "I crossed kingdoms to be here. I *changed* to be here. Despite everything, I have *earned* my right to be here. Whomever I place by my side will be someone who shows their dedication through action, not title."

Faythe knew she'd drawn attention to Reylan with her words, unable to stop the rising need to defend him without saying his name. Awareness at her back made her twist her head, only to catch the last glimpse of silver hair before Reylan left the room inconspicuously.

Her gut twisted and her heart withered as she wondered if she'd said too much. He didn't want this—the war with lords, the politics, the crown. Faythe realized in that moment she'd never asked him how he felt about it all; had never given him the chance to back away from what would come of her exposing who he was to her and who he could become to the people.

"As Faythe has said," Agalhor said to calm the tension she'd stirred, "though no marriage is arranged, the prospects are open. I hope you look forward to our Comet Ball, Lord Zarrius."

"Very much so," Zarrius said with a tightness that could have been down to her making him an awkward spare part in minutes. Though Faythe didn't take him for one to give up so easily on a vision that could still transpire in his favor.

She tuned out of conversation then, wanting to go after the general with her heavy heart. She tried to ignore Malin's stare but gave in, meeting his cool, loathing look that spoke of nothing but accusation.

If it meant sparing Reylan from this battle, maybe Faythe would lay down her protest.

It didn't take long to track Reylan down. He hadn't gone far, and in her turmoil, she didn't think before barging into the drawing room. His conversation with Livia halted, the cool, calculating lines of his face smoothing out instantly. It only wrecked her further that it seemed he wanted to conceal his feelings.

"I'll leave you two," Livia announced, her voice stripped of its usual cheerfulness.

Faythe noticed she still wore her black combat suit, best suited for incognito work. "Have you found any leads?" she asked as Livia went to pass.

Livia hesitated, but her face displayed a distress that left Faythe feeling guilty for being so caught up in her problems here that she hadn't followed up with her sooner on Evander. "I've been tracking the Raider activity. I haven't found him yet, still only whispers," Livia answered briefly.

Faythe wanted to press for more, but Livia spared a look to Reylan as though handing over the task of explaining.

"I'm worried about you," Faythe blurted. There were so many people she was concerned about that Faythe felt as though she were failing them all.

"Don't be," Livia assured her, resting a hand on Faythe's arm. "I can look out for myself."

"That's not the point," Faythe argued.

"She's telling the truth," Reylan interjected. "But I'll explain more."

Faythe nodded at him and exchanged a small smile with Livia, almost feeling the pull of an embrace, but the commander brushed by her before they could yield to it.

Turning to Reylan broke Faythe's frenzied thoughts. "I'm sorry." This seemed to surprise him. "I shouldn't have said all those things in there without considering how you felt about all this. The role of being with me would take—"

"Faythe." He took her face after a careful scan behind him, keeping his voice low. "Do you think I haven't considered all that?"

The sharp edges of her panic smoothed out. "You left, and I thought…" She wanted to slap herself for the conclusions she'd jumped to.

"I saw Livia by the doors. It seemed important."

Faythe rubbed at her temples, the constant doubt and mental tug-of-war starting to exhaust her.

"I've never wanted power," he said. "Never seen myself fit enough to help rule a kingdom. It still seems a ridiculous notion, but I've always known what being with you means. I don't choose a crown, but I choose you, Faythe. Every damn time, no matter what."

She leaned into his palm, letting his thumb brush her cheek. "You already do help run this kingdom. You don't get half the credit you deserve, Reylan—least of all from yourself."

He smiled in appreciation, though not agreement.

"You leave tomorrow?" Somehow, she hoped plans might have changed, but his nod made her shoulders slump.

Reylan tipped her chin back, lips pursing as if he were debating his next words, but he spilled them into her mind nonetheless.

"I want to show you something."

CHAPTER 76

Tarly

TARLY CLOSED THE door to his rooms behind him after bathing across the hall while Nerida washed up in his rooms. He slung on low sleep pants and lit a fire while she finished up. In the mirror, he checked over his wound, wincing at the ghastly sight of the blackening skin and protruding veins. He caught her in the reflection wearing only a short cotton robe, her wet silver hair hanging free of the braids that usually kept it half back. Her brow pinched as she fixed her concerned gaze on his shoulder.

"Do you really want to know," she whispered, "how long I predict before it reaches your heart? And from then…I can't be certain."

Tarly gave a small smile. "No," he said honestly. "I can't enjoy a moment of life if I know the countdown."

"You want to enjoy life?" she said as though she believed the opposite to be true.

He thought for a second, but now she'd seen him at his most vulnerable and still stood before him, he feared less about sharing the inside of himself. "Before the Great Battles, losing my mother, and what happened with Isabelle, I did enjoy life. Now every day there's a fleeting moment of *want* that quickly becomes an impossible feat. I guess I was just waiting for it all to be over."

She fiddled idly with her sleeve, traveling elsewhere for a second, and he wanted to know what troubled her. Wanted to erase it all so she might laugh for him instead.

Nerida wiped all sorrow from her face, perking up as she went into the dining area. "I brought what books I could find. After you left, I made sure the guard you harmed would suffer nothing more than a nasty headache when he awoke."

"How did you know where I was?"

Her gaze met his with a smile. "Katori wanted me to follow something, and in the stables I picked up on your scent. I met Chief Zainaid first. He told me where your rooms were."

"You didn't think I'd left you?"

"It never crossed my mind, no."

"Why?"

"I don't know."

Intensity shot between them—or at least, it did through him—but Nerida's attention caught on something else, and her expression lit up as she skipped around the table. "You had it this whole time?" she said, pushing off several small books until the large tome revealed itself.

Tarly shivered involuntarily at the sight of it. "The Book of Enoch?"

"Yes!"

"Tauria was supposed to take it with her before the events that unfolded," he offered.

"What did she hope to gain from it?"

"Information on the dark fae, I suppose. Anything that could give us an advantage."

Nerida hummed as she heaved open the heavy book. "I'm hoping so too. This is not just a book on the dark fae, but a book on all species. I'm also thinking there could be something on what Marvellas is. I want to know exactly how the Transition works."

Tarly marveled at how engrossed in the text she became.

"I read a tale once, about a goddess who had forsaken her duty to walk a realm of mortal beings for a human she'd fallen in love with. But it was a trick. She was romanced and convinced to give up everything only to become a slave to their creations."

That piqued his interest, and he leaned his hands on the table. "Creations?"

"Humans into fae. It required her blood. I thought it all to be a fable, for it was told as a work of fiction, but what if all great tales are inspired by some note of *history*?"

"It's possible. But Marvellas has been raising an army of dark fae."

"That's what puzzles me. I think she chose the dark fae to create creatures that would be bound to her. They're not like the Born. The Transitioned are more like demons with a lifelong thirst for human blood. But I think some can find salvation if they can control it."

"You sound like you hold hope for them," Tarly observed. Admirably, as she couldn't help her nature.

"I have seen it," she admitted. "Both the Born and Transitioned. They're led to believe they're far more wicked, but in truth…they feel just like you or me; they just won't admit it because of how they've been raised. Nature versus nurture, so to speak."

Tarly bounced his thoughts. "So you think this book you read could be about Marvellas."

"It's plausible. If her blood creates fae of humans…whose blood is creating the dark fae?"

A nagging idea formed in his mind, as if the answer should be there yet he couldn't draw it.

Nerida thumped the book shut. "We'll need to take it with us when we leave."

Us. Such a simple word, but it was inclusion.

His chest tightened. Maybe she wouldn't realize she'd included him in her plan; her journey.

Nerida's eyes briefly flashed over the table. "At least now I have a pretty good idea of what you like to read," she teased. Then, smiling to herself, she found distraction enough to hold up one of his books. "Gasteria?"

Tarly crossed his arms. "She's very well-known and an excellent writer."

"I know. Also known for her enthralling romances."

"Those are never the focus of the plot."

Nerida grinned, and then there it was: her light laughter fluttered through the room. It only lasted seconds as her gaze met his, but he captured it, stored it. Tarly moved as if gravity were directing him, without breaking their stare. Around the table until there was only a torturous slither of space, a noticeable cool breeze between them. Her head angled to his, and she didn't move away.

"Why did you come find me on the rooftop?" he asked quietly.

Her large eyes fluttered with sorrow. "It felt like you needed someone," she said, equally as hushed.

"Is that part of your healing capabilities?" he pondered. "Being able to feel others."

"Not really. I got to your rooms, I saw the balcony doors wide-open, and Katori was whining, restless, and there was a brief moment when I believed you'd…I mean, I thought you might have—"

Guilt washed over him at her quickening pulse as he realized what the scene and his absence could have implied.

"I looked down first. Tarly, I don't know what I would have done. I've never felt this before, and it terrifies me." Nerida backed herself against the desk, hands curling around it as though her confession would make her flee now it was out.

Tarly could hardly move, though he wanted to close that distance. "Me too," he whispered. He took the one tentative step toward her. "Just tell me if this is too much, angel."

He'd thought it the moment he saw her in the woodland clearing. How the sun shone its glittering rays through her silver hair, reflected in her large hazel eyes, and glowed against her golden-brown skin. Nerida was angelic in every sense of the word.

Her lips parted, and he was drawn to them with an overwhelming burst of need. Slowly, in case she desired distance at any

A SWORD FROM THE EMBERS

second, his hand rose to her cheek. Sparks ignited as he felt her skin beneath his palm, traveling to erupt his pulse. Her chest rose and fell deeply, nervous, but he remained as slow and patient as she needed.

"I really want to kiss you," he said, his voice no more than a quiet gravel.

Her brown eyes flashed to his mouth, to his gaze, as though restraining herself. "I want that too."

He was seconds from becoming completely and wholly undone by her. The sensation was so effortless it was madness.

Tarly's other hand cupped her cheek, and when her fingers grazed his bare abdomen he had to stifle a groan. Inch by torturous inch he leaned down to meet her, then something seemed to blissfully snap as she pushed up on her toes to close that distance herself.

When their mouths met, it became an explosion of color in his monochrome world. They moved against each other, their bodies answering to each other so seamlessly, obsessively. Their lips and tongues clashed as they lost themselves to desire as if neither of them had felt its true effects in so long that it was breaking them. He craved more of the taste of her; wanted to leave no inch of her untouched by him. With her soft moan, Tarly's hands dropped, and he leaned in to scatter the books from the table before hoisting her onto it. The feel of her thighs around him could have made him lose it right there, seconds from climbing onto the table with her. His lips met her jaw, her neck.

"Tarly..."

His name as her breathless plea made him tighten his grip on her with a growl of satisfaction. It became hers, his *real* name, for there was no one else he wanted to hear it from. No one else who could make it sound like a new breath of air. It was hers to scream and call out, and he would answer to it. In pleasure, while arguing, to tease. He enjoyed it too much, needed to hear it again and again. It became a token of being alive. A reminder of being *wanted.*

He breathed her in deeply, needing to fill his senses with every note of her scent to memorize it, but something sparked within. A flickering beacon. Itching at a recognition that he couldn't think to make sense of until...

Tarly pulled back abruptly. They breathed hard, but he couldn't ease his look of bewilderment. Utter disbelief at first, but complete confusion when it dawned. The reason why since the moment he'd met her she seemed so familiar to him. It snapped through him like he'd always held the piece, just shy of finding its place.

"You're—"

She reached over his mouth to halt him. Her brow pinched with her eyes as she straightened, not pushing him away but trailing her fingers over his lips before bringing them to rest on his collar. "I hoped you wouldn't realize," she whispered, barely able to meet his eye as though she thought he'd retreat immediately. "But if you need an explanation, this has to end. It is not knowledge that should be free when it could hurt someone."

"Hurt someone?" he repeated, incredulous. He backed away despite the flinch of hurt in her eye. "How is this even possible?"

Tarly didn't want to believe he was staring at a stranger all over again with the knowledge that flooded his mind. History, tales...his mind searched and plucked but came up blank for answers, yet his senses couldn't erase what blared right before him. A scent that made every outward piece of her so *damned* obvious he wanted to slap himself for not seeing it sooner.

"I can't tell you."

"Why? This isn't just about you."

"It is," she snapped, slipping from the table. "Because I'm the only one who's had to live with it my entire life." Her voice broke, and so did every argument from him that formed in defense of someone else. "You see, I am the shield to the harm it could cause. Only I bear the burden, so long as it remains unheard."

He was wrong to have seen one so bright with sunshine and think her immune to becoming overcast. Tarly thought her rays of light could pierce through anything, but right now...he couldn't fathom the sorrowful story behind her spirited will.

"I don't understand." He shook his head, eyes turning pleading. "It changes nothing of what I feel for you, but I can't simply *forget* this."

"I tried to walk away." Her voice rose, but it cleaved through him to watch her tears glitter. "I've walked away so many times, but with you I couldn't. Every time I wanted you to keep following, and when you didn't...I turned back." A tear fell, and his knees could have followed. "I've never turned back before."

"You wanted away from me the moment you knew who I was. You didn't want to get too close to me..." he realized. "You knew I'd figure it out."

They matched tense, hard breaths for a long stretch of silence that allowed him to ponder.

"What changed your mind?" he asked.

"I'm so tired, Tarly." Nerida paced to the wall. Her back slumped against it, head tipped to the ceiling as though she were asking the Gods, "Why this cruel hand?" "I'm so, so tired of moving. I've never felt at home. I've never fully known who I am. I might never, and I'm also afraid."

He approached, but she didn't track him. "You didn't answer my question," he said quietly. Tarly slid down the wall slowly, and he cast the same question to the answerless sky.

"You feel..." Nerida barely whispered, but she paused.

Tarly resonated with the way her words failed her. Perhaps they lingered on the surface, cried out in her chest, or ached in her throat. He'd read many wonders of the world, both in fiction and in history, and he knew words could devour parts of a person more furiously, irretrievably, than any weapon, and time was a wicked accomplice. While flesh would heal, words could condemn for a lifetime.

She went on quietly. "You feel like a place worth coming back to. So I did."

His existence exploded, only to mend slowly but with a new clarity, wrapped in pieces of her. Whatever was to come, Tarly would be dedicated to her. He'd never felt like this before, and it shook his world with so much confusion he didn't know what it meant.

What *she* meant.

She'd stumbled onto his path, and now he couldn't picture the road ahead should she stray from it.

He turned his head, and so did she. They sat there on the ground near touching. He *had* to touch her to be sure she was real when this gift seemed too perfect to be true. His arm slipped around her, and when Nerida's body eased into his side, she rested her head on his shoulder. Nothing had ever felt so complete.

This current between them became undeniably strong. It was a cruel taunt in his mind and a wicked torment in his soul that cried one word. One impossible phrase.

Mate.

Why couldn't it have been her when this need for her came stronger than anything he'd ever felt before?

"You feel like home too, angel," he said at last. With hesitation in case she retreated, Tarly took her hand. He studied her beautiful brown skin against the tanned complexion of his, slipped their fingers through each other's, and his brow pinched. "You matter to me—more than I expected. I didn't know I was still capable of feeling like this. But you deserve far more than the affections of a fractured soul."

Her hand squeezed his. "I'm fractured too."

Tarly gently rested his head atop hers and their silence became liberating. He wondered with a flicker of longing if the cracks in their existence could somehow align. If two unlikely halves could forge something whole. Perfectly imperfect.

"We should get some sleep," Tarly said softly. He didn't wait for an answer and stood, taking both her hands to pull her up too. Then he watched as she slipped under the covers, which he pulled back for her, unable to place the emotions that washed over him to see her there. This bed that hadn't known a long, restful slumber. That had felt the claws of his night terrors and the restlessness of his conscious mind. Now it didn't seem like a place of torment with her in it, but it coaxed him in.

Tarly had the urge to say, "I don't know how many months or weeks or days I have left. But until you say otherwise, I'm not going anywhere."

Nerida's eyes creased as she shuffled down, laying her head softly on the pillow, her silver hair spilling over it. "Years," she said quietly. "Like it or not, I'm going to make sure you have so many *years,* Tarly Wolverlon."

Tarly had long believed the seeds of his life were always destined to grow weeds. He'd tried to find beauty in the times a flower would sprout, but they were always a guise, not anything real. A momentary deceit. Then she had come, the first sure bloom of such vibrancy and hope, and he knew…

It was worth suffering the lifeless seasons for this one true flower.

Tarly shifted before he lost himself again. "You can sleep here. I'll take the room across the hall." He released the covers when her soft hand closed over his.

"Stay."

One word…like an arrow that struck him, only to wrap him entirely with something he didn't know he yearned for. *Stay.* A desire for his company. In those seconds, he realized it had been so long since someone wanted him enough to ask for more. It terrified him. He had an urge to deny and flee and turn into the ice that kept him from feeling so it could never hurt. She could walk away at any moment, and he would let her go even though her imprint would forever mark him. And this truth he knew about her wouldn't stop rattling through his mind, and he needed a silent space to try to comprehend it.

"Not tonight," he said.

He hated himself with every step away he took for having killed that one treasured word with two. He'd already gone too far, and regret creeped in that he should never have kissed her. This line they'd met on balanced at a height that could shatter them both in the fall.

CHAPTER 77

Reylan

ANY TIME HE was confident the halls were clear, he couldn't stop his fingers from finding Faythe's. Her presence was an energy that vibrated through him; a sharp current that was thrilling, but also calming. He couldn't help his need to touch her.

He led her up several flights of stairs, and to his surprise, she remained silent, asking no question of where he was taking her though her nature had always been curious. That fact gripped his heart and squeezed.

They came to a familiar narrow, winding staircase, and the nerves that had been itching since they left the drawing room raked at his skin. This section of the castle remained deserted, unguarded, when there was little of any importance this way.

Reylan halted below the stairs.

"What's wrong?" she asked, her voice so soft the melody of it soothed his anxiety.

He brushed away a strand of hair that had come loose from her braid. "I've missed you."

The corners of her mouth upturned, never failing to stop time. He took her hand fully and led the way up the spiral stairs. As he fetched a key from his pocket, all reservation left him. He twisted the lock, and though it was once a space that had only known one face, he pulled Faythe inside.

It had been some time since he'd slept in this room, but it was his sanctuary for many decades. It wasn't much, the room small, but the tower was peaceful. Setting the key on a chest of drawers, he turned to watch Faythe carefully, heartbeat picking up an uneven tempo as he wondered about her thoughts as she scanned the room.

She moved slowly as though not wanting to miss an inch, examining everything with careful attention, running her delicate fingers along some of the furniture until she stood by the bay window overlooking the city. She didn't utter a word.

"I've never brought anyone up here before," he said quietly.

"Kyleer and Izaiah?"

He shook his head. "No one."

Faythe's brow pinched, but he couldn't read her sadness. Reylan almost winced at it, watching her scan the made bed thoughtfully, then the few items littering the table by the small fire pit. Nothing lavish—not like the rooms she slept in down below. Nothing compared to what she deserved.

"You could have any room you desire in this castle," she hushed out with some emotion he couldn't decipher, but it tugged within.

"I liked it up here," he explained, taking slow steps until he joined her, looking out from one of the highest vantage points of Ellium. "It's peaceful."

"Beautiful," she whispered.

Reylan tried so hard to keep his hands off her, to refrain from pulling her into him as it was the only time he'd ever felt such *happiness*. He had pitiful willpower. She cast those glittering amber eyes to him, and he lost his fight.

Taking her hand, Reylan gravitated toward an old dresser. He paused, wondering if this was foolish, but he unlatched the small box anyway and dipped his hand inside. He didn't look at her eyes, only at her fingers, and simply the idea of it adorning her hand flared something within him.

He had to make it real.

Her breath hitched when he slipped the ring onto her center finger. He couldn't settle on what raced his heart at seeing the two delicate golden butterfly wings and the white opal center against her skin. Frustration rushed in as something blared so strongly right in front of him, but he could only see through frosted glass.

Faythe slipped her hand out of his, and he met her look in fear he'd overstepped. "I can't take this." Her wide eyes spoke something like panic.

Reylan eased his fingers through hers as if she'd move to snatch the ring off. "Please," he said.

"Why?" Her eyes glistened.

"Because for the longest time it has felt lost." He brought their hands to his chest, taking a step closer to brush his palm across her face. "And with you, I am found."

He couldn't bear her pain, which inspired the notion it was a mistake to give it to her—but selfishly, nothing had ever felt so freeing. Her gaze fixed on their joined hands, on the ring, and as Faythe broke into a sob, Reylan's brow pinched tight with regret.

"I'm sorry—"

She shook her head, closing her eyes, and his thumb brushed away the tear that fell. Faythe said nothing, and while he wished for her words, he wouldn't push for acceptance.

Reylan led her over to the window instead. Sitting, he twisted sideward, bending a knee, and Faythe tucked herself in close, her back flush to his front. They sat in silence for a few blissful minutes, his fingers idly tracing the golden markings on her arm, leaving it for Faythe to speak. Even if she chose not to again that night, he was at peace watching the sky welcome nightfall wrapped in her presence.

"Why did you move from this place?" Her voice wasn't whole, and the hollow notes unsettled him.

"Isn't that obvious?"

"You moved across the hall as soon as we got back from High Farrow."

Reylan titled her chin until she was peering up at him. Faythe tried to blink back the sheen that coated her eyes. "I loved you long before then." He kissed her once, but as he pulled back, he couldn't tell what made her gaze drop. "What's the matter?"

Faythe subconsciously fiddled with the ring, and Reylan couldn't help but study what seemed a natural habit. Her change of mood since she'd left his room without an explanation had kept him on edge, only with agony she could be keeping something from him. Maybe she had doubts about him. Perhaps bringing her here had only added to them. He was a general with no one to care what he did or where he stayed. No wealth to offer—nothing but himself. And she was a princess with the weight of an entire court on her shoulders. He wished he could take that burden, share it, and there was a moment when he believed he could... until the council meeting. Hearing it all dawned on him a new clarity, and now it seemed laughable to present him as a favorable match.

Yet he couldn't let her go.

"I have to tell you something," Faythe said quietly.

"You can tell me anything."

She leaned away, twisting to sit sideward over his lap. His arm curled around her bent knees. With a long breath, she asked, "What did Farrah look like?"

It was the last thing he expected. Reylan took her hand, curious as to why she wanted to know as he watched sorrow and fear clash in her amber irises. "Blonde," he told her. "The kind like pale gold. Clear blue eyes. She was small in form, so delicate I thought I could break her with one wrong move."

Faythe nodded with a sad smile.

"Why do you ask?"

She almost looked away, but Reylan caught her chin, not wanting to miss a flicker of what troubled her. "I visited the memorial you gave her in Fenher," she confessed. "I-I should have asked if you would be okay with it or waited for you, but we were there, and I saw the memorial field, and I—"

"Faythe," he cut her off. He pulled her hand, and she shuffled over until she was sitting sideways on his lap. "It makes me happy you did. That you wanted to."

"It's perfect for her, where it is," she said.

He squeezed her thigh with gratitude.

"I hope we can go back together."

He smiled. "I'd like that."

For a long moment of silence all they did was watch the city in perfect contentment. Reylan knew he could spend hours like this and feel not a second of time had been wasted. He stroked her skin, her hair, marveling over every touch he would never get enough of.

"Has Livia really not found anything more about Evander?" Faythe asked quietly.

Reylan took a deep breath. He had no reason to hide anything from her.

"We knew he would be hard to find if he's remained a shadow this long. He rarely uses that name, and Nessair likely would have met his end by my uncle for letting it slip in his arrogance when he thought he had you trapped." He didn't want to doubt Faythe for a second, but in attempt to ease both their minds, he said, "Perhaps there's someone imitating him. He was a legacy to those crooks. I didn't think anyone could survive what I did to him."

"I hope so," Faythe said, barely a whisper that told him she didn't believe that.

There came tension of guilt that seized him with the ripples of Faythe's fear she tried to suppress. For a moment he wondered if it was in fear of him. Horror as he remembered that fact of his past. Regret that she'd ever thought it was something she could accept.

Faythe lifted her head to hold his eyes with such conviction it hypnotized him. "Not even for a moment," she said, quiet but firm. Reylan realized he must have opened his thoughts for her to catch them. "Not even for a second have I ever feared you or your past or what you're capable of. What I fear…" She paused. "Is myself. For the *worse* things I could be capable of if he is alive."

Gods, the agony in his chest could kill him.

"We don't know that yet. The state I left him in…I didn't believe anyone could have survived that, and if he did, his revenge has been building for a long time. All I can think about is there is only one way to hurt me, Faythe." Reylan stared into her eyes, his weakness and his strength. "You."

To his surprise, she gave off nothing of shadowy dread or horror or anything that indicated she was afraid. Faythe's fingers slipped through his hair, and he relaxed with the pleasure of it. He studied her features: thoughtful, but strong and confident.

"If he's alive, he'd better hope to never cross my path. Seeking me to get to you would be the end of all that time spent building retribution. A waste, really."

Reylan's pride exploded with his utter incredulity at the beauty of her dark side. Though the thought of her and Evander ever coming face-to-face had become a new terror at the forefront of his mind, he blessed the Spirits for a mate who was growing into such confident skin. He was continuously in awe of her, undeserving, but *damn*, if he couldn't stop being a selfish bastard and just enjoy every piece of her.

"I want to spend the night with you," he blurted before he could rethink for her best interests. "If I'm going to miss how exquisite you look at the Comet Ball, I want you for one whole night. Tell me no. Tell me it's reckless and it could risk the spell on these damn bracelets right when it matters the most." His hands slipped up her waist in anticipation with her long, searching pause.

"I can't," she whispered. "I want that more than anything." She angled her head to kiss him, and he almost erupted, wanting to take her right then. Everything about her should be a temptation out of reach, yet here she was, *wanting* him as much he wanted her. Nothing in this world was ever easily gained or there for the taking; it had been a fight, a will, a demand to keep striving.

For her, he would never stop.

"We could stay here," she said, pulling away.

Reylan shook his head. "There's no washroom."

"I don't care."

"I do," he said softly, wanting to give her the world. "We can come here again. Anytime you want to escape or see the city as high up as possible. Here, maybe we can forget and just be."

"I like the sound of that," she agreed. "Thank you for showing me this piece of you."

"There's no part of me that isn't yours now, Faythe."

CHAPTER 78

Faythe

FAYTHE'S PULSE QUICKENED her breath as she stood there in her robe. It was just a mirror. Just a damn reflection. She hadn't glanced at herself since her world was shattered and reformed. Not once in months had she looked at her new powerful body, her delicate pointed ears. Faythe was riddled with nausea and unease to finally confront her fear.

Reylan was preparing for bed in the washroom, and in her moment of alone time, she wanted to face it. Face herself. It seemed ridiculous, and she'd tormented for months over why she found it so difficult to look in the mirror. As if seeing *what* she was would change *who* she was.

Faythe wasn't afraid of seeing what she had lost. She was afraid because she had never felt more *alive*. In this body that was strong and powerful. And she *enjoyed* it. Was it a betrayal to her human heart? To want everything that came with being fae. To feel free and powerful.

But she was also frightened to face the woman who'd died long ago and see that no amount of power or strength or goodness would pull her from her own shadow's grasp. It was determined to hold her to her failures.

With a deep inhale she moved toward it, but Faythe's eyes clamped shut instantly. When she knew she was standing right in front of her reflection, she paused. Just to breathe and remember that no matter what she saw, she was Faythe Ashfyre. As human, as fae, as both. She had lived and fought to be here. She had loved and lost to survive. She would fight and rise to reign.

With a flare of defiance, her head straightened, and her eyes slid open.

Faythe's chest rose and fell deeply with the drumming of her heart. Her mouth parted as she stared and stared at herself. Her eyes burned, but she didn't blink.

She looked just as she did before—except *more*.

One face, one soul, but two stories to tell.

As fae, her hair was waved like silk, no dull snapped ends. Her features were sharper, skin so smooth and free of imperfections. Faythe looked to her pointed ears, but while she expected to feel horror, all that struck her was *awe*. As if she were only now realizing...

This was who she was always meant to be.

This body was always hers. It changed nothing but gave her the means to fight a fairer battle.

Then her eyes trailed to her hands, and she twisted her palms to see the gold Spirit symbols within them, attached to a vine of another language that led to someplace she still didn't know. Her robe covered her arms where it snaked around them and past her shoulders.

In her focus, Faythe didn't hear Reylan emerge from the washroom, but she caught the flicker of movement in the mirror. He was still, his stare hard to decipher. His bare chest was so glorious her eyes couldn't refrain from trailing down his sculptured abdomen. Every impressive contour of the warrior's tanned skin was highlighted beautifully by the warm glow of candlelight. They watched each other through the reflection as he took slow steps toward her, a hunger darkening his sapphire irises that flushed her body with heat.

Her eyes fluttered on a sharp inhale when his body pressed against her from behind, his breath caressing her from her temple down her neck as she inclined her head a fraction. Slowly, Reylan's hands trailed over her waist, and the eye contact they shared was an electrifying challenge. He torturously undid the tie of her cotton robe, and Faythe's breathing stuttered with her rising lust. His fingers slid into the folds, moving up until he reached her shoulders in a slow, entrancing seduction. She said nothing when he paused—an opening for her to object—and then with purposeful attention slid the robe from her.

Reylan didn't suppress his groan. His eyes closed for a long second upon first glance, when the material came away and dropped from his grip, exposing what she wore underneath. His voice was pure traveling gravel then as he leaned his mouth to her ear, drinking in every inch of her skin that tingled under his stare. "You're going to be the end of me, Faythe Ashfyre. But what a blissful end it will be."

Faythe stood in a similar crimson-and-gold lace underset to the one she'd once spotted and teased him about in the outer city Sloan Market. "It's not the same one," she said. Her breath hitched when his hand grazed her abdomen. Reylan pressed her tighter to him, and she felt his desire at her back heating her core.

"No. It's so much better." He pressed his mouth to her neck, and Faythe bit her lip to suppress the noise that caressed her throat. "Don't do that," he mumbled, his fingers trailing over her ribs, shooting sensations straight to her breasts, which were torturously caged behind lace. It was an effort not to come undone in his arms. "I want to hear you. Every sound I can draw from you. *Gods,* Faythe, you are the most exquisite thing to have ever lived." His eyes once again locked with hers in the mirror as his lips grazed the point of her ear, and she moaned softly with the blissful torment. "As human, you could have brought a man to his knees. As fae, you could make the world bow before you."

Faythe tried to twist around, but his grip tightened. Reylan's slow smile skipped a beat of her heart, sending a tremor down her spine that rattled her whole body. "Please," she breathed, holding his gaze as it devoured her whole.

That smile stretched to a grin. "I want you to watch as I worship you, Faythe. I want you to see that as human and as fae, every inch of you is perfect." His hands trailed over her arms, fingers tracing that ancient vine of script. His gentle grip at her shoulders guided her to turn. Her hands met with his firm abdomen, sparking a heat that raced from her fingertips. Her eyes stayed fixed on the impressive contours of him, soaking in every inch as her hands trailed upward. Over his chest, marking every scar she remembered. Reylan's breathing came hard, his heartbeat picking up a delightful tempo at her touch.

Then sapphire met gold, blazing like fire and ice. Reylan claimed her entirely with that gaze. His attention flashed back to the mirror, and when Faythe glanced over her shoulder a short gasp left her. The two vines on her arms met in the middle, and Reylan's fingers traced down her spine where all three Spirit symbols adorned her shoulder blades, wrapped in a design so beautiful it quelled her horror at seeing the markings.

"Exquisite." Reylan's other hand lifted to her chin, guiding her face back around. "Powerful." He closed that distance inch by torturous inch. "Mine."

A desirous tremble shook her, the inexplicable need for him sending her to desperation.

"I need you to tell me to stop, or I'm seconds away from damning everything this night."

There was nothing Reylan seemed to value more than his honor and loyalty. Except her. Faythe knew what she should say. For both of them, it was best they kept apart—at least until after the ball when they could figure out something to keep the lord and Malin at bay. But thinking of them only roused her defiance. Everything she wanted was right here. Everything they deserved after all they'd been through.

"Kiss me, Reylan."

He needed nothing more.

Faythe unraveled the moment he crashed his lips to hers. A soft moan left her at the glorious friction of their bare skin, and Faythe strained on her toes to match his ferocity in the way he claimed her mouth. Her hands slid up, but he caught her wrists before she could tangle her fingers in his hair. Reylan pulled out of the kiss abruptly, his eyes so dark they devoured the sapphire, so wild her whole body shivered.

Without warning, he spun her back around to face their reflection, but he didn't waste a second before his hands were upon her. They dominated her waist, and Faythe could do nothing but lean against him, one of her hands reaching up to his nape, needing something to grasp so she wouldn't give in to her weakened knees. Her fingers tightened in his hair, and she moaned louder when he massaged her breast over the red lace, his gaze turning primal as he watched her come undone for him—watched everything he was doing to her that clouded the room with both their desires.

"Look at you," Reylan admired, his voice near unrecognizable in his lust. His other hand reached lower. "You feel incredible."

Faythe's back arched, and she failed to bite back her noises when he reached her apex over her underwear. His fingers only teased and massaged, a wicked torture. Watching his hands on her, roaming and mapping and igniting—it was an unraveling she'd never felt before, like he was determined to leave no inch of her untouched by him that night.

His lips grazed her shoulder, pressing once to her throat. "You have no idea how glad I am to see that creature's bite gone, so that someday you will only wear mine."

Faythe noticed then how the skin had healed completely from the unruly scar. She shuddered with the memory of the gruesome dark fae attack. Her eyes pricked, overwhelmingly relieved. The thought of his mark there sparked such primal need, and a hopeful promise for their future.

Reylan moved around in front of her, his gaze holding her submission, reading it. Without breaking that intense stare, he reached down. Faythe's arms instinctively wrapped around his neck, her legs around his waist—a position that was quickly becoming a favorite as she flashed the thought of him taking her this way. He walked past the bed, though not toward any wall to fulfill her fantasy. Reylan headed instead into the next room, and a wild thrill shot straight to her core when she realized his destination without looking.

Faythe sucked in a sharp breath when her skin met with the cold bite of the grand piano. He released her with deliberate slowness.

"Lie back for me, Faythe," he said, so quiet, but with a lustful command that pricked her skin.

She obeyed. Palms against the smooth, polished wood, Faythe shifted herself before reclining. On her elbows she paused, but as she read Reylan's dark look, another shallow gasp left her when her shoulders touched the cold. It arched her back, and she turned her head to watch Reylan begin to stalk around the piano, the hunger in his eyes devouring every piece of her with his slow walk. The reaction she invoked became utterly empowering. There were no lit candles in here; only the moonlight flooding through the balcony doors illuminated her spread out for him.

"Nothing comes close to this," he said.

Faythe had seen him lost to lust and claimed by love before, but this… She couldn't place the emotion in his voice, nor what was etched in his attentive look. Something more enchanting than awe, deeper than adoration. It skipped her pulse and raced her blood.

"No sight or sound or feeling," he continued. Reylan let go of a long breath and came around the piano until she couldn't incline her head to see him anymore without moving her body. "Nothing compares to you, Faythe." His breath whispered across her ear as he planted his hands by her head and leaned in close. *"Fuck,* I love you more fiercely than I thought any person could be capable of."

Faythe's eyes fluttered closed when his lips pressed to her bare shoulder. She almost twisted, needing to touch him back, to *show* him how much he meant to her. His hand ran along her throat, tilting her head back to look at him upside down.

"Stay as you are," he commanded, pressing a soft kiss to her lips.

Her chest was bursting, needing some outlet, but Reylan knew there were more ways to convey his feelings. She listened, knowing his intentions. Behind her, she heard him sit on the bench and fold back the piano's cover. The pause of silence as she held her breath for the music he would flood the room with drifted her burdens afar. Then he began to play, and the sting behind her eyes reminded her how deeply she had longed to hear this again.

Faythe let her head fall back as she stared out through the glass doors, fixing her sights on the starry night sky while Reylan swept them away in song. A gentle melody, but it wove around her heart with a calming promise she couldn't explain. Soundless tears slipped down for the precious memory of when she'd first heard him play. He'd lain so much bare for her without knowing she was becoming completely and wholly his all over again. That night when she was nothing more than a human consumed by fear and overwhelmed by power—not within, but in title. Before she knew just how deep and binding their bond was.

Now so much was different, and it struck Faythe with freedom to realize she didn't miss who she was. She'd spent so much time doubting she could accept herself, but now she wasn't just going to embrace it; she would rise to it. As the Heir of Rhyenelle—as someone who held enough power to stop Marvellas—she was ready for it all. And it hadn't been without Reylan taking every uncertain and dark step with her that she'd gotten here.

Faythe's hands ran over her navel, feeling the song shimmer over her, and she gave herself to it completely. One hand dipped lower, and she closed her eyes, tipping her head back as her body bowed off the piano. Not through lust; Faythe was so entranced by his song that touched her body with stars.

"It's beautiful," she whispered.

"It's yours."

Faythe couldn't fight the need to see him. The moon rays highlighted every contour of his battle form, his tattoos catching mesmerizingly in their glow. He didn't miss a note as he met her gaze through long, dark lashes.

"You wrote that for me?"

The song tapered off gently, the last note settling in her heart. Reylan's fingers stayed poised on the keys until the final echo of that note faded completely. Then he slowly closed the cover, never once breaking eye contact. "I missed you," he said in answer. His fingers combed through her hair.

Her voice lowered with the emotion that burned in her throat. "Can you play it again?"

"As many times as you want me to. Until you hear it even when you're far and you remember I'm yours."

Faythe swallowed hard, wondering how she'd ever convey how much it meant to her. Everything he'd done for her. Words weren't nearly enough. The ache that swelled in her chest was a welcome pain. Real and all for him.

"Come here," Reylan said softly.

Pulling herself up, Faythe slid around on the smooth piano surface and shuffled over until her legs eased down in front of him. Reylan's hands wrapped around her calves, and he set her feet on the cover while she reclined, bracing on her palms. He watched her while his touch traveled higher.

Faythe let go of all her shyness at the way he devoured her with a mere look. He stood carefully, propping one knee on the bench as he leaned into her. Faythe's breath hitched as she thought he was going to kiss her, but he halted, and her lips tingled with the near touch of his while his fingers grazed along her thighs, racing heat between her legs.

"I wish I could taste you in more ways than one tonight." His gaze flashed briefly to her neck, the implication surging her lust. She wanted it so badly—for him to mark her. As her teeth pinched her lips at the thought, she stifled her shock. She had yet to get used to the reaction. Tasting him back…it was a desire that was so new and wild.

Reylan's fingers hooking under the band of her underwear drew a sharp breath. "I still plan to fulfill my first promise. Do you remember?"

Reading his movements, Faythe lifted her hips and let him drag the material away, the cool air against her slickness giving away how easily she came alive at his words and torturous grazing touches. He guided her legs farther apart, his breath continuing to blow across her jaw, and her head tipped back with an ache for him to relieve the tightening of her core.

"Do you remember, Faythe?"

"Yes," she rasped. His touch ignited up over her ribs, and with little effort he maneuvered the fastens between her breasts, which she'd fidgeted with for so long to figure out how to secure them. "You've done that before," she observed.

His pupils devoured most of the sapphire as the material came away to expose her completely. "Never," he admitted.

Then his mouth descended on her.

Faythe's fingers wove through his hair, tightening when his assault amplified, and she pushed her chest into it. His arm circled her back, taking her weight then lowering her until she was flush against the piano once more. Teeth nipped at her peaked breasts. Her legs wrapped around him, and soon she was shamelessly grinding against him, desperate for any friction below.

He grabbed her wrist, slipping the bracelet from her before reaching for his own. "Tonight you are mine," he growled. "I want to scent every piece of me on you."

The bracelets ricocheted off the ground where he tossed them, a liberating sound.

"Yours," she breathed.

Reylan kissed her ribs, down to her navel. Her hands slipped through his silver locks, desperate to guide him right where she wanted him.

"Look how ready you are for me."

He didn't lick; he devoured. Faythe cried out, her back arching off the piano when he didn't tease or go slow or tender. Instead, he alternated between sucking her hard and giving long laps of his tongue, which he'd dip inside her, deeper than she imagined. Faythe saw stars. Her fingers fisted his hair. When she couldn't stop her hips from undulating, Reylan slipped two fingers into her, knowing she was beyond needing to adjust.

"Come for me, Faythe," he groaned, the vibrations of it sending her right over the edge. Reylan continued to work her precisely while she trembled violently, slowing his strokes before removing his fingers to continue to devour her whole.

Constellations broke and stitched themselves back together again. She came down from the high of it breathing heavily, fingers easing out of his hair, and she wondered if her tight hold had been painful in her lack of awareness.

"Stay right there," Reylan commanded, his voice pure, thick lust.

Faythe didn't think she was capable of doing much else. She submitted easily to everything he—*they*—desired.

Reylan braced a knee on the piano cover, and in a few short seconds he was hovering over her. One hand planted on the black polish while with the other he held himself at her entrance—but he paused, glancing up to catch her eye. Faythe answered by running her hands up his chest with a barely-there nod, nails scraping just enough that his neck tensed with pleasure.

"I need you."

He plunged into her in one long glide, straight to the hilt, then he stopped with a groan that shivered over every inch of her. It made her tip her head back on a deep inhale of absolute bliss at the fullness she felt, which she'd been craving from him for a lifetime. It shot through her far more powerfully than before, consuming her entirely. In this new body it was like experiencing him all over again, a changed range of desire that drew out a wild, feverish need.

"Do it," she panted, knowing what he was refraining from. "I want it, Reylan. Hard."

He swore and adjusted his position, one hand hooking under her thigh to lift her. Then he let go. She let go. Reylan drove into her endlessly, and she could do nothing but cry out for him—clawing his skin, gripping the piano edge, not knowing what to do with her hands when she was splayed so completely at his merciless assault.

She was so lost in the moment she never wanted to see an end, so when he pulled out her eyes snapped open at the abruptness. Faythe had never felt more torched alive, buzzing with exhilaration for what he would do next. She wanted to explore with him, thinking they could do this a million times and it would never be the same. She craved his touch, his taste, his scent—everything that had become a map with infinite paths but always ended at the same destination.

Reylan's chest rose and fell deeply as he looked over her, claiming every inch of her with those blazing sapphires. "No amount of you will ever be enough," he rasped. He took her hand, helping her to sit as she felt so heavy and light at the same time. "Even buried inside of you doesn't feel close enough."

Faythe's arms circled around his neck, their lips near grazing as he lifted her. Turning, he sat on the piano bench, spreading Faythe's thighs over his. His hands roamed over her sweat-slicked skin. Her brow pinched with the waves of adoration he peered up at her with. It was all she could do to keep from bringing her mouth firmly to his.

"I can't stop needing you," Faythe said. "Not now, not in any lifetime. I am yours no matter what."

Reylan's head angled to meet her, and Faythe moaned with the trace of his tongue up the column of her neck. "Take what you want, Faythe," he said, words like embers shooting over her skin.

For the first time, she hesitated. "I've never done this before," she confessed. This position, relying on her to satisfy them both.

His forehead pressed into her shoulder, and she thought that fact aroused something in him. That he was her first for this too. She treasured the knowledge like it was everything.

"You know there's nothing you could do wrong, right?" he ground out, hands adjusting her hips.

Like a magnet she answered to his touch, beginning a slow, torturous slide along his length. Faythe bit her lip as the shoots of pleasure hit her apex, but it wasn't enough.

"Hands here," he whispered, guiding her wrists until her palms were splayed over the cover behind him. Instinctively, Faythe lifted herself just enough for Reylan to position himself for her. "Brace, then take what you want."

Her thighs sank back down, the new angle hitting deeper than she expected. With the need to feel it again and again, her pleasure drove her movements. Relaxing his light hold, he submitted to her entirely, tipping his head back against the piano, eyes closed in a state of bliss invoked by *her*. She wanted to capture the sight of him, godly and utterly mesmerizing. His face glistened against the moonlight, brow pinched tightly while short, fast breaths shot through his parted mouth.

Her pace turned demanding; a race toward pleasure that tingled through her.

"Just like that," he rasped, head lifting to watch where they joined. "Gods, you have no idea how much torture it's been waiting this long to fuck you again."

As much as her body begged to reach the ending that came so close, her mind didn't want that yet. It was Faythe's turn to stop. Slipping off him, she shuddered. She'd surprised herself with the idea, but she wanted to sate her need to have him in every way she craved.

Reylan rested there like a perfect sculpture, and her thoughts rejoiced. *My mate.* It was all she could hear with euphoric pride. Neither time nor distance could change that. Not their greatest foe, nor their most perilous conflict.

Not even death could keep them apart.

His eyes met hers with fiery question. She only dropped to her knees before him.

"Faythe..." Her name left him on a breath.

"You said to take what I want." Her pulse skipped, hand curling around his length.

Reylan's jaw flexed with her long, tight strokes. His hand came up to her face, thumb tracing along her bottom lip before pressing lightly, and she opened her mouth, flicking her tongue over the tip and drawing out his low groan. Then he straightened and stood, fingers angling her head back before trailing down her neck.

"This is what you want?"

Faythe nodded, swallowing hard at the darkening look in his eyes.

"Open and relax your throat for me."

Faythe tried to do as he asked, bracing her hands on his thighs and allowing him to guide himself into her mouth. He went slow, easing in inch by inch, and Faythe only focused on her breathing—on not allowing the size of him to rouse her panic. She had done this before, but it was short, and that had been with *her* fear setting a limit. She trusted Reylan and wanted to experience him fully unleashed in every way. Teasing him herself—it pushed boundaries that thrilled her to explore.

Tenderly, he brushed away her hair before holding it back. Faythe flashed her eyes up then, and he watched her with a glaze of amazement. "Perfect," he ground out.

He began a slow thrust, and Faythe adjusted to the foreign sensation so deep in her throat. When she showed no protest, his pace quickened, and soon, Faythe was matching him, answering to him. She enjoyed every second, the sounds of pleasure it brought from him, the flex of him, feeling her own arousal climbing and climbing but just lacking.

"You feel incredible in every damn way."

His approval only tightened her legs, and she could have whimpered with the height of need.

Reylan pulled out with such a loud growl she thought he might be close to spilling himself but wanted to prologue their desires after they'd been denied each other for so long. She took a second, hands braced on her knees, to gather her breath, grappling with the threads of need that untangled all at once. Him inside her, his mouth over her, his hands exploring her…

"I need you," was all she could get out, wondering how it could ever be enough. Knowing it wouldn't ever be.

This need for him was eternal. And insatiable.

Breath left her when she was scooped up and cradled against Reylan. Her head leaned against him while he carried her. She was lain upon soft sheets, and the comfort brought on a sleepy kind of lust.

"I'm a selfish bastard for this," he said, his hand slipping over her side, kneading her breast, before settling over her collarbone. "The thought of his hands on you has been driving me wild, Faythe."

"It means nothing." Her hand fisted his hair. "But you mean everything, Reylan."

He groaned when she brought her lips to his. Faythe's mouth opened on a silent cry when his hand slipped between her thighs.

"I want you to think of me when you're with him," he growled, picking up the pace as he circled her apex, and all she could do was writhe beneath him. "Think of how you feel when I'm inside you. That's it, Faythe."

She came loudly—an eruption from nowhere when she'd been teetering on the edge for such a short time. As she trembled with the aftershocks, she knew this wasn't the end, nor did she want it to be despite her heavy eyelids.

"One more time for me. Can you do that?" he whispered over her skin.

Her eyes remained closed, but she nodded.

She would do anything for him.

"Turn around."

Faythe rolled onto her hands and knees, a new thrill sparking through her with clear awakening at the position. She felt him behind her, but he didn't enter her yet. Instead, he leaned over her, every touch he made so slow and with such attention—over her breast, up her chest, curling lightly around her throat, and then he guided her up until, on their knees, her back was flush with his front.

It was then she discovered a new favorite, giddy with electricity at the intimate hold. He slipped inside slowly, and her brow pinched, back arching to give him a better angle on instinct.

"No one could fit you as perfectly as I do."

"No one," she echoed.

He answered by pulling back nearly all the way before plunging in with a punishing thrust. Faythe repeated the words: *No one else.* Over and over, each time he gave her what she craved, until he set a pace and all she could do was claw at his forearm holding her upright, the sound of their skin meeting mixed with the cries that came from her unchecked and the primal groans he let out that shot straight between her legs. His fingers rubbing circles over her apex was the final push, and Faythe erupted. From the inside out she ignited. Her magick entwined with his and her golden tattoos glowed as she finally reached the pinnacle of absolution.

Reylan came with a roar and one final mighty thrust that dropped them both to their hands and knees, panting hard, skin to skin, slicked in the aftermath of a bliss unlike anything she'd experienced before. His harsh breaths blew her hair, and her head angled to look at him.

"You were really holding back before," Faythe rasped. "In the waterfall cave."

Reylan breathed a laugh. "You were far more breakable then. Trust that this is not the limit of what I've thought about doing with you. Not even close. But tonight, you surprised me in more ways. It thrills me to no end, Faythe."

She shuddered with the scandalous thoughts he stirred in her. Most prominently, his teeth in her—marking her. He pulled away, and her body tensed with the breeze. She slowly lowered herself until she was lying contentedly on her stomach.

Reylan was silent for long enough that she eventually peered down at him. He stood at the end of the bed, a blanket in one hand, but he remained still.

"You are a Goddess, Faythe Ashfyre."

She smiled for him. "Come here," she said sleepily.

Reylan dipped onto the bed, dropping the soft material over her as he came to lay beside her. Faythe lifted up just enough to fold herself into the perfect space between his neck and shoulder.

"The dance with the lord means nothing. It's only a means of satisfying them for now," she mumbled, needing to be sure he knew it again and again. "But I wish it were you."

Reylan kissed the top of her head. "It would not be to their pleasure to see a general leading their princess."

"You are more than that," she said quietly. "So much more."

He didn't respond, but she felt the echoes of his gratitude.

Faythe was distracted by the dip in her stomach. "You hate dancing."

"I do, but it doesn't feel like a tedious routine with you. It feels like what we just did—intimate. A moment when the world fades and the barriers fall. That first time in High Farrow, I would have danced with you that whole night if you'd asked."

The memory flared in her chest with a wave of emotion. Her fingers idly traced the tattoos on his chest as she remembered what it felt like—the moment the realization locked in her heart that there was no letting him go.

Faythe lifted herself up onto her elbow, watching her fingers trailing over his markings. One set called her, hypnotizing her with the pattern she traced over and over, until she stopped. Her lips parted. She couldn't unsee it. No longer a decoration, but a phrase her mind translated so suddenly her eyes pricked.

"You said these were memories of your parents," Faythe said vacantly.

Reylan frowned. "They are."

Most of them, Faythe thought. All except this one, yet he wouldn't know.

He remained confused by her interest, but Faythe only smiled, leaning down to kiss him. A soft moan escaped her when his hand hooked her thigh, pulling her over him completely without breaking them apart.

"I don't think we're done here," he muttered huskily.

"I hoped not." Her desire ignited all over again with every hard inch of him beneath her.

As she glanced once more at her favorite marking on him, Faythe scanned his beautiful face. "No matter how long it takes, or what name, or what title, I will find you endlessly, Reylan Arrowood. If you only remember one thing, always remember that is my promise."

CHAPTER 79

Zaiana

Her eyes flew open, yet Zaiana froze with panic upon meeting a storm that cracked and whorled around her. She was awake, or at least she felt conscious, yet…something wasn't right.

Scrambling to her feet, she swayed, disoriented, but gravity didn't weigh the same here. This place was sorrow and anguish, a pure, dark energy, allowing little light through with the black clouds that raged, making hairs fly across her vision when she tried to squint to find something solid.

She wanted out.

More than anything, and her hands clamped over her ears and her eyes scrunched as though blocking it all out would take her back the bleak cell she was certain she fell asleep in. This place taunted, choking her lungs with misery. Hatred—so much self-hatred—and she realized at once…

This place was *her*.

"Zaiana Silverfair." A dominant male voice echoed through the whip of wind. It rang with a distant familiarity until she pinned a face to it seconds before he emerged across the void.

King Agalhor Ashfyre of Rhyenelle.

Her knees became weak, threatening to make her bow before him as the realization of what he was doing finally dawned. The violation that stripped away the last piece of herself she had left.

"I didn't expect you to be able to awaken here. At least not as surely as you are," he observed. "Like a Nightwalker."

Zaiana tried to focus and push him out, but a heavy weight as sure as her Niltain steel clamped around her mind. He seized control of her entirely, his power slamming over her leaving no room for her to mistake she was at his mercy within her own mind. She knew Agalhor Ashfyre to be legendary in his Nightwalking ability, and this helpless terror drowned her with an unfamiliarity that stung her eyes.

"Please," she whimpered pathetically. She had nothing left.

"Did my daughter beg when you tried to take her life?" he taunted.

Zaiana hung her head, but that wasn't a submission he accepted, and he commanded her gaze back to him. She clenched her teeth, managing to bite her nails into her palms to hold back the tears that threatened to spill. Her rage pulsed so tangibly she thought it could break his spell. She felt him push back to fight her.

"You can't say you didn't expect this," he went on. "You could hold the answers to everything, and once I have them, I will end your miserable existence. Isn't that what you truly want?" He stalked around her, observing every vulnerable inch and reading her far deeper than anyone had before. Seeing everything ugly and twisted she was within. "I feel you, Zaiana—your true desires—and I may even pity you. Is it not a mercy for me to end this storm?" He looked around the whirling mass of her subconscious. Lightning cracked ferociously while the black clouds raged. Maybe she agreed on some level, and he knew it.

Faythe had lied.

She had retreated like a coward and instead passed the task off to her father.

Zaiana would kill them both.

"You only prove my need to kill you, Zaiana. I will not allow you to even think of another threat toward her again. Though if it makes you feel anything in that cold heart, Faythe kept to her word and knows nothing of this."

How could she believe him? It could be a desperate attempt to save Faythe from her wrath. It wouldn't change anything.

The king took her chin, and she was helpless to jerk out of his hold. "Listen," he ordered.

At his command, a rhythmic thump echoed through the space. Distant at first, until it built, strong and sure. A heartbeat.

"Yours," he said.

Zaiana could have laughed at his absurd claim, but she wondered what kind of twisted joke he was playing. Then she felt it. In her chest that movement terrified her, but the more that terror grew, the harder it slammed, the faster it sprinted, and she couldn't take it, straining helplessly against a cry with a rush of need to tear it out.

It's not real, she chanted. It had to be a manipulation. *Make it stop.*

There were times when she'd allowed herself to dream of this. What it would feel like to own a heart that *beat*. That could translate to so many wondrous, hidden things with careful attention in its ever-changing harmony. As she focused on the illusion of how it thrummed in her chest, Zaiana began to calm, holding this fluttering, sure thing that felt *beautiful*.

Until it was snatched from her as quickly as blowing out a candle, and she whimpered.

"I plan to find out what caused its stillness. Perhaps it could be the key to ending you all."

"I will kill you," she promised through clenched teeth. He'd been marked from the moment she set foot in his castle, but now he'd lit the fire ablaze for her to carry it through.

"You will not wake from this. I am not heartless; I will ease your passing in here."

Color began to form out of the misty clouds. Voices echoed and Zaiana slipped her eyes shut, unable to face her own past, succumbing to her defeat. She couldn't bear to watch another mind witness all she was and all she had done, plucking and picking parts of her he had no right to see. She tried to tune out the voices, but she couldn't. Even in consciousness she begged, but what she could never do was disconnect from her own cruel mind.

Her home, her prison, her cage.

The crack of a whip lashed through her. *How much of your blood must we spill before you learn? Your defiance will be the end of you.* Another crack before the echo of Nephra's sinister voice faded.

The reel of her memories played out, skipping weeks, years, decades. Agalhor took his fill.

Which of them hurt you?

Her brow flexed at Maverick's voice, almost enough for her to steal a glance, but instead she whispered her own words on top of the memory.

"All of them."

All of the masters and everyone she had ever crossed paths with. They would always betray her. Or lie or cheat or hurt. Zaiana trusted no one. Not completely. And in turn, she didn't expect anyone to trust *her*.

"So you *can* feel," Agalhor mused.

Zaiana drew more blood from her palms at hearing Kyleer's voice next. Her cheeks burned hot, humiliation straining her movements as she wondered if her sheer will to kill the king could break his spell. "Burn in the Nether," she spat.

Just as she roused something of anger to help her climb out of her pitiful state, her gaze lifted to the one scene she couldn't bear. Ice laced her spine, locking her whole body, which she knew would kneel here without his influence.

"Stop," she begged vacantly, though she couldn't look away.

Her own dark, merciless eyes pinned the surrendered dark fae she'd wounded enough to take his fight. On his knees he panted, clutching a deep wound on his abdomen that spilled silver blood over his hand. She hadn't forgotten this day. Not even a second of it. Yet in here it was like *living it* all over again. Zaiana's body vibrated with a haunting caress, staring and staring at the broken sight...

Finnian.

"*Why?*" her past-self demanded through her teeth. Pain, so much pain, flexed in those purple eyes that fought the silver that lined them.

"*I didn't have a choice,*" Finnian rasped. "*I can't— I can't control—*"

Zaiana's mouth parted on a choked scream as she watched her past-self, so consumed by betrayal, kneel with him...and plunge her sword straight through his chest. "*Kill or be killed, right?*" she whispered to him.

He spluttered in agony, yet he didn't show anger, only so much pain and regret. His mouth floundered as though he were trying to say something.

"*I...I would never...*"

He faded in her arms slowly, the light in his green eyes flickering.

She would never know the end of what he wanted to say. And that unfulfilled sentence would forever linger like a ghost.

Zaiana watched herself tear a strip from his shirt, a token for the weakness that had almost gotten her killed. She tied it to the hilt of her sword so she'd never be granted a moment to forget.

"I was right to stop your claws from sinking into my commander more than they already have," Agalhor said darkly. "Your love is deadly."

"You had no right." Zaiana felt the slow build of a wrath so charged she hoped it could kill him. Her tears fell to the black ground. "You had no *right!*" She screamed the last word, her head exploding with an affliction that blackened her vision instantly. She was falling and falling, and she didn't care if the final piece of her shattered when it stopped.

As long as she took out the King of Rhyenelle with her.

CHAPTER 80

Nikalias

NIK ARRIVED AT the stables Tauria had indicated to him. His senses were heightened to a dangerous point at being parted from her, but while she boldly took the main route to the castle with Mordecai, this was his only way to follow her inside. He checked back for Samara, his hand hovering on her back to guide her into the hidden passage first.

"What will we do here?"

He gauged her question to be nothing more than something to fill the silence and distract her from her unease.

"Keep hidden and find out what *he* is doing here," Nik answered, barely able to offer any warmth or assurance.

"I'm sorry," she blurted.

That stole his attention from his simmering anticipation. He thought on her apology for a moment, guessing it was for more than one thing. "You are forgiven, Samara. It can't have been easy to feel as if your survival depended on you attaching yourself to whatever allegiance seemed strongest."

Her silence seemed contemplative, and he glanced over to find her fidgeting with her sleeves. "I'm not strong like Tauria. Or really that brave."

"I don't think that's true."

"Why not?"

"You're here. You didn't have to agree to this plan."

"You would have killed me otherwise."

"Is that the only reason you agreed?"

Her pause was answer enough. Nik took a deep breath, feeling he had nothing to lose with his next confession. "For what it's worth, we would not have killed you."

"But I tried to kill you."

"Did you truly love him?" Nik couldn't figure out how she could have fallen for Zarrius, whom he'd never seen show an ounce of affection to anyone.

"I don't know," she admitted. "I think…because I don't know what that *means*. You once tried to explain it to me, and I think then I wondered if it was love or if I was too afraid to be nothing without him. If I didn't kill you, he planned to leave me. He said I was weak and that he needed someone he could trust. I don't think—" Samara hesitated.

"You don't have to tell me more," Nik said softly, "but I hope you know you can trust me."

They walked past the scene of the carnage, sparing only a glance at the ruined ceremony room that chilled Nik with dark memories.

"What happened?" Samara breathed in horror.

His touch on her shoulders urged her to keep moving. He didn't want to lose a second. "Mordecai almost forced Tauria into a marriage once before."

"He doesn't seem all that truly evil."

Nik huffed a sour laugh. "Monsters can take many faces. Don't be fooled by the ones they wear to lure you in."

They exchanged a look, and Nik could have pitied her naïve heart, thinking there was a sadness to the revelation.

"I wasn't attracted to him," she said. "Zarrius, I mean."

Nik smiled. "There is nothing wrong with that."

595

"I wasn't attracted to you either."

His chuckle vibrated quietly through the narrow passage.

"I just mean... I don't know. I'm confused, and I'm scared I won't ever get the time to figure it out. I've made so many mistakes in thinking a figure with high power meant safety, but maybe I don't care about that anymore. Maybe I want to try danger, or the unknown, if that's what it is to *live.*"

Before they reached the end of the passage, he pulled her to a stop. "Where is this coming from?"

"I've been sacrificed my whole life, Nik. From my parents to Zarrius. From Zarrius to you. From you to Mordecai. I kissed him, and for the first time I felt *free*. I almost broke to tell him everything because there's often this voice in my head that just wants to *break.*"

"To find what you truly desire," Nik assessed. "For someone to hear you." A whole new side to Samara had opened wide before him, and he should have *seen* her sooner.

She dropped her eyes. "I'm not a lady of the court anymore. I thought I'd feel ashamed as it's all I was taught to value. Yet I'm glad, and I'm not afraid anymore."

His hand reached out to her arm on impulse. "You are brave, Samara. It's only taken you until now to embrace it."

Her mouth upturned with liberation, and while he was glad for the weight that lifted between them, which he didn't know had grown so heavy, he didn't have time to bask in it. "Come on," he pressed gently, taking the lead this time to peer first into the abandoned room.

As he slipped out from behind the bookcase, he was hit so powerfully with the memory this room held that the world around him faded away. Rooted to the spot, his eyes trailed from the couch to the wall, and his heart fractured, his soul cried, and it was sheer will that kept him from falling to his knees.

Nik hadn't allowed himself to grieve a moment for the severed bond they'd created in this very room. He had to be strong for her. While it changed absolutely nothing of his love and adoration for Tauria, he couldn't deny the pain of having sampled a gift between them only for them to be cruelly robbed of it.

"I'm so sorry." Samara's quiet voice pierced through his plummet into sorrow enough to find a grapple, but it would take time to reel him back from this loss fully.

He took a long breath to ground himself. "We will have our revenge for everything they've stolen from us."

CHAPTER 81

Faythe

IT HAD BEEN so long since Faythe felt light and free. Parting with Reylan would always be a strain on the tether that kept him selfishly by her side, but the night they'd shared had opened a bright new freedom within her. She heard Izaiah's teachings, but her mind kept drifting back to it. She twirled the bracelet on her wrist nervously out of fear the lord, who was due to arrive soon, would detect the other scent so thoroughly entwined with hers in the aftermath should she remove it.

"Apologies for my delay." Zarrius's voice rang out.

Faythe tensed but faced him with nothing but pleasant reception. "No matter. It gave me extra time to practice. I must warn you I am not so experienced in dancing."

Izaiah muttered under his breath, "That's putting it lightly."

Faythe sliced him a subtle look, but her friend focused hard eyes on the lord, who fixed his attention on her. "Then you chose your partner well. I am confident with my expertise. We will put on quite the performance together."

She hadn't *chosen* him, nor would he even make the top ten list of dance partners she'd consider. "I hope you're right. I won't make the intended impression by fumbling on the dance floor."

Faythe's palm slipped into his when he extended it to her. Everything about his touch felt wrong—repulsive even. The gleam in his eye twitched her ire, and she wondered if he was aware of the condescension he bore onto her with that look alone. She couldn't protest when his arm slipped around her waist and he raised his palm for the opening stance.

"I'm very much looking forward to having this dance with you, Faythe Ashfyre."

She didn't have it in her to return the false sentiment. What Zarrius looked forward to was making his importance known to her court without a second of wasted breath.

So Faythe only smiled sweetly, and they danced.

"It pains me to say this, truly," Izaiah drawled when it was once again just the two of them finishing up in the ballroom, "but he's going to show you up big-time if you don't match his energy."

"It's hard to find the enthusiasm," Faythe grumbled.

His smile was all-knowing as he rested a hand on her shoulder.

A spike of panic rippled across her nape seconds before Kyleer marched into the room. Faythe was already walking to meet him.

"I need your help," he rushed out.

"Did you find out something about the library?" she asked hopefully, but his quick shake hollowed her stomach.

"Not that. I can't explain it, but they won't let me access the cells on Agalhor's orders. I need you to check on her for me."

Faythe's brow furrowed. "Zaiana? I thought you were her overseer."

He exchanged a look with Izaiah at that, jaw working as though he knew the request he'd come to her with was a step out of line. "I'm hoping it's nothing, but I can't be certain what his plans are with her. If he has already…" Kyleer didn't finish the thought that washed his face with dread.

Agalhor wouldn't kill Zaiana, she wanted to tell him. At least not until they exhausted her for information...

Faythe drew a sharp breath, the puzzle sliding together with the pieces Kyleer had brought to her. "He plans to Nightwalk through her."

"I tried to persuade him otherwise, to tell him we were making progress, but I fear he's taken matters into his own hands now, and when he's finished..."

He would have no reason to keep her alive.

Faythe was already striding with a hurried pace, her heart sprinting. Her father wouldn't do that—not if he knew Faythe had ordered everyone against it so she could try her own methods. If he crossed that line with the dark fae, there would be no gaining back the small kernel of her trust, and Faythe couldn't shake the feeling it was important. *Zaiana* was important.

Jogging now, the slow coating of cold fear she'd felt since her attempt to infiltrate Zaiana's mind had her *praying* Kyleer's hunch was wrong. She wanted to believe Agalhor would come to her first, that he'd hear why she was against this method.

Guards immediately blocked her path. "We're not to let anyone see the captive, Your Highness."

Faythe didn't slow her marching pace. "Get out of my way."

"Orders of the king."

Her teeth ground, palms prickling with heat, and Faythe slipped into their minds effortlessly in her rush. Without overthinking what she was doing, she figured a quick way to send them into unconsciousness was the least invasive attack. As if feeling the wall for a lever, she flicked it, blackening their minds in an instant. Stepping over their fallen bodies, she couldn't feel guilty for it.

Her steps finally slowed, but her pulse sped up when she spied the mass curled on the floor. She inhaled through her nose, a hint of salt catching in the air.

Faythe knew then that she was too late. Though she shouldn't care, a splinter snagged in her chest.

The dark fae lay facing the wall, huddled in a black cloak that had been torn at the bottom to fit her height. Faythe scented it to have belonged to Kyleer. Her head rested against the cold, abrasive stone, midnight-black hair spilling down like ink. Utterly still and soundless.

"Zaiana," Faythe whispered to the eerie silence.

Nothing changed for a painstakingly long few seconds.

Then: "I hope you got what you wanted." Her answer came devoid of any emotion, the whisper of a ghost.

"He shouldn't have done that—"

"Spare your breath, Faythe Ashfyre." She cut her off. "While you still have time to draw it."

"How can I make this right?"

Zaiana shifted, pushing up weakly as though she'd spent days in that immobile position against the unforgiving ground. "You think you are the heroes. The *good*, the *fair*. But you are no less willing to do what it takes to *win*." Her dark hair shielded most of her face as Zaiana shifted to her knees, still not turning to her fully.

"He didn't kill you," Faythe said, more as a relief than to counter her words, but Zaiana gave a breathy chuckle of pure, bitter resentment.

"It seems the notorious Nightwalker is not as powerful as he thought."

Faythe wondered how it could be possible. If Agalhor had infiltrated her mind, how Zaiana knew, and how she'd survived given all Faythe had heard of her father's ability. In that moment she didn't care—she was *glad* of Agalhor's failure, though it came as a stab of betrayal. All this time she'd fought to prove herself—to the lords, to the court—thinking one of the few people who believed in her was her father. Yet though Agalhor may not have seen it, this act erased his words. Faythe closed her eyes, breathing through the simmering rise of anger. It wasn't charged to a reckless force; instead, it gave her a steady sense of clarity.

She'd tried to fit in, tried to *bend* to what they wanted, but she should have known it was a mold she could never conform to. She didn't want to fit really. All she'd been doing was biding time.

Now she was going to do things her way.

Before she stormed from those cells, although Faythe owed the dark fae nothing, she let her last thought linger aloud.

"Or perhaps your will to survive is simply *more* powerful."

CHAPTER 82

Faythe

FAYTHE ASHFYRE DIDN'T spare a breath despite the warning she was given that the king was not alone. She barged into the council chamber. Many eyes pinned her, but she only sought one, and she found them, held them, *targeted* them.

"You should have been announced first, Faythe," Agalhor said with calm irritation.

Faythe opened her arms, coming to a stop. "What do you consider this?"

The air became thick with tension at her brazenness.

"You have something on your mind," Agalhor guessed carefully. She didn't miss the warning in that tone. "Let's talk in private."

More silence. More rules. She should have seen it sooner, and she almost shook her head now she'd seen her father in another light. On some level she knew he'd always had his doubts about her though she'd clung to his hollow words with a child's clutch.

The lords and Malin, whom she caught sight of briefly, shuffled to leave.

"Wait," Faythe commanded.

Everyone froze as that single word fell with the weight of a gauntlet. Agalhor turned to her fully, the flex of his eyes voicing his displeasure, but he didn't stop her. Her heart pounded. Hard in its cage, loud in her ears, thumping to a beat that canceled out all thoughts except for her determination.

"I need to know if I'm wasting my time here," she began. "Because I will not be another court's pawn."

It was Malin who spoke next, as though she'd given him the perfect opening. "You're emotional. You're contradicting yourself with this outburst and it's clear you can't make a balanced judgment. You are not a pawn, but an heir too volatile to be trusted with power until you can be taught."

"Taught? You mean tamed and controlled."

"Not my words."

"But your meaning." Faythe's smile was all challenge. "You once said it was unjust of me to execute a fae in the town of Desture, but have you bothered to send soldiers to find out how that town is faring? Did you ask who they have to thank for their nights without terror and provisions that arrive safely?" She left a pause—not through arrogance, but to be sure every word she spoke was heard. "Their Phoenix Queen."

From their shared looks, Faythe knew she'd made an impact even in the minds of the high-born fae.

"About that," Malin interjected, the song of his voice chilling. "Perhaps we should let our princess know what gathered us here today."

"That won't be necessary," Agalhor warned.

Malin only smiled, not removing his gaze from her as he said, "Many texts on the Firebirds, on the effects and powers of Phoenixfyre, were stolen from a well-guarded section of the library a few days before the massacre."

Her next breath stuttered, and she couldn't hide her guilt as the accusation became inescapable.

"They were found in your rooms, Faythe, after the break-in."

"I-I didn't steal them," she defended. "I borrowed them. I had nothing to do with the murders."

"We know this," Agalhor cut in once again. Yet as Faythe frantically scanned every hard set of eyes that pinned her, she couldn't be sure that was true. Even without further evidence, Malin was turning their suspicions.

"Of course," her cousin said. "I only wonder how someone would know she possessed the books. Even then, it seems a high risk for an intruder who'd already gained the main prize to infiltrate again. What were you doing with them anyway?"

Her blood pounded with the confrontation she didn't expect. Everything Malin did was meticulous and cunning, but she'd been blindsided by his boldness this time. He met her bewildered look, and his words were clear.

She'd threatened him first, and this was his countermove.

Faythe had a choice to make and no time to deliberate. To deny her actions felt wrong when she had nothing to hide. She was done being so easily shaken.

"The Phoenix feather was real."

Her declaration filled the room with gasps and murmurs. She ignored them to bring her magick forth, igniting a red flame that drew wide eyes to her fingertips before she sent it for the unlit candles.

"I didn't steal it; I took back what was once stolen from the greatest Firebird of all time—Atherius."

"A desperate child's tale," Malin sneered.

The lords looked at her with outrage and indictment, but Faythe held firm. She almost smiled at her cousin's dark look as for once she'd caught *him* off-guard by admitting her guilt. Though she was not clear of charge yet.

"The murders were only an act of vengeance because I got to the feather first. I planned to come forward with what I'd found once I was certain, yet my rooms were infiltrated, and what was left of the feather was stolen. Judgment is yours to make as I tell my truth now, but I hope you will ask what I have to gain in condemning myself. Someone killed innocents within our walls, and that person"—Faythe dared to hold Malin's stare—"knows exactly what the feather is capable of in the hands of our enemies."

The power battle between her and Malin had reached its climax, and while she felt the energy of hatred and malice, there were no more cards to play.

Malin was seething as he said, "We cannot simply take the word of a girl not even born in this kingdom. A girl whom we have invited into our home and let betray our trust. Faythe Ashfyre should be trialed for the theft and the murders in the library."

"You forget yourself, son." Agalhor spoke calmly, stepping toward him and laying a hand on his shoulder. "Though there is much discussion to be had, there is a bigger threat looming while the rest of the feather remains unaccounted for. Rest assured, I agree with you there is some consequence to be bestowed upon Faythe here for her actions, but not under the judgment of criminal court. I shall settle this matter privately."

Faythe flexed her fists, barely able to look at the king. Disappointment bubbled to the surface as she remembered why she came here. If she didn't have his confidence in her decisions, she had nothing when the council accepted her by his judgment. For that reason, it wasn't to Agalhor she said, "If you do not see me as fit to rule based on all I just lay bare, speak now, and I revoke my claim."

Every flicker of attention made the hairs on her arms stand.

"This is not a discussion to be had now," Agalhor protested firmly.

"The majority of the close council is here. I trust your judgment right now to decide if this should be taken to a larger vote."

"Where is this coming from?" Agalhor asked.

Faythe's eyes sliced into his. Her stomach churned with hostility toward him—not as a king, but a father. She'd craved his praise and belief all this time, and she could only blame herself for thinking it would come easily because they might be blood relations. So much lost time kept them as mere strangers, and that fact squeezed her heart. She felt orphaned all over again.

On Agalhor's face she saw the moment he seemed to realize what had fueled her brazen visit. She ignored him to address the room one final time.

"All I ask is that you consider actions, not words. Power is not in a name. Strip me of it and see nothing more than what I would sacrifice—not just for this kingdom, but for the world beyond it. I have given my life and I came back to give it again. With or without this crown. To choose me is to choose *faith*." She hoped they felt even an echo of how strongly the last word pulsed in her chest, near upturning her mouth with sheer pride for her companions, who'd built up her unshakable strength enough that she could face this moment.

To live like death is a game, love is a prize, and danger is desire.

"Nothing about me is certain." She came down from the high of her speech. "But neither is every day we brace ourselves to face the unknown of tomorrow."

The beating drum of verdict pounded heavy in the air. Faythe didn't move, looking over their firm-lined faces with falling hope the longer the silence lingered. Then someone stepped forward, and she cast her attention to the red-glowing Phoenixfyre.

"You returned from a place none of us could fathom, and you returned to be here. I would be a fool to turn away from that miracle though you have much to learn. You require help and guidance. But that is why I chose to stand with you, Faythe Ashfyre."

His words relieved so much burden. She was about to utter her gratitude when another joined him.

"I stand with you, Faythe Ashfyre."

Then came a humming murmur of those same four words attached to her name, granting purpose and pride. They barreled into her one after another, until the agreement spilled from most of the lords standing in that room. Faythe's shoulders squared with such appreciation and gratitude. She looked to Malin. She wouldn't let his cold, hateful eyes pierce the new confidence she'd *earned.*

"Thank you. I hope to lead *with* you, and for you," Faythe said, giving her own nod of respect.

Agalhor's expression she found hard to decipher, and she didn't drop his intense stare, staying still when he dismissed the room. Soon what pulsed between her and the King of Rhyenelle felt like a test.

"I'm doing all I can to make sure you're seen as a viable candidate for my throne. This is not how it is done. Care to tell me what caused your reckless outburst?"

Faythe itched at his tone. "You don't have to speak to me like I'm a child."

"You won them over this time, my dear. Don't expect your passion will always be taken so kindly."

"Did you ever truly believe in me?" Faythe's heart broke with the thought. "Or did you only see me as your blood and guilty conscience?"

"You know what I see in you."

"You knew it was on my order that Zaiana's mind should be left untouched."

His chin tilted with confirmation that boiled her blood.

"You undermined that anyway."

"I am the king, Faythe. Do not forget that."

"And I am your heir, but only by your terms?"

"Stop this." His voice switched with a softness she knew, from king to father, and Faythe struggled to find the balance. Agalhor took steps toward her, but she raised her hand to halt him.

"You are a great king. A fair and just ruler. I still wonder how I could ever follow in your footsteps. But this time, your overruling was wrong."

"I am not always a fair and merciless ruler," he admitted, a darkness easing into his tone she'd never heard from him before. "I do not give second chances when lines are crossed by the enemy. She crossed the line that protected you. Zaiana is nothing more than a plague in my land, and I didn't care for her pleas when she did not care for yours."

"You're wrong." Faythe shook her head. "She spared my life. You know that."

"She was the reason it ever hung in the balance. I treasure your golden heart, but you can be too forgiving for your own good."

"Wrong again." Faythe looked him in the eye, owning her words. "I killed a captain who hurt me greatly. I killed another fae who saw nothing but cruelty and taunted my name, *tainted it*, with the blood of another. I would kill again. Maverick, for what he did to me. Anyone who comes for my friends. I am not wholly *good* either. You made a grave mistake with Zaiana—she is different though she will never admit it. Day by day we are discovering more of her, and as an ally...she could have changed the tide of this war. Instead, now we have a storm collecting inside and out."

"She may have been able to push me from her mind this time, but she will not again."

"You are right." Faythe knew it was dangerous to test her tone with him. She didn't know if the king would stand for it. "Your Majesty—"

"You do not have to call me that."

"I do because I speak to you as a king for this. As the one with the power to hear my advice and take it. We need her. No matter what she has done or what she is, we can't lose her to their side. I can't explain it further, other than I hope you trust my judgment on this and choose to take a risk."

Her anticipation sharpened. Faythe believed she saw his will to give her this, but the way he cast his eyes away sank the rejection.

"I believe in you, Faythe. More than anything I have before. Don't ever doubt that again. But I think your actions with the Phoenix feather show just how much you still have to learn. Being a leader is to hear opinion, to weigh matters, but sometimes we must make judgments against those we believe in. I am sorry."

Her jaw worked, fingers flexing. "Then it is on you when the walls of this city tumble from the inside out."

Faythe twisted on her heel, acid burning her throat for the words she'd spilled too quickly to reel back. Perhaps he didn't deserve them, but she couldn't shake the jittering sense of foreboding. It felt like it was too late now anyway. She couldn't rest her mind with the awareness something was coming. Something dark and unstoppable. All they could do now was stand, brace, and fight.

CHAPTER 83

Tarly

TARLY CREPT SILENTLY back into his room. He halted for just a second, his breath stolen completely at the ethereal sight of Nerida fast asleep. Her silver hair shone against the moonlight that flooded her brown skin. Adrenaline had caused him to intrude, but now it calmed to capture her beauty. He didn't want to wake her, but he didn't believe they were safe here anymore.

As gently as he could, he put his hand over her mouth in case the shock caused her to scream. It was necessary: Nerida's eyes flew open, the flash of terror on her face hitting his gut, until she blinked rapidly and recognition replaced it.

"Sorry," he whispered, leaning off her while she shot up.

"Tarly, Gods above—"

"Shh," he encouraged, pushing back the covers to help her out. He'd forgotten the shortness of her nightgown and how high it rose in her sleep, and he had to bite down on his rush of thoughts as he glimpsed the smooth, long length of her legs.

"What is it?" she asked, voice hushed but alert.

"We need to leave," he said, wandering into the closet where he'd left her new clothes, which had been fetched by Zainaid earlier.

"Tell me what's going on."

"We have company."

At her silence, his eyes flashed to her. He pulled on his shirt, suppressing a smirk at her cross-armed stance and scowl. "Angel, if you could dress, please." He grabbed a pair of pants and boots before giving her some privacy.

Nerida emerged not five minutes later, and Tarly trailed his gaze over the impeccable sight of her in form-fitting leathers in place of her usual cotton gowns. It shone a new light on her, giving her exterior the fierceness he knew lived within her. He approached as she pulled shyly at the material.

"You'll find the journey far more practical in these wears," he explained, not thinking when he drew arms around her and fastened the black cloak at her collar. "But if you're uncomfortable—"

"I'm fine," she assured him. Her gaze lingered on his hands before she met his close look. "It's actually more comfortable than I thought." Her voice quietened at their proximity, but before the electricity could charge between them, he stepped away.

Grabbing a pack filled with provisions, Tarly slung it over his shoulder before holding Nerida's out to her. It held her medicines.

"The Book of Enoch," Nerida said, rushing into the next room to retrieve it.

When she was back at his side, Tarly took her hand on instinct and crept to the doorway.

"Are you going to tell me what *company* you're so concerned about that we couldn't catch one night's rest?"

The hall was clear as expected, and he didn't let go of her as he guided them stealthily. "The dark fae high lord, Mordecai."

The surge of her fear echoed through him. He unlatched the window he knew well before turning to Nerida, focused completely on getting her to safety. She didn't need his words to catch his every implication. He pulled up her hood, and then, hands on her waist, he helped her up and through.

A SWORD FROM THE EMBERS

"This is a rather inconspicuous route through your castle," she remarked as they shuffled along a narrow ledge and across a flat roof. "Should I ask why you're so accustomed to it?"

"Probably not," he said.

They crossed a couple more roofs and scaled down. When they came to the window that he'd long ago made accessible from the outside, he showed her inside, and they arrived in the passage that held the forgotten room and the escape route.

"Could we not have simply moved cautiously *inside* to get here?"

"Yes, but this is far quicker and there's less risk."

Nearly to the door, a spike of awareness pricked his nape. It appeared so fast his instinct had him hooking an arm around Nerida, forcing her behind him. Tarly retrieved his bow in the same breath, drew an arrow, and pointed it right into the face of the one extending a blade to his chest.

He exhaled hard, his laser focus turning to a stunned stare instead. It was mirrored back to him as he trailed the length of the Niltain steel, right to the unmistakable Griffin pommel.

"Well, fuck."

Hearing his voice finally slackened Tarly's bow. Both of them lowered their weapons and pulled down their hoods. Nik didn't look best pleased to see him, but he reserved his usual insufferable glare. Tarly scrambled to conclude why in the Nether he was here. Nothing short of the world going to shit seemed plausible.

"What are you doing here?" Nik asked, sheathing his sword, and only then did Tarly snap out of his stupor.

"Me?" An incredulous laugh escaped him as he dove a hand through his hair. "You're in my home, you asshole."

"Have you been here the whole damn time?"

Tarly didn't take well to the insinuation, but the shuffle of movement behind Nik caught his attention, and two things sprang to mind at once but clashed so unexpectedly that he found himself looking for Nerida first.

"Hello, Your Highness."

The voice that greeted him did not belong to anyone he

expected. Tarly pinned the fae, unable to return her timid greeting as accusation flared, and he targeted Nik.

"Where in the Nether is she? What have you done?"

His shift toward the High Farrow king didn't go unchallenged. Nik's dominance and wrath combined with Tarly's to stir a dangerous energy.

"Watch yourself," Nik warned.

It only enraged him. Tarly's near step halted with the gentle curl around his forearm. Nerida's touch smoothed the sharp edges of his fury, calming him so quickly and easily he found himself taking a step back instead. Nik's attention was drawn to her, and though Tarly knew he was no threat to Nerida, he didn't like the ugly flare of defense that wanted to make him tear his gaze from her.

"Pleasure to meet you…?" Nik drawled in a way that prodded at Tarly's irritation.

Her head dipped for him. "My name is Nerida, Your Highness."

Tarly couldn't explain how her discomfort unsettled him. Her wariness around royals, especially Nik, was justified. The king studied her for too long, and Tarly's pulse raced with the flickers of what he knew once resided on his own face, and in his own mind.

"Where is she?" Tarly asked, firmer this time to attract his attention.

"My name is Nik." He responded to Nerida first, flashing a goading look at Tarly. "And this is Samara."

Tarly knew the lady from her short visit the past summer, though he couldn't fathom her being here now when their marriage alliance was no truer than his to Tauria.

"Tauria is here," Nik confirmed. "With the high lord."

A flash of hot rage had him nocking the arrow back into place and taking deadly aim. "What have you done?"

Nik's eyes narrowed with cool annoyance at the threat. "Put that down."

His jaw clenched. "Not until you tell me what in the *Nether* is going on."

Tarly felt the invasion in his mind too late, and in his utter bewilderment over how it could be possible, he didn't have it in him to rise a defense against the infiltration. He let out a strained sound as he fought the command convincing him to lower his arms, slackening the bow. He gave in, letting it fall from his grasp completely, and it clattered to the ground before the presence retreated entirely.

As he gasped, Nerida touched him in concern, but Tarly's gaze snapped to Nik with such hatred he didn't know what to do with it. Not at this revelation. Now he was doubly unsure of what Nik was capable of.

"You're a mind manipulator now. Just like that human friend of yours."

"Something like that," Nik said calmly.

"Don't ever do that again," Tarly spat.

"Don't give me cause to."

Tarly wanted to hurt him. Badly. There had been very few instances in his life that had surged this kind of rage. Nik's presence caused many of them.

"How is that possible?" Nerida wondered.

Nik assessed her as if deciding if he could trust her. "Phoenix Blood," he said finally.

Tarly had become in tune with Nerida's shifts in mood, though her intrigue wasn't surprising, nor was the fact she seemed to know what he spoke of. "I ask again...how?"

"I don't have time to explain that right now. We're heading up to keep track of Tauria with Mordecai."

"That you need to explain," Tarly snarled.

"If you're leaving, I don't have to explain shit to you."

They stared off, and Nik seemed to find his answer but added, "If you're coming, I'll tell you on the way."

He didn't wait to see if they would follow.

Tarly didn't move right away, turning to Nerida with a surge of conflict. He wanted to get her as far away from here as possible with the dark threat lingering through the halls above. But he couldn't abandon Tauria if she was in danger.

"You don't have to come. We can decide on a meeting place, and you know the way out." He wanted to take the fear and turmoil from her, knowing this was no easy choice for Nerida to make.

"I'll come with you," she decided. "I can't leave her if I could help."

Tarly nodded, though he didn't like it, the thought of her backtracking toward the danger they'd almost evaded. "Was it true what you said?" he asked carefully. "You've never met Tauria."

"No. I mean, yes, it's true. I've never met her." Nerida wrung her hands, and Tarly reached out to her arm.

"We'll just make sure they know what the Nether they're doing."

She nodded vacantly until he took her chin to meet his eyes.

"But angel, I'll leave with you the moment you say."

CHAPTER 84

Faythe

THIS NIGHT, FAYTHE became the Phoenix meeting the sun.

She waited, overlooking the city peppered with the bright crimson of banners and real flames, listening to the distant town rejoicing in celebration of the Comet. Part of her wished to be among the humble setting—to taste the air infused with bonfire smoke and sweet scents from the market stalls. Her venue for the evening would be far grander, more polished, and filled with the expectation she would match its grandeur.

Faythe looked the part, draped in pure gold. Silk poured like liquid down her front, the high slit allowing her legs air and movement. From her waist more extravagant layers fanned around her, glittering and mesmerizing. The best part she could not see, but everyone else would: the feathers that peeked over her shoulders but came to life as crimson-and-gold wings across her shoulder blades. What followed became an illusion of a fiery waterfall: long embroidered Phoenix tail feathers.

In the reflection of the window, she admired the halo crown in her elaborately braided hair, golden as the new dawn rising behind her.

"No words would be enough to describe how you look tonight."

Faythe twisted to Kyleer, whose wide eyes traced her form, and she gave a sad smile. "Reylan?"

His expression fell with her, and he gave a small shake of his head. "I haven't heard anything of him making it back."

Her stomach hollowed out, though she knew the chances were slim. To distract herself, she admired the commander in his fine wares. All-black but fitted so perfectly they accentuated every angle of him. His hair had a wet sheen, side-parted and combed back, giving an even more beautiful appeal to his waves. "You look good," Faythe mused, deliberately downplaying just *how* good.

He scoffed. "Honestly, I can't wait to be away from the formality."

Faythe chuckled, looping her hand through the arm he extended to her. "It suits you."

Just then, Izaiah came around the corner, a hand raised to his heart as he examined every inch of her. "There's our Phoenix Queen," he said in awe.

Faythe blushed with the attention and the name, her nerves rising as she remembered they were heading to a ballroom full of court members and citizens, who were waiting for her to arrive and open the ball with her first dance as tradition dictated.

Izaiah's genuine warm smile eased her tension. "You're going to be incredible in there. I may have been a harsh teacher, but in truth, you've been nailing this dance for weeks."

Faythe didn't think that was true with the errors she'd made this week alone. But something told her it wasn't just the routine Izaiah spoke of.

"Time to fly," Kyleer said, and Faythe relaxed in the best company as they headed to the dance.

With a nod of pride and assurance, they left her alone at the ballroom doors to slip in first. Faythe paused to gather breath and tame her trembling hands, reflecting on her life with incredulity that events had brought her to this point.

A loud squeal sent her heart up her throat, still thumping

wildly when she spied Jakon and Marlowe. "Look at you!" Marlowe beamed, unhooking her hand from Jakon to rush over.

Taking her hands, Faythe shook her head, observing her friend's stunning blue gown that coated her like a crystal sea. "Me? Look at you!" she gushed, then she extended a hand to Jakon. "Both of you."

"No longer street rats, huh?" Jakon mused.

Faythe choked on a sob, her tears stinging. She'd been thinking the same thing. She never would have believed she'd go from owning one single gown, gifted by her best friend, to standing in the most elaborate, most expensive dress she could have imagined. Though it wasn't really the wears or the food or the home that made her so overcome with emotion. It was that they'd all taken that path together. Everything around them had changed, but never their hearts; never how they felt about each other and the new friends they'd made along the way.

Jakon's calloused palm came up, wiping away a stray tear. "We can't have you going in there all red-faced and puffy-eyed. I hate to tell you this now, Faythe, but you're not a pretty crier."

She breathed a laugh, and he smiled.

"I'm so damn proud of you."

Jakon and Marlowe slipped into the ballroom, and Faythe took one last pause to stare down the hall. Her heart yearned, and she wondered if she could summon Reylan with the sheer ache in her soul alone. The one person missing who mattered the most, and she couldn't stop feeling that this wasn't fair. Her resentment grew that it was no coincidence, no urgent matter nor sheer bad timing. Her cousin simply hoped to shake her confidence or dampen her spirit with Reylan's absence.

She would not let him win.

Everything exploded to life before her. The room she'd danced in countless times now seemed far too huge filled with so many bodies, so much color and music, and so many voices. She didn't know where to land her attention. The first eyes that saw her triggered the nudge that led their companions to look up to, and then the murmurs hushed slowly. With no anchor to grasp, all Faythe could do was walk and focus on putting one foot in front of the other though her racing pulse wanted her to pass out before them, her scrambling thoughts wanting to trip her. Her magick hummed to her distress. Maybe her palms were glowing—they certainly tingled, so she flexed her fingers to disperse the sensation.

Faythe knew where she was headed then. When the crowd began to part and Lord Zarrius headed toward her. He was far from who she desired to see, but nonetheless he was the partner she sought begrudgingly. Her hand slipped into his with a pleasant smile for the court that settled to watch them.

"You look absolutely divine, Your Highness." His words she believed, though they were not spoken with endearment. His green gaze sparkled as though he were eying his next investment. "I hope you will allow me the great honor of leading you through this first dance."

Poetic words expertly rehearsed. Just like her own.

"The pleasure would be all mine, Lord Zarrius."

Faythe forced her feet to move before they rooted themselves in defiance. This was wrong. In her heart she knew this dance wasn't right. When they stopped, she took one second to collect herself, eyes tracing the intricate red-and-gold patterned marble floor now ingrained in her memory. So many people bore attention on them. The silence was nerve-wracking. The small band in the corner looked to be bracing for their song, and she recited the steps over in her mind one last time. Faythe looked to the lord who was waiting expectantly for her to step forward in their opening stance, and her mind chose now to protest it.

Faythe was about to fight herself when her near step faltered.

What stilled the air and slowed time was an embrace of warmth and safety. It was home. It encircled her from behind, and it was all she could do to keep from forgetting the lord who stood with his hand poised to lead her through that first statement dance as they had practiced. None of it mattered. She couldn't stop the twist of gravity that answered to that presence.

Until she saw him.

The sight of Reylan took her breath away.

He didn't try to stand out, but he did. Not because of what he was to her. Not because of his domineering presence that always trumped a room. Reylan Arrowood wore no leathers, no steel. He was dressed impeccably in fine wears of crimson, black, and gold. Rhyenelle's colors. What struck her in that moment was something she might have always harbored in her mind, but there in plain sight, the concept blazed into clarity.

And he didn't even know it.

He stood among the masses by a pillar as though he hoped she wouldn't know he was there. He would have watched her dance with the lord despite the hurt it would cause. Their gazes locked, and his face smoothed out as all she could do was stare. She wondered how he was here, but her elation and relief left no room for caring.

The crowd started to ease away from him as they caught onto who she'd settled her attention on. Reylan Arrowood stood poised, but not like a general.

Like a ruler.

"Your Highness."

The lord's voice snapped her back to the present, bringing the room of spectators' attention back to him like a lashing, but Faythe was too stunned to be embarrassed by her delay. She tore her eyes from Reylan to twist back around and meet Zarrius's knowing look. Her mouth opened, but her thundering heart gripped her words. She knew what she wanted to say, yet the fear of judgment and the audience's reaction had her stumbling. She found herself sliding her gaze to Agalhor at top the dais. Her throat was bone-dry as everyone watched her with confusion and irritation, and she knew in that moment she had to make a decision.

The lord's eyes darted between her and Reylan, mouth twitching with distaste, and she supposed it was logical to assume Malin would have shared his suspicions about her and Reylan with Zarrius. His hand jutted out again in an irked prompt, and her stomach knotted with dread, the cage of her chest close to breaking if she chose to refuse.

"We mustn't keep them waiting," he said quietly.

She couldn't do it.

Instead of taking the step forward, Faythe took one back. "Thank you," she said, out of nothing more than politeness, to ease the speculation of the court, "but I cannot have this dance with you."

Fire blazed across his gaze, his anger and humiliation like a blow to her gut. But as Faythe found the will to turn from him, a hand lashed around her forearm before she could walk away. Quiet gasps and murmurs broke out at the bold move. Reylan jerked forward with a murderous gaze, but Faythe kept calm.

"Don't let this become a scene," she warned in the lord's mind. Then she turned back to him, furious. "If you ever try to come for my friends again, your last breath will be mine."

That made him drop his hold, but not without a score of fiery resentment as she left herself open to him, needing to know how volatile he could be or if there was any part of him she could salvage. All she felt was *hunger*. A desirous, powerful hunger that would stop at nothing.

"You're making a grave mistake," he muttered, so dangerously quiet, with a hint of threat that sent chills down her spine.

Faythe didn't balk; she locked their firm gaze. A mark made. Then she twisted, and he did not stop her this time.

Her guilt lifted with each step she took, reservations slipping away at the knowledge of who she was headed for. Reylan remained exactly where he was, his expression dropping with concern as she closed the distance between them while the crowed parted entirely. Her heart raced with adrenaline. She was going against a plan that had been set in motion for months.

This was her defiant stance.

She halted before him, and the few seconds they spent matching hard heartbeats were electrifying. "Are you going to ask me to dance, General?" It came out breathlessly. She couldn't tame the building need to feel him and damn the eyes that judged them.

"Are you sure you know what you're doing?" Reylan sent her privately.

Faythe's smile was a partial smirk. *"Not at all. Just yesterday I stepped on the lord's foot, and I think he was running out of ways to politely tell me I can't dance."*

Reylan smiled, showing teeth with a burdenless ease. Suddenly, she wasn't afraid to voice all that rushed to the forefront of her mind at seeing him standing in this hall for the first time. She wanted the world to know what she saw, *felt*, about the great General of Rhyenelle who was so much more but lived in the shadow of his own title. Esteemed, but not nearly enough. She wanted everyone to find the same clarity she did when they looked at him.

"It took until now to remember why I chose to be Rhyenelle's heir. It wasn't to sacrifice my heart, but to lead with it. It wasn't to bow to customs and ideals that have far overstayed their welcome. I wanted to show this kingdom devotion like my mother and protection like my father—neither of which I would have had the strength to embrace within myself if it wasn't for you, Reylan. Your belief in me, your dedication to this kingdom…you're everything our people deserve. I choose you, Reylan Arrowood. This kingdom chooses you."

Those sapphire eyes held her with such pride and liberation. Reylan surveyed the crowd, their people, whom Faythe knew were in agreement, or at least open to the notion of him. She wondered why she'd let her spiteful cousin's seed of doubt grow at all. Reylan upturned his palm, and her stomach burst in a flutter when her skin met his, publicly, showing everyone she wasn't afraid of what they might think of him.

"Would you do me the extraordinary honor of having this dance with me, Faythe Ashfyre?"

Faythe didn't scan the onlookers; didn't care if the lord was watching or if Malin was throwing daggers of hatred, or even if her father might be voicing his protest. She would challenge that too. Reylan's hand slipped across her waist as they positioned themselves in everyone's view. Faythe leaned into that hold, one hand on his bicep while the other hovered close to his palm.

"You came back," Faythe said.

Reylan smiled softly. "I wish I could say I never left this time, but I did. Only for a few days before I had to turn around, and I didn't care about the speculation or punishment it would cause. I couldn't miss seeing you tonight."

The song began, and like clockwork, her steps matched each note with him.

"I would never get this night back. By the Gods, Faythe, I don't think you realize how devastatingly perfect you look tonight. I never would have forgiven myself if I'd missed it."

The melody didn't echo through the great hall; it wove around them, so personal and close the bodies around them seemed to fade away one by one to leave only two souls as one on that dance floor.

"I'm so glad you're here, Reylan," she sent to him privately when emotion clogged her throat. *"It feels right."*

She knew in the way Reylan held her full attention that she hadn't needed the endless hours of practice—not with him when her movements came so effortlessly at his touch, his guidance. Faythe led the dance as practiced, but it was because of him she did so with a fluid grace. Their gravity became a seamless force that dipped and twisted to the musical cadence. His hands on her, his near touches, sparked embers over her skin, igniting a passion that grew, quickening their pace to the crescendo of the song.

"You caused quite the stir, and we'll have a lot of explaining to do."

"I don't care," she answered honestly. *"But I care for* you."

Faythe took spin after spin, giving life to the flames of her dress, but her gaze snapped to the night sky of his irises without faltering. She felt as if she were dancing in them, dreaming in them, loving in them. Those eyes she would always seek across time and space.

He continued to talk to her mind. *"Do you remember our first dance?"*

"Of course."

"The moment I saw you that night I knew you belonged here." His arm hooked around her waist, and they twirled weightlessly, bodies flush and warm. *"The moment you stepped into my arms I knew you belonged with me."*

Her eyes burned. *"I think I knew it too."*

His strong arm dipped her low and he leaned in close, their breaths mingling as the song tapered off. Her leg slipped free, and his fingers trailing from her knee up her thigh parted her lips. This wasn't part of the dance, but it also wasn't scandalous enough for detection. Then the strings grew to a mighty climax, and he straightened with her, spinning her once, hooking an arm around her, side by side, and the song exploded as he lifted her, turning slowly. Their eyes never broke contact as she looked down.

As the song came to an end, it was like being drawn slowly from a blissful dream. Her pulse thrummed to the tempo of his, until they stilled with the euphoric high of something unexplainable that was *theirs*.

The murmuring around the room filtered into her senses with the music gone. They didn't release each other. She couldn't step away as he captured her so entirely with his blazing eyes. Her hand slipped over his chest, and she felt the strong, hard beat of his heart in her palm. Reylan's hand came up to close over it, holding it there. Faythe needed nothing else. As she pushed up, his other hand took her face, their mouths met, and never before had she felt such a release of burden.

In that second, they declared to everyone that they were one.

He kissed her fiercely as though sealing his want for this. For them. No matter what, they would face it all together.

Faythe heard the music start up again, a far softer and much tamer song, and people began to flood the dance floor out of courtesy, dispersing some of the attention from them. When they broke apart, her whole world expanded before her, held by those sapphire irises and seeing a new weightless *happiness* in them. No road seemed too far to travel, no hill too high—not with him by her side for every obstacle they could face.

Reylan's hand on her back guided her off the dance floor, and though the music and bodies flowed, the attention of the court clung to her like a film over her skin. Faythe dared a look around, finding people smiling, whispering, some gushing, others curious, and the lack of any distaste dawned the realization she'd been so afraid for nothing, allowing the lords and Malin to fill her head with unfounded doubt.

"Excellent performance, darling Faythe. We should thank your teacher." Izaiah scanned the area sarcastically. "An unexpected twist to the night, but damn if it wasn't the best scandal to have happened in the court. Should we start calling you both 'Your Highness'?"

Faythe bit her lip to keep from giggling, glad to see the light jest even brought a smile to Reylan's face.

Reylan looked over his shoulder then leaned his mouth to her ear. "I'll be right back." His lips pressed lightly to her temple before his warmth breezed away from her. The exchange felt so casual and open and *right*.

Faythe followed him with her gaze to where he headed, finding Agalhor watching them, and she couldn't decipher his firm stance and cool expression.

"So begins the consequences of your public affection," Izaiah drawled as they twisted to observe the party.

Faythe found her two friends on the dance floor, and her smile widened to a grin at their laughter, neither one caring that their steps didn't match the fae around them as they didn't know any of their dances. Jakon and Marlowe moved to their own rhythm, and Faythe found herself chuckling along with them from afar.

"I haven't seen Reuben," she observed.

Izaiah gave a hum as he joined her quick search. "Me neither. I haven't seen him around much at all these past few weeks, come to think of it."

"He said he's been spending a lot of time in the outer town among the humans," Faythe relayed vacantly. Something distant unsettled her, but she explained it away as her own guilt at being too consumed by court life to really check in on him. "Jakon and Marlowe keep him company sometimes, but I thought he'd be enjoying the celebrations here."

Izaiah squeezed her arm. "I'm sure he's simply enjoying the night like the rest of us, no matter where he is."

She cast him a grateful smile, but then she realized something. "Where's Kyleer?"

Izaiah gave a stiff shrug, swiping a glass of wine from a passing tray. "Slipped out about halfway through your dance."

Faythe wondered—though not for long when the conclusion seemed obvious. She said nothing but hoped in her heart she was right. This was the one night the guards would be sparsely posted to allow as many as possible to enjoy the celebrations. Hopefully, those sparse postings included the cells. Izaiah must have guessed where he'd headed too from his disgruntled shift. She wondered for a second why he hadn't followed his brother, though more than once now she'd caught Izaiah stealing glances across the hall, and just as often, a stunning fae male with dark blond hair looked their way.

"Is one of you going to ask the other to dance, or will you both just throw flirtatious looks across the room all night?" Faythe's grin spread slowly at his quick defensive reflex, but Izaiah seemed to know it would be pointless to deny it.

Something like determination pinched his eyes, and then he swore, downing the rest of his wine. "I suppose you could say you've given me the confidence to be bold tonight, Faythe." He flashed her a wink, and then he was heading over to the male who straightened, scanning around as though there could be someone else her friend had fixed his sights on.

A giddiness rose in Faythe as she watched Izaiah pass off his glass, approach the fae, and extend a hand to him. Awe wasn't enough for what overcame her as the fae accepted and they seamlessly, beautifully, blended into the ongoing dance.

Faythe leaned into the warm force that snaked an arm around her waist. "Is he outraged?" she asked Reylan, peering up.

"He's concerned. Might have lain down a few threats to me. But I think he sees your happiness above all." He curled her around to face him, scanning every inch of her expression. "No regrets?"

Faythe's hand lay on his chest. "None."

Reylan entwined their fingers. "Come."

She ignored the crowd that eased away from them as he led her through it, onlookers still tracking the touches they shared and whispering their thoughts. It all quietened as they left the ballroom and slipped into a hallway.

"We'll miss the comet," Faythe said with little objection if it meant time alone with him instead.

He cast her a soft look, and the shift in him was so precious it didn't fail to ripple through her with bliss. She followed him, their hands joined, up several flights of stairs. She could only remember one time he'd led her up so high in silence. Yet they weren't heading to his tower.

Out the door they walked onto a long stretch of path, an ideal location for archers to defend the castle, but no one was here. He didn't stop there, taking her up one final narrow set of outdoor steps, and then they emerged onto a flat roof bursting with surprising color.

"Any other secret spots you've been keeping to yourself?" Faythe breathed, eyes admiring the plants and flowers.

"Maybe," he mused. "One by one I'll show you them all." He hooked her to him, planting a long, single kiss where their hands joined between their chests. "We have forever. Right now, this is the happiest I've ever been, and you continue to amaze me—to make me *want* things I never thought I would. It's all for you. And for this kingdom. You're changing the world every day, Faythe, however seen or silent."

Faythe's fingers tangled in his silver locks, bringing his lips to hers since words failed to convey the feelings that erupted within her. She barely registered her backward steps until her back met something firm, but she only arched further into him, needing something that felt imminent, yet would be life-changing by design.

That thought snapped her out of his entanglement. Breathless, she caught his eyes. Nothing had ever felt so sure and promising.

"I want to claim the bond tonight," she said. Promised. She needed no more time to be certain, though her nerves rose that he might.

A primal darkness expanded over his sapphire eyes. His palm

slipped across her cheek and Reylan took a deep breath to regain control. "There is nothing I have wanted more in my existence. Nothing I will want more than to be yours." Then his brow pinched with a pain she knew. "Words are failing me right now to describe how much you mean to me and how I feel for you. All I know is that this is eternal. As sure as the stars; as anchoring as gravity. You are a need, not a want. An obsession, not a simple desire."

"Yes," Faythe whispered, for she felt every feeling he spoke of.

Reylan took her wrist, sliding the concealment bracelet off then removing his own. He looked at them with resentment, and Faythe's hand closed around them. Dragging forth her magick, she recalled what it had felt like when she held the watches. How all she'd wanted was for them to no longer exist and torment her. She breathed steady at the heat and pulse under her palm, watching in admiration as the metal turned gilded before slowly crumbling off in a shimmering gold dust, beautifully broken by the raw power that lived within her. Until her hand met Reylan's and the shackles between them were no more.

"Never again," he growled, claiming her with his mouth. His lips moved to her cheek, her neck, her collar. Faythe's skin pricked everywhere he trailed his passion, marking his scent where he could, and she wanted more.

So much more.

They moved, and she could hardly track one step—only his hands on her body and the heat of his breath on her skin, never wanting this moment to end. Her back leaned over stone, and Reylan's fingertips slipped into the cut of her dress to trace up her thigh, dragging a soft moan from her.

"It would be wholly inappropriate for me to do what I'm thinking," he blew out against her lips. "Right here, where anyone could trespass."

Faythe drew needy gasps. "Probably."

Reylan grinned, the sight never failing to skip her pulse. "You look like a queen tonight, Faythe Ashfyre." He took a deep breath as if to be sure he still could. "My Phoenix Queen."

He pulled her over to a small patch of grass, so out of place for how high up they were, but a beautiful contrast nonetheless. She watched him sit then lie back, completely relaxed.

"We'll get the best view of the comet passing over us shortly," he explained, reaching out a hand.

Faythe smiled broadly, shifting the layers of material to settle in close beside him. And there they lay watching the stars, listening to the distant revelers, feeling utterly at peace and finally complete.

CHAPTER 85

Tauria

TAURIA COULDN'T PLACE her feelings now she was back within these walls. She maintained her composure, but her throat tightened with the suffocating reminder of her imprisonment. Her wind surfaced to prick her skin, and she freed enough manipulation to weave idle cooling wisps between her fingers.

Mordecai walked close by with Lycus following behind him. "Your ability is most impressive," the high lord remarked.

Her fist clamped, an itch she had to suppress.

"There aren't many with such a talent left," he went on. "I have great confidence you would manage to hold onto it if you Transitioned."

Tauria's head snapped to him. He only spared her a sidelong look of amusement.

"You will not be forced," he said. "But perhaps you could be persuaded."

"I have no desire for a bloodthirst and to have my memories taken."

"Why see only what you will lose, and not what you could gain? A chance to forget you ever had a bond at all, a new start to be all that you were supposed to be in your reign. It would be legendary."

"I plan to mark myself in history without the need to Transition."

That earned her something akin to his respect. "You are powerful. I saw what you were capable of when last we met in this castle. Tell me, have you ever been in contact with one of the Spiritual Ruins?"

Mordecai offered the topic so casually she replayed it to find the test. This was why she was with him. They'd lost their bond in the hope of securing the ruin, and it was *working*.

"I briefly felt Aurialis's when Faythe found it in High Farrow. Can I tell you something I haven't admitted to anyone before?"

His eyes held a sparkle of intrigue. Not darkness, but the faint warmth of surprise. "I would be honored for you to share yourself with me."

"It has fascinated me since, the call of power from the ruin. I've been longing to feel it again. Perhaps answer it."

Approval curled his mouth, lighting up his face with a thrill that chilled her. "That excites me very much, to find out what you could be capable of with it. Though you should know, not all those who tempt its power survive its touch."

"I have heard. But I can't explain what I feel around it, only that I believe I have the strength not to fall victim, but to *pair* with it."

His gaze shifted straight ahead, his deep inhale contemplative. "Marvellas would be pleased to hear this. There is only one other who has successfully mastered the ruin, as I knew she would. It takes some time. It is not kind or easy in the slightest. To wield that velocity of power... It will try to break you, challenge you. It will hurt—*more* than hurt. The Spirit of Souls hasn't stopped trying to push others with abilities to learn how to wield the ruins should her ability fail."

Tauria soaked up every morsel of information. "Is it here? Dakodas's ruin?"

"No."

Her jaw worked as she tried not to pry and risk suspicion. "I hope we don't stay here long then."

"I assure you this will be quick, and you will be pleased with where I take you next."

Tauria didn't want to hope, but she did. She clung to it so desperately she couldn't bear the tension of not knowing if her conclusion was right. "Can you tell me?" she asked quietly.

"I'm taking you home, Tauria. It's about time you stood on your lands again."

The ruin was in Fenstead.

Her steps faltered. Time stopped. Tauria stared at nothing in particular while her mind processed the truth. She would be going home.

Home to Fenstead.

Yet she knew the lands would not be as thriving as she knew them, nor as hopeful as they once were. Tauria blinked back her tears but struggled to suppress what it meant to her. Despite the company—despite everything—she wanted this so badly she didn't care about anything else.

"I hoped that would please you," Mordecai said with an unusual gentleness.

"It does," she breathed. "Very much."

"Then come. Let's not delay our departure."

As he turned to continue his walk, Tauria exchanged a hopeful look with Lycus. He kept his forehead creased with concern, but he gave her a small nod to confirm he felt the same spark of hope to go back.

Tauria's feet pressed on, and she remembered all at once what choosing Fenstead would mean. She thought of Nik. *Oh Gods...* If Mordecai took her, would he follow? Her heart splintered knowing he would, but she couldn't let him. It only spelled danger and more time away from High Farrow.

She pushed those thoughts aside for now. After she was finished with Mordecai, she would take to her old rooms to rest, and Nik would come to her then to devise a new plan with all this in mind.

Lycus's arm pressed her to walk on. Her mind reeled, her

blood thrummed, and her wind rejoiced. Over a century and she couldn't believe how close she was to standing on Fenstead soil again.

Through her new spike of adrenaline, Tauria realized they were heading toward the throne room. In the next hall they passed, waves of sadness lapped at her. She didn't want to look, yet her eyes were drawn out through the glass doors. The garden remained black and defiled. The phantom scorching of nature tore through her, and flame reflected in her eyes.

"Tauria?" Lycus's voice snapped her back. His touch kept her walking, and she gave a hollow smile.

"That was Varlas's own doing, to make you suffer that," Mordecai said.

She didn't know what this knowledge meant. It changed nothing when she knew the high lord was capable of far worse forms of torture. Alarm began to creep up her spine at the thought, and she found herself glancing at Lycus to remember she wasn't alone. But in times of conflict, she feared him being near when she wasn't certain of the high lord's plan.

Tauria nearly stumbled when they rounded into the great throne room, crafted beautifully with stone arches and sheltered by a glass dome roof. The patter of rain against it became the only sound. As his gaze locked on her, Chief Zainaid's surprise slackened the hard lines of his dark skin.

She often wondered what had become of the chief in the aftermath of the battle here, yet as he stood proudly to address them where the king would have once sat, Tauria realized she'd never expected *this*.

"Welcome back," Zainaid greeted them, his attention flicking back to Mordecai—but assessment lingered there as if he were deciding what to make of them *together*.

The dark fae around the hall bowed for Mordecai, and he stopped tall, hands clasped behind his back, yielding no reception.

"Any progress on the task?" the high lord asked.

"I'm afraid not. The prince remains unfound, as do the former queen and princess."

Tauria's lips parted at the mention of Tarly. It wasn't confirmation he was alive, but Mordecai had to be greatly suspicious to be actively searching. She also felt relief at the confirmation Keira and Opal remained out of his clutches.

"I see." Mordecai spared one look, and it was enough to make the hall erupt with singing steel.

Tauria startled back at the sudden threat. Every dark fae who answered turned on Zainaid, who only stared down at the high lord with a flex of his eyes—the only indication he knew why so many blades were angled toward him.

"We agreed to let you live—let the city remain untouched under your temporary rule—in exchange for your loyalty," Mordecai explained. "Yet you are either withholding information or your efforts are severely lacking. I'll admit, both of these conclusions disappoint me greatly, and in truth, I have little use for you when I couldn't care less about this kingdom falling to terror and chaos for a while."

Tauria's pulse raced as she watched the pure darkness and threat emanating from the high lord. This was who he was: a leader of no mercy. He would kill without thought and held no regard for innocent lives.

"My people are human, unlike you," Zainaid said.

Mordecai answered, "I have provided you with many warriors."

"Forgive me, high lord," Zainaid yielded. "I have been using them to restructure the people here. Without their king, many guards and soldiers rebelled. Citizens were wary of their presence, and it has been no easy task to keep the city from chaos. You might not care for it, but all I ask is that you trust this benefits us all."

"I do not trust, for you have given me little reason to, other than this show of kinghood that may be a position too far out of your depth."

"You are right. Being king is not my desire. Might I ask why it is so important the prince is found?"

"Because he *will* be king. As soon as Varlas is disposed of."

"Why keep him alive?"

Mordecai gave a smile that Tauria thought was meant to be cruel, yet his eyes portrayed only a hollow void. "As punishment. Marvellas doesn't take kindly to allies who fail her. They are no better than enemies to her." He advanced forward one step. A warning. "Now, how is it my own spies caught wind of the prince in a nearby town and yours did not?"

Tauria didn't know why she looked to Lycus at the news Tarly was alive. Her eyes pricked with relief—so much relief. She'd spent months in an exhausting denial that he might not have made it.

The general shared her comfort with a small smile. "I apologize for the oversight. It will not happen again."

"No, it will not."

Mordecai gave another silent command, and bodies moved faster than Tauria could calculate a way to stop them. Two dark fae approached the chief. One struck him hard across the face, another struck his abdomen, and he was forced to his knees. The reckless brutality stunned her still, until the glint of a rising blade finally tore her voice free.

"Stop!"

The hall silenced and all attention snapped to her. Tauria breathed hard, unsure of how to appeal to Mordecai without showing him a weakness he could exploit.

"This gains us nothing," she said, turning to him with anger. Not for what he was about to do. No—Tauria had to match his firm leadership.

His eyes tightened with her interference. "I have little tolerance for those unable to do what is asked of them, princess."

"I am a queen," she asserted for the first time.

His eyebrows eased from their deep frown.

"I chose to become *your* queen, not to stand idle and let you wreck alliances on impulse. We need him to maintain order here until the true king can be crowned. Zainaid is the only one who can do this. Marvellas won't be pleased if you make a wild playground out of Olmstone for her to clean up later."

Mordecai backtracked to her, and Tauria kept her chin held high though his proximity repulsed her. "There you are," he said calmly, and for the first time a flicker of wonder gave way in those onyx eyes. "I was wondering how long it would take for you to break into the powerful leader you could become. This glimpse is most exciting. What should we do, Tauria Stagknight?"

She took a few calming breaths of deliberation. In those seconds, she felt him. Tauria didn't know how with their severed bond, nor did she have the sense without it to know exactly *where*, but Nik was near. "I was close with Tarly." She thought quickly, trying in the few seconds she had to pull together a plan that could separate them but keep Mordecai on her side. "Perhaps I could stay here. Word could travel of my capture, and Tarly would come. If he believed I was in danger, he would give himself up."

The idea sickened her, but she spilled the words of betrayal to her friend in the desperate hope it wouldn't come to that. This would only keep Mordecai's suspicions at bay.

His hand reached for her face. "I don't like the idea of being parted from you. We have so much to do together."

Her stomach clenched painfully as she wondered what that meant. "This will only be for a while," she forced out softly, cupping his hand over hers, and it worked to relax his cold eyes. "Then I will come to Fenstead. I want that more than anything."

Though her stomach sank at having come so close to going home, she could wait a while longer if it meant figuring out a way to find Tarly and keep him far from the high lord's reach.

"We could use her help," Zainaid cut in.

"Let him rise," Tauria said to the high lord.

He stepped away from her, giving one nod for his guards to retreat. It pained Tauria to see the legendary leader reduced to his knees in front of his people, who were also scattered around the hall.

"I would say this is a fine plan..." Mordecai's tone turned to darkness. The foreboding kind, and Tauria stilled. The air cooled. Lycus shifted closer. "Except you must take me for a damned fool, and you know how I feel about that, Tauria."

It all happened so fast she didn't know where to direct her attention. The struggle that surrounded her gripped her still.

Horror seized her entirely. A blade rested along Zainaid's throat, Lycus was detained by three dark fae, and then…

Tauria couldn't turn around at the commotion entering through the doors. She knew it was him without looking. In this damning situation that had become of them, she was all that remained untouched. The only one who had the small hope of halting any impulsive command Mordecai could make to end them all.

"What is this?" she asked calmly, knowing no amount of fear or protest would get through to him.

"You think I wouldn't know I was being tracked?" He stalked to her with a predator's grace that should have had her balking, but within, she felt Nik's presence and could have whimpered with the relief.

"I'm right here, love."

Tauria's shoulders squared when he stopped, towering over her intimidatingly. "Why won't you look at him?"

"Why should I?"

His hand gripped her chin, and she winced at the force. She gave him nothing, clenching her teeth as pure hatred coursed through her.

"You expect me to believe you knew nothing of it?"

"I expected you to be smarter," she snapped. That stunned him just for a second, enough for him to relax his grip, and she jerked out of his hold. "You should have known he wouldn't have accepted our bond snapping so easily. *You* should have anticipated he would come after me and made sure he couldn't."

Mordecai searched her eyes for the deception. Tauria's nerves had never sharpened so much at the realization he might find it.

"And what of them?"

Her breath caught in her throat when he whirled her around by her shoulders. Wisps of hair appeared in her vision, and when they fell…she couldn't believe it.

His name tumbled from her lips. "Tarly."

Their eyes locked with a longing sense of sadness. They'd been parted so suddenly, and she'd never had the chance to tell him she understood…that she knew he wasn't the monster she'd thought him to be. *Gods,* she was so sorry, and it took everything in her not to move with the urge to embrace him after all they'd been through.

Tauria eyed the blade at his throat, then Nik's, then Samara's, until her gaze fell on a female fae. She couldn't be certain what caused her need to blink several times. Her face creased in confusion as if she should know the fae, but her mind was conflicted. She was certain she had never seen this fae with stunning silver hair against golden brown skin before, but at the same time she seemed familiar. The fae only stared back, hazel eyes wide with fear, and Tauria saw the blade threatening her life too.

"Let them go," she said. A vacant response. She had to gather herself again as her mind tunneled into a stupor. The ground didn't feel so solid, and a small voice questioned if this were a nightmare instead. A twisted conjuring of the impossible and the worst of her fears.

How had they been caught so easily?

"We can leave." She spun back around to Mordecai. "I have no need to stay here now. We can go together. Let Zainaid detain the prince and send Nik back. There is no gain to be had from making a martyr of him for High Farrow."

Tauria studied every flicker of his expression, knowing he was contemplating her words.

"You are not going with him," Nik growled in her mind.

"You have to think reasonably. Listen to me. The ruin is in Fenstead, and he means to take me there," she sent back.

Everyone was silent for a long, tense moment.

Mordecai locked eyes on Nik behind her as he approached, and the taunt in those onyx depths seemed to rouse her mate's rage right until his gaze fell to her…and she read the test.

Tauria's heart squeezed. It splintered. His vile hands took her face, and she knew his intention. Knew she couldn't pull away or it would all be over. Right here in front of Nik, he'd decided to shatter the last piece of her broken bond.

Mordecai's head angled to meet hers, and tears formed, which she closed her eyes against. Tauria slammed up her mental barriers, unable to stand Nik being able to slip in and say anything—*feel* anything. Though he couldn't hear, she chanted her apologies to him while a sickness so awful consumed her for what she was about to do.

Mordecai's lips grazed hers…

Then Nik broke with a cry of rage and revenge.

Before all Nether broke loose.

She spun to see Nik fighting with his sword, seizing minds for an advantage in numbers. Tarly reached for countless arrows, and as he aimed one at Mordecai, Tauria acted on impulse.

She cast her arms out and the wind answered, sending a current to intercept Tarly's arrow, knocking his aim completely. Tauria didn't waist a second as she unleashed a storm. Her steps were weightless, her arms dancing as the room became hers. Without air, they would be nothing in minutes.

Collecting her tornado, she sent it down, then skyward.

The dome roof shattered, and Tauria redirected her currents to spare those she could, but it had to be believable. She might never forgive herself for the shards that rained over her friends, her mate, but she hoped one day they would understand.

The rain began to slick her skin, and Tauria breathed against the surge of unleashed power.

"You saved me." Mordecai's voice held a note of surprise she'd never heard before. He looked at her now with a new trust and awe.

What caught in her eye she followed, and Tauria's mouth dropped open as she watched the rain gathering together. It was *suspended* in the air, then it traveled toward something, and when Tauria's gaze fell, she couldn't believe her eyes.

A Waterwielder.

She had never encountered the talent before, and the spectacle was mesmerizing. A beautiful kind of weapon as it answered to the fae's firm stance, the way her arms moved akin to Tauria's own style.

Who was this fae?

A SWORD FROM THE EMBERS

Tauria didn't have time to remain in her moment of wonder. Her attention shifted to Nik taking down one dark fae after another as they swarmed in through the doors. Tarly aided him with his bow. Samara had taken shield behind the Waterwielder who didn't attack, only braced as though this were her last resort.

Tauria had to help. Too many dark fae surrounded Nik even with his ability.

She took her first step to him.

A cool metal snapped around her wrist, and she cried out at the sharp bite that threw a blanket over her senses. She already knew what it was, and she didn't look to the wrist Mordecai held having attached the Magestone cuff. Nik spun to them with a fury so dark it frightened her more than the high lord. She wasn't scared for her safety, but Nik's. Because Mordecai's action stole his focus while peril raged around him. She pulled against Mordecai's hold, her eyes wide and mouth parted to call out to him.

But she was too late.

The most soul-shattering sound she'd ever heard pierced her like the blade that ran through him.

Tauria couldn't hear the scream that tore out of her. She hunched over in absolute shock when the blade through Nik's abdomen was retracted. Slick with his blood, it was raised to strike again, and Tauria pushed deep against the Magestone to find her wind. She felt it, but not nearly enough.

Tarly's arrow struck Nik's assailant's throat.

She strained again, but an arm encircled her waist, and she cried out as she watched Nik fall to his knees. Crimson poured out from his wound, and Tauria became numb at the sight. Helpless. Her heart wasn't breaking; it had been obliterated all at once.

"*Stay with me!*" She sent the thought so loud, hoping he could hear her despite the agony he was in from a weapon partially crafted of Magestone. She couldn't live with any alternative. "*You can't leave me.*"

If Nik died...so would she.

The Waterwielder went rushing over to Tauria's mate, and she didn't know why she felt relief, nor how she knew this fae could help him.

"Tell them to stop attacking," Tauria said. They were the words of a ghost as her body trembled, so cold and distant she could grapple with nothing to find some footing in reality.

Mordecai listened to her, but she couldn't surface any calm. The fighting stopped, but all she could do was watch as Samara and the other fae tended to her mate. Nothing had ever overcome her so wholly with despair. It should be her by Nik's side when instead she stood in the arms of another.

"*I love you,*" she thought over and over, but she heard nothing back. "*As eternal as the moon, I love you, Nikalias.*"

His groans of pain formed her tears that fell silently.

"Are you ready to come with me now, Tauria?"

Every bone and nerve and muscle locked tight in protest. Every thought screamed against it; every instinct cried out to deny. But this had to happen. She had to go to Fenstead, or it had all been for nothing.

"We have to make sure he lives, or it will mean war," she tried —one last attempt to at least know without a doubt that Nik would be okay before they were torn apart.

Too much blood. She begged for it to stop, seeing each measure he lost as a countdown to his fading life.

"You come with me now," Mordecai warned, his body pressed to hers from behind, "or I resume the attack in my belief you still side with them."

"I saved *you*, not him." Tauria found the bite of her voice, only out of her devastation at watching Nik lie back with aid at the Waterwielder's instruction. Some of the cuts on his clothing, his face, she had allowed with her rainfall of glass.

She had harmed him. It was a truth she would forever harbor like a permanent wound.

"*I'm so sorry. I'm so, so sorry, Nik.*"

"*Love.*"

She perked up at hearing his voice in her mind.

"*Don't go with him. Please.*"

Nik was in so much pain, yet still he fought for her. His head lolled, the panic in his emerald eyes striking so deep.

"*I'll come back. I'm smart, remember? I can do this, and now he trusts me. I'll find the ruin and I'll come right back. You stay alive. Do you hear me, Nikalias? You stay alive for me to find home again.*"

Though she was headed to the land of her birth and reign, it meant nothing without him.

"I'm coming with you," Lycus cut in from her side.

Tauria shook her head. "When the time is right, I will send for you. It may be a while as I assess the state of the kingdom before we reintroduce our citizens and make them believe it is safe again in my rule. Tell no one of my whereabouts. Your role right now is to keep this a secret."

She spoke the command only for Mordecai's sake, the wreck of her mind, soul, and heart crying out for Nik to understand her next move on the board. They were so close.

Lycus's face twitched with a protest, but as he held her eyes, he saw her silent plea.

"*Tauria,*" Nik said to her mind quietly as he faded into unconsciousness, and she realized the Waterwielder had retrieved some tonic that was taking him from her.

Tauria captured his fluttering gaze. The air wanted to choke her. The ground threatened to swallow her. She felt she had failed him so truly she didn't know how she would ever repent.

"*You are so brave. I...I'm going to come for you. I promise.*"

Those were the last words Nik spoke before his eyes slipped shut and her world was silenced with them.

CHAPTER 86

Zaiana

ZAIANA SAT WITH eyes closed, head tipped back, while the moonlight caressed her face. She listened to the music she could hear faintly if she focused. The celebrations for the comet were well underway. There was peace in the songs they played, and while she listened her mind drifted afar. She allowed her thoughts to run wild just for one night.

She'd once believed her pitiful notions could be locked away and no one would know. That solace had been taken from her now.

Still, she couldn't tame her thoughts of fantasy with the music that coaxed them out, and she imagined what it would be like to dance. She'd seen it before—the clumsy but joyful type in small-town inns; the elegant and whimsical movements she'd spied through castle windows; the intimacy of two lovers who'd stolen a moment in the night, slow and without any care for specific steps, only what moved them as one. Zaiana wondered what it would feel like to be held in such a way. To step out of her combat leathers for the first time to wear something beautiful and glittering.

Her childish whims were snuffed out like a candle.

Zaiana's eyes opened with the shuffling that started down the passage. She kept her eyes on the brilliant moon, hoping her lack of attention would get him to leave as quickly as he stormed to her cell.

"You're missing out on the celebrations," she drawled to Kyleer.

A rattle snapped her attention, straightening her head, as Kyleer jammed the key into the lock. The resounding *click* of it opening stunned her. She used her back against the wall to rise but barely got to her feet before his hand gripped her chains, the other wrapping around her throat.

It all happened so fast she blinked with bewilderment as he held her to the wall, green eyes blazing while he pushed out hard breaths. Her bound hands stayed locked above her head.

Neither of them spoke for a few long, electrifying seconds. Her chest rose and fell deeply to have him so close with no bars.

"You've been gone for weeks."

"They forbade me from seeing you."

"Then you shouldn't be here."

"He should never have gone for your thoughts," he snarled.

His anger stunned her. She waited to see the trick, yet his fury wasn't directed at her.

"You shouldn't care."

"I can't stop," he confessed, the sharp lines of his face easing to something far softer. His hand over her neck slowly moved around her nape. "I am undone by you. Annihilated by you. I can't stand it."

"I have done nothing."

"You don't *need* to," he ground out. But then his forehead creased with pain before it fell to hers. "I want to kill you because the only way to find peace is to know I cannot *find* you. Then just as quickly as I imagine that possibility, I want to follow right after you."

Heat gathered, and she swallowed hard.

"I thought you were smart, commander," she whispered.

Something wild flared in his eyes when he pulled back, his

fingers curling in her hair, but not in a painful grip. "I don't want to be smart with you. I want to be reckless and daring, and I want you to fight me at every turn, because nothing feels more alive than this." His nose grazed her cheekbone, breath breezing across her ear. "You feel it too."

The answer rushed in too fast, too certain, for her to fight it. The agreement that curved her body into his subconsciously. She didn't want to slip away from his shield, though she could have.

She said nothing. Did nothing.

"I want to be the last," Kyleer went on in a low, husky murmur, "to ever lay a hand on you." Rough fingers trailed her hips, under her sweater, to graze her bare skin. Zaiana's lips parted with the warm vibrations. "To ever bring you pleasure." Up over her ribs, and she didn't want him to stop climbing, but he paused under the curve of her breast, his thumb brushing between them. "You have no idea how much it makes me hate you."

"Then you have your answer. Kill me, Kyleer."

It was a dare for him to try.

His eyes narrowed, then something in him let slip his final tether of control. *"Gods*, you are insufferable. Exquisitely, punishingly insufferable."

Kyleer's mouth slammed to hers, his body molding with hers against the wall, immediately drawing out a moan, and as she opened her mouth his tongue slipped inside. She unraveled, she exploded, feeling a warmth that grew at the feel of him; a frenzy that reacted to the taste of him. It became a beautiful wonder how everything that had plagued her for days, that had her plotting revenge on them all, dissipated for him. She only cared about what he gave her in that moment.

She shouldn't feel this way. He was just one male. One who'd tormented and tortured her mind, but also offered it a reprieve. One whom she despised, the enemy, yet who had become a presence she didn't want to admit she yearned for.

Kyleer let go of her chains. Her arms dropped around his shoulders, but still bound she couldn't tangle them in his brown locks like she'd so desperately wanted to do for months. His tall, built form made her feel so small, but it fueled her lust. She wanted to feel every contoured part of him, yet she was unable to do anything but surrender.

His large hands hooked around her thighs and her legs wrapped around him. The angle, his broad body—she clung to him as though he could shield her from the world and douse her in bliss for eternity. Zaiana kissed him as if she were nothing more than a dark fae with a burning passion. It didn't matter what she was—the color of her blood, the fact she could unglamour her wings, that she would always be his enemy and they would never be accepted beyond this cell. It didn't matter, but Kyleer deserved better. She didn't expect to grow feelings for him as she lured him right into her trap.

She certainly didn't expect to fall *with* him.

Love was a fickle thing, a master of deception. A powerful force with a silent snare. Zaiana didn't want to believe the beginning of such a cruel attachment was what had started to creep through her defenses. She wanted to deny, to feel the lust but not the breakable emotions that attempted to entangle her.

Yet she was tired of fighting. So tired of the war in her mind that never ended.

Her eyes…they burned. Hot and with such a distant feeling that when the tear fell, she whimpered. She deserved to feel its pathetic ache.

Kyleer pulled out of the kiss, his forehead resting against hers while he panted, cupping one of her cheeks in his calloused palm. A palm that had felt cruelty just like hers, but which had dealt it far more in return. The pad of his thumb brushed away the betrayal that she cared. For him.

She had allowed herself to care, and it had carved a new void that would never heal.

"I want to take you right here, but you deserve better."

She didn't. She didn't deserve anything.

Her stomach twisted and twisted. Was this guilt? It felt vaguely familiar, but she'd never had it root itself so deeply and spread so rapidly.

Her eyes dropped, and her lips pinched together to stifle her sob.

Kyleer spoke so gently it was unbearable. "We're going to do this together, Zai. You and me. We'll convince the others you're on our side."

Zaiana shook her head, and her exhale tunneled her into the coldest detachment of her existence. "I'm not on your side," she whispered. "I can never be."

It was time.

Zaiana moved fast.

With a cry against an agony far deeper than the cut of metal, her wrists pulled apart with such force she snapped the chain between them. It wasn't without great effort and resistance that she dragged her magick forth, past the blanket of the Niltain steel on her wrists.

Then she struck.

With a hand on his chest, her lightning heated to the surface and gripped him fully. Kyleer fell, and she with him. They crashed to the ground, where she straddled him. His hands took her wrists, but his strength was diminished with the shockwaves she pushed through him.

She could kill him—*should* kill him. It was her order.

More tears gathered as she watched his bewildered eyes fill with so much pain, but not from her lightning.

He pinned her with betrayal.

"Look at me, Kyleer," she said through gritted teeth, failing to keep her voice from wavering at the stab of her chest. "Really look at me. I am not *good*. Not like you. Not like them. I am a monster, and I'm only disappointed you fell for the beautiful guise."

"How?" His choked voice pinched her brow.

"I've been building a tolerance to Niltain steel since the day I found out it could harm me over a century ago. I wore it. Small pieces at first, until I could stand pretty bracelets like these. Then I trained through them. *Gods*, it was agony, but it was nothing compared to how the material could be used against me if I didn't master it first. When I could build back my strength and speed, it was a harder challenge to surface my magick past its restraints. But I never stopped until I conquered that too. All I had was time. And sometimes, it was nothing compared to what I would endure under the masters' hands anyway. At least my own torture made me stronger. Brought me to this day right here. Put you right at my mercy in thinking I was vulnerable."

Zaiana should have killed him and made her escape already; she was wasting precious time. Yet she couldn't stop herself from leaning in closer, trembling as she watched his fierce, beautiful face contort with the electricity she coursed through him. It bounced flashes of amethyst across his features, and despite everything, hatred and anger were not written in those pleading eyes.

"What would we have done?" She spoke softly, the question one of sorrow, for herself as much as him. "There would have been no place for us. No acceptance for a villain with a hero." She took his hand and placed it on her chest. "Listen, Kyleer. I don't have a heart to give."

"Why didn't you escape sooner?" He strained for the words, but she didn't ease her attack.

Zaiana held those green eyes, wishing they were filled with loathing or revenge, yet all they gave her was a sadness and disappointment that threatened to stop the air from reaching her lungs. "You have all been unaware of the plans that have been in motion around you this whole time, and it was my pleasure to watch you all try to figure out what was right in front of you." She should have stopped there, yet those mossy irises she'd come to find peace within dragged forth more words faster than sickness. "And maybe because even monsters can fall to weakness..." she confessed, knowing they would never face each other again, and what would it matter anyway if they did? "For a moment, perhaps you became mine."

She didn't know when she had allowed herself to care for him enough that the thought of taking his life *hurt*. She had lived through torn flesh and cruel punishments, but this pain touched one place very few had before.

Her heart.

The withered, cold, black thing that occupied her chest cried out at the thought of killing the warrior beneath her.

Hurt. It cleaved through her so deeply she might have believed she had a soul after all as she pictured the light of hope and longing in his hopeful irises winking out forever. Even now, through his hate and pain and betrayal, he still looked at her with a slither of a plea, as though he clung to something she could never give him.

"I expected better of you, commander." A cold detachment washed through her all at once, steeling her expression and darkening her mind. She looked to him now with nothing but indifference. "Goodbye, Kyleer."

Zaiana's hand curved around his neck until she found the spot to send a precision shock that gripped the right nerve. Kyleer's whole body tensed, his final wide-eyed look one that would brand itself in her memory.

Then he fell limp.

The silence rang loud. She breathed heavy, unable to tear her eyes away from how peaceful he looked despite her attack. He was beautiful. But Zaiana had to go, had to leave him, because there was no telling how much time she had.

Yet she couldn't move.

Her hands fisted his jacket, and she leaned her forehead down to his chest. Then, for just one moment, she broke.

She stole a kernel of time to surrender in her war, accepting that misery would always be a product of cruelty. That no matter how many triumphs she made, it would never be enough to balance the sacrifice of feelings she was told she couldn't have. Right now, they were barreling down on her, drowning her, torturing her, but she accepted it all for the warrior beneath her skin who didn't deserve to fall victim. This was the single time she'd been consumed with regret not only for what she'd done, but for *who* she was. Who they'd made her.

Zaiana took three long breaths.

One to entomb anything she'd felt within this cell.

A SWORD FROM THE EMBERS

One to sever the attachment that had begun to thread around her.

One to welcome the darkness once more.

Zaiana straightened, dipping into his pockets, though she thought it was a long shot. She patted him over before groaning in frustration when she didn't find her iron guards. Without another minute to waste, she had one last place to search.

She stood and exited the cell, locking the door and taking off with the keys down the dark hall. With the celebrations in full swing, the guards were sparse, but she didn't bother to be cautious, knowing she would be the least of their worries any moment now.

Coming up behind the first guard, Zaiana clamped both hands on his shoulders, her thumbs pressing into the precision points on his neck. "You have two other prisoners—where are they?" she asked calmly.

The other guard was halfway to drawing his sword when she cast her hand toward him with a lethal blast.

"I have very little patience," she said in the fae's ear.

His fear vibrated through him. Seconds ticked by, and she was just about to snap his neck when he spoke.

"This way, darkling."

The voice that called through the darkness she knew. With her lightning, she sent the fae under her grasp into unconsciousness before begrudgingly following the sound. Zaiana found him, only a flood of moonlight streaking across his hard face while he stood with his hands in his pockets.

Izaiah Galentithe.

"Are you sure you know what you're doing? There's no going back," she taunted.

"You upheld your end of the deal; I've upheld mine," he said coolly.

"That remains to be seen."

Instead of replying, Izaiah twisted, and she marched after him. They came to a cell, and when the occupant spied her, he shot to his feet.

"About time," Tynan groaned.

"Yes, it has been a rather strung-out torture," she remarked, jamming the key into the lock.

Zaiana knew they wouldn't have set them free. Not with their knowledge of Faythe being alive. Her plan had only been for them to survive captivity with her—something she wasn't certain would happen until an unexpected ally came to visit.

"Where's Amaya?" she snapped at the commander.

Izaiah's *wince* pierced her with cold wrath. "Down three blocks," he said, hesitating before adding, "I tried to help her as best I could, but she's weak, and moments out of the Niltain steel hardly did any good. You might want to work on that if she survives."

His familiar green eyes clenched like a fist in her chest. These ones held the type of cool hatred she'd hoped his brother would have surfaced for her in his final moments. It would have at least made what she did to him far easier to live with.

She contemplated doing the same to Izaiah with no remorse, but Zaiana had one last urgent matter. She jogged down the dark halls, sending her lightning into the locks of the steel doors, until she saw her.

The darkling lay so still that *fear* threatened her balance as Zaiana slowed to a walk. There was no heart to confirm life, no movement she could detect, and her voice came as barely a whisper of dread.

"Amaya."

The first shift could have been mistaken for her own desperate illusion, but so painfully slowly, the darkling began to peel herself up in her helpless state. Zaiana didn't waste a second, twisting the key in the lock as Amaya held herself up on trembling arms, barely getting her head to turn before she fell. Zaiana caught her head before it could crack off the stone. Dull green eyes met hers, and despite everything, her dry lips cracked a small smile.

"I knew you would come back."

Zaiana pinched her eyes closed for a second. Guilt became a storm she wanted to claw from her chest. When her lids slid open, she met Tynan's gaze. Neither had to say a word before he scooped the darkling up in his arms.

"What now?" Izaiah leaned in the cell doorway, lingering a look on Tynan she didn't probe into. "You tear down the wall—then what happens?"

Zaiana spoke to Tynan first. "Take her above. Find somewhere comfortable and get a healer if you can."

"I want to fight with you," he protested.

"Not this time," she said firmly. "That was an order. Go."

His eyes flexed, but Tynan knew this was what she needed of him.

Izaiah watched them leave until silence settled between them. She couldn't decide if she admired him greatly or thought him to be the most foolish of them all. Only time would tell.

She finally answered him. "This city will fall, and you need to let it."

"Did you really have to drag him through your mess?" Izaiah's voice cut like a knife. His loathing she'd never doubted was true since he was the first to see what was happening with his brother.

"I can't be blamed for your brother's weak heart," Zaiana defended, though it tore something within her.

"I see right through you, Zaiana. But I understand, and for your sake, you'd better hope no one else finds out about your lapse of judgment."

"Do you really think they'll forgive you?" Zaiana asked, needing to sway the topic to anything but that.

Izaiah huffed, beginning to walk away. "Forgiveness involves understanding. From now on, who knows how all this will unfold?"

CHAPTER 87

Nikalias

NIK STARTLED AWAKE. In an instant he knew this living nightmare was far worse than anything he could conjure in his sleep. He groaned with the sharp pain that erupted in his abdomen. Someone touched his sweat-slicked shoulder as if to coax him back down, but he couldn't. His blood roared with violence, answering to the relentless pounding in his head. His vision swayed, but he blinked rapidly.

"Where is she?" he asked no one in particular, scanning the room and not registering any face—not even the one he sought desperately. His memory started to trickle back, and he couldn't bear the agony. Twisting off the bed, he stood, catching himself on the post.

"You're gravely injured, Nik. You need to rest."

He knew that voice. In his rage he snapped his head to Tarly. He didn't direct his anger at him for once, but he hated the insinuation he could rest another second without knowing.

"Tauria," he ground out. "You let him take her?"

"She went with him," Nerida said quietly. When Nik's unhinged attention fell to her, Tarly shifted, and Nik wasn't so far gone to miss the shift of his scent. Protective, dominant. The kind that drew some conclusion about them, and he would be a fool in his state to prod at it.

He remembered slowly, so heartbreakingly slowly, what his love had said only to him because only he could hear. *Gods,* he had let her be taken as though she were a piece to be sacrificed, and that was never his wish. Never would he have left her alone.

Tarly inched toward Nerida subtly as she rose from the bed. Nik noted then all the blood-soaked bandages. While his abdomen remained tender, it shocked him all at once that he was even able to stand at all from the near-fatal wound that appeared raw but had at least been naturally stitched together. His eyes widened with horror, and he wasn't sure why he looked to Samara.

"How long was I out?"

"Only for a day," she confirmed quickly.

That wasn't possible.

"Nerida is a healer. A rather brilliant one," she explained.

In his disbelief his attention returned to the silver-haired fae. Gratitude rose within him, but nothing felt like enough to thank her for saving his life.

"I know you don't want to hear this," Tarly began carefully, "but this could work to our advantage. She's got the trust of the enemy, and you have your bond."

The world collapsed all over again as his eyes slipped shut. Any outward wound was nothing, absolutely nothing, compared to the frays of his bond that were slowly fading out thread by thread. "I don't," he said, making his way over to the balcony. He needed air, and the air inside was too hot, too thick, to breathe.

"What do you mean?"

"I mean just that," he snapped, whirling, but his balance wasn't right. Everyone flinched, but he caught himself on the door. His eyes burned as he cursed his pitiful, weak state in front of so many. "Marvellas broke our bond. It's gone."

Nerida's sharp inhale twisted something in him as Nik stumbled outside.

"How did that happen?" Tarly's voice came surprisingly soft. Nik couldn't decide if he despised his pity more.

"Mordecai never would have trusted her with ties to me. We sacrificed the bond willingly. Because it didn't matter... It was perfect and true and beautiful. But I loved her unquestionably long before it." The cool air wrapped around him, and he shuffled over to the balcony rail.

"Maybe I could try... I mean, I don't know. I haven't encountered a severed bond before, but—" Nerida stopped herself. "I'm so sorry that happened."

She sounded so sincere. This fae was no more than a stranger to him, but she didn't feel like one. He twisted his bowed head to her. The sight of Tarly's hand on her, the look he gave her...it was selfish of Nik to sink further into despair as it touched on his yearning pain for Tauria.

She was so far from him.

Nik looked up at the moon. Full and bold. The sight squeezed and squeezed in his chest, but he had faith she would remember. Held hope that she would be staring at it too as often as she could while they were parted. So they'd never truly feel alone.

"Do we at least know where he's taken her?" Tarly asked.

"Fenstead." Lycus made his presence known for the first time.

"I'll be leaving as soon as I can," Nik said.

"You'll need a few more days rest," Nerida interjected.

"I don't have a few days." Nik cut her off. He gave them all his back, clutching one hand over his tender abdomen that was a sure conflict against his words, along with his balance that relied on the stone to keep him upright.

"We can leave tomorrow if you're up for it," Lycus offered.

All Nik gave was a shallow nod. He would be no matter what tonics he had to take to numb the pain. He wasn't at risk of bleeding out, and that was health enough, *time wasted* enough, to go after Tauria.

"Can I come?" Samara's quiet question was unexpected.

"It would be safer for you here," Lycus said.

"I want to help. I don't know this kingdom, and really, I'm tired of courts."

Nik wouldn't stop her if she thought she could handle herself. In such a small amount of time, the guise of a perfectly poised lady, all she was forced to be, had turned out to be a mask she felt brave enough to let go of.

"I want to come too," Nerida said.

Nik turned to her fully then, leaning back against the railing. He couldn't decipher her nerves. Nerida's golden-brown skin glowed with a familiar beauty. Even her eyes tugged at something within, and he could hardly stand to look at them through no fault of hers.

"You don't have to." Tarly spoke to her softly.

Nik didn't particularly like the prince—that hadn't changed. Though he observed a different side to him he'd never glimpsed before that shone in this fae's presence.

"He's right. I thank you for all you have done for me, but you have no reason to risk your life on this quest."

"I do."

Their silence pinned her. Nerida wrung her hands, and Nik knew it was the sign of a lingering confession. His heart rate spiked.

"You owe them nothing," Tarly said quietly.

"I spent my life hiding, watching and yearning only in my cowardice. I owe this to myself, and to her."

Nik's alarm rose. "What are you talking about?"

More silence. Yet it was not enough to curb the weight of knowledge that crashed down on them all at once.

"Tauria Stagknight is my half-sister."

CHAPTER 88

Faythe

THERE WAS NOT a single moment in her life that Faythe had felt such otherworldly bliss. A bliss she knew wouldn't last forever, so she clung to every precious second of it. In Reylan's arms, lying peacefully away from all the flamboyance, and with the starry night sky blanketing them, she didn't feel the chill of the night within his warmth. His hand caressed her arm while he whispered so many words of promise and adoration and nothing of the possibilities they would face in the aftermath of tonight, only what they knew for certain.

Each other.

A flicker of light caught in her vision. A giddy excitement awoke as it expanded to diffuse the night. She watched the blazing core cross the sky like a brilliant shooting star.

"I lay right here for Matheus's Comet last time," Reylan said. "I never thought I would admit this, nor that I would care to remember, but I made a wish."

Faythe didn't tear her eyes from the comet. "What did you wish for?"

"I can't explain the hollow feeling I've carried, like something was missing but I didn't know what it was or how it was taken. I committed myself wholly to training the moment I stepped into Agalhor's service. Punishingly, when I thought that was all it was. I needed a purpose, and so I climbed the ranks to general faster than most would, but it wasn't enough. I got to where I wanted, and still it wasn't enough to fill the void."

Guilt tightened her throat. "I'm sorry."

Reylan's mouth eased a soft curl. "Don't be. I knew Farrah as a friend during it all before we became anything more, and she helped for a time until I lost her too." He paused, and Faythe's nose crinkled against the sting. "After that, I became very distant from life. I focused all I could into my new role. I earned my reputation pretty quickly, because in my grief and hollowness I didn't care what became of me. I fought ruthlessly, mercilessly. It was similar to when I worked for my uncle, but at least there was honor in how I used my skills then. Often, I would take leave and wander, always drifting as though I would somehow stumble across what had been missing all this time." Reylan propped himself up to glance over her face. Those starry eyes touched every inch as if he were drawing a subconscious pattern and he didn't even realize it. "My wish was answered, Faythe. With you, the nights are no longer so tormenting, and the days are not so dark."

Faythe touched his cheek, the swell in her chest coming close to flaring. "I'm sorry I took so long."

He leaned down to kiss her, muttering against her lips, "You're here now."

Reylan deserved more answers he didn't know existed, but for now, she breathed light in his happiness.

"I wish for a hundred, maybe a thousand more comets with you. Right here every time."

Reylan smiled, broad and without restraint. "To a thousand more."

Faythe opened her mouth to say something, but when Reylan's gaze flashed back to the sky, alarm seemed to stiffen him. He pulled them both up, and her pulse spiked as she scanned around them, then up.

She saw it. Flickers of amber like falling embers, except they held direction.

Then, so distantly, her blood went cold as she heard it.

Screams.

Faythe was pulled to her feet with Reylan as he rushed over to the ledge.

"What's happening?" she asked.

Reylan didn't answer right away, and his stillness froze her with trepidation. She watched his face as he calculated—a look she'd seen before, but one that inspired her worst dread. It was a face he only wore when...

"We're under attack."

Those three words dawned a reality so frightening her balance faltered for a second. Faythe watched the alluring fire soar like stars, until it landed and began to devour. Fire arrows. Knowing this day could come didn't make the reality any less terrifying.

She was dragged from her refusal to believe it as Reylan moved, gripping her hand to guide her in a hurried pace that almost had her tripping. Faythe bundled the front of her dress, slowly coming out of her stupor.

"Is it bad?" she asked him, not really expecting a sure answer but needing some assurance.

Reylan said nothing. His face was hard, his eyes tunneling away as though he were calculating a hundred measures of defense in his mind. Her whole body jerked at the loud clang that tremored through the hall, the castle, the entire city. The bell announced the battle that was coming to them.

They were jogging now, hand in hand. Servants began to rush through the halls; guards were moving and calling to each other. She didn't know where they were heading, but suddenly Reylan pulled them to a stop in a wide hallway. His chest rose and fell as he scanned around until he turned to her firmly. A hand slipped over her cheek, and Faythe braced for what he would ask.

"I know where I need to be, but you have never been a part of that protocol." His jaw worked, a slight surfacing of his panic that riddled her with alarm. "I need you to listen to me and not go against my words. I won't focus for a second if I don't know you're safe. Go to your rooms, Faythe. Change, be ready, but stay there until I or someone else comes for you under my orders. Lock all the doors. Answer to no one unless you're certain I sent them. Can you do that for me?" He must have read the protest in her hesitation because he took her face between his palms with such fierce urgency. "Please."

Faythe couldn't stand his worry, and this was no time to keep him here. She nodded, and while a quick flash behind his eyes revealed he didn't believe her, he kissed her firmly.

"Reylan," she called when he broke away, shifting into the fierce general he was. "Come back to me."

"Always," he said to her thoughts.

Gods, the ache that pulled at her chest was unbearable. They locked eyes in a promise, and then he was gone.

Faythe stood for a second longer staring after his ghost, physically restraining herself from going after him. She would be of no use to anyone in the lengths of her dress. She took a long, deep breath, ignoring the rush of frightened humans and fae around her. Then she headed to her rooms as he had asked, but the rope that lassoed her heart squeezed tighter and tighter with the knowledge that while her people fought, she could not sit idly by.

CHAPTER 89

Zaiana

Zaiana smiled at the toll of the city bell.

It had begun.

The guards in front of her were alerted to it before they could twist to fear her first. This night of lax protection and stealing wine on duty would be their last. To her blazing fury but great delight, Zaiana recognized them both. She dove her hand through the back of the first, fingers clenching around his shuddering heart. The second male reached for his sword, but her lightning sent him crashing into the wall.

"I'm glad we got the chance to meet again," she hissed cruelly in one's ear, enjoying his final floundering look. "Do you want to count down the last of your heart's beats before I tear it from your chest?"

She gave a squeeze, and his eyes bulged. His silence was to her displeasure even if it was inspired by terror.

"Count for me," she whispered against his ear.

His lips parted. "Y-you witch—"

Zaiana tore the heart out through his back, unfurling her fist to let it drop with him. She was upon the second fae in a flash.

Humanity left her as she clawed his face and chest, taking her anger out on him. She hadn't forgotten for a second how many lashes they'd watched their companion strike her with.

When she stopped, he lay choking on his own blood, and Zaiana wore it. With her fingers poised and pointed down, she snapped her lightning over them. His trembling hand rose as if to beg. She struck his heart with the full force of her power, seizing him whole until he stilled.

As she examined her skin, she hardened herself to the thick, sticky blood dripping from her fingers. Her mouth watered with the temptation, but her grip on control was strong enough to snap out of the trance. She stormed from the cells, spiraling up and up, killing two more with little effort and no attention.

Zaiana calculated her way to where she thought she'd find Kyleer's room. It was too quaint to be in the main halls, so she headed back down. Screams and hurrying bodies began to catch in her senses, but she didn't slow her marching pace, willing to kill anyone who realized she was a loose enemy in the chaos. A double take that would be their death. Most didn't notice, too busy scrambling to lock themselves away, and the guards rushing to their posts didn't understand the threats were already inside.

And she wasn't the worst of them.

Zaiana still wore Kyleer's cloak. She'd spent weeks wrapped in his scent, which she tracked when she reached a far more humble quarter of the castle. She opened door after door, finding nothing but startled humans who blanched at her. She grabbed the next guard rushing past and slammed him to the wall.

"The commander Kyleer's room—where is it?" she asked with thinning patience.

The fae's face turned ashen as he raised a shaky hand down the hall. "There's a lone room far down that hall on the left."

Zaiana debated killing him, but she let him go roughly before striding away instead.

This city didn't stand a chance.

Bursting into the room, she didn't expect to be so hit with grief. It stunned her like a physical blow. Zaiana walked to the bed, tracing slow fingers over the wooden posts, trying not to imagine herself lying there wrapped up in him and how that night she'd slept better than she had in a century. The whole room was doused in his scent. The air became thick guilt to breathe.

Her sword was not propped up by the fireplace where she had seen it last; instead, it lay out of its scabbard across his desk. She studied the polish of the blade, wondering why he would have cared to tend to it. It was sharpened to a lethal perfection, especially given the caution that would have gone into sharpening it to avoid the pain of the Magestone it was partially crafted of. The strip of fabric remained exact, to her relief.

Next to the blade, Zaiana took a long breath of relief as she found two of her iron finger guards. She slipped them onto the middle and pointer fingers of her right hand and found herself crouching down to reach the book splayed next to them. As her fingers traced the ancient script, she bit her lip hard. Why would he care to study the language her sword's name was plucked from…? She couldn't figure it out.

Why, why, why?

Kyleer would remain an unsolved puzzle that had somehow scattered its vibrant pieces in her mind. She had collected them, fitted them together without trying, each one drawing her closer and closer to him, and over time it became a thrill to know what the full image of him would present.

She would never find out. Didn't *deserve* to.

Zaiana gave a quick scan around, but she couldn't find the matching guards for her other hand, which flexed irritably with weightlessness in comparison. She hastily opened a few drawers but gave up with a groan, accepting they were gone.

Equipping her back with the scabbard and sliding Nilhlir inside, she left without a glance back.

Take to the rooftops.

She could abandon that order and do what she liked, but if it meant she might find it safe to unglamour her wings and fly after months of torture, it was exactly where she wanted to be.

After one short detour.

Zaiana roamed the castle as if she'd conquered it. She had one person on her mind, and when she found him, her face twitched with distaste.

"Malin Ashfyre," she called down the hall.

The prince's back locked stiff, but Zaiana didn't falter a step. He barely got to twist around before her hand clamped over his shoulder. Pulling the handle of a door that led to somewhere or nowhere, she shoved the prince inside.

"You cannot treat me like this," he barked, rolling his shoulder.

Zaiana slammed the door and stalked to him slowly. Without the bars between them, he appeared every inch the frightened mouse he was. "Are you going to stop me?"

Malin backed all the way to the wall. "What do you think you're doing? This was not part of our deal."

"I'm here to collect," she said with enough cold warning to portray her lack of patience while the battle raged on without her.

"The wall still stands," he said. "I tell you nothing until you *fulfill* your end of the bargain."

Zaiana was upon him in a flash, hand curled around his throat but keeping distance from him as much as she could. "How does it feel to betray your own blood?" she asked, head tilting as she observed him. She tuned in to his heart: fast with a stroke of fear, but it held a broken beat. He hated so much of the world; so much of everyone.

"They betrayed me first," he hissed.

"How?"

"I was to rule this kingdom, and I will."

Zaiana's smile curled, slow and predatory. "You are nothing more than a puppet who tied his own strings."

"Do not insult me."

"Or what?" His rage was so palpable Zaiana had to stifle her lightning that begged to hurt him.

"You're a wicked witch," the prince spat.

Zaiana dropped her hand, hooking a brow in amusement. "At least I'm not a false king with a hollow crown."

A slam ricocheted off her mind. The absolute fury that overcame her at his attempt to infiltrate her thoughts damned her to whatever punishment she would face as her lightning lashed out. Malin tensed with strangled chokes of pain, lowering slowly until his knees met the ground. It was sheer willpower that made her retract the purple bolts crackling over him.

He breathed hard as he came around from the aftershocks.

"Don't ever try that again," she warned in a deadly tone. Zaiana crouched, observing the pitiful being. "Though it's good to know your plan worked, I suppose," she mused. "Is it true then, what the Phoenix Blood can do?"

"Burn in the Nether," he breathed, not meeting her eye again.

Zaiana straightened. She had nothing more to gain from him yet.

At the door, she paused. "I will uphold my end of the bargain, and when I come looking for you, the Nether will seem like a paradise compared to what you'll endure if your information doesn't uphold yours."

As she slipped through a window, the bell rang with a piercing cry. Through its intermittent echoes, the city scattered into chaos. Zaiana stood when she reached a tall, flat rooftop. Most of the damage she'd faced so far was within the outer ring—blazing houses and slaughtered humans. She couldn't deny the sight heated her skin with adrenaline. It had been so long since she last saw the destruction and tragedy of war, but it would never fail to inspire a pinch of sorrow.

The enemy Rhyenelle had unwittingly let within the outer city gates would reach the inner ring soon if their plan was carried out seamlessly. The king didn't stand a chance this time. Zaiana watched the event that would mark history.

The city that had never fallen; the kingdom that had never been claimed...

Conquered.

A SWORD FROM THE EMBERS

They were winning.

Something in her withered a little more, turning a shade darker than black. She tried to expel the image that haunted her, tried not to replay the second the light in Kyleer's eyes died out. That light had shone even on something so soulless and heartless.

She planned to take off running, maybe to kill, needing something to stop the threat stinging in her eyes. Spinning, she halted her near lunge, stumbling as if a wall had formed in front of her with the shadow that fell and blocked her path. Her lips parted in utter shock, though she shouldn't have been shocked at all. The tail blast of his wings blew past her like an embrace. He straightened and Maverick stood tall, his face firm, all lethal like she remembered, but with an edge of calculation as he looked over her.

She didn't know what caused her stillness. The familiarity of him tugged at something she wanted to ignore. Perhaps she should surface some cruel remark or insult, deny she was even remotely glad to see him...

But it would be a lie.

Maverick took slow steps toward her, his eyes scanning every inch, and neither of them spoke. Right in front of her, he dipped into his pocket. They didn't break electrifying eye contact, not even when he reached for her hand, but she gave a shallow gasp at the cool metal sliding onto her fingers. Only when the familiar weight adorned both hands again did they look down. She didn't know how he'd found her missing guards, only basked in the relief that they weren't lost to her.

Maverick's thumb brushed the thick abrasions on her wrists. "What happened?" His tone was all hard threat. When she met those dark orbs, a shadowy chill shook her. "If you ever try something like that again, I'll kill you myself. But damn, if it isn't good to see you, Zaiana."

She opened her mouth, but no words came out. It was so unlike her, but her cold arrogance faltered completely as she wondered if he saw her desperate shoveling within. She was trying to dig a deep enough grave for any feelings she'd felt before he stared for long enough to decipher her foolish lapse of judgment.

His hand gripped her chin, and she couldn't deny his touch made her skin tingle but raged a conflict inside. He searched her gaze, and something like understanding softened the edges of his. He didn't know what she'd reduced herself to with the commander. Perhaps the only conclusion he made was that her torture had been brutal enough to cause her pitiful frozen state.

It was a partial truth. What she'd done just a moment ago struck her with a pain worse than anything she'd endured in her lifetime.

"Get yourself together, delegate," Maverick said, soft but with a firm command.

Normality would be to bite at that remark, but all she felt was a snap back to reality at his words. Her title. Who she was and what side of the battle she stood on. Zaiana nodded slowly, tunneling into that persona she had trained her whole life to be. The ruthless killer. The merciless enemy.

She turned from him, letting ice freeze over anything warm and darkness cloud any hint of compassion. She had one last person to kill, and her task remained unfulfilled as she stared at the inner-city wall still standing, lined with an unwavering defense of soldiers and weapons while the outer city gates were opened by the human rat.

Zaiana rolled her shoulders, stifling a moan at the sheer bliss of feeling her wings expand from her back. The weight of them was far more endurable and welcome than the glamour she'd carried for so long.

"What's the plan?" Maverick asked.

"I'm going to tear down the damn wall," she said, more to herself.

Maverick braced for flight with her. "Then make it storm, Zaiana."

CHAPTER 90

Faythe

FAYTHE PACED HER rooms equipped in her combat leathers with Lumarias strapped to her back. She warred over not wanting to defy Reylan's wishes and knowing she had to. Her anxious pacing was only in calculation of where she was headed. Imagining the humans in the outer city, Faythe could only picture her humble town of Farrowhold, and in flooded a surge of need to protect it.

The first people on her mind were her human friends. Her best bet was to scour the castle for them.

Just as she stepped to the door, it swung open. Faythe lunged into a defensive stance, hand flying behind her to draw her sword, when—

"Gods above, you could have knocked!" Faythe choked on the words to Jakon and Marlowe in her fright.

"I figured under the circumstances you wouldn't mind," Jakon answered, closing and locking the door. Faythe frowned. "We happened to pass Reylan a while ago. He said to make sure you'd locked it."

Faythe refrained from rolling her eyes. "Where's Reuben?"

Marlowe's expression was concerned. "He wanted to enjoy the celebrations like he did back home."

A cold dawning washed over Faythe even before Marlowe continued.

"He's in the outer city with most of the humans."

Right then, her plan fell into place. Now she knew for certain her destination had to be on the front line. Faythe spun to the balcony.

"I know what you're thinking, but there's no way—"

"Jak," Faythe cut him off, having no time for this argument. "You can't stop me."

"Then I'm coming with you."

She spun to him. "I'm fae now. Stronger, faster, and I have a power that can protect me out there. I can't afford for you to be another person I have to worry about. I need you to trust I'll be okay."

Faythe swore internally at his hard look of protest—so damn familiar, his commendable courage—but she didn't have time.

"Faythe..." The brokenness of Marlowe's voice snapped both of their attention. "I'm so sorry. I did what I had to, and I didn't know how soon this would come. You have to believe me that I'm sorry, I'm sorry—"

Crossing the space, Faythe took hold of Marlowe's upper arms in her panic. She searched her glittering ocean eyes with trepidation. "Can you tell me, Marlowe? Please," Faythe begged. She needed to know if she knew something, had *seen* something

"I did what I had to. And what comes next..."

Faythe heard the words as if they were someone else's twisted reality. She listened to every one, trying to stand firm against horror and heartache.

"I don't believe it," she muttered.

But she did.

Marlowe spoke of things she had suspected but never wanted to believe, yet some of these revelations Faythe never could have anticipated. They weighted her eyes from being able to look at

Marlowe; she couldn't push aside the twist of betrayal. She *wanted* to understand, but she needed a moment.

To calculate.

To breathe.

To think there could be some other way out of it all.

"I need to go," Faythe said vacantly.

Though he was an accomplice, knowing everything yet keeping silent too, Faythe couldn't walk away without turning to Jakon. Their eyes locked in knowing. How could it have come to this? Yet her promise to him remained, and she would never break that. She would never make him—either of them—choose.

She couldn't help herself when she took quick strides toward him, wrapping her arms around his neck. He held her tightly, face angled to her neck to breathe her in.

"I'll be okay," she whispered—not a promise, but a hope.

"You'd better be," he mumbled back, squeezing her a little tighter before they released each other.

Marlowe's ocean eyes were hollow, and despite everything, Faythe drew her arms around her next. Her friend released a sharp sob of relief, and while Faythe still struggled to accept everything Marlowe had brought to light that night, they'd gathered too many precious memories for their friendship to be erased by a war they'd all been thrust into.

Then Faythe left her dearest friends, heavy with burden and sorrow and guilt, but she didn't look back.

Her new agility had never been put to the test quite like scaling the sides of Rhyenelle's castle. She drowned out the cries of the city, the distant commotion of steel and fire and all things heinous that descended upon her people. Faythe made it to where she'd hoped. Jumping down, she landed on the wall and didn't pause for one second before she was sprinting the perimeter. It took careful maneuvering as the wall was teeming with soldiers in their lethal focus. It seemed everyone in the inner city knew exactly what to do in this situation.

"It's the princess," she heard a few mutter as she raced past.

They shuffled from their stone stances as though debating whether to break protocol and go after her. A few tried to call, but she couldn't pause in her urgency. Mercifully, no one chased her, but she wondered how effective their communications were, and knowing Reylan, how quickly they could get the word to him. She couldn't afford to think of that. For the sake of keeping him focused, she hoped he was far enough away to delay anyone from reaching him before she found Reuben and headed back.

Faythe sprinted the perimeter wall, dashing and twisting, not flinching at the screams that grew louder, nor the ash she tasted on her tongue. At the halfway point soldiers lined the whole wall, and ahead was barricaded by many more bodies, but also a set of closed doors. She should have anticipated it, and knowing it would take too long to plead her case for them to open a key defense, Faythe eyed the height instead. It wouldn't be an easy climb, but she'd grown up on the streets of Farrowhold scaling buildings, and she would attempt it now with her reckless, coursing adrenaline.

When she got close enough and a few of the soldiers braced to block her, Faythe turned, hoisting herself up the wall before hopping and running over the structure of it. Battle raged to life beside her, but she couldn't look down without risking her confidence.

"Your Highness!"

A few soldiers barked; others hissed for them to be quiet as they risked announcing to the enemy there was a key target within range.

At the gate, Faythe threw all caution to the wind. Her fingers clawed and slipped on the abrasive stone. Her feet found the smallest of crevices to hoist herself further up, and it was sheer determination that had her managing the climb.

Exertion caught up with her all at once. The heat, the terror, the panic. High and overlooking it all, any idea she might have had that she was prepared to see and hear and feel true battle was nothing compared to the stilling horror of this moment. Soldiers in pure black tore through the streets, killing and wrecking with such barbaric chaos her blood raged. She closed her eyes for a second to breathe, dropping into a crouch to make herself small. She had to find Reuben, and she prayed to the damn Gods he wasn't among the bodies; that his blood wasn't painting the streets like so many others.

Faythe leaned out to gauge the distance down. She thought she might tolerate the impact.

"You shouldn't go down there, Your Highness," a guard warned.

Faythe spared one look at the wide-open outer-city gates across the long expanse. She ignored him to ask, "How did they break through?"

He hesitated, and then trepidation crawled her skin with the dread in his voice. "They didn't. It's like someone let them in." He balked a little at the incredulous look she snapped to him. "We don't know who or why," he added quickly.

It didn't make sense, but at the same time, it did. With the feather going missing this was no coincidence, but her mind demanded to know *who*. Even Malin wouldn't attack his own people—that would never win him the crown…

Faythe shook her head, trying not to overwhelm herself with too many tasks and questions. One at a time, and right now her attention was fixed on her friend.

"Keep defending the wall. Alert no one. This is not the time to care for one person over thousands."

A wave of dizziness lapped her so suddenly Faythe thought she was falling. Her mind pulled away from body as if it had been lifted to another void that hushed the terror around her. A vaguely familiar tingling coated her skin. Then she heard a voice.

"Oh, my dear Faythe," Marvellas cooed. *"Trust that I take no pleasure in knowing how this has to happen."*

She tried to get back to consciousness. Color came in and out of focus. Flexing her fingers, she felt the stone and heard a real voice so close. Someone was cradling her.

"*You can stop this,*" Faythe pleaded in her mind.

"*It will end—have no fear of that. This way, there are less casualties. Only those of weakness, and those who rebel.*"

"Your Highness!"

The guard's tone boomed over her, snapping her awake, though the presence in her mind lingered. He must have caught her before she could fall the other way. He helped her to sit, and Faythe wasted no time in getting to her feet, leaning on the wall for stability.

"*Show yourself,*" Faythe hissed.

"*Soon. So very soon.*"

Just then, Faythe spotted her father. She hadn't expected to find the king in the thick of the battle, figuring he would be commanding from afar. He fought valiantly, and pride stuck her so truly, giving her the strength to climb up onto the wall once more.

"I should advise you against this plan, Your Highness!" the young guard called up to her.

"*Who will you choose, Faythe?*" Marvellas goaded, and her blood began to chill. "*What if I told you my sister seeks out your mate as we speak?*"

The world around her was canceled out. Faythe turned, seeing the castle she had left, and somehow, *somehow*, she knew Reylan was back there.

"*But there is also a particular threat with a vengeance set on the king.*"

Faythe had never felt the harsh tug of two strings before. She thought they might tear her apart before she chose to give in to either.

"*It's time to choose, Faythe Ashfyre.*"

"*I won't,*" she breathed, yet terror became a clock that ticked too fast, racing toward a decision she could never take back.

"*Then you will lose both.*"

"Me," Faythe rushed out, her eyes scanning the flickering amber night, over the smoke, up to the stars, around the bloodied chaos, as if she would find the Spirit who taunted her. "Take me. I'll go with you if you stop this."

"*A tempting offer. But understand this is beyond my lone desires now. I still plan for us to be together again. First you must see what it takes to reform the world piece by piece."*

Faythe clenched her teeth, her fists, so tight as if it would still time for just a moment. She glanced at the battle, gasping as she caught sight of the person she'd been looking for.

Reuben tried to fight off a fae, but he was faltering. The king cut through many with his warriors, but there were so many fae—dark fae—that Faythe couldn't tell the difference with the sheen of red, silver, and black that began to spill across the streets.

A loud rumble made her halt then rocked her balance.

"THE WALL!" a guard barked, causing an immediate disruption to all those who were armed upon it. Faythe saw it in the far distance a second before he chased his words with, "IT'S COMING DOWN!"

"Time is never in our favor when we desire it most."

Those were the last chilling notes that circled, *taunted*, her mind before her connection to Marvellas severed completely. There wasn't a second for Faythe to think beyond pure, desperate impulse. Exchanging a look with the warrior behind her, eyes wide in fear of death as the wall began to crumble and bodies piled under the mass of stone, Faythe decided what she had to do.

"Get everyone off the damned wall!" she ordered, and then she leaped.

Gravity flipped her stomach, taunting that she'd break her bones. But she wasn't a human anymore. The fall ended in four heartbeats. Her teeth clenched against the harsh vibration that exploded through her, her palms pressed to the ground…but she had made it unharmed.

Only instinct drew forth her magick, pulling it like roots from the very earth. It built and built with pressure, and she didn't know how it would be released. Faythe sprinted a few meters away. Twisting, she gave a battle cry, barreling the force of her magick into the wall. It shot out like a brilliant flare of gold dust, meeting the stone and spilling over it with a glittering hue. Faythe's breaths came hard at the sweltering heat on her skin, igniting in her veins, as she felt the wall's resistance with whatever else was blasting into it to make it crumble like no more than a wooden shed. Casting her gaze, she saw soldiers still frantically passing over it, scrambling to get down before she couldn't hold it any longer. Her magick became the sole thing keeping it upright, trembling every nerve, but she couldn't let go. Her vision began to turn gold around the edges. Faythe clamped her eyes shut, shifting her stance and turning her knees weak against the surges of pure power that coursed through her.

"You have to let go, Your Highness!" the same guard called from above.

Faythe only shook her head. Her palms burned the most, but the lines over her arms, the markings on her spine, shone the brightest they ever had. This velocity of magick she had never tempted before, and in it she found no good nor evil; she found herself.

Faythe challenged that power, gripped it and claimed it, unlocking the height of all she'd been too afraid to face. What lived within her was every triumph and transgression, who she was, and what she wanted to be.

She was Reylan's strength.

Nik's wisdom, and Tauria's resilience.

Jakon's courage, and Marlowe's knowledge.

And while she fought a power of familiar might that dragged forth her own frightening will of vengeance and defiance, Faythe realized one other thing she was too.

Zaiana's darkness, and deeper, cloaked in shadow, her light.

"You can let go now." The guard's voice drew a gasp from her at his closeness, and she snapped her eyes to him. "You saved us all."

Faythe had to be sure. Though her body was slick with sweat and vibrated with a consuming rage, she scanned the weakening wall.

No bodies were above it.

With the next blast to challenge her, Faythe yielded.

She tried to slowly ease back, allowing her magick to reel itself in as gently as it could. It took an incredible amount of focus, and when she slipped with a shooting pain, the power sucked back into her all at once with a punishing lash.

Faythe stumbled back, caught by the guard. She tried to draw breath, but she swallowed it like flame.

Large rocks thundered over the ground. They curled into themselves as debris flew past them. It seemed endless when all Faythe could imagine were the casualties she couldn't prevent this time. Some of the stone hit the ground and exploded into gold particles with the remnants of her magick, small bursts of devastating beauty among the tragedy.

Until everything stilled.

"Phoenix Queen," he muttered, bearing her whole weight while she felt utterly boneless.

Coming around from her surge of energy, Faythe found her feet, still leaning on him but finding her balance carefully. "What is your name?" She could barely speak, but he heard her.

"Terran," he answered.

To her incredulity, she looked around and found many soldiers on one knee, all staring at her. "Do me a favor, Terran," Faythe rasped as she straightened off him.

"Anything."

"Lead these warriors. The fight is far from over. Defend the citadel, but should the worst happen, your surrender is not a betrayal. Do what you have to do and stay *alive.*"

She met his warm brown eyes. He was too young, though she couldn't guess exactly how old in fae years. He reminded her too much of one other, and she almost broke into a whimper as she remembered he didn't make it.

"Stay alive," she repeated in a whisper.

Terran gave a nod of determination. "Where are you going?"

Faythe battled herself. Battled the sheer helplessness and soul-deep twist that she had to do this. Agalhor was right here, and so was Reuben. Faythe didn't see it as a choice because she'd already stacked her dark retribution on Dakodas should she make it back and find the Spirit had harmed Reylan in the slightest.

I won't choose.

It was all she could do to turn away from her mate's direction. "*I will come for you,*" she sent to Reylan, knowing he was likely too far away to hear it without their bond complete.

They had come so close.

Faythe took a deep breath to silence her torment and numb her heartache. "I gave you an order. Now go." She used as much authority as she could in her command, straightening as all the soldiers stood and began to form their new defense around the castle now the wall no longer offered it safety. Faythe watched them all with a stroke of pride, but as they climbed over the avalanche of what was once an unshakable barricade, she tried not to lose hope completely.

With her cloud of thoughts at the worst moment, Faythe only caught in the nick of time the attacker who raced for her, retrieving her sword just quickly enough for it to clash with his above her head. The dark fae gazed down at her with no life, only fury, blazing in those black orbs. His weight pushed down, and she yielded an inch closer to her face. His strength alone was too much.

In a surge of memory, Faythe felt for the formation of her Firewielding ability. Blue sparks licked over her blade, and with focus, she amplified the heat that had the fae crying out and dropping his sword. There was no time for mercy—not when innocent blood painted the stone beneath them.

The slick glide but firm force as she ran her blade through his chest was a feeling she would never forget, and never apologize for. Her sword dripped with black blood, but Faythe was running again before his body could fall, the unnatural color churning her stomach. She headed to where she'd seen Reuben first, but as she skidded into the square, she halted at the worst alarm rang in her ears, canceling out all else.

It was too quiet here.

Though she was sure she had seen the place raging with battle and her friend in the thick of it. She *knew* she'd seen Agalhor among the masses close by. Breathing became difficult as she thought the worst. Thought of how easily Marvellas had slipped into her mind, how she'd realized far too late. Had she underestimated how easy it was for the Spirit to manipulate her mind when it was all an illusion?

Faythe had chosen wrong.

Her weight shifted with the dawning of that doom. Did Marvellas know Faythe would come this way at seeing the immediate danger she could stop before the threat toward Reylan? Those weren't just words. They were a trap to lure her farther away.

And she had fallen for it.

She scanned the square again as though she could be wrong and the fight had simply moved. It was left as a wreckage—destroyed instruments, stalls turned into blazing bonfires, torn celebration banners now defiled with the blood of three species. There were no bodies. The place was eerily deserted.

"Faythe!"

Her whole body tensed as she angled her blade. She recognized his voice, yet her skittish mind flashed between what to trust and what wasn't real.

"Reuben," she breathed, spying him across the square.

That hadn't been wrong; he was here. With vacant steps she headed for him, but she couldn't drop the unease that coated her, expecting to look up and find an audience. She snapped her head in every angle as though an opponent would barrel out.

"You're okay," she thought out loud. Scanning him, she saw he was completely free of injury or blood or anything of the devastation that surrounded them.

He drew a dagger as he jogged up to meet her, frantic eyes darting all over until they met in the middle. They had to get out of the open vantage point.

Yet something halted her. A dark, sucking energy drew her attention down to what Reuben held.

The blade was pure iridescent black. Her mind screamed at her to retreat, but too late when, with a flash of movement, in her utter shock at who wielded it, agony erupted over her chest, her shoulder, and her neck, gripping her whole with an immobilizing enchantment, though she couldn't be sure it was entirely the effects of the stone. Faythe's wide-eyed disbelief snapped to Reuben, yet who she was looking at was someone else entirely. Those cold brown eyes belonged to a stranger; the harsh lines of hatred to a monster.

"You are *weak*, Faythe. You always have been," he said, low and without a shred of remorse. When he let go of the blade he'd lodged close to her shoulder, Faythe's trembling hand rose to the hilt. Her mind raced with what to do, but a numbness started to coat her from within, and the golden glow of her palms sputtered like a dying candle.

"Why?" she breathed, knowing she would get an answer she couldn't comprehend. No conclusion she could draw would ever ease the tearing of something far deeper. "I trusted you. I... We—"

No words. There were none she had that could explain it, and maybe she didn't want to know the truth of his betrayal. Didn't want to hear what she had been so naïve not to have seen this whole time.

This whole time.

Faythe swayed. In her utter heartbreak she fell to one knee.

"You led the dark fae right to us...on the quest." She fitted it all together, each new piece drawing her closer to a clear image she struggled to believe.

"Your observations come far too late." He spoke with no emotion. It was like talking to a ghost in her friend's body.

"It's not you." Faythe chose denial when reality came so close to collapsing the world around her.

Reuben crouched, but she couldn't look at him, unable to bear seeing the face of her childhood friend bearing such hatred upon her. "It is me, Faythe." A cruel amusement slipped into his tone. "The one you undermined, underestimated. The one you all treated like a simple fool. Do you know even my own mother favored you, Faythe? She always thought you were brave and good and destined for great things. Me? I was set up for nothing but disappointment. No ambition, no will to fight. Yet look where we are now. You lose, Faythe. You will always lose."

"No." She shook her head. This couldn't be him.

Somehow, the words felt familiar—perhaps with the crushing ache in her heart, her soul.

Reuben straightened. "You got to the feather before I could, but it was Malin who suspected you, and to douse you with guilt, he sent an assassin to kill the library masters you left vulnerable."

Faythe couldn't lift her head from its bow of submission.

"I went to your rooms to find the feather when I saw you leave that night. Your handmaiden saw me and foolishly decided to follow me. Why couldn't she have just let it *be?*"

Through her blurry vision, Faythe thought she caught a glimpse of the boy she once knew. An expression eerily similar to the one he wore the day she'd helped him stow away to the unknown. He was terrified. "You didn't mean to," she said, trying to forgive him.

"I did," he whispered. "I didn't want to kill her, but I *had to*, Faythe. And I need you to tell me where the ruin is. It's all she wants, and it's all I was looking for. I searched everywhere, but you've hidden it on someone else. I sought the feather for Malin knowing he was working with her."

Faythe tunneled into so much grief in her silence.

"I need the ruin, Faythe. Tell me where it is." His voice took on a sharp edge she didn't recognize on him.

Faythe shook her head weakly. "I can't do that—"

Her cry turned to a gasp when the pain in her shoulder exploded to immobilize her. Reuben seethed as he twisted the handle while the blade was still lodged deep.

"I don't want to kill you," he begged with so much fear and conflict filling his brown irises. "But she's going to kill me. Kill us all if I don't have it."

Faythe should have seen it sooner. Seen *him* sooner. The guilt of failing him called out to her defeat. "You don't have to do this," she pleaded. "I forgive you. We can fight her together."

That turned his expression to stone, wiping all she knew of her childhood friend in an instant. "You are pitiful." Reuben let go, and Faythe braced a hand on the ground. "It has to be in the castle, and with you out of my way I will find it."

She watched his boots leave her vision, alone and vulnerable after he'd lured her right here. Bait. That's what Reuben was, and she had to find a way out before the real predator came.

Teeth clenched, she wrapped a shaky hand around the blade, knowing the blood loss would be dangerous but the Magestone could spread its poisonous effects faster if she left it submerged. Her heart pounded in her ears, a dizziness fogged her mind, and her body was slick with sweat and a fire that raged deep in and around the wound. She took one deep breath, and then, with a loud cry, pulled the blade free.

The pain exploded. Faythe sobbed. The blade clattered to the ground just as her other hand reached out to catch her from falling through the sweep of darkness she fought. She didn't get long to succumb to her agony. Many footsteps sounded around her in every direction, trapping her in the square. Faythe tried to search for her magick, forcing some to the surface, but like a burned-out wick her flame wouldn't catch.

Her fingers shuffled over the sandy stone, inch by inch, until they slipped over the hilt of her sword. At feeling the familiar leather grip, a new fight sparked within her. Before everything, she'd had this. Her blade. Lumarias. If that was all she had to go out with, it was enough.

Despite what felt like iron shackling her to the stone ground, she gripped Lumarias tight, and Faythe rose. Sheer adrenaline kept her from sinking back down with the wobble of her knees. She breathed steadily, forcing herself to look out over the damning odds, and she braced with her sword.

Those few seconds of suspense were measured in erratic heartbeats when no one moved. The first commotion ensued behind her, but when she whirled, it was not their advance that caused it. The soldiers behind her were all turning to face some threat at their backs.

A gust of air had Faythe whipping back around, and at seeing who was straightening from their crouch, reality spun away farther than it already was.

"Zaiana."

She wasn't sure if she spoke the dark fae's name aloud, but her partially predatory smile shone at Faythe's reaction. She'd grown accustomed to seeing Zaiana without wings; had almost convinced herself she was like them or could be. Yet now she was free, it was clear the side she had always stood on.

"We have to stop meeting like this," Zaiana drawled. "But I must admit, it is rather thrilling."

If Zaiana was free…

"What did you do to him?" Faythe asked in cold-set terror. Kyleer had been with her when the battle started. That had to have been where he'd headed.

A darkness so frightening blocked out every possibility except death from the dark fae's expression. "You and your foolish hearts," she answered. "It was his that became his end. Just as it will be yours. Fitting, really, how one by one you bring about your own downfall."

Her words replayed, desperate to find a new formation, but Faythe's hand was already clamped tighter around her sword, raising it a fraction higher. "You didn't kill him." She offered the chance for Zaiana to deny it, yet all she gave was a sinister look of challenge.

Her physical pain numbed to the anger and grief that consumed her in that second. Faythe's sword ricocheted off the dark fae's before she'd even noticed her steps to erase the distance. She didn't stop, using every ounce of strength she could find to parry with Zaiana, but it was like she wasn't even trying. The dark fae watched with an unreadable gaze while she humored Faythe's weak attacks.

Even in her new fae form, even with her new power, she was *weak*. One second of betrayal stripped back everything she had survived to be. Her eyes burned, but she still pushed on.

"Your fight is admirable," Zaiana said so quietly Faythe wondered if she even meant to let it slip.

She only surged with the condescension. It took her right back to the first time they battled, and Faythe was not enough then, and nor was she now. "You are the weak one, Zaiana," she spat. Ignoring the searing pain in her shoulder, she pushed harder, moved faster. "You see deceit in all good things that come before you."

"Better to be prepared than blindsided like you."

"He *cared* for you!" Faythe shouted, unable to accept Zaiana could have killed Kyleer after what she'd witnessed growing between them. "He saw something in you none of us wanted to."

"And he was *wrong.*" Zaiana pushed back.

Faythe had hit something in her. Their blades slipped off each other's, singing their rage and anguish above the noise of the battle around them as they paused, matching hard breaths.

"He wasn't," Faythe admitted. And then she saw the way to break Zaiana down was not with steel or hatred. "The biggest betrayal you will ever face is yourself. The biggest war within yourself."

"Being the hero is easy, Faythe." Zaiana's nostrils flared.

A delirious laugh escaped Faythe's lips. "Sure doesn't feel like it." She winced, trying to shift her injured shoulder. "I guess I'm not qualified for that role."

While they stood, Faythe tunneled into her magick, feeling it there but with an unsure numbness that convinced her it was stifled. Throwing everything she had into it, she cast her palm out toward the dark fae, expelling a brilliant gold flare that struck Zaiana and sent her flying backward, crashing through the falling structure of a home that swallowed her whole.

Twisting her blade, Faythe reeled into combat when the enemy lines broke to attack. She moved on instinct, but she wasn't alone when at last Rhyenelle soldiers joined her and the odds began to ease her seed of doubt. She had to get back to the castle; had to find Reylan before either vengeful Spirit could.

"You should not be here."

Faythe gasped at the deep, rough voice. Pulling her blade free from the gut of her enemy, she spared a quick glance at Agalhor who fell another. He met her bewildered look with blazing eyes—not out of anger at her, but at the many threats that targeted them.

He was here. This was real.

"Arguably, I wouldn't have expected you to be on the front line either," she commented, twisting around him to clash blades with another.

His laugh was so far from humor. "Go back to the city, Faythe. Soldiers will take you—"

"I won't leave you here."

"I have fought many battles, my dear. You have not."

"Nor will I if I'm kept from them."

Their conversation was short through the focus they kept on fending off the relentless attacks. Her blade slicked through black and silver blood of both the Born and Transitioned. Her next assailant let out a shrill cry when her blade came down on his wing, but it was a huge mistake as the steel lodged in the thick cartilage and she was forced to let it go. Faythe stumbled back at the sheer agony and wrath the dark fae spun to her with. Her stomach lurched when his head tumbled from his shoulders in one sickening swipe. She caught sight of the golden flicker of the Ember Sword.

Agalhor met her blanched look with a look that said, "This is not the battle for you." Her face steeled to protest, and she reached for her blade. It took the grim act of digging her foot into the dark fae's back to dislodge Lumarias.

Yet in the few seconds they faced off, Agalhor's expression eased to one of understanding.

"It terrifies me to see you here, Faythe. And I have every power to see to it that you aren't." Her protest rose until he spoke again. "Yet more so, it strikes me with the pride of my life."

Her face pinched at hearing that, awash with a determination she feared she was losing. This was confirmation she hadn't made a grave mistake in following her instinct here.

"How touching," a beautiful voice mocked.

Faythe turned her attention to Zaiana, finding the soldiers around them leaving this fight to her.

"Father and daughter going down together in battle. Poetic really." Zaiana retired her sword, but Faythe knew the most lethal weapon was already in her hands instead. The elegant point of those two metal-adorned fingers that sparked with alluring but deadly purple bolts.

"Faythe, go back to the inner city," Agalhor warned, not taking his calculating gaze from Zaiana.

"You might want to do as he says." Zaiana matched his stare, two opponents targeting each other with vengeance. "I don't think you want to witness your father's death."

"Your fight is with me," Faythe flared.

"You were never my fight, Faythe, only a mark to capture. Your father became my fight the moment he decided to infiltrate my mind."

Her heart couldn't be tamed, but she was ready to stand with him whatever it took. Agalhor couldn't die. This kingdom needed him in the aftermath of this battle, and for the greater war to come. *She* needed him, as a child who didn't get enough time. It was that urgency that pushed her forward, trying to gain Zaiana's attention, which had locked on the king as though Faythe were not there anymore.

"He shouldn't have done that," Faythe agreed. "But if you kill him, there is nothing that will stop me from coming for you."

Zaiana didn't flinch, nor did she give a single indication her words meant anything. "You had your warning to flee," was all she said, the lightning growing, her stance shifting. "You can't say I am not merciful when it is you who chose to witness this."

Zaiana sent her lightning for Agalhor with one hand, and sheer impulse had Faythe casting her own power out. It clashed with her second flare. The first must have struck Agalhor, but she couldn't turn back to look.

Faythe stiffened her legs against the pulsing blast they held. Her will to protect roused a violence that threw a blanket over *weakness* and made her believe in the impossible. Bracing, she sent their joint current skyward. Thunder boomed overhead, illuminating the entire sky.

Agalhor groaned, shuddering with the waves of electricity as he got to his feet. But Zaiana was fast, already braced with both hands, summoning a current that could kill.

"Please!" Faythe yelled, having nothing else, *nothing* that could stop her before she struck. "Please. He's all I have left." Desperation drew her plea, her knees near buckling if that was what it would take.

Zaiana wasn't entirely unfeeling. She wasn't devoid of care. Faythe had seen it many times, though thanks to her cruel upbringing, the dark fae would never see it. It was what made her hesitate in this moment, braced with the current to kill but hearing Faythe's cry. Her gaze finally tore from her target to meet Faythe in her final verdict.

"You're wrong," Zaiana said quietly. "You have far better."

All Faythe heard was the sealing of Agalhor's fate, the dark fae's mind made up despite the seconds she'd managed to buy. Faythe moved faster than she ever had in her short life, damning everything to step into the path of Zaiana's flare, which grew to a deadly current.

Before she could unleash her storm, time slowed to a crawl.

Then stopped.

Through the stuttered breath that left her she refused to believe what she felt.

Heard.

The bright amethyst charge in front of her began to fade until the light on Zaiana's face switched from white to the amber glow of the natural fire that destroyed it. Rain began to fall, but Faythe couldn't feel it. She only watched it start slowly until it became a filter between her and Zaiana, who hadn't dropped eye contact. With the second choke that struck her spine hard, the ground was pulled from under her, and she forced herself to turn around and see what her mind had clouded with complete denial.

Faythe saw him.

Them.

Saw the glint of the steel and Magestone blade slick with crimson protruding through Agalhor's chest.

Her stare locked on the talons of the towering wings that led down to the face of her nightmares.

There were no words to describe what overcame Faythe in that second. She didn't believe she'd ever recall the moment she erupted from the inside out. A violent scream tore up her throat though she didn't hear it. The edges of her vision were diffused in gold. Fire devoured her. Then expelled from her. Not in flame but something beautifully lethal. Gold dust that blasted through the entire square, hitting everyone but him.

Her father.

Faythe's palms splayed wide and trembled by her side. Her hair whipped around her, and the rain couldn't touch her. She kept screaming until the vibrations of the ground no longer trembled through her. She became weightless. Power surged through every internal piece of her, and for a moment she believed it would destroy her.

Until the sound that lifted from her throat died out. Her vision began to bring back the real grim colors of her world that had turned gilded before her.

Then everything stilled at once.

She was falling.

Falling.

Falling.

The snap back into herself whipped like a lashing. Faythe pressed her cheek to the wet stone as she slowly came to, scrambling her thoughts to gather who she was, where she was, and what she had done.

Her whole body shook with tremors. She dragged her hands up to brace herself. The symbols within her palms slowly died out and exhaustion began to sweep in, taking the place of the power she'd summoned in reckless, raging desperation.

One thing slipped through her memory as she pushed herself up.

The reason *why* she had done it.

Faythe found Agalhor lying still against the cold, wet ground, no other bodies around him as though the gold particles the wind and rain swept away were all that was left of the fallen. She forced herself to stand. Walked to him on weak legs. Her sword caught her like a crutch a few times. Her steps dragged slow, begging for him to get up before she could make it there and discover the worst.

Get up. Get up.

Faythe might have slipped the words aloud, as if her need alone could raise the king.

Not a flicker of movement answered her.

She gave in to her boneless knees, falling by his side. "You'll be okay," she said, shaky hands going over his. Faythe pressed down on the wound, but blood flooded over her fingers. Her mouth opened and closed. She didn't know what else to say.

Think.

She had to *think*.

A blank mind mocked her, but she shook her head against it. Scrunched her eyes shut. She listened, straining hard through the pulse of her eardrums that felt stuffed with cotton.

A heartbeat.

Her lids snapped open.

Alive.

Shuffling on her knees, Faythe applied more pressure, frustrated when he kept *bleeding*.

"Help." The word was a weak croak. Her breaths came hard as she looked over his peaceful face, and her jaw flexed with the desire to glare at the sky for the rain that disturbed him. "I'll get help."

That was all they needed. A healer. He would be just fine as soon as they got to one.

"Faythe."

Her name, his voice, erupted in her chest. No matter the strain, he was alive.

The king's head lolled weakly to her, but that didn't matter— he would be up in no time.

"I'll need to leave you here just for a moment, but I can be quick." Panic began to seize her with his consciousness only half-there. "One time I raced my friend, Jakon. I beat him by no competition," she laughed, tears falling, but she sniffed hard to plaster on a brave face. Agalhor's eyes fluttered, but she gripped his hands as if they were tethering him here. Keeping him with her. She forced a smile. "You didn't get to hear half the antics we got up to in Farrowhold. I think some would make you laugh."

"Faythe—"

She shook her head, eyes pressing shut for a moment. "Mother didn't like it when I would climb trees," she rushed out.

Time ticked loud, raced too fast, and she begged it—*begged it*—to slow, but it sped *faster* with the dawning realization that there were so many things he didn't know. Pointless things, childish things, but she wanted to tell him everything.

"Because I...I always went too far...too high. A-apples, I...I was always reaching for the apples, but the best ones were always the most stubbornly placed." She huffed a shaky, delirious laugh. "Why is that?" she thought suddenly. "Why are the things we want the most always just out of reach?" Faythe kept blinking her blurry vision, hoping he couldn't distinguish her tears from the rain. "It's as if life tries to tell us some things aren't meant to be, like when I fell and broke my arm once, passing so many apples on the way down, but there was only one I wanted."

Agalhor tried to smile, but his response came as barely a croak. "I bet that didn't stop you from reaching again."

Faythe shifted closer, trembling stiffly. But her smile broke to a grin for him. "You would win that bet."

He huffed a laugh, but it twisted to agony as he stared up at the sky. "It's your turn now, Faythe."

She shook her head vigorously, tightening her eyes in utter denial. "Don't. Don't say that."

"Listen, my dear—"

"I *can't*," she broke. Like a flood Faythe sobbed in complete helplessness, unable to accept his fading life beneath her. "I'm not ready. This kingdom needs you."

A SWORD FROM THE EMBERS

"Not when it has you."

Faythe's cries were unlocked, arriving hard and with a grieving pain that tore her soul deep.

"Shh," Agalhor tried to soothe, but she couldn't stop. This couldn't be all they had. She still had so much to learn from him, so much to tell him and show him. He couldn't *leave* her. "Did you know this was where I met your mother?"

That forced her to painfully clamp down on the sobs that cut off her airway, tightening her lips against their harsh escape. Agalhor raised a hand to point, shaking so badly she couldn't bear it. She bit down on her lip hard to taste blood, but no pain short of her own life would be enough to counter this agony.

"Right there. She sold the best pastries in the city."

Faythe wiped her sniffling nose.

He met her gaze with a twinkle of joy—each harboring different memories of her mother but the same love. Agalhor reached for his sword, taking her hand to wrap it around the hilt.

"You'll know what to do with it."

Her sobs couldn't be silenced anymore.

"If all seems lost then it is not the end, Faythe. Lead our people to that world you dream of. Make it rise from these ashes. From the moment I saw you…I knew you had it in you. Knowing you and watching how much you have grown since coming here…it has been my life's joy." His hand almost couldn't make it, so she took it, resting her cheek in his palm though it cleaved her heart in half. "My daughter."

"We didn't have enough time," she whispered.

"You have to believe your mother is watching all that you have become. I am ready, Faythe—I have been for some time—to see her again. Keep telling me your stories and know that we will both be with you in every step as you rise to all you were destined to be."

Faythe didn't look at his peaceful face when his eyes slipped closed for the final time. Her teeth clenched so tight they might break, and her body jerked in silence with the urge to release her violent sob—but she didn't want it to be the last thing he heard.

"Thank you, father," she said in a high-pitched voice, taking a moment to breathe through the suffocation. "For believing in me."

She stayed with him until the very end. Her tears fell in silence while she rocked, holding his hand and filtering out the rain to count his weakening heartbeat. Faythe stilled as the last thump resonated to a silence so cold and final she could do nothing but kneel to the mercy of fading hope.

She doubled over, arms folding into herself, unleashing a cry that shook the earth in her loss. It tore from her relentlessly, the grief of all that dawned in that second.

A fate sealed.

A kingdom on the brink of collapse.

An heir thrust into power too soon.

Agalhor Ashfyre, the King of Rhyenelle, was dead.

CHAPTER 91

Zaiana

IN THE SECONDS she had to react to Faythe's explosion, Zaiana chose the only thing that might spare her wings over everything. She threw up her glamour and summoned a lightning shield in the nick of time. It saved her from incineration, but not from injury.

Zaiana groaned, coughing dust from her throat in the heap of debris, her attempt to move blocked entirely from all angles. She found herself buried under wood and rocks. A pounding battered her head and agony tore through her limbs, but she began to claw at what she could.

With a sharp cry she realized a thick wooden pole had speared her side and fell back down. When a clamor started from somewhere nearby, Zaiana's instincts brought lightning to her fingertips. Light flashed across her vision as a large piece of debris was shifted to grant her an opening. She raised the threat of her bolts until the face blinked into clarity.

Maverick swore, carefully shoveling and maneuvering debris until he kneeled beside her. His hands curled around the wood. "I've dreamed about you crying out for me again," he said, and her complete incredulity at the comment distracted her the second he pulled the rod free. Agony clawed her throat. "Though not quite like this."

She didn't have the energy to voice the string of profanities she wanted to. But damn, if she wasn't chanting them in her mind over and over as she did nothing but accept his help.

Zaiana peeled herself up, desperate to be free. She was saved from a lot of effort as he pulled her from the wreckage instead. She didn't fight the warm force of him holding her tight while she regained full conscious and reoriented herself. His hand stroked her nape while they caught their breath. Her ear pressed to his chest, and it was so still, so quiet. Yet in her own way, she knew its familiar echo.

Pulling back, their closeness, those pitch-black eyes, inspired a conflict of so much reckless, dangerous emotion. Zaiana scanned him, noticing his wings were also gone, black blood smeared across his face, which she almost reached for.

She hated him. *Hated him.*

"He was mine," she snarled, pushing away from him, and their battle returned. "The order to kill him was *mine.*"

The skin around his eyes creased. "You hesitated."

"I would have killed him."

"I know."

She couldn't decipher what crossed his face, but rage flexed on hers knowing he'd caught her flicker of weakness. At hearing Faythe's plea, a part of her had given a second thought to what she was about to do, but her mind hadn't changed. Not with what he'd done to her.

Zaiana stepped up to Maverick, near touching him though he stood a foot taller. "This is the last time you undermine me," she warned, letting as much threat to his life as possible seep into her tone.

His fingers grazed her waist, a distraction that caused them to detect the energy too late. Power blasted into them, sending them careening into the wall. Maverick took most of the impact with the arm he hooked around her. When they met the ground again,

Zaiana was already up, charging her lightning while Maverick took a moment to recover.

What stood before them was neither fae nor human. A familiar face but harnessed by something frightening that they had unleashed.

Pure, undiluted energy radiated from Faythe, emitting a golden outward aura. The tattoos in her palms and through the cuts of her leathers burned as brightly as the suns glowing in her irises, barely broken by the defiance of her pupils.

Blue fire shot for her, yet with a mere raise of her hand, Faythe caught it and added to it before sending the huge ball of flame barreling toward them. Maverick stepped out to disperse his element, but not without challenge.

The two of them erupted.

He darted away, calling Faythe on a chase. For the first time in her life, Zaiana was completely baffled about what to do. Her shock paused any immediate reaction as she watched the rage unleashing in Faythe's attacks. She was using a power she would suffer for later, but she didn't seem to care.

Agalhor was dead. He had to be. It was the only reason Faythe would care to come after them so vengefully. After Maverick at least, because it was as if Zaiana didn't exist in this battle despite being close to going through with it herself.

Watching them…she knew Maverick would lose. What the heir was in that moment was an unparalleled force. A power Zaiana could only compare to the ruin itself. She should let Faythe kill him —let her have that revenge that would never know rest until it was done.

Yet something in her own selfish, foolish mind had already decided she couldn't stand by and watch.

Her lightning formed, but she waited, gathering, knowing it would take no small attack to stop her. Maverick and Faythe darted around the open space, blue flame shooting among golden bursts, an otherwise magnificent spectacle. Maverick's cry snapped the tether on Zaiana's control as he was brought to his knees, and it was all she could do to stop herself from running toward them and sending her lightning straight for Faythe.

She might have caught Zaiana's intention before she even acted. Her hand cast out, and though Zaiana winced for the impact...Faythe *absorbed* the bolts, curling into herself while she watched the purple snap over her hand, adjusting to its feel.

"If you want to live, you damn bastard, *go!*" she barked at Maverick.

Maybe together they could take her down, but Zaiana had decided now wasn't the time to test it. Both of them unglamoured their wings, ready to shoot skyward as their only means of escape.

Yet just as Maverick splayed his wings, Faythe called out: "*Callen!*"

Her tone was as striking as the lightning she played with, but Faythe had no concept of how to wield the ability Zaiana had foolishly unlocked within her. It slowly winked out from her grasp.

That single word—a name, she thought—was enough to halt Maverick from his flight, and Zaiana could have killed him herself.

"So you do remember," Faythe said.

The rain pattered down enough to weigh down their clothes, but not enough to diminish the fires around them that danced with anguish. Maverick gave no response, but Zaiana studied the recognition that tightened his face. Now it was her turn to be stunned with a flicker of familiarity...a missing piece that was right there but she couldn't find its place.

"I hoped you wouldn't," Faythe went on. "At least then maybe I could understand that fae died and a monster replaced him. That fae who had a kingdom and a mate he loved."

"Stop," Maverick growled. "You don't know a *thing.*"

Zaiana had never seen him so threatening and *vulnerable.* Two contrasting feelings that whipped through her, and she didn't know what to make of the exchange.

"Go. Now," Zaiana ordered. Her wet skin crawled with the anticipation that the two of them were seconds away from exploding again.

Faythe's head tipped back against the rain, her eyes slipping closed as though she were...*elsewhere*. Meeting eyes with Maverick, Zaiana blazed her order once again through that look alone.

He had a chance to flee, yet he was hesitating.

What caught Zaiana's attention almost made her stumble back. It did cause her to move several steps away from Maverick.

Faythe was drawing fire. Not like Maverick's—not the cobalt kind of magick. This fire blazed a shimmering red, the sight calling out to a familiar impossibility that lay just out of reach. Zaiana watched in astonishment as it began in Faythe's hands but didn't grow there. It crawled like a smoky veil up her arms, touching between her shoulder blades, where it began to gather...and *form*. She couldn't tear her eyes away though the urgency that screamed at her to retreat because their one advantage was about to be matched.

Wings.

Zaiana couldn't believe the wings of flame so blazing and bright that began to expand from Faythe's back. Fire of a kind she had only seen once before.

From the Phoenix.

"*Go!*" Zaiana yelled, and Maverick didn't falter this time.

Neither did Faythe.

Shooting skyward, she lagged behind them only for a second to test those ethereal wings, but then she crouched, and Zaiana mirrored her, and it became a race to get to Maverick.

It shouldn't have been possible for Faythe to fly so well even with the means to do so, yet Zaiana couldn't rule out anything when it wasn't just her storming with vengeance through the skies. Now she was something *more*.

The rain hit harder, and as they were swallowed by angry clouds visibility became a hurdle. Zaiana tracked Faythe by the brightness of her wings and the tattoos that shone through their grim surroundings. She caught flickers of pure black—Maverick attempting to lose her. Gold charged in Faythe's palms, and before she could send it hurtling for him, Zaiana reacted on instinct, conjuring her lightning and striking it at Faythe.

Just in time, Faythe twirled in the air, her gold blast meeting amethyst in a beautiful but staggering explosion. They both let go at once, and Zaiana faltered, falling a few feet before pulsing her wings to stay in the air. She panted hard, quickly reorienting herself and recharging while she snapped her gaze up. Faythe blazed eyes of no mercy at her. Zaiana's chest faintly wrenched to see it. How deeply Faythe had to be hurting to have come to this...

"This is what you wanted," Faythe cried, the echo of her voice sounding otherworldly. "To match battle in the skies. Well, here I am, Zaiana."

Yet it wasn't for Zaiana to choose when Faythe attacked again. Her wings beat hard, and she strained her shoulder blades to narrowly miss the gold flare. There was no pause for breath as she found herself outmatched. Panic began to rise, but she honed every ounce of her battle focus to survive.

"This isn't you," Zaiana called out, twisting and darting when Faythe didn't relent. "You don't want to kill me."

Faythe chuckled—a dark, foreign sound from the fae she'd spent time trying to figure out. She'd even somewhat admired what could lie under the surface of her kind composure. But this...it was reckless power, heartache, and rage, fueling actions that would not stitch the wound that would continue to cleave her from within even when she achieved her task. Zaiana knew this.

"You would have killed him," Faythe seethed through her teeth, rain spraying from her mouth with harsh breaths. She couldn't hold it much longer—the wings, perhaps the power. Zaiana thought she would falter soon. "You are no better than Maverick, and I know what you mean to him. If you are foolish enough to offer yourself in his place, so be it."

Faythe charged a frightening light. From her palms, which faced each other, grew an orb of energy so dangerous it rippled through her even from a distance. It charged the air to stand every hair despite the rain. Zaiana wouldn't survive the strike of it. Maybe neither of them would. Panic drew her quick breaths as her mind grappled with survival.

Zaiana winced, calling out in utter fear, "You were right!"

A SWORD FROM THE EMBERS

The blow never came, and she dared to meet the gaze of one so close to erupting the force of the sun, uncaring if she went down in the blast.

"I did care for him."

Words, confessions, were all she had left now that Faythe's power was unmatched.

"You betrayed him," Faythe said, her voice low, trembling with the orb she held ready to destroy them at any second.

The clouds began to disperse with the piercing light chasing them away. Zaiana looked down to see the destruction the invasion had caused. Buildings still caught fire, but the streets were empty and quiet, not like the screaming and chaos she expected. It was as though the citizens knew how to find shelter; knew how to surrender.

"I didn't want to," Zaiana said, not caring anymore if Faythe could hear her over the rain and magnetic hum of her magick. "He didn't deserve it." The void in her expanded, flashing the image of Kyleer's last look of horror and heartbreak.

"For a moment I thought there was a chance with you. I had a fleeting vision of what could be if you chose our side. But I realize now," Faythe said, her final words indicating she'd made up her mind, just as Zaiana had in the seconds she ignored Faythe's plea, having every intention of taking her father from her, "you have no allegiance. This…this is doing you a favor. And by killing you, I'll hurt Maverick far more than his own death sentence ever could."

Zaiana turned, spying the open courtyard of the castle and making out the many bodies gathered there. She wondered if they were watching their spectacle in the sky. Yet she had to blink the water from her eyes as she recognized one in particular straining against the many fae who held him. He might have been calling out for his mate, but Faythe gave no indication she could hear him above all that consumed her.

Time was measured in a countdown of breaths. Feeling Faythe's charge building, Zaiana reached to the very depths of her well for one last strike. Maybe it would be fitting for them to go out together after all they'd been through.

As Faythe's undiluted magick surged for her, Zaiana threw her all into an attack in a clash of power. The moment gold met amethyst....

The world erupted.

Energy surged through her in a burst of stars. Every nerve cell exploded. Right down to her bones she absorbed a power like she'd never felt before. Both her palms splayed and shook violently against their joined current, and she pushed with everything she had, but it wouldn't be enough. Faythe was stronger. She was winning.

If this was how she would go, Zaiana was surprised at the emotion that rushed, flooded, *drowned* her. One word screamed on repeat.

Sorry.

She was sorry for so much. For so many people. But most of all, she was sorry to herself. For not becoming anything. For not finding her freedom when she didn't know what the word truly meant. What she wanted and dreamed... *Gods,* she was sorry for not allowing herself to dream more.

Only when time raced to a final beat did she realize she didn't want to die. Not when she hadn't *lived*. Only when she thought of what could have been did she regret not trying *harder*.

Over three hundred years and she could count with one hand how many days held a memory worth remembering.

Zaiana wanted to feel. She wanted to love—something foolish she had been denied for so long, yet she knew its touch of blurred madness and euphoria. It was a drug she had craved since she got her first taste, but she'd worn shackles that had bound her from reaching for it again.

Now...it was all too late to know what would happen if she dared to break free.

A flicker of blue caught in her vision before the fragments of her reality obliterated. That blinding, reckoning current that connected them surged skyward, severing as if she'd been cleaved in two. Then she was falling, the fire within still devouring her despite gravity and time and element.

A SWORD FROM THE EMBERS

Zaiana cut through the sky like a sharpened blade, deserving to have her bones shatter on the ground. She couldn't feel her wings or her limbs. Her misery numbed her to feel nothing but the air that wrapped around her.

The darkness called, and she didn't fight it, taking its hand as she fell to a still, depthless oblivion.

CHAPTER 92

Reylan

REYLAN KEPT HIS orders calm though he knew what they faced was no small battle. While directing soldiers and making sure they stuck to protocol no matter how many stages had to be skipped, he was internally calculating how they could have gotten so far so fast.

The conclusion was blaring, so his next merciless thought was *who*.

The city of Ellium was strategically built. A long wall ran along the perimeter as the inner and outer city defense, and Reylan had gone to the half that hadn't been infiltrated from the main city gate. They ushered as many citizens as they could through the middle city gates before they were sealed and soldiers set out to fight there. Meanwhile, Reylan was seeing to it that the evacuation took place.

This half of the city was silent, all fires snuffed out while the back city gates opened and the citizens began to leave, heading for the outskirt towns. Reylan couldn't let go of the itch to be on the other side fighting with his warriors against the enemy that rained terror on his kingdom.

"General, the city is almost clear," a lead commander informed him.

That lifted his shoulders with relief. "Send a legion to join them. Everyone finds shelter and safety. And if the city is taken, they surrender."

The commander nodded, and Reylan was unable to stand the desolate look that cracked his firm composure. He felt it too. No one had ever made it this far for the protocol to be enforced. Surrender and disband...

No, they still had a chance to fight.

He didn't waste a second now he could head to the other side. Reylan marched along the silent wall, reaching another commander.

"Once the last of the citizens are out, lock the gates. The rest of the soldiers, send them across the wall immediately."

"Have we lost, General?"

"Never," Reylan said firmly. "Even if the city falls, it will not be for long. Even if they triumph this night, Rhyenelle will never last in malicious hands."

He was sure of that. No matter what happened, they would always have the means to take the city back, and he would delight in the opportunity to tear the unlawful suitor limb from limb.

Reylan was moving again, leaving the commanders in charge on this side of the wall while he raced to lead the true battle. His skin crawled as he thought of Faythe. When he had retrieved his sword, he would check on her.

A rumble halted him. It started as a low vibration, but then it stole the night with ear-splitting thunder. He knew exactly what it was when he felt it beneath his feet and *saw* the wall coming down.

"Get everyone off the wall!" he barked.

Warriors began scrambling for a way down, some leaping, others taking the painstakingly long flight of stairs, and he cursed, unable to move until he was sure everyone had made it off. He extended his magick, feeling and *hoping* to the Gods that luck was in his favor.

Pain shot through him, so powerful and consuming he had to brace a hand on the rumbling stone just to draw steady breath. *Faythe.* It had to be her. He cast his gaze up to find a faint dusting of gold in the distance and knew immediately what she was doing. Buying them time. *Gods,* she was brilliant.

Reylan forced himself to straighten with clenched teeth, but his balance didn't last for long when the wall began to come down around his fumbling steps. He reached out one last desperate time, and just as he was falling, he found it.

Reylan pulled the Shapeshifting ability from the direction he found it, not knowing who it came from, but that it was enough for him to shift into an eagle. He tried desperately to fly out of the path of the debris.

A rock clipped his wing, and then Reylan was falling, tumbling and barely able to find flight again with the agony that tore through him. He kept trying, beating his wings against the desire to falter. He flew over the dividing wall toward the castle, and that was as far as he made it before he had to let go.

Reylan shifted on the courtyard, clutching his arm when it twisted to an awkward angle. Falling to his knees, he removed his jacket just as a soldier came rushing over.

"General, you should get inside. Shall I fetch a healer?"

He shook his head, sweat coating his body. There was no time for that. He had to get to Faythe. "I need to you fix it back into place."

At the fae's silence, Reylan met his blanched look with firm command, and the fae shifted around to Reylan's side. He bit down hard, gave one short nod, and braced.

The sound was worse than the pain, but it was also a relief since his arm no longer felt disconnected. Reylan didn't hesitate to rise, trying to flex his arm and willing his healing to work *faster.*

An echo came to him. Her voice. Yet it was not elation he felt when he couldn't make out words, only feelings. Love. Apology. Both doused him with utter dread at whatever Faythe was planning.

Just as he was about to take off, a fiery figure obscured his path. Reylan straightened with the blaring acknowledgement of who was advancing for him. Alone, her red hair complimented the amber that torched the night sky. Her ruby gown made a mockery of Rhyenelle wears, her legs exposed in combat leathers, which only told him she didn't plan to stand idle. She had come prepared to participate.

"Reylan Arrowood." She drawled his name, and something about the way she spoke tugged with a familiarity he couldn't place. "Look how you thrived without her. In status, in name. Pitiful how you couldn't stay away."

"Marvellas," he said, only to be sure he could speak, and when the name spilled from him, he had to fight against his confusion at having been here before.

Her slow, elegant walk halted a few paces away. The Spirit's head inclined curiously as she studied him, and her assessment curled her red-painted lips. "I wondered for some time if you would recognize me when we came face-to-face."

Reylan shook his head to clear the nagging confusion. He did recognize her, only with a blaze of desire to kill her for the harm she'd inflicted on Faythe.

Marvellas went on. "Though it seems she is far stronger in her gift than I originally thought all that time ago. You should have resisted, General. You should have seen this coming."

"I saw you coming," he growled. Reylan extended his senses. "And I'm glad you sought me out first."

Her chuckle vibrated over him with a haunting caress. "Some things never change, and you will never learn. If I can't have her, Reylan Arrowood, neither can you."

"General, I can't—"

Reylan heard the panic of the guard who'd helped him just in time to step out of the path of his blade. Muttering a quick apology, Reylan twisted around him, landing his elbow to the guard's head as the quickest means of sending him to unconsciousness.

He didn't get a second to think beyond survival when he knew what Marvellas was capable of. The pull of strings had him snatching up the guard's fallen blade. Tuning in to the arrow's flight path, he pivoted on his heel, swiping his sword in the nick of time to slice through the arrow midair.

"Impressive, but we're just getting started," Marvellas called out.

Nearly a dozen guards ran toward him with horror-struck looks at their ally target, but their movements were not their own; Marvellas stood with cruel amusement, driving the attack in their minds. He gritted his teeth, overcome with rage and a will to charge for her, but he wouldn't make it to her first. Reylan felt over the courtyard and seized the rippling essence of Firewielding.

Instinct took over, but it required far more focus because he couldn't kill his own warriors. Faces he'd trained with; males who trusted him. No matter they'd been manipulated to kill him—he couldn't target the same back.

Blue flame licked along the blade he clashed with, and the guard cried out at the heat scorching his palms. Reylan winced with guilt at every blow he had to deal to get them to stop. His movements became impulse, his surroundings a blur. One by one he fell them, catching arrows that soared for him, and no matter what, he did not falter.

Faythe was out there, and he would do anything to get to her. Or at least to make sure Marvellas couldn't get there first.

On his next spin, Reylan didn't anticipate he'd be staring into blazing amber eyes. For the first time he stalled, only a second before his mind realized they weren't Faythe's. But something else caught him off-guard.

The hatred emanating between them felt...*rekindled.*

The distraction was enough that he didn't detect the next arrow until pain ripped up his side. Marvellas pushed off his blade, striking from his shoulder to his abdomen. The pain fell him to one knee. She could have run him through, but she didn't. Reylan clutched the arrow protruding out of him, gathering a few deep breaths of preparation before he tore it free. His vision swayed with the agony, but he cast his gaze up to find what had made her hesitate.

The loathing eased from her face as she tossed the blade aside. "If I kill you, she will never come with me. She will never stop fighting." Marvellas seemed to be thinking out loud. She crouched slowly. "Instead, I will use her own cunning to get her to remember what we had before you ruined it all. *You—*" Her hand lashed out to his jaw with a surprising grip. Reylan jerked out of it, but he was weak to defend himself when his wounds bled freely, and his energy was dwindling. "This is all your fault. She didn't need your poisonous influence when she was safe with me."

Reylan couldn't make full sense of her words, but one thing was certain. She was speaking of Faythe.

His Faythe.

And that was enough to cancel out his pain with sheer adrenaline and determination. He lunged for her. Marvellas choked when his bloodied hands wrapped around her throat. He squeezed, the urge to kill her coming seconds from shattering her windpipe when a shadow cast a veil across the courtyard.

"You cannot kill a true immortal being," a dark feminine voice called over them. "But the same cannot be said for this one."

Reylan looked up to find an impossible number of bodies had Shadowported here. There could only be one with the strength to transport several dozen fae. The daunting conclusion dawned upon him.

The original wielder.

Reylan's hands slackened on Marvellas as Dakodas emerged from the center of her shadows. Slowly, they began to ease back to her as if she absorbed the darkness. As if she were made of it.

Marvellas stood livid with fury, touching her neck but in need of no recovery from his attack. Reylan fixed his stare on the snakelike elegance of the one whom the Dark Spirit walked with. All she brought forth in him was an all-consuming rage...a patchy memory of the temple. He'd wanted to kill her then, and as the reminder of how Faythe's life had been sacrificed for her to walk these steps toward him, his wrath and vengeance returned to him so violently he trembled where he stood.

"Reylan Arrowood," she drawled across the space. Her black-painted lips curled cruelly. "I've been looking for you."

It wasn't her voice but the soft cries that followed it that torched his blood. The cruel hand gripping Livia's arm pulled her along, and Reylan could only picture ripping apart the one who held her limb from limb. He wore a full-black mask, but Reylan would never forget a thing about him. His insufferable swagger, his sickening scent. Reylan's fists already trembled, refraining from a reckless explosion.

His uncle had surrounded himself with dark fae and raiders. It had always been him. Reylan could never forgive himself for foolishly overlooking the greater mastermind who'd been tracking them for so long. What Livia and Faythe and all of them would pay the price for.

Coming to a halt a few paces away, the air between them grew so thick he could hardly stand to inhale. "Evander," Reylan bit out through gritted teeth, not leaving him the chance to dance around his denial.

"I've waited a long time for this." His uncle spoke, each word like a razor over his skin. A voice of pure loathing he thought he'd never hear again. "After all I made of you, what a pitiful thing you have become. Even when given a second chance you allowed her to weaken you entirely."

Flashes of the night he'd last seen him filtered through Reylan's mind. Threatened his composure. Only fragments. He couldn't recall every hit and break and slice he'd made in the rage that had snapped him.

"Let her go." Reylan tilted his chin to Livia, not breaking their intense stare. "Your fight is with me."

Evander's vile hand stroked her hair, and Reylan flinched with a snarl.

"I'm going to enjoy killing you again," he growled.

"You have made quite the name for yourself, I must say.

General Reylan Arrowood, famous white lion of the south," he drawled in sheer mockery.

"Why do you hide?" Reylan taunted. "Are you afraid to show them what is left of you by my hand?"

A sudden tug within him drew out the most damning rage. Never before had he been faced with two dire urgencies. His will to go to Faythe tore at something that shook his confidence in the confrontation he faced now. Reylan could evade them. Outrun them. Kill them. Do whatever it took to get to his mate.

But he couldn't leave Livia with the monster of their past.

Hold on, please, he begged into a vast void that felt too distant from her, but he didn't stop chanting all he could in the hope she would hear him and not be alone.

"You want to see what you did to me?" His uncle's dark tone rippled the air as he reached for the back of his mask. As he peeled it away, even Reylan was struck by the horror of the sight.

The missing flesh of his lip permanently exposed a few bottom teeth. He kept both eyes, but one lid could barely blink closed. His skin was a lattice of raised scars, not an inch untouched. A part of Reylan turned in revulsion to know he was the hand that had inflicted such lifelong injuries on a fae—but the far more dominant part of him sought satisfaction in the fact, knowing everything worse his uncle had done to others. Including him and Livia.

"If I were you, I would have stayed dead."

"You didn't kill me," Evander spat.

"Did you come here for your revenge—is that it? After all this time, you still think of me."

"Yes. What kept me going was picturing the day I'd get to face you and inflict it all back upon you, so I can leave you to heal and do it all again and again. I've had a long time—who knows when I will be satisfied? Or…"

Once again, Reylan had to fight against a violence so consuming when Evander took Livia's chin, her eyes widening with a fear he'd so rarely seen since she took her life back with vengeance.

"You can have me," Reylan barked. "Trade my place with hers."

That earned him a sinister smile. "I don't know, nephew. I see how much she means to you. I am well aware of your impressive physical endurance, though there remains something to be broken in you. But perhaps the way to do it…is through her."

"Evander!" Reylan growled.

Reylan was so close to snapping that it was all he could do to halt Evander's wicked assessment of Livia. It was as if he were eyeing the weakest spots to know how to make the biggest impact with the least hits. Reylan could disarm one of them—that was all it would take, and then he would cut through them all one by one if he had to. He didn't calculate numbers, only movements.

"Make the trade."

The cold voice eased out from behind him. Reylan's shadowy gaze slid to Malin Ashfyre with nothing short of fury. He should have known. On some level he always suspected the bastard would turn on them all if the prize was right. And that had to be Faythe's crown at the end of this.

"You traitorous bastard." Reylan took one step toward him but halted as if he'd connected with stone. The prod in his mind felt oddly, *damningly* familiar… "You stole what was left of the feather," he concluded. It was the only explanation for the ability akin to Faythe's he now harbored. Who he'd found to make and activate the Phoenix Blood potions seemed insignificant, yet that question too was answered when a blonde head stepped out, lingering by the castle doors, as always accompanied by…

Reylan shook his head in disbelief, unable to comprehend what Faythe could have done in their eyes to be deserving of such betrayal. Marlowe tried to appear confident; it was only in Jakon's eyes he might have seen an apology, but Reylan couldn't accept a single note of it.

Marlowe had created the potions.

A deadly weapon now wielded by the greatest foe.

"Unfortunately, it doesn't last long," Malin decided to share.

Dipping into his pocket, he pulled out a vial of glittering crimson. "Fortunately, however, we have a lot of them."

"You can't expect a kingdom to bow before a betrayer."

"A savior," Malin corrected. "They will not know of this, only that I was the one to put an end to the terror before the city could fall completely. What the lords will see is that they were wrong to believe in Faythe when *she* is the betrayer."

Reylan resisted the urge to claw the triumphant chuckle from the prince's throat.

"She thinks she won them with her poetic tale of the Firebird and her fitness to rule, but she has given me exactly what I need. A culprit. How shameful they will feel for believing her word for a second when she stole the Phoenix feather, brought our kingdom to the brink of ruin, and killed her own father, their beloved king. This entire kingdom will despise the day she ever set foot on Rhyenelle land."

Reylan recoiled, the darkest trepidation of his existence coiling in his spine. Tightening at the sinister gleam in Malin's smile as he relished in how everything had been turned in his favor.

"You did not know? Agalhor went to aid his foolish daughter when word got out that she'd wandered to a place too out of her depth of experience."

She went to find Reuben. Reylan drew the conclusion quickly, having known the human was out there when he passed through the city on his return earlier that night. *Of course she went for him.* He cursed himself for not remembering sooner. It was a fatal error he was all too familiar with, and the haunting grip of his past threatened to undo him helplessly.

He couldn't lose her again. *Fail* her again.

"The girl is a walking, bleeding heart. And now the death of her father is blood on her hands."

"That's not true," Reylan snapped. There would be no bringing her back if Agalhor died and she believed herself to be at fault.

A loud blast sounded distantly, and everyone became alert. A gold light laced with amethyst flared skyward and sent the earth trembling before breaking into rainfall. Faythe's power was unmistakable, and the other...

The odds stacked slowly, tipping the world, and Reylan struggled to grasp the tethers of his composure wondering how the dark fae got out—but more so, what she could have done to Kyleer. He was not where Reylan had expected him to be in their protocol.

So many lives, everyone he held dear, and he had nothing. Nothing but himself to offer up to whatever Gods held a shred of mercy to take him.

"The trade." Reylan drew their attention back. "You get me, you let her go." He turned to Malin with such hatred every muscle strained against the urge to kill him. "You end this terror, but you let Faythe leave with Livia. You will have the throne."

"It's good to know you can calculate with an ounce of brains instead of brute force," Malin drawled, sparing a quick look at Evander with the last words. "You heard him."

His uncle's jaw worked with reluctance, as though he'd hoped to gain both of them. It was unusual to watch him submit to authority. Why he cared to answer the pathetic fae under a false crown Reylan couldn't quite figure out.

"Come here then, nephew," Evander growled.

"Release her first."

He looked to Malin in protest, but the prince gave a nod. "I have missed you, daughter," Evander said to her cruelly. "I hope this is not goodbye."

Reluctantly, he released her. Livia didn't move for a few long seconds, and everything in Reylan tensed with anticipation that wouldn't know relief until she was in his arms, however fleeting the embrace.

"I have never been your daughter," she said coldly. Reylan admired the courage she dragged forth, now standing face-to-face with him as the worst of her living nightmares. "You look every part the monster you are within, and I am glad to have had the chance to see you in your true form. I don't fear you, Evander; I *pity* you."

She walked away from him, steps hurried until she fell into Reylan's arms, and the relief it offered meant one less burden.

"Take a new route out through the castle. I'm hoping Izaiah or Kyleer will have found Faythe and will take her out of the city." He leaned in close to whisper the specific instructions to the posted commanders. "You'll find each other, I know you will. Tell Faythe I'm sorry and that it's not her fault—none of it. Tell her—"

Gods, agony wasn't enough to describe what tore through him at the thought of being taken from her.

"I can't leave you with him," Livia choked.

"You have to. You know you have to." Her arms tightened, but he pulled her back. "Go now. They're not patient, and I can't risk him going back on his word."

Livia was one of the bravest, most resilient people he knew. She had risen from the depths of a desolate upbringing and made herself into one of Rhyenelle's most esteemed commanders. She knew when it was right to surrender and not feel guilty for a retreat that could save many people. Yet beneath it all she was still just a fae. With a loving heart behind the steel.

"Go," Reylan encouraged her once more.

Livia nodded slowly, swiping away a tear. "We're coming back for you," she promised.

Reylan had no room to argue as she slipped away. Knowing she would be safe, he turned to his uncle with new defiance. Stepping out into the rain stung his skin, and every movement tore. He walked steadily toward his uncle, not giving him a shred of satisfaction with any emotion.

Faythe would be safe. Livia would be safe. Kyleer and Izaiah would be safe.

That was all that mattered. If this was what it took to buy them time, Reylan would gladly face it.

Standing right before Evander, he tensed for the impact of his fist, which he saw twitching seconds before it connected with his face. Reylan spat the blood pooling in his mouth, letting out a breathy chuckle.

"I see you've gotten better at your punches now you don't have a personal hit man to throw them for you," he taunted.

A second punch came to his face, then another to his gut.

Reylan's voice strained as he tensed his muscles against the impact. "Still weak as a faeling, however."

A fourth to his jaw, a fifth to his cheek, and he surrendered to the impact that fell him to one knee. Reylan braced for the next when a smooth feminine voice called out from behind them all. He panted through the throbbing of his face.

"Enough."

Marvellas eased out from the crowd of parting dark fae, a creature of blazing red flame against the night. She moved as if the rain couldn't touch her, the red cloak and gown she wore still dry and her fiery hair perfectly intact. His bloody handprints still marked her neck to his satisfaction.

"I didn't say you could harm him yet."

Her hand rose and Evander started clawing at his throat. Not from any physical touch, but the manipulation she worked in his mind to make him believe her real hand were squeezing at his airway. Seconds ticked by, and Reylan believed she might kill him. Then, just before he could fall into unconsciousness, she let him go and he fell to his knees, reaching for his mask as if it could hide the fear he felt.

Marvellas approached, tilting Reylan's chin and searching his face with wonder. "I should have killed you a long time ago," she said, more to herself as though thinking out loud. Perhaps she was reassessing her plans, and no matter what it would mean for him, it became a relief. That whatever she wanted he would do it, even if it took every drop of power to achieve. As long as she no longer needed Faythe.

Thunder cracked overhead too loud, and sudden alarm gripped him entirely. His and everyone else's heads angled to the sky.

What Reylan saw stole gravity.

Faythe.

Unmistakably, *unbelievably*...

His Phoenix was *flying*.

Were it not for the dark fae hovering parallel from her in a deadly standoff in the sky, he would have basked in a moment of pride. Wings of fierce red fire kept her there, but even from this distance he saw the brilliant gold flare expanding from her palms. Reylan tried to rise, but four fae gripped his arms. He fought them without taking his eyes from Faythe, overcome with something unexplainable that canceled out all else but the raging urge to go to her however he could. She needed help.

His breath caught in his throat as he watched her send that brilliant flare then saw the full charge of purple lightning that answered it.

When their powers met...

A current blasted with the force of a hurricane, shooting down to tremble the earth, rumbling with an ear-splitting boom that knocked everyone back. Reylan braced just in time as the power sent the fae holding him sprawling. It continued to pulse in waves of energy that made him squint, arms raising. Marvellas stood as if she couldn't feel it at all, her chin tilted with incredulity and awe as she watched the battle erupt in the sky.

Reylan thought to take her distraction to his advantage, but with his next glance at Faythe, what gripped him in that second was a helpless sense of failure. He could do nothing but watch in terror and agony as new wings shot for Faythe.

Maverick was fast, shooting one dart of blue flame that struck Faythe unawares. The gold-and-purple flare shot skyward, and then they were both falling from that severed connection. Maverick flew impossibly fast toward Zaiana, but he didn't care. Reylan moved as if he could run to her, as if he could somehow catch her, though the impossibly of that outcome tore a scream from him. Fae tried to grab him, but he fought, unable to accept the plummet that would seal Faythe's fate. He watched the red flaming wings die out and his Phoenix falling and falling.

And there was nothing he could do.

A shrill cry pierced the sky.

While the fae loosened their hold on him, Reylan only straightened, praying to the *damn* Gods what he heard was not a desperate conjuring of his own mind.

It was hope.

Hope that came to fiery, blazing clarity as it burst through the clouds in an explosion of embers. Reylan fell to his knees, begging it would take her far from here.

He didn't struggle against the fae who took his arms; didn't care for whatever they were about to do as they restrained him. Reylan watched his Phoenix soar and prayed to every forsaken God that Faythe *lived*.

CHAPTER 93

Faythe

FAYTHE FELT THE warmth of Phoenixfyre like a slow awakening. Right when she needed it most, the power came to her, and she reached back. She knew it was Atherius, had listened to a familiar bond tugging within, but she couldn't figure out how it was possible to feel her but not see her.

Until now.

After her collision of power with Zaiana was severed, exhaustion made it futile to try to recover the impossible wings she'd conjured from the Phoenixfyre. They dissipated as glittering embers around her while she cut through the air, beauty in bleak misery.

Something screamed at her from within, trying to reach out.

Reylan—his name burst through the dream state she'd tunneled into. All she could do was chant her apology. Meeting her end wrapped in the soul-destroying force of his terror became the most punishing reality. Only her desperation to spare him had her directing the last of her strength to close off that distant tie.

Faythe focused everything now on summoning another bond as her last hope.

Last chance.

Last salvation.

She begged for it to save her, if only so she could return to him.

The air whooshed from her upon impact, but the landing wasn't as unforgiving as she'd braced for. It dipped to her descent, and she sank into surprising softness.

Faythe forced her body to turn, her arms to tighten, and her hands to clutch the silken feathers tightly.

Atherius had caught her.

While she drifted in and out of consciousness, Faythe couldn't give in. The Firebird soared away from the city, and Faythe wasn't sure where she thought to go.

"Take me back," Faythe said aloud, her voice barely audible, but it wasn't the common tongue she communicated with anyway. She adjusted her position to sit, taking a second to breathe in complete awe at the sights, the air whipping through her as she clung to Atherius's red feathers and watched embers travel around her from the long wisps of the bird's crown. Breathtaking. Exhilarating. For a second, the inferno within her extinguished. The poison dulled, and Faythe echoed her gratitude to Atherius for the temporary reprieve.

Her grip tightened along with the clamp of her legs when Atherius dipped before turning slowly in an elegant glide.

The destroyed half of the outer city expanded below her, and Faythe's reality came tumbling back around. Atherius swooped down to exactly where Faythe needed to be, for she had one last ask of the Firebird before she left.

Atherius tipped her head back, and Faythe winced as the firebird's cry trembled the ground. Her eyes pricked, doused in mutual grief and waves of piercing sorrow. Faythe couldn't turn around to the body of her father. Instead, she sobbed at the pain shooting through every inch of her body, inside and out, as she reached down to retrieve the Ember Sword.

"Take him," Faythe whispered. "Take him somewhere peaceful. Where the Firebirds found peace, so he can fly with them."

A SWORD FROM THE EMBERS

Powerful gusts blew past her, scattering flames across the blood-stained ground. She tuned in to the loud beat of wings, trusting Atherius would know exactly where to take Agalhor's body, and that she would grieve, just as Faythe did, for the loss of one of the most powerful, fair, and kind rulers of the Ashfyre name.

Faythe stood unmoving until the wind calmed and the rain fell straight. Fatigue began to creep over her, but she wasn't finished. *Reylan.* She needed him. It was all that drove her to take heavy steps against the threat of crumbling into nothing more than the debris of homes, stalls, playgrounds...safe places.

A depthless gravity beckoned her—one that could make her forget the shreds of her heart. One that could cool the inferno raging within as the Magestone slowly coursed through her blood, infused with tiny needles. She tried so hard to keep going, but her knees wobbled and gave out, cracking off the stone, though she barely felt it. Her vision came and went, only seeing blurry embers that rained like stars among the wreckage.

She had to get to the castle. Had to find Reylan and tell him...

Gods, how would she tell him of Agalhor's death? Some part of her was numb to the truth. She recited the words in her mind, but her throat tightened against the lie.

He's dead.

The one who was in some ways more of father to Reylan by bond, not blood.

With a cry, Faythe forced herself back to her feet. She had to keep going. She kept an iron grip around the golden hilt of the Ember Sword, barely able to lift its mighty weight. All she could do was drag it. Metal scraped the stone as she began to walk again, giving her something to focus on so she'd stay conscious and keep moving.

Agalhor Ashfyre is dead.

She kept trying to believe it, accept it.

The King of Rhyenelle is dead.

Amid all that had been invaded and defiled, this was the final collapse. Their savior, their leader, their *hope*...it was all gone.

Step. *Scrape.* Step.

I wonder who you will choose.
A spark of incredulity hit her.
Scrape. Step. *Scrape.*
Pause.
Or perhaps you will be too late to save either.
The Dresair's words.
Faythe had been a fool. Such a damned *fool* not to have seen the trick. In giving the device over to the mirror she'd received what she said she did not want. Wrapped in a twisted taunt, the knowledge was right there.
This night. Her choice.
And she had chosen wrongly and now risked losing both.
Faythe was close to falling again when something large came pounding toward her. The black panther felt somewhat familiar, and with a quick rattle around her mind, she almost cried with relief.
Izaiah didn't shift back; his large head caught her stumble forward, and she needed no other coaxing before he lowered enough for her to grip what she could of his sleek coat and clumsily climb onto his back. Her face buried into him, clutching tightly as he took off running. Faythe began to cry all over again, not knowing how to tell anyone what had happened. Still branded with the image of her father lying so still she ached with the impossibility of reversing time.
She just had to make it to Reylan.
"I hope you can hear me, Faythe."
Her consciousness fogged. She wasn't sure the echo of Izaiah's voice was real.
"Gods, I hope so. I need you to know I'm sorry, that this is the only way, and I've known it for a while."
Nothing made sense, but some part of her knew these words were important.
"Tell Kyleer, for once in our lives, I was one step ahead."
Kyleer. Faythe broke down all over again. How could she tell Izaiah that he was right...that his brother had fallen victim to the beauty that lured him right in as bait? Her head pounded with so

much grief and agony she wanted to give in to the sweeps of darkness and never awaken. All that kept her from it was a flicker of silver and sapphire.

When the jostling stopped, her alarm returned. Faythe tumbled off Izaiah, and he shifted just in time to catch her head before it could meet stone. Her face crumpled at meeting familiar green eyes. Her mouth parted, but she couldn't say it. Any of it. She clung to it all as an unforgiving, unfathomable nightmare she could still awaken from.

"You're going to be okay," Izaiah said softly, helping her to stand.

She trembled against him when his arms wrapped around her.

Then Izaiah's whole body tensed.

"You don't want to turn around. Please tell me you won't," Izaiah said.

Faythe tried to pull back, but his arms tightened.

The groan of pain from behind her tightened in her gut, raising the hairs on her nape. Within torched a raging urgency, and despite his strength, Faythe pushed away from Izaiah. But what she saw made her mouth part on a silent scream. She watched the rise of two fists that would fall on Reylan again—Reylan who had surrendered on his knees, bloodied and beaten, while two fae held his arms outstretched.

Faythe did scream then—something between a cry for them to stop and a roar of wrath. At another blow, she lurched, but Izaiah caught her. Faythe fought him, searching deep for any flicker of magick, but only dark laughter echoed back. Her skin was so hot, her mind exhausted, and the Magestone finally nullified the last of what she could feel. She knew her magick was there but was unable to drag it forth. A small kindling was all she needed, and some desperate part of her believed it kept taunting her, rising and burning out just before she could reach for it.

She whimpered, going limp in Izaiah's arms.

A male in a black mask caught in her vision, and Faythe swayed at the sight, having seen it before. She'd questioned who it was that had tracked them, wondered if he were real, yet now it was so clear, so obvious, that Faythe felt like a failure for not figuring it out before now.

It was Evander, Reylan's uncle. Their encounter in the town...

Flashes of memory boiled her blood, and it all made sense now.

A white rage flashed across her vision, and she was about to reach for her sword to end him despite every physical barrier that stunted her.

Until a voice stopped her fight.

"Faythe Ashfyre."

The silken delivery of her name tore her eyes from Reylan, who didn't look up. When Faythe found the source, it was like an answer she'd searched an eternity for blazed like a beacon before her. One that torched anything of mercy and reached some impenetrable darkness within her.

"Marvellas," she breathed, more to herself just to know she could speak.

To know this was real.

"Or should I tell them all who you really are since in your cowardice you cannot?"

Faythe nearly doubled over as the sickness rolled through her gut.

"Please."

"I taught you better, Aesira."

That name became a key Faythe didn't know she'd been searching for. Hearing it spoken aloud placed her in a hallway with so many doors she didn't know where to begin. Each one led to a life she didn't know she wanted to have back.

Aesira knew Marvellas. What flashed to her, but which she immediately wanted to expel...was that once, that fae might have harbored a twisted love for her. But in this life, Faythe had long hoped Marvellas was nothing more than a fable, a ghost.

Not the returning nightmare from her past.

"I've been looking for you." Marvellas's tone became so warm, unexpectedly soft, as she took slow steps forward as though she were wondering the same thing: if *Faythe* were real. "Then there you were in High Farrow. How craftily your mother hid you, but you revealed yourself to me because destiny cannot be fought. I mourned your sacrifice no matter how long I had to prepare for it. No matter that I despised you for your betrayal long ago. Then my sister brought you back, so unexpected and powerful, and I thank her for that gift. You and I, along with Dakodas...you would be fooling yourself not to see the alignment of a great fate."

Faythe couldn't breathe.

"You brought her to me." Marvellas flicked her golden gaze to Izaiah.

No. Izaiah hadn't known who they were to face. He wouldn't—

"Only for her to see what's at stake if she plans to fight."

A ringing filled her ears—an attempt to block out the words, change them, *fix* them. They were wrong. So wrong, and Faythe was falling into a depthless pit of despair. She couldn't get a grip to keep herself from plummeting.

Izaiah released her, and without any support Faythe fell to her knees. All she could do was look to Reylan across the stone courtyard, wondering how they'd gotten here when they'd come so close to having everything.

"I'm so sorry," she sent to his mind in her utter heartache. Everything was because of her. So much of what he'd suffered was by her cause, and she should have set him free, yet instead, she'd anchored him to her once again.

Izaiah walked right up to Marvellas, dipping his head. "I hope you will accept me on your side."

Disbelief wasn't enough for what carved out her chest.

"Very well." A triumphant smile sounded in her voice.

Faythe didn't look up; didn't look away from the hard glare of rage laced with pain on Reylan's face. She tracked every mark on him: the cut along his jaw, the bleeding of his lip, the bruise forming on his temple. Faythe committed it all to memory for the vengeance she would unleash.

He was still alive. She was still alive. It was not the end.

Izaiah went to stand by Malin on the portico. Her cousin was near grinning at her hopeless state. She felt nothing. Her gaze immediately caught on Jakon and Marlowe.

It was over. Faythe had nothing left. No one left.

"Tell me it's not them," she said in denial.

The Spirit chuckled with soft amusement. "Believe it or not, I have no influence in any of their minds. How does it feel that while you remain in your defiance, those you care for have chosen to believe in my vision for this better world?"

"Reuben?" she dared to ask. "All this time?"

"Yes, Faythe. He has told me everything. And you were the one to send him straight to me—do you remember?"

Lakelaria.

Faythe wished to wake up in the high peak of Rhyenelle's castle, having fallen asleep in utter bliss in Reylan's arms, both of them lying there on that patch of obscurely placed grass that seemed as if it had been planted especially so they could have that night watching the stars, witnessing their first comet of many. As rulers, together. The prospect of that future crashed down around her now like the broken fragments of all that could have been.

"I heard you out there, you know," Marvellas said, her voice low and personal, speaking…as if she *cared*. "You said he was all you have left. But that's not true. You have me."

The wave of grief at having her last plea thrown back at her made Faythe bow her head. Marvellas needed no steel, no weapon, to know how to strike deepest.

Marvellas took to her mind again to say, *"You will always have me, Aesira. I created you."*

With the anger that seeped from her, she found her voice enough to hiss back, *"That is not my name. And the only thing you created is your own downfall."*

Softness turned to darkness so fast it was frightening. Marvellas only looked back, giving one small nod that had a dark fae positioning to strike Reylan again.

"Stop! Please, please *stop!*"

Marvellas raised a hand. Faythe splayed her palms on the ground, trembling violently, her mind racing, dizzy with thoughts of how she could get them both out of this alive. It was easy to believe while wrapped in the bliss of each other that what they had was unbreakable. Untouchable. That what had forged between them could defy anything. But it was all an illusion from the high of being drunk on him. His scent, his taste, his power, which always hummed and entwined with hers when he was near, as though ready to take on the world.

Yet they had been blindsided, ambushed by the forces that surrounded them, and their bond was not enough.

All that mattered was protecting it.

Faythe was glad then. Glad their incomplete mating bond remained protected so the Spirit of Souls could not reach out to snap it. It was now a promise she clung to with new reverence; a fierce will and determination to end the war no matter what she had to do, if only so they could have what had been stolen from them.

If that made her selfish, if she had to burn the world to do it, then so be it.

"I'll go with you," Faythe said in defeat. "Just let him go."

"No," Reylan snarled.

She looked up in time to see him topple the second fae who held him. Reylan moved so fast and powerful, fighting for her, yet there were too many. Faythe sobbed, begging for it to stop. For him to stop fighting and allow her to do this. Her world cleaved in two knowing he never would. Until the very end he would fight for her.

"Tell them to stop hurting him," she pleaded.

Marvellas said nothing. They kicked him and beat him until they'd restrained him back on his knees, and each hand they lay on him she felt like a branding on her. Her rage and retribution could do nothing against the defeat. She couldn't reach him.

Suddenly, they all choked at the display of Marvellas's magick. Faythe watched Marvellas's invasion of their minds as she effortlessly seized them all and realized she had done that before. She was merely a product of the evil entity before her. No better, and no worse.

"It's not enough this time," Marvellas said. "Why let him go when I have this chance to set you free once and for all? To give you back the memories we had, the life in which we were happy. Before *him*. He won't stop getting in the way, and you won't stop wanting to go to him. I see now what I should have done a long time ago. When I'm finished with both of you, it will be as if you never met at all."

Dread coiled in Faythe's stomach. Her eyes closed for a long few seconds, but she found the will to part her lips. Anything else… she would have accepted any punishment or sacrifice but her memories of him, which she gathered anew and swore to return to the both of them *somehow*.

"You won't have to do that. I will be yours—I won't fight it. Please." Faythe rose to her feet, wiped her tears, and took one deep breath of courage and strength. For him. He made the choice easy.

Just as she took her first step, smoke surrounded her, and she cried out at the grip that clamped around her middle.

"Not this time, Faythe."

She gasped at the voice, momentarily forgetting everything in her sheer relief and joy. "You're alive," she breathed. Her lip wobbled, needing to see him.

Faythe twisted her head when he didn't let go, and Kyleer's brow pinched with the release of her sharp sob. Despite it all, this was a gift. Kyleer had become someone she couldn't stand to picture a world without.

"We both are. And we're getting the Nether out of here," he said.

Faythe shook her head. "You have to let me go."

"Not going to happen."

Relieved he was alive but annoyed at how he'd chosen to intervene, Faythe tried to break out of his hold. Kyleer remained unyielding, and Faythe's panic started to rise with her plea, knowing any second, he could take her from the courtyard completely with his Shadowporting ability. She whirled back to

Reylan with a frantic desperation that had her thrashing against Kyleer, fighting him. She couldn't leave.

She wouldn't leave Reylan.

"Let me go!" She chanted it over and over, anxiety pounding in her ears to cancel out all else.

"*Listen to me, Faythe. Just for a moment.*"

And like that, Reylan's gentle voice in her mind silenced the world.

"*We didn't get enough time in this life. Not even close. But there is another, maybe infinite, in which we will have that time. Without war and conflict; without a crown or a name. I promise to stand by you. Always.*"

She sobbed, still straining against Kyleer's hold, but she listened.

"*Go with him, my Phoenix. You're not done flying. I love you. This day until the end of days. Say it back to me.*"

There was never a more helpless agony that tore at her soul. She shook her head. She couldn't… She couldn't say those words.

"Please," she whimpered, but she was already weighed down with defeat. "Don't let them take him."

The cries of the frightened city returned to her senses. The smell of ash and devastation smothered the air. But only his words were enough to invoke any reaction in her desperation.

"*Say it back to me,*" he tried again, so gentle and calm it was unbearable. But in those sapphire eyes he pleaded with a need for her to hear it.

"*I love you,*" she said to him within. Against all the protests that tightened her lips at the finality of the words, Faythe sealed a new promise to him. "*I won't stop finding you. Until the end of days.*"

For a second, the relief on his face was worth the hollowness that opened in place of her heart.

Then came the final command from her fierce, selfless warrior.

"Get her out of here, Ky."

They were so close to having everything, to having each other in every perfect, complete way. And now what had bound them was tearing and *tearing*, and Faythe became helpless to defy it.

This couldn't be happening.

Her grip slipped on the Ember Sword, and Kyleer caught it.

"Along with Agalhor, your reign is over, Faythe." Malin's words surfaced a wrath, a determination, so all-consuming it stole her physical fight. She straightened her poise, pinning her cousin with a promise she bonded to the very earth.

Faythe broke away from Kyleer only to stand tall. "You have yet to glimpse my reign, but it is not a crown you should fear falling to me." Her cry resonated over the courtyard, stilling everyone so they could hear. "I will rain down the stars so you may never dream upon them. I will rain down Phoenixfyre to burn all you build to ash. And I will rain down the might of the Ashfyre name to avenge the bloodline you betrayed. You are staring into the face of your deepest fear, Malin. For when I am finished with you,"—her chest heaved with a promise so final, words that struck like a declaration from the Gods—"you will yield all to me."

Faythe sealed it all in that stare she pierced him with. Then, with careful attention, she looked to Marvellas, who stood by in awe and delight. Dakodas looked hateful and bored. She let them decipher what they wanted from her. It wouldn't matter when she ended them too.

Who she couldn't bear to see were her friends, unable to witness them standing on her enemy's side with the fear her mask would crumble.

Faythe felt the light touch of shadows beginning to reach for her. Instinct fought against it first. Her face crumpled. Then within…her flame caught. It was a faint kindling of magick, and without thinking Faythe reached for it before it could be snuffed out again.

Panic slipped time through her fingers like sand. Gold met sapphire, and she promised them both it would not be the final time. Reylan remained on his knees, surrendering, and as the embrace of Kyleer's Shadowporting ability began to creep over her, she jerked as Evander's fist connected with Reylan's face to break their stare. Her mouth parted with a silent scream of horror as she caught him land another, then another.

A SWORD FROM THE EMBERS

Faythe gave in to the familiar pull of magick, engulfing herself in its shadows before she knew how she was doing it. Only her power answered her last dying call.

When the ground formed beneath her feet a heartbeat later, she did not feel it. All Faythe knew was that her hand was clamped around Evander's throat.

Squeezing. Crushing.

The fae in her grip couldn't fight because she'd seized his mind too. Everything became a white blur of hot rage, and she didn't know who she was in that moment as something else took over. His skin became diffused with the golden glow from her palm, and Faythe removed his mask to reveal the monster, only to watch him shrink into the pitiful male he was in his last dying moments of terror.

The scars mapping his face delighted her. Reylan's marks of retribution.

"I remember now," she said with a cold sense of calm. "Not everything, but I remember this. My promise, though you never got to hear it."

He managed to claw at her hand, but she felt nothing, staring into such hateful blue eyes she knew nothing warm had ever thawed. He wouldn't have stopped chasing his terror. His vengeance toward Reylan never would have ended, and that made her act easy to shoulder.

She *enjoyed* it. The power. His struggle. She took *pleasure* in it. This darkness she had felt before but had never embraced so freely that it became her. Faythe's heart beat through shades of black, and she embraced it, wanting him to be hurt by her hand. She squeezed *harder*.

The choking stopped. His hands slipped away. Faythe let go a few seconds later, and he fell to the ground.

Evander was dead.

Maybe one day she'd look back and be horrified by how easily she'd taken his life. But right now, knowing those hands could never again rise to harm Reylan, all Faythe could surface was relief.

Knowing her seconds were precious, she fell to her knees, taking Reylan's face in her palms, though he was still stunned in his stupor. "I hope you will forgive me," she whispered, holding those sapphire eyes with such conviction. "I want to give it all back to you."

"Faythe…" He breathed her name, but she couldn't be sure what emotion was most dominant in him. Agony, shock, awe, terror. Then a staggering rage. "You're hurt—"

Faythe's lips pressed to his, and she drifted faraway with him, canceling it all out. She touched his rain-slicked shoulders, his chest, trailed her hands down his arm to slip the metal from her wrist onto his. He held her face tenderly. Faythe ignited with every touch she could steal and wished the seconds could stay suspended as minutes. Minutes to hours. She wished time were a force that could be fought and reversed, but all it did was mock her fantasy.

"Take them both," Marvellas commanded.

Dakodas approached, and Faythe sobbed as her shadows reached for Reylan.

"Let me go," he said softly.

She shook her head, but he took her wrists, prying them from around him when a new arm hooked around her waist and she felt the transportation pull.

Not with him. *Away* from him.

She didn't tear her eyes from Reylan. Misery wasn't a big enough word for what obliterated her heart, her soul, as Kyleer's shadows snaked around her and engulfed them in a heartbeat. With one final effort, she pushed everything she had into the bond. It was incomplete, but she'd heard him in another realm, and all she could do was believe he heard her now as she didn't stop repeating her promise so he wouldn't stop remembering it.

I will find you.

As her body was Shadowported she didn't register the movement. She didn't yearn for the light in the darkness that encased her. Because when it dispersed, he would not be there.

She would have missed it if she'd allowed her lids to blink.

A SWORD FROM THE EMBERS

Everything stilled just as brutally fast, and when the hold on her eased, gravity pulled her to the ground.

Cold, numb.

Her eyes hadn't moved a fraction from where she'd held them on her mate for as long as she could. The ghost of Reylan's image faded rapidly, only to be replaced by a dark, depthless woodland. Timber bodies stood before her instead of flesh. The contrasting silence rang out at a high pitch, swallowing the echoes of steel and cries.

She didn't know where Kyleer had taken them.

I killed Evander.

She didn't care. Faythe would do it again. It had done nothing to ease her flashes of hot anger that still haunted her with the image of his hands striking Reylan. Suddenly, she was *angry* with herself for killing him so quickly.

Her tears flowed as she struggled to accept all that had unfolded.

Against the odds, she wanted to face them, just to be by his side.

"We have to go back," she whispered. How could she have left him?

"Faythe—"

When she finally snapped her head up to him, Kyleer grimaced at her grief-stricken face. "We left him. What will she —?" Faythe couldn't finish her sentence. Nausea overcame her in a strong wave that had her bracing palms on the cold woodland floor. Wood splinters snagged in her skin; rocks cut her palms as she squeezed so tightly, but apparently not tight enough.

She was weak. The Magestone raged, and she had to tell Kyleer, not knowing if it could kill her, because that couldn't happen. Not until she found him. Faythe rubbed her wrist, so used to spinning the amulet—the eye of the Phoenix—but it was bare. Her gaze snapped to Kyleer, who propped up the Ember Sword. Seeing her attention on it, he stepped forward to extend it to her, but Faythe shook her head.

"It's not mine."

"By rights it is. He would have wanted you to have it."

"No." It had been her last hope, and she prayed Agalhor's tale of the ruby stone was true. "It will take us to him."

"I'm sorry," Kyleer said, as broken as she. "I wasn't strong enough to test my ability on Dakodas's claim, and I had to get you—"

"It's not your fault," Faythe said quietly. She reached into a small, concealed pocket of her leathers, whimpering when she felt it, so overcome with gratitude that she'd decided to take it with her in the heat of the moment. Her eyes dropped to her clenched fist. Despite the agony, she opened it to glimpse the wooden butterfly Reylan had carved, the image of it beginning to blur. Then she twisted her hand to see the ring that was a promise forged so long ago.

"I tried," she said, quiet through clenched teeth—not in pain, not in sadness, but with a wrath so consuming it vibrated her whole body. Her fist closed again around the carving. "I tried to be good. To be better. To be fair. To be kind. But they took him, and I see…those qualities are not what will win this war." What overcame her was something she had felt before; something she had battled with. "Sometimes you have to fight fire with fire," she whispered, still hearing the screams of the city, tasting the ash in the air. *"Fire with fire."*

They'd killed him, her father. They'd killed King Agalhor Ashfyre.

Faythe rocked back and forth, repeating it as amber flashed across her vision, burning the innocent. Her head tipped back while her eyes closed. Tears slipped down her face, over her ears. Her palms heated in response to her grief, but it sputtered out, the Magestone numbing what she could unleash.

"I could kill them all and I would not be sorry for it. I could find everyone who harmed him, and I wouldn't just make them hurt—I'd make them beg for death as I lay them at its doorstep." Between flashes of the hands that hit him…Faythe breathed steady. She opened her eyes, turning her head to Kyleer, who stood

A SWORD FROM THE EMBERS

watching her intently. "Tell me I'm a monster, that my revenge would be immoral. Tell me I'm no better than them."

The lines of his face became firm, their seconds of silence tense and heavy. Then he took the few steps toward her, reaching out a hand. "I cannot, for I plan to follow you, no matter what course, to get him back. And to avenge Agalhor."

Faythe found the will to accept his palm as it rose, and they locked eyes with cold, simmering determination. "We do this, and we do it together, whatever it takes. If not better, then worse."

Faythe swayed, and Kyleer took her into his arms. "Magestone," she rasped.

Kyleer swore. "We're going to get you help. Just hold on."

Faythe would. For him—for Reylan—she would fight because she'd made a promise. Her lights were dying out, her legs were swept from under her, and then she was cradled in Kyleer's warmth.

Faythe Ashfyre sealed the promise one last time before the darkness claimed her in another temporary reprieve from her shattered heart…

I will find you.

END OF *A SWORD FROM THE EMBERS*

The story will continue.

ALSO BY CHLOE C. PEÑARANDA

AN HEIR COMES TO RISE SERIES

An Heir Comes to Rise

A Queen Comes to Power

A Throne from the Ashes

A Clash of Three Courts

A Sword from the Embers

NYTEFALL

The Stars are Dying (coming soon)

PRONUNCIATION GUIDE

NAMES

Faythe: faith
Reylan: ray-lan
Nik: nick
Jakon: jack-on
Marlowe: mar-low
Tauria: tor-ee-a
Kyleer: kai-leer
Izaiah: i-zai-ahh
Livia: liv-ee-a
Reuben: ru-ben
Zaiana: zai-anna
Maverick: mah-ver-ick
Mordecai: mor-de-kai
Tynan: tie-nan
Amaya: ah-mah-ya
Lycus: lie-cuss
Tarly: tar-lay
Nerida: ner-eh-dah
Marvellas: mar-vell-as
Aurialis: orr-ee-al-iss
Dakodas: da-code-as
Augustine: au-guss-teen
Ashfyre: ash-fire
Arrowood: arrow-wood
Galentithe: gal-en-tithe
Zarrius: zar-ee-us
Katori: cat-or-ee
Asari: ahh-sa-re

PLACES

Ungardia: un-gar-dee-a
Farrowhold: farrow-hold
Galmire: gal-my-er
High Farrow: high-farrow
Lakelaria: lake-la-ree-a
Rhyenelle: rye-en-elle
Olmstone: olm-stone
Fenstead: fen-stead
Dalrune: dal-rune
Fenher: fen-er
Ellium: elle-ee-um
Niltain: nill-tain

OTHER

Riscillius: risk-ill-ee-us
Lumarias: lou-ma-ree-as
Yucolites: you-co-lights
Dresair: dress-air
Magestone: mage-stone
Skailies: skay-lees
Fyrestone: fire-stone
Phoenixfyre: phoenix-fire

ACKNOWLEDGMENTS

My dear readers, I've been so excited to come to this book. To reveal so many things we've been building upon since book one. Thank you for sticking with me. None of this would be possible without you and I find myself taking so many moments to reflect how far we've come and the support you have followed me with. From the bottom of my heart, you'll never know how much it means to me.

To Lyssa, you've been with me from the start and I can't thank you enough for how hard you believed in this series and me. This book is yours. For the endless messages we shared about it, and for listening to all my stress and doubt. To the best chaos co-ordinator there is!

To my mum, it doesn't matter how old I get, I'll still call you first for the most trivial things. Thank you for always being my rock.

To my family, I wouldn't be the person I am without you all. I may not see you as much as I should while I lock myself in other worlds, but I think of you everyday, and I'm forever grateful for the support no matter what.

To my dogs, Milo, Bonnie, and Minnie, the loves of my life and the daily tests of my patience.

To all the help on the launch team for this book, you know who you are, and you are amazing! Thank you for helping spread the word for this next leg of the journey.

To my brilliant editor, Bryony Leah. Five books down! How time has flown so fast and I'm so grateful to have you sticking with this series. Thank you for bringing out the best in these books time and time again.

To Alice Maria Power, go team Rocket! I hope you don't tire of hearing this because we're all in awe of how you continue to make these covers incredible.

Printed in Great Britain
by Amazon